THE FISHHOOK
REBELLION

THE FISHHOOK REBELLION

HAWAI'I 1847

A SWIFT & DANCER
ADVENTURE

DAN GOODER RICHARD

INKSPIRATION
MEDIA

Maps and illustrations by Rhys Davies/www.rhysspieces.com
Interior book design by David Wu/DW Design

Publisher's Cataloging-In-Publication Data
(Prepared by Cassidy Cataloguing Services, Inc.)

Names: Richard, Dan Gooder, 1947- author.
Title: The Fishhook Rebellion : Hawai'i, 1847 / Dan Gooder Richard.
Description: Arlington, Virginia : Inkspiration Media, [2022] |
Series: A Swift & Dancer adventure | Includes bibliographical references.
Identifiers: ISBN 978-1-939319-34-0 (paperback) | 978-1-939319-35-7 (ePub)
Subjects: LCSH: Women war correspondents--Hawaii--History--
19th century--Fiction. | Spies--Hawaii--History--19th century--Fiction. |
Treasure troves--Fiction. | Betrayal--Fiction. |
Hawaii--History--19th century--Fiction. |
LCGFT: Thrillers (Fiction) | Historical fiction.
Classification: LCC: PS3618.I33374 F57 2022 | DDC: 813/.6--dc23

Library of Congress Control Number: 2022915932

For my Father and Mother
whose storytelling instilled my love of adventure tales.

And for the demigod Maui
who pulled the eight Hawaiian Islands from the sea
with his magic fishhook.

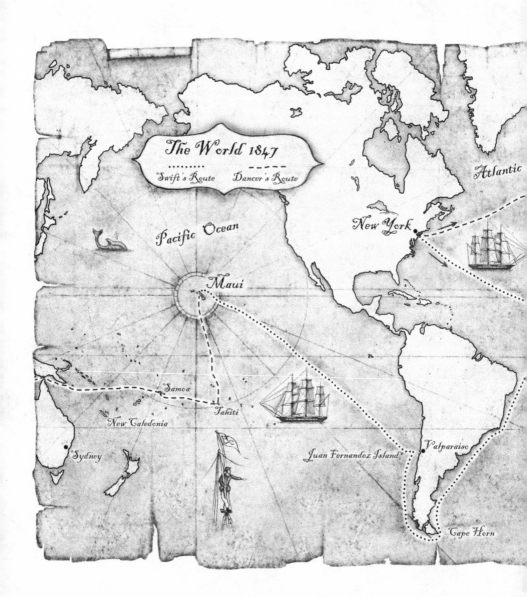

The World 1847

········· Swift's Route   ‒ ‒ ‒ Dancer's Route

Atlantic

Pacific Ocean

New York

Maui

Samoa

Tahiti

New Caledonia

Sydney

Juan Fernandez Island

Valparaiso

Cape Horn

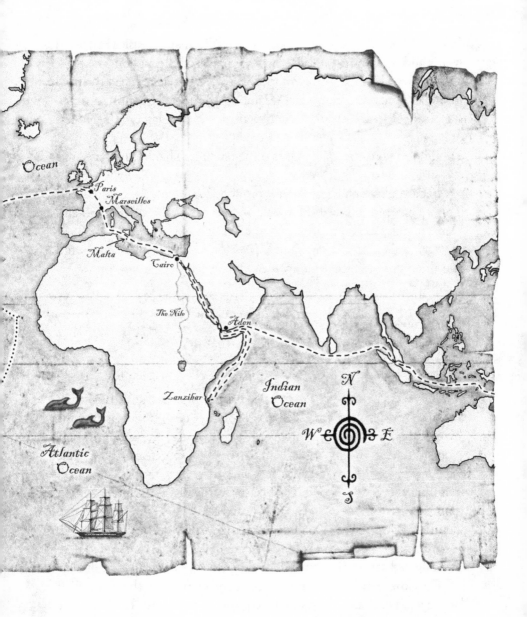

HAWAIIAN PRONUNCIATION GUIDE

HAWAIIAN words can be tongue twisters. To make it easier Hawaiian words and other non-English words are italicized throughout the book and followed by their synonym in English. This style reduced the need for a dictionary and eliminated requiring you to refer continuously to a glossary. Palace and place names are set in regular type regardless of language.

Pronouncing Hawaiian takes some practice. Thankfully there are a few simple rules.

Separate letters: Every letter is pronounced separately. For instance: The *a*'s are pronounced separately in the town Kapaa (Kap-ah-ah). Here are samples of proper names spelled phonetically.

• Hawai'i (ha-VAI-ee) (Note: *Hawaiian* is not a Hawaiian word and thus is not spelled with an *'okina*.)

  • Pi'ilani (PEE-ee-lan-ee)
  • Maunakili (MAW-nah-kee-lee)
  • Kahekili (KAH-hee-kee-lee)
  • Kamehameha (Kah-MAY-ha-MAY-ha)
  • Pilikua (PEE-lee-koo-ah)
  • Pālā'au (Pah-LAH-ow)

'Okina: The *'okina* (') is a character (not punctuation) that causes a glottal stop between vowels as when you say "uh-oh." Sometimes the *'okina* can change the meaning of a word. For example: *kou* means "yours" and *ko'u* means "mine." Similarly: *moa* refers to a chicken while *mo'a* means cooked. We kept the *'okina* to reflect the oral Hawaiian tradition — even though in today's usage the *'okina* is often deleted (particularly in modern signs and printed text). Any time you see two identical vowels next to each other you can assume an *'okina* is missing.

Kahakou: The *kahakou* (line over the vowel) causes a vowel to have an elongated sound (Example: Pālā'au Cliffs — Pah-LAH-ow Cliffs).

Consonants: There are seven consonants in the Hawaiian language. They are all pronounced the same as in English. The consonants are *H. K. L. M. N. P. W.* Sometimes the *W* is pronounced like a *V.*

Vowels: There are five vowels. All are pronounced the same as in English except for the "i"—which is pronounced like a long "e" as in *me*. The vowels are: *A* (ah). *E* (eh). *I* (long E). *O* (oh). *U* (u).

There are more rules of course and more explanations. Particularly how the oral Hawaiian language was changed and simplified by the early missionaries' intent to translate their Christian Bible into text. These starter basics help make reading easier.

PROLOGUE

CITADEL OF QAITBAY
RASHEED/EYGPT
1 AUGUST 1798

VICE-AMIRAL GAGNON LEGRAND stepped onto the gallery of the Citadel's minaret. A Mediterranean breeze blew through the evening's heavy air and cooled the sweat on his face. While climbing the one hundred and four counterclockwise steps to the top of the cylindrical tower suffocation had crossed his mind. The ancient shaft acted as a chimney to expel the hot air the Egyptian climate trapped in the mosque's prayer hall far below.

LeGrand studied the small man in front of him who faced Aboukir Bay to the west. His somewhat delicate hands jammed against the narrow *muezzin* gallery. The man was lean and stood squarely with a calm and serious bearing. LeGrand's mind flashed back to the argument in March he had heard the officer ambitiously orchestrate in Paris with the French Foreign Minister Talleyrand. All listened spellbound by the man's decisive grand plan for a French invasion of Egypt. His cheekbones were pronounced. All the muscles of his face moved when he spoke...even his nose to an astonishing degree.

"With victory in Egypt...France will cut the communication line of the British to their colony in India." The man stared directly at Talleyrand as he argued. "Then we will join with the Tipu Sultan of India's Seringapatam to drive the British from the subcontinent."

Talleyrand knew victory in Egypt would strangle the British treasury. The dream of choking the life from that little island kingdom was too ripe to resist. Ultimate French victory over Britain meant everything. Talleyrand gave his blessing. In the months since that spring day France had captured the vast treasury of Malta in June. Landed at Alexandria in Egypt by July. Then three weeks later defeated the Ottoman Turks and their enslaved Mamluke cavalry in Cairo at the Battle of the Pyramids. Now only ten days after that victory the critical naval strategy of the Egyptian campaign had unraveled. Britain's Rear Admiral Horatio Nelson's fleet had found the French fleet near Alexandria in Aboukir Bay.

The commander kicked the balcony rail. His hair plastered to his temples was worn long: A flattened pigtail reached to the middle of his back. He paused. Then turned and ground the heel of his boot into the minaret's dust at the top of the Citadel built by Qaitbay. The venerated Mamluke Sultan of Egypt. The ancient tower three hundred years later still commanded the mouth of the Nile where it emptied into the Mediterranean. Aboukir Bay — now illumined by a setting sun — cut into the shore here between the river and Alexandria. For eons the great river's opalescent black water carried silt and sewage here to form the river's delta. That rich land spread like a table below the two Frenchmen with nothing to slow an army but a web of irrigation ditches. Heavy smells rose to greet them in the humid dusk. Egyptian incense. Thick jasmine. Wood smoke. And dung.

"First" — LeGrand nodded northwest toward the bay — "Vice-Amiral Brueys moved the fleet from Alexandria harbor to the Aboukir Bay."

"He should have kept the fleet in open water." The short general snapped his reply. His face loomed more oval than round. After a moment the small Frenchman arched his eyebrows and continued: "Then — when Brueys' captains insisted the entire fleet be anchored in line of battle fifteen hundred meters from the shoals — he did not overrule them...the fool."

LeGrand shifted uncomfortably. A bead of sweat hung on his temple. As he waited he noted his commander's masculine mouth and chin — which were especially strong and roundly contoured.

"Then Brueys made it worse by cabling every warship stern to bow to form a one-sided battle line facing the sea." The perceptive officer's disgust sharpened the line of his curved nose. "He called his battery an 'impregnable barrier'…the stupid peacock."

The general recited his admiral's errors like an indictment. "Brueys did not prepare the landward guns for battle. He assumed — wrongly — that the British would attack broadside to broadside only from the Mediterranean side of our line." LeGrand nodded gravely. "The British can slip between the shore and the backside of our fleet. Then Nelson can send more ships to set up in the gaps between our anchored ships…where we will be fired upon but cannot reply. The British will attack from all sides at once. Our ships will be defenseless." His voice was cold with contempt.

Dusk darkened the plains…the thunder of cannons had rolled across the bay for three hours. Somewhere in the distance a *muezzin's adhan* called the faithful to sunset prayer. Without warning a giant red fireball erupted into the air over distant Aboukir Bay. The contours of the bay were faintly visible from the cylindrical tower. Yet soon enough reports would reach them with disastrous details: How splintered wood and broken bodies rose high in the humid August air. How the concussion ripped open seams in close by ships. How debris rocketed over the surrounding ships. How the flaming wreckage of flagship *L'Orient* dropped in a huge circle into the sea.

These details would prove redundant after the sound of the devastating explosion reached the two men at the Citadel. Then silence. As the guns paused. Held in check by the unimaginable blast. The two men knew nothing remained of their greatest French warship. And its commander — Brueys — had disappeared under the shallow waters off the shoreline a little more than twenty-five miles west of Rasheed.

The two men stood shoulder to shoulder on the *muezzin's* gallery. Beneath them the silent waters of the River Nile swirled into the Mediterranean Sea. The small erect officer muttered to no one in particular. "Who knows…five thousand casualties? Four thousand captured? Ships of the line destroyed — including our greatest warship

L'Orient? I can imagine ships of the line captured…frigates destroyed." He fumed. "Nelson has won this Battle of the Nile. But the war is not over."

In a rush the men descended the Citadel minaret. LeGrand kept up as best he could. The supreme general confided in LeGrand as they crossed the great prayer hall: Expecting Nelson's attack he had ordered the entire treasure captured at Malta offloaded from his *L'Orient* flagship. And replaced with gunpowder. "That is why the treasury of Malta is safely in Cairo. Far away from the dirty grasp of Nelson and the British."

The two soldiers slowed as they walked along the outer parapet wall. In the near distance where the river met the sea the hastily restored walls of Fort Julien were dotted by picket torches.

The shorter figure explained brusquely as his face hardened in determination: "From Malta we captured a treasure beyond imagining in gold and silver and gems…plus priceless objects and gold plate and jewelry collected by our lieutenants. At all cost — that treasure of Malta must be preserved. It holds the key to France's victory…and Britain's defeat."

"How can we feed our army in Egypt?" LeGrand questioned.

"The riches of the Pharaohs will sustain my army against the coming British attack."

LeGrand then asked the critical question. "With Nelson commanding the Mediterranean…how can the treasure get back to France?"

"*Oui*…the Mediterranean may be Nelson's lake for now." The commander's answer was emphatic. "That is why we must — as we did at our victory at Leoben in Austria — use strategy and bluff and keep our boots dry to outflank Nelson. LeGrand" — he nodded — "remember: War is a lie that only tells the truth in victory."

LeGrand's commander then outlined the secret escape plan he had devised for the treasure. LeGrand must race up the Nile to Cairo. "Since we fought at the pyramids the Mamluke slave-soldiers realized their Turkish Sultan is no match for French muskets. The old Ottoman fool." The general swept his arm across the southern horizon. "In the last weeks the Ottoman flotillas have been cleared from the Nile." He pronounced his assertion confidently. "Wagons are waiting for you in Cairo. From there you must haul the treasure overland to the Red Sea."

"The Red Sea." LeGrand noted the destination in a somewhat surprised tone. "How vast is the treasure?"

The commander paused. "A pope's ransom." He smiled. "Gold. Gems. Silver. Collected for centuries at the gateway to the Mediterranean."

His hand shifted to the golden hilt of a jeweled dagger at his belt. "We also captured the Sword of La Valette...This dagger was a gift of gratitude from King Philippe of Spain to the Knights of Malta for defeating the Ottomans." His eyes narrowed. "La Valette held out for three months—one of the greatest sieges of all time!—until help arrived to push the Ottoman Turks back. Invincibility travels with me always in his dagger."

The French officer with deep-set eyes mapped out his vice-admiral's mission. LeGrand must sail around Africa to land at Brest on France's Atlantic coast. Home port to the French fleet. "That way you will avoid Nelson's Mediterranean and his Gibraltar blockades."

LeGrand nodded.

"Loaded wagons are waiting for you in Cairo. And three ships are standing by at El Suweis in the Red Sea. Nelson may have blocked our front door"—the liberator of Egypt squeezed the dagger's hilt—"but this Frenchman never attacks without having an escape plan."

The two men reached the Rasheed riverfront where it lapped at the Citadel walls. A glow from the torches of Fort Julien shone in the clear night sky not three miles away. Tied to the landing before them was a single two-masted *dahabiyeh* riding high in the water. Its sweeping triangular sails and oarsmen waited at the ready.

"LeGrand...go! Live true to your name: 'Gagnon'...the guard dog. You cannot fail...you *must* not fail. The future of the empire—and France—rests on your shoulders." The general moved close to LeGrand. "Your mission must meet more success than Brueys' or those worthless charts of the lost La Pérouse expedition in the Pacific."

LeGrand saluted and jumped into the *dahabiyeh*.

"LeGrand." The commander called out harshly. "The French empire is doomed to die with you if you fail."

"I will not fail you...or France." LeGrand saluted again.
"To France!"

"France's entire future and fortunes go with you...LeGrand."

"Until Brest...*mon* General. *Vive la Republic! Vive Napoleon Bonaparte!*"

LeGrand turned away as the hired *dahabiyeh* boatman unmoored the shallow-bottomed craft and slowly steered it into the dark quick currents of the Nile.

PART 1

NAPOLEON'S TREASURE

A SWIFT *&* DANCER
ADVENTURE

CHAPTER 1

PARADISE PALACE
NEW YORK CITY
21 NOVEMBER 1846

IT WAS — bluntly speaking — a stunt. S. Thomas Swift squared her shoulders as she looked at her alter ego in the bordello's gilt-framed mirror. Even with hair dyed dark. Stage makeup. And a silk hibiscus bloom behind her ear she looked more Polynesian than she felt. Her mother's sea-green Welsh eyes and auburn roots were two giveaways. She had learned to hide her slightly bookish look with a beaming smile. Even though her lithe body was decidedly not an islander's shape.

"Don't worry…honey." The island princess next to her spoke warmly. "The Paradise Palace is neither palace nor paradise. But it's a step above most of the bawdy houses in Paradise Square…and the Five Points district."

The painted face of an Irish girl appeared behind Swift in the mirror. "Of all the parlor houses I've worked off Broadway — this one beats the Dutch." The strumpet's voice paused before continuing offhandedly: "Take away the palm fronds and the fruity rum drinks…and the 'Randys' all want the same thing: the fantasy of getting a little hogmagundy with an island girl."

"It all fantasy." A Filipino girl added a fake mole to her upper lip. " 'Step right up. Enter new world...far far away. Leave your life outside red door.' "

"Welcome to your fantasy!" Aussie Kate sounded like a carnival barker as she slipped a colorful *lei* around Swift's neck then gave Swift's bare arms a squeeze. "Add more eyebrow blackener and red carmine shadow around those sea-green eyes and Missy"—she winked—"you'll be fair dinkum."

Swift reached for the blackener. Stole a glance around the room. Almost half the girls in the place were Polynesian. Asian. Or Hawaiian. The world of human trafficking and the opium trade surrounded her.

Swift knew the other girls were part of an international ring. Just exactly how that ring operated was what she had to prove. Beyond a doubt. Before she could unmask the trade in her newspaper exposé. Around the *Brooklyn Daily Eagle* she was lauded for her investigative reporting. "Stunt journalism" the other papers called it. Yet she had gone under cover to expose patent medicine clinics peddling heroin disguised as cure-alls. Sanatoriums where rich husbands discarded unwanted wives as mad. Sweatshops that worked children to death. And filed behind-the-lines dispatches from the Mexican War in Matamoros last spring. All those risks had been worth it. After three weeks under cover in the Paradise Palace Swift had almost threaded the needle. She knew that island girls. Opium. Whale oil. And some of New York's most powerful financiers were tied together. All she needed now was proof.

"Chop chop. Queen Tin'a want you." The tattooed henchman's image leered in Swift's mirror. His entire face masked by a fearsome tattoo. What the Maori of New Zealand called a bird-of-prey *moko*. His expressionless eyes made his face look as deathly savage as a vulture. The Maori terrified the other girls. And made Swift's blood jump. She followed him down a narrow hall to a thick oak door where he turned like a guard and jerked his head for Swift to pass into the presence of Queen Tin'a.

"That Tonga slut smoke too many pipes again. You take greeting duty tonight." The madam of the Paradise Palace gave Swift her marching orders. "You know drill. Greet gentlemen. Make sure they post the pony. Business before pleasure. Put money through safe slot in door behind desk. Escort randy gent to parlor. Make gentleman comfortable with island girl. Bring 'em drink. Paradise Palace not just any New York rum-hole. Make 'em happy. They wait turn to visit Hall of Paradise." Queen Tin'a was all business. "Now walk me. Show you Hall of Paradise. My masterpiece." The seductive Polynesian madam's painted lips parted slightly in a cunning smile. Swift walked in lockstep beside the island procuress.

"Learn this from Mama Samoa when we work New Orleans." Queen Tin'a clutched Swift's elbow in sharp talons as she spoke. "Took while. But you know right people in business. Anything possible." Swift's heart skipped a beat. Mama Samoa was a name she knew. And Swift assumed Mama Samoa knew her from New Orleans only a few months before in the spring. Their paths had not crossed amicably in the lead-up to the Mexican War along the Rio Grande. Did Queen Tin'a suspect? Had the madam gotten word from Mama Samoa? Was Swift's stunt about to blow up in her face?

The two women continued their trek. Up the main staircase. Past the great hall landing. Up onto a mezzanine balcony. Unexpectedly a furtive figure opened the door of a cabinet beside the railing. He shielded his face behind a bowler. Ducked past the two women. Like a roach scurrying for cover. Swift glanced down past the concealed cabinet at what looked from above like it once was a large ballroom. Standing by the rail Swift's gaze took in giant palms that reached the balcony railing where she was standing. The ceiling above her was painted a light blue with violet clouds like a Pacific sky. Part sunset. Part sunrise. A subtle aura gave the room a timeless sensation. Doves cooed from gilt cages. A rhythmic pool in the far corner splashed water like waves on a beach.

A square-walled space constructed of raffia-mat walls occupied the center of the great hall below her. The space was divided into four equal apartments plus a diamond-shaped dressing room in the center. The dressing room shared a diagonal wall with each of the four corner apartments and trimmed a corner off each of those four rooms. In each of the four shared walls a door provided access from the dressing room into each apartment. A carpeted walkway ran around the square perimeter defined by the exterior walls of the four apartments:

The walkway was tucked neatly between the great hall's interior walls and the raffia-apartments' exterior partitions.

Swift was able to observe the entire layout of the apartments — and the dressing room — from where she stood on the mezzanine balcony: There was no roof above the squared-walled space or the centralized diamond dressing room. She noted that in addition to the door set into each apartment's shared diagonal wall all four apartments had a door on each of their two exterior walls.

Queen Tin'a proudly pointed out every detail to Swift. And Swift locked them all into her investigative memory. Each of the four apartments was furnished with a washstand and a fainting couch. Wide enough for one patron…but narrow enough for the lady of the hour to take her client astride. And keep her feet on the floor.

The center dressing room contained a narrow wardrobe that held street clothes. A hat rack held evening capes. One corner was occupied by a porcelain wash basin with water pitcher and champagne bucket. An open shelf held various venereal-related preventatives. Pregnancy pessary suppositories. And douching syringes. White hand towels were stacked beside a wicker laundry basket. And — oddly — a wooden annunciator with numbered shutter-drops and four levers on one side that was mounted on one of the walls.

Swift's gaze followed as Queen Tin'a pointed to four wires connected to the cabinet. Each wire ran atop a partition to a short pole extended outward from above one of the exterior doors of each apartment…and from this support hung two colored vanes like Philadelphia railroad signals. One red. One green. Swift saw these signals were switched into position — one at a time — by whichever attendant ushered the gent to that apartment. The girl turned a lever mounted on the outside walkway wall. She pushed it up or pulled it down. Which moved the signals — a piece of painted glass — up or down like flags. A footlight fixed behind the colored disc illumined the selected signal. The action also pulled the wire. Which activated a pulley-and-pivot system. Which raised or lowered the numbered shutter drop in the cabinet on the central dressing room wall. A closed green shutter indicated an unoccupied room. A red background alerted the *femme galante* on duty which apartment would soon be next. Swift realized the levers on the sides of the annunciator box could also reverse the glass signal discs in the outside walkway.

Queen Tin'a said in a proud voice: "We only sell one thing here. More we sell…more better I do. My secret? Not sell slow—not to one Randy one time—but sell fast to many…as many as you can. All the time." She nodded confidently then confided: "Keep moving. Like merry-go-round. No let up."

Extending one tattooed hand from her Hawaiian *mu'umu'u* dress the madam pointed. "Guest escorted up main stair there to walkway. Shown to corner apartment." Queen Tin'a indicated one of the two doors on the exterior walls of the closest apartment. "Gentleman enjoy his visit. Go out there." She indicated the room's other exterior door that led out to the perimeter walkway. "Last guest never see next guest. They like that. 'Specially politicians and bankers and policemen and lawyers. Not mention stockbrokers and merchants and traders. All men same. Want screw. Then run away. Dauber between legs." Queen Tin'a chuckled loudly at her own joke.

"No beds?" Swift gestured toward the corner rooms with nothing more than a fainting couch.

"Beds?" Queen Tin'a scoffed. "Too slow. Too much clean up. Sheets only for hotel. Not for Hall of Paradise. Attendant girl greet guest. Help him…as we say…get ready. Wash him with blue carbonic. No need spread French pox in Queen Tin'a Paradise Palace. They get soon enough from competition. When he horny she go to dressing-room door and move slide other way. Slide cover in dressing room shows green." Again she pointed…and Swift only now noted painted panels in the interior doorway of each room—the door in the shared diagonal wall. Again red. And green. Just like the signals outside the exterior doors. "Walkway red tell other girls room is occupied—not to bring next Randy to room yet. Center door green tells harlot in dressing room client is ripe: time for her to do her magic." Queen Tin'a winked slyly. Unconsciously the madam rapped the band of a huge diamond ring several times against the mezzanine railing then continued: "See no ceiling? Mat walls? Mama Samoa teach me. Sound travel. Sound from other cribs help raise next client…how you say…anticipation."

"What happens then?" Swift asked innocently.

Queen Tinʻa motioned that Swift pay attention. Rapped the railing next to Swift. "Best girl on duty for that hour enter from center diamond room. When Randy done girl return to dressing room and pull lever box. Signal show green. Attendant outside enter. Take Randy into hallway. Show ʻround to saloon. Thirsty work…this happy ending. Some crackers down couple drink. Quick like. Good money. Other Jonathans smoke opium pipe afterward. All go into night…happy."

"And your best girl moves on to the next guest…" Swift said casually.

"You got idea. New girls take forever." Queen Tinʻa snorted. "Take fifteen minute to do one circuit of four room. One tell Queen Tinʻa…ʻartists can't be hurried.' Bunkum. Nonsense. Best girl take ten minute…do whole circle. Me? Queenie best time six minute twenty-seven second. Nobody come close. As I say…time is money. Faster we turn Randy…better I do. Island girl best. Exotic. Randy think they in paradise. Fantasy come true." Queen Tinʻa cackled heartily. "Only at Paradise Palace."

Queen Tinʻa led Swift past her office and private chambers then down a back stair to the reception area. Swift took her station at the welcome foyer. She checked her latte-colored powder and eyepaint in the hall mirror. Then she caught the eye of a girl named Kikilani who served the front parlors. With a stab of doubt in her stomach Swift realized what both she and Kikilani knew. This was the night. Tonight. One chance. Now or never.

Queen Tinʻa unexpectedly moved beside Swift. Too close for comfort. In her hands she held her Blue Book. Its well-turned pages contained the names of her regulars. "No riffraff. Only rich. Powerful. High-rank gents. They keep Paradise Palace in business." The madam spoke sharply as she stroked her book.

Swift realized Queen Tinʻa and the names in that Blue Book had an understanding that paved a two-way street of patronage and nonenforcement.

"I have special client tonight…." Queen Tinʻa softly whispered her confidential information. "For him last night in town. Bath. Shave. Champagne…." Her voice trailed off. "So Queenie want no disturb. No problem. No commotion. Just paradise — or Missy…your pretty face no look so good with Maori tattoo."

Swift did her best not to reveal the chill that ran down her bare arms. Dressed in island costume she wore a calf-revealing *pa'u*-wrapped skirt of *kapa* bark cloth and a sleeveless bloused shirt. Swift adjusted her *lei* necklace then fussed idly with the fragrant ferns she wore as *kup'e* bracelets and anklets. To the evening patrons she looked the vision of a fetching hula dancer.

Queen Tin'a nodded to her Maori bouncer. He gave Swift an untrusting look. Then unlocked Paradise Palace's giant front red doors.

"Let game begin!" Queen Tin'a exclaimed.

CHAPTER 2

KIKILANI SMILED as she passed by an octagonal mirror framed by a bacchanalian orgy of lusting satyrs and naked sprites. The reflection showed her lustrous black hair fastened behind one ear: Her island coiffure was punctuated by a large five-petaled blossom. Her brown eyes shown. Yet were overwhelmed by the radiance of her innocent smile. Kikilani moved silently on bare feet into the parlor. Served round after round of rum punch with pineapple slices to the stream of men primed in the front of the Paradise Palace.

Three hours later — just before midnight — Samantha Swift slipped up the back stairs unnoticed. Using a pass key Kikilani had copied Swift ducked into Queen Tin'a's outer office off the mezzanine. She listened. In the boudoir through a closed door she heard a cork pop. Seductive giggles. Bath water splashed. A masculine voice stroked the room like a double bass. Swift's eyes quickly fell on a refined *bureau à cylindre* rolltop desk that dominated the space. *My my.* Swift recognized the desk's style from spending hours in her father's library. *That French desk would be right at home in Marie Antoinette's palace.* She moved silently toward the ornate desk. Then froze. The elaborate rolltop desk with its gilded bronze mounts and expensive inlay stringing was closed. Locked tight.

Gingerly Swift tested the tamboured-slat top. It didn't budge. Next she tried a small key copied by Kikilani. Slowly the lock turned. At the same time she reached under the front panel emblazoned with the symbol of the French queen's royal cabinetmaker. There her fingertip found a push-button release. With both hands on the tambour knobs Swift gently lifted the oak curtain. The heavy rolltop opened a crack. Then raised on its track more than halfway. On a back shelf Swift spotted Queen Tin'a's Blue Book tied with a white ribbon. She slid the book out. Stuffed it into the back of her wrapped skirt. Then fluffed her blouse over the bulge. The soft leather felt cool against her moist lower back.

Swift turned back to close the desk. Too late. The heavy lid of the rolltop desk slammed closed. *Clatter! Rattle! Thump!*

"Who's there?" shouted Queen Tin'a.

A face jutted through the boudoir doors. Queen Tin'a's special client. Swift froze. Their eyes met. Swift recognized her nemesis from only months earlier during her adventures on the frontier of the Mexican War. She quickly put the side of her index finger to her lips. Pleaded for silence.

"No one here…Queenie." Her confidant turned and called over his shoulder: "One of your Nancy-boys must have knocked over a potted palm on the mezzanine. I'll look. You sit tight…Sweetness. Be right back."

The clean-shaven man was half-dressed in what remained of an elegant traveling suit. Trousers still tucked into knee-high polished boots. He pulled on an ironed but slightly damp shirt as he ushered Swift out the office door. His scent was a mixture of tobacco and Queen Tin'a's body powder.

"What the hell are you doing here?" he demanded in a hoarse whisper.

Swift flushed. The questioning tone made her jaw clench. Yet in an instant she sensed an ally.

"I'm undercover for an exposé on sex trafficking." She whispered her words angrily. "A Hawaiian girl…Kikilani…was abducted and I'm trying to save her. What are you doing here?"

"I'm shipping out for Paris tomorrow. The boys in Washington want me to check out some connection between the Rosetta Stone and the Louvre Museum."

Swift gave Dancer a questioning look. "Isn't the Rosetta Stone in the British Museum...in London?

"Is it? Crazy. But who knows? Wouldn't be the first wild-goose chase the boys sent me on." Dancer gave a shrug and a disingenuous smile that hinted to Swift there was more to the story. "Orders are orders." Dancer lifted his shoulders again. "So I stopped in for a tub and a rub on their tab."

Jack Dancer looked carefully at Samantha Swift. "Been a coon's age since I last saw you...Swift." He recognized for the first time that she was dolled out like a Polynesian princess. "You don't look bad...for a highfalutin newspaper heiress."

Swift shot back: "You don't look bad...for a common Randy." Her quick glance took in his oiled brown hair. Waxed moustache. Suntanned hands. And the galling way his polished knee-high boots added to his look of certainty. "Nice boots. You're probably in Queen Tin'a's little Blue Book. Anyway...no time to chat. I've got to find Kikilani and get out of here now."

At that moment Kikilani came around the corner of the mezzanine. "Sam...are you okay?"

Dancer in a flash realized the danger Swift was in. Kikilani too.

"You two get out of here through the Hall of Paradise. I'll wake some snakes with a ruckus. That will give you cover."

Swift eyed Dancer uncertainly as she questioned whether he would truly help. *Whose side is he on?* One look at Kikilani's pleading expression made her decision. Swift grabbed Kikilani's hand and the two ran down the back stairs. At the bottom they turned and made their way into the Hall of Paradise labyrinth.

Dancer slipped back into the office. As he reached for the ostentatious brass doorknob to return to the boudoir the door flew open. Queen Tin'a filled the doorway. Fixed him with a suspicious stare as she smoothed her disheveled hair and pulled a nightgown around her shoulders. The next moment Queen Tin'a pushed past him. She ran directly to the rolltop desk...as though having already gleaned the true cause of the earlier commotion. Threw open the lid. Madly rummaged among the papers. Then shouted incredulously: "My Blue Book! Some slut stole Blue Book! I'll kill her!" Queen Tin'a yanked the alarm cord in the office. Moments later heavy boots pounded along the hollow mezzanine floorboards as they bounded toward them. "Stop her! The hostess slut! Bring her to me!"

In the Hall of Paradise one floor below Swift and Kikilani ducked into a green-lighted room. On the couch an expectant banker quickly snuffed out his cigarette. Kikilani smiled. Swift reached outside the door and flipped the red-signal lever. A moment later one of the Maori's henchmen threw open the door. "Beat it!" the corned toffer shouted. "Two's enough. Ain't leavin' till I'm ready." The surprised henchman slammed the door and moved on.

The island twosome smiled seductively. And poured the man champagne from a bottle by the sofa as he settled back onto the couch in anticipation. Swift cooed: "Be right back...Sugar Britches." She and Kikilani ducked into the diamond room. Flipped the three other wires to drop the red vanes outside every corner room. Both slathered on *Crème Celeste* moisturizer derived from the waxy spermaceti extracted from whales. Then hastily toweled the cosmetics off their faces. Swift grabbed one of German Hilda's oversized red-silk Parisian gowns from the wardrobe. Kikilani fastened the back as Swift stuffed the Blue Book behind the front stomacher panel of the bodice. Then contained her hair under a rakish plumed hat. And jammed her feet into front-lace Balmoral boots almost too small.

Kikilani reverently placed their *leis* inside the wardrobe as an after-performance offering to the hula goddess *Laka*. Like a matador she donned a hooded evening cloak as disguise. Secured it at the neck. Pulled on a smart pair of elastic side-gusset boots. Then Swift pulled two levers and turned two opposite-corner room signals green.

From overhead a cacophony erupted. Swift and Kikilani looked up. Half hidden by the peekaboo cabinet Dancer leaned forward and swung two wooden fire-alarm rattles as hard as he could. The noise from the lead-weighted rachets raised the roof on the Paradise Palace.

The banker next door yelped. Scrambled for the exit. In an instant everyone panicked. Randys scattered...clutching their pants. Girls bolted. In and out of doors. Patrons shouted. Pandemonium! Kikilani and Swift pulled more signal levers at random. Green flags. Red flags. Just before the Maori burst into an outer room Swift and Kikilani stepped into the opposite room then closed the door behind them. The Maori raced into the center diamond room. His flat wooden *mere* club raised to strike. Only to find it empty. He pivoted and raced out the way he came.

As the warrior burst into the hallway he was engulfed by a headlong stampede of patrons. Floozy mawks. Wagtails flashing their drumsticks. Drunk lushingtons. Server girls. Eunuchs. Child attendants. All struggling to cover themselves and race to the doors. The Maori grabbed one Polynesian lass by her *lei* necklace. Flower petals flew into the air as the *lei* snapped.

"Where are they?" the Maori shouted as he tossed aside a fist of flowers.

"Who?" yelped the startled Polynesian girl. "The coppers? The fire brigades? They're everywhere!"

The Maori pushed her away. Rounded the corner and rushed into the next room. He confronted Kikilani—who now was caught like a doe in the torchlight. Swift from behind the door rounded on him with a half-full bottle of Dom Pérignon champagne. The thick bottle smashed into the Maori's head but did not break. The warrior staggered. But was not out. Kikilani wound up and busted a water pitcher over the Maori's head. His knees buckled. And he fell like a sack onto the velvet fainting couch. Swift doused him in champagne. Then took a drink for herself.

"They'll think he's corned." Kikilani giggled while sharing the champagne.

Swift flipped the signal cable for their room back to red. And the others to green. Like lemmings the ruckus raced around the Hall of Paradise. From the hallway into the rooms and back from all directions.

At that moment they looked up. Queen Tin'a stood at the mezzanine railing. "There! There!" She pointed. And screamed: "Get them!" Her voice quickly became lost in the chaos.

From the hallway hidden below the mezzanine Dancer again spun his fire rattles into the din. Two clamorous loud cranks.

The melee of the Hall of Paradise exploded into a higher state of panic.

"Let's get out of here before the chief wakes up!" Swift shouted.

"Or Queen Tin'a catches us!"

Swift tilted her feather hat toward the balcony above them. "She's already as mad as a March hare."

From all three doors of each of the four rooms other patrons tripped. Shoved. And poured past each other in every direction. Fighting to get in. To get out. To get free. Down the main and back stairs they spilled. All made haste to escape.

Into the bedlam Swift and Kikilani blended. Flowed with the mayhem. Ducked out through the back saloon into the back alley. One Randy hopped down a side alley. He held his waistband. One leg in his pants. The other leg bare as he tried drunkenly to run and dress at the same time. Both feet pounding naked on the gritty alley. Cats yowled. Dogs barked. He crashed into a cluster of coal-dust bins. Tripped over a pig and fell into a pile of filth. Someone screamed. A girl laughed madly at the sight. Wild madhouse chaos.

In the alley far to one side of the Palace's back door a closed four-wheeled brougham carriage with polished red doors waited. A stocky man with a shaved head and the thick look of a boxer stood nearby holding the horse's bridle firmly. The man was dressed in the full fig of formal butler clothes. No sooner had Kikilani and Swift scrambled into the alley but the man stepped forward. Calmly he beckoned to Kikilani. "Miss! Come this way!"

Something about his authority convinced Kikilani instantly. She sprinted toward the carriage. The man guided Kikilani to the step plate — and gestured to stay low on the floor of the carriage…unseen below the window. He tossed a blanket over Kikilani. Then eased the door handle closed behind her.

When Swift looked up she realized she was alone. She froze in place. Caught between the carriage and the back door of the Paradise Palace. Unsure of her next step.

Dancer loped through the back door. Emerged into the alley. Stopped next to Swift. Grabbed her by both shoulders.

"What are you doing?" Swift seethed.

Dancer said amusedly: "You're my alibi."

"What do you mean?"

"Slap me!" he said to Swift.

"What?"

"Slap me. *Hard.* Make it real!"

Swift walloped Dancer across the face. He reeled. A small trickle of blood rose on his lower lip.

Just then the Maori and his man stumbled out. They saw Dancer nursing his lip. Beside him Swift stood in her red gown and plumed hat. Graceful. Elegant. As if the opera had just let out. The butler came around and held an evening cape for his lady. Frozen as if in a living tableau the three looked questioningly at the Maori.

Holding his aching temples the Maori growled. "Where'd they go? Where are they?"

"Who?" Dancer feigned.

"Two Hawaiian tarts." The Maori hissed as he regained his balance.

"Could be just about any of the girls that work here." Dancer spoke in a deadpan manner.

"Look like hula girls." The tattooed warrior's words were raspy.

"Oh…those two. Nasty business." Dancer dabbed his bloody lip with a sneezer embroidered with *MM*. "Tried to stop them. One smacked me. Vicious little tarts." Dancer worked his jaw.

"Which way!" bellowed the Maori.

"They ran up the alley that way." Dancer pointed toward the street. "You can catch them. Only half a minute ahead. I saw them turn left. Toward the river."

The Maori and his henchmen took off running up the alley.

Dancer helped Swift up through the carriage's crimson open doorway. As the butler mounted the front driver's seat.

"Sorry to say good night…but I must tend to Queen Tin'a inside." Dancer bowed. "Always a pleasure…Miss Swift."

Samantha Swift massaged her hand. "The pleasure was mine."

Jack Dancer touched his eyebrow in a mock salute and closed the carriage door. The four-wheel broom clattered down the alley. Turned the opposite direction away from the river. And disappeared into the night.

CHAPTER 3

THE SECRETARY OF STATE crushed the custom receipts report in his fist. "Damn. Damn. Double damn." He shook his head. "America is going to need some serious wildcat money to pay for this war... or we're finished."

Secretary James Buchanan clasped his hands behind his back. Gazed east out his office window with his one farsighted eye. The view framed the new center hall and east wing of the Treasury Building on 15th Street. At that moment the white granite in the Greek Revival money temple appeared rose-colored in the setting sun. As he inhaled the crisp fall air the bachelor Secretary muttered: "Couldn't come at a worse time."

Buchanan's mind ticked through his impressions schooled from the first nineteen months of James K. Polk's presidency. *Yes...Polk is secretive. Yes...he's suspicious. And...yes...he's made his entire cabinet sign an oath not to seek the presidency.* Buchanan knew Polk had demanded the pledge so the Secretary would not run against Vice President Dallas — Secretary of the Treasury Walker's brother-in-law. *That retirement promise is Polk's biggest mistake to date.* Buchanan continued musing as he refreshed his glass of the Madeira wine he favored for afternoon "tea breaks." *Took the bite out of his bark with Congress. The man works day and night. He hasn't left Washington for a day in over a year and a half. But he has gotten results.*

Buchanan rubbed his left eye. Which was pitched higher in the socket than his right. *Got to give Polk credit. He has accomplished three of his four biggest objectives.* The Secretary checked off a mental list of successes. First…Polk supported his personal diplomacy to get the Oregon Treaty with Britain negotiated. That settled the boundary between the Oregon Territory and Canada. And ended the prospect of a border war in the northwest. *No more bellicose slogans like Polk's "Fifty-four Forty or Fight" balderdash. Not to mention Polk got the Senate to ratify the treaty five months ago in June.* Then Polk got a reduction of Tyler's protectionist import tariffs in July. Plus Congress gave him the Independent Treasury Act a week later. Which let the government keep its tariff money in the Treasury building and other "sub-treasuries" like Corcoran & Riggs across the street. No longer spread about in a handful of "pet" state banks. *All before that hell-fire August drove everybody out of Washington and its pestilent Foggy Bottom swamp.*

Buchanan caught a reflection in a windowpane of his silky gray hair swept up and back. The last of President Polk's objectives. And the most important. Now consumed all the cabinet's attention: the defeat of Mexico and the acquisition of the territory from Texas to California. The Secretary's wine glass stopped short of his lips as he considered that risky adventure. Before he could exhale someone knocked on the door of his second-floor corner study. The door opened quietly.

"Mr. Secretary." The aide politely cleared his throat. "Secretary of the Treasury Robert Walker and the new Senator from Texas are here to see you." He paused. "I mean Senator Houston. Sir."

The Secretary of State turned back to his desk. Straightened his high collar and white neckwear. And stole a glance at his Swiss Patek pocket watch with his nearsighted eye. "Is it teatime already?" Before the aide could respond Buchanan barked: "Never mind. Send them in."

Sam Houston was first through the door that led from the diplomatic receiving area of the Secretary's two-room suite. He wore his signature wide-brimmed hat and carried his heavy-tipped hickory cane. Made of wood from his mentor Andrew Jackson's Hermitage estate near Nashville in Tennessee. "Old Buck"—Houston drawled as he slapped Buchanan on the back—"hope this isn't too much of a surprise."

"Nothing compared to your surprise of Santa Anna at San Jacinto…Senator." Buchanan's retort was unassailable.

"That was a rip-snorter…warn't it?" Houston said. "Got the drop on the Mexicans durin' thar siesta. And concluded the whole affair in eighteen minutes. Worked out well I dare say. 'Cept for taking a bullet in my ankle."

"That's what I call a short war…even for The Raven." Buchanan paused for effect. "Maybe Zachary Taylor can duplicate the feat this time around with Santa Anna's Mexicans." He turned his head. "Good evening…Walker."

Behind Houston's large frame stood a small man. Bald. Thin. Angular. With the irritable look of someone with perpetual indigestion. Barely five feet tall. Almost a foot shorter than both Houston and Buchanan.

"Could have used Sam's boldness when Marcy chaired the Mexican Claims Commission." Treasury Secretary Walker's tone was sour. "Even for an ardent expansionist like me…right now I'll settle for keeping Zachary Taylor and Winfield Scott from stabbing each other in the back. If you have any suggestions on how to keep two generals apart— one old rooster and one preening peacock—let me know."

"Give 'em each one of my canes and have at it." Houston half joked as he tossed his hat and cane onto a chair. "Worked for me with the rascal Stanbery…that no-account Ohio congressman."

"Maybe a better place to start is a little Washington camaraderie?" The urbane Buchanan gestured toward a carefully chosen cluster of bottles on a polished mahogany table. "On my Sunday ride I collected a ten-gallon cask. Compliments of Jacob Baer's Distillery. Can I interest you gentlemen?"

"A little nerve tonic is always a good thing." Houston smiled as he poured a hefty snort of "Old J.B. Whiskey" for himself and passed two smaller glasses of the prized rye to Buchanan and Walker. As was the custom in the complex of four brick buildings that surrounded the President's Mansion on Pennsylvania Avenue business was often done informally. Especially in President Polk's inner circle. The four

undistinguished buildings with identical floor plans occupied the
corners of the executive compound. Each building painted leaden gray
with white trim housed an executive office. In clockwise order: State.
Treasury. Navy. War. Walkways connected all four to the executive
mansion in the center. On the rare occasions Polk left his office the
others knew he walked the four paths within the quadrangle.

Houston launched the topic. "Why'd yah call this here husking
bee…Buck?"

At that moment the outer door opened and in walked an aide who
handed the Secretary of State several folders. When the Secretary
turned standing in the doorway was President James Polk.

"At ease." Polk nodded as the aide flattened his back against the wall
to let the President pass.

"What now?" The President growled like a stern taskmaster
addressing his subordinates. "I've got a pile of field reports to read from
General Taylor in Monterrey. Hope it's better news than that damned
two-month ceasefire Taylor handed that Mexican General Ampudia.
A general's job is to kill the enemy…not make deals."

The President poured a small brandy for himself. "Mrs. Polk
doesn't abide spirits in the mansion….Here's to Andrew
Jackson…gentlemen. May Old Hickory rest in peace."

Walker gave a quick glance at the President. "I know high finance
can make our eyes glaze over…but hear me out." The homely
Mississippian continued as if addressing a class of children: "The
government receives payments from custom duties. And the
government issues Treasury Notes that pay interest in times of crisis —
like the Panic of 1837…and our Mexican War. These are IOUs or what
we call 'Bills of Credit.' Mostly holders use them to buy public lands.
As you also know about four months ago Congress ratified a new
schedule classification with lower import tariffs. They also allowed
importers to warehouse their goods in our ports and not pay duty until
those goods were sold to a buyer."

Polk nodded. "The New York City warehouse owners are very
happy with that arrangement."

Walker finished his J.B. Whiskey. "The upshot of these changes is
the United States Treasury's funds are the lowest they have been since
Jefferson repaid Hamilton's debts thirty years ago."

Buchanan went right to the point. "You mean the Treasury is broke?"

"Not broke...exactly." Walker equivocated: "Just temporarily short of funds. That Great Havana Hurricane last month that wreaked havoc to our ports from Florida to Maine cut receipts too."

Houston shook his head. "Just when we need powder and shot for Taylor's army in Texas."

"We can issue more Treasury Notes...but our creditors are more and more demanding to be paid in specie—in gold and silver. Flat on the barrelhead. No notes. No promises. We're not penniless. But if we want to press the war with Mexico we need gold and silver...now."

Polk paced slowly back to a long oak table covered with military reports. In an alarmed voice the President blurted out: "If we lose the war with Mexico that will endanger our westward expansion in one stroke."

Houston swirled his whiskey. "And John O'Sullivan's vision we're so proud of promoting as our *manifest destiny* will evaporate like a San Francisco fog."

Walker fidgeted nervously. "Not only America's high destiny—but it could bankrupt the United States Treasury in the bargain."

"Is there some cache...some treasury of money our spies don't know about?" Polk asked.

Secretary Walker looked at Buchanan. Then back to the President. "There is one possibility."

The President's expression demanded details.

Secretary Walker cleared his throat. "We've known of a long-rumored trove worth millions in gold and silver specie for some time now—perhaps not enough to pay off all our creditors...but it would buy time until the lower tariff schedules we're putting in place increase our revenues. There's one complication." Walker paused. "As I say... we've known about the trove for some time. But its whereabouts are currently unknown."

Polk glared at the Secretary. "What good is a treasure trove that we can't find?"

"Sir"—Houston butted in—"there is an old story about the loot. We have traced its history back to Napoleon. He stole Malta's treasures in 1798 to bankroll his Egyptian adventure. The treasure was known to have passed through Rasheed — what is now Rosetta — the site where the famous stone was discovered. The trove is worth millions in gold and silver specie — as Secretary Walker says. We just need more time to follow Napoleon's trail and track down the treasure."

Walker assured the President: "Prosperity is just around the corner...I'm convinced!"

"Like that fair trade bunkum." Buchanan snorted under his breath. "Reduce tariff rates to collect more income...Sounds like sleight-of-hand to me."

Polk's pronounced widow's peaks gave his penetrating look at Walker the gravity of an eagle's stare. "So? That treasure was never recovered...was it?"

"No. Not a trace. As far as we know...Mr. President." An unexpected gust of wind from the open windows ruffled the reports on the long oak table. Treasury Secretary Walker looked at the storm clouds forming outside the window. Then raised a sperm-oil lamp to lighten the gloom. He turned to face the president. "The trail has been cold for almost fifty years..."

President Polk's expression hardened. "If we can find Napoleon's treasure — that is...find it before some other treasure hunter finds it — then we have a prayer of a chance to supply boots and powder to Taylor's army."

Sam Houston perked up. "And whup the Mexicans."

"Plus take California to fulfill our westward expansion...." The President brooded.

Secretary Buchanan buried the finance reports under some papers and put a second lamp on the long table as the President glanced at each of his men. "Do we have any clue how to find this lost treasure of Napoleon?"

"Not exactly." The Secretary of State smiled. "But we have our best man on the trail."

"Who is that?" Polk asked.

"Known him since he saved my life in Texas." The President looked at Houston quizzically. "Darndest thing. I was riding hell-bent to catch up with a Mexican spy back in '36...'bout ten years ago now. Just after the Alamo. Didn't know I was headed into an ambush. This American scout dropped my horse with a rope snare. Damned near broke my neck. But he pulled me and my horse into the mesquite. Just then one of Santa Anna's Mexican patrols rode past. If that scout hadn't slipped my horse…I wouldn't be here today."

Buchanan chimed in: "And likely Texas wouldn't have been annexed as a state last December 29 either."

Then Walker added: "Of course my annexation platform helped. Kept Texas out of the hands of Britain too."

Polk nodded as he recalled how Walker had brought about Polk's nomination at the Democrat's convention two years before. And rounded out the ticket with Vice President Dallas—Walker's brother-in-law. The President shook his head. *The Treasury job was Walker's payback.* He always had disliked the man.

Houston raised his glass in salute. "I'd set store by that scout…gentlemen. That man is the best we've got. On my *bone fide* that scout now is on your payroll…Mr. President."

Polk nodded. "What's his code name?"

"He goes by his given name." Houston took a sip of his Old J.B. "Dancer. Jack Dancer."

For the President's benefit Walker added: "He's paid off the books like the other dozen or so agents in what we call the 'secret service fund for foreign intercourse.' No receipts. No vouchers. All beyond the nose of Congress. And paid by Treasury on your presidential certificates."

Polk set down his unfinished brandy wine. "Good. Glad we kept that fund secret from Congress last April. That blasted House wanted receipts and records for all the secret services hired by Secretary of State Daniel Webster under the last administration. I'm the only national officeholder. I'm the true representative of the people. Not those self-interested sectionalists in Congress. Nothing but harassment. Pure politics."

"That fund was created for George Washington…sir. Grown quite a bit since then. Wouldn't be very secret if we had to make public all our accounts…would it?" Walker chuckled.

"Where is this agent of ours now?" the President asked.

"New York City. Just got a telegram that he will ship out on a steam liner today for Paris."

"Paris?" Houston frowned. "Why Paris?"

Walker answered: "Our other secret service agents—that is *your* agents...sir—report there is a connection between the Louvre Museum. The Rosetta Stone. And Napoleon's treasure."

"What?" Polk said in an irritated tone.

"The trail must start somewhere." Buchanan patted his sizable paunch. "We know it's a long shot...but it's all we have."

Silence fell across the room as a distant thunderstorm rumbled out of the west.

The Secretary of Treasury confided: "As you all know...every last resource has been dedicated to winning the Mexican War. And I mean everything. We don't have a worthless bungtown copper available to finance the Mexican War...or pay interest on more Treasury Notes."

Seeds of doubt again grew in the silence.

"Don't fail us...gentlemen." The President's warning was as solemn as it was direct. "The destiny of the United States of America rests on your success."

Before any members of the President's inner circle could answer he turned and walked out.

Once again behind closed doors all three men stood near the shuttered window a short walk from the President's house. They heard the roll of thunder from the rising storm.

"How in the world can one man have a prayer of finding a treasure lost for fifty years thousands of miles from our shores?" Walker quietly shook his head.

Houston spit in the direction of the fireplace. "Dagnabbit. Any shoplifting hoister would have better odds of ransacking Young Hickory's presidential mansion over yonder than locate this treasure single-handed." His tobacco juice had not yet finished sizzling when the storm outside finally broke. Within moments dark low clouds engulfed the view over the capital.

CHAPTER 4

ROYAL HALE/HĀLAWA BAY
MOLOKAʻI/MAUI
NOVEMBER 1846

When a man is uncommon by nature — no matter half his blood be common — his mana *is to rise up to make himself chief of other chiefs.*

The ancient crone Queen Piʻilani repeated that mantra into her great-grandson's ear as he bit hard on a twist of coconut husk while lying prostrate in the queen's *hale* palace. Two royal tattoo artists were finishing the application of their ancient magic across his body.

The Queen had droned her words into the great-grandson since he was in her granddaughter's womb. But the child was grown now. A mountain of a man. That is how he came by the name Maunakili. Man mountain of the line of Kahekili.

Kahekili. The last King of Maui. Queen Piʻilani's brother...and the forefather of her two sacred granddaughters. As was the old way of the purest royal bloodlines. For brother and sister produced the most venerated offspring.

Queen Piʻilani had waited. Patiently.

More than fifty years ago — in the ʻĪao Valley — she had escaped murder and butchery. The slaughter by King Kamehameha the Great. The conqueror of all the Island Kingdoms — and the King of the new

Kingdom of Hawai'i. She had escaped. She…and her granddaughters. Then waited. Yes. Patiently.

The first of the Hawaiians had come ashore. Their skin reeked of rancid coconut oil and their strange customs. They talked in tongues. Then the traders had crowded the harbor with their fancy clothes — and their fancy money. Engineering schemes to enrich themselves. Trading trinkets for valuable tools and supplies. But in the morning they were just like all the others: Their bodies littered the sidewalks outside the brothels and the grog houses. Their clothes stunk of cider.

Yes! She had waited. Pacing the *lanai* of her house. Through the dry season. Through the rainy season. Every morning watching the sun break through storm clouds over the distant mountain peaks only to soon be hidden again. Waiting to rid Maui of all foreigners. Traders. Worst of all — the missionaries. Her eyes narrowed as she recalled the pious young man who had approached her on the street last week. He thumped his Bible and smiled through his shining American teeth. Now the skin on her fingers crinkled like thin parchment and her fingernails unfurled like talons. Queen Pi'ilani was ready to let loose revenge on the Hawaiian usurpers.

Maunakili lay prostrate on a mat-covered low platform. His great-grandmother perched by his shoulder. The two royal tattoo artists finished applying their fearsome magic. An attractive chosen girl sat on a short stool nearby: In her lap her small hands held a stained bowl filled with ink. The work had begun weeks before. As the artists worked Maunakili bit hard on the coconut twist to stifle the pain. A warrior's pain. The pain of initiation. A pain he had been raised to endure. For as *akua* the god he now received the anointment of his station. Bestowed by his pure lineage from Kahekili: the last Maui king. Through King Kahekili and his sacred sister-wife Queen Pi'ilani. Through their two granddaughters — the public and visible Keopuolani — and the hidden princess Alohalani. It was the loins of granddaughter Alohalani that produced Maunakili to be Kahekili's great grandson.

A half-body *pahupu* tattoo would soon be Maunakili's rite of passage. Right face. Right neck. Right chest. Right arm. Right leg. Right foot. The warrior cut in two. The tattoo was his *mana*. His armor. A replica of Kahekili's tattoo. The mark of a king. The black swirling *kakau* design rose across the side of his neck. Face. And head: A ferocious bird of prey took the place of the man. Every inch intended to awe enemies. To strengthen his weapon-bearing right side. Queen Pi'ilani knew also this terrifying *kakau* symbol of the god of thunder would command allegiance from all commoners.

For how many hours had the needle-sharp combs and mallet driven the black dye into his flesh? He had lost track. The burned *kukui* nut ink disguised a purple birthmark on his right inner forearm… a birthmark that looked like a three-limbed sea turtle. Afternoon came. Then darkness. Now morning light returned to the single window in the crude batten-and-thatch walls of Queen Pi'ilani's *hale* palace. A cool tidal breeze brought in the salt smell from Hālawa Bay. Outside the *royal hale* the pure water of the Hālawa Stream passed down the valley from the volcano above. Inside Maunakili's body the pain was dulled by a now-empty bottle of opium spirits. Somewhere beyond…Queen Pi'ilani's voice droned on with the story of his making.

"Originally your father—a foreigner—sailed for Europe but was blown off course and shipwrecked on Maui. He was carrying a treasure that was lost in the shipwreck. Without the treasure…he could not go back to his king empty-handed. Instead he stayed on Moloka'i under my protection. Over the years your father grew to be a demigod. He spoke Pi'ilani and Hawaiian as well as an islander. Cultivated the traditions of the small chiefs like lost brothers. He had many run-ins with Kamehameha. Whenever your father saw an opportunity for a new enterprise Kamehameha would stop him outright…or grant permission only for an exorbitant price."

She repeated the tale as a storyteller might: referring to herself in the third person. "Upon Kamehameha's death in 1819…Queen Pi'ilani saw her chance in the debauched orgy following his death. The Hawaiians justified their defilement as the rites of the triumph of life over death. Ha! Wanton sacrilege…a licentious rampage…nothing more. Queen Pi'ilani bred her secret granddaughter—Princess Alohalani—with your father. You—Maunakili—are the result of that union. That is why the people of Maui love Maunakili as their *akua*. Their god. That is why Maunakili must take back the kingdom. For the good of the people. The little people. Maunakili's people. When Maunakili is the true King of Maui—independent from Hawai'i—

we at last will be severed from the venomous poison spread by the alien missionaries. From the imported evil of the outlaw merchants. All protected by their foreign powers."

Maunakili winced as the tattooists performed their irreversible work. To give into the pain and leave the work incomplete would bring an unthinkable lifetime of shame. The pain was excruciating. And exquisite. As the ink on the razorshell stylus penetrated his body Maunakili felt the power of the *kakau* rise within him. The power rose to fill his destined *mana*. To embrace it. Then merge with the power of his great-grandfather. The great Kahekili. Maunakili felt the power swell up from deep within through the haze of pain. He knew.

"Maunakili will be king."

Queen Pi'ilani's eyes closed and her body swayed as she chanted: "It is Maunakili's destiny. Only Maunakili has the legitimate bloodlines. And — do not forget. Maunakili's father also was a great man. Though of French blood he was an *amiral*. A trusted confidant of the great French commander. Napoleon.

"Now" — she returned to her vengeful plan — "all Maunakili needs is the cannon to succeed. First Maui…then all the Sandwich Islands…to be 'King of Hawai'i.' Ever since Maunakili was a teenager he has known that was his calling."

Maunakili's giant body — when erect — stood greater than his *anana* was wide — his wingspan from fingertip to fingertip. His body welcomed the pain of the tattoo artists' work… welcomed the *mana* into his being.

"No man ever lived who crossed Maunakili." The hag queen's cadence rose as she proudly recounted her great-grandson's feats: "In boxing…he crushed men twice his skill by strength. They began to call him *Pilikua*…The Giant. Once Maunakili killed a man with his bare fists. The fool wouldn't go down. So Maunakili taught him a lesson for all to see. Do you remember? Afterward Maunakili said he enjoyed the feeling. The power. The right. It is his calling to rule. Maunakili is smarter than any man or woman. He spots a man's weakness instantly. When the second King Kamehameha died — the older brother of today's king — Maunakili killed two chiefs that wanted his *moku*." Here the old queen bent down to speak softly into Maunakili's ear. "Tied them up…tossed them from the sailing canoe.

Then Maunakili took the bones of King Kahekili and hid them. Soon all the Pi'ilani chiefs — the *ali'i* chiefs — will do as Maunakili commands. As Queen Pi'ilani has taught Maunakili" — the ancient schemer leaned back again and raised her voice — "Maunakili's right as the victor is to take their wives as his wives whenever he desires. Maunakili will use the Pi'ilani genealogy that flows in Maunakili's veins from his mother and from her grandfather — Kahekili."

The prospect of spoils was...enticing. Maunakili clenched his jaw in a forced smile.

Like a witch his great-grandmother continued in that tedious tone as geckos skittered across the floor mats. "The polluted Kingdom of Hawai'i is a hollow shell...the weakling King kisses the shoes of any foreign power that walks ashore in Honolulu. Why? First the missionaries feasted on the kingdom's souls...then the foul whalers took the Hawaiian women...Now the traders and soldiers peck at the defiled pieces. The King's false bloodline will die with him...and beat in the wind like a shredded death shroud...never sung...never remembered in the *mele* chants of storytellers. Maunakili will fill that gap...fill the *mele* with high-blood children and allow Queen Pi'ilani's own storytellers to *oli* praise on the new history...the new king...Maunakili...the rightful *ali'i nui moi* — the highest chief and king — as Maunakili will be called."

Silently the artists nodded to the comely girl sitting on the stool nearby. She dripped more black ink from the lava bowl onto their seashell needle combs. Then to the lips of each artist in turn she tipped a gourd of cool stream water.

Queen Pi'ilani poured her concluding words into the prostrate warrior's ear: "Legitimacy means opportunity...all are ready for Maunakili to play his hand: At last the way is open...The weakling King abandoned Maui when he moved the capital from Lahaina Town to Honolulu — where his foreigners and his missionaries pull his strings like the puppet he is....The door is open...Maunakili is ready. Rise up! Now is the time to take back the kingdom of Kahekili...to again become the chief of all chiefs."

The royal tattooists rolled Maunakili onto his clear left side. Queen Pi'ilani pressed her lifelong scheme. "First you will shut down Lahaina...end the debauchery of the whalers and traders. All permitted by the King in his greed…and his weakness. The King has forsaken his kingdom to foreigners—allowing them to run our islands like alien proxies."

The harpy Queen clutched a protective ivory death totem in her bony fingers. Her words drifted in and out of Maunakili's brain. The would-be king spit the saliva-soaked coconut husk from his mouth. "Every knife in the trade carves a morsel from my pig." He growled. "The weakling King is too coward to oppose me."

Nodding assent the Queen quieted Maunakili with a light touch. "When the British Captain Paulet came to Honolulu in 1843 the so-called King wet his pants." The shriveled Queen hissed. "Then his entire privy council peed on themselves like dogs…and rolled over. The King signed away the Sandwich Islands as a protectorate of England. Then within five months the word arrived from London that England didn't want any colonies—and the English frigate sailed away to Chile."

Maunakili sneered. "The King will backslide again…as sure as a dog returns to its vomit."

In that moment the artists again signaled to the attractive girl. This time she brought an open gourd of saltwater to them. The two artists each took a large ladle from the vessel then generously poured the water over Maunakili's body and gently massaged the raw skin to work out the impurities—and the inflammation—of their work. Maunakili grimaced. And stuffed the husk wad back between his teeth.

The crone repeated the end of her tale for the hundredth time. "At last…the hated Hawaiians will be deposed from Maui by the rightful Pi'ilani…and you—Maunakili—will be the Pi'ilani King…You will reign as sovereign. The Pi'ilanis will hail you as their true king because you hold the old bones of their dead king—Kahekili—and the strongest Pi'ilani bloodline is yours…true and legitimate…Your subjects will call you King Maunakili Pilikua. You will be the rightful heir to the lands of Kahekili."

Revenge. Maunakili's twisted soul matched the dark ambition of Queen Pi'ilani. *A tooth for a tooth.* Above all else…he knew he must kill the King whose father Kamehameha slaughtered his great-grandfather's people in Maui's 'Iao Valley. A golden ring—said to be worn by Kahekili—hung from his ear.

Silently like spirits the royal tattooists and maiden withdrew. Maunakili rose slowly to his full height. Mused to himself behind a veil of pain. Nothing could stop him. Soon he would be king of the Maui. Then Hawai'i. Then all the islands. *Yes!* Soon all the shipping of the Pacific would flow through his pockets. And the traffic in rum. Women. And opium. But first he must right the greatest wrong.

Maunakili tightened his right fist. Vowed to himself: *As King of the Maui...I have one true purpose: to revenge the death of my only true love—my princess—that the bastard King—her blood brother!—despoiled and drove to her death.* For that crime alone Maunakili vowed the King must die...by his own hand. And with the King's death he would restore the rightful order. Expel all foreigners. All missionaries. All traders who unlawfully stole Maui by force.

Only Maunakili can bring back the true origins and old gods of Maui...the true mana *of Maui...ruled as one kingdom...by one rightful king...Maunakili.*

CHAPTER 5

NEWSPAPER OFFICES/THE *BROOKLYN DAILY EAGLE*
BROOKLYN/NEW YORK
28 NOVEMBER 1846

THE INNER DOOR of the offices of the *Brooklyn Daily Eagle* slammed smartly. On the door's frosted glass the word *EDITOR* in gold letters quivered. Samantha Swift and Kikilani sat anxiously in the no-man's-land of the outer office. Through the open transom rose angry noises. Shouting. Cursing. Two shadowed figures ranted back and forth. Magnified behind the frosted glass.

Transfixed like the condemned Swift and Kikilani watched the angry shadows. One silhouette held a manuscript in its two separate hands. Read the story. Clucked. Whistled. Tsked. Dropped a fist of loose pages on a desk. The other figure flipped through journal pages. Forward and back. Then stiffened. Head tilted toward heaven. A bound book smacked on a desk.

"What were you thinking...Swift? Get in here!" an angry voice roared.

Swift and Kikilani entered the sanctum of the *Brooklyn Daily Eagle*. Isaac Van Anden — the *Eagle*'s publisher — exploded.

"You're barely back from the Mexican War! That stunt in Matamoros last spring could have ruined the paper! I *told* Whitman you'd be trouble! Now you're working in a brothel!" He fumed as spittle sprayed from his mouth. "Not just any bawdy house but the most infamous brothel in Five Points! Disguised as an island girl no less!" He glowered at Swift. She met his gaze steadily. Tried to appear as confident as she felt in her favorite tweed traveling jacket sporting velvet lapels.

Samantha Swift defended her stunt. She had gone undercover in early November. No one knew her face. Sex trafficking was right up there with the worst ugliness of society. "We report on violence and war. We cover the rapaciousness of Manifest Destiny. Just look at the ghastly conditions in our slums. Our prisons. Our asylums. Our factories. Not to mention the abomination of slavery!" Swift shot back.

Editor Walt Whitman intervened. His arched eyebrows gave his face an open expression enhanced by the surround of his graying whiskers trimmed in a Shenandoah chin-beard style. "She has a point...Mr. Van. And you have to admit—the ugliness of society sells papers. Swift's dispatches from the Mexican War put the *Eagle* on the map. Now this."

Swift clenched her hands. "Kikilani isn't the only girl the whalers kidnapped...."

The publisher shot Whitman a hard look.

Whitman explained: "Kikilani is a Pacific Island native. She was drugged and kidnapped from Maui. Brought here on a whaler. Sold to a brothel. She had no papers. No money. Nobody knew where she was. She contacted Swift after seeing her name in the *Eagle*." He turned to the discarded journal on his cluttered desk and tapped it with his finger as though to emphasize his words. "Kikilani told Swift her story. About the other girls. The trafficking. The opium. The rum." He settled his pale eyes on the native girl and softened his tone. "Without Kikilani's help...this exposé would never have been possible."

The publisher looked at Kikilani as if seeing her for the first time. "There were other girls? Tell me what's going on."

Swift began. "It happened almost two years ago in Maui..."

Van Anden hushed Swift with a gesture. "Let's hear this straight."

Swift reached over and touched Kikilani's arm. "It's okay. You tell your story."

Kikilani took Swift's hand and inhaled a deep breath. "In Lahaina a red-haired sailor told me my cousin Loki was aboard an American whaler in the harbor. That is how I knew to go to that ship. I wanted to talk to her. It was the first of May. I'll never forget. They gave us sweet tea...and we fell asleep."

Swift blinked. "You were drugged? And...Loki...?"

"Sweet...dear...Loki." Kikilani gave a heavy sigh. "When I woke up the ship was at sea...and Loki was gone. For all I know she's dead now."

"Then — two of you were kidnapped?"

"And who knows how many more....Without Sam's help I'd still be a prisoner." Kikilani turned her gaze to the floor. "All I want now is to go home."

Before Swift or Whitman could speak the publisher ranted again: "You're in trouble...Swift. This exposé is a powder keg. It could blow the *Eagle* right out of the water."

The publisher shook Swift's manuscript pages like a rattle. "Whitman...do you stand by this story?"

Swift squeezed Kikilani's hand in anticipation.

"Already checked most of the facts. Looks rock-solid. I say we launch Swift's piece with a multipart front-page series. Then...when the 'good ol boys' start to howl...the denial headlines should be good for weeks of follow-ups. Not to mention reactions from vengeful wives...and amused mistresses."

Publisher Van Anden pulled absently on his black beard. "Keep stirring the pot until the big bugs sour on raising a ruckus...."

"Exactly." Whitman took a stand. "I say we run with it...Mr. Van."

"Wouldn't mind taking those elitist libel mills across the river down a peg." The publisher mused to himself for a moment. "Okay. On one condition. Get Swift and this native girl out of town before the story breaks. Not for our sake. For theirs." With that pronouncement the publisher of the *Brooklyn Daily Eagle* turned and then slammed the door to his editor's office behind him. Silence filled the room.

"No question there is some serious shecoonery here." Whitman ran one hand through his self-barbered hair and with the other gestured toward two wooden chairs beside his editing desk. "But we need iron-clad proof...and some collaboration with additional sources." Swift squeezed Kikilani's hand — this time in triumph. "Even then...we can't hold this beyond a few days. Day-after-day-after tomorrow at the latest. It's too hot."

"You mean too good." Swift smiled. Her light Welsh complexion flushed. "What can we do?"

The editor looked at Samantha Swift as if his mind was lost in a meditation. Here was the heiress of one of the largest newspaper fortunes in America. The *New York Examiner*. Says she wants to prove herself. Wants to be an investigative reporter. A foreign correspondent no less. He thoughtfully looked out his window onto the gritty streets of Brooklyn and rubbed his hands together as if washing them.

"Van Anden is right…You've got to leave town now."

Swift shot back: "I can't leave New York. That's impossible. If I leave town my dear father's scheming brother will find some new way to steal my *New York Examiner* from me."

"That bastard Jacob Swift is a piece of work." The editor freely admitted the truth about one of his archrivals. "But if you don't leave the only thing you'll inherit is an early grave…like your father."

Kikilani looked pleadingly at Swift. "Only you…Sam. Only you can take me home—and get to the bottom of the traffickers that kidnapped me."

The somewhat disheveled editor interrupted: "True. Kikilani would never make it back without you…Swift. As to the smuggling network…sounds farfetched. But maybe there is a connection between trafficking girls and smuggling opium and shipping magnates…or whoever is behind this ring."

Whitman's ink-stained fingers pulled on his black neckcloth loosely tied over his high unstarched collar. Then brightened as a new idea formed. "Remember that old report twenty years ago? About that Nantucket whaler—the *Essex*—being sunk by a vengeful whale?" Whitman paused then continued as he paced: "Then three years ago the court-martial trial of the commander of the Wilkes Expedition was big news…Just last year Lieutenant Charles Wilkes published his *Narrative* about his four-year-long voyage…discovering Antarctica and touching almost every island in the Pacific?"

"He was that tyrannically harsh captain…wasn't he?" Swift said—although she was uncertain why Whitman had brought up the subject. "Didn't he flog his men constantly and wouldn't let islanders come on board ship unless fully clothed? If I recall…his so-called *Narrative* of the expedition was mostly a compilation of his officers' journals."

"Pure plagiarism. That was Wilkes." Whitman frowned at the affront.

"Made his men shave off their moustaches just because he considered moustaches to be immoral." Swift's widely read memory began recalling the details. "Got off with only one conviction out of seven charges. While his accuser — the ship's assistant surgeon: Charles Guillou — was sentenced to dismissal."

Whitman shook his head. "Rarely pays to be your superior's accuser." After a moment his gray eyes brightened. "Remember that new fiction book out last spring? *Typee*. By that first timer...what's his name?"

Swift answered with alacrity: "Melville. Herman Melville."

"That's right. First published in London in February...I believe. Then here in New York by Wiley & Putnam in March. Only eight months ago. The street can't stop buzzing about the Pacific Islands. Cannibals. Mutinies. Every copyboy and typesetting clerk is dreaming about naked nymphs coming aboard wearing nothing more than gardenia flowers in their hair." Kikilani threw Whitman a disapproving look. "Not to mention this year more whalers will land in Lahaina...Maui...than ever before. One report predicted over four hundred and sixty ships for 1846." Whitman stroked his uneven beard. "Whalers. Paradise. Trafficking. There's a story there...People always make better reading than events...."

Swift returned the conversation to the point before Whitman could rhapsodize on schooling his readers. "Look in Queen Tin'a's Blue Book. There's a list of captains and the girls they trafficked. Doesn't that prove the connection with sex trafficking and the whalers?"

The editor sank into his chair. His hand caressed the blue-leather journal. "Damn good stuff...Swift. Nothing like a madam's ledger book to stir a hornet's nest. But...as they say...we need a smoking barker...not just a bag of nails."

Kikilani looked at Swift uncertainly. Swift whispered: "Direct evidence...not everything in confusion."

Whitman opened the stolen Paradise Palace ledger. His thick rounded brows raised as he flipped beyond the list of captains to the section labeled *Expenses*. Down a column his finger ran past the charitable contributions. Past orphanages. Schools. Churches. Skipped the legal fees and fines. As Swift and Kikilani looked on he read a list of recently ordered notions. "Bubble bath salts. Body lotions. Women's preventatives. Champagne. Bathrobes. Combs. Powder. Cosmetics. Perfumes. Evening wear. Oil paintings. Brussels carpets. Red plush parlor furniture. Items of silver plate."

Kikilani looked at Whitman and smiled. "We used things like that at the Palace."

"True." Swift moved to the edge of her chair to be closer to Whitman's desk. "But none of these items were ever delivered to the Palace. They were crated and sent to a ship about to sail for the Pacific...the *Black Cloud*. That's what I got Madam Tin'a to tell me."

Whitman scratched his ear beneath his long hair. "The *Black Cloud*? It's a whaling transport — isn't it? Looks like Madam Tin'a was planning to exchange this cargo for more island 'merchandise' for her Palace. These trade goods are her barter."

The editor's attention returned to the ledger. "Swift...what does this last column mean — the one with the tally marks under the 'New Year's' header?"

He handed Queen Tin'a's Blue Book to Swift. Who showed it to Kikilani.

The island native explained the matter succinctly: "That's the number of visits since last New Year's."

The editor reached over and pointed to some marks. "Some of the entries are crossed out. What does that mean?"

Swift flipped through the pages. A look of comprehension came over her face.

"These crossed-out names are either moved...deceased...or castrated by their wives. Either way they're no longer clients."

Swift's finger stopped at one particular entry. *Jack Dancer. Rub & tub. Charleston. Profession unknown. Kentucky Straight Bourbon. Any champagne. Black Oscuro cigars. "My boots will travel."* Swift noticed there were four marks in the 'New Year's' column. And three stars.

"This one's dead. No question." Swift smiled and crossed out Dancer's entry.

Now we're even...Dancer.

She handed the ledger back to her editor. Whitman turned in

his chair. Leaned down. Shoved the book into his safe. And spun the tumbler.

He paused. "But that doesn't change the fact that your life is in danger as soon as this story hits the streets. Every Gothamite will be out for your blood. You've got to save yourself…Swift. Think of Kikilani too."

"How should we do that?" asked Swift as the inevitable began to dawn on her.

"That's your job…Swift. You're good at undercover stunts. God knows. Become a missionary or something. Do what Darwin did on the *Beagle* in 1833. Present yourself as a self-funded supernumerary on a literary expedition."

"You mean a ticketed passenger with a cover story?" Swift retorted.

"Exactly." Whitman looked at Swift. Then Kikilani. Then back to Swift. "All these trade goods Queen Tin'a assembled…the one thing they lack is a madam…a supercargo." He looked at Swift.

Swift's expression conveyed her reaction. *Not me…no way.*

Whitman persisted: "It's a natural cover. All you do is reprise your roles from the Palace."

"Too risky." Swift deflected the proposal without hesitation.

"Your pick…my dear. As soon as this story hits the streets…*bang*. Every Randy and official and policeman and two-bit thug in New York City will be gunning for you. Not much choice…Swift. At least not as I see it. Get out of here…now. It's your skin I'm worried about. But you better hurry."

Swift and Kikilani exchanged alarmed glances.

"Why?"

"The *Black Cloud* sails for Maui in three days. December 1. It's the only ship that carries passengers and freight…not like the whalers. It's the last transport ship out of New York. No more ships are scheduled this year."

"Three days? That's not enough time."

"What you don't have is time…Swift. The voyage to the Sandwich Islands takes about four and a half months. With luck you'll get there by late April. No transport can arrive at Lahaina after May."

Kikilani's face brightened with anticipation as her fingertips touched her lips.

Walt Whitman continued: "In spring the whaling fleet returns to Maui from the Sea of Japan. As soon as the whalers can reprovision and recruit…they leave."

"Where do they go?"

"They leave Maui for the summer whaling in the Arctic waters after the ice leaves up north." The editor eyed his young protégée frankly. "Swift…if what you think is true then late spring will be the height of any smuggling activity. That's when the whalers pass their catch to the transports. The transports—like *Black Cloud*—ship the oil and baleen bone back to San Francisco and New York. Every ship. All the whalers. The transports. The suppliers. All will be gone by end of May. You have only a small window—May 31st at the latest—to get this story. Miss it…and this story dies."

Swift frowned. *And I may die with it.*

Kikilani beamed at the editor who looked far older than his six years' seniority over Swift. Her face glowed in the hope of returning home.

Swift shrank slightly against the straight-back chair. Rubbed both temples. Glanced at Kikilani. Her friend radiated hope and innocence. Swift considered the alternatives. Quickly weighed the consequences. Methodically ticked off each positive and negative. Then took a long breath. And exhaled deeply. Her decision was made.

"Lahaina it is."

Whitman had the last word. "*Black Cloud*. Wharf 13. Bring anything you may need for your cover. Perfect your story. You'll need to honeyfuggle your way around those sailors for months. Whatever you do…don't let anybody blow this stunt. Your lives depend on it."

CHAPTER 6

RATTER DAWES felt the hair on his neck bristle. Before he pushed the door open to The Tombs he glanced both ways along Little Water Street. A babble of poverty rose from the overcrowded Old Brewery tenement on Cross Street a short block away. No one had followed him from Paradise Square. The scuffed door to the tavern's entryway opened. A pitch-black hallway stretched before Dawes. As he stepped into its maw the closing door cut the only glimpse of light he had moments before. In utter darkness the first mate ran his fingertips along the wall. Ahead a door with a smoked glass window led to the tavern. Before the sailor pushed through the opaque door he smiled.

The familiar stench of blood and dead flesh seeped down through the floorboards of the Sportsman's Hall from the arena above. In the echo of the hallway he could hear the terriers pitted against giant rats. The thick boards muffled the high-pitched screams of slaughter from the rat pit. Stomping boots and blood-thirsty shouts came from the liquored men betting on the contest above.

Beyond the door stretched a crude oaken bar that supported beer kegs without a glass in sight. Sailors from every nation pushed for a turn at the rubber tubes connected to the barrels. A barker shouted: "Three cents. Drink from the tube. Until you run out of breath." Clearly some denizens had perfected the art of circular breathing to maximize their turn. They lay slumped under the bar. One with his fist dangling inside a rancid spittoon. Another crumpled in a corner. Pockets turned inside out.

On a table stood a sign: *Two nickel beers. Free lunch!* Beside the sign was what appeared to be two slices of bread with a brick between. Blue-green mold had devoured the bread — if that was what it was — weeks before. Something wriggled between the two slices. Beyond the bar to the right was a dance hall. Irish girls passing as German barmaids maneuvered among the tables where paying patrons played cards. With fists full of beer steins the barmaids moved oblivious to the taunts and gropes elicited by their short skirts and red boots with tinkling bells. A polka band played off key. To the far side was a target practice range with live ammunition.

Dawes' nose detected a toxic brew being served. A pigtailed Teuton beckoned. "Want some punch…Mistah?" He'd seen the concoction before in other seaport dives. Some whiskey. Maybe hot rum. But surely cut with camphor. Benzene. And cocaine sweepings. All for only six cents a glass. The attraction wasn't the low price. It was the resulting oblivion.

Dawes pushed past the barmaid. Moved toward some booths in the back hidden from curious observers by heavy curtains. Outside one chamber three of the meanest-looking cutthroats you'd hope never to meet stood guard. As Dawes approached one meater with a neck like a bull signaled him to come over. The thug pulled back a stained green-velvet curtain. At a table illuminated by a whale-oil lamp on the wall sat an uptown gentleman. The man Dawes had been summoned to see.

"Mr. Dawes? Be seated. We have some business." The man spoke with a slight Welsh accent.

Dawes slid into the booth. He knew better than to ask for an introduction. This was not the place or the man to ask questions of.

"You are the first mate of the *Black Cloud*?"

Dawes nodded.

"You come recommended to me by my associates." The gentleman's head gave a tilt toward the green curtain.

Dawes looked at the man. He had the fixings of a highfalutin squire.

"Before this rum-hole deposits a smell on both of us...I have a proposition for you. A business proposition."

Two beers appeared on the table before the men. Dawes downed half his stein in one draft. The man's eyes never left Dawes. The second beer went untouched.

"There's a young woman on your ship. She is sailing with a native girl. They have booked for Hawai'i. Maui to be exact."

Dawes replied that he had seen their baggage come aboard.

The gentleman continued: "Let's just say...destiny suggests that a young woman like that may not complete such a voyage."

Dawes finished the beer. Wiped his mouth. "Why she sailin' on the *Black Cloud*?"

"Probably some stunt for the *Eagle* newspaper. No matter." The man with the Welsh lilt leaned forward. He reached inside his tailored overcoat and produced a significant sack of coins. He dropped it heavily on the table.

Dawes understood. He licked his lips. "A ship can be a powerful dangerous place. Passengers 'av been lost at sea afore. 'Specially young women travelin' alone."

Dawes reached for the bag of coins.

Abruptly the city gentleman's strong hand grabbed his wrist. The Welshman then continued: "If that were to happen...you could find yourself master of your own ship...Mr. Dawes. And a very very wealthy man. Very wealthy indeed." The grip relaxed.

Dawes removed a coin from the sack. Bit it hard to prove it was gold. The gentleman with the slight accent pushed the second beer toward Dawes. He saw Dawes steal a glance at the distinctive sapphire pinky ring on his left hand. The gentleman turned the band slightly with the gloved thumb and second finger of his right hand. Then retrieved the left glove from the pocket of his neatly tailored Kashmir wool overcoat and worked his fleshy ring hand into the fine kid-leather.

"You will be rich enough to have all the women you want that go with rings like that."

Dawes stuffed the coin sack into his peacoat. Kept his hand clutched around the leather pouch in the patch pocket.

"Can you rid us of this pest...Mr. Dawes?"

Dawes smiled malevolently. "They don' call me Ratter Dawes for nothin'."

"Then we have an understanding. Make it look like an accident. But don't dispose of her right away. Wait until the ship is well removed from New York. Perhaps the seas at Cape Horn would be such a place...." The gentleman laughed. "Don't want her body washing up on our shores...and questions being raised." The Welshman gave Dawes a direct look. "You'll earn my gratitude if the young woman doesn't survive the outbound journey. Ten times that bag of coins will be yours."

Dawes kept his seat as the gentleman stood up. "Should'na be a problem." The murderous-looking thug outside the booth extended his gnarled hand to hold the green curtain back for his boss. Then Dawes raised a tentative finger. "Just 'un question."

The gentleman paused beside the drawn curtain.

"What's her name?"

The man fixed Dawes with a long penetrating stare and replied with a dismissive snort.

"Samantha Swift."

As Dawes downed the last of the second beer the gentleman and his menacing entourage disappeared into the darkness.

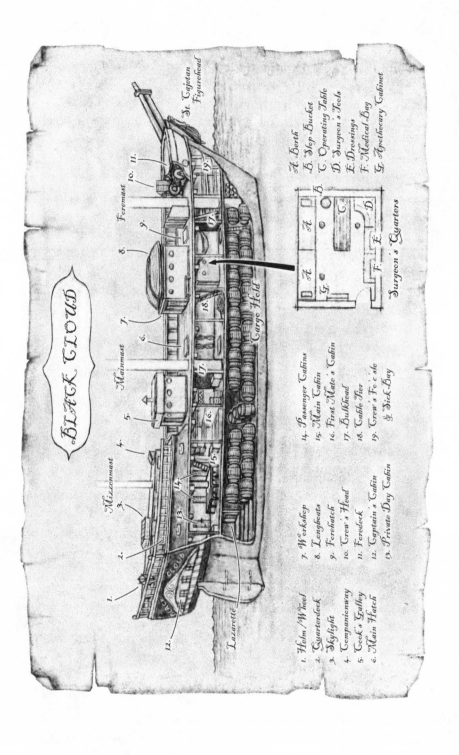

BLACK CLOUD

St. Cajetan Figurehead

Foremast 10. 11.

8. 9.

Mainmast 7.

6.

Mizzenmast

3. 4. 5.

2.

1.

12.

Lazarette

Cargo Hold

A. Berth
B. Slop Bucket
C. Operating Table
D. Surgeon's Tools
E. Dressings
F. Medical Bag
G. Apothecary Cabinet

Surgeon's Quarters

1. Helm/Wheel
2. Quarterdeck
3. Skylight
4. Companionway
5. Cook's Galley
6. Main Hatch

7. Workshop
8. Longboats
9. Forehatch
10. Crew's Head
11. Foredeck
12. Captain's Cabin
13. Private Day Cabin

14. Passenger Cabins
15. Main Cabin
16. First Mate's Cabin
17. Bulkhead
18. Cable Tier
19. Crew's Fo'c'sle
& Sick Bay

CHAPTER 7

ABOARD *BLACK CLOUD*
NORTH ATLANTIC
10 DECEMBER 1846

TO A MAN the *Black Cloud*'s veteran seamen smelled of tar and rum.
Ten days before — on a raw early-winter afternoon — the *Black Cloud*
was towed through the Hell Gate narrows. Sailed down the East River
past the South Street docks and off Sandy Hook into the open sea.
Those first days on the North Atlantic seasickness sent the landsmen
and greenhands retching at the bulwarks. "Downwind! Loo'ard
side...you lubbers!" The old shellback put a mocking edge to his shouts
at the inferior mortals hugging the rails. In the seamen's fo'c'sle Captain
Hyram Head knew folk remedies were exchanged between purges.
Some tried eating raisins or vinegar and salt while others stuck to tea
and dry biscuits. *Mal-de-mar* preventatives against the nausea and
associated vertigo and giddiness ranged from beer or a sweet caudle
drink among the sailors to brandy or champagne or frothy bottled
porter in the passenger cabin. After a bulwark dash others favored
distilled creosote tar mixed with bitter-sweet almond and apricot kernel
oil. Or forty-five drops of laudanum opium. Or simply chloroform in
water. The ship's cook offered the Captain's cabin cayenne in warm
soup or Willmott's Antalgia with its harmless ingredients.

With some irony Cook was fond of calling through the door of the head on the foc's'le deck as he sidestepped the ejecta outside: "A good purge rids the body of excess bile! You'll be much better for it afterwards!" Among the forms lying miserably in the seamen's bunks below many used an eye mask or girdle tightened around the abdomen for relief. One severely stricken young farm lad cried out when his nightmares were tormented with primordial Leviathan and tentacled Kraken in deadly combat with a multiheaded serpentine Hydra. Since setting sail Samantha Swift and Kikilani kept close to their berths—and a shared spew bucket—until the sea and their stomachs settled. With a wan smile Swift read from Darwin's 1832 letter to his father: " 'If it were not for seasickness the whole world would be sailors.' "

Unexpectedly one day the seasickness disappeared.

Now the *Black Cloud* bore southeast on course toward West Africa. The fully rigged ship romped at speed as it leaned on the winds of late fall.

For Captain Head this passage was a matter of life and death. No alternative was known. The only route to the Sandwich Islands was around the tip of South America at Cape Horn. There the driven master knew icy seas and howling winds churned the Horn into a graveyard for ships and sailors. When experienced deep-water mariners spoke in hushed tones of danger…no place held greater dread for them than Cape Horn. Not Africa's distant Cape of Good Hope or the English Channel. Not North Carolina's Cape Fear or Cape Hatteras. Not the boiling shoals of the Potato Patch approaching the Golden Gate of Alta California.

Captain Head could see it in every old salt's eyes. No other hell was worse. Tides. Currents. Winds. Rocks. All brought the full fury of the raging sea to bear on ships and men. Nowhere was life ended more often than Cape Horn. The master knew nothing must go wrong. For Captain Head had staked more than his fortune on this one last voyage.

From the aft helm the Amish-bearded Captain cast a steely gaze over the length of the *Black Cloud*'s upper weather deck. The large and bulky cargo ship was an impressive behemoth of the sea. Three-masted. Square-rigged. Triple-decked. The Captain buffed a toe of his new black boots against a black trouser leg. The thickened heels gave him added authority whenever he walked the boards. With an enigmatic smile he looked down at the peaked skylight almost close enough to touch before him: The thick glass allowed sunlight and air into his dining area below.

The master's knob-knuckled fingers worked their way through his black chin-curtain beard. He nodded with satisfaction as his steely eyes surveyed his domain from the quarterdeck to the bowsprit. Beyond the skylight rose the mizzenmast from the roof of his trunked cabin. At the quarterdeck break before the mizzenmast the covered hatch of the companionway sheltered the ladder from the officer's mess below. The companionway doors opened onto the flush main deck. On a good day Cook could reach these doors with only a few steps from the galley house. Moving toward the bow—between the mainmast and the foremast—the captain's gaze noted how the wide midship's waist allowed room for the main hatch. Then an expanded carpenter and cooper's workshop between the mainmast and the foremast. The captain nodded approvingly. *Barrels and spars are more profitable on a transport ship than tryworks to boil blubber.* Facing him in the center of the workshop's aft side the double doors had been hooked open to provide air to the companionway down to the cable tier on the tween deck below.

Farther forward—hidden from view between the workshop and the foremast—a flush lift-away cover over the booby hatch on the foredeck took up the space. Then came the crew's fo'c'sle ladder housing. Before the foremast on the fo'c'sle head the windlass held the anchor chain. Around both sides of the workshop the Captain's limited view revealed three steps at each rail leading up to the small wedge-shaped anchor deck. He frowned as the longboats stowed on the workshop roof blocked his inspection of the heavy anchor flukes secured to the buffalo rail and the shank ring secured to the cathead timber on the bow. Rising into his sight the bowsprit thrust ahead as it emerged above a carved black-robed figurehead of Saint Cajetan— patron saint of good luck and gamblers. Captain Head's pale blue eyes seemed to be fixated on the fortune to be had beyond the horizon....

From the stove-crammed galley Captain Head inhaled the smell of woodsmoke and grease. Below the Captain and before the raised quarterdeck the galley or caboose was the domain of Cook. Here he concocted meals for fifteen crew and five passengers. Salt pork and salt beef alternated. Undistinguished from salt ham and salt fish. A meager larder filled the other food groups. Flour. Corn meal. Hardtack. Occasionally accompanied by dried beans. Dried fruits. Pickled vegetables. Or desiccated potatoes. As Cook himself muttered: *Not bad with lard and salt.* Even the recently patented stove — that did not need to be put out in rough weather — did not improve Cook's repertoire.

Cook's thin-skinned pride reigned over a two-dish repertoire he prepared from his ingredients. First was *lobscouse.* Known to the Captain's men as "scouse." Derived from a Norwegian *lapskaus* stew. In Cook's hands it was little more than a hash concocted from what was once salted meat. Potatoes. And hardtack. Second was *switchel.* The same scouse hash but now disguised with molasses. Vinegar. And indeterminate spices. Which excuse for victuals was presented any given day depended on the volume of yesterday's leftovers. And how much rum Cook had consumed.

Below the helm — at the stern — the Captain's quarters boasted a velvet settee in the sitting room. Adjacent to this sitting room on the port side a day cabin was trimly outfitted: a retreat purpose-built originally for day use by a captain's wife. Vacant now but not so intended by Captain Head for the homebound voyage. At the master's order the ship's carpenter had installed a staple hasp and padlock on the outside of the cabin door to secure the space — and close off any future occupant against prying eyes.

By custom other occupations should have shared the next cabins. Cooper. Shipsmith. Carpenter. Sailmaker. But on this voyage the Captain had displaced the senior seamen from their cubicles to provide berths for paying passengers. And renamed the mess room space as the Main Cabin. The spartan berths lodged the Reverend Jedidiah and Mrs. Wise: a newly frocked young missionary and his even younger bride. Another given up to Angus Macomber: the American Consul in the Sandwich Islands. Square port holes gave these coveted cuddies welcome light and air on calm days.

At the opposite side of the master's sitting room was his stateroom. Word had long ago spread of the Captain's gimbaled bed that moved with the roll of the ship. Four compact steps led from the stateroom up to the Captain's private privy over the stern. Abutting the Main Cabin was the stateroom of First Mate Ratter Dawes; the room was furnished with a writing table to record the ship's logs. Beside the First Mate's stateroom — and forward on the starboard side — was the Captain's pantry. China. Tableware. And the Captain's select personal food and drink were secured here.

Beneath the skylight at the center of the Main Cabin — between the pantry and the other cabins — stood the Captain's dining area — dominated by a curbed mahogany table with two center bumpers that kept plates and mugs corralled. The master. His mates. And select passengers took their meals here. If they stomached eating at all. The varnished Captain's table was divided into two distinct seating groups by the great white shaft of the mizzenmast.

From the exposed helm the Captain's gaze followed the mizzenmast down from its uppermost shrouds. His mind's eye tracked the shaft to where the great spar ran through the quarterdeck between skylight and aft companionway — through the Main Cabin — down to the cargo hold deck below. There — as the Captain knew — in the noxious bilge area belowdecks all three masts were stepped on the keelson. Underneath the Captain's quarters in the cramped stern after-hold — the dingiest area of the ship — was the *lazarette*. This low chamber served as a quarantine when disease broke out. And as a brig or jail for troublemakers — or anyone Captain Head turned against. The Captain himself forbid trespass to the cargo hold on the lowest deck. As sole commercial officer only he himself — acting as both supercargo and jailor — had access.

Captain Head pulled on his black beard as his eyes focused on the quarterdeck break where the Main Cabin companionway emerged onto the main deck. The companionway's doors and flat slide-cover opened onto the caboose galley and the mainmast. The steep stairs were built against a bulkhead that separated the Captain's quarters from the midships cable tier. In that tier the crew stowed coiled racks of rigging. Spare sails. And splicing tools for repairs. Months of provisions were jammed in the cable tier alongside dock fenders. Spare blocks. And iron-banded seamen's chests. Captain Head knew the two bulkheads that sealed off the cable tier maintained the command hierarchy required of a profitable ship: No one seeking to pilfer supplies from the cable tier could pass from the stern area of the *Black Cloud* — or the crew's fo'c'sle at the bow — without first climbing to the weather deck and being seen. Similarly: No escape from the cable tier was possible without stepping on the main deck.

The master's dark eyes narrowed as he pictured the segregated space in the midship cable tier where the ship's owners had constructed the afterthought of a surgery over his objection. *Nothing but a waste of valuable cargo space.* The compulsive Captain insisted the surgeon's quarters be little more than a dark dispensary with an impromptu operating table rather than a regulation cabin. In the end he conceded the insertion of three glass prisms into the low deck overhead that begrudged a murky daylight into the sea surgeon's area below. A post the Captain thought rostered. But at the last moment in New York the sea surgeon failed to join the ship's complement due to a not uncommon shoreside dispute that ended in blood: his own.

The master clenched his jaw behind his black whaler's beard as he recalled the fully provisioned surgeon's space billeted at the last moment to two strikingly different women from Philadelphia. Where else could the Captain stow two unaccompanied skirts? The notion doubly galled him because the quarters had four bunks. Much to the annoyance of the other ranking mariners: Carpenter. Sailmaker. Shipsmith. And cooper—who was convinced he was the best barrel-man on the seas. Again they were displaced—first from the officer's mess and then from the surgeon's quarters—and now in the ultimate indignity relegated before the mast in the fo'c'sle. They seethed from being ostracized by an uncaring master to a voyage amidst the endless watches of the common seamen. And assigned berths adjacent to the curtained-off bunks of the sailor's sickbay.

Rarely seen on the deck—until now—the two women appeared on the second Sabbath at sea sporting long city dresses fashioned in the style often seen around Philadelphia society. The tar and rum sailors openly ogled both ladies: The men's indispensable tobacco pouches hovered over their clay pipes and rolling papers. The crew's youngest member—Duffy Ragsdale—was a fair-faced country boy with a mop of unruly straw for hair. Young Ragsdale envisioned in the beautiful native woman the original Eve in the Garden of Eden. She had large brown eyes. Olive skin. A radiant smile and black luxuriant locks.

In Ragsdale's captivated mind her loveliness was the ultimate of innocence...and beauty.

The native woman's traveling companion was equally captivating in the imaginations of the crew. Yet her brashness. And her confidence. Left a note of intimidation that called for caution. Distance even. Rumors circulated among the crew: The traveling companion's letter of introduction said she was last of Philadelphia. Scuttlebutt gossip had exaggerated her story as a "business" associate of Queen Tin'a of the Paradise Palace of New York. One wag tapped his clay pipe and swore the cargo the bold young woman had brought aboard was "tools of the trade." Intended as a delivery to a "related" enterprise in the Sandwich Islands.

"Working girls?" Samantha Swift scoffed as she and Kikilani mingled with the crewmen around the scuttlebutt placed on the forward anchor deck. "My word. No. No. No." A surly sailor ladled water into a tin mug and passed it to Swift. She gratefully took the offering. Eyed the cloudy liquid. "Lads"—she took a small sip and forced herself to swallow—"I dare say your imagination has run away with you." She returned the mug to the barrelhead. "No. My companion and I have never been to New York. Except to board the *Black Cloud*...of course. I'm simply chaperoning my friend on her return to her adopted missionary parents. And acting as supercargo for another acquaintance's possessions. Simply common notions. Nothing more."

The older salts made wagers. Whomever ended the voyage in Swift's favor would have first dibs among the native girls in the Islands.

Samantha Swift intended to cultivate her ruse. Especially on Sundays—which faith set aside as a day of comparative rest from the unending tedium of work. As Swift and Kikilani made their rounds they saw some crew mending or washing clothes. Or washed themselves with a cupful of precious fresh water from the rainwater butt. One old salt carved whale ivory into intricate jagging wheels used to crimp the edge of pies. Still another weather-beaten sailor etched a scrimshaw carving. Kikilani joined a small group watching an ebony-and-ivory dominoes game between two sailors. As the two matched their pips in a line of play Kikilani brought forth a pair of honed surgeon's sheers and pitched in with haircuts for the onlookers. Then provided two leathernecks with shaves in the open air using a curved bistoury knife — a scalpel found in the surgeon's tool kit that Woodall's medical guide prescribed for amputations.

One foreign seaman named Moses Smidt stood a head taller than any other crewman. And was thought to be half as smart. On this day the hulking Prussian asked Swift to explain a word he didn't understand in his Bible — a prized miniature volume he carried everywhere. Then asked Swift to read aloud a tract from a Scriptures page oft folded by his thick fingers: It lived deep in his seaman's jacket.

On this Sabbath another homesick sailor approached Swift. He sat down beside her on the bench in the lee of the workshop facing the main hatch — then requested Swift write a letter home to his three brothers. "How shall I address it?" Swift asked. The young sailor gave this some thought as he tried unsuccessfully to smooth the wet disaster of his self-rolled cigarette. "Address it: To those who stay at home."

Swift paused before dipping her pen nib into the ink bottle held in her writing box beside her. A pang of nostalgia crossed her features as she remembered what seemed to be faraway days in Beaumaris — her family's Bleeker Street brownstone. Then the correspondent brightened. *As father said…everything is copy.*

One man — a harpooner with forearms of steel — stood out among the seamen. Swift gave him a sidelong glance. His powerful chest rose almost straight to his head without as much as a howdy-do for a neck. His pate glistened. Shaved clean. A secret to the other crewmen. Until this day. When in a rare moment he removed his knit cap. Once every six-hour watch this seaman held a spool of rope above his head while standing at the taffrail beside the helm on the quarterdeck at the *Black Cloud*'s stern. Then cast into the following sea a knotted long line with a triangular chip-log board fastened at the end.

Swift moved closer along the starboard rail and watched as the mariner's knotted line played out. Beside him young Duffy Ragsdale held a thirty-second sandglass ready to signal the moment when time expired. As the line lengthened the bald mariner counted the knots as they passed between his fingers. When the last sand grain dropped Ragsdale called out: "Mark!" At that same moment the harpooner wrenched the spool to a stop. Then turned to shout toward the waiting first mate. "Seven knots…sir!" The Jack-tar hauled the line in hand-over-hand and the recruit respooled it. Ready to heave the chip-log again for the next recording.

Swift stepped closer to the harpooner. "Does this mark our speed...sir?"

"Aye...ma'am. Without landmarks 'tis the only way to gauge our speed. Only way to navigate by dead reckoning." His voice gave Swift a comfort she had not felt since her frantic last-minute departure from New York.

"As you may know...there is one knot on the line every eight fathoms...or forty-eight feet." The harpooner demonstrated as the unworldly Ragsdale listened intently. "The number of knots played out in thirty seconds is the number of nautical miles per hour the ship is moving. That's why seamen call it 'knots.' Mate Dawes keeps the log. Only way to know if our arrival will be on time...or tardy."

As Ragsdale stowed the log line spool — and the mariner and Swift moved closer to the quarterdeck ladderway — the harpooner directed more words toward Swift. "Good that you've gotten your sea legs...Missy. You'll need 'em when we challenge the Horn." The harpooner gave Swift a searching look. "There hundred-knot winds and sixty-foot seas 'ave sent many a sea dog to the cold deeps of Cape Stiff. They's the reason behind that name." The harpooner shook his head. Then in a respectful whisper he made sure the apprentice seaman heard as well. "We all must be ready to fight the fury of Cape Horn."

Swift paused and looked at the seaman carefully. "Have we met? Perhaps in New York...Were you a butler by chance?"

"Not to my knowledge...ma'am. 'Spect a bloke like me would remember an important woman such as yourself." The harpooner touched his woolen cap politely.

At that moment Swift noticed young Duffy Ragsdale lurched past them toward the quarterdeck steps and hurried toward the gunwale. The morning switchel was apparently not sitting well. Abruptly Swift said: "Excuse me...sir." And hurried off to direct the young greenie to the opposite downwind leeward rail.

CHAPTER 8

JACK DANCER looked like a mouse in a maze. Without the cheese. A murmur of French nuns rustled past Dancer in the Cour Carrée courtyard. Then he stepped inside the largest museum in the world. The Louvre. The boys in Washington had asked him to find a connection between La Valette's fancy dagger and Napoleon's treasure. Only one problem: The prospect of finding any particular object in the Louvre was so preposterous it would make a stuffed bird laugh. Dancer shook his head. What kind of treasure hunt was this? He checked the small *Carte de Musée*. He wandered into the Egyptian Antiquities Department on the second level. What the French called the first floor. Coffins. Tombs. Chairs. A cat-headed woman sculpture. Caskets for mummies. Sacred bulls. All arranged in chronological order by the first and late curator Jean François Champollion. Dancer quickened his step as he passed the colossal statue of a seated King Ramesses II. From behind the King's mashed nose a smug glare seemed to follow Dancer's every step.

Dancer climbed the stairs at the end of the Colonnade wing. What was it about fortresses that become palaces that turn into museums?

At the third level he glimpsed the River Seine below. Then he looked down the hallway. *Through there...then left? Or is it right?* None of the rooms had numbers. The American turned left into a labyrinth — leaving behind the inner halls of the museum of Charles X. He entered the outer wing of the Campana Gallery. Turned right toward what he hoped was the *Objets d'Art* section. Beneath his feet the seldom trod parquet floor squeaked. Dancer wandered into another room of armor and goblets. There he stopped short. Bathed in the fading twilight from the floor-to-ceiling south window — was what Dancer hoped to find in Paris. The sword of Valette.

He moved closer. The sword's inlaid grip was small. Room only for perhaps three of Dancer's fingers. The ornate cross-guard delicate. Clearly ceremonial. The exhibit card explained:

> *This gift was in thanks from the Spanish king to Grand Master Jean de Valette of Malta for breaking the Great Siege to his island by the Ottoman Turks in 1565. The defeat of Suleiman the Magnificent was the salvation of Christendom in Europe.*

Dancer considered the words. Suleiman's defeat had indeed saved Christendom in Europe. *And* — Dancer reminded himself — *kept the hordes from invading Spain next.*

Dancer stood in front of the case and looked at it for a long time.

Beside the fragile sword stood an empty bracket. Designed to cradle a small object. Dancer eyed the empty brace uncertainly. *Where is Napoleon's dagger? The lucky charm worn by the Emperor himself?* Scanning the museum label was again unhelpful. Napoleon had ransacked the sword and dagger — along with a fortune in coins. Jewels. And other precious objects — from Malta in 1798 to finance his invasion of Egypt. Napoleon then sent the sword to France...but kept the dagger. And the treasure. When Napoleon died in 1825 the dagger was inherited by his son. He donated the dagger to the Louvre in 1840.

Dancer looked again at the empty bracket. *So where is the dagger now?*

"More important...what happened to the rest of Napoleon's treasure?" Dancer asked the display plaque in irritation. "No dagger. No treasure. Now what?" Dancer circled the glass case. The enigma of the missing dagger's meaning remained a mystery.

From a distance a chime echoed throughout the museum. Closing time.

Dancer made his way outside. Crossed the square-sided Cour Carrée. As he passed under the gold-hued Parisian limestone of the Marengo archways on the north side he paused. Bought roasted chestnuts from a tattered vendor. He juggled the hot nuts from glove to glove as he walked. Out into a wet Place de l'Oratoire. Peeled one chestnut with his teeth. Strolled forward along Rue du Coq. Moved a short block north to the east-west through street. Before him the Rue Saint Honoré ran past the Royal Palace. Two hundred yards to his left. Immediately Dancer almost gagged. The reek of horse dung and city filth assaulted him. He cupped his hand over his mouth. Two chestnuts dropped from his hand and disappeared in the gutter ooze. *Gay Paree. Mostly gay horse shit if you ask me.* The aroma of hot chestnuts diluted the stench. For Dancer the early-December drizzle had turned Paris cold. Wet. A busted inside straight. Dancer hiked his wool collar closer to his ears. The River Seine slid darkly by two blocks to his back. He stepped to the curb of the Rue Saint Honoré.

Dancer heard the iron wheels on cobblestones echo off nearby building walls. He turned to his left. A four-horse Hirondelle stagecoach pounded down the wet street. From the team's flared nostrils steam clouds blew like a *chemin de fer* engine. Luggage stacked on top. Driver hunched low in his elevated seat. Behind the splatter board. Blinded by rain he had let the team go. End of the last city-center run that day. To his left Dancer became aware of a hurrying figure. A woman. Her cape hood pulled forward against the rain hid her face. She stepped into the street. Unsuspecting. The oversized coach was bearing down on her from not ten yards away.

Without thinking Dancer jumped into the street. His expedition boots skidded in the gutter muck. Snatched the woman in his arms. His momentum lifted her off her feet. A surprised yelp left her lips. Onward charged the thundering vehicle. With all the leg strength he could muster Dancer pushed hard. His boots slipped on the slick cobbles. In a last straining effort he leaped toward the banquette. Braced for impact. Mud splattered his backside as the heavy stagecoach thundered past — the smaller leading wheel just inches from Dancer's boot.

Still in one piece Dancer settled the woman on the paved sidewalk.

Alarm showed in her now mud-spattered face. Her eyes large. She stared at the coach receding into the gloom. Then stared into the face of this stranger. Looking at her Dancer realized she was exceptionally tall. Yet slender. Roughly his age. Early thirties. He had lifted her without effort.

"*Monsieur.*" Slightly breathless she folded back her hood. "*Monsieur…merci. Merci beaucoup.*"

Dancer replied in his street French. "*De rien…Mademoiselle.*"

"*Américain?*" she queried.

"*Coupable.*" Dancer smiled. "Guilty. Are you all right?"

"*Oui.* Thanks to you." She gathered herself. In the dreary dusk her flushed complexion glowed above the cowl of her cape. Smudges of mud on her chin. Nose. Cheeks.

"Here." Dancer offered his kerchief.

She dampened the cloth on her wet cheek and cleaned her strong chin and nose. She offered his soiled handkerchief in return.

Dancer touched the brim of his hat. "Keep it. Pleasure was mine."

In a voice stronger than she felt she asked in lightly accented English: "How can I repay you?"

Dancer replied simply. "I'm looking for an address." He took out a scrap of paper. "Twenty-seven Rue de Grenelle. Do you know it?"

Her blue eyes blinked. Widened slightly.

Dancer read from the paper. "At the intersection of Rue de Grenelle and — "

"Rue Coquillere." She had finished the sentence for him.

Dancer squinted into the darkening dusk. "Is that far?"

"*Non…Monsieur…*not far."

Water drops fell from Dancer's hat brim. He looked puzzled.

"I know it well. That is my father's apartment."

"Monsieur Jacques Joseph Champollion? Keeper of manuscripts at the Bibliothèque Nationale?"

"*Oui.* The national library here in Paris. I am his daughter…and assistant…Zoë Champollion." She spoke with a sense of pride.

"Zoë. What a lovely name. From the Greek…is it not?" Dancer said.

Zoë smiled. "That's what happens when your father is a scholar of languages."

Dancer repeated the name: "Zoë. It means 'life'...I believe."

"I was named after my mother." Zoë gave a slight nod that seemed to say she accepted this American as one to be trusted. "Come...I will take you."

They crossed the Rue Saint Honoré. This time without incident. Then bore right on Rue de Grenelle. Passed Pelican Ally on the left as their footfalls made little sound in the city silence. Passed the covered arcade and shimmering gilt of the Galerie Véro-Dodat. Zoë led single file on the narrow sidewalk. Little air or light reached the old medieval street. Passed a closed *boulangerie* and *charcuterie*. Passed a *bistro* and print shop and tailor. All shuttered now after hours. Before they reached the first intersection at Rue Coquillere Zoë stopped abruptly at a large double door wide enough for a carriage. She turned the lever handle. Then stepped through a narrow pedestrian door. Dancer ducked and followed her into a dim passage. The passage opened onto a small courtyard. Barely large enough to turn a one-horse *cabriolet*.

Zoë led them to a staircase labeled Stairway B. Inside she ran a hand up the iron railing as she began to ascend the stairs that spiraled up into the five-floor building like a serpent. Dancer admired the slim figure before him. As she rounded the second landing a heavyset man bounded down the stairs. His bulk slammed Zoë against the railing. Tail over teakettle she lost her balance. Her body toppled backward over the stairwell chasm. Two floors below. Dancer lunged. Grabbed whatever he could in a bear hug. His head buried in a cloud of warm petticoats and perfume. Zoë's knees reflexively clamped around Dancer's ears. Her weight yanked him forward. Bent almost double Dancer jammed one knee under the railing. His trailing leg shot backward as a counterbalance.

At that moment a second man rattled down the wooden steps. Dancer's leg tripped him with the heel of his boot. The man somersaulted down a flight of steps. At the bottom his bulk bounced off the curved wall. He ricocheted down another flight. With a hollow smack he landed on his face. Slid across the foyer tile. Until his head collided with a protruding pillar. A brown leather notebook shot from his hand. Then spun to a stop on the foyer tile.

In a dialect unfamiliar to Dancer the first man shouted: "Get up! Get up! You stupid son of a pig's whore!" The big man stooped.

Grabbed the notebook at his feet. And bolted for the courtyard. The second man held his head. Rose up. Scrambled after him. Out into the passage.

Zoë locked her fingers onto the stairwell railing. Together she and Dancer struggled to withdraw her from the deadly drop to the foyer below. Zoë unlocked her knees from around Dancer's head. Dancer eased her down to her feet. Admired the strength in her supple body. She blushed. Recovered.

Zoë pointed down to the entrance foyer. "Thieves!" she shouted. "That notebook...it is my father's!" Dancer raced down to the tiled entry. Sprinted across the courtyard. Through the passage. Onto the street outside. Dancer shot a glance left. Right. Then exhaled regretfully. The thieves had evaporated into the night. *Too many escape routes.*

Dancer returned to the entry. Seeing him empty-handed Zoë ran up the stairs. Dancer galloped up the stairs after her. Two steps at a time.

At the third landing an apartment door was ajar to the left.

"Pappa!" Zoë called.

They hurried inside. Papers everywhere. Books scattered across the floor. Shelves empty. Manuscripts thrown helter-skelter like confetti. Chairs toppled. A *papier-mâché* terrestrial globe spun crazily in the middle of the hardwood floor. Then came a groan from the next room.

Zoë raced into the study. There on the oriental carpet a man lay splayed out on the floor. He struggled to rise on one elbow. Fell back. Blood coursed from his temple. "Pappa!" Zoë cried again in anguish. Quickly she cradled him in her arms. Withdrew Dancer's damp kerchief from her sleeve. And pressed it firmly to her father's wound.

Dancer found towels and a water cistern in a tiny kitchen alcove. Returned with dry and wet towels — and a brandy bottle. Zoë cleaned the wound and tore towel strips to tie into a rudimentary bandage. Now propped up in his favorite overstuffed armchair M. Champollion of Figeac blinked groggily. He sipped the welcome brandy.

"Father...this is my American friend. He saved me on the Rue Saint Honoré...and just now in the stairwell. He has come to Paris in search of you."

Dancer nodded. "My name is Dancer…sir. Jack Dancer. Gather yourself. No need to talk."

Jacques Joseph Champollion was more shaken than hurt. The blood did not soak through the bandage. And he revived steadily. Zoë served them all hot tea mixed with honey milk and brandy.

"Should we notify the police?" Dancer asked.

"*Non.* The *garde municipale* police are no friend of the people. And the *garde nationale* are mostly unarmed bourgeoise." Champollion shook his head. "*Non.* This is our own business."

Zoë sighed. "What happened…Pappa?"

Champollion took a deep breath and explained. "They were at the door. I thought it may be you…Zoë. Returning from the museum…searching for your key. When I opened the door…they rushed inside and grabbed me. At first I thought they were simple robbers. Since the potato blight last year and the failure of the wheat harvest this year there have been frequent tax and food riots."

Dancer nodded. "The Rouen newspaper was full of the riots near the Faubourg Saint-Antoine in the fall over the high cost of bread."

Zoë adjusted a blanket over her father's legs. "Begging and theft are common in Paris streets. Especially among the poor in the quartier des Arcis between the Louvre and the Hotel de Ville—or as you say City Hall."

The elder Champollion grimaced as he felt the lump on his head. "To my surprise they demanded my notebook. 'Why?' I asked them. 'Just give it to us…old man!' they shouted. One held me while the other turned the apartment upside down. My eyes must have shown them where I kept it. They grabbed my notebook. Then the leader hit me with my miniature Luxor-obelisk. The next I remember you arrived."

"Did you recognize them?" Zoë asked.

"*Non.* They were strangers to me. Foreigners."

"What is this notebook they were after?" Dancer asked. "Why steal just that?"

Zoë reached across. Gently touched her father's shoulder. And gave him an imploring look.

"Do you think it has to do with your Malta research?"

"*Oui.* I'm sure of it." Champollion drained the last settling mouthful of hot milky brandy. "The Malta coins are the key."

CHAPTER 9

DANCER MOVED TO THE EDGE of the worn dining chair and leaned forward. His brows knit to take in every word.

Champollion began: "Let me explain. You know Napoleon ransacked Malta in 1798 on his way to invade Egypt?"

"Yes." Dancer nodded. "I learned that today at the Louvre. The Sword of Valette."

The curator opened his palms as if reading from a textbook. "With that treasure Napoleon invaded Egypt."

Dancer tilted his head with a quizzical look. "Where the Nile empties into the Mediterranean — near Rasheed." Zoë resettled the globe on its stand and pointed to the location. "He ordered a small garrison to rebuild Fort Julien closer to the sea. And he changed the Arabic name of the city — as he often did. Rasheed was to be Rosetta in French."

Zoë's father balanced his brandy on the upholstered arm of his chair. "At Fort Julien a French lieutenant discovered a curious stone tablet. When the British drove the French out of Egypt that stone tablet was sent to London. It eventually went on display at the British

Museum. It's called the Rosetta Stone…a large…curious stone. On it a
text was chiseled in three languages: Ancient Greek. Ancient Egyptian
hieroglyphs. And Demotic — the common script of Egypt at that time.
Although the three scripts described the same decree they were not
direct translations. No one could decipher the hieroglyphs. Which
made it a greater mystery."

Zoë couldn't restrain her enthusiasm. "Copies of the script were
distributed to scholars and museums throughout Europe."

"But no one could break the code. Is that right?" Dancer recalled.

"*Exactement.* Not for twenty years. Until my younger brother —
Jean-François Champollion — did it in 1822." The older Champollion
lifted his chin with a touch of French pride as he drew himself straighter
in his chair. "Single-handedly Jean-Francois Champollion broke the
silence of the ancient world…and created the science of Egyptology."
The curator's voice cracked slightly.

Zoë continued the story as she stood with one hand on the back of
her father's reading chair. "But in 1832 my uncle died before he could
publish his hieroglyph grammar. Father and I — and my brother —
worked for years. We gave order to uncle's papers and published his
great works in 1840 and 1843. Today an English colleague of my
uncle — an orientalist named Edward William Lane — continues the
work in Cairo. His sister — Sophia Lane Poole — is a very interesting
woman. Very independent. Two years ago she published a book about
women's roles in segregated Egypt. *The Englishwoman in Egypt.* If you're
ever in Cairo" — she gazed at Dancer warmly — "give Monsieur Lane
and Madam Poole our warmest greetings."

Dancer nodded. "That's an incredible story. But how does that
connect with the two thugs tonight?"

Champollion resumed the tale: "While my brother focused on
deciphering the ancient Rosetta Stone we uncovered a trove of
documents. Some ancient. Some modern. All about Napoleon's
Malta treasure."

Zoë measured a double spoonful of laudanum painkiller into
her father's cup. "Being curator of manuscripts at the National
Library helped."

Champollion took a sip then continued: "We collected every
papyrus document and letter and reference that seemed to refer to

Napoleon's Malta treasure. Over the years I transcribed those into a leather-bound notebook. It was that treasure notebook that was stolen tonight." Champollion's attention drifted.

Zoë picked up the thread. "A scrap here. A reference there. Occasionally a symbol or chart or *graphique*. Anything we came across Father added to the notebook. It was a curiosity at first; gradually it became more like…how do you say…?"

"An obsession?" Dancer suggested.

"*Oui.*" Champollion brightened. "We have the same word… *la passion.*"

Dancer asked the key question. "Is your notebook valuable?"

Champollion glanced at Zoë.

"Not to an amateur." Zoë put a gentle hand on her father's shoulder. "The entries were incoherent. Disjointed. Notes over time. They were difficult to make sense from…even for me. For years these random objects and documents and minutiae fed my father's notebook. Until one day several coins came to the library anonymously. How do you say? A gift from the gods?"

Champollion corrected his daughter: "Three coins…to be precise."

"Coins?" Dancer looked at Champollion and Zoë. The two scholars in turn looked at each other.

Zoë nodded to her father as if to give permission. "Tell him…Pappa. Monsieur Dancer saved my life this evening…twice. I believe we can trust him."

"Three coins. All different. From different places. Two gold. One silver. We were told they were confiscated from an Arab slaver on the East Africa coast. Typically when the French authorities caught slavers at sea…the slaves were released on the mainland—and the slavers imprisoned on Madagascar. Any loot or treasure in the cargo was returned to Paris."

Zoë shrugged. "No one cared. So the coins were passed along as an afterthought by the Louvre's Antiquities section to my father for his safekeeping."

"What more can you tell me about the coins?" Dancer asked.

"At first we thought they were simply coins from the Indian Ocean trade. No one knew exactly. Then we realized how the coins were connected…they all came from the treasury at Malta."

"The same treasury Napoleon looted in the Mediterranean?"

"Yes." Champollion rubbed his throbbing head.

Zoë opened a locked drawer hidden in the study shelves. She withdrew a small coin collector's envelope. "These are the three coins."

Zoë handed the stiff envelope with three slots to protect the coins to Dancer. "One Greek. One Assyrian. One Lebanese." She repeated her father's earlier statement: "All from different places. All from different times. Given the dates and origins…the only place they could have been collected was at the treasury in Malta."

Champollion gave a weak gesture toward the envelope. "For over two hundred years the Knights of St. John used their strategic location on Malta to dominate the Mediterranean. From trade. Conquest. Tribute…the Knights amassed a huge treasury — until it was looted by Napoleon in 1798. It's a mystery how these three coins all came into the possession of the same East African slaver."

"Did any other coins from the Malta treasury ever surface?"

"*Oui.* A few. We recorded them all in my research notebook." Champollion shrugged. "Without the notebook I cannot say. What I do know is these three coins came from the slave coast of East Africa. The others? Just rumors. You must find the notebook to find an answer."

"Can I keep them?" Dancer requested.

"Yes. You may keep them. They are of no use to us without the notebook."

Dancer reached down and inserted the collector's envelope in a secret pouch inside his right expedition boot. Then paused.

"Before I leave you. Tell me. Who were those two men?"

"Thieves?" Champollion guessed.

"The one I tripped was European. The bootblack on his skin smeared off when he hit the wall. And his boots were European."

"The first?" asked Champollion.

Zoë replied: "Arab. Definitely. When that first figure yelled at his companion he used an obscene expression." Zoë blushed. She hesitated to say the words. "We heard it used by the camel drivers in Egypt. And I've seen it in military reports from the African coast. Is it important?"

Champollion smiled and repeated the Arabic phrase. " 'You son of a pig's whore.'" He turned to Dancer. "Zoë is correct. It's the greatest insult an Arab can make."

"Probably lost on that European ratbag." Dancer paused. "Anything more?"

Champollion nodded. "The words are Arabic. But the dialect is Omani….It is an obscene curse peculiar to the Arabic spoken in Oman."

Dancer chewed on that fact.

Champollion added a key to the puzzle. "The Omani — and their pirate henchmen — run the slave trade from Yemen to Mozambique."

"Along the east coast of Africa?" Dancer asked.

"*Mais oui.* The Sultan of Zanzibar controls the slave trade now from Stone Town…the capital of Zanzibar."

Dancer tapped the pouch in his expedition boots. *Looks like the trail leads to East Africa. So much for Gay Paree.*

Champollion pressed trembling fingertips to his temples. Dancer and Zoë could see Champollion was fading. "*Je regrette…*I cannot be of more assistance."

Zoë stood up. "Thank you…Jack Dancer. Thank you for saving my father — and me." She gave Dancer three meaningful kisses. Slowly. On alternating cheeks. In the Parisian way.

"Would you do one thing for me…Zoë?" Dancer asked.

"*Certainement.* It would be my pleasure to return to you the favor." Zoë touched his hand.

"Could you guide me to lodging for the night? That inn where I've slept for three nights wouldn't even pass as a manger at Christmas."

Zoë gave Dancer a perplexed look.

"It's a dump. Tomorrow I hit out at reveille for Marseille."

Zoë smiled. "It will be my pleasure. I know just the place."

Dancer helped Zoë support her father as they trundled the professor off to bed. When they returned to the foyer Zoë put her fingertips to Dancer's lips. "Shhhhh."

She held the dancing light of a chamberstick candle holder in one hand and in the other used her untied *fichu* scarf to lead Dancer up a narrow steep staircase to her cozy sleeping room in the attic. Under the low garret roof a simple chair occupied a dormer nook beside a bed covered by a thick eiderdown *duvet*. In the candlelight Zoë's eyes sparkled playfully as she turned Dancer to sit on the chair and coaxed off his jacket. Expedition boots. And trousers. While Dancer pulled off his shirt—Zoë's clothes dropped to the floor. In one motion she slipped under the white cotton cover and held open the comforter. Wearing nothing besides her sheer rose-pink *fichu* neckerchief... Dancer joined her.

The next morning dawn reveille came and went.

CHAPTER **10**

SURGEON'S QUARTERS/*BLACK CLOUD*
CAPE VERDE ISLANDS/OFF WEST AFRICA
16 DECEMBER 1846

EVERY HARD-BITTEN SEAMAN knew the way of ships. Not so the naïve farm lads set on world adventure. Nor the unwary immigrants or waterfront lowlifes kidnapped into service at sea. All were easy victims for the blood trade of the crimps and body mongers back in New York's Battery. A trade well paid by unscrupulous sea captains like Hyram Head desperate for crew. The fresh-faced Duffy Ragsdale soon found himself an innocent greenhand set amongst a crew of sea stiffs and old salts. In short order the *Black Cloud's* full complement had a harsh reality kicked into them by Mate Ratter Dawes — under the approving eye of Captain Head.

Dawes hammered home his lessons watch after watch. The *Black Cloud* had almost thirty miles of rigging and as many as five hundred separate lines. Everyone on board had to "know the ropes." That included name and exact position of every line. Even on the darkest night. On the roughest sea. The daily routine was hard. Every man mastered a range of skills. Each needed to keep the *Black Cloud* seaworthy. Their lives depended on it. One loose knot. One broken foot rope…From the top gallant almost one hundred feet above the sea a mistake like that could mean the death of a half-dozen men. Yet injuries were inevitable.

"If a man can stand…'e can work." Such did Mate Dawes often bellow as his cure-all. Or else — as he knew…*I'll 'av to answer to the Cap'n.*

Samantha Swift recalled a saying her mother oft repeated: *Every unopened book is a challenge that contains further challenges.* Swift hefted a well-turned medical book in her hands as she moved under the meager cones of light emerging from the three hexagonal prisms set in the deck above their surgeon's quarters. Neither Swift nor Kikilani could have imagined how the medical guide they discovered would change their lives.

Swift sat on the three-legged examining stool inside the open door of their cramped space. John Woodall's *The Surgeon's Mate* rested in her lap. She gave a tender look at Kikilani on the far side of the cuddy's solid oak table. Seated on an empty cable spool her cabinmate dried the wicks of two tallow candles with an absorbent lint. After last night's rain they prevailed on the sometimes-sober carpenter with his caulking mallet to pound oakum — hemp fiber soaked in pine tar — between the deck boards over their berths to reduce the drippage. For his efforts Kikilani exchanged a dollop of laudanum opiate to soothe the veteran seafarer's aching shoulders.

At that moment men's crude voices penetrated through the bulkhead divider from the crew's forecastle to the surgeon's quarters.

"Water I can work with…air and noise is beyond my control." The ship's woodworker paused. "Your door is directly beside the cargo hold grate where the bilge air is foulest…and here forward where the rocking is greatest. Best keep your tools wrapped in oilcloth. That bilge water will tarnish gold and silver in an instant."

The woodworker pointed toward what looked like a woodpecker hole in a support timber above the surgery's center table. Then dug at an earwax plug with his little fingernail. "Drive a sticking iron into these notches. Shipsmith made 'em to have moveable candle holders on hand. The iron's spike'll drive right into the wood. Least that's what I do when I have to saw off a leg…or an arm. That's where the bucket goes that collects my work." He pointed to the fold-down arms attached to the bulkhead. "That is…'til it's time to toss 'em overboard." A wicked smile crossed his sunburnt lips before he touched his temple and stepped out of the cabin. Four stiff strides…and he pulled himself up the main-deck stairway. Swift closed the door behind him and slid the bar bolt into place.

As Swift often did in duress she had turned to reading the book of knowledge after the carpenter left. Since New York she devoured *The Surgeon's Mate* cover to cover: The life-saving medical guide was first published in 1617. Almost two hundred thirty years earlier. Swift gave a slight inward smile. *Appears little has changed in sea medicine since then.* The book listed instruments and medicines…detailed two-hundred eight-one remedies. Treatments for everything: Injuries. Diseases. Afflictions. Wounds.

Now Swift gripped the medical book tighter. During her three years of Latin in finishing school—before being expelled when the headmistress found a man in her room—Swift had translated Caesar and Horace as well as Latin grammar and rhetoric. But never had she faced a medical text. Swift pondered this now as she scanned the ten-by-twelve-foot quarters while Kikilani twisted a lit candle into the sticking-iron's holder. Beside her lay a candle snuffer just in case.

Swift leaned back against the unpainted beadboard of the cable-tier wall. From her stool she put her left hand on the apothecary cabinet beside her. Its upper shelves had guardrails and dividers to keep items from falling out. Below the shelves was a counter for preparing medications. Beneath this counter were several latched drawers. The entire unit was built into the aft wall perpendicular to the keel— the carpenter told them—to prevent items from flying across the cabin when the ship pitched and rolled.

Swift had translated from Latin all the labels on the glass-stoppered bottles in the apothecary's cabinet. These she arranged in alphabetical order in the medicine cabinet. Then she read Woodall's instructions aloud while Kikilani blended ingredients of particular usefulness. Treatments for scalding from boiling tar. For maiming from the backlash of the capstan. Cut forearms. Crush injuries. Knife wounds. Swift prayed that worse wounds would find their fate in God's hands. Urinary problems or fever called for various mixtures: Tinctures of spirits. Salts. Wormwood. Vinegar. And quicksilver mercury. Opiates were Woodall's remedy for bites from serpents. Mad dogs. Wild beasts and creeping crawling things.

Kikilani added her own island remedies. Chamomile flowers to soothe headaches and to ease kidney problems. To clear mucus from the bronchial tubes Kikilani concocted a syrup. The mix included various ingredients: Almonds. Red roses. Saffron. Lemons and other plants.

A recent margin note handwritten in Woodall's guide recommended a daily ration of lemon or lime juice for scurvy. While a dose of mercury was preferred to battle syphilis. That is…until mercury poisoning caused weight loss. Drooling. Foul breath. And all manner of side effects. From blurred vision to slurred speech and poor balance. And soon killed the kidneys along with the sailor himself.

Swift's gaze took in two raised double bunks next to the apothecary cabinet and against the outer hull. Beneath each lower bunk was room for two sea lockers. Swift reminded herself that she and Kikilani were fortunate to have a place to store the clothes and books they had packed in New York. Attached to the wall and bulkhead at opposite pillow ends of each coffin-shaped box was a lantern candle.

Beside Swift's lantern a robe hook held her night coat and a towel: both serviceable rather than clean. To the right and well below the hook a circular frame was mounted on the bulkhead that dropped down when needed. Into its opening a bailing bucket could be placed for rinsing…or collecting amputated limbs. An open water cask sat under the scrubbed-wood table that jutted out from the wall: about the length of a bunk or a man. Above the table from another bulkhead peg a stained-canvas table cover hung like a sleeping ghost. Swift ran her fingers along the wide gaps between the worn planks of the table. Then her eye paused on the saw-blade cuts along the table's edges. The marks seemed more fitting for a carpenter's workbench than a dining or operating table. *Probably seen its share of pain in either use.* A jute bag of sand and sawdust swung from the underside of the table: ready to absorb vomit or blood.

Swift fingered the bookmark ribbon in the thick guide as she recalled reading that Woodall forbid administering alcohol before surgery — for fear it would weaken the patient's heart. Swift nodded to herself. A drunken patient could make a difficult operation even worse. Instead: Poppy sap was to be administered for pain relief—but only after surgery. In Woodall's world anesthesia was little more than a flat stick to bite and the strong grip of a fellow seaman to hold the patient still during blade and saw and sutures. Or so the ship's old workshop sawbones liked to tell Swift.

To the right of the table along the bulkhead Swift studied a solid cabinet that curved around—and ran along—the wall to the cabin door. Swift followed Woodall's guide as she reviewed the three cupboards. The first cupboard contained the Surgeon's Kit. Drawers held every tool needed. Most wrapped in oilcloth to fight against rust. Kikilani followed Swift's gaze and moved to the tool chest. From a drawer she removed an oilcloth bundle. Spread it open on the cabinet counter: Knives. Razors. Cauterizing irons. Probes and spatulas for drawing out splinters and shot. Syringes. Stitching quills and needles. Cupping glasses. Blood porringers for letting. And more artful tools for pain and healing.

Both Swift and Kikilani hoped they never needed the skull saws. Or to treat broken bones from falls. Or that they must someday hurriedly crib the section titled *Amputation*. Those emergencies they reserved for the carpenter or shipsmith…depending which man was tolerably less drunk at the time. Kikilani gave a slight shake to her head that suggested these instruments were best packed away. She rolled and tied off the protective cloth then put the lumpy bundle back in its latched drawer.

In the next cupboard was the Dressing Box. Here the drawers and cupboards held the surgeon's dry goods. Kikilani opened the doors to show Swift how she had organized like items. Plasters. Pledget pads. Compresses. Ligature twine. Absorbent lint. All the linens needed by a sea surgeon.

Kikilani stepped to her right. In the cubby at the bottom of the last cabinet nearest the cabin door Swift eyed a two-handled canvas medical bag. The bag held common tinctures and salves. Pills and lotions. All arranged in a removable tray that held a double row of small medication bottles. Kikilani withdrew a bottle containing an astringent mixture of vinegar and water. The label read: *Use to stop bleeding.* Beneath the tray half the bag held splints and needles prepared to close wounds. Stuffed in the other half was a compartment for dressings. Kikilani closed the medical bag and returned it to the cabinet by the door: ready to see service on sickbay rounds in the fo'c'sle. Or an emergency call from the captain or passenger quarters.

Kikilani squeezed around Swift seated on her stool and crossed the dim cabin in three short steps. Then dropped into her bunk box next to the medicine cabinet. The prism light faintly illumined her warm features. She turned her head toward Swift and gave a long heavy sigh. "We may have found our calling in the surgeon's quarters. But I fear for when we must answer that call."

Swift swept a glance around the surgeon's quarters. "Luck has given us this surgery outfitted with everything...except a surgeon." She placed the essential Woodall's guide on the examining table. "With a well-stocked medicine chest the only thing we can do is improvise. Who knows? Maybe disease and injuries and amputations won't happen on this voyage." Swift gave Kikilani a wistful look.

Just then the *Black Cloud* creaked loudly as the ship rolled in the sea. Followed by a waft of bilious air that belched through the floor timbers. *Will our cabin be friend or enemy?* Swift wondered. She wrinkled her nose and shivered involuntarily—as if an invisible door had opened somewhere.

CHAPTER 11

DANCER BLEW ON HIS HANDS and opened the railroad car's shutters. He smiled to think of Zoë. He smiled whenever he thought of her...as he had often since he left Paris seven days before. He stretched his body as he lay on the hard leather seat. Beyond the shutters the winter brown fields of Provence slipped by in the steely early morning light. *Railroads.* The French called them *chemin de fer.* Dancer laughed to himself. An iron highway? *A horse is faster.* Still it beat a stagecoach. He was traveling first class from Avignon to Marseille. *They'll choke at this expense in Washington.* Nothing was too good for an agent on a foreign mission.

The American moved toward the salon seating at the front of the car. Took a seat on the sunnier side. Perhaps it was warmer. Across the aisle a young woman sighed heavily. Pinched a drip from her nose with a colorful Avignon kerchief. She looked like she had cried for days. Dancer stood from his seat and fetched two mugs of coffee from the café vendor near the conductor's seat at the rear. Almost spilled one on a traveling priest when the car rocked sharply around a bend. Then sat down opposite the distraught woman. When she turned he

offered her the steaming mug. She took it with a grateful—
if distracted—expression.

"*Êtes-vous américain?*"

"*Oui.* Guilty as charged."

"Then I must practice my English." She took the steaming mug
in both hands and held it with kid-skin gloves. Dancer realized she
was pretty. With large eyes. And the doe-like expression of a maiden.
His act of kindness opened a sea of emotion in her.

"My father is dead."

Tears reappeared in her eyes. Her nose snuffled. Dancer handed
her a clean napkin. And she placed her untouched coffee on the
window ledge.

Dancer's expression invited an explanation.

"My father owned an *indiennes* textile mill in Avignon. He drove
the workers to create new designs. Use bright colors. That endless
invention of new patterns was the secret to his success. But it made
him…how do you say…an angry man. We lived across from the mill
on the Rue des Teinturiers. Only two houses away from Jean-Henri
Fabre—the famous insect writer. Even the popular Fabre spent only
short pauses with father for tobacco or coffee."

Dancer swirled the last swallow in his mug. "The textile dyers'
street with the canal and the shady plane trees?" He paused. Frowned.
And amended the words in his mind. *At least they* might *be shady if the*
mistral *had not stripped them bare.* "Charming. I walked that way from
the river wharf to the train station this morning. I was told the *indiennes*
makers of Marseille were banned in 1686. All their wood blocks
destroyed…mostly at the instigation of the other textile makers. The
river-steamer captain told me some fabric printers moved to Avignon.
As a papal possession King Louis XIV's edict couldn't be enforced there.
Is that true?"

She pushed a tight curl of hair from her temple and looked out the
carriage window at the River Sorgue. Its clear waters flowed west into
Avignon along the fabric makers street. She lifted her coffee and took a
tentative sip. "*Oui.* The printed cottons are light. Low cost. Easier to
wash than silk. Seventy-five years after the edict clandestine mills
appeared in Aix and Arles and Nîmes. Now today—another eighty
years later—Avignon's *indiennes* fabrics are famous. As you saw…

the Canal de Vaucluse that runs through the Rue des Teinturiers has many waterwheels to power the looms. That day my father's master dyer was away." Her voice caught with the raw emotion. "The mill was famous for its careful and colorful Avignon patterns. But if one color is not washed at just the right moment the entire cloth is ruined. My father took the fresh-dyed cloth to the lower level where the water canal ran. It was less than a fortnight ago. They say he slipped. Got twisted in the long cloth…then the current pulled him under a wheel. Gone. In a moment."

Tears again streamed down her face. "Now I must find my mother's sister—my aunt—in Marseille…if she will take me in. But I have never met her…or been to her house. They have not spoken since mother died when I was small." She shivered with the memory. "Not after the scandal." A forlorn expression filled her face as she dabbed at the grief that gripped her.

Dancer held the woman's gaze. "Marseille is no place for a young woman." *Or any honest person for that matter.* "I will escort you to your aunt's. That's the least I can do to help."

The young woman blinked at the unexpected news. "*Merci* monsieur. My name is Mercedes. You are most kind."

"My name is Jack. Jack Dancer. We will find your aunt's home together. I will take you. You will be safe. Dry your tears. It won't be long. We will arrive in Marseille just after midday. Sleep now." Dancer stood then draped his greatcoat over the disconsolate maiden. Her eyes closed immediately. She curled under the heavy coat like a relieved kitten. Dancer looked out the window and idly noted the hazy light as the train passed through the Provence valleys. His thoughts drifted to the kindness Maybelle and Tony showed him and his brother Jace— and a dozen other orphans in Charleston—when they took in the boys after their parents died in a cotton-factory fire.

The train squealed to a stop in the Gare de Marseille just inside the old wall of France's second city. Dancer gathered his luggage and Mercedes' small valise from under their seats. Together the travelers moved down the open platform. Soot and cinders whipped their faces as they passed through a cloud of steam expelled from the engine. Their stiff steps eased as their traveler's kinks loosened. Dancer grasped the handle of one cumbersome traveling case in his left hand and wedged the second under his armpit. Leaving his right arm free. Then tapped his right foot against his left lower leg where the bulge of his Bowie knife filled the scabbard inside the shaft of his cowboy boot. His Walker Colt pistol packed away in the case would be no use in a street fight. *Any knife-wielding* nervi *working the Vieux Port won't find easy pickings here.* Being forewarned helped lessen the atmosphere of fear that was Marseille. Or at least he hoped.

Dancer carried Mercedes' small valise in his left hand. And Mercedes took his other elbow. They picked their way around iron girders laid out to become the station roof: The station itself was still under construction. In moments they emerged from the side entrance hall of the temporary building…and stepped onto the street. The infamous *mistral* wind of Provence hit them full force. Dancer lowered a shoulder against the onslaught. *Damn. This wind could blow the ears off a donkey.* Both travelers bent forward. It was one hell of a blow: The wind roared down the Rhone valley to the Mediterranean Sea.

Sharp and cold *Le Mistral* drove the innocents back inside. Gusts of thirty miles per hour that could knock a man off his feet. Dancer sinched the belt on his greatcoat. Pulled Zoë's fine pink silk-cotton scarf tighter over his face. And breathed deep. *Wish you were here. Or better yet…I was there.* A week of stagecoaches. River steamers. A hundred twenty kilometers in a cold train. All in the name of Napoleon's lost treasure. *Or so they want me to believe.*

Dancer was bone tired. Hungry. And cold. The *mistral* hit them again. Dancer raised his shoulders to his ears. Stepped toward the first hackney carriage in the queue. If you could call the two-wheel dog cart a carriage.

"*Ou?* Where to?"

Mercedes pulled a yellowed letter from her jacket pocket. She steadied the flapping paper with two hands in the bitter wind and read the faded address: "La Canebiere. Number 114. *S'il vous plaît.*" Dancer extended his hand to guide Mercedes into the carriage.

As the taxi navigated the streets downhill toward the harbor Dancer glanced out the window. Buildings were stained with soot. Bird guano. *Is that a huge rat gnawing at that tow rope?* The buildings were built close. As if the mountains and the sea constrained the city. As well as the stone battlements of the city's walls. *France's second city.* Dancer shook his head. *Maybe I'd have to be a Marseillais to love it?* All he needed was a ship to Alexandria.

The carriage came to a stop before No. 114 La Canebiere Boulevard near the harbor. The great iron gate presented elegance and wealth within.

Mercedes and Dancer climbed from the carriage. Then approached the extravagant double door. Dancer rapped the heavy knocker. Twice. He and Mercedes sheltered near the door against the intense wind. From some distance inside came the muffled sound of steps advancing across a marble foyer. When the door opened Mercedes curtsied toward the woman before them. The woman looked at Mercedes. Swept an assessing eye over Dancer.

The aristocratic woman then looked back at Mercedes. "Don't tell me. Your father is dead." A hardened expression passed over her face. *I hope the godless bastard suffered.* Just as quickly the courtesan's expression softened as she gave Mercedes an appraising look.

Mercedes burst into tears.

Dancer looked at the tall figure before them. He saw a woman whose beauty had faded. But only somewhat. *As her wealth grew is my guess.* In a blink Dancer took in a flamboyant woman who entertained elite men...men who — in turn — kept her in style. Pleasure-loving. Single-minded. Dangerous. A mistress forsaken by respectable women who unsuccessfully tried to keep their husbands on a short leash. Who knew only a married society that forsook an underworld unknown by righteous folk: An underworld presumed to include a pantheon of sins. Drink. Drugs. Gambling. Theatre. Ballet. Horseraces. Actresses. A world where the men spent themselves into debt...which led to ruin. And a world of promiscuity...which led to disease. She drew a proud breath. *The textile makers' wives sniffed at women like me...Women who inhabited that world regardless of their riches and social standing.* She scoffed at herself. Déclassée *the wives called us.*

Something suggested to Dancer that Madam DuFour — for that is how she had introduced herself — was an enterprising woman who endured the ostracization...and survived to thrive. *You will be in good hands...Mercedes.* Dancer knew that Mercedes — as a *protégée* to her

Madam Auntie—would learn elegant manners. Deportment. An eye for the latest becoming fashion. And how to value jewels. All to prepare her for a life to please gentlemen who would provide her a beautiful lifestyle. Or misery.

"And you…Monsieur. Tell me your name and your business in Marseille."

"Jack Dancer…madam. Here to find a ship to Egypt as soon as possible."

"Auntie"—Mercedes stared warmly into Dancer's eyes even as she addressed her aunt—"Monsieur Dancer helped me. Without him I would never have reached you."

The madam of La Canebiere assessed Dancer again. And recognized a man of pleasure. Adventure. Action. In a word: They understood each other. "Interesting. I may be able to help you both. But do come in. *Le Mistral* is not our friend today."

With that welcome Madam DuFour held one of the double doors open just enough to allow them to pass. And Mercedes stepped into a world in which her life would be changed forever.

Madam DuFour slowly dripped iced water over a sugar cube placed on a flat pierced spoon that rested on the rim of a glass of absinthe. The sweet water turned the green licorice-tasting alcohol a cloudy white. She handed Dancer the glass and repeated the ritual for herself. Conversation turned toward the Le Panier district. The oldest district in Marseilles…near the docks. "You will need a shipping agent to secure passage." She handed Dancer her calling card with an address handwritten on the back. That introduction—when presented to the appropriate personage in the Vieux Port or Old Port—was the key to Dancer's passage on a Mediterranean steamship bound for Alexandria later that evening.

After a nap and cold dinner Dancer readied himself for the port not five or six streets from Madam DuFour's fine mansion. On the wall of his bedchamber an old map of Marseille made the port look like the open jaws of a great crocodile—the docks its extended teeth. Mercedes found Dancer as he latched his cases. She had enjoyed some rest. That—and artful powder and rouge applied by the experienced madam — allowed Dancer's gaze to take in the stunningly pretty young woman who now stood before him.

"Monsieur Jacques...how can I repay you?"

With a flick of his hand Dancer dismissed the idea. "My honor — and duty — to help a damsel in distress."

Without a word Mercedes presented a neatly folded square of prized Avignon *indiennes* cloth. "From my father's works."

Dancer brushed away a tear that formed in the corner of the young French woman's eye. "Thank you. This is more than enough for my small service."

At that moment Madam DuFour appeared in the chamber doorway.

"Godspeed...my little one."

With a nod and knowing smile toward the Madam of Marseille Dancer took his leave.

◎   ◎   ◎

Dancer stepped down from the madam's carriage to the wharf. The cacophony of the busy port rose up from all sides. Languages of the Mediterranean and beyond melded with the patois of the sea. Carts pulled loads. Crates were shifted and hauled onto ships tied to the wharf. Dancer walked down the line. The *mistral* had disappeared. Now the clear blue sky of Provence with its unique luminous light bathed the harbor buildings in a low early evening glow. Violet clouds raced high in the sky beyond the harbor mouth. Dancer's gaze looked beyond the old port. Across the blue Mediterranean. To beyond the horizon...where he imagined Algiers stood on the far southern seashore.

Algiers. The other "white city" controlled by the French through their Mediterranean system of trade and dominance. From his vantage point above Dancer saw the harbor's outline indeed looked like the open jaws of a giant sea monster. Swallowing and spitting out tiny ships continuously.

Dancer spotted his ship near the end of the last pier. The SS *Rosetta* had seen many voyages. And better years. Through many seas to many lands. How many more voyages did the old ship have left in it? Dancer prayed: *Saint Christopher...all I need is one!* Dancer climbed the gangway. His nose caught a tang in the air of saltwater and olive-oil soap. He stowed his gear in a private cabin. Looked around the cramped quarters. *At least it has a porthole. Even if it doesn't open.* Then he stepped outside to the second deck rail. Above him the steamship's smokestacks released dark smoke that rose toward the brilliant violet clouds.

At that moment the sound of a fight below jerked Dancer's head toward the wharf. A drunken sailor was being beaten by two men. A large heavy-set thief viciously kicked the sailor in the ribs. While the thinner man ransacked the sailor's ditty bag. Dancer ran down the gangway. Almost caught his heel on a tread ridge. Righted himself on the handrail. Bent low to his left boot and raised his Bowie knife. Then sprinted toward the three men not thirty yards away. "Hey! You bastards! Leave that man alone!"

At Dancer's voice and the glint of his blade the skinny man froze. His fist deep in the sailor's bag. The heavy-set thief looked up. Saw the knife. Reached for his own curved *khanjar* dagger. Thought better of it. Gave the drunken sailor another kick…which glanced off his thigh. The larger thief thumbed his nose at Dancer. In a low voice he snarled at his companion. "Let's go! *Adhhab!*"

The big thug pushed the skinny thief into the shadows between stacked shipping bales. Then paused at the edge of light. His *khanjar* glinted in his hand. From under his chin he flicked two fingers at the American infidel in an obscene gesture. "Next time you die…you son of a pig's whore." Then he disappeared into the darkness as he silently followed the skinny thief's path.

Dancer knew that voice. It was the same thieves he and Zoë had surprised at Champollion's apartment. The thugs had traveled to Marseille. *Why Marseille?* Dancer peered into the darkness where the two men had disappeared. *Are those two cutthroats following the clues in Champollion's notebook?*

The drunken sailor tried to regain his feet. Groaned. Dancer grabbed the man. Settled him on a nearby salted fish cask. "Are you alright?"

The old sailor shrugged. Tested his various parts. Winced when he touched his right ribs. "I've had worse from these *nervi* maggots. Gives the true Marsellais a bad name."

"You're English."

Dancer gathered the man's ditty bag. The sailor snatched the bag from Dancer's hands. "Don't insult me. I'm Aussie. Through and through."

"What did the thieves want?" Dancer asked.

"What do they ever want?" the sailor returned. "Money. That's why I never carry any…at least not after I spend my last sou at the house of the lovely Minette—a gifted student from the school of Madam DuFour." A wistful smile crossed his face. He spit a glob of tobacco and blood on the cobblestones. Wiped his chin with a hand missing half its index finger. "Can you help me to my ship?"

"Which one?"

"There at the end. The *Rosetta*."

"Happy to oblige." Dancer nodded. "I'm a passenger on the old tub myself. Maybe the captain can give you some assistance?"

The sailor gave Dancer a look as if the American was daft.

"McKee is the name." The men shook hands as the sailor limped beside Dancer and headed toward the ship. "The *Rosetta* has a lot of runs left in her…but she's no virgin on this passage. I know. I'm the captain."

CHAPTER 12

DANCER JOLTED from an unsound sleep. The last echoes of disturbance faded away as he carefully monitored the darkness. *Was that the sound of cannon?* He returned his Bowie blade to its boot scabbard and keened his ear toward the sound. Beyond the steady drum of the steam piston and beat of the side wheel outside his porthole the SS *Rosetta* offered no answer. He stuck his head out the door of his narrow double-bunk first-class cabin. Only a single smoking lamp lit the steamship's low-ceiling central saloon. He inched past the other louvered doors to the companionway that led up to the aft bridge deck. Where he called out a friendly greeting: "Ahoy on the bridge. May I come aboard?"

A cigarette sparked then pinwheeled over the rail into the darkness. "Aye. If youse not a miserable bandicoot...and 'ave a bottle to share."

When Dancer stepped onto the bridge Captain McKee greeted him with a scowl. "Collision is the most common danger at night. Got to keep an eye myself. 'Specially when passing Malta." The Australian Captain raised the chin of his full gray beard toward the starboard side. "Even the salute cannon don't help. Any blind Freddy could see that."

Dancer looked into the gloom. In the distance to his right passed the silhouetted dome and ramparts of Valletta.

"So that's where Napoleon snatched his treasure on the way to Egypt?"

McKee shot Dancer a sidelong glance. "You've heard of Napoleon's treasure?"

"Been on my mind lately." Just then a waft of coal smoke from the forward single stack engulfed the bridge. Dancer coughed. Pulled a brandy flask from his inside jacket pocket. Uncorked the flat bottle and handed it to the Captain.

"You're not alone." Captain McKee took a hefty slug and placed the bottle within easy reach. Then gave Dancer a withering glance and bit a hangnail in scorn. "Rarely a season goes by that we don't get a treasure hunter or two on this run to Alexandria. You may be the bravest American I've encountered — and God knows I appreciate the help on the Marseille wharf — but getting mixed up with Madam DuFour qualifies you as a witless infant. Did you cover the Madam or one of her charges in 'the Phocean City'?"

"Damn it. That's a fine howdy-do." Dancer scoffed. "What a question!"

The Captain nodded. "I thought as much. Tell me my friend... how many women of easy virtue have you coupled since you arrived in Europe?"

"What the devil do you mean?" Dancer demanded.

"How many? Be honest...as a favor to an old man."

"What's it to you? I landed in France not a fortnight ago." He turned away — intending to go back to his cabin. Then thought better of it and took another swig. Wiped his mouth with the back of his hand. After a long moment he finally spoke again. "Well...since you ask..." He came back to the helm. Handed the flask to the Captain. "There was a maid in Gay Paree..."

"Aye. My guess is a man like you has fornicated more times than I have pissed in a pot." McKee chortled as he took another swallow from Dancer's brandy. "And just because they were accommodating...did you trust them? Did you think they were in love? Hardly. I enjoy my time with Madam DuFour...and Minette — but I don't think for a minute that I am beloved. They're no more trustworthy than those *nervi* scum on the dock."

Captain McKee peered into the darkness. Made a slight adjustment of the tiller. Then downed another brandy and handed the flask back to Dancer. "Take Madam DuFour...for example. She is a notorious seductress. Beds kings. Prime ministers. And wealthy married men across Europe." McKee gave a knowing laugh. "Then she ruthlessly blackmails them. Maybe you were next?"

Right or wrong—tonight didn't seem to be the best time for Dancer to test the question. Instead he took a different tack. "You mentioned Napoleon's treasure. This is the exact route the general took...have you heard stories?"

McKee lit another cigarette. "I've sailed the Mediterranean nigh on ten years—ever since steamships were put into service. Circled the Adriatic more times than I can remember. Brindisi. Venice. Corfu. Bumped around the Aegean from Crete to Istanbul. And now I hump this old wooden-hulled steam packet back and forth from Marseille to Alexandria—ever since my company got the London-to-Alexandria mail contract in 1840." The white-haired mariner took another long swallow. "From Gibraltar to Sevastopol...I been there. And remember every port. Almost." McKee took a deep breath and gave an even longer exhale. "Even squired some English swells on a dredging mission last season to Aboukir Bay—where Napoleon's flagship *L'Orient* met its end under Nelson's guns. Told them they were looking beyond the black stump."

Dancer gave McKee a quizzical look.

"Beyond the known world. Beyond civilization." The Captain held the wheel with what remained of his index finger and took another swig. "Nothing there to find."

"What makes you so sure?"

McKee gave a contemptuous snort. "When youse been in as many ports as I have...shared a bottle with as many sailors and adventurers and swindlers as I have...you come to know a thing or two. What I know is that Napoleon's treasure never got blowed to kingdom come. Never got spent in Egypt. And never came back to France." McKee waved vaguely toward the darkness. "They say it's out there... somewhere. What's the chances of finding it? I'd say it's Buckley's and none. As good as impossible."

From a tin case inside his jacket Dancer lifted a stubby black

Oscuro cigar and passed it beneath his nose. The fermented notes of black pepper and sweetness cleared his mind. *My only hope is to discover LeGrand's trail.* But how? Dancer blew smoke into the wind and risked he could trust the Captain. He then shared the stories he'd heard. About the Sword of Valette. The Rosetta Stone. About a trail of coins. "You know those *nervi* that jumped you?"

The Captain stretched his shoulders back and rubbed his sore ribs. "Go on."

"I recognized them. They were in Paris. Caught them stealing a notebook — of all things — from a professor. They used that same Omani oath about the skinny one's mother being a pig's whore."

"Same *nervi* you say? Sounds like you made a couple of mates while you were in Paris."

"Real lovebirds those two."

McKee turned serious. "It's a fair go they're shadowing us right now." He gestured into the blackness to the south. "Arab types from Marseille take boats that hug the Barbary Coast along the North African shore. Algiers. Tunis. Tripoli. They don't have regular steam packets like the *Rosetta*. Gotta keep hopping from one coastal dhow to another. If we're lucky — not saying we are — we may beat them to Alexandria."

"What makes you think they're headed our way? You said no one knows what happened to Napoleon's treasure."

McKee combed three and a half fingers through his full beard. "True." He gave Dancer a steady look. "But there's one story I've heard more than once that rings true."

Dancer returned the Captain's gaze. "What have you heard?"

"You mentioned a trail of coins. And those two Arabs spoke Omani." The expatriate Captain adjusted the ship's wheel a degree to the southeast. "May just be a shag on a rock — but the one tale that seamen repeat 'bout the treasure is that slavers used those Malta coins to buy trade goods. Arab slavers. From Zanzibar."

"Zanzibar?" Dancer almost squeaked the word. McKee's scuttlebutt fit with Champollion's research. "That makes sense."

"My guess is those two thugs are racing to beat you to Zanzibar — and I doubt it's to give hugs and kisses to their granny."

Dancer shuddered in the chill night air…and at the stories he'd heard about the Sultan of Zanzibar and his dislike for foreigners meddling in his profitable interests. *Maybe this goose chase isn't such a wild thing.* "Zanzibar. Has an adventurous ring to it...doesn't it?"

The Captain muttered into his beard: "Except for the murderous Somali pirates along the path." McKee shot Dancer a strange look. "If you value your white hide keep your swag tight — and that Bowie knife even closer. Especially when you work your way down the African coast."

Dancer watched as the grizzled seaman opened his worn logbook and withdrew a well-traveled calling card. Under the narrow cone of light from the compass lamp McKee crossed out the name on the card. "A recent listing in the shipping news reported the longtime American Consul Richard Waters was replaced by a Charles Ward...I believe." The Captain wrote Ward's name on the tattered card. "But consuls change like a carousel...so these names may mean nothing."

As the *Rosetta* chugged onward like a painted courtesan beyond her prime the Captain sketched a crude map on the back of the card showing where the consulate was located. "Should you reach Zanzibar make the American Consul your first stop." The Aussie scoffed. "I've heard the new man's as useless as tits on a nun. But only the consul can get you an audience with the Sultan." Dancer took the card and tucked it into his cigar case lid.

At that point the sound of boot steps came to their ears. Time for the first mate to take his trick at the wheel.

The Captain tucked Dancer's bottle inside his coat. Then saluted the first mate and lowered his voice to a whisper.

"Zanzibar...my friend. No dillydallying. It's the only place you'll find the trail to your treasure."

Dancer gave an emphatic nod. "Zanzibar it is."

CHAPTER 13

DANCER LEANED HIS BUTT against the Citadel's low parapet wall. The great River Nile slipped behind him into the sea. He wiped his forehead with a section of Avignon cloth as he looked across the open keep and up the yellow stone mosque walls. He shaded his eyes as they ascended the Citadel to the narrow minaret tower high above the mosque. Climbing the one hundred and four spiral steps to the *muezzin's* balcony at the top of the tower had been almost a mountain too far. Coming down was even trickier. Again he wiped his forehead. And sighed. *Happy to put that chimney behind me.* Four days on the SS *Rosetta* and an overnight on a horse-drawn track-boat from Alexandria along the Mahmoodeeyeh Canal left him more than ready for solid Mother Earth.

Dancer scratched several flea bites his ankles had collected on the canal boat. He inhaled the humid delta air of Rasheed. Tangs of wood smoke. Dung. And incense tickled his nose.

Dancer muttered to himself in a low voice. "Napoleon was no fool. That's why he must have taken his Malta loot off his flagship. Judging from the terrain here—and because he had just taken

Cairo—the treasure must have been shipped up the Nile. To Cairo. And then on to Zanzibar…like the trail of coins suggests?" Dancer shook his head. "The lads at the State Department will love this wild-goose chase."

The American agent walked along the Citadel wall and down the steps to the boat landing. He paid for passage to Cairo. Then stepped aboard the ancient sidewheeler most recently christened the *Jack O'Lantern*. He looked at the rotting deck and shabby crewmen. A brazen rat gnawed at its fleas near a coil of ropes. *Makes the SS* Rosetta *look like the swank SS* Great Western *in comparison.* Dancer took a seat under the awning of the upper bow deck to make the most of Egypt's coldest month of the year. A chill breeze made him pull his great coat around his neck. But it wouldn't be long before the Egyptian sun made it time to trade the heavy coat for something cooler.

At dark the mosquitoes drove Dancer to his cabin. Within moments he clapped at the buzzers inside his netting like a demented operagoer. Then wiped his hands clean of more than a dozen smears. He fell asleep to a nightmare of getting lost in the desert between Cairo and El Suez…then being cut into pieces by Arab pirates who used a jagged two-man crosscut saw to shave off his limbs somewhere near Zanzibar. With a jolt he sat up. Crushed the last mosquito inside his netting. Looked at the pest's blood on his hand and laughed. *Take that…you son of a pig's whore.*

At breakfast Dancer tucked into just baked *baladi* flatbread with yogurt. A fava bean *ful.* And a boiled egg. Olives on the side. He let the too-hot-to-drink cup of sugar and finely ground coffee settle before attempting a sip.

After a few moments an Egyptian man came onto the bow deck where Dancer was eating. He ducked beneath the upper deck awning and settled like a busy hen across the communal table from Dancer. With a glance Dancer composed the man's story. Egyptian…but white twill like an Englishman. Ink on his index finger. Frayed right cuff. *Suggests a man of letters. A scholar?* The man clutched a leather briefcase as if it contained a pharaoh's jewels.

The Egyptian looked up. Caught Dancer's gaze. Nodded a

greeting and slid along the bench to sit closer to the only other first-class passenger.

Without pause the man of letters spoke in a slight Oxford accent: "Good morning. I suspect you have an interest in Egypt...or perhaps The Levant in general? Otherwise why are we on this ship?" Dancer expected the man to give him time to answer...but the Egyptian continued enthusiastically. "May I introduce myself. I am Ibrahim al-Disqui. Scholar of manuscripts. Just returning from the great Alexandria library...what remains." His expression only now invited Dancer's response.

"Dancer. Jack Dancer. American abroad. On my way to Cairo...then Zanzibar...on a spice-buying venture for my New England benefactors."

Dancer nodded. The scholar smiled and touched his heart in a cordial Arabic greeting. Dancer opened the conversational door a bit wider: "I hope my buying venture is as productive as your manuscript search." His eyes indicated the nervous man's case.

The Egyptian clutched the case closer. Dancer removed his hands from his pockets to show deference. Then tried a different tack.

"Do you think this paddler will make it to Bulac wharf on schedule?"

"Oh yes. Every time I am going on this fine ship I am reaching Cairo on schedule. Most definitely...except once." His voice trailed off with the memory. "That was five years ago...when Mr. Lane came out to Egypt for his third travel and we took this very voyage. As luck would have it — or misfortune if you are that turn of mind — the ship broke down about halfway. I was dismayed. Not Mr. Lane. Reveled in the adventure. He said to me: 'Come...Ibrahim. Let's walk and ride on land with the people...not like the Pharaohs in their palanquins.' And so we did."

Al-Disqui held the case to his chest with both arms. "Mr. Lane — as you may know — is fluent in many languages...especially Arabic. He prefers to live like an Egyptian among the people rather than with the 'Franks' — as he calls the expatriates. The journey from village to village and across a lifetime of irrigation ditches in the sweltering humidity took us four days. I was exhausted. Not Mr. Edward William Lane. No...he was exhilarated."

As the fond memory poured forth the scholar relaxed. The briefcase now settled on his lap.

"Did you say Edward William Lane?"

Al-Disqui bobbed his head. "Why yes…We are working together on a great lexicon of the Egyptian and English languages. Do you know him?"

"We have a mutual friend: Jacques Joseph Champollion."

At the mention of Champollion's name the professor brightened. "You know Monsieur Champollion?"

"When I was in Paris not two weeks ago he and his daughter asked me to take their special greetings to Edward Lane and his sister…Sophia Lane Pool."

The professor leaned back and closed his eyes almost in rapture. "Champollion oversees the greatest manuscript collections at the Bibliothèque Nationale. I can only dream of the treasures that surround him." A moment later his demeanor darkened. He clucked. Shook his head.

"A sad story. Not Mr. Lane…I mean his sister. Mrs. Poole. She is estranged from her husband in England. Is it not wrong for a wife to abandon her husband? Mr. Lane encouraged her to get away and come to Cairo. Now she — like Mr. Lane — lives among the people. Wears the Egyptian costume. Never leaves the house unless fully swathed and veiled. Now she speaks Arabic as well as I do. Miss Sophia has made inroads into…how do you say…the places only women can go. She is the confidante of the highest and lowest ladies. They tell her stories. Share what life is like for a woman in the land of Islam…"

The professor's description piqued Dancer's interest. "And I understand Mrs. Poole has just published an insightful book…What is the title?"

"*The Englishwoman in Egypt.* Twenty-eight letters from Cairo. Quite amazing. Harems. Bathhouses. Apartments where only women are allowed. Miss Sophia Poole is what we say *ya dahwety!* She walks on the edge of disaster. But amazingly her letters are genuine. Sincere. Heartwarming. Despite her tragic situation."

At the mention of harems and bathhouses Dancer lifted his sweet coffee to his lips to disguise his wry smile. "Sounds fascinating. I would like to meet this Mr. Lane and Mrs. Poole."

"I will ask Mr. Lane. Perhaps it can be arranged...good sir."

Dancer rose. Shook the scholar's hand. Then excused himself to improvise some sort of shoulder straps for his government-issue traveling bags.

"I will find you this afternoon...Mr. Dancer...as we approach the Bulac wharf in Cairo. The *Jack O'Lantern* makes the same journey in a day that takes a two-masted *dahabiyeh* three days against the current. It will be my privilege to show you the way to the British Hotel. May the peace and mercy and blessings of God be upon you."

With that kindness the scholar made his way to his cabin.... still clutching his case in two hands.

CHAPTER 14

BRITISH HOTEL
CAIRO/EGYPT
24 DECEMBER 1846

THAT EVENING DANCER ORDERED white champagne on the
hotel verandah. A waiter wearing a red *fez* brought the bottle in an
evaporative terracotta vase...where the champagne stood gently cooled
by several inches of water. When the waiter presented the dripping
bottle he held it against a white napkin draped over his forearm. Dancer
took note. *French.* He nodded approval. As the server poured a glass
Dancer surveyed the verandah of the British Hotel.

The potted palms did not move in the windless evening. A layer of
fine dust coated every leaf and frond. The hotel felt like a *caravanserai*
along the Silk Road—rather than Christmas Eve. Dancer raised his
glass and toasted his safe arrival at the elegant hotel with a slight nod.
After all that was the hotel's purpose: an oasis of New World order
surrounded by a desert of Old World chaos.

Dancer's dinner of passable beef. Carrots. And potatoes drowned
in brown English gravy sat well enough. From across Cairo he picked
up on the nightfall calls to prayer. From every district the *muezzins* in
their rotation sent the same word to all four compass directions.
Dancer leaned back into the pillow of the wicker and cane chair.

Nothing like a tub and a shave to revive the spirit in the City of a Thousand Minarets. Overhead a straw-mat *punkah* fan moved the air languidly. Its pulley system operated within earshot of Dancer by a deaf *punkah wallah.* Dancer relaxed in his newly acquired cream-colored full-cut linen trousers and white cotton shirt with splayed collar. The clean clothes felt crisp next to his skin. *Lucky to meet that London-bound fellow in the barber's shop. A straight-up exchange for that heavy greatcoat was more than fair.* In the gentlemen's salon Dancer had asked the hotel's barber to wash out the pomade the man — without asking — had mistakenly spread on Dancer's thick black hair. But he kept the touch of beard oil to curl his trimmed Lord Bryon moustache.

Dancer inhaled the night air and settled into the high-backed chair. When he reached for his glass his attention was distracted by a commotion near the hotel's entrance. There a native woman covered head to toe in a black *burka* and full veil moved to enter the verandah. The *maître d'hôtel* stepped forward to stop her. Recognized the figure. Exchanged whispered words. Then gestured toward the far end of the palm-lined space.

The woman crossed the portico with a determined stride. She came directly toward Dancer's table. Past potted dwarf orange trees. Lemon trees. And pomegranates. Her black robes flowed behind her as if blown by a desert wind. Her large brown eyes peered out at him from a narrow rectangular opening above the mesh breathing panel in her veil. Her upper eyelids were painted with black *kohl*; her lower lids were colored green. The effect was exotic.

The harridan stopped short of Dancer. Leaned forward as she set both hands on his table.

"Jack Dancer... I presume." Her voice spoke in a cultured British accent.

Dancer raised his eyes to meet the apparition.

"Ibrahim al-Disqui said I would find you here." With that declaration the woman reached up to her headpiece. Took hold with one henna-dyed hand. The practiced movement revealed a sheen of lustrous straight black hair. Trimmed square across her eyebrows in the fashion of an Egyptian queen. She dropped her headpiece on the empty chair at Dancer's table. With both henna-patterned hands she moved her palms over her head and smoothed her tousled hair. Her lips were red ochre.

"I'm Sophia Lane Poole." She gave Dancer an expectant look. "Are you going to ask me to sit down?"

Dancer pulled a third chair over for Mrs. Poole. As the attractive woman took her seat she spit out a single word: "Monstrous."

Dancer signaled the red fez to bring a second glass. "What…what is monstrous?"

"Marriage…of course. Suffocating in England. But in Egypt it can be a death sentence."

The astonishing Mrs. Poole held Dancer in rapt attention.

"Among the upper Egyptian classes the condition of female slaves is — in one respect — preferable to that of wives. While the wives are in constant fear of divorce the sale of a slave is reckoned highly disreputable. Especially if the slave has long been with the family. And if the slave is a woman who bore a child to her master to sell her is illegal!" The woman squeezed her strong hands into fists. "Wives on the other hand can be beaten or divorced at will. Among the lower and middle classes both wives and slaves are often treated brutally. The wives often cruelly beaten and the slaves not unfrequently beaten to death! Monstrous."

Dancer attempted a first sip of champagne but the tirade prompted him to put the glass down. He ran his tongue inside his mouth in unfulfilled expectation.

Mrs. Poole continued unabated: "Why…our neighbor has ten wives now. Several others already divorced. When we asked he said he would marry ten more but he cannot afford twenty wives! Once divorced the castaways cannot return to their families for the shame. A few survive on the streets…but many throw themselves into the river in despair. Marriage is an abominable trap for women! Truly monstrous!"

Dancer ventured the question. "And Mr. Poole…?"

Sophia Lane Poole set her jaw. "Thank God my brother brought us out to Cairo. Without that escape I fear a jump into the Thames may have been my destiny too." With that confession she fell quiet. For a moment. "And thank heavens my two sons were released too — instead of starving on the withered vine of their father."

In the uncomfortable silence the sound of a waltz drifted through the hotel's faux pointed arches…filtering onto the verandah from the interior central courtyard. Earlier the courtyard had served as the main dining room. Now it had been transformed into a ballroom for the early nighttime hours. At Dancer's table the music seemed to soothe the woman's irrepressible nature.

Mrs. Poole turned her gaze beyond the verandah balcony. Toward the great pyramids that rose in the endless desert beyond the city and the green zone of the Nile. "The city has the appearance of having been deserted for a century. Suddenly repeopled by persons who are unable — from poverty or some other cause — to repair it. Unable to clear away its antiquated cobwebs." Her voice drifted for a moment. "Cairo." A note of affection in her tone. "I love it."

The bold woman slid her chair partway around the round table. "Professor al-Disqui tells me you are bound for Zanzibar."

Dancer dissembled his true mission. "Yes. I've always been intrigued by the island's spices." *What the devil?*

The beguiling Englishwoman turned a penetrating gaze on the well-barbered new arrival. To Dancer her mysterious eyes looked somewhere betwixt an Egyptian temptress and she-devil.

Her henna-painted fingertips hovered tantalizingly close to the breast-shaped bowl of her coupe glass. "Then some advice from one who frequents the harems and bathhouses and learns the *true* power behind closed doors." She flicked her flute to make the bubbles dance and looked at the American. "Beware the Shieka Sharife of Zanzibar."

Dancer tilted his head slightly as he studied the *burka*-covered creature beside him. "Shieka Sharife? Who — or what — is that… pray tell?"

"Misguided men will tell you the Sultan is the power of Zanzibar. But don't be fooled. Women rule that world in unknown ways. Be advised: The real power behind the sultanate is the Sultan's daughter: the Shieka Sharife." Sophia Lane Poole gave her long charcoaled lashes a languorous blink. "The whispers of Cairo's bathhouses are rarely wrong. Understand one thing: The Sultan is *very* protective of his favorite daughter."

"Good to know. I'll keep that in mind when — or if — I travel to Zanzibar."

The inscrutable face ran her eyes over Dancer and gave a slight flare to her nostrils as if she scented something. A twinge of discomfort shot through Dancer. *Is that the look of the quarry…or the hawk?*

Mrs. Poole gave her black bob a shake and leaned even closer to Dancer's ear. Then continued in a husky voice: "Whatever you do…don't initiate contact directly with the Shieka. And absolutely never look at the Shieka without being in the presence of a court official or chaperone." The surprising woman raised her glass off the white linen. "Men have lost their heads — in more ways than one — simply by looking at Shieka Sharife. Consider yourself warned."

With that admonition Sophia Lane Poole stopped talking. Gave Dancer a direct look. Then abruptly stood up. With one flamboyant motion she slipped the black *burka* robe over her head. Then dropped it atop her headpiece on the extra chair. Beneath the robe she was dressed in a white *kalasiris* sheath. The linen hugged her body from her torso to her ankles. Elegantly simple yet embellished with edging of embroidered gold. Two wide straps over her shoulders held up the dress. The upper edge rested just above her fulsome breasts. Dancer's glance concluded that her attractive figure had not thickened from motherhood.

In front of Dancer stood a vision that looked as if she had stepped from a wall fresco of a royal tomb in the Valley of the Kings. A jolt of excitement hit Dancer's gut. The woman had transformed herself from a native harpy to a royal vision. Astonishing.

Sophia Lane Poole reached down to the table and raised her untouched glass. "White Champagne. The one thing the French get right."

Dancer noticed a playful expression crossed her face…magnified by her exotically painted eyes. He admired how the brown henna dye on her hands and wrists formed a delicate design — like laced gloves. She tilted the raised glass toward Dancer in a toast to the evening. Then drained the wine in one swallow. She exhaled deeply. Replaced the shallow-bowl glass on the table. As a lively tune came from the courtyard the Champollions' exotic friend gave Dancer a long look that seemed to suggest approval.

"Shall we dance?"

"It will be my pleasure."

Dancer settled his wide-rimmed glass on the starched tablecloth. Smiled quietly to himself. *''Twas the night before Christmas' after all.* Then he returned Sophia's glance and rose to his feet. A wry smile lifted one end of his rakish moustache. Sophia Lane Poole's black-green eyes glittered as she extended her hand.

"The pleasure will be mine."

CHAPTER 15

TREASURY SECRETARY WALKER received the message sent from Paris. Mrs. Walker's New Year's Eve ball would have to wait. Why did the woman insist on a prize for best costume? Walker tapped the inexpensive face of his wooden shelf clock and grimaced as he rubbed his dyspeptic stomach. The biweekly cabinet meeting would convene momentarily with President Polk. Secretary of State Buchanan. And the irrepressible Senator from Texas: Sam Houston.

As the President's Inner Circle entered Walker's spartan office the little man from Mississippi unfolded the single sheet written in the graceful hand of a woman. This was the only message they had received from Dancer in weeks. No other word. Nothing.

Walker glanced at the other three then cleared his throat. "Gentlemen: Finally a message from that agent we sent to Paris. Appears to be dictated." He held the sheet at arm's length with a faint expression of distaste. "*Napoleon escaped Egypt. Returned to France without treasure. Was treasure lost with the* L'Orient *flagship? Spent on Egyptian war? Bribes? Buried? Nobody knows.'*" Dancer's hastily composed note ended abruptly: "*"Trail of Napoleon's gold as cold as*

Napoleon. Paris is a bust. Following a hunch. Dancer.'"

The message was dated December 12. Dispatched almost three weeks before.

Houston thumped his hickory cane. "What the hell does that mean? 'Following a hunch'?"

"What's going on? What's happening?" Polk's voice sounded tired. His deep-set eyes looked darker and his white mane fell farther past his collar.

Walker voiced his worry. "Maybe we sent Dancer on a wild-goose chase?"

"Now I've seen the elephant." Buchanan scoffed. "Is this what you said was your best man...Walker? The future of the nation's treasury hangs in the balance...and we're no closer to finding Napoleon's treasure than we were back at Thanksgiving! What's all this about a cold trail? Paris being a bust? If you ask me...it looks like one step forward and two steps back."

Polk paced. Buchanan stared out the window. Walker dropped Dancer's message onto a pile of abysmal year-end tariff reports.

Houston said what everyone was thinking. "Perhaps the greatest mystery is" — the Texan pointed to the discarded message — "what's become of Dancer?"

PART 2

SANDWICH ISLANDS

A SWIFT & DANCER
ADVENTURE

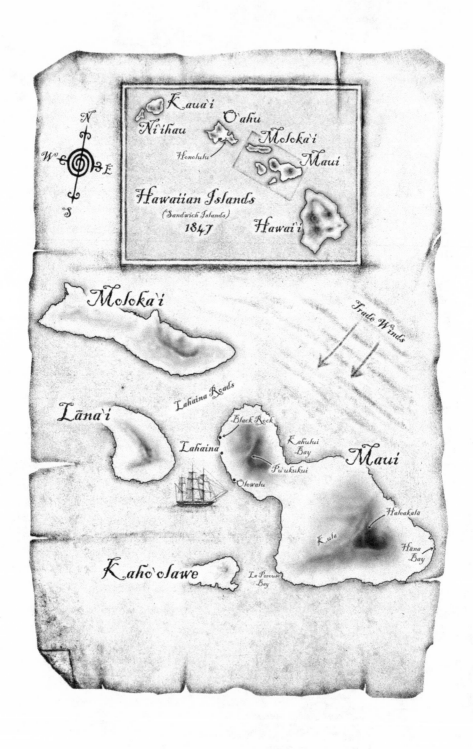

CHAPTER 16

OFF KALAUPAPA PENINSULA
MOLOKAʻI/MAUI
1 JANUARY 1847

MAUNAKILI towered over the swivel gun mounted beside him. His white shark-tooth necklace and white human-bone anklets contrasted with his fearsome tattoos — the black designs covered the right half of his body. A golden cloth encircled his waist. On the other side of the bow-mounted gun sea-hardened Englishman Bull Shaw steadied himself. Squinted in the relentless North Pacific sun of Molokaʻi. Maunakili's two-masted sailing canoe crested the outer breakwater chop. One of the fastest canoes in the islands. The double hulls cut through the waters of the Molokaʻi Channel. Like a two-headed sea monster with wings. Hālawa Bay was quickly left behind as a gaggle of chiefs sat on the woven platform between the hulls of the canoe — their wives and women separated near the stern. Soon off to the south the great canoe raised the flat lava-tongue of the Kalaupapa Peninsula. The dark silhouette of distant Oʻahu Island — where Manuakili's spies reported the Hawaiian King sullenly brooded — was a vague hump across the open water not fifty miles to the west.

Maunakili privately reveled as he stared toward Honolulu. *Your claim to our occupied kingdom will die soon…little king. Our title to our*

Maui land cannot be extinguished...our righteousness goes back to Kahekili and before...to the great origins of our creator. Wakea. God of Light.

Even as a young boy Maunakili was bigger and more powerful than much older boys. As he grew on Molokaʻi under the watchful nurturing of his great-grandmother she embellished his nickname. *Pilikua.* The Giant. Now the *mele* song called him *Pilikuakili.* Giant in the bloodline of Kahekili. His feats of strength were legion. Repeated without end by Queen Piʻilani's storytellers. *Pilikuakili.* His name taken from his bloodline. From his great-grandfather. The Great Kahekili. His renown embodied Piʻilani history.

Maunakili Pilikuakili. A giant mountain in the line of Kili.

The sailing canoe tacked toward the dark Pālāʻau Cliffs. Lava ridges protruded like stern eyebrows overlooking the peninsula. The cliffs frowned impassively at the mortals in the near distance as the racing vessel slowed. Then settled into the gentle waves far from shore.

Maunakili turned toward the chiefs seated between the hulls. He fixed the attention of these *aliʻi*: they were among the last survivors of Maui nobility. He stroked an ornamented *ipu nui* gourd cradled in the crook of his left arm.

"Do you know what I possess?" Maunakili shouted. The chiefs stared. Eyes wide.

Maunakili took one step closer to the chiefs. Raised the revered gourd over his head. "These are the sacred ashes of your royal ancestors. These are the remains of Kahekili!"

A murmur of alarm swept through the chiefs. Then silent attention.

"Yes. I possess the very ashes that came to me from the King's sacred burial cave." Maunakili paused for effect then shouted: "Today you have a choice! You can forsake your ancestors—as the false King in Honolulu has done. Or...you can choose to obey the laws of your race. You can choose to obey your true king: Maunakili! For I am the only one who has the true *mana*...the true power of Kahekili!"

The chiefs sat dumb. Waiting to hear more from the man who would decide their fate.

Without warning Maunakili stepped to the side of the central platform. He extended the sacred gourd out over the ocean waters. The highest-ranking chief of the group leaped to his feet.

Maunakili fixed the chief with a malevolent stare. "Here is your choice: Keep faith with the bloodline of our ancestors...or I will dump the worthless ashes of Kahekili into the sea forever."

An elder at the edge of the platform went white. Another elder beside him outstretched his arms. Pleaded to save the ashes. Behind the *ali'i* chiefs the women gasped. All eyes had swiveled to stare at the gourd Maunakili held so precariously over the water. A distinguished white-haired noble rose to his feet. Beside him in a mirrored pose his eldest son — not yet eight years — stood as straight as his father. The highest chief spoke. "We stand with our ancestors...Maunakili. Without those ashes we would drift endlessly across the shoals of time. Never to live. Never to die. Wandering souls. Forever in search of deliverance. Forever without rest."

Acquiescence overtook the faces of the gathered chiefs. A general assent rose from the terrified nobles.

"Words are nothing." Maunakili's voice was commanding. "Only action will carve your words in stone." As he stepped in front of the highest chief he hissed. "Here is your choice...high chief of Maui *ali'i*. To stop these ashes from being lost forever to the sea you must prove your loyalty. You must show me your conviction." His voice had become menacing. "I will dump these ancestors — the dead from the great battle of 'Īao Valley and the ashes of our forebear...King Kahekili himself — or to prove your loyalty to Maunakili you must cast your own son into the sea."

A gasp rose from behind the chiefs. A young woman holding her son loosened her grip on the boy who often frolicked with the high chief's son. The lad quickly huddled by his father's side. The men exchanged startled looks from chief to chief. Then wife to wife.

Maunakili bellowed: "These ashes I dump into the ocean...unless the highest chief proves his loyalty to me and our ancestors by sacrificing his only son in place of these ashes." Maunakili spread his feet in a powerful stance. His giant frame stood well above all others. Half black. Half brown. The warrior cut in two. Terrifying. He began to beat time with one heel. His anklets of bone rattled ominously. Almost as if the bones of the chiefs' ancestors were present.

"These ashes of sacred ancestors can only be redeemed" — he paused for effect — "if your highest chief obeys my command and casts his only son into the ocean."

The great war canoe lifted and dipped in the gentle waves. At that moment a fresh breeze chilled the sweat on the elders' temples — and the dignified high noble made his choice. He knelt and solemnly held his son close to his chest. Then with a distant expression turned the lad to face the others. The august chief steadied his son's quaking shoulders. With lengths of husk rope and ballast stones taken from one hull the others reluctantly tied the boy's wrists and feet without a word of protest from the boy. Bull Shaw watched as a cold expression that suggested greed played around the mercenary's mouth. In the relentless sun the chiefs handed the restrained boy back to his father. The dumbstruck high chief stood. Extended his long arms over the water. Dropped the boy into the sea.

The boy sank into the realm of his ancestors. Forever. In despair the high chief fell to the deck. Prostrate before King Maunakili. The others shuffled to one side. Only then did they notice Bull Shaw had turned the swivel gun. Ready to rake the deck with shot if a mutiny arose.

Maunakili moved beside a round studious urchin of a man. Kapu the Ugly. Maunakili's loyal messenger. Crier. And royal storyteller. His faithfulness forbade speaking out. He had not resisted. To others his simple presence swore fealty to the rebel king. Maunakili whispered to Kapu the Ugly: "You too made a choice today. You have chosen to obey our ancestors…to be loyal to Maunakili. If you fail me…I will put a curse on your children. A curse that will break your bloodline forever. Do you understand?"

Kapu the Ugly nodded. Of all the lore he knew from repetition of the ancient *mele* story-songs and honorific *oli* chants none held greater terror than that of a king's curse. Yes…Kapu understood. He bowed his consent.

"Say it!" Maunakili sneered. "Say it out loud. Your king must hear the words."

Kapu pledged: "I will obey."

In that moment Maunakili knew he owned Kapu. Forever more. Kapu had given his word. He would be obedient to Maunakili… or Kapu's broken word and public shame would be forever reviled by a royal curse.

Maunakili held the ashes high overhead. Chanted that the *mana* had passed to him. "The Hawaiian King had no right to rule over our race—the Pi'ilani of Maui…He lost his *mana* by becoming Christian…The old gods now pass the *mana* to Maunakili to be the true King of the Maui…I am the Great Kahuna." Maunakili handed the sacred gourd to Kapu the Ugly.

Maunakili gave a thin smile and closed his eyes to see his great-grandmother's approving visage look down at him from her place in the afterlife among their ancestors. Only six weeks had passed since Queen Pi'ilani had droned her wishes into her great-grandson. But now the time was right. A great foreign power would soon send warships to Maui to be Maunakili's ally. Now he must execute the plan for which he had been groomed over decades. *Now is my time.* Maunakili knew this. *I will restore the ancient Maui kingdom…with Maunakili as King of Maui.*

The afternoon sun dropped lower behind them to the west. Maunakili directed the royal sailing canoe away from the shore below the Pālā'au Cliffs.

He stood beside the foresail. The words of his great-grandmother at his tattoo initiation came to him as if on the wind. *Produce a male heir through the highest Maui princess. No other ali'i chief will then be able to question the bloodline of your heir apparent. At last your line will be most pure!* The rebel king inhaled deeply. *The usurper Hawaiian King will fall as the false occupier of our land…our Kingdom of Maui. And forever you will put to sleep the foreigner's defamations: their lies that you are nothing more than a* hapa haole…*a half-breed.* Maunakili lifted his broad jaw toward the sky. *Only you today—and your heirs tomorrow—are the true rulers of the sovereign Kingdom of Maui.*

Maunakili moved toward the swivel gun and motioned for Bull Shaw and Kapu the Ugly to lean in close. With his back turned toward the huddled chiefs the king spit out his scheme.

"To enshrine my kingdom I—Maunakili—will produce a male heir from the direct bloodline of Kahekili and Queen Pi'ilani through her granddaughter Alohalani…my mother."

Shaw broke the silence. "Where can we find such a pureblood Maui princess?"

Kapu the Ugly—the storyteller—explained: "There is an *oli*

chanted about a maiden from 'Iao Valley. The song says she was as pure a line as the waters of the sacred valley."

"Who is this princess?" demanded Maunakili.

"The *oli* says she was the true Princess of Maui. Great-great-granddaughter of Kahekili and Queen Pi'ilani." Kapu paused. "The *oli* says she was your niece. Daughter of your sister. Conceived after your father had died."

Maunakili smiled. "Where can I obtain this niece-princess?"

"That is no longer possible." The storyteller squirmed. "She is gone. Left this world."

Maunakili grabbed Kapu the Ugly. And elevated the plump storyteller by the throat. His toes dangled above the deck. "I—Maunakili—must find her at all cost. She must be mine. Is she dead?"

"No." The storyteller gasped for breath. "But the same as dead. Perhaps worse."

Maunakili released the storyteller. Kapu the Ugly crumpled to his knees. Coughed for breath. "Kidnapped…by white whalers…a year and a half ago. In the spring. Taken in their ship to the other world." The storyteller dropped his voice. "From the other world no woman kidnapped has ever returned."

The giant warrior closed on Kapu the Ugly again and growled. "What was the name of this princess-niece?"

"The *oli* chant tells her story…and says she has a birthmark like a sea turtle on her neck." Then Kapu the Ugly lied. "But the song does not say her name."

Maunakili gritted his teeth. "Maui princess…daughter of my sister…wherever you hide: You will be mine. You belong to me… princess. It is Maunakili's right as king."

CHAPTER 17

MAIN DECK/*BLACK CLOUD*
EQUATOR/ATLANTIC
NEW YEAR'S DAY 1847

DAWN ON THE EQUATOR broke to a nonexistent wind. Even the
landlubbers sensed anticipation in the motionless air. The ship was
snug. Tops'ls were set. T-gans'ls hauled up and furled. In the equatorial
doldrums flying fishes and porpoises leaped into the air. Raced past the
becalmed ship. From her bunk in the surgeon's quarters Swift heard the
morning still suddenly split by the boatswain's shrill pipe to quarters.
All hands poured on deck. The steerage passengers joined the assembly.
On both siderails — and leaning against the workshop — veteran
seamen gathered for the proceedings. A sense of mirth filled the air.
Captain Head and First Mate Dawes watched from a distance where
they perched beside the quarterdeck wheel like a black pair of ravens:
master and enforcer.

When Swift and Kikilani emerged from the companionway to join
the festivities they were dressed as comely sea surgeons in men's
pantaloons — except for their long tresses. Their manly style was met
with applause and whistles of approval. To the audience's gathered
attention Swift returned haughty waves. Then gave a pat to the bone
saw strapped to her belt. Kikilani led Swift up onto the side bulwark.

Then they climbed the ratlines to take a bird's-eye seat on the roof of the carpenter's workshop. Swift's boots and Kikilani's bare feet dangled over the extraordinary scene that greeted them.

In the gathering Swift saw that many among the shellbacks cross-dressed as painted mermaids — oft with beards. Several of these paraded before the royal company in the manner of a saucy burlesque. Somehow being costumed like seamen no longer felt strange. From their lookout Swift gave Kikilani a fleeting smile. Kikilani returned the thought with a radiant smile. "Turkish trousers suit us both...Sam."

Swift heartily agreed. "These trousers are like my riding breeches. Much more practical on ship than a society dress and petticoats." But again she smiled weakly. *And if swept overboard...the dead weight won't pull us under. Like mother.*

Swift bumped Kikilani's shoulder with hers — and the duo knew a pact was made. For the duration of the voyage the two supposed businesswomen from Philadelphia would stow their long dresses. Instead: Both would go about their days dressed comfortably like sailors.

Above the main spar deck Swift saw that a sail had been draped to create a shaded space. Under this cover and before the mainmast three water kegs faced amidships. On these kegs sat a cluster of bizarre creatures. As if arrayed on a royal throne.

Upon the elevated center barrel sat Rex of the Seas: King Neptune. Swift scribbled notes as she gave the King a long look. None other than the *Black Cloud*'s most imposing shellback was costumed from foot to crown. Literally. His legs tar-blackened under short trousers. A double-ruffled shirt. Over which a long fishnet covered His Royalty like a cape. His cheeks vermillion. A gray horsehair wig and attached beard reached from head to sandal like a regal headdress. On his head a tin crown rested. In one hand the symbol of Neptune was held: a golden trident. The King's attire was both terrible and imposing.

Swift jotted everything down. At one side of the seated Neptune stood Davy Jones. His regalia covered in barnacles. His face painted deathly white. Played by the boatswain with a stern air. At the other hand stood the Queen of the Sea: Amphitrite. Neptune's consort. Cast half-dressed and half sober for this day by the rail-thin Consul Macomber. Coconut shells for bosoms. The Queen's lips a seaweed green. Her golden locks held branches of sea coral and stiffened starfish. Her crown was a cracked and inverted flowerpot. In her arms she held in swaddling cloth a squirming piglet.

A seafarer just below them guffawed and pointed. "Neptune's royal baby."

Off to the side of the royal entourage lay stretched a small sail. Secured from the gunwale railing to a boom. This canvas created a hammock with a four-foot deep hollow. This hollow was filled with a saltwater bath colored green with some noxious agent. A plank hung over this pool.

Davy Jones stepped forward. Pounded his staff for silence.

"Hear ye...hear ye!" Jones boomed. "All those among you...known as pollywogs...step forward. You are untrustworthy slimes who have never crossed the equator...who never had your seaworthiness tested. Step forward and face your subpoena!"

The assembled seamen pushed four young sailors before the royal court. Among them stood wide-eyed Duffy Ragsdale.

Davy Jones raised both arms and thundered: "You are today summoned into Neptune's court." The ghastly figure turned toward the gathered audience. "Before this court you are commanded to answer the charges brought against all green pollywogs." The creature from the ocean bottom paused before he detailed his indictment. "That you are only *posing* as sailors. That you have not paid proper *homage* to the God of the Sea...Neptunus Rex."

A clamor burst from the gathered sailors. "Neptune! Neptune! Neptune!"

Davy Jones quieted the rabble with a gesture. Solemnly the deathly specter of the sea floor continued as he faced the four pollywogs. "You are charged with disregarding the traditions of the sea. What's more you are charged with taking licentious liberties with the subjects of His Majesty. Indecent liberties with tuna. With bonita. Dolphins. Mermaids. Whales. And other dwellers of His Majesty's deep."

King Neptune thumped his trident three times heavily on the deck.

"Test! Test! Test!" chanted the surrounding mariners.

Each young sailor was given a bowl of switchel.

"Eat your breakfast!"

Never an eatable delicacy...this particular batch of switchel had

been doctored with the hottest chilies. Ragsdale swallowed hard.
The other three young sailors spit out the first spoonful.

"Not a good sign!" bellowed Davy Jones as barnacles rattled in
his finery.

A chorus rose from the rambunctious mariners. "Not good! Not
good! Not good!"

A second mate stepped forward. Snatched the bowls from the four
novices. Then upended the bowls on the deck. Into this mass he broke
several handfuls of rotten eggs. Then irrigated the mess with the filth
from a chamber bucket.

Any previous levity had by now left the faces of the four
pollywog initiates.

"Before your next test" — Davy Jones thrust a whitewashed finger
toward heaven — "there first will be a truth serum." Cook stepped
forward and placed into each wog's mouth a peeled hard-boiled egg.
What once was a white egg was now discolored a noxious yellow
green. "Enjoy this delicious gift! Do not fail Rex Neptune! Now that
you have eaten...strip your clothes and put them on backward and
inside out!"

Catcalls rose from the sailors. The young missionary Jedidiah Wise
tried unsuccessfully to shield his bride's wide eyes. The four young men
stripped to their drawers. Put their clothes on as best they could. Inside
out. Backward.

Davy Jones' foot slipped in the mess on deck but he caught himself.
"Now on your bellies...slide like the slimy wogs you are!" The
disguised boatswain bellowed his commands. "On your bellies through
that delectable breakfast you just refused. Mop it up carefully! Nary a
morsel must escape being attached to your clothes like a mop."

The unfortunates slid forward on bellies and elbows and knees.
As they passed along the deck veteran crew whipped them hard on their
backsides with wet ropes and canvas twists. Rotten mushy potato peels
landed in the mess. Two greenhands gagged when they swallowed a
mouthful of rotten egg.

When the unfortunates reached the royal throne Davy Jones
boomed another commandment. "Kneel before the King!" All four
greenhands took a knee.

"Now kiss the royal baby's belly!"

The golden-locked Amphitrite thrust forward the piglet. The grease and tar slathered on the pink porker was now mixed with the rotten eggs on the puckered lips and faces of the wretched pollywogs.

"Kiss the foot of the sea hag!"

Consul Macomber extended his foot. Toes wiggling.

"And the ring of King Neptune!"

All four complied one by one after wiping their mouths with damp sleeves.

Neptune rose from his keg throne to his full height. Waved his golden trident and pointed toward a plank suspended over the hammock bath. "Sit and be judged!"

One by one the four youths mounted a short stepladder and slid on their rumps out onto the center of the plank. The privileged son of a ship owner went first as always. Next the freckle-faced cabin boy inched slowly onto the board. Followed by the slight Irish lad who rarely spoke but whose large eyes darted about the precarious scene. And finally landlubber Duffy Ragsdale awkwardly took last place on the plank. One of Neptune's constables shoveled the rotten leavings from the mess deck into the hammock's green slime. Another emptied into the mix a gunnysack of living bilge rats.

"Guilty! Guilty! Guilty!" sang out the shellbacks pressing forward around the main deck.

A cord was pulled that dropped the plank. All four wogs fell into the toxic bath. Slipping and sliding. Lost footing. Several flagons of beer were poured over their heads by Her Highness Amphitrite. The dregs of the last flagon mostly finished down Angus Macomber's gullet. But much overflowed his naked chest.

Davy Jones somewhat quieted the spectating crowd. "All rise in Neptune's Court!"

King Rex planted his feet apart. Thumped his trident for silence. His full-length gray beard and wig stirred in a slight breeze. "By the powers vested in me...stand!" All four greenhands rose to their feet as best they could in the muck. Supported each other. Slime dripped from every surface. Several rats scrambled down bulwark scupper holes.

"By the Order of Neptune...you have been summoned for your crimes into my court. Crimes committed against me...Neptune Rex...God of the Sea." The burly seaman raised his trident over his head like a thunderbolt. "Before this day...you were virgins! Not one amongst you had crossed the equator line. Now you have witnessed the baptism of the line. From this day forth you griffins will forever be known as shellbacks. True mariners of the sea!"

A chorus of huzzahs rang from all aboard. Forward on the anchor deck both salute guns fired. "Hip...hip...hurray! Hip...hip...hurray! Hip...hip...hurray!" The voices of a dozen men rose as one over the listless ocean.

Into this circle the Captain stepped forward. Took center stage. The master swept a black look over every man. An uneasy silence settled over the *Black Cloud*'s crew. "This diversion will be your last." Captain Head commanded their attention. "For the next weeks...we have but one course. We furrow the sea toward an element not destined by nature for the residence of man. If we are not to enter the dominions of Davy Jones forever...we must prepare." The Captain gave the assembly a cold half smile. "Before us lies Cape Horn."

In the silence Swift heard the death squeal of a rat. She and Kikilani turned their eyes toward Ratter Dawes. He stood behind the Captain's shoulder as he twisted the head off a rodent's body.

Then tossed the parts overside.

Dawes mirrored the malevolent glare of his Captain over the crew then bellowed: "Back to stations...ye dogs!"

CHAPTER 18

PERSIAN BATHS
STONE TOWN/ZANZIBAR
8 JANUARY 1847

JACK DANCER'S fingertips touched the cool metal in his inner
pocket. Inside the cigar case was the card with the rude map Captain
McKee hastily scratched that night on the SS *Rosetta* near Malta not
three weeks before. *Better to follow a hunch than do nothing.* Dancer's
mind flashed on his last eight days. Overland by staged omnibus from
Cairo to Suez on the Gulf. Peninsular & Oriental steamer *Hindostan*
the length of the Red Sea to Aden in Yemen. Finally down the East
African Coast on local packets and coastal *dhows* to Zanzibar.

Was he following the trail of Napoleon's treasure? Or was his hunch
nothing more than futility headed for a shipwreck? From Aden the
powerful winter monsoon winds drove him south...into the hands of
the Sultan of Zanzibar. Dancer knew the Sultan was one of the richest
and most feared traders of the Indian Ocean. A man said by seafarers
and secondhand newspaper reports to trade anything for a price.
Particularly slaves.

Last night in Zanzibar Harbor Dancer had hunkered under a scrap
of canvas aboard ship. The heavens descended in torrents. Rain so
heavy a man could barely stand against it. Then as quickly as it started

the monsoon deluge stopped. A thick miasma filled the air like a suffocating blanket. The smothering night filled with a cloud of mosquitoes. Dancer shuddered at the memory. *God damn gallnippers.* The insects' incessant bloodthirsty whine had only occasionally been dispersed by a feeble breeze. By morning Dancer eagerly made shore.

Being a stranger in Stone Town Dancer rehearsed the Aussie captain's advice: *Seek out the American Consul. Not that he is noteworthy. More a necessary evil. The consul can get an audience with the Sultan…and only the Sultan can help you trace the coins.* But by all means…avoid the scourge of Stone Town: Lahl Paatel.

In the tropical heat Dancer found his way to the diggings of the American Consul. Only to be told Consul Charles Ward was out of station. Now Dancer edged through Stone Town's old quarter. Tiny winding streets so narrow gossip easily carried window to window across opposite sides. Tongues wagged about the *mzungu* foreigner below. Evil had soon pressed at the white man's heels. The hair on Dancer's neck prickled. *Feels like hunting Comanches in Texas…and being hunted at the same time.*

Dancer sensed he was being followed. Ever since leaving the American Consul's lodging the menacing crowd behind him had grown in number. At every turn more sandaled feet multiplied the threat. When he stopped…they stopped. When he lit a cigar…low voices soon rose from the swarm. Steadily the mob grew through the twisted narrow streets of Zanzibar's Stone Town. Murder was on their mind. Not only the murder several days earlier of an Arab merchant by three American whalers…but Dancer's murder as well. Eye for an eye. A white man must die. Tit for tat.

Dancer hopped up on a long stone *baraza* that hugged the exterior of most of the houses along the street. The benches formed an elevated sidewalk. A lifesaver when the monsoons turned the narrow streets into maelstroms and impassable torrents flowed toward the creek on the east side of Stone Town. He pressed his back against the coral ragstone wall of a broad three-story house. *Mji Mkongwe.* Old Town. The Swahili words shot through Dancer's mind like an epitaph. He braced himself to face the robed mob. Rehearsed a conciliatory phrase or two in Arabic. Yet checked the razor-edged Bowie knife in his snake-hide cowboy boots. Then sidestepped into a doorway arch. His back braced against the brass-studded mahogany door. *If this is where my road ends...so be it. But not without a fight.* Tit or tat? Dancer would be neither.

The murderous-minded sons of the dead merchant and their mob came around the corners from both directions. *Trapped!* Blood lust filled the narrow alley four abreast. Dancer looked to his left...then right. There — in the center of the murderous mob — was the heavy-set Arab thug from Paris. Beside him covered in Berber drag was his skinny partner. *Well...well...if it's not the pig brothers.* Several curved *khanjar* blades flashed. Clubs raised. Without warning the ornate double door that supported Dancer gave way. A strong hand grabbed Dancer's arm. Jerked him inside. The heavy door slammed shut behind him. The bolt rammed in place. He spun to face his foe.

A ravishingly beautiful face greeted him in the half-light of the narrow passage. Whoever the woman was she set her fingertip under her nose...then pursed her lips against the finger. *Be silent.*

Dancer blinked. The woman before him was stunning. Her eyebrows seemed lengthened with paint. Blackened lids made her blue eyes seem wider than they actually were. She was almost as tall as he. At first she had appeared to be virtually naked...but no. She was draped in a diaphanous robe of sheer netting. The same requisite gauze that served as nightly defense against Stone Town's mosquitoes. The netting gave her voluptuous figure an almost ephemeral turn...

"Come!" she whispered.

Dancer sheathed his blade. The young beauty led him along an arched hallway. Shortly they stepped into a second larger chamber. Dancer inhaled a thick humid atmosphere. The domed room was octagonal. Seven large whitewashed sitting nooks encircled the chamber. Each nook formed by a Persian pointed arch and illumined by a high central window. In the center of this space was a pool. A step-over lip led down two steps into waist-deep water filled from a burbling spout. The woman's bare feet noiselessly led Dancer's echoing snakeskin boots carefully around the black-and-white marbled walkway. The two figures stepped carefully between patrons mingling on the walkway or sitting on the lip of the pool...dangling their legs into the water unconcerned.

Dancer's eyes adjusted to the translucent light as he and his guide made their way around the pool. The milky glow filled the space through the windowed nooks and the domed skylights above. A stimulating scent of citrus mixed with eucalyptus filled the air. As Dancer's eyes adjusted the modest light revealed the vague figures around the pool. Women...All women. Some in see-through net gowns. Others half-covered behind finely spun cotton towels.

Dancer's eyes adjusted farther. Women. From Oman. Persia. Assyria. Nubia. Ethiopia. Mozambique. And — Dancer realized — the most highly prized of all...the Russian Caucasus. Again he looked at the woman who was leading him. Earlier — on the deck of the *dhow* — he had heard stories of the Sultan's harem: a dozen free wives. A dozen more concubines. Three dozen children. But the Sultan's most beautiful daughter was a somewhat brazen princess. And a renowned beauty....

Dancer's guide led him onward. Smiles. Titters. Flashing eyes. Yet the bathers appeared not in the least disturbed by Dancer's presence.

Dancer's guide led him into a coral-stone staircase. The steps twisted upward. Dancer kept his eyes on the strong legs before him. The beauty's oiled skin filled his nose with a provocative fragrance of jasmine and clove....

They ducked under a low rounded arch. More steps deposited them before a doorway. The exotic woman poked her head outside. Then led Dancer out onto a roof and along a third-floor verandah. Through a doorway leading into the next building. Down worn steps. Then along a passage above an atrium court shielded from view below by an intricately carved rosewood screen. They stopped at a landing. Breathed heavily before a carved-teak door. The woman opened the door. Turned. Smiled. Placed her palm on Dancer's chest. And gently pushed him through the door.

The bolt slipped shut behind him.

Dancer faced the Zanzibar sunset. A languid sea breeze cooled his face. His gaze took in a panoramic view over the rooftops of Stone Town. The Old Fort below. Beyond the treetops of the Forodnani Gardens the sea glistened in the setting sun. The coral buildings took on a pinkish glow in the low light. Dancer turned slowly. Froze. There before him was a seated figure. Cross-legged on a raised divan. Smoke rose from a silver hookah. The scent carried slowly past Dancer on the evening air.

"Mr. Dancer…I presume." The greeting came in Indian-accented English. Dancer gathered enough wits to say — nothing. He bowed slowly toward the voice. Held a respective beat. Then straightened.

"Lahl Paatel." Dancer's observation was said with sincerity. "I've heard so much about you."

The Indian merchant rose. Zanzibar's wealthiest Gujarati wore his thin beard trimmed at the jaw line. An even thinner moustache graced the Banyan's upper lip. Dancer's eyes took in a trimly cut *sherwani* jacket with high embroidered collar. Gold buttons only to the waist. Under the expensive jacket he wore baggy crimson *chrono* pants. Tight at the ankles and rumpled to the knee — as if the pantaloons were a foot too long for his legs. On his feet were curl-toed brocade slippers. On his head a tightly wrapped turban clasped his ears to his temples. And accented the magnificent ensemble of crimson. Orange. Green. A triple chain of fine gold beads surrounded his neck. For effect a scarlet silk scarf was thrown over one shoulder. Drawn forward under the opposite arm and draped casually over his forearm. The entire effect was opulent wealth. Elegance. Decadence.

Paatel nodded. "I see you have met the Sultan's daughter. Dazzling beauty…no?"

Without waiting for a reply Lahl Paatel sat back down and tucked his legs under him. "The pleasure is mine…Mr. Dancer." He was the Sultan's customs collector and principal merchant who monopolized all Zanzibar trade. Paatel proffered a hookah tube and indicated that Dancer should join him on the divan. "Please…"

Dancer sat. Then took a deep draw of the mildly flavored *shisha* tobacco.

Paatel gave Dancer a sly sideways glance. "Nothing quite like Persian baths on ladies' harem day."

Dancer exhaled. The Indian trader answered with a half-smile: as friendly as a cobra ready to strike at the slightest movement.

"The wives and concubines and servants enjoy the soothing waters." Paatel took another pull on his pipe. "Today Shiekha Sharife" — he paused…and smiled — "the Sultan's daughter: She sent word that the scorpions were restless. That is her term for the undesirables among our *coolie* laborers. Some of the lowest *thuggees* have been known to ignore the Sultan's rules that confer 'most favored nation' status for American visitors."

Paatel exhaled a white cloud into the rising breeze that freshened the rooftop retreat. "Before we continue…unless you think you are going somewhere?" he said with a cold tone. "Tell us exactly why you are here…Mr. Dancer."

CHAPTER 19

TRADER PAATEL'S ROOFTOP
STONE TOWN/ZANZIBAR
MINUTES LATER

DANCER MADE a split-second calculation. *Honesty can wait.* If Paatel wanted him dead...he would have left Dancer on the street. But the Indian merchant apparently wanted something more. Something greater than credit for turning over a white man to his coolies.

Dancer again gave a long exhale of smoke. Then turned to face Paatel with an expression of open frankness. "My purpose is simple. I'm sent here by a cartel of Texas planters who have more cotton than they have hands to pick it. My mission is profitable trade."

Paatel nodded. "Yes. First the Dutch and then the Portuguese tried to rule the Indian Ocean. Now the British and French want to control our trade. That is why the Sultan of Oman signed a most-favored-nation treaty with America — not the Europeans — in 1833. And why he moved his sultanate to Zanzibar in 1840. The arrangements we've enjoyed with your previous consul — Richard Waters — have been...how shall I say? Most profitable...."

Dancer nodded. "Exactly. My country — and Texas — offer an alternative to the imperial dominion of Britain and France. We offer profits. No strings attached. Our only interest is trade. Not colonies."

"I am listening." Paatel's voice was cool.

Dancer spoke confidently as he fabricated. "But the Sultan has signed a treaty with the British. A little over a year ago…wasn't it? Yes. 1845. About the same time my beloved Texas joined the Americans. Now His Highness the Sultan — and some minor Zanzabari merchants — have second thoughts about the British. Instead they want to expand trade with the French to offset the British influence." Dancer paused. He threw a casual look toward Paatel. "But my cartel suspects that you want to protect your trade with the Americans — and keep your cozy monopoly to yourself. Are we right…Mr. Paatel?"

Paatel shifted uncomfortably. Then gave a reluctant head waggle of agreement. "Look what the British did to India. They dominated the land. And they froze Oman — and the Sultan — out of direct trade with India. We must navigate the trade waters very carefully. Both the British and French are tiresome. First the British banned the slave trade. Then they claimed the Indian Banyans in Zanzibar were British citizens! As if that gave the British the right to rule the Sultan." Paatel twisted his legs under himself almost into a knot. "Now the French set up a so-called 'Free Labour Emigration System' for Africans. Hypocrites! Just a ruse to steal slaves from our territory on the Africa coast. Territory that belongs to the Sultan's authority! A blatant attack on the Sultan's sovereignty. Without Paatel's heavy tariffs on the British and French" — the man spoke of himself in the third person — "the Americans would no longer enjoy the low prices they are so found of." Paatel gently tapped a bound ledger beside his hookah.

Dancer probed. "Now that Mr. Waters — and his codfish aristocracy from Massachusetts — are gone…I understand Consul Charles Ward is not up to the task of peddling their overpriced Yankee notions."

Paatel almost gagged on a chaw of betel nut. "The fool is an officious ninny! Nor does Ward take the hint. First his lodging rental was canceled by a merchant. Then his house was stoned for more than twenty nights. No one will translate messages for Ward from the Sultan. Even his firewood was stolen. One day he shoved a merchant over some slight — and was beaten by the merchant's slaves. Two weeks' recovery!" Paatel raised two heavily jeweled fingers. "What does Ward do?

He writes your Secretary of State Buchanan long letters. Ward doesn't have the first idea how Mr. Waters and I ran our little…arrangement."

Dancer inhaled slowly from the hookah. "The Indian Ocean trade is not made by nations. The trade is created by the sea…by ships… It has a maritime identity. A system of traders — not states…Is that not true?" Dancer bluffed. "Waters told me you were the kingpin behind the trade for the Sultan."

Paatel beamed. "For almost eight years! 1837 to 1845. The arrangement was simple. Waters encouraged ships from Salem to bring their goods to Zanzibar. Paatel arranged a palaver at Waters' lodging. He brought the Yankee captain and his sample goods. Cotton *merkani* cloth. Mirrors. Chairs. Perfume. Gold thread. Hardware. Whatever our spice plantations needed. Paatel brought the merchants of Zanzibar. Paatel translated. The conduit. The captains dealt with Paatel…and Paatel alone. The planters and merchants dealt with Paatel…and Paatel alone. The best price was agreed for the inbound cargo. That price was paid with goods for a return cargo…such as gum copal from the Swahili Mrima coast…the Sultan's territory from Tangate to Kilwa in East Africa."

Dancer leaned in. "Gum copal from East African trees….The resin is a key mineral ingredient in varnish and shellac?"

Paatel's head waggled. "Yes. Our resin is in great demand. Furniture. Ships. Carriages. The Sultan controls the world trade in gum copal. Your country now gets almost two-thirds of the shipments. Germany takes the remainder. Paatel always supplies cases of the highest quality gum copal…cleaned for varnish."

"But sometimes lesser merchants slipped in dirty 'jackass' copal?" Dancer said as he pricked at Paatel's overblown self-importance.

The Indian held up both hands in protest. Then dismissed the trifling allegation with a backward flip of his fingers.

Paatel continued his description of his trading monopoly: "Paatel's return cargos also included bales of leather hides for shoes. Persian carpets. Ivory tusks for carving. Sacks of coffee from Mocha. Spices from Zanzibar. Cloves. Even…" Paatel paused.

Dancer finished his sentence: "Even slaves."

"The captains knew what to ship to Zanzibar…and Paatel knew what they wanted in return trade. Of course — as customs collector for the Sultan — Paatel had to collect taxes on all imports…and all exports. And — of course — Paatel must pass along the coolie-hire fees necessary to offload the cargos and store the goods in my Customs House. Also necessary were the coolie costs to transfer the export goods of the local Banyans to the ships. Paatel's records were perfect. For the Americans' benefit Paatel set taxes and fees much higher for the French and British. They rarely came back. Plus…Paatel's palaver got the best prices from the local traders — who appreciated Paatel's conduit. Without Paatel and Mr. Waters…neither side would have prospered."

"Of course." Dancer spoke offhandedly. As if he stated the obvious. "You simply greased the slips."

Lahl Paatel took a satisfied draw on his hookah.

Dancer returned to his point. "As always…America and the Sultanate of Zanzibar are on the same side. We are both small fish. That means we must be smart…efficient…resourceful…and swim quickly where the big fish of Britain and France cannot follow."

"You've described the harbor of Stone Town precisely… Mr. Dancer. Too shallow for big ships. Very profitable for Americans. Please continue."

"I'm here to offer you an even bigger Texas trade than you had with the Salem merchants. Have you heard of Texas? We are the newest state in the United States. Joined up just a year ago. Like I said…December 1845." Dancer paused. Then set the hook. "Texas is a huge land…as large as the territory of Tanganyika over yonder. Cotton. Sugar. Cattle. Plantations everywhere. But not enough hands to work the fields."

"How is this important to me?" Paatel asked.

"One thing…my friend. Slaves. Texas is a slave state. For our economy to reach its potential we need slaves. Now. As soon as possible. As many as we can buy. Shiploads of slaves."

"But you Americans outlawed importing slaves. Now you breed your own — especially in Virginia — and sell them to the Southern States 'down the river'…as you say. That undercuts our prices."

Without asking Paatel's permission Dancer reached out and flipped over the slave trader's tariff ledger. Opened it to a blank page. With a pencil stub he used broad strokes to sketch an outline of the United States and the territories west of the Mississippi River. Then drew Texas in the lower center. "Best thing about Texas is our coastline. Our Gulf

Coast. Ships drop the slaves directly on Texas soil. No need to worry about abolitionist eyes. No need to worry about delivery fifteen hundred miles overland from Virginia. Not in Texas. Not when you know how to run Padre Island." Dancer smacked his palm on the map. Then raised the ante. "We send our own ships to you. Transport is our expense. Any die-off is our problem. Your profit is higher."

The merchant smiled cunningly. Untangled his legs. "Dancer" — Paatel sat forward on the divan's edge — "how many do you need? Ten slaves a month?"

"No. More."

"Twenty slaves a month?"

"No. Not enough. Many more."

"Thirty?"

Dancer shook his head. "Nope. Tell you what. I've got a number here. When you're tired of guessing...I'll show you my number."

Lahl Paatel hesitated. Dancer handed him a scrap of paper. The Indian's eyes popped.

"That's right. Two hundred a month for the first year."

Paatel sucked at his teeth. Impressed.

Dancer artfully closed the deal with a gambler's nonchalance. "And that's just for starters. We can make each other rich...my friend. Very rich. Do we have a deal?"

The merchant haggled. As Dancer knew he would. "The French buy every slave Paatel can acquire for their coffee and sugar plantations in the Mascarene Islands east of Mozambique. And for the Seychelles."

"But the French pay in common *merkani* cloth. Trade beads. China plates. And less than they pay on Africa's West Coast. What I have to trade doesn't compare...not even close." Dancer half smiled. He knew the trade competition as well as Paatel himself. This irked his host. The merchant shrugged.

Dancer played his monte card. "In payment for your human cargo...Texas doesn't pay in cloth. Or trinkets. We pay in guns. And powder. And shot."

Paatel straightened.

Dancer continued. "Not those worthless secondhand British Brown Bess muskets. Never. We ship only the best. Double-trigger Hawken rifles like our mountain men and buffalo hunters use.

Plus only the best Whitneyville Colt Dragoon revolvers. Your little African slave-gathering raids to the Swahili coast will be more productive. Very much more productive indeed."

"Perhaps we can reach a deal...." The Banyan smiled. His teeth stained red from his habit of chewing Indian betel nut. With his words Paatel replaced the hookah pipe. Stood. Then beckoned to Dancer.

"Come." The merchant gestured. "There is something you should see."

CHAPTER 20

PAATEL'S PLEASURE ROOM
STONE TOWN/ZANZIBAR
A SHORT WHILE LATER

DANCER FOLLOWED the figure of Paatel's embroidered jacket into a candlelit anteroom. The ornate chamber was clearly the Gujarati's pleasure room. Sculptures. Statues. And plasters of unclad goddesses and naked women adorned every inch of the space.

"Why wait until heaven to enjoy these virgins?" Paatel half joked as he ran his fingers slowly over the polished curves of a voluptuous marble figure. The trader stepped to an Indian rosewood table where a silver tray held his extensive collection of Kamasutra cards with miniature Rajput paintings of sex positions. Paatel paused to admire several cards. With an approving head waggle he selected a graphic card and handed it to Dancer. The picture showed two turbaned princes ravishing a naked maiden on a divan. Dancer tucked the gift into his jacket pocket.

"Will you do one thing for me..." Paatel asked without asking. The merchant retrieved a brown leather notebook from a drawer in a gilded sideboard table. Then he extended the notebook toward Dancer. Dancer looked at the notebook without touching it: Paatel held it upside down and backward. The open edge faced left—just as the

Quran in Arabic would open.

"What is this?" Dancer asked. He took the notebook and stepped closer to a brace of candles. Turned his back to Paatel. Then opened the journal. It was indeed upside down: When he flipped it over he found pages of writing in a trained French hand. Sketches of antiquities that had been carefully drawn. Maps of Egypt and the surrounding area. He turned through several more pages. And stopped only when he came to a page with a sketch of three coins from the treasury of Malta.

He stared at the sketches of the coins. The realization struck Dancer like a thunderbolt. Whoever sent the pig brothers to ransack Professor Champollion's apartment ordered them to take the notebook to Zanzibar before him. Dancer was playing catch-up.

He was about to turn back to Paatel when a second realization struck him. Paatel had handed him the volume the wrong side up: He had no idea what he had. He couldn't read French.

Dancer again drew the notebook to the candlelight. And continued turning through the pages...Who sent the two thugs to steal Champollion's notebook? Whoever brought the notebook here knew Zanzibar was a critical stop on the trail of Napoleon's treasure. Who was it? Even if the trader could not read English...did Paatel know Dancer knew the origin of the leather notebook?

Dancer took a deep breath — unsure of his next move. When in doubt...bluff.

Dancer flipped the notebook upside down and backward again. Turned back to Paatel. Fanned through several pages back to front in the Arabic fashion. Finally Dancer shrugged. "Okay...if you like this sort of thing. Personally I prefer your Rajput drawings." Dancer tapped his jacket pocket with a slight leer. "What you have here is a coin collector's notebook. See these sketches? Mostly coins. Some old...some French. Are you a collector...Paatel?"

Dancer returned the book to Paatel who placed it back in the drawer he had withdrawn it from. From that same drawer the merchant pulled a tiny bag. From the bag four or five coins fell into his hand. The Indian proffered the coins to Dancer.

Dancer immediately recognized the coins. Clearly part of Napoleon's treasure. Still...he examined each briefly. Spit on one. Cleaned it on his pants. Rubbed it with his thumb. "Yup. Old coins.

See how they are worn almost smooth? Not worth much unless you are a museum…or a jewelry maker." Dancer dropped the coins back into the bag. And Paatel dropped the bag into the desk drawer.

"Interesting hobby." Dancer continued to feign disinterest. "Now back to business. Do we have a deal…Paatel? Two hundred slaves a month for a year…in exchange for guns and powder and shot?" Paatel haggled the details. Dancer held out. Paatel demanded gifts — ostensibly for the Sultan. Spermaceti candles. Reams of letter paper. Refined sugar. Music boxes. Chandeliers. Dancer pretended to balk. Then reluctantly accepted the exorbitant price. "Still a bargain compared to Africa's western Slave Coast along the Bight of Benin. Even the children there bring a fine penny…let me tell you."

The Banyan's eyes narrowed. "Throw in your cowboy boots…and we have a deal."

Dancer laughed. "If that's what it takes. I'm in." Dancer pulled up his right pant leg. "My Arkansas toothpick ain't included." He smiled…then openly transferred the Bowie knife to his belt. Then pulled off his boots. Handed them to the merchant. Paatel stripped off his curly-toed slippers. Jammed his feet into the snakeskin cowboy boots. In a poor imitation of a Texan at high noon Lahl Paatel clumped across the marble floor. The heels thrust his posture forward. He turned at the door. A forced smile seemed frozen on his brown face.

"Let us drink to seal our agreement."

Paatel poured wine into two silver goblets on a heavy carved table next to Dancer. "Drink!" But he was sloppy in his pouring: Some of the wine spilled down the sides of each goblet.

Dancer noted the spilled wine. He nodded to Paatel as he reached for his goblet. "Show me that Texas walk one more time…pardner." While Paatel crossed the floor Dancer adjusted the positions of the goblets on the table: He shifted each goblet slightly so it sat off-center on the same wet ring that had formed at its base when Paatel spilled the wine. Then Dancer pretended to admire a freestanding mermaid-shaped bronze candlestick nearby.

Paatel returned to the table. He noticed the slightly off-centered position of each goblet and assumed Dancer had switched them. Awkwardly with one hand he reached for the far goblet…meant for Dancer. And with the other hand stretched for the near goblet…intended for himself only moments before. Then he extended the near goblet to Dancer. Both men drained their wine.

Paatel's mouth turned up in a malevolent smile. His eyes locked with Dancer's. An instant later Paatel's face froze. His body stiffened. His heels jerked backward against a cylindrical pillow. Then his body toppled over the pillow backward to the floor as stiff as a plank. The senseless body came to rest…with Dancer's cowboy boots high in the air.

"Can't hold your liquor…Paatel?"

Dancer hastily pulled open the desk drawer. Grabbed the leather notebook and tiny coin bag. Stuffed them inside his shirt. Then stripped off Paatel's gold-brocade slippers. Pulled on his own boots. Then leaped to the door. Dancer yanked the long mermaid candlestick from its base…scattering the burning candles across the polished floor. Jammed the sculpture through the arched-maiden door handles. Then ripped a curtain cord off its fixture. And tied the candlestick and door handles quickly together.

Dancer ran to the balcony doors. Pulled down the curtain rod holding up gossamer curtains. Stripped the sheer fabric off the rod. Found the middle as he dragged the cloth onto the balcony. Stuffed the ends of the doubled curtain around a balcony baluster. Then clambered over the railing and slid down the curtains like a rope. At the same moment Paatel's guards pounded through the Pleasure Room door. Intent on slitting the American's throat.

Dancer dropped the last feet to a dim back alley as guards raised the alarm above him. He sprinted down the dark alley. Rounded a corner. Looked back. Just then strong arms grabbed him.

Hooded and overpowered…Dancer was dragged helplessly toward oblivion.

CHAPTER 21

FOR SWIFT AND KIKILANI the day started like all the other days before. But today—after thirty-nine days at sea—the *Black Cloud* would finally cross the Tropic of Capricorn. A muffled knock came at their surgery-cabin door. Followed by a miserable groan. Through the opened door stumbled a young greenhand hugging his belly with both arms—Duffy Ragsdale. He croaked in misery: "Got the gripe somethin' awful. Maybe somethin' I 'et."

Ragsdale grimaced bashfully at Kikilani and Swift. Swift unstoppered a bottle that contained a watery solution of flavorings. Cinnamon. Licorice juice. And concentrated peppermint essence. Swift poured a quarter tot of Woodall's general cure for belly gripe. Vomiting. And hiccups. Then handed the mixture to Kikilani. Ragsdale accepted the elixir from his Island Eve with shy gratitude. Then sheepishly confessed to the Philadelphia ladies: "My name's not really Duffy. It's Malcolm. That's the Christian name my mother gave me on our farm on Long Island." The lad raised a sunburnt hand and sipped the medicine while holding his midsection with the other. "My mother always said I was a huckleberry above a persimmon—and that I could be anything I wanted if I set my mind to it. She died from typhus when I was ten. Rest her soul. Then my father died last spring. My uncle took the farm. That's why I went to sea. And also for the adventure."

Kikilani gave the uncomfortable wog an encouraging smile. But Ragsdale's shared grief of orphans unexpectedly flooded over Swift in anguished memories. Her mind flashed on the day her mother drowned in that canal. And her father died too soon after from a broken heart.

A coldness shot through Swift. Kikilani noticed. Swift struggled to find a response to the loathing she felt toward her uncle…Jacob Swift. He had wooed her mother. But soon lost the Welch beauty to his younger brother…Thomas Swift. A smarting loss that drove Jacob Swift's revenge. Still to this day.

After a brief hesitation Ragsdale babbled on. "Nobody never met a real sailor named Malcolm. That's why I signed on as Duffy. Sounds like a real sea dog…don't it? Been practicin' my seamen's knots since I was a pollywog." The guileless Ragsdale showed Swift the uniquely braided safety cord he hung from his belt and used in the watch-rings. "Cain't be too careful when you're in the rings atop the mainmast watchin' for a whale to blow. That is…once I git to see my first one in the Pacific. I'll 'bout 'ave turned seventeen by the time we reach the islands."

Ragsdale emptied the medicine tot and stood to leave. Then bent closer to both Swift and Kikilani. "Beware of Ratter Dawes." Ragsdale lowered his voice to a soft whisper. "I overheard some talk in the crew mess. Dawes was passing out the midday tots from the rum tub. He and his rum bosun gave themselves double rations. 'Splice the mainbrace' they ordered…for their own good service." Ragsdale drew away. And glanced both ways outside the cabin. Then leaned back in. "Dawes said you and Kikilani are nothing but whores. He bragged he planned to take his pleasure on you both. Be warned."

"Don't worry about us…Duffy." Swift spoke confidently. "These are tight quarters…and help is always near at hand. But thank you for your kind warning. We will keep our guard up."

Ragsdale bobbed his head. Then stepped outside and closed the surgery door.

Some hours later Swift found herself enjoying the midday calm whilst sitting beside the ship's cook and transcribing a letter for him on the main deck. The calm was abruptly broken by the call from the lookout atop the mainmast. "Ship ahoy! The *Condor*! Flying the flag of a hen frigate! She signaled a request to gam us...sir!"

Swift's gaze followed every pair of eyes on the cloudless Sunday in the South Atlantic. All on deck turned toward the approaching whaler. The ship's cook sitting with Swift hastily signed the letter she had scribed for him.

"Tell me...what is a 'hen frigate'?" Swift inquired.

The mostly sober chef returned the letter to Swift. "That's a blubber hunter with a woman on board...miss. Probably the captain's wife. She'll want to come aboard the *Cloud* to greet us. And exchange the news. If they're headed to New York...can you give her my letter?"

"I'd be happy to."

The Captain gave orders to hove to and put their head into the wind. "Prepare to accept visitors!"

Sails were backed. The crest from the bow wave dropped. Gradually the ship hove to a near standstill. Shortly the American whaler came about. As the *Condor* settled astern the *Black Cloud*'s waist the New York-bound whaler dropped its own sea anchor. Soon with the vessels no more than a ship's length apart the *Condor* lowered a whaleboat. The double-bowed craft was rowed toward the *Black Cloud*. A short portly man with a white beard and the look of a master sat in the bow. An even shorter and stouter woman in black holding down her ruffled bonnet weighed down the stern. She projected the rigid bearing of a bollard post. As the whaleboat drew alongside Swift watched the crew of the *Black Cloud* lower a wicker gamming chair. The dangling contraption seemed a cross between a basket chair and a porch swing. The heavyset lady was the first to be lifted aboard. Her husband—the ship's captain—then climbed up the side on a Jacob's ladder as quickly as the swaying rope-and-rungs—and his girth—allowed. Followed nimbly by the *Condor*'s first mate...who sported a bush of flaming red hair.

Captain Thomas Hunter introduced Mrs. Hunter to Captain Head. First Mate John Salt—who came aboard on the heels of Captain Hunter—warmly greeted Ratter Dawes. As old acquaintances the captains and mates adjourned directly to Captain Head's quarters. Mrs. Hunter extended her greeting to Reverend Wise's wife. The pale woman made her best curtsy. Then turned abruptly and scampered back down the passenger companionway—either from seasickness or morning sickness. Her husband followed. From the corner of her eye Swift saw that Kikilani looked equally distressed before she too disappeared down the cable-tier ladder.

Mrs. Hunter turned a stern gaze toward the only other woman passenger on the deck of the *Black Cloud*. "If we may…" The whaling Captain's wife frowned and made a gesture that suggested she and Swift go belowdecks.

The duo made their way to the surgeon's cabin. Where they greeted Thomas—the freckle-faced cabin boy—coming out of the surgery after he delivered coffee and fried pan bread. "Compliments of the cook." As the cabin boy ascended the companionway and Mrs. Hunter inspected the surgery Swift hung back in the cable tier passageway. Kikilani stuck her head out from behind a curtain of rope skeins hung beneath the companionway stairs. She looked terrified.

"What's wrong?" Swift asked in a whisper. "Did you see a ghost?"

"I know that ship. The *Condor*. And that Captain and his mate."

"What do you mean?"

"That is the ship that kidnapped Loki and me from Lahaina twenty months ago."

Kikilani trembled at the memory of her encounter.

"How can you be sure?"

"I'll never forget that redheaded first mate. They call him Red John." Kikilani tried to control the cold memory that ran up her spine. "That's the same sailor who told me Loki was aboard the *Condor*."

"That was Red John?"

Kikilani shot a terrified glance up toward the companionway doors that opened onto the upper deck. Crossed her arms and shuddered. A wan expression froze her face. Unable to speak.

Swift wanted to ask more questions but realized there was no time. Thinking quickly she made a plan. "Hide in the forward cargo hold. You'll be safe there. Stay behind the kegs but near the hatch. When we feel the ship is underway and it's all clear I'll rap on the grate three times."

Swift and Kikilani lifted and slid back the wooden fore hold grate. "Take this sticking-iron and matches. But don't light the candle…except as a distress signal." Kikilani took the objects Swift held out to her. Then climbed silently down to the cargo deck that held the *lazarette* cell at the opposite end. Swift replaced the forward hold's cover.

Swift rejoined the whaler's wife as the nosey woman closed Woodall's guide on the apothecary counter and tapped it with a plump finger. Swift gestured for her visitor to pull the examining stool from under the table and take a seat. She looked quickly at Mrs. Hunter. The plain woman was stuffed into a black silk dress and corset. Above her deep-set eyes a weathered forehead receded to a white streak in her dark hair as severe as Moses parting the waters. The remainder of her hair was pulled taut behind her neck and mostly hidden by her old-fashioned Sunday-come-a-calling bonnet. Swift asked herself if the Captain — or his wife — administered the strictest discipline aboard the *Condor*.

From across the narrow table Mrs. Hunter gave Swift a severe look. "I see the missionary's wife is properly escorted. Are you…?" The austere woman let her question hang in the air as she cast a disapproving eye over Swift's banded-collar blouse and Turkish trousers.

"Oh…yes." Swift had answered the stern woman confidently. "My traveling companion and I have each other."

Mrs. Hunter coughed. Then gave a sour smile…as though she'd swallowed something that did not agree with her.

Swift moved the cabin boy's coffee and fried bread within the woman's reach. Mrs. Hunter ignored the coffee and selected the largest slice of pan bread. After a fulsome bite the Captain's wife's demeanor softened as she chewed. Then she gave Swift what passed for a thin smile.

"Perhaps life cooped up in that day cabin put a few too many barnacles on my manners." She washed down the cook's slightly burned offering with a sip of coffee and wrinkled her nose as if the bitterness disappointed her. "My apologies." After a moment the flinty preacher's daughter reached into her bag and presented a book to Swift. "Please accept this copy of Daniel Defoe's *Robinson Crusoe*. I take it on every voyage to read to the lads. On the outbound journey they appreciate the story of a castaway." She gave a doleful half smile. "But by now they are more in the mood for penny dreadfuls. Seems the tedium of the ship's work has worn away the excitement of the chase. I'm afraid loneliness and boredom have taken ascendency with the men. Rollicking blood and buxom wagtails are all they dream of now."

Mrs. Hunter handed the volume to Swift. Then reached for another fry bread. "For me the discomforts of life at sea are preferable to years of separation. Once had to navigate when Captain Hunter fell ill. And another time I helped the crew put out a shipboard fire from an over-stoked try-pot furnace." Sun-baked crow's feet showed in the corners of Mrs. Hunter's knowing eyes. "That book has been well used on this short voyage. A bit worn around the edges...perhaps a bit like me. But the men enjoy the story when it's read to them."

"Do you always accompany your husband?"

"I try. But not the voyage before this one. When the *Condor* left New York I was in the family way. That was April 1844. Little Thomas had just turned one year old when the ship returned in September 1845." The whaler's wife gave Swift a look that suggested an unanswered question. "Don't know why...but that voyage was one of Master Hunter's most profitable." The stout lady shook her head and gazed around the surgeon's quarters.

Swift took the opportunity to try to glean more information from her guest. "Does your husband sail with the same crew always?" she asked.

"Oh...heavens no. Not at all. Entirely a fresh set of hands this time. Except for John Salt. The mate."

"The one with red hair?"

"That's Red John. Don't cotton to him myself...something of a bad egg who never proves as good as his promise. But Master Hunter swears by him...so I make do."

Swift nodded with a smile and pulled Melville's *Typee* from her shelf. "Here. Take this book in return. It's a new story about a South Sea princess and a castaway. I've read it twice during the crew's after-supper social hour. It's been published since you set out on your voyage. Also...here are several New York newspapers. As you see they're from late November. But I suspect the news and fashions will be new to you."

Mrs. Hunter accepted the book and newspapers graciously. "Is there anything I can do for you…my dear? We should reach port in about forty days. About the same time you have been at sea."

"There is something."

The two women stood up. Swift opened her journal bag hung from the apothecary cabinet…and took out a tied packet. "Would you be so kind to post these letters for the men when you reach New York?"

"Yes. Certainly." Mrs. Hunter put the letter bundle into her drawstring reticule bag. "We women of the sea need to help each other in every way."

"You're too kind." Swift gave Mrs. Hunter a warm smile. "Also…here is a diary I've kept about the voyage so far. Could you see it reaches Mr. Whitman at the *Brooklyn Daily Eagle*? I'd be very much obliged."

Mrs. Hunter blinked at the name of that across-the-river newspaper but added the addressed journal to her promise. Then made ready to leave the surgery.

"Oh…by the way…I do have one other curiosity." Swift spoke offhandedly as she reached for the surgery's door. "What was your Captain's good fortune on his previous voyage?"

"That's a good question: he never rightly said. Something about 'special cargo' that 'brought a pretty penny'…whatever that means." Mrs. Hunter then turned to Swift and spoke softly not to be overheard. "It's never easy to be a woman in a man's world…as I'm sure you know. Be prudent…my dear. And give heed to the scuttlebutt of the ship." Her eyes raised a glance toward deck to assure herself the stairway was clear. "In my experience men gossip before they reveal unwanted attentions…shall we say."

Swift shook hands firmly and the women exchanged knowing glances.

"Thank you…Mrs. Hunter. As you say…I'll watch out."

They walked together to the companionway. Swift then raised her hands…bracing herself against the bulk of Mrs. Hunter's backside as she pushed while her visitor strained to ascend the ladder to the deck. Moments later—as the boatswain positioned Mrs. Hunter's substantial girth in the wicker gamming chair—she motioned for Swift to come closer.

"Be sure you take to heart what I said." Mrs. Hunter clutched the wicker supports as the windlass hoisted the gamming chair off the deck. "Where you are going"—she had to raise her voice now—"you'll need it."

Sunset soon brought the end to the unsettling Sunday. Swift retrieved Kikilani out of the forward hold: Together they returned to the surgery and closed its door behind them. As a distraction they busied themselves with Woodall's prescriptions. Then stowed their medicinal herbs and tinctures. Returned the plastering supplies to the dressing chest. And settled into their berths. Their whispers took another turn in the candlelight when Swift asked what Kikilani expected when she got back home.

"Who knows?" Kikilani shrugged innocently. "I was a commoner before I left...so I will be a commoner when I return. But I can't say for sure. It's not clear. I might find myself an orphan—I have no knowledge of my parents."

"You don't know?"

"The truth is...for generations storytellers kept my people's genealogy alive with *mele* chants...but many *ali'i* storytellers died from the *haole* foreigner's diseases. So many that much of our oral history died with them. By now my bloodline—whatever it might have been—has been forgotten too."

Swift leaned forward with her arms wrapped around her knees. "A matriarchal lineage."

Kikilani ran her palm along the wooden edge of her boxed berth and smiled shyly. "Everyone knows who their mother is." Kikilani blushed. "But not necessarily who was their father."

Swift felt a stab of loneliness again.

"How did you get kidnapped?"

"In Lahaina Harbor I went to the *Condor* to fetch my cousin Loki. *Loki* means 'rose' in my language. She always wore a fragrant tube-rose flower in her hair. But we were drugged...only to wake up at sea. I was trapped. Loki was gone."

"What happened to her?"

"Maybe she died from the drugs...and they threw her overboard?"

Kikilani murmured in a low voice as her eyes welled with tears. "The mate—Red John—told me she jumped from the ship in despair. His tone made it clear his intention was not an explanation but a warning." Kikilani shuddered. And pulled a thin blanket under her chin.

Swift held her knees tighter. *Drowning. My worst nightmare.*

"When the *Condor* reached New York the first mate hauled me to a warehouse on the wharf and sold me to a pimply man reeking of fish. He took me to a seedy bar in Five Points—and from there an uptown gentleman took me to the Paradise Palace." The stricken Kikilani shook her head at the memory. "I quickly learned how to fake disease. What some called 'the French Pox.'"

Swift reached across to the other bunk and squeezed her friend's ankle under the cover. "That's one way to give those Jonathans the mitten. Nothing like the pox to keep them at a distance."

Kikilani expelled a heavy sigh. "That's why Queen Tin'a made me a hostess instead of working the men. Every day my only prayer was survival. Simply survival. One day—after fourteen months—another island girl read me your newspaper story."

"The one about unwanted wives committed to the madhouse by their husbands?"

"That's the one. You exposed the truth about those trapped women. That gave me my first hope. I began to dream I could maybe someday get out of that madam's madhouse...That I could truly return home."

Swift listened into the dusk as the *Black Cloud* beat a steady course toward Cape Horn. She learned of the decimation of Kikilani's people from disease. How the traditional *kapu* system was broken in 1819 after the death of King Kamehameha the Great.

"*Kapu?* What's that?"

"*Kapu* is our traditions. Taboos. Our laws. Rules. *Kapu* tells us what is sacred and all the things you cannot do."

"Like what Christians call the Ten Commandments?"

Kikilani nodded and gave a forlorn sigh. "The old *kapu* rules were thrown away. All order was lost. Into that void came the whalers. Then the missionaries. Both brought disease. One of the body. The other of the soul."

Swift nodded sympathetically as Kikilani told how the reigning Hawaiian King was torn between old ways and new realities.

"A council of foreigners persuaded the young King to move the royal capital from Lahaina on Maui to Honolulu on O'ahu. One old *ali'i* told us the American missionary advisors argued for the King to relocate his throne. They insisted: Be near the British. The French. The commercial hub." Forlornly Kikilani chewed her thumbnail. "Fearful for his kingdom's weakness without old gods to protect him the young King relented."

"That was almost two years ago…wasn't it? 1845?"

"Yes. Just months later Loki and I were abducted. Red John and Captain Hunter were the men behind it. I'm sure."

Sometime later just overhead from the fo'c'sle deck the ship's bell sounded eight times. After they snuffed the feeble glow of their solitary candles Swift lay back in her bunk and tried to put her thoughts in order. Surrounding them were the ghostly sounds of groaning timbers and strained rigging as the *Black Cloud* swept on. Toward the deadly seamen's hell called Cape Horn.

CHAPTER 22

RECEPTION *DURBAR*/SULTAN'S PALACE
STONE TOWN/ZANZIBAR
9 JANUARY 1847

OBLIVION SMELLED of jasmine and clove. Dancer's mind floated up from its well of unconsciousness. From somewhere a thought formed. *If I've died...I've gone to heaven.*

Gradually Dancer became more aware that he was not alone. Gentle strokes grazed the back of his hands. Rubbed his feet. Cooled his forehead. His eyes fluttered open. His blurry gaze became filled with a halo of faces. Angels. In the center—as large as life—Shieka Sharife smiled down at him. The most angelic countenance of all.

In a moment the face withdrew. Another face. Brown eyes. White trimmed beard. A royal face crowned by a blue-and-white checked Omani turban fringed with broad red borders. Around the figure's waist was tied a cashmere shawl of equally bright colors. Over a long white *dishdasha* undergarment the man wore a black *bisht* robe trimmed with gold. Splendidly embroidered at the shoulders. A curved *khanjar* dagger with gold and silver filigree decorated the rhino-hide hilt protruding from his waist shawl.

"Welcome back...Mr. Dancer." The Sultan of Zanzibar smiled slightly.

"Where was I?" Dancer quavered.

"It is a calming potion we often use for unruly chickens… and slaves."

Dancer drew his fingers across his brow to clear the grogginess. "It works."

"I am Said bin…Sultan of Zanzibar. You are safe now. You are in my palace. You are in my care…and our American friend."

The Sultan moved across the reception *durbar* with a slight limp. Caused by a ball still lodged in his thigh from a battle forty-years past. Legend claimed the Sultan took the ball when he saved an English artilleryman during the victory over the Wahahbi from Saudi Arabia. Neither the wound nor the war's memory had healed.

Dancer pushed himself up by both elbows. An explosion like a thunderbolt slammed between his temples. He sank back onto the cushions with a groan.

"Drink this." At the Sultan's direction Shieka Sharife drew a small handleless *fenjan* cup to Dancer's lips. "Zanzibari coffee with cardamom and clove is the elixir that solves all ills."

Dancer's eyes gradually adjusted to the room around him. He discovered he was propped on a rolled-arm couch in the *durbar* chamber where the Sultan apparently held court. The American's gaze focused on the Sultan and his daughter…Sharife. The blue-eyed Shieka returned his gaze with an intrigued look of curiosity. Then Dancer noticed there was a third man in the room who looked like an ancient beachcomber shriveled by sun and groveling hardship. Dancer screwed up his eyes to look at the gaunt survivor who clutched a brown leather notebook—Champollion's notebook— in his bony fingers.

"*Excuse moi…mon ami*. Allow me…" the wizened visage began. "*Je suis* Rene LaFleur." The tattered mariner giggled slightly as he introduced himself. His glance darted furtively from the Sultan. To the window. To Dancer. And to the door…like a rat listening for a dog. The Sultan cleared his throat—bringing LaFleur back from his reverie. He continued in a heavy French accent: "*Les* Indian Banyans *pour qui'ls gagnet leur vie vendre les* slaves. They get top money from the Amazons for selling white men. Only by the grace of the Sultan do any men escape."

LaFleur's age was as indeterminant as the man himself. Dancer guessed seventy-five. If not ninety.

Dancer sat up with an effort. Drained the last of his spiced coffee. The Shieka placed the cup on a heavy side table where she had also placed the foreigner's cigar case and metal flask. All faces in the room seemed to inquire why Dancer had come to Stone Town. Dancer wanted to know why the castaway held Champollion's leather notebook.

Dancer made another split-second calculation. *This treasure hunt will remain a mystery unless I have the Sultan on my side. Deal straight.* He got right to the point. "I'm in search of a legend."

"You mean a ghost?"

"In some ways…yes. Though part legend…part ghost."

"And what is this legend — or ghost — you seek…Mr. Dancer?" the Sultan asked.

"It is the story of Napoleon's treasure. Stolen at Malta. Shipped from Egypt. Never seen or heard of again."

LaFleur's eyes flicked toward the Sultan. The Frenchman received an imperceptible nod. Evidently he had a story to tell — and the room fell silent. All Dancer could do was wait.

CHAPTER 23

WITH THE AIR OF ONE unraveling a secret held for ages Rene LaFleur began. "In 1788—now fifty-eight years ago—I was a common sailor in New Caledonia in the Pacific. I was ordered by Comte de La Pérouse to sail back to France as supercargo on an English naval ship—with a secret message for my King of France."

Dancer leaned forward. His mind snapped to high alert. "La Pérouse led a French expedition of discovery around the world. When was it? About 1785 to 1788?"

LaFleur's head bobbed excitedly. The ancient mariner performed an animated two-step...like a schoolboy promised a honey cake.

Dancer continued on as his mind snapped the pieces into place. "La Pérouse set out from Brest...France...to complete Captain Cook's discoveries and map the Pacific. He was the first Frenchman to visit Chile. Hawai'i. Alaska. California. Plus East Asia and Japan. After two years he landed in Russia. From Russia La Pérouse sent his ship's logs and charts back to Paris with the French Consul de Lesseps. De Lesseps traveled overland from Petropavlosk...Russia...for almost a year."

"Ah..." The Sultan was impressed. "You know your history... Mr. Dancer."

The Shieka poured Dancer a second coffee. "Where is this place 'Paris' you speak of?"

Dancer gave Shieka Sharife a mistrustful look. *Sophia warned me about this one.* The Shieka had saved Dancer from the street mob. But also delivered him to Paatel.

"Paris? I was there a month ago. It is a great city in France."

The dazzling beauty knit her brows as she caressed the warm coffee urn. Then murmured: "I have never been beyond these palace walls....and the baths."

The Sultan gave his willful princess a stern look then picked up the narrative. "It was a year later — after continuing the expedition to Australia — that La Pérouse sent a second batch of maps and journals back to France...under LaFleur's care in 1788. Unfortunately — after LaFleur sailed — La Pérouse was lost at sea. His original maps that showed trade routes — and suitable bases for French colonies in the North and South Pacific — were lost with him. Some say La Pérouse failed. That is not for me to judge."

Dancer snapped his fingers. His forefinger jabbed the air. "But some of La Pérouse's journals and charts were finally published in 1797."

LaFleur licked his sunburnt lips. Shieka Sharife supplied the Frenchman his accustomed goblet of wine from a dusty bottle. After a long drink the beachcomber resumed his tale.

"*Je*...Rene LaFleur...was entrusted. Only I carried the *message privé*...the private message for the King from La Pérouse...and his ill-fated expedition. But I...Rene LaFleur...was castaway in Zanzibar by the bastard British captain of the warship *Alexandria*. If 'e would have waited only one day...my fever would have broken! But *non*... 'e abandoned Rene LaFleur on this island. I was not yet eighteen years. 'e said 'e had better things to do than...*comment vous dites?*... nurse-maid some papist frog."

Dancer smiled wryly. "My guess is you hate the British."

LaFleur crooked his arm. Slapped the bend in his elbow. And made an obscene gesture meant for all British. "LaFleur was the only Frenchman in Stone Town. This Sultan's father found me useful as a translator. Ten years later—in 1798—that's when I met LeGrand."

Dancer looked at LaFleur with astonishment. "LeGrand?"

"*C'est exact.* That is correct."

The Sultan confirmed LaFleur's tale. "Vice-Amiral Gagnon LeGrand. Napoleon's right hand in Egypt." Again the Sultan fixed his gaze on LaFleur. "The time has come…LaFleur. Tell us what LeGrand told you in confidence…under pain of death…just as you once told my father."

LaFleur shrugged indifferently. Closed his eyes to recall the hazy memory. Then told Dancer what LeGrand told him almost forty-eight years ago: Napoleon had loaded the treasure ransacked from Malta aboard his flagship *L'Orient*. Once the armada reached Aboukir Bay near the mouth of the Nile the treasure was offloaded from *L'Orient*. Once the treasure was ashore Napoleon stored it at Fort Julien. Then replaced the treasure that had been aboard *L'Orient* with gunpowder.

"Fort Julien?" Dancer said. "The place Egyptians call Rasheed on the Nile?" He could hardly believe it. "I've just come from there." The Sultan raised an eyebrow in surprise. LaFleur was momentarily unsure what to make of the news. Shieka Sharife looked at Dancer with open astonishment as well.

The castaway fidgeted. "*Oui.* The place the French call Rosetta… and where they found the Rosetta Stone while rebuilding the fort in 1799. But I get ahead of my story." LaFleur took a second goblet of wine. "Napoleon stored his treasure at Fort Julien…then transported it up the Nile to Cairo once the Mamlukes—the slave-soldiers of Egypt's ruling Ottomans—were defeated at the pyramids. That is what LeGrand told me. *C'est vrai?* Is it true? I cannot say. What I know is Nelson cut off the Mediterranean from Napoleon. Before the treasure was sent to Cairo…Napoleon kept for himself the *magnifique* dagger…from the Sword de La Valette. A talisman of good fortune… or so LeGrand called it."

"LeGrand told you about the Valette dagger?" asked Dancer.

"*Oui.* Napoleon always played the *grandiose role…non?*"

Dancer considered the Frenchman's words. Knowledge of the dagger proved LaFleur told the truth about LeGrand…and Napoleon's treasure. Several parts of the puzzle were beginning to fit together.

LaFleur continued. "After leaving Rosetta...LeGrand sailed up the Nile to Cairo. Then by wagon to the Red Sea port of El Suweis...what you *Anglais* call Suez. Napoleon's three ships were waiting. If you can call them ships. To the last shipworm...they were not seaworthy. LeGrand had orders to sail all *trois* ships from El Suweis in Egypt. Through the Indian Ocean. Around Cape Hope at the tip of *Afrique* destined for Brest...France...where the French Navy headquartered." The Shieka listened to LaFleur's narrative with rapt attention. "Arabs in the north encouraged LeGrand to follow that course. What they didn't tell LeGrand was the easterly monsoon winds from Oman and India would force LeGrand against the shoreline. Against the *Africain* coast. That route was...*comment vous dites?*...thick with pirates in the North. And British warships patrolled Madagascar in the South...hunting for French prizes. Only thing worse than a pirate to the British was a Frenchman."

Dancer nodded. "The Arabs sent LeGrand right into a trap swarming with their Abyssinian pirate brothers."

LaFleur hopped about animatedly. "*C'est vrai*. LeGrand fought his way down the coast. Fought the winds! Fought the pirates! Fought the miserable ships the Mamlukes sold Napoleon!" The effort exhausted LaFleur. Spent by the tale he slumped into one of the *durbar's* elaborately carved armchairs.

The voice of Said bin Sultan filled the silence. "After a last chase LeGrand's three ships limped into Stone Town. My father— the Sultan bin Ahmad— saw a chance to make a new friend and stab an old enemy in the throat. He gave LeGrand shelter. He convinced LeGrand to place a token of the treasure in his weakest ship. Just enough to buy time. That ship— crewed by my father's men— sailed toward the African coast to our west as a decoy. It soon was captured by pirates. The other two ships were given shelter in Stone Town Harbor. Though the wild dogs circled— none dared test my father...Sultan of Zanzibar and Oman. In this safe harbor LeGrand cannibalized the second ship to outfit his remaining ship. The strongest and fastest of the three. In tribute my father received these."

Said bin Sultan pulled a doeskin pouch from a pocket inside his robes. Loosened the braided tie and held the soft leather in his palm.

Then turned the leather pouch upside down. Jewels and coins spilled onto the heavy side table beside Dancer's flask and cigar case. Precious stones. Coins from Malta. Egypt. And across the Near East. Only a glance was needed for Dancer to confirm these valuables came from the treasure of Napoleon.

The Sultan resumed in a matter-of-fact tone: "Winter passed. Word of course spread to the pirates that LeGrand was at Stone Town. LeGrand was trapped. If he sailed south — as the winds demanded — pirates would pick him apart...or the British would blow him out of the water. Yet if he remained on Zanzibar...spies were certain to give away his weaknesses. With every day LeGrand's position became more vulnerable. Time was running out. Until LeGrand made a fateful decision...."

The room went silent. A bead of icy sweat trickled down Dancer's ribs. Even the feeble sea breeze from the high windows died in the tropical heat.

LaFleur rose unsteadily. "LeGrand decided to cast his fate to the winds. 'e could not surrender. 'e would sail. His duty commanded. That last night LeGrand gave me this letter. 'e made me swear upon my life as a Frenchman to keep this letter secret. Under one condition — and one condition only — could I reveal LeGrand's letter: If word of his death reached Zanzibar."

Dancer nodded gravely and tapped his heart with two fingers.

LaFleur stared at him for a moment. Then the grizzled Frenchman pulled forward a tattered tote-on-a-string. From this satchel LaFleur withdrew a folded yellow parchment. The red wax seal still intact. In the seal the bold stamp of a signet-ring's monogram — *LG* — was clearly readable. LaFleur gave the letter to Dancer. Upon releasing the paper the decrepit beachcomber giggled. Smacked his lips. Clapped his palms. The old man looked as if he expected a jack-in-the-box to spring from the letter. Then cavorted from foot to foot in glee. A lifetime curse had been lifted.

"Rene LaFleur kept his *promettre.*" He giggled. "No word of LeGrand's death ever reached Zanzibar...until today...That is why I can give up this letter...*comprenez vous?*" Wild-eyed LaFleur danced his crazy jig and moved murmuring across the *durbar* chamber. The great weight of a great secret seemed lifted at last. LaFleur collected the dusty wine bottle and skipped down the tile stairs of the Sultan's palace. Out into the blinding sun of Zanzibar.

◎   ◎   ◎

Dancer broke the seal on LeGrand's letter and translated with minimal embellishment:

My General Napoleon...

Against all odds your treasure is under my command. Only a small sum was sacrificed as tribute to the African pirates. The winds now come from the northeast. Those northeasterlies trap us against the coast of Africa. When we sail we'll be easy prey for pirates or British or both. Our one hope is to hold out until the sudden seasonal monsoon winds shift to come out of the southwest. Those summer monsoons will take us east. Only then will the winds blow us away from our enemies. Excellency...with all speed and your God-given authority we sail east. Our best hope is to avoid Australia and the English penal colony in Sydney. Give us your grace to bear toward eastern Oceania. Then south around South America's Cape Horn. Finally north through the Atlantic to Brest. That is my plan. My duty is clear. Return the treasure of Napoleon that will support your divine rule forever.

If you are reading this then I have failed.

All hail! General Napoleon! God speed to the empire!

— Your humble servant. Gagnon LeGrand.

Dancer's thoughts spilled out into words. "Whether LeGrand succeeded or failed—we now know LeGrand's plan. He sailed east toward the Pacific...not south around Cape Hope and Africa."

Dancer rose to his feet. Shieka Sharife reached out to steady him. Her touch to his waist and arm shot strength through his body. The Sultan's daughter bent over the ornate side table. Picked up Champollion's notebook where LaFleur had left it. She felt the cool leather under her fingertips. As her frown deepened and her color heightened she handed the worn volume to the American. Dancer blinked to clear his mind. Then quickly opened Champollion's notebook. Flipped to the last section. There his finger located a sketchy list of coins Champollion had drawn up. Each entry indicated where a particular coin had been discovered. The next to last entry struck Dancer as particularly remarkable. In 1801 a handful of coins from the treasury of the Knights of Malta was reported. Hearsay claimed the coins surfaced in French Polynesia in the South Pacific. But that flimsy thread was never confirmed. Still—the evidence was indisputable. *Clearly the coins are from Napoleon's cache.*

Dancer's finger traced the list down to the last reference. The strangest of all. One coin—struck in Malta prior to Napoleon's arrival—was found embedded in the belly of a totem carved from a large coconut shell. The notebook recorded the only fragment of knowledge gleaned from research: The fertility totem was unique to the Navigator Islands northeast of Australia.

Dancer rubbed the sketch of the totem like Aladdin had stroked his lamp. But no genie appeared. Dancer frowned as he considered the meaning. Had LeGrand bartered the coins for supplies? Or lost the treasure in a shipwreck? But where? Asia? Oceania? Napoleon's treasure could be anywhere in the vast South Pacific.

Again Dancer touched the totem drawing. Impulsively he decided to cast his next move to the monsoon winds—to leave his fate in the hands of that desperate straw—like LeGrand before him. Immediately the president's best agent gambled on his instincts. Within twenty-four hours his trusted compass had set him on a fateful course east for the Navigator Islands in the western Pacific.

CHAPTER 24

SULTAN'S PALACE
STONE TOWN/ZANZIBAR
NEXT AFTERNOON/10 JANUARY 1847

THE SULTAN OF ZANZIBAR placed his hands on Dancer's shoulders after the midday meal. "Tell His Highness...Secretary Buchanan...that Zanzibar will honor our American Treaty for as long as the world endures." The bearded patriarch looked Dancer in the eye. "Safe travels my friend...*mushiiyat Allah*...God willing."

Final preparations were complete. The Shieka had prevailed upon the Sultan to order his finest brig—*Al Sultanah*—to take Dancer north to Aden in Yemen. There Dancer would meet the Peninsular & Oriental steamer to Ceylon and continue to Singapore. From Singapore sailing ships were frequent to Sydney in Australia. And from Sydney Dancer could sail to the South Pacific islands of Oceania wherever the cold trail of LeGrand led him.

As Dancer turned to leave the palace atrium Shieka Sharife blocked his path. Her beguiling smile and gold ear drops dazzled in the brilliant sunlight.

Dancer touched his steepled fingers to his lips. "I owe you a word of thanks." As the Shieka lowered her chin slightly Dancer reached out with a curled forefinger and thumb. Then gently lifted her face toward his. She blushed at his touch. Dancer wore an honest look of appreciation. "Thank you for saving me from that mob on the street."

Shieka Sharife's eyes glistened. Then from the folds of her colorful kanga dress she raised a scrolled document. Dancer recognized the Sultan's official papyrus. The Shieka handed Dancer a passport issued by the Sultan. Dancer glanced at the illumined document opened in his hands.

This letter comes from Said bin Sultan — Sultan of Zanzibar.
Greeting to all subjects. Friends. Governors.
On behalf of Mr. Jack Dancer…the American…behave well
to him and be everywhere serviceable to him.

Dancer slid the rolled passport into his kit. The Shieka pressed closer. She put her arms around his waist. Positioned her lips to one side of Dancer's cheek. Her jasmine-clove perfume was as intoxicating as her touch. She whispered into his ear. "Take me with you."

Out of the corner of his eye Dancer thought he saw movement. Behind the carved rosewood screen above them on the first balcony. When Dancer looked up a dark shape moved back from the light. *Was that the flash of a white beard?*

Sharife sank to her knees. Arms encircled Dancer's legs. Her seductive face turned up toward him from his waist. She clung to him for an answer.

After an eternity of temptation Dancer gently lifted the princess to her feet. He dried a tear from her moist blue eyes. In a lapse he kissed the gold-filigree tiara that sparkled against her velvet smooth forehead.

Dancer spoke sincerely. "As much as I want to…I cannot take you." Her eyes again glistened as she searched his face. Dancer let his shoulders sag and gave a sigh of profound disappointment. "Your father has not given us permission to marry." He paused for effect. "I cannot take you with me…if it is not first arranged by your father's wishes."

The Sultan's favorite daughter blinked. She understood. Tradition overruled passion. As she knew: Unions must first be agreed by the fathers. The Shieka straightened. Took a half step back. Lifted her chin bravely. Then brought forth from the folds of her traditional dress a small object wrapped in blue silk. The bundle was knotted with a braided gold ribbon. She pressed the gift to her lips. With no further words the Princess of Zanzibar gave the object to Dancer. Then stood aside.

Dancer pressed the blue bundle to his heart. Then tucked the silk offering into his travel kit beside the Sultan's free passage scroll. With a smile and a nod Dancer stepped through the palace's raised portcullis gate into the oppressive heat.

And into the deadliest test of his life. Against hopeless odds.

CHAPTER 25

FRENCH PRISON COLONY
NOUMEA/NEW CALEDONIA/PACIFIC
MID-JANUARY 1847

HENRI MALBEC burned an *M* into the leather brace on his wrist. Slowly. Artfully. With a red-hot tool. The singe of the scorching leather gave Malbec's mouth a tight smile. *Henri Malbec. Commandant. Colonie Penitentiare du Nouvelle-Caledonie.* His eyes narrowed in pride as he savored the pain. From where he sat on a flattened log bench beside the blacksmith's forge his cold eyes swept his prison yard.

You...Malbec...You are the inspiration for what the incos call "The Game."

Incos. Incorrigibles. Hardened cases. Prisoners driven by hard labor. Heat. Life sentences. Hopelessness. Driven to play The Game. They drew three straws. The short-straw prisoner was killed by the other two. A merciful death. As painless as possible...or so they promised. For the two remaining a singular hand-carved die assigned their destiny. In their fetid cell a higher number earned one the role of "witness." For the other the lot of "killer."

The two survivors alerted the guards. A judge was summoned to Camp Brun. "Guilty!" For the killer a slow death by *oubliette.* For the witness...freedom for his cooperation. *La belle liberté!* Simply *La belle* in prisoner's slang. A beautiful freedom in the dreams of all three. Freed by death. Freed from Camp Brun. And freed from Malbec's tortures.

Malbec dropped the branding iron into the smith's quenching tub. Then walked across the yard to the cell blocks. High above Malbec an albatross with enormous wingspan soared. The bird looked down at Noumea. Its harbors were shaped like a giant mouth in full scream. The harbor to the north was the Baie Moselle. While the port to the south was the Baie des Citrons. A promontory called the Artillerie formed the soft palate between. Two ancient calderas created the twin deep-water ports of Noumea. Capital of the New Caledonia prison colony. Or as the French called it…*Grande Terre*. The Rock. Twelve hundred kilometers east of Australia. The spine of this 350-kilometer-long island was defined by a mountain range of fifteen-hundred-meter peaks. The range split the sides of the half-green island like the spines of a giant lizard. The evergreen forests on the wet eastside inspired Captain James Cook in 1776 to name the island after his beloved Scotland. Caledonia. The dry westside was a desert.

Hugging the dual gullets of Noumea a sketchy town grid spread sparsely along the thinly populated shore. At the northern edge of Baie Moselle a narrow spit connected the mainland to the peninsula prison island of Nouville. In the whispers of up-island work gangs they referred to this hell on earth as *l'abattoir de Nouville*. The slaughterhouse of Nouville. From the southern shore another barren lip curled around Baie des Citrons and formed the peninsula known as Camp Brun. Here steady winds from the island blew west. And carried out to sea any sounds from the prison sheds. But every prisoner knew. The true name was not Camp Brun. It was Sang du Camp. Camp Blood. Last home to any incorrigible. Every *incos* knew there were only two ways out of Nouville prison or Camp Blood. As a corpse. Or as a witness to murder. A life-saving charade. And desperation odds.

Malbec entered the horseshoe-shaped cellblock building. Before the commandant in one stained cell were three empty bunks. Malbec smiled as he stared at the empty space. *Soon three fresh incorrigibles to discipline.* He liked The Game.

Henri Malbec was a tall man. Thin. As deliberate as a surgeon. "Cold as a scalpel" — so his dossier recorded. A gray complexion fading to a soft *café au lait* made his thin eyebrows barely visible. Before his receding hair perpetual beads of perspiration gleamed. His mean mouth appeared to have no defined lips. Especially when he postured a determined expression. No teeth showed when he spoke. His voice was a pitch high. Reedy. Given to sarcasm. Yet his lean body was tight muscled like knotted ropes. The dominant impression he gave was the look of a large bird. An evil bird of prey.

Malbec stepped back out into the yard. Squinted northeast toward the harbor. *Why has the admiral not called upon me?*

He twisted his branded wrist brace back and forth as he mused. *S'il vous plait. No more artists please…or poets for the up-island road gangs. No more political exiles for the isolation of the Isle of Pines.* Even though the Island of Pines was the only island in the Pacific where captains could obtain a new mast from the old-growth pines. Yet a world away. One hundred twenty kilometers to the southeast of Noumea and the Grande Terre. *Send me men who are not weaklings.*

Malbec's mouth tightened into a determined lipless slit. *No petty recidivists this time. No repeat offenders from the Paris food-market riots. No bread thieves or grain robbers. No street beggars. No vagrants. A waste of my time! Too often they cut off a thumb to get out of hard labor. But mostly they committed suicide. What difference to hurry one's destiny? They must know that. There is no escape…except Malbec's divine escape.*

Certain their God had abandoned them. Certain of the penal colony's unending labor. And dead certain of Malbec's punishments of despair. For the *incos* Malbec was their judge. Jury. Executioner. Hardened men would succumb. At last. Freed from the pain. Sweet relief. *La belle.*

Sooner…not later. So Malbec mused. Why pretend? They will welcome death…my sweet certain death.

CHAPTER 26

"MALBEC!" the admiral barked as the prison commandant entered the stateroom. "Attention!"

In a show of rank — and some distaste — the admiral had waited a day to summon the commandant once the man-of-war and prisoner convoy had reached New Caledonia. *Why spoil a record ninety-one-day run from Brest?*

Admiral Messimer stood tall at the flagship's stern gallery window in the admiral's quarters. Before him Malbec struck a somewhat insouciant pose as if he looked down on the High Commander of the French Navy in the Pacific. Malbec acted like the dominant shark in the room. Sleeves rolled up. Hands clasped behind his back. Messimer walked slowly around the commandant. Inspected Malbec's strength and character. Judged if Malbec could execute his orders. In that moment the Admiral noticed a purplish mark on Malbec's inner-right forearm. The stain appeared to be in the shape of a turtle missing a forefin.

Messimer pointed at the mark. "Is that a tattoo…Malbec?"

"I would be proud of a tattoo." Malbec unrolled his sleeve to hide the blemish. "That is a birthmark." His tone was indifferent. "I was born in Tahiti. But I was raised among French clergy."

The Admiral picked up a scroll sitting on a large map of the Pacific Ocean spread on his grand table. As an officer and aristocrat Messimer had little respect for Malbec. After all Malbec was colony-born. Nothing more than a petty-bourgeois official with much pretention.

The Admiral tapped the map with the scroll. Then swept his right hand in an arc over the vast territory of the Pacific Ocean. His point was emphatic. France intended to rule the Pacific. The *entire* Pacific. In the west New Caledonia was secure. And showing a profit. In the South Pacific the Marquesas Islands were already controlled. Tahiti was under treaty. French Polynesia was taking form.

"Next is the Sandwich Islands in the North Pacific." The Admiral opened the parchment scroll illustrated with royal crests and writing in a florid script. "These orders come directly from the King of the French. King Louis Philippe himself."

Messimer took a deep breath. "The King is sending you — Malbec — and a corvette fighting ship. First to the Marquesas Islands to enhance the prison there. Eight weeks. No more. Then you are ordered to sail north and claim the Sandwich Islands for France. Work with the rebel natives and their chief — Maunakili — to gain advantage where you must. But attack Maui if resisted. Those are your orders."

Malbec's face reflected nothing as he savored the Admiral's idea.

"In the meantime...Malbec: A secret messenger will take word to the rebel chief Maunakili on Moloka'i. The messenger will arrange for you and Maunakili to meet four months from now on neutral ground at the Place of Refuge in Kona on the Big Island of Hawai'i. You must not miss that rendezvous. Louis Philippe's plan depends on it." Admiral Messimer tapped a smaller scroll held by royal seals. "The date is set: May 21. Do you understand?"

Malbec made a rapid calculation. One month's sail to the Marquesas. Two months purging undesirables at Nuku Hiva. Then a month's voyage to Kona on the Sandwich Islands...for more prisoners. A malevolent sneer crossed the commandant's tight mouth. Malbec toadied to appear agreeable to the King's plan. "Their Maui canoes are nothing to our cannons."

The Admiral fixed his eyes on Malbec. "For Maunakili and the Pi'ilani of Maui there is a *cher prix*—a high price…Malbec. They must pay. A payment equal to Napoleon's treasure…or no deal."

Malbec put on a nonchalant expression. "The old reports said that Napoleon's treasure went missing…did it not?"

"*Impoyseebla!* Rumors! Lies!" The Admiral gave a mocking look. "A treasure that large doesn't just vanish. The King's orders are clear…Malbec. Accept no excuses from that Maui pretender—Maunakili. Payment in full is the price for the services of the French Navy. Or we will take Maui for ourselves by force. Make no mistake…Malbec: The second empire of Napoleon will be built on the return of Bonaparte's Egyptian gold. And then…it will be my personal pleasure to settle old accounts with Nelson's navy."

Malbec's eyes seemed to darken. "What we will need for the conquest is a prison frigate—especially for our return…if the natives resist." Malbec's cold expression grew more cruel. His smile seemed like the blade of a saber. "After all…the corvette is too small to represent the supremacy of France…my Admiral." Already Malbec envisioned his stinking *cachot noirs* dungeons filled with native islanders fresh for his torturing devices. "There are losers in every war."

The Admiral measured the prison commandant through narrowed lids. "Losers? It is true…The *transportes*—the prisoners shipped to New Caledonia—are criminals. Exiles. Political traitors. Multiple offenders. Tried and found guilty."

The Admiral paced as he warmed to his lecture. "Yet…all these prisoners are victims of their circumstances. Their crimes are crimes caused by their destitution. By where they were raised. By their environment. By their circumstance."

Malbec objected. "Ah…that is not my experience…Admiral. These *bagnards*—the prisoners we serve in Nouvelle-Caledonie—are defective beings. Inherently they are destined for crime. They are a curse on society."

"Do you not think they can be reformed with work? That with discipline and reflection they can be rehabilitated and returned to French society?"

"You may know ships…Admiral. You do not know criminals. Let me assure you we must avoid the mistake such naïveté leads to."

Malbec raised his eyebrows pointedly. The commandant touched his chest with the fingers of both hands in feigned astonishment. "Rehabilitation? Never. Return? Unthinkable. The only solution is to separate these flawed lawbreakers from the genetically pure…from the law-abiding citizens of France. As you know prisons in the homeland are too expensive. The best solution is to execute the defectives. But the *liberati* would howl. And there are not enough guillotines in all of France. So…if not the guillotine…what?" Messimer gazed at Malbec oddly. Flecks of spittle formed in a corner of Malbec's mouth. "What then? Purge them. Exile them to a colony. Look at what the British have accomplished in Australia in the last sixty years. Botany Bay near Sydney saved English society from a beastly scourge. The solution is simple. Purge the pus. And the body recovers."

The Admiral threw up his hands in exasperation. "Surely the system of *doublage* is abominable." Malbec's expressionless face suggested the Admiral's reasoned argument made little impression on the penal colony commandant. "As you know…if the sentence is under eight years the prisoner must stay on New Caledonia for an additional time equal to his original sentence! What reform value can there be to double the punishment?"

"Under my care…some are submissive…not violent. For those we have jobs such as gardeners. Bakers. Carpenters. Stonemasons. Even musicians. Why…one prisoner assists me as my private secretary."

"Yes. I'm sure his family paid a pretty penny for that privilege."

"It is true I responded to the entreaties of his family. But — as the guards say — Caledonia is not an assignment to be requested. For the guardians to ease the life of prisoners — in exchange for a few five-cent *sou* pieces — that small technicality can be overlooked for the larger sake of the homeland."

"For the sake of brutality is more like it."

Unmoved Malbec shrugged. "We take in prisoners. The worst rejects from society. Thieves. Murderers. Rapists. Repeat offenders with multiple convictions. They soon learn life in my colony can be — how shall we say? — much healthier than the guillotine. Or an island near Brazil. Here our climate — and their cooperation — make an acceptable sentence. For the *incos* — the incorrigibles — that is a different story."

The Admiral's smile became a mocking sneer. "Your reputation — though we have just met — precedes you…Malbec. They say that a *transportes* sent to New Caledonia is more certain of an early death than if a man had cancer."

Malbec shrugged again. "With time here you will see it is as obvious as it is to anyone who can see the sun is shining…Admiral. There is nothing wrong — would you say — with enforcing our laws with order? What can be wrong with that? The law caught them. And…the law found them guilty. We must enforce the sentences or the rule of law becomes meaningless. The ability. The power. The legal requirements of enforcing the laws will reduce crime in France. And cast out the undesirables. That is our highest calling…*non*? Malbec is ready to meet that challenge."

"*C'est vrai.* It is true laws must be enforced."

Malbec raised his chin. "There is only one thing I hate…Admiral. One thing above all else. That is — anything that is not French. Take the native Kanaks of Caledonia — and all the Pacific Island races. They are beneath civilization. Vile savages. Licentious. Our women are in constant danger. The natives do not work. They die in droves at the slightest discipline. No…Admiral. The natives are subhuman. Beneath contempt. Animals. That is the law of nature. And natural law is absolute."

Malbec concluded as his eyes bored into Messimer. "The less their blood is mixed with the blood of pure French…the better for our country."

Seven days later Admiral Messimer stood on the rampart of Camp Brun. Through Noumea Harbor before him passed the *Némésis*. A fully rigged three-masted prison frigate. The battery on the Artillerie peninsula fired the first salute. The salvo was answered by six booming guns from the frigate. The Admiral caught sight of Malbec's dark figure standing alone on the aftercastle of the large ship. Feet braced. Elbows cocked wide. Chin thrust toward the figure on the rampart atop the cliffs of Camp Brun.

As the King's Representative Malbec struck as brazen a salute as his tall frame allowed. Into the wind Malbec bit off his words. "With

Emperor Napoleon as my witness…I will do whatever is needed to help the *incos* play The Game at Nuku Hiva. Then enforce this 'treaty' with Maui's *metis*—that half-breed rebel…Maunakili." Below Malbec on the tween deck four cages were ready with shackles to hold sixty prisoners each. Eighty if tight packed. After all…Malbec knew a ten-percent death rate was the rule with "black bird" ships. Sometimes fifty to seventy percent when disease broke out.

The Admiral returned the special envoy's salute as the *Némésis* passed beyond the harbor. In a hoarse whisper the unimaginable escaped the lips of the high commander of the French Navy in the Pacific. "God save the natives in Maui. They will be begging to die."

CHAPTER *27*

THE NOON RUM RATION began as always. At a bench beside the galley the second mate shouted: "Up spirits!" Then the assembled sailors eagerly replied: "Stand fast the Holy Ghost!" Swift took a position near the midships rail to view the scene as a whole. As was custom the first sailor in line poured a portion from the coconut shell-and-whale tooth dipper onto a small sample of gunpowder. To this mixture he touched a burning punk. Followed by a moment's hesitation. Then the powder flashed into smoke and flame. "'Tis one hundred percent proof!" the seaman shouted to the others. "The rum is true...not watered grog."

Under the watchful eye of Ratter Dawes the rum bosun measured tots for each sailor.

With a shuffle the queue surged forward for their daily share of rum. Swift saw each pour included a dose of lemon juice. At the back of the line the lone temperate seaman turned to Duffy Ragsdale. "None for me...mate. If you wish you can double the rum tub...and take my share."

Duffy Ragsdale squared his shoulders. Pleased to be singled out.

Even though he was a greenhand. After he had taken his tot and returned the mug the young sailor got back into line for a second. The abstaining seaman handed his tin tot to the unsuspecting lad. When Ragsdale again reached the rum tub the bosun filled his unmarked tot. But before Ragsdale could turn away Dawes grabbed him. Threw him to the deck. The tin tot clattered into the scupper opening in the bulwark rail.

"What's this? A wog doublin' the grog tub! Tha' earns you the lash…boy!" Dawes lorded his rank over the boy curled at his feet. "Bend 'im o'er the rail!" The bosun and mate yanked Ragsdale to his feet and pulled him toward the gunwale. Forced him to his knees with his chin over the bulwark and pinned his outstretched arms along the rail. Dawes untied the whip from his belt and uncoiled his cat-o'-nine-tails.

Swift started to step forward but was prevented by the large harpooner reaching out his calloused hand and placing it on her arm.

Dawes drew his arm over his head. Then flung the cat-o'-nine-tails down on Ragsdale's back as he called out: "One! Two! Three!" Ragsdale's shirt was cut to ribbons by the nine knotted lines. "Three! Four! Five!!" All knew Dawes had not kept count on purpose. "Four! Five! Six!" Ragsdale's cries succumbed to a whimper. His back flayed. "Six! Seven! Eight!" Dawes' face turned red as a faint smile rose from the corner of his bloodless lips. "Nine! Ten! Eleven!" True hatred and vehemence rose in his expression as he wiped red splatter from his chin. The last lash rained down with two-handed ferocity. "Twelve!"

Dawes shook the blood from the lash. Tied the coiled whip to his belt. "Take 'im to the *lazarette*!" The mate turned on the crew. "And let tha' be a lesson to you all! Daily ration or not! One tot per man! No more! My cat longs for the next man who tries to double his rum tub! Damn your eyes! Back to work…ye rascals!"

Ragsdale was dragged away. Barely conscious.

The temperate seaman caught the first mate's eye and received an acknowledging nod from Ratter Dawes.

CHAPTER 28

KIKILANI AND SWIFT pulled back the forehatch grating outside their quarters and slipped down the cargo hold ladder. Swift strained to replace the hatch cover. Then joined Kikilani at the bottom step. At once an overpowering smell hit them. The stench rising from the bilge made them gag. The reek was part maggoty sewage. Part decomposing rat corpses. Part vermin hatched in the filth. All sloshed about in a black resin-tar ooze between the ship's frame timbers. From this noisome atmosphere a putrid steam barely exhaled from the watertight hold through the deck boards low above their heads. Swift dabbed mentholated camphor on both their upper lips to hold back the retching.

Together they picked their way through cordage and detritus dropped on the grating that formed a removable platform above the frames. Quietly the twosome navigated between looming barrels in the pitch-black hold. Here — below the waterline — light and air rarely reached. Both held a whale-oil lamp: a cutaway pewter mug with a screw lid. Double wicks provided them each a meager cone of light. From the darkness left and right came squeaks and chatter from the disturbed mischief of bilge rats. Too quick to be caught in the scant illumination the lamps cast about.

Kikilani led the way as she found a path that snaked along the keel line. Past barrels packed tight: Fresh water. Cargo. Provisions for the five-month voyage. Seawater from the hatches and uncaulked deck boards ended in the humid bilge. Cautiously they made their way toward the stern after hold — where Ragsdale suffered in the *lazarette.*

"What are the chances someone will see us?" Kikilani whispered over her shoulder toward Swift.

"Almost impossible. We'll hear them first." Swift applied more camphor. "We can hide amongst these barrels. Or just act innocent — like we're checking our cargo...or treating Duffy."

Kikilani slowly exhaled as she cast her light before them. "This way."

They stepped past the curved oak of the arched ribs of the ship's skeleton. Tiptoed gingerly past the angled knees hewed from New England hackmatack. Ran their fingers along the shutter plank. The last plank on the ship's hull that bound all the forces to support the structure like a keystone in a stone arch.

Ragsdale's moans reached them over the bilge wash and hissing rats.

Kikilani discovered the *lazarette* wasn't locked. She smiled wanly. *Where is there to escape?* As they entered the low cell — wedged between the built-up keel and the berth deck — an advancing rat plague skittered away into the darkness.

Swift called out gently: "Duffy? Duffy?" The young sailor's eyelids fluttered. Swift's eyes met Kikilani's — and she knew her friend was thinking the same as she. Duffy was lying on his stomach. His back a raw wound. Kikilani tipped a water flask she had brought from the surgeon's quarters to his dry lips. She then bathed the cuts and dabbed his flesh with dry linen. Swift had read Woodall's remedy. The *Surgeon's Mate* instructed the physician to close wounds with an astringent powder made from agave and rattan palm. Now she searched in the upper tray of their dressing bag — also brought from the surgeon's quarters — for the brownish-red powder labeled *Dragon's Blood*. It also worked well to make varnish for violins.

Swift applied the stringent salve. Then covered the wounds with a surgical lint plaster. This revived Ragsdale enough to attempt some hardtack softened with molasses. The neophytes wrapped his torso in clean muslin. Then helped him pull on a clean shirt. A spoonful of poppy sap completed their treatment.

Kikilani managed to work a small vent hole open in the stern for air. Swift took out a candle stub. And placed several Lucifer matches nearby to light it. A blanket was last spread over the young adventurer's fetal-curled form. And Ragsdale fell mercifully asleep.

Shortly after Swift and Kikilani worked their way back toward the forward-hatch ladder. In this area Swift's whale-oil lamp illuminated stack after stack of barrels. From cargo deck to the above tween deck these barrels were jammed into the hold. Kikilani touched the drippings from a barrel. Sniffed her fingertips. "Rum." She sampled the seepage from another barrel. "Dark Caribbean rum… from Martinique or Saint Kitts. I recognize the scent from the Paradise Palace."

Swift cast her lamp over several barrels. Oddly every barrel was boldly stenciled in white letters: *PAINT OIL.* The two looked at each other: Paint oil? Clearly the outbound cargo of the *Black Cloud* was rum. Why was all the rum mismarked as paint oil?

"Rum." Swift muttered in a low voice. "How better to profit from the Pacific whalers?"

Kikilani lifted her light to show her own face. "And what better commodity to trade for island women."

Swift counted the rows and height. Made a quick calculation. "There must be a hundred barrels here."

"Enough to get the entire whaling fleet drunk for months." Kikilani's expression held no humor.

Carried along by excitement Swift patted her friend's shoulder. "Once we survive Cape Horn we'll have quite a story to report." Within moments they ascended the ladder through the forward hatch to the cable tier. Replaced the cover. Swift ducked into the surgery cabin to stow their lamps and medical bag in its cubby. She wiped camphor from her upper lip with an absorbent flour-sack towel while Kikilani made her way up the workshop steps to the main weather deck. Unsuspecting their every step had been shadowed.

Kikilani stepped on deck first. She turned to give Swift a hand up the companionway. Without warning and from nowhere the bludgeon end of a belaying pin knocked her momentarily senseless. Swift bent forward to help...and was grabbed by two strong arms. Kicking and flailing she was dragged from the stairs onto the deck. Her screams muzzled. Helpless. Feet kicking air. She was carried toward the port rail. The galley house hid her from sight of the rear wheel or starboard watch. Swift felt the two strong arms lift her over the side. From somewhere she heard a commanding voice.

"Stop right there...Dawes. Or you die."

Dawes' head snapped around. He lost control of Swift. Swift wrenched herself free. Dawes in a crouch spun to fully face his challenger. At that instant a harpoon drove through Dawes' coarse-wool peacoat...and lodged deep under his armpit. The razor-edge single flue buried its iron head into the solid oak bulwark.

Just as Dawes wriggled out of his jacket two powerful hands grabbed him by the scruff and belt. Then flipped him spread-eagle on the wrong side of the rail. Dawes turned his head down to see the racing black sea below.

"Should I feed you to the fish?" the harpooner asked as Dawes kicked in vain dangling over the abyss. And certain death.

Swift stepped beside the harpooner and bent over the rail. For a long moment she watched Dawes flail in the air. "That depends on him." Swift leaned over and shouted into Dawes' ear. "Tell me... Dawes...since we've barely passed a word...I suspect someone put you up to this mischief. Who hired you to kill me? Be quick. Your words could save your life."

Dawes squirmed. He tried desperately to find a ledge or handhold to stop his fall — should the harpooner let him drop. Nothing stood between him and the racing sea.

"I don't know what yer talkin' about!"

"Let me refresh your memory." The harpooner shook Dawes and feigned dropping him to his death. "My grip won't last much longer. Tell us about The Tombs in New York."

Dawes went limp. A glance made his dilemma stark: Answer or die.

"I don't know who he was. It was dark." Dawes' voice combined insolence with evasion. "We only met for a few moments. He did'na say his name. A fancy gentleman. I...I...dun know."

Swift came around the harpooner and Dawes looked at his tormentor with his black rodent eyes. Swift demanded an answer. "He hired you to kill me. Is that right...Dawes?"

"Aye." Dawes finally answered in the tone of a man accepting defeat when the harpooner again feigned a loss of grip as he held Dawes outside the bulwark. "Aye!" The mate's palms slid helplessly against the wet hull.

"Not good enough...Dawes." The harpooner shook Dawes' body like a rag doll.

"Look in my peacoat...there's a pouch sewed inside the lining!"

Swift felt around the harpoon shaft and found the pouch. She withdrew the bag and brought it to the rail.

"The fancy gent...he gave me that."

With one hand Swift opened the purse. Coins spilled out. The glitter bounced off the rail—and Dawes' prominent ears—and dropped away into the nothingness of the tempest below.

"Tha's all I know. I figured he was her pimp...or summat. The only thing I saw was his ring. Big oval sapphire. Surrounded by diamonds. Gold band. Wore it on 'is pinky finger. That's the truth...I tell ya!"

Swift was about to reply. But just then Kikilani came from the starboard deck where she landed after Dawes had clubbed her. Rubbing her head she asked Swift: "Do you know the ring?"

"Yes." Swift's voice was decisive as she told them both of the ring's history. "It was to be my mother's engagement ring...until she rejected the suitor."

Kikilani looked at Swift. "Who was that?"

"My uncle...Jacob Swift." Swift put a hand on the harpooner's shoulder. "I know that ring." She leaned over the rail so that Dawes could hear. "That was my uncle—Jacob Swift—that hired you." Swift turned again to the harpooner. "Pull him back."

Dawes fell in a crumpled heap on the deck. Panting. Sweating in fear. He looked like a rat trapped in a corner as his shoulders twitched and his eyes searched for an escape. To no avail.

The powerful harpooner kept Dawes quiet by holding the point of his knife at Dawes' throat. Kikilani rolled her head to clear the cobwebs from her brain as Swift explained. "That ring was the engagement sapphire my Uncle Jacob gave my mother. She refused him. He told her to keep the ring…in case she changed her mind. She never wore it. When my father died…my uncle stole the ring. Along with my home and my newspaper."

Swift turned to the first mate. "That truth-telling saved your life…Dawes."

"Try this again…my friend" — the harpooner sneered in Dawes' face — "and you'll answer to me first." With that warning the harpooner kicked Dawes toward the aft companionway and the mate's quarters on the lower deck. Dawes slunk off as if his tail was between his legs.

The harpooner helped Kikilani steady herself.

"You know your way around a harpoon…sir." Swift shot the seafarer an appreciative look. "Thank you."

"Nothing…ma'am. Glad to be of service." He touched the brow of his wool seaman's cap with a forefinger.

"May I know your name?"

"My name is Flute. Mr. Flute is what they calls me."

"Do you have a given name or a forename…Mr. Flute?"

"No…ma'am. No first name. As I says…my friends call me Mr. Flute. And so does my enemies."

Mr. Flute worked to free the single-flue harpoon from Dawes' jacket still pinned to the bulwark. Then tossed the torn peacoat into the ocean. And after it…Ratter Dawes' cat-o'-nine-tails lash.

A deathly silence fell over the *Black Cloud*. Punctuated ominously by the ghostly creak of stanchions and the groan of blocks as the ship bore into the darkness toward its fate at Cape Horn.

Mr. Flute turned to watch Swift help Kikilani down the workshop companionway and over to the surgeon's quarters between the bulkheads. He eyed them stoically. *Safe for now. But keep your guard. As every whaler and seaman knows: There is no God west of the Horn.*

When Swift slipped the cabin's lock behind them she became fully aware of their precarious situation. The fear must have shown in her face because Kikilani gave her a worried look.

"I hope we don't regret this."

CHAPTER 29

LOUIS PHILIPPE distractedly stroked the queen's pet Pekingese. He stood at a western window in the Diana Gallery on the second floor of the Tuileries Palace. The King of the French faced the dull February afternoon. Below was the King's private garden. Icy statues and barren beds took up the space behind a small fence. A stack of roof slates nearby.

The Tuileries. Louis Philippe laughed to himself. *What an odd name for the residence of kings.* Built almost three hundred years before on a site where roofing tiles — *tuiles* — were once made....*Les Tuileries.* A royal city within a city. *Even though the palace lacks modern comforts like running water.*

Outside the window — to Louis Philippe's left — was the River Seine. Flowing away past the Quai des Tuileries. Pack ice jammed the riverbanks like a frozen confection.

The King's gaze traveled across the brown Tuileries Gardens. Along the main promenade. Through the Place de la Concorde. There in the western haze the gold-pointed Luxor Obelisk stood like a bayonet. Surrounded by snow. The phallic stone guided his vision like a rifle site along the broad Avenue des Champs-Élysées. Past leafless trees. Up to the top of the hill. To the Arc de Triomphe nearly three kilometers away. Completed only eleven years before. This axis was the spine of Paris. The backbone of His Majesty's monarchy.

The Tuileries Palace defined the western edge of the Louvre complex. The Louvre. Rich with the treasures looted by Napoleon. Steadily becoming the greatest repository of art in the world. The King smiled at the thought...even as he felt the presence behind him — in the Place du Carrousel — of Napoleon's victory arch. Reminiscent of Rome.

The King of the French talked to the queen's Pekingese as if it was his closest counselor. "Paris.... my native city. I named my first grandson the comte de Paris. I walk the streets with nothing but an umbrella. My people adore me. To my people I am the popular king. Their citizen king. Just as Lafayette advised after those three glorious days in 1830 when the Bourbon monarchy was overthrown. Ah...my July Monarchy...."

The Pekingese squirmed. The King persisted. "My monarchy was established here. In Les Tuileries. No longer is there the old corruption of throne and altar. Today my people never see me going to church on Sunday. I refuse. King Louis Philippe. Our House d'Orléans will live forever."

A sudden gust of wind rattled the windows of the gallery. The Pekingese twisted free. Then leaped to the floor. Ran toward the King's chambers on the opposite side. Across the Diana Gallery the foreign minister cleared his throat. "Your Majesty. If I may..."

The King turned and walked across the sumptuous yet narrow stateroom. More than forty-five meters long. The walls. The ceilings. The doors. The entire space lavishly decorated in Baroque gilding and forty-one mythological painted scenes. The queen had counted them. The *Diana with Pan and Endymion* tableau was her favorite. The splendid ceiling was crammed with human figures. Rendered in various stages of undress — which also pleased the queen's Neapolitan blood. Blue skies. Verdant trees. All lit by a row of giant rock-crystal chandeliers.

Minister of Foreign Affairs Francois Guizot touched his moist brow with a fingertip. Blew on his other fingertips in the overheated King's private apartments. Then beckoned the King into the chambers on the east side. Here Napoleon had slept. Worked. And plotted forty years before. At one of a dozen gilded mirrors Louis Philippe passed his fingers gently over his stylish side whiskers that started out narrow and got wider at the jaw. Admired his embroidered high-collar uniform. Then stepped into the Salon de Service overlooking the Place du Carrousel. From their chairs aides de camp and chamberlain advisors snapped to attention. The Louvre loomed in the distance through the eastside windows.

Without a glance the King strode across the room to the far corner and the paneled doors leading to the gilded Salon de L'Empereur. The Foreign Minister followed trying to control the twisting Pekingese in his arms. The King brushed past the doorkeeper and moved into the opulent room: the royal audience chamber. Minister Guizot stepped inside this last room of the outer apartments. Only the King could pass to the *sanctum sanctorum* of the next inner study and bedchamber. The minister released the dog to the parquet floor as the keeper closed the gilt double doors behind him.

At an oval *gueridon* pedestal table beneath the large easterly window the King paused. Selected a decoratively shaped Lombart chocolate from a silver platter. Wrinkled his nose upon discovering the drop didn't contain nougat cream. And slipped the leftover morsel to the queen's lapdog. The King moved behind a heavy armchair at one end of a dark rosewood table inlaid with light sycamore and lemonwood around its edges. His hands rested impatiently atop the chair's curved back. Minister of the Navy and Colonies Ange de Mackau stood at the far end.

Minister Guizot wasted no more time and took up a position between them. "Your Majesty. The reports are troubling."

Before the King could dismiss the news his Foreign Minister continued. "The scribes say they may someday call this the 'Hungry Forties.' Deprivation. Unrest. Possibly revolution. The wheat and rye harvests were a disaster last fall. Now the severest winter in decades has your people in its grip. Already the bakers are reporting flour shortages. If the people cannot eat...if there is not even the barest sustenance...We will see pillaging. Stealing crops. Begging. Hoarding. Market riots are possible soon."

"You speak of hunger. You are wrong. I see no hunger among my people. The ice of winter is inevitable. As winter turns to spring this too will pass. As inevitable as there will be a change in the weather."

The ramrod straight Admiral Mackau spoke up. "They say across the channel entire villages of Irish peasants are dying. A blight on their potatoes...they say."

"Yes...Admiral." Minister Guizot nodded in agreement. "Some say a million people may die in Ireland alone. And there are more reports. The same to a lesser degree in Prussia and other districts on the continent. No bread. No potatoes. A catastrophe is coming."

"Can we not repeal the Corn Laws like the English?" the King protested. "That will allow the country peasants to hoard their grain."

Minister Guizot coughed lightly into his cuff. "There is little to hoard. Already the decline in food is seen to hurt France's rising manufacturing revolution...Your Majesty. Plus the high cost of cotton hurts even more of your working people in the cities. People who now labor for wages."

"The Crown certainly cannot be blamed for the price of cotton. Didn't you tell me it's related to a shortage of raw cotton coming from the slaveholders in America's South?"

"You are correct...Your Majesty. That is partly to blame. In Britain...the parliament repealed the requirement that banknotes only be issued with full gold backing. The loss of that financial protection will almost certainly lead to more commercial distress and financial panic."

Absentmindedly the King's attention was drawn to a large bowl of Spanish grapes beside the chocolate platter on the pedestal table beneath the window. He glanced out at Napoleon's Arc de Triomphe du Carrousel in the courtyard below. Then brought the grapes and chocolate with him and sat in his armchair at the council table.

The Foreign Minister tried to simplify his message. "Local versus global. Economic versus political. Rural versus city. Agriculture versus workers. The conflicts are multilayered."

"Whatever the causes that worry you...my popularity will calm the masses. There will be no crisis in my monarchy." The King fished a gold snuff case from his vest pocket and placed a pinch into a flared nostril.

"Yes...Your Majesty. Of course. Yet whatever the causes—

traditional or modern — this spring could release a disaster. We can expect protests."

The King dabbed his nose. "*Mon Dieu*. Can that be? What do your informants tell you?" The King smoothed his signature pompadour reflected in a gilded mirror on the wall behind Mackau.

The Minister of Foreign Affairs paced back and forth along the inlaid table. "Almost anything could happen. Blockades. Forced sales. Local riots. False talk of speculation. Rumors of nonexistent stockpiles." Guizot stopped pacing and clenched his fist. "Then fear takes hold. The people panic. Peasants are terrified food won't be in the markets. The laboring classes take their fears and rumors into the streets. The authorities crack down. Then the cycle repeats. But with a vengeance." The Minister opened his hands toward the frescoed ceiling. "Shortages drive grain and bread prices higher. Rumors run unchecked. More speculation! Hearsay! The starving masses direct their wrath on millers. Bakers. Traders...Even the Palace. Uncertainty. Inequity. Unemployment. The slightest spark could turn *les misérables* into a mob."

The King pondered the dark report. As one of France's richest men he valued the connections he maintained with the wealthy bourgeois class. The banking houses. And liberal opposition groups. "They should thank me. In my reign I beat down the aristocrats. The establishment. The elites. The church. I did it for the good of France. But above all...the King must defend the law." Louis Philippe paused to select a bulging sprig of grapes from the bowl before him. "When order breaks down...only the power of an iron hand can save France. Dissent must be stifled. Worker insurrections must be put down. And of course the lawful rich are the true rulers of France — not the lawless little people. That is the natural order." The King popped a particularly large grape into his mouth. "The poorer classes may resent me at first. For some there will be short-term pain. But in the end we will all gain. And the people will learn only I am right. They will thank me. After all...they are not men of property. Only the propertied class knows best." The King flicked the grape seeds toward the ornate fireplace blazing to his left — opposite Guizot. With an embroidered handkerchief the King dabbed his lips. "If the lower classes object they must be put in their place."

"We have two options…Your Majesty." Minister Guizot paused. "First—as you say—we must keep law and order. We must use the army to enforce the laws. Any protesters must be found guilty and exiled as criminals."

"Are you suggesting the penal colony in New Caledonia?" questioned the King.

"Exactly. That is our first defense." The Foreign Minister's tone was firm.

He turned toward the Admiral. "As for the second option… I pass our strategy over to the Minister of the Navy and Colonies. He commands our navy. And he has a brilliant solution."

CHAPTER 30

EMPEROR'S SALON/TUILERIES PALACE
PARIS/FRANCE
MOMENTS LATER

ADMIRAL ANGE DE MACKAU took control of the meeting. Before the royal attention drifted as the King eyed the handmade chocolates on the table and settled into the curved arms that enfolded him in his favorite armchair. Mackau knew the King's years in exile in England made him nostalgic. Even reluctant to consider a bold solution. All the more reason to press an insistent case for France's opportunity. Perhaps the last opportunity for the King to restore the honor of France. The last opening to put the name of Louis Philippe on the lips of every Englishman. The last chance to keep the Americans contained on the eastern edge of their little continent. This opportunity would never come again. Or so the Admiral insisted.

"The Marquesas. Tahiti. New Caledonia. Each stepping-stone is in place that allows France to strategically dominate the South Pacific — or French Polynesia...as it will be known." The Admiral looked sternly across the table as the King lowered his hand to let the Pekingese lick a smear of nougat cream from his fingertips. "By adding the North Pacific...France can dominate Indochina. Loosen England's grip on India. And control all trade with the Orient. Best of all: When France dominates the Pacific...France can bleed the American whaling industry dry by denying ports of call. Their ships will rot in New Bedford and Nantucket."

The Admiral gave a look of heavy-lidded disdain at the Royal Pekingese in the King's lap. Then leaned pointedly onto his palms set at the edge of the Napoleonic table. "Only then can France strike the *coup de grâce.* Then France can launch attacks on California and Oregon. Take back the Louisiana Purchase from the Pacific coast to Louisiana on the Mississippi River...Proclaim it New France while the defenseless Americans consume themselves with their internal conflict between North and South."

Quickly the Foreign Minister chimed in. "The Americans are overextended...Your Majesty. They cannot defend the west coast until they recover from Polk's Mexican War of aggression. That is why the Americans compromised with the British over the Oregon Territory border. The Americans will not...cannot...fight a second war. We still have allies in the Northwest...in New Orleans. And the Southern slave owners will help us — just as they sent money to support the Mexicans against Polk. Plus...the rebels in Texas who miss their own republic are easily persuadable. Imagine...Your Majesty. *Nouvelle France!*"

The King listened distractedly. His mind drifted. Yet he leaned toward acquiescence with every argument. He dabbed a gleam of perspiration with a scented handkerchief in the overheated room and stuck it back in his sleeve. *Nouvelle France... a tribute to the French...and my greatness.* The King mused absently as the Admiral of France pressed on.

"England rejected accepting a treaty with Hawai'i to be its protectorate in 1843. Now the Hawaiian Islands will fall as easily as the Pomare Kingdom in Tahiti. And the annexation of the Marquesas Islands before. We must seize this opportunity. We must destroy our enemies by leveraging France's renewed protectorate treaty the Hawaiian King signed last summer. We must move now while Hawai'i's King is weak. While the English are uninterested. And...while the Americans are preoccupied."

King Louis Philippe's attention again drifted to the fine Parisian chocolates. And fed a solid dark drop to the queen's lapdog under the table.

The Admiral thumped his fist on the table. "The clock is ticking…Your Majesty. We must be in position by May…or all is lost. All the American whalers will have left for the Arctic by then. The Hawaiian King will be cowering faraway in Honolulu. Maui will be low-hanging fruit for Your Majesty's warships."

The King waffled. "Adventurist empires are expensive….Given our reduced tax collections this scheme could break the banking houses. Even the Banque de France."

"Not when we use Napoleon's treasure."

With a confused look the King turned toward Foreign Minister Guizot who said: "You recall the story of Vice-Amiral LeGrand and Napoleon's Maltese treasure?"

The King recalled the story vaguely. "Captured by pirates…never heard from again…."

"Until now. Your Majesty…let me introduce a visitor."

The Minister stepped to the double door he had entered from the King's service salon and knocked twice on a decorative panel. The usher opened the door from the outside. In walked what looked like a newly dressed scarecrow. Whom the Foreign Minister warmly welcomed as the King rose and moved around the table to the intense fireplace. "Your Majesty…let me introduce a special messenger. Recently of Zanzibar. Monsieur Rene LaFleur."

LaFleur's ancient sun-ravaged body shuffled into the small salon. His knee cracked when he bowed deeply. The beachcomber's ragged appearance had been upgraded by the smart brocade of a wealthy man of trade. A bath. And a threat—if he did not perform—to end the little time his long life had to offer.

The King returned his perfumed kerchief to beneath his nose.

With eyes lowered LaFleur reported. The Americans were sniffing around. An American Treasury agent was on the trail of Napoleon's treasure. The agent had stopped in Paris in December…only a few short blocks from the Palace. Then he followed LeGrand's trail to Zanzibar—and there recovered a long-lost letter. This letter proved what was previously unknown: LeGrand sailed east with the treasure. Napoleon's trusted admiral followed La Pérouse's expedition maps from 1797. Landfall by landfall across the Pacific.

The Admiral shot LaFleur a point-blank question. "How do you know about this American?"

LaFleur quaked in his new pumps. "*Avec mes propres yeux*. LaFleur saw the agent himself…in the Sultan's Palace."

"Where is this American agent now?"

LaFleur shrugged at the impossible answer. "*Qui sait?* Somewhere between Australia and Oceania? Who knows?"

The Admiral smote the ornate arm of his chair. "In the name of *Nouvelle France*…we must stop this agent before he discovers our Pacific Strategy."

The King picked up a piece of chocolate but did not taste it. He knew the sooner he gave the Admiral and the Foreign Minister what they wanted the sooner they would leave him alone.

Guizot touched LaFleur's elbow and rasped in his ear: "*C'est tout… pour le moment.*" The Minister knocked twice on the corner door. With a deep and elaborate bow the spy from Zanzibar withdrew backward out the open double door. His uncomfortable pumps scraping across the parquet.

The King considered the royal cocoa tidbit in his fingers. "So be it. Do what we must to conquer the Hawaiian Islands."

The Admiral and Minister looked at each other. And relaxed. "Excellent…Your Majesty. We agree. Your grasp of the situation is excellent. As you wish — your dispatch will reach Tahiti before the American agent. We can send instructions for a spy to assassinate the American pest."

Always one to turn first to conspiracy the King muttered: "We will defeat the Americans from the inside. A Trojan Horse." The King understood intrigue. "Our spy must be a native English speaker…to avoid suspicion. Keep low. Be an observer. Anticipate the American agent's next move. Strike when an accident presents itself."

With disingenuous courtliness Admiral Mackau and Foreign Minister Guizot congratulated the King of the French on his decisiveness.

"*Exactement*…Your Majesty. As you command. Your orders will reach our French fleet in Tahiti…before they move on Maui. A messenger pouch dispatched to Brest in Britany and sent via a Dutch clipper ship will travel at speed all the way around the Horn to the

Pacific. That fast opium clipper will deliver your instructions to Tahiti. Trust us...your orders will arrive in time." The Foreign Minister and Admiral again exchanged smiles. Knowing they had dispatched Admiral Messimer from Brest in mid-October — almost four months before. Only the unexpected arrival of the long-forgotten spy from Zanzibar had provided them this opportunity to manipulate the King.

The King paused then turned to Guizot. "What is the name of this American agent?"

The King's Foreign Minister pursed his lips and there was a malicious gleam in his eyes: "Your Majesty. His name is Dancer. Jack Dancer."

The King bit in two the fleur-de-lis-shaped chocolate nougat he was holding.

"Then that is the man we must kill."

CHAPTER 31

"*DAILY EAGLE* EXCLUSIVE!"
NEW YORK CITY
22 FEBRUARY 1847

NEWSBOYS FLOGGED the special edition of the *Brooklyn Daily Eagle* at every corner and tavern. Their voices rang through the streets.

"Read All About It!"

"*Eagle* Exclusive!"

"Latest From South Atlantic!"

"Correspondent's Official Report!"

Newspapers flew from their hands on the streets of New York and Brooklyn. Pennies soon weighed down their pockets. The headlines sold themselves.

Just Published!!
Special Dispatch to the Brooklyn Daily Eagle
40 DAYS BEFORE THE MAST
RED-BLOODED LADS LUST FOR ADVENTURE
CORRESPONDENT BECOMES SURGEON
NEXT—THE TERROR OF CAPE HORN

Part One in a Three-Part Series
TROPIC OF CAPRICORN. SOUTH ATLANTIC—
At what latitude or longitude did the adventure of sail turn to
the tedium of the sea? Your correspondent cannot put a sextant
to it. Perhaps during the tumble and toss of the first sickening
weeks on the North Atlantic? Perhaps after our shore-blown
kiss when we raised the Cape Verde islands off West Africa?
Or during the oppressive doldrums of the equator when our
ship lay motionless on a sea like molten glass? Or perhaps after
the Tropic of Capricorn in the South Atlantic from which this
OFFICIAL REPORT was passed to a homebound ship.

For the ordinary seaman quartered "before the mast" in
the cramped space of the forecastle—or fo'c'sle as they called
it—the working life aboard ship had not changed a flick since
Richard Henry Dana Jr. exposed the life in his 1840 memoir:
Two Years Before the Mast. *Life is hard at sea…Dear*
Reader. Unending work. With long days of tedium. And in a
gale…moments of terror.

As Dana wrote: "The world's great books are foreordained:
They have this mission. Their propagation of goodwill go on.
Perchance. To the end of time." Having taken that declaration
to heart this reporter offered to read to the ship's company from
*Herman Melville's new book—*Typee. *As oft as not sailors*
cannot read. You then can imagine your scribe's surprise.
Not three but a half dozen copies of Melville's A Romance of
the South Seas *emerged from hiding by boy and grizzled*
sea dog alike.

For many Melville's tale published in February 1846 was
their spark. The raison d' être *of their escape. The essential*
vision of adventure that drove them from field to wharf
last December. Now after one month of tossing without rest on
waves of salty freedom…the company shared a common
yearning. A felt need to smell the tang of fresh-cut hay. Or press
a fist of moist farm earth. To drink cool water. Fresh from
a streamlet.

As Melville detailed…our own destination to the Pacific
Ocean conjured thoughts of lovely houris. Cannibal banquets.

Tattooed chiefs. Bamboo temples. Sunny green valleys. Carved canoes. And fiendish rites of human sacrifice upon heathen altars. These thoughts now fill the daydreams of most men aboard the Black Cloud. *And their slumbering visions.*

Last night beneath the moon above and sea all round your correspondent read out loud the following passage from the first pages of Melville's tale. You be the judge…Dear Reader. Picture the described scene of dozens of naked and dripping native girls climbing aboard the Dolly *in the storied Bay of Nuku Heva. A scene many worlds away at an unfrequented island in the Marquesas. Where missionaries abandoned their work. Admitted defeat to the idols of wood and stone. Once aboard…the maiden sylphs dried and combed and oiled themselves. Wrapped their waists in variegated kapa cloth. Beautiful in the extreme. They danced with abandoned voluptuousness. Welcomed the* Dolly's *sailors to join. Would not Melville's passage—despite its dissembling prudence— not peak any red-blooded lad's lust for adventure?*

Read for yourself in Melville's own words:

> Our ship was now wholly given up to every species of riot and debauchery. The grossest licentiousness and the most shameful inebriety prevailed with occasional and but short-lived interruptions. Alas for the poor savages when exposed to the influence of these polluting examples! Unsophisticated and confiding they are easily led into every vice. And humanity weeps over the ruin thus remorselessly inflicted upon them by their European civilizers.

Civilizers. Indeed! And that merely Chapter Two! The three-word title of Melville's next chapter foreshadowed the adventure to come: "Resolve to Escape."

As we fair wanderers progress across the rolling South Atlantic—where sail and steady wind do our bidding— more chapters will be read by your scribe. During the last watch…and for Sabbath respites. Yet fret not…Dear Reader. Melville's tale may unwind. But the Holy Grail will not budge.

Forever etched in the minds of every shellback and greenhand aboard our ship…One dream. One resolve. One thought has taken hold. Escape.

Whether Melville's paradise island still exists—or ever did—your faithful correspondent will soon report. It's a settled thing. The Black Cloud *cuts water toward the Sandwich Islands in the North Pacific. The last-century name bestowed by Captain James Cook on our destination. In today's modern age the true name is: Kingdom of the Hawaiian Islands.*

But first the course we shape is toward Cape Horn. What some old salts call the "worst hell in the Seven Seas." If perchance…fair reader…this is the last dispatch you receive from your adventurous rover…then Godspeed. Until then! Full sail to Cape Horn!

S. Thomas Swift
Foreign Correspondent
Exclusive to the Brooklyn Daily Eagle

With this dispatch and each edition of the *Daily Eagle* Jacob Swift's blood boiled. The angry publisher of the *New York Examiner* crushed the latest copy of the *Daily Eagle* between both hands. Several club members raised their eyes as he tossed the ball into the red-hot fire grate beside his favorite chair. He knew street sales of his *New York Examiner* plummeted. Tepid interviews with geography professors and retired mariners published in the *Examiner* held no match. Nothing matched the magic next to S. Thomas Swift's seafaring true adventure in the *Daily Eagle.*

Along with Jacob Swift's anger grew a gnawing discomfort. His scheme to end the career of his dead brother's heir seemed not yet to have found its mark.

He whispered to himself as the *Daily Eagle* burned: "Never fear. That wretched guttersnipe isn't home safe yet! Not by any means. Don't hang up your fiddle…my friend. It won't be long 'til that girl adventuress meets her match…and ends up on the little end of the Horn."

CHAPTER 32

BELOW DECK/*BLACK CLOUD*
CAPE HORN/AT THE BOTTOM OF THE WORLD
23 FEBRUARY 1847

SWIFT AND KIKILANI avoided hidden corners of the *Black Cloud*. When they ventured beyond the surgeon's cabin to the fo'c'sle on their daily sickbay rounds Mr. Flute shadowed them. After the incident with Ratter Dawes the harpooner moved his seaman's chest to the cable-tier and tied his hammock to the deck beams just outside the surgery within striking distance of the workshop ladder. Swift and Kikilani felt comforted when his tobacco smoke drifted into their dispensary. Yet their minds were tense. Alert. On the defensive.

In the sickbay or surgery Swift treated rope burns. Bruises. Cuts. And fingers pinched in blocks. With visceral experience she saw the crew's daily work was always hard. Now nearing Cape Horn it became backbreaking. Every minute of every day every man had a job to do. And then some. The fair-weather sails were taken down. Rolled tightly to preserve space. Then lowered by windlass to the cable-tier. Raising the heavy-weather sails required all hands. A single sail could weigh a ton. Hoisting these behemoths to the courses and tops'ls yards demanded many straining turns of the windlass. Aloft sailors and mates wrestled the massive canvases into place.

Swift regarded the men as they overhauled the smallest parts of the rigging. Ropes were spliced. Tarred. Countless ends were carefully seized with bights of twine: one and a half times wider than the rope was thick. Mr. Flute's gnarled hands whipped the lines into knots. Then showed the young sailors in step-by-step slow gestures how to perfect their crafts of the sea. Any less and Dawes' boot made the men do it again. The work was demanding. But survival at Cape Horn meant it had to be done. Patience and perfection were the only answer in the coming battle for survival.

After having been some months at sea the men became used to the work. Even the hapless carpenter sat still for Kikilani's solution of mineral oil and warm water to flush his plugged earwax. At their stations the seamen acted like a piece of machinery. Each man depended on the other. The sea would kill them if they shirked their tasks. Now the ship and company must become a single living thing. Together they would face the fury of Cape Horn. Their salvation lay with each mariner's skill and the strength of their ship.

Swift concentrated on her journal entries as the *Black Cloud* beat south. As one weathered mariner told her: "Call it superstition. Or call it fate. What lies ahead is neither celebration nor ceremony." She realized the stark elements of sea and gale and tides and rocks were the ultimate truth. Work for those before the mast was unending. Sleep and nourishment were jettisoned. Soon fatigue stalked the men. *Like an enemy.* Only ingrained routine survived. The company forged ahead mechanically. Rote repetition rendered their instincts doubly acute. Discipline was each man's only defense against chaos and terror.

Approaching the gray headland at the end of the earth all hands were fraught with the test to come. In the fo'c'sle Swift overheard the young sailors repeat the old salts' hearsay: Thousands before have vanished in these seas. Bodies never recovered. Many a grave back home holds no coffin. Marked only by a tombstone: a grim admission by a wife or mother or sweetheart that their men would never return. Some small towns had seen a generation of seamen lost. Yet the sea would call them still. And Cape Horn would cast them asunder.

On this day in late February the *Black Cloud* sailed in sight of the Horn. Braced against the foremast beside the windlass Swift swept her gaze across the steep headland the old-timers called the fiercest place in all the seven seas. For almost two hundred fifty years — since a Dutchman named the Cape after his birthplace in Hoorn Netherlands — the scene had not changed for mariners. In the best of seasons Swift was told February promised calmer summer weather in the Southern Hemisphere. But this February Neptune's fury rose up.

Rain mixed with salt spray stung Swift's face as she tried to steady herself on the foredeck. She shielded her eyes as she stared into the near distance to the west where waves pounded the rocky shore into geysers of white lather. Her riveted gaze searched the shoreline for hidden frothing reefs. With a leg braced against the windlass and her left hand clutching a halyard: Just then the *Black Cloud* pitched into a white-topped wave. With little warning the violent surge drove the ship like a walnut shell toward the shoals of the Chilean coasts.

Despite the promised Southern Hemisphere's summer warmth — the passage was dotted with icebergs. Each block calved from the glaciers in the southern Antarctic. Into this tempest Swift saw the ship approach the Horn in the close company of perhaps another half dozen whalers and two China-trade clippers.

Swift looked again to starboard through the sea spray. There — between the *Black Cloud* and the headland — two nearby whalers without warning tacked dangerously close to each other in the crosswinds. A ship's bell clanged. Both helmsmen cranked the wheel. On the wind Swift heard a rending crash as the first ship collided with the second. Its port rigging ripped away in tatters. The offending ship instantly — uncontrollably — careened toward the rocks. The vengeance of the Horn's ferocious weather now commanded the damaged ship.

From the *Black Cloud* Swift watched helplessly as the hull of the first careless whaler shattered on the rocky coast. Hours before a living vessel...now pounded to splinters. All hands surely lost. The second damaged whaler valiantly managed to stay afloat. Yet Swift could see the vessel no longer steered effectively. That captain and his crew battled to force her about. Their lives held by a thread of hope: to limp downwind toward the Falkland Islands three hundred seventy-one nautical miles distant — or die.

Under her feet Swift felt the *Black Cloud* suddenly shudder. In the black water overside Swift caught a glimpse of a granite-gray shape as it rolled to the surface. The rending scrape of an iceberg ground along its hull not eight feet below where she stood. She listened. Frozen in fear by the sound just below the waterline. Unseen belowdecks water squirted from under the shutter plank as the rock-frozen berg fell away in the ship's wake. Cold rain like lashes whipped Swift's face. Her world pitched and rolled. Above her she sensed men clambered aloft to reef a tattered sail. Icy rigging crackled beneath their thin boots. To break free the frozen sheets she knew the coated canvas felt like ice blades to the crew on the lines.

Swift twisted her neck around to look back past the workshop toward the quarterdeck. There her limited gaze saw both Head and Dawes strained to control the traveling tiller. Head's wind-whipped black beard flapped over one shoulder like Methuselah. Both struggled with the sluggish controls as the minimal heavy-weather sails propelled the ship forward. Wind buffeted from one angle. Currents pushed from another. Headway was survival.

As spray stung her eyes Swift now saw a short four ship lengths away the sea churned against the formidable headland. What seemed like inch by inch the *Black Cloud* pressed onward. A gale roared through the square-rigged ship: tossed and driven by the wind. The ship strained and screamed in an agony of wood and rope. Wind vibrated the lines over Swift's head into a siren's song.

Into Neptune's roar Mr. Flute appeared. Together his strong grip and Swift's unencumbered legs guided her in several slippery steps around the workshop deck to the cable-tier companionway. Mr. Flute forced open a half door. Wedged against the gale he pushed Swift onto the drenched stairway and leaned under the transom as he shouted above the din: "Best help Kikilani batten down the surgery. We're in for a blow."

From out of nowhere a mountainous wave slammed amidships. The sweeping wash obliterated the deck with foam...exactly where Swift and Mr. Flute had stepped only moments before. The mariner used his shoulder against the half-open companionway door to fend off the sea. But the ship's luckless carpenter emerged a second too late from his hiding place in the bow privy...and was swept to his doom. His muffled scream lost in the remorseless cacophony of wind and sea.

Unhearing the carpenter's cry as the ship pitched forward Swift tumbled onto the cable-tier deck. Kikilani extended her outstretched hand from the surgery door. And pulled Swift into the dripping cabin.

Just then the ship tossed up. Heeled to starboard. Then rolled violently to port. In that instant another giant wave drove the ship's prow headlong into a dive that buried the fo'c'sle in freezing brine. Where Swift had stood just a minute before.

Again the ship tossed and tumbled as if some great millstone was rolled up a slope and down another. From outside the surgery came a horrible furor. The play of barrels in the hold. Timbers cracked. Spars rattled. The wind howled through the shrouds. Overhead the confused shouts of the ship's crew came through the deck boards — along with the seawater. Heavy boots pounded back and forth along the deck. From deep inside the ship came the incessant clanking of the chain pumps.

Closed inside the surgery Swift and Kikilani fended off the examining stool as it ricocheted around the cabin. Until they lashed the possessed stool to a table leg with dressing strips. Petticoats casually stowed in upper bunks flopped over the rails like damp laundry. Books with the look of ravenous bats flew in the air at their heads. Glass tinctures shattered like missiles. Swift and Kikilani wedged dressings into drawer gaps. Stuffed soggy blankets into open shelves. Kikilani grabbed their chamber pot as it spun across the floor. Then they crammed the porcelain and lid back into its low cabinet using the canvas cover from the operating table. Both then jumped into Swift's narrow bulkhead berth. Back-to-back they locked elbows. Jammed their legs quivering against the bunk's corners. Gripped the berth's leeboard rail.

At that moment all stopped.

Time stood still for what seemed like forever.

The slow motion of fate took over....

The captain and mate fought to hold course. A feeble human effort against the outcome of destiny.

Sometime later — just as suddenly as the apocalypse had risen at the bottom of the world at Cape Horn — the heavens broke. Winds subsided. The gale fell behind. Sunrays appeared in the deck prisms as if angels had been summoned.

The deck found an even keel. Excess water escaped from the scuppers. Even the bilge rats ceased their squealing.

Swift and Kikilani cautiously crawled out of the berth. With an arm around each other's shoulders they surveyed the chaos around them. From the floorboards Kikilani swept shattered medicine bottles. Swift crawled under the examining table and freed the stool. The chamber pot was returned to its rightful place. Waterlogged dressings and lint were recovered in a bucket for drying. Kikilani righted what was left on the shelves. And in the cabinets. Everywhere their life was a jumble. Then Swift realized: Woodall's guide was missing. After a frantic moment Swift found the lifesaving book wedged safely behind the medicine cabinet. When some order was restored the two women straightened up. Neither missed the slightest detail of the scene. And then they laughed. Hearty. Full throated. A laughter of relief.

Ahead lay the Pacific Ocean.

The *Black Cloud* bore onward....Near the square-rigged transport ship several seagulls bobbed in the sun on gentle waves. Unconcerned.

Swift's diary (once located) held one simple entry that night:

23 February 1847: 85 days at sea. Doubled the Horn. And survived.

CHAPTER 33

SECRETARY'S OFFICE/DEPARTMENT OF STATE
WASHINGTON DC
25 FEBRUARY 1847

SAM HOUSTON shook the snow off his walking cape. "Don't know how you Northerners weather this cold." Houston tossed his cape on a hook. And walked toward the two men huddled over a large map. Their derrieres warmed by a meager coal fire. President James Polk faced the fire across the map table and blew into his hands.

Secretary of State James Buchanan pointed to the detailed map of Northern Mexico with one hand and held three dispatches in his other. Treasury Secretary Robert Walker and the President looked on.

Buchanan began in his Philadelphia courtroom voice. "This first dispatch just came in from New Orleans with a report from General Zachary Taylor in Mexico."

"What's Old Rough and Ready got to say for himself?" Houston piped in as he poured himself a J.B. whiskey. "Doctor's orders. Best way to keep a scratchy throat at bay is a healthy anti-fogmatic. Cheers...y'all." Houston took what looked like not his first combustible of the February evening.

"Same to you...Senator." Walker tried to straighten his threadbare suit jacket.

"Not good news from Mexico." Buchanan frowned as he skimmed Taylor's dispatch. "Since Matamoros in May…Taylor camped upriver on the Rio Grande for the summer. He lost about one third of his command. Over a thousand deaths. Mostly from cholera. Another third was walking dead. In the fall Taylor advanced about three hundred miles into Mexico due west from Matamoros. He was darned lucky to win at the battle of Monterrey in September."

"No army would follow that Pedro de Ampudia even if you paid them…which they don't." A slight smile formed on Houston's craggy features. "But going three for three in the enemy's territory is a feather in Old Zach's hat. If I reckon…he should have moved about fifty miles west of Monterrey by now. Somewhere south of the town of Saltillo… near Buena Vista."

The President ran his finger over the Mexico map and stopped. "That would be about here."

"Treacherous terrain that area." Buchanan's hand hovered over the rectangles formed by the map's unfolded mountain-valley creases. "Ravines everywhere. Like a giant fan. We expect General Santa Anna is going to bring everything he can beg. Borrow. And steal against Taylor any time now. Dispatch says Santa Anna outnumbers Taylor about three to one."

"Don't worry about Old Zach. He's whupped his weight in wildcats before. And he'll do it again." Houston swirled his rye. "Lucky we captured this map of northern Mexico at the battle of Resaca de la Palma last May. Otherwise we wouldn't know the first thing about Santa Anna's backyard." For emphasis Houston drew back his head and propelled a chaw of tobacco into the fireplace.

"Wasn't that map captured by one of your agents?" Polk asked Secretary Walker.

"That's right. Same agent we sent to Paris in November. Got the map — as I understand it — with help from a newspaper correspondent. Out of New York. A woman of all things."

"What was her name?" Houston asked.

"If I recall her *nom de plume* was just a last name. Something like Gift…or Miffed?"

Houston drawled: "That's right. *Swift.* Not bad work for a little woman. Next thang ya know the ladies'll be pushin' temperance on us."

"God forbid…Sam. The end of the world as we know it." Buchanan's tone had turned droll.

"Swift? New York? Ain't that the little stunner that writes for that paper that turned the tables on all the politicians and cops a few months back?" Houston stroked his bushy side-whiskers. "If memory serves…their wives and mistresses got a nasty Christmas present when they read the ole boys were listed in that madam's little Blue Book."

"That's the one." Walker's mouth had formed the suggestion of a smile. "S. Thomas Swift. Writes for that Walt Whitman fella at the *Brooklyn Daily Eagle*. She sure stirred up a hornet's nest with her December series about how New York's high-and-mighty collected bribes — and favors — at that pleasure palace."

Houston chuckled. "They say Swift got out of town while the gettin' was good."

President Polk hit the end of his patience. "Let's stay focused…gentlemen. The missus has us off to the Methodist church for candlelight Vespers in the next hour. Then we must greet the unfortunates at the South Portico. If we run too long…she'll be in a fine pucker."

"No way I'd cotton to giving any missus a wraithy turn. No…sir. Never pays." Houston shook his head dourly.

Secretary Buchanan held up the other two dispatches — one in each hand — in the direction of the gathered cabinet. "This dispatch is from our American Ambassador in London. Says his office has gotten wind of a conspiracy to take over the Hawaiian Islands. Someone is plotting to control the islands in the name of the local chiefs — and to 'protect' the chiefs from foreign powers."

Houston raised his glass. "Like us."

"I thought they called them the Sandwich Islands?" Polk asked.

"Yes…sir. Most folks do. That is…ever since Captain Cook named them that in 1778." The polished Secretary of State expanded his lesson. "Then about a dozen years later — in 1790 — a powerful chief from the biggest island of Hawai'i conquered all the other island kings — and eventually created one kingdom for all the islands by 1815. That chief was King Kamehameha."

Buchanan tapped the globe at the end of his map table. "Jump forward — past twenty-five years of missionaries and whalers:

The King's second son — King Kamehameha the third — signed up for a constitutional monarchy in 1840. Since then...Mr. President... the Sandwich Islands have been officially called the Kingdom of Hawai'i or the Hawaiian Islands."

Houston raised his glass. "Old names die hard."

Secretary Walker nodded his assent toward Buchanan. "A British naval commander signed up England as the protector of the Hawaiians in 1843. But the British Parliament rejected the commander's colonial acquisition within months...leaving the Hawaiians without a protector."

"To make matters worse this just arrived from Paris." Buchanan cocked his head to the left and extended his arm past a candle to help focus his nearsighted reading eye. He read the last dispatch aloud. "This says the King of the French — Louis Philippe — secretly signed a trading treaty with the King of Hawai'i last March 26...little more than eleven months ago."

Houston took out a clump of chewing tobacco and inserted it in his cheek. "Goldarnit. Guess bad news don't travel as fast as they say."

"Does that mean the French have leapfrogged the British?" Polk asked.

"Not unless the Brits changed their minds...Mr. President." Buchanan continued: "The French got most-favored-nation status...with minimal tariffs...plus rights for its Catholic missionaries...and no taxes at all on imported French brandy and wine." Buchanan scanned ahead in the text. "To sweeten the deal the French returned a bond worth twenty-thousand American dollars they had extracted from the Hawaiian King in 1839. Back then it was to ensure French priests were allowed into the kingdom."

Walker noted: "Makes the French look like real swells to the islanders."

Houston smirked with amusement. "Ah...the talking power of money."

President Polk irritably pinched the bridge of his large nose that separated his deeply set gray eyes. Walker put his empty glass aside while Houston poured himself another Old J.B.

Buchanan's farsighted eyelid twitched as he continued. "The Paris dispatch says the plot is to project naval and military power to control the Pacific."

All four men sat in silence as they contemplated the disastrous repercussions.

"The British have a longstanding interest in the Pacific. Plus they've been sending about three thousand criminals a year to Australia." Walker nodded in acknowledgment.

"I reckon that's what you call 'cleaning house' …Shame we caint do that with some Congressmen." Houston chuckled into his snifter.

The Americans hovered together over an ornate world map laid on top of the Mexican map on the long table.

"Who's behind this plot to take over Hawai'i?" the President asked.

"I wouldn't put it past the British." Buchanan dropped the dispatches on the map table. "They weren't happy about losing the Oregon Territory."

Walker added: "The French and the Spanish know we've got our hands full with the Mexicans. And the French already have the trust of the Hawaiian King with that most-favored-nation trade treaty."

"And I wouldn't rule out the Russians or Portuguese or even the Chinese." Buchanan growled.

"Who? How?" demanded an agitated Polk.

The two secretaries exchanged glances uncomfortably.

"We don't know the who."

"For the how…the foreign power wants an arrangement with the kingdom. What the power covets is a 'protectorate.'" Buchanan's fair complexion looked a shade paler. "In this case—if the foreign power has its eyes set on Hawai'i—they'll take advantage of the fact the island populations have been decimated by disease over the last thirty years. Today in many places the kings and chiefs have only one-third the population they had before the foreigners came…the foreigners being mainly New England whalers."

"So the Hawaiians are scared?" Polk asked as he ran a hand over his unruly gray hair worn long.

"Scared white…you might say." The little Wizard of Mississippi spoke without irony.

Buchanan tapped two fingers on the map. "Local royalty and their chiefs are easy marks. They're outnumbered. And they know they can't win in a fight...so they take any deal they can get. The big powers know this. That's how the French took over Tahiti and the Marquesas in the South Pacific."

Houston interjected as he studied the map. "The South Pacific is a far piece from Hawai'i in the North Pacific...."

"We know all those countries." Buchanan swept his hand over the map as he identified each nation. "England. France. Spain. Russia. Portugal. China. All of them have warships operating in the North Pacific. The South Pacific. The South China Sea near Hong Kong. Or the Coral Sea off eastern Australia."

"Who—and how—they plan to hit in the North Pacific is anybody's guess. As to where...Our sources tell us it will indeed be Hawai'i...and soon. Very soon."

"What's their next move?" Houston wondered aloud.

Polk clasped his hands behind him. Straightened his lower back. Then moved around the table to warm himself at the meager fire...whose warmth barely reached half the room. "American whaling interests would be cut off without a port to our name. Merchant routes to the Far East blocked. The winner could dominate the China opium trade. California and all our western territories would be within striking distance." He shook his head.

The Treasury Secretary interjected. "My guess—the entire plot to dominate the Pacific depends on money. Lots of money. Ships are one thing...but money is critical. Whoever it is...they must have money to pay for the operation. Pay for bribes. Pay for cooperation of the chiefs."

"What do you mean?"

"With enough money...anybody can buy off island chiefs and a king's allegiance."

Houston drawled: "Or fill an empty treasury vault....Won't be the first time some foreign power wanted to be the biggest toad in the puddle."

At that moment the outer reception-area door opened. A State Department assistant brought in a fist of papers that looked like three documents. A telegram form. And an illustrated calling card. The aide handed the batch to Secretary Buchanan.

"What's that?" Walker asked as he nodded at the first document.

"Looks like a reimbursement request from your agent."

Buchanan handed the document to Walker.

With a perplexed look Walker read the bill out loud item by item.

"Jack Dancer. British Hotel. Derb el Barabra. Frank District. Cairo. Egypt.

"Lodging with sitting room…3 nights

"Hot bath in room & lamp in sitting room with candle: Extra…3 nights

"Board…27 meals

"White Champagne…9 bottles

"Claret…7 bottles

"Port…3 bottles

"Tub and rub…1

"Laundry (Lady's white linen gown. Wine stain removed)…1

"Surgeon visit…1 (Donation to Sisters of Mercy)

"Bootmaker (Modify right snake-skin cowboy boot)…1

"Tobacconist (Oscuro Cigars)…3 boxes."

Walker's eyes popped when he saw the amount. Then he read the details regarding reimbursement.

"PAID IN FULL. 25 December 1846 by Sophia Lane Poole. Forward reimbursement immediately to Sophia Lane Poole/Author. Hotel d'Orient. Northside El Ezbekiyeh Gardens. c/o Edward William Lane/Orientalist. Cairo. Egypt."

Buchanan handed Houston the illustrated card. At first the senator could not believe his eyes. Then he laughed as his gaze comprehended the colorful miniature Rajput Kamasutra painting that vividly depicted two turbaned princes as they ravished a naked maiden on a divan.

Houston passed the painted card to Walker. "Looks like your boy is on the tail — I mean *trail* — of something." He snorted. "Jus' not our trail."

When the Treasury Secretary recovered all eyes turned back to Buchanan.

"Interesting." Buchanan glanced at the packet from Dancer. "The routing slip indicates Dancer's pouch left Zanzibar on 10th January instant" — Buchanan read off the entries — "then north to Aden in

Yemen. There it was given to the Peninsular & Oriental Steam Navigation Company to carry to Suez Egypt. Then overland to Cairo. Down the Nile by river steamer to Alexandria. And on to Southampton England by a Mediterranean P&O side-paddle steamer. In Southampton the dispatches were delivered to the Cunard Line's *Britannia*...which steamed to New York in a fortnight." Buchanan paused. Flipped the routing sheet over. "There the packet was handed to our New York custom office. Last night the office put the documents on the overnight train to Washington. Then sent a telegram this morning by Samuel Morse's Magnetic Telegraph Company. An hour ago the telegram was received at Morse's office in the Main Post Office on Seventh Street here in Washington. *Voilà*. The telegram and dispatches just arrived together. Elapsed time...forty-five days."

"Impressive." The bald Walker clucked. "Wasn't it just seven years ago when the Sultan of Zanzibar sent his royal yacht from Zanzibar around Cape of Good Hope to New York?"

Buchanan traced the route on the globe. "The newspapers wrote the Sultan's son caused quite a stir. You're right...Walker. The *Al Sultanah* made the sailing voyage in eighty-seven days. Dancer's dispatches made it here in almost half the time....forty-two days faster."

Polk marveled at the accomplishment. "What a small world we're living in."

"Zanzibar?" Houston asked. "Where the hell is Zanzibar?"

"Zanzibar is an island off the east African littoral. In other words...the central coast of East Africa. Opposite the main port of Dar es Salaam. North of Mozambique. South of Mombasa." Buchanan traced the region on the State Department's globe.

"Better question is what the hell is Dancer doing in Zanzibar? Thought Walker sent him to Paris?" Buchanan relished a tweak to his rival. "Told you...We should have sent a diplomatic man for this mission."

"Glad he made it." Polk nodded. "What's your agent have to say...Walker?"

Secretary Walker read out loud from the longhand telegram form:
NAPOLEON SENT LEGRAND AND TREASURE AROUND CAPE GOOD HOPE BARELY MADE ZANZIBAR LOST TWO SHIPS ESCAPED SAILED

NORTHEAST TOWARD INDIA NO ONE KNOWS WHERE SOME CLUES NOW ON TRAIL LEAVING ZANZIBAR POSTHASTE = THESE BOOTS WILL TRAVEL=DANCER

Buchanan opened the other two dispatches. They proved to be a letter in French and its translation. "LeGrand's own words confirm Dancer's telegram. LeGrand escaped east with the treasure. Parts unknown."

Polk ran both palms over his prominent widow's peak. "Tarnation. We've got our hands full paying for the Mexican war without this Pacific intrigue. Taylor is stuck in northern Mexico. Santa Anna is headed toward Taylor's walking dead with an army three times the size. Major General Scott—Old Fuss and Feathers—is primping and playing blockade in the Gulf of Mexico: too timid to mount a landing in Vera Cruz. Or march on Mexico City. Now it's February. And we still aren't any closer to locking up Napoleon's gold in Walker's Treasury vault than we were in November! Now we find out some nation is plotting to outflank us in the Pacific. Yet not the slightest inkling who the conspirators are! Who said the new year would bring good news?"

Secretary of State Buchanan summed up all the doubts that hung in the air: "No treasure. No clue who is going to strike in the Pacific...or when or where. No time...and no way to warn Dancer— even if we knew where he was."

The President muttered through clenched teeth:

"How in the Sam Hill could things get any worse?"

CHAPTER 34

ABOARD *BOUNTIFUL*/AMERICAN WHALER
SAMOA/NAVIGATOR ISLANDS/PACIFIC
MARCH 1847

CAPTAIN HAMILTON POST was a man of his word. And bound by it. Post stood only six inches over five feet. Built as sturdy as any keel-worthy oak from his beloved New England. His strength always a surprise to mischief makers. One day on the rough Boston docks years before Post became a ship's master a big mean stevedore overheard Post make a promise. The brawny fellow laughed. Spit. Stepped in front of Post…and challenged his word. The roustabout said no more: Post hit him square under the jaw…and the man dropped like an anchor. Over the stretched-out form Post spoke: "Challenge me…but never question my word." Then Post remarked to the dock men who pressed forward: "Take your friend away…and when he comes to his senses he best remember to be more respectful." From that day Post won a name — and was known among the tough class of seamen and stevedores as…"Hammerhand." Which became a name as familiar to him as his own.

Post's thumbs rested easily in the folds of his ivory-linen knee-button pantaloons. At his waist a broad belt held his seaman's knife close at hand. In colder climes Post sported a matching ivory vest with gold buttons. On this day in the South Pacific he wore a cotton shirt. White sleeves rolled to mid-forearm. Collar deeply open at the throat below a rakishly dimpled chin. Kept clean. A mirror of his Yankee conscience. His widespread eyes and dark brows somehow fit on his large head. The combination tended to give his face a brooding expression.

Post's one nod to vanity was his rich black hair. Always trimmed about the ears and sideburns. Curving locks at the front perpetually fell across his right temple. He fought this losing battle with bay-rum hair tonic. But to no avail. Below his hat line. Behind his neck. He wore a braided rattail. This singular affectation was held by a storied black ribbon that curled the braid back into a small loop at the end. Not a man aboard risked pressing the Old Hammerhand for an explanation.

Whaling had been good this voyage for the American Captain. For his ship *Bountiful*. And for his polyglot crew. The winter pods in the Sea of Japan filled over a hundred barrels with the finest whale oil. Now secured in the ship's cargo hold. Even better was the haul of baleen whalebone. The coveted "teeth" that bowhead and baleen whales used to filter tiny krill crustaceans by the ton. Baleen plates once extracted and dried were cut into long flexible rods. Many baleen plates in the *Bountiful*'s winter catch measured over ten feet and close to two hundred pounds. Much sought after in fashionable down-east ports for a range of products. Anything needing spring and strength used baleen. From back-scratchers to collar stiffeners and buggy whips to corset stays.

It was Captain Post's word that brought the *Bountiful* to Samoa on the spring return voyage to the Sandwich Islands. Even though Samoa was out of his way. Located in the Navigator Islands. Thirteen hundred nautical miles east of New Caledonia and halfway to Tahiti. He had promised to make a delivery for Mama Samoa. And Captain Hamilton Post always kept his word.

That duty accomplished in the port of Apia to the northwest...the three-masted *Bountiful* now gently entered the port of Pago Pago. Truly a fine ship. Purpose-built for the whaling trade she had much dark mahogany in her craftsmanship. Master Post saw she was frequently oiled in neat harmony with her gray teak decks. Varnished spars. And white canvas stowed aloft. In contrast Pago Pago's craggy black-lava escarpments dropped directly into the sea. The dramatic contrast of green jungle meeting blue water was broken by occasional slashes of tan beach. Thatched Samoan huts dotted the shoreline breaks. *An extra day or two — perhaps to savor some tuna or shore time for my men — won't hurt.* So the proud Captain thought. The Stars and Stripes hung limply from the gaff in the gentle South Pacific air.

Post was about to give orders for relaxed watch rotations and shore leave when the first mate called out.

"Native canoe approaching...sir!"

Captain Post looked up as all eyes turned toward shore. There a solo canoe with single outrigger cut toward the *Bountiful*. In the bow a white man applied himself vigorously to his paddle. In the stern a native girl — hair streaming behind her naked torso — paddled equally furiously.

"Appear to have a native greeting party...Captain." The mate smiled.

All hands moved toward the bulwarks on the bay side to watch.

The canoe cut a rapid course toward the whaler's half-furled sails. Perhaps a hundred canoe lengths distant.

As the entire crew watched the sound of a drum rose from the shoreline five hundred yards farther up the beach behind the two paddlers. The sound throbbed across the water like a war cry. At that moment two score native men raced toward the water's edge. Lifted two great war canoes effortlessly and drove them into the surf. In that fore canoe a warrior chief took his place. A mountain of a man. He braced himself against the surge of his paddlers with the shaft of a spear. Its tip barbed with a fearsome array of shark-tooth points. A lethal war club in his other fist.

The white man and native maiden stole a single glance over their shoulders. Then redoubled their efforts as if their lives depended on it. Closer they pressed toward the *Bountiful*. Sixty. Fifty. Forty canoe lengths. Their early advantage quickly shrank as the war canoes gained momentum.

Captain Hamilton Post saw the sweat pressing through the American's white shirt. A circular headdress of flowers flew from the woman's brow as she paddled furiously.

Post muttered to himself: "This is naught a welcome committee."

The mate replied dryly: "Looks more like a hasty escape."

Within moments the white man and the woman came within hailing distance of the whaler. Then closed even farther on the *Bountiful.*

"Permission to come aboard!" the man shouted in one burst.

Replied Post: "Guests are welcome who come in peace."

Over the bulwark a seaman hastily rotated a davit arm. Then dropped a cargo net just short of the waterline.

"Mr. Russell…shake out those topsails." The Captain's command was spoken low-voiced to not raise alarm. "Be ready to turn about and be away…Mr. Russell. All taut?"

"Aye…sir…All taut." Mr. Russell went quietly about his business.

The white man stood in the outrigger. Turned. The woman deftly stepped forward to within arm's length. Then kissed the man. Passionately. Locked in love's embrace the canoe drifted within two lengths of the *Bountiful.* At that moment the woman looked again toward shore. A sharp gasp escaped her lips. Onward the monstrous chief bore down on them full tilt.

With a deliberate gesture the woman slipped a crimson pandanus key necklace from around her neck. Then over her head. Paused. Then placed the royal-red ceremonial *ulafala* necklace over the man's head and onto his strong shoulders. The back of the man's fingers tenderly caressed the woman's cheek and neck. She clasped his hands between her maiden breasts. Over her heart. A sudden calm came over her. A realization. She retreated to her place at the stern of the outrigger: a comely vision of natural perfection. With a single stroke she guided the canoe forward to the ship's waterline as gently as a kiss.

The white man tossed three cylindrical traveling cases into the cargo netting lowered from the davit. Then stepped into the net himself. The shift of his weight pushed the canoe a length away from the whaler.

The maiden's chest heaved less from exertion. Sweat trickled down her neck. Then tears of loss cascaded silently down her cheeks. She pulled a red bougainvillea bloom from behind her ear. Kissed it gently. Then let the flower drift from her hand into the lapping waves of the bay.

Moments later the man clambered up and over the rail. Nimble as a cat. The wooden heels of his new bucket-topped Cavalier boots rapped the deck.

When the warrior chief saw his objective was no longer in danger he growled an order. The battle canoes back-thrust their paddles against the water. The menace of their brightly ornamented crafts slowed eight lengths short of the drifting young maiden.

Calmed by her epiphany the long-haired beauty swept her paddle in a wide arc: forward toward the bow. The graceful sweep pivoted the canoe. Another stroke moved her craft into the path of the oncoming war canoes. The canoes swiftly parted for her. The scowling anger of the warrior chief sent a murderous last glare toward the white man's ship. Then the great war canoes crossed right-about and escorted the maiden back to shore.

Every agog whaler and seaman aboard the *Bountiful* placed the brown-skinned nymph in their dreams as a princess of paradise. For she was. To a man they watched the princess of Pago Pago retreat into the distance. Captain Hamilton Post stepped toward the white man at the railing. The man turned. Without hesitation the two Americans stepped forward and embraced each other. Slaps across the backs were traded. Hearty claps that could knock the wind from a lesser man if not prepared.

"Captain Hamilton Post" — the man smiled broadly — "am I glad to see you!"

"Sink me if I don't travel halfway 'round the world…and I still can't get rid of you." Post's reply was quick and warm. "Appears my lot in life is to save your rascally skin once again. How did you come to Samoa…Dancer?"

"Bit of a story. But the best part is seeing you…Captain."

Captain Post didn't hesitate. He turned to his crew. "Bos'n! Tell the lads shore liberty is canceled. Mr. Russell! Crack on all sail. Get us out of this cursed water. Take us past the Fatumafuti headland…then bear east. Give us some distance from those war canoes. Mr. Russell!" Post again barked crisply to the first mate. "I leave the deck to you!"

And so it went. Canvas fluttered out. Sheets hauled home. The lines overhauled. Braces tended. Set taut. In no time the *Bountiful* cut a path that raised the Samoan headland. Canvas straining. And Mr. Russell handled the helm in sweet fashion.

Captain Post shouted for his cabin boy. "Young Smythe!"

"Yessir." The lad snapped his presence loudly.

"Stow our visitor's plunder cases in the pantry cabin next to mine. Be sharp...ye danged pup! And tell cook to put on a meal and a bottle of Madeira. Make that three. We may be certain — there's a story behind this day...and an equally long night." The lad hefted the American's cylindrical cases — which were the size and length of four or five stacked hatboxes. Unusually each riveted case was covered with a different African beast's hide: Zebra. Cheetah. Crocodile.

Captain Hamilton Post turned again to look upon his latest project. "A story...indeed."

"By your leave...Captain. You've always been a man of your word." With that Jack Dancer clapped his hand again on Captain Post's back then went to tend to his luggage.

CHAPTER 35

POST TOSSED THE BUTT of his cheroot out the aft-gallery window. The cigar died in a sparking pinwheel as the swift twilight of the tropics merged into the gentle Pacific night. Dancer took out two black Oscuro-wrapped cigars from his well-traveled tin case. Then rose to offer his friend a dark fermented smoke. He took care to bob his head around the master's low-hanging wine wheel. Of no worry for the shorter Captain Post.

Post leaned forward. "How the dickens did you ever get to Samoa...Dancer?"

With two fingers Dancer tapped off his Oscuro ash. "As you know...my friend...I soldiered for Houston and Texas for years. My military skills at the Charleston Arsenal paid off. When Texas was annexed as a state in December 1845 I returned to Charleston. Before Houston went to Washington in February 1846. The Raven...as the Cherokee called him. Houston put in a word for me to work in President Polk's secret service group. Officially I'm a Treasury agent. Unofficially...I report directly to the President."

Dancer skimmed lightly over his experiences in New York. Paris.

Zanzibar. Then brought out Champollion's notebook and explained about the lost treasure of Napoleon. About LeGrand. La Pérouse.

"To be honest...I'd do anything...even go to hell across lots to solve this." Dancer shook his head in frustration. "But I'm at my wit's end. I've read and reread the notebook for weeks since I shipped out from Zanzibar. Talked to captains. Old-timers. Every ancient mariner with a memory. First Aden. Then Ceylon. Singapore. Sydney. Samoa. Nothing panned out. Finding LeGrand's trail after almost fifty years is about as likely as catching a weasel asleep. I'm desperate...my friend. Even following a cold trail to Tahiti or Easter Island is no better odds than a hopeless dead man's fix."

Dancer paced the Captain's well-appointed cabin. "Then where? Chile? Cape Horn? Even if I retraced La Pérouse's log stops...what are the chances some clue about LeGrand will surface? Fact is...I've found nothing to go on. Going forward is a wild-ass guess." Dancer removed a phosphorus Congreve match. Snapped the airtight metal box closed and lit another Oscuro cigar "The only thing I know is I've come too far to turn back."

"Trouble." Captain Hamilton Post mumbled the single word. "You're either in trouble or you attract trouble. That's all you are... Dancer. Trouble. Pure and simple. And ye know I hate trouble like the devil hates holy water."

The dilemma hung in the air like a muddle. Gradually Captain Post let the cigars and a third bottle of Madeira—that is: let friendship and necessity—overrule his duty and honor. Post let the moment get the better of his judgment. "Don't hang up your fiddle yet...Dancer. The *Bountiful* is short three men. Seems the pleasures of Japan had more appeal than whaling. If we sail to Tahiti maybe I can recruit some seamen..."

"You might have a fix of trouble trying to recruit on Samoa just now." Dancer winked.

"Blast you...Dancer." But Post's admonition was quite warm. "Alright. Blame your cigars. Blame your honeyfuggling story." As he cuffed Dancer smartly on one shoulder he added: "Dad-blame it. My duty as your friend will take you east. As far as Tahiti. But mind... no farther. We'll tell the lads that you join me in the wardroom as a land officer. Just remember. From Tahiti I sail north to the Sandwich Islands to cash out our oil and baleen with a homebound transport. How you get to Easter Island from Tahiti…how you retrace LeGrand's log stops in Chile…That's up to you…Dancer. Tahiti with the *Bountiful*. Halfway. That's it."

Dancer soft-punched his old friend in the chest. "Tahiti it is!"

Post's word was his honor. But already he regretted it. "You're nothing but trouble…Dancer. Tahiti is the lion's den itself. Sailing into Pape'ete will just pile on the agony. We'll be lucky if the French don't trump up some excuse to confiscate our entire season's catch. Just like the French to look for any excuse to flex their new protection agreement. And show how useful they are to Queen Pomare."

Captain Hamilton Post shook his head. "For an American whaler to get into Pape'ete will be trouble enough." He frowned. "Getting off French Tahiti will make escaping Santa Anna's Alamo look like a stroll in Charleston's Marion Square."

CHAPTER 36

MAIN CABIN/*BLACK CLOUD*
RAISING CONCEPCIÓN/CHILE/PACIFIC
11 MARCH 1847

ANGUS MACOMBER looked like a lapsed missionary. For his first ten years in the Sandwich Islands he supplied the missionaries. And handled all mission financial affairs. Three years ago Macomber cashed in his connections. And went to the other side. He became a merchant. Landowner. Customs officer. And now U.S. Consul on Maui at Lahaina.

Macomber's lanky reach took up space for two on the *Black Cloud*'s aft salon benches. With each summerlike day in the South Pacific the American Consul's noxious tobacco further enlarged his presence. To any passing audience he ceaselessly held garrulous court as the ship rode before a steady breeze toward Valparaiso Chile. By now Swift's journal put the terror of Cape Horn seventeen days in the past.

When Swift descended the salon's aft stairway Macomber gestured expansively for Swift to join him on his bench. Macomber reached for the pewter coffee carafe sitting inside the table's divider fiddles. "Diplomats and consuls. We all play a vital role." Macomber poured a mug of boiled coffee for himself without offering Swift any. Then placed the pot back on the table between the bumpers. And leaned back against the mizzenmast that separated the passengers' mess from the captain's table. "The difference you may ask? Well...miss. It can easily be summed by the difference between courts and ports."

Pleased with his word play Macomber blew a satisfied puff of smoke toward the open skylight. Swift kept mental notes for her readers.

"Two different worlds entirely." Angus Macomber gilded his self-importance. "Diplomats are career men...generally. Work for the State Department. Ambassadors tend to be born into the position... if you get my meaning. Aristocrats. Monied families. Old school. Different type of man altogether."

Swift nodded politely. Mused to herself as her gaze took in Angus Macomber. Gangly. Severe. Bowl haircut. No part. No moustache. Oversized ears that stuck out. *He makes me think of Ichabod Crane.* A slight smile passed over her face as she recalled listening spellbound to her mother read about the awkward schoolmaster in Washington Irving's *The Legend of Sleepy Hollow*. The one dissimilarity was Macomber's patchy beard...trimmed below his lower lip in missionary fashion. Yet—unlike the guileless Ichabod Crane—Macomber did not disguise being out to grab whatever he could with his mercantile schemes.

"Bostonian by birth. Been in the islands for thirteen years." Macomber turned his head to one side: The missionary's long snipe-like nose above his spindly neck reminded Swift of a weathervane showing the direction of the wind. "Speak Hawaiian. Write Hawaiian. Read Hawaiian. Some say I know Hawaiians almost better than they know themselves!" The trader hmphed proudly. "Fact is...I've made quite a fist for myself in the islands...if I dare say so."

As the self-made American droned on in tedious unison with the ship's gentle roll Swift looked up as the missionary's pale wife appeared in her stateroom doorway. The suffering woman pressed her mouth with her fingertips. "I'll just step on the quarterdeck to take the air." Swift rose to let her pass between the polished bench and the curbed Captain's table. Then Swift settled back and poured herself some coffee. She positioned herself to face Macomber with her nose upwind...toward the sea air coming from the trunk vents above.

"Now...consuls...like me...." The narrow-shouldered Macomber warmed to his new audience. "We are merchants. Noncareer men. We are the agents of great trading and mercantile houses. Yet we are paid a pittance. Expected to cultivate relationships with local merchants. Foreign traders. Sea captains. Even ordinary sailors. Why...the fee I'm paid for the consulate doesn't amount to enough to furnish stationery!" He spoke to Swift in an injured tone. "'Tis why we're given 'unusual privileges' for smoothing the wheels of commerce...as it were."

"Is there ever a temptation to...say...bend the rules?" Swift drank a little of her bitter coffee to disguise a knowing smile on her lips.

Macomber's expression grew animated as he went into details. "Did you know four hundred and twenty-nine ships landed in Lahaina last year? That's why I had a canal and marketplace built in the harbor — so the chase boats wouldn't capsize in the channel. Now I sell whatever the seafarers need. Fat beef. Hogs. Sheep. Sugar. Syrup. Lard. Turkeys. Firewood. Limes. And the biggest seller of all: Irish potatoes." He crossed his long arms triumphantly. "Rules...you ask? Little lady... this is the frontier. The 'Wild West'...as it were. In the islands a man's honor — and the Good Book — are our constant guides. Bend the rules? Absolutely not. No. Never. Totally beneath my station." Macomber tried without success to tug a short white cuff from his rumpled jacket sleeve toward his long bony wrist. Then with a sly look from the corner of his eye he added a caveat: "Of course...if the occasional opportunity came one's way..."

"To promote American commerce..." Swift wore a matter-of-fact look of prudent skepticism.

"Ahem. Yes. That would be completely within the scope of my mission. Certainly." Macomber pulled back one rumpled coat lapel. Placed a finger and thumb into the watch pocket of his ill-fitting vest. Then raised to his lips his odious cigarette...pinched between his ringed forefinger and thumb. He half closed his eyes against the smoke.

"Let me tell you — it's a thankless job sometimes." Macomber's large ears seemed to almost flap as he spoke. "Take the British. Or the French. They're both just as bad. They undermine American commerce with stories planted in their colonial newspapers. Claim we are interfering with trade. Can you believe the cheek? Just because we favor American captains and American trading houses!" The consul gave an affronted look. "Then they say we're interfering in the affairs of *their* subjects. Who happen to be living in *our* ports and *our* islands.

Rubbish. Foreigners just trying to justify their colonial warmongering to force the locals to work with them. 'Protection' they call it." With bony fingers the ex-missionary stubbed out his smoke into a sand tray lying on the table. "Other times the rogues make wild claims…like consuls deliberately burn dispatches sent from our State Department. Not to mention stirring up the ungrateful local traders. They holler that some great spirit manipulates prices! Then whine that they must sell low…and buy imports too high. That's the free market…I say. The American Way."

"Do the foreigners ever escalate their ill will?"

Angus Macomber put a blazing Lucifer match to his latest handmade. "Ever? They do it all the time. If they get the ear of the local king…they say you are the wrong man for the job. That you 'aided and abetted' and undermined this treaty — or that agreement — with their government."

With that the man moved his gangly frame along the bench…toward Swift. And let his scarecrow fingers fall near her sleeve. She pulled her arm back discreetly. Macomber leaned in. "Ever heard of the Great Mahele?" Swift shook her head. "It's a land division scheme…Ingenious! The King's advisors cooked it up. All in the name of progress." Macomber gave Swift a crooked smile. "Don't tell anybody you heard it from me."

Swift nodded as if in assent and coyly crossed her heart. *The Great Mahele. What is this?*

Macomber wrung his hands in anticipation. "Up to now only the Crown and chiefs controlled the land. Commoners were traditionally allowed to cultivate and live on a parcel where they had responsibility — or *kuleana* — for that plot. Foreigners — even longtime residents like myself — were forbidden to own land. The King's Great Mahele puts an end to that islander-only land system." A twinkle came into Macomber's eyes. "With this land division the old way will be as short-lived as the native Hawaiians in a small-pox epidemic." The consul smacked his thin lips. "Won't be long before resident aliens — that's what they call us foreigners who live on the islands — can own and sell land in Hawai'i." Macomber leaned back like a conquering hero. "The natives won't know what hit 'em."

At that moment Kikilani came down the aft companionway and stepped into the salon looking for Swift. "We have a call." She nodded formally toward Macomber. "Two sailors were hoisting a sail with a quad block. The line slipped. One sailor's hand was pulled into the block. Looks serious. Can you come to the surgeon's quarters?"

Swift nodded. Then turned to her talkative companion. "Excuse me…Consul Macomber. I hope we can continue this another time."

Macomber lifted the empty coffee carafe. "Duty calls." He waved the pitcher at the cook with the presuming expression of a paying passenger.

As Swift hurried from the salon a strain passed through the ship's hull as it tacked against a rising wind. Macomber's green eyes followed Swift's form up the stairs. Then he thrust out a long hand to block the sand tray before it shot between the table's bumpers like a carrom. Farther aft—outside the ship's workshop—the put-upon barrel cooper—whose workload doubled after the loss of the carpenter—called to the sick bay ladies as they passed: "Mind the watch… weather coming."

◎ ◎ ◎

Duffy Ragsdale waited his turn outside the surgery while the two young women splinted the other sailor's fingers. Shortly Kikilani beckoned the greenhand to take his place on a keg that passed for an examining chair. He had tried to hold the t'gallant halyard as it ran toward the block. The racing line burned his hands like a hot iron. Ragsdale lost his grip near the end. Miraculously he was near the deck. And not aloft on a yard. His singed pride taught him a seafaring lesson as much as his burned palms.

Kikilani applied a native poultice to his scalded hands. Swift looked at Duffy's uncut locks hanging down his neck. "Folk cures aren't Kikilani's only skills." With a nod from Swift Kikilani wrapped her barber's chair cloth around Duffy's neck. Then clicked her sheers against a well-used shell comb. In relief Ragsdale volunteered the scuttlebutt he had heard in the seaman's fo'c'sle as his hay-blond locks fell to the floor. Then he told Swift of the dangerous conditions and mistreatment common among whaling-ship sailors by some corrupt captains.

Swift observed the young Ragsdale as she made careful notes. "Most sailors…like myself…are greenhands when they start a voyage from New Bedford or Nantucket or Westport…or even New York. Treatment…good or bad…all flows down from the master." Duffy dropped his voice almost to a whisper. "Captain Hyram Head…master of the *Black Cloud*…is one of the worst of all…they say. Cain't prove nothin'. Only hearsay. Two men who sailed with Head on two separate voyages say he has a reputation to flog the crew."

Kikilani snipped the coarse yellow hair around Duffy's ears.

"Dawes enjoys giving the floggings. Often adding extra lashes…"

Swift shook her head with an air of disgust. "We saw Dawes miscount on purpose over that trumped-up rum tot affair."

The unashamed seaman looked Swift in the eye. "That warn't the only time an innocent sailor was on the wrong end of one of Dawes' joyrides."

Kikilani put a soothing hand on the country-lad's shoulder.

"We saw it too…Duffy. His time will come." Swift's voice hit a comforting tone as she thought of Dawes' peacoat skewered by Mr. Flute's harpoon.

"Dawes is mean enough." Duffy gave them a worried look. "But he's not the one who tormented the sailors on those voyages. That was Cap'n Head. Head cheated everyone at every turn. Some seen him do it in petty ways—like cheating cards…or shortchanged transactions. Another time Head destroyed letters of introduction meant for his safekeeping. Makes it nigh impossible for a sailor to sign on with another ship without a letter." The lad blew on his bandaged hands. "Worst of all…the most experienced seaman said he heard Head bragging to Dawes. Head said he falsified cargo transshipment records from Hawai'i. That way he stiffed the ship owners and increased his take…and shortchanged the crew for their lay share too."

Ragsdale gave Kikilani a long look. His heart ached as he looked into the island maid's beautiful dark eyes. She held his gaze unperturbed. Then adopted an air of open purity. "Is there anything a sailor can do about it?"

Ragsdale made sure Swift had closed the surgery's door. He shrugged his shoulders under the barber's cape. "If anyone crosses the

Cap'n…the complainer is 'lost at sea.' No other cap'n has a higher 'lost at sea' record than Head."

In a whisper Ragsdale shared with Swift another report—whether true or rumor—that claimed Head smuggled rum and whale ambergris 'off manifest.' Swift listened closely as Duffy Ragsdale said the goods were often disguised as something else to avoid custom duties. The *Daily Eagle*'s correspondent nodded. *Smuggling seems to be a way of life for Captain Head.*

Just then from a deck prism came a sudden light that fell on the farm boy's cropped hair as Kikilani removed the barber's cloth. Ragsdale continued divulging what he knew about Captain Head's illicit activities. "The big money is in the opium…and the traffic in native girls." Swift and Kikilani exchanged meaningful glances. "Profits are sky high. And they get away with it. Because cap'ns are a law unto themselves. No one can question them."

Holding his hands aloft Duffy rose from the examining keg.

"Thanks…Duffy. That's the most damning report yet." Swift closed her notebook. "Keep your ears open. And we'll do the same. But go slow. We can't be too careful."

Kikilani closed the cabin door behind Ragsdale. She shook her head then quietly asked the key question: "Dawes is dangerous. But if Captain Head is a cheat and a smuggler…do you think he is just as dangerous?"

Swift sucked in a breath through her teeth: "As dangerous as a hornet." Unexpectedly the ship heeled to one side. Swift steadied her balance against the operating table. "And we seem to be sailing inside the hornet's nest itself."

CHAPTER 37

WEATHER DECK/*BLACK CLOUD*
SOMEWHERE WEST OF VALPARAISO/CHILE/PACIFIC
IDES OF MARCH/FOUR DAYS LATER

AN UNEXPECTED SQUALL LINE from out of the east bore down on the *Black Cloud*. There was no escaping the threatening seas: All aboard the *Black Cloud* knew a monstrous tropical storm would threaten the ship. Driven west before the wind the original intention of raising the haven of Valparaiso was snuffed by the tremendous gale. Beset by the onrushing blackness Captain Head straddled the stern post to control the wheel. "Send only the best hands aloft...Dawes! Keep the salts near the ropes for now! All others below deck!"

The hunted Captain frowned as he cast his gaze beyond the ship's wake at the thunderhead that bore down on his ship. "Trim the top gallants! Reef the mainsails! Leave the storm jibs to carry us before the wind! Step lively...you devils! Before this gale drives us beyond redemption!"

Dawes yelled at the petty officer stationed near the starboard ladderway at the bottom of the quarterdeck break. "Pipe the first watch...bos'n!"

As a few men scrambled on deck Dawes sent select seamen aloft. When Ragsdale reported he showed his bandaged hands.

"Your own fool fault...sailor!" A mocking sneer crossed Dawes' lips. "You and me get the top gallant. Make it fast!"

All other nonessential souls hunkered below deck. Hatches closed. Vents shuttered. The atmosphere below deck was airless. Humid. Dark. Suffocating. In the fo'c'sle seamen rolled from one side of the ship to another. Duffy's young bunkmate clutched his bruised shoulder. Seamen's chests tumbled back and forth. Rum tots pelted the men. All but the oldest salts were afflicted with seasickness.

Shortly Captain Head came below to the passenger salon. His black beard glistened with sea spray. Tersely he delivered his blunt assessment: "All will be done to save the ship. But this freak gale is the worst I have ever seen." Without warning the ship tossed and plunged. Angus Macomber lost his footing and landed in a pile like a cattywampus scarecrow. Nearby the newly minted missionary gripped his doorframe with white knuckles. Inside the cabin his pregnant wife clutched her hymnal but could not utter a word amidst such peril. After a slight hesitation the Captain turned back to the maindeck ladder. From the second tread he twisted around and shouted toward the cook and cowering passengers: "If any of you have not made your peace with God...you better do it now!"

By the pounding of boots above and the violent change of motion in the ship the terrified denizens below deck understood their fate was no longer their own. Kikilani and Swift battened down the surgery as best they could. Then locked arms back-to-back in a cramped bunk as the ship pitched and rolled and dipped into troughs. Only to be tossed on the highest wave by the wind.

Into the dismal howl Ragsdale climbed the shroud rigging. Nimbler now from months of practice. Yet his fingers took a lighter grip to protect his stinging palms. Dawes followed. The *Black Cloud* rolled hard to port as the wind drove through the cables. Ragsdale pushed ever higher up the weblike ratlines. Pursued by the voice of Dawes dogging him at his heels.

All at once the wind filled with blinding rain. Ragsdale's trailing foot slipped on a wet rope rung. He caught himself. Continued higher. Hand over fist. Dawes shouldered past the greenie. Rain coated the rigging. In the maelstrom they reached the spar that held the sail at the height of the topmast. With his back to the bow and bent over the yard Dawes inched his way out on the spar to his right. Ragsdale mirrored the mate's moves. Both were engulfed by the howling gale that struck them in the face like needles. Every roll of the ship amplified the swing of the mast over the mad sea below.

Two Jack-tar sailors joined them on the yard footropes to their left. Ragsdale had the third position from the mast. Dawes was the farthest outlier. His boots balanced on the Flemish horse at the outermost yardarm end—a separate footrope—where the port mainbrace was fixed to the tip of the main yardarm. Painstakingly they bundled the heavy canvas tightly on top of the yard. Then looped the gasket lines over the sail and tied the gaskets off to the Jackstay cable fixed along the top of the spar beneath the heavy canvas. Methodically they moved. One hand working. The other clung to the Jackstay lifeline ninety feet above the sea.

Once the topsail was stowed Dawes signaled the deck hands below to square the sheets and the fore and aft mainbraces. Without warning the rain now mixed with a swirling fog that engulfed the *Black Cloud*. Ragsdale looked down at the deck. Nothing but whiteness. Visibility was now less than the length of a man's arm.

Dawes bellowed at the two seamen clinging to the Jackstays. "You two lubbers! Off you go!" In an instant the other two topmen disappeared like black squirrels into the white clouds that surrounded them. And made their way down the lines to the deck below.

Ragsdale was next. He made it to the second quarter of the yard—partway to the mast rings—with his boot pressed against the footrope's vertical stirrup. Just then a giant wave slammed into the beam of the *Black Cloud*. Dawes' boots slipped off the yardarm footrope. He lost one grip on the Jackstay. One leg caught the line behind his knee. Wildly Dawes spun around. He dangled like a monkey by one hand only…and his knee. Ragsdale reached his right hand for the mate. Grabbed a fist of peacoat. Pulled Dawes back into balance on the Flemish horse footrope. Then reached his hand for the Jackstay.

Violently the trough of the huge wave rolled the ship back in the opposite direction. The sudden movement ripped Ragsdale's right fingers from their grip. He looked at Dawes. Only his bandaged left hand held a loose gasket line. Helplessly the young sailor extended his free hand toward the first mate. Their eyes met. Dawes' expression turned to triumph. Instead of assistance the mate put his boot on the lad's footrope—and bounced his weight on the line. The sudden vibration broke Ragsdale's feet from their balance. His last bandaged grip slipped. His hands flailed in the air. Caught nothing. He fell back. Screamed. But his voice was lost in the howling of the gale. In a moment he was gone. Swallowed by the fury of the storm. The next moment from below came the sickening thud of a body slamming into the wood deck. Like a 120-pound sack of potatoes. Hollow. Still.

"That 'ill teach ya to spy on the master." Dawes spit at the deck below. "One less witness…and two more to go." A fleeting smile of intense malice crossed his salt-spattered lips.

Dawes descended the ratlines quickly. There was great commotion around the mainmast. Several old hands bent over the lifeless form. Nothing to be done. Hearing the commotion Kikilani and Swift braved the weather and came on deck. Kikilani raced to the side of the body. And shuddered.

Dawes hopped from the shrouds to the deck. Landing next to Captain Head he gave the Captain a furtive sidelong glance. "He should never 'ave gone aloft…sir. His hands still raw and bandaged. But 'e insisted."

Captain Head shrugged and touched the still body with the toe of his black boot. He muttered to no one in particular: "Just a bad-luck Jonah. Some landsmen aren't cut out for the sea."

Dawes knelt and lifted one of the dead sailor's hands as if that was proof of some kind. "Told 'em to go below. Lost his grip. I seen it." Dawes toadied to the Captain. "Always carried a jinx with him. Ask the other topmen."

A tear came to Kikilani's eye. Then anger.

Swift glowered at Dawes.

The squall still gripped the ship. "Smidt!" The Captain bellowed above the storm. "Take this accident to the cable-tier! We'll send him to Davey Jones when the skies clear! Back to stations! Now!"

With a grunt the hulking Prussian seaman stepped forward. Never far from Head's side: His obedience made his brawn useful. Smidt slung Ragsdale's dead body over his shoulder. And descended the workshop stairway. At that moment green seawater sloshed across the deck. Then an eddy of white froth flowed away into the scuppers. With that motion the sea erased the crimson puddle where Duffy Ragsdale died.

Dawes caught Swift's eye. With a sinister lift of his blunt chin Dawes pointed at the spot where Ragsdale's body had been as if to say: *But for the grace of God…that could be you.*

Swift and Kikilani withdrew down the stairs where Smidt had gone. And made their way to the surgery cabin door as the storm continued to unleash its fury.

Mr. Flute followed.

In the cable-tier just outside the surgery Smidt dumped the body on a hastily placed plank between two water casks. Then returned to the weather deck for further orders. Swift whispered under her breath. "Why is it always the good ones?"

Mr. Flute stepped up to the plank. Then put Duffy Ragsdale in the repose of the dead. With gentle care the mariner took out two large cents from his pocket and placed a copper coin over each closed eyelid. In a quiet voice — almost unintelligible — Mr. Flute explained: "These are to pay Charon the ferryman to carry this seaman across the River Styx to the afterlife. May he rest in peace." Mr. Flute returned his knit cap to his shaven head and turned toward Swift and Kikilani.

Swift stepped forward to the bier. She mouthed a silent prayer then placed Duffy's knotted safety cord like a cross in the grasp of one bandaged hand. Kikilani moved to the other side of the plank. Two large tears coursed down her unblemished cheeks. Her lower lip trembled. She wiped her cheeks with the back of her hand. Then brought out from her pants pocket a carved chrysanthemum blossom. Swift recognized the secret-admirer's gift Kikilani found one morning hanging from the handle of the surgery-cabin's door. With the natural grace of an island Eve Kikilani placed the wooden flower under Duffy's other hand next to the braided cord.

After a moment Mr. Flute placed a bag of ballast stones between Duffy's feet and tarped the body in sailcloth. Then lashed the sailor's remains smartly inside its shroud. This he covered with a rough blanket. Then raised a pocket flask of rum with lemon and bitters: "Skaal! Never fear...lad. I will watch over you tonight. Someone must. That first mate is mean enough to steal the pennies off a dead man's eyes." After a healthy draft he handed the flask to Swift and Kikilani.

"The Ides of March...an unlucky date for sure." Swift slowly gave a long-exhaled sigh. Then took a small sip. "That is the date my mother drowned...and the same date two years later when my father died."

The two women comforted each other. Then stood in silence.

"Aye." Mr. Flute replaced the pewter flask inside his jacket. "It's hard to lose a friend. Even harder to lose one's parents...or a brother or sister. Life is rarely fair." Swift and Kikilani looked at the weathered seafarer as he returned their glance. "But that's the challenge...ain't it? The dead are gone. It's up to the survivors to carry on in this world. To soldier on. To remember them. To honor them. And to live life fully for those we've lost...and for yourself."

As Mr. Flute spoke the rolling and pitching of the storm raged. And the *Black Cloud* was driven west into the trackless Pacific.

CHAPTER 38

SURGEON'S CABIN/*BLACK CLOUD*
RAISING JUAN FERNANDEZ ISLAND
THREE DAYS LATER

DUFFY RAGSDALE'S BODY slid off the plank. Kikilani and Swift watched as the bundled remains of their friend disappeared. A brief splash rose from below the taffrail at the stern of the *Black Cloud*. Captain Head closed his black Bible. Already his roster log was annotated: *D. Ragsdale. Ordinary seaman. Lost at sea. Accident. 15 March 1847.* In the distant western sky Head watched the monster storm blow toward the open ocean. A satisfied smile passed above his long Shenandoah beard as the storm's fury and death pushed west by northwest into the equatorial Pacific.

No longer sure of their north-south longitude the Captain ordered a course due west. A course that traced the horizontal latitude where he guessed the *Black Cloud* would encounter Juan Fernandez Island. Captain Head busied the crew with mending sails and splicing ropes and endless turns at the tar bucket. Experience taught him the regimen of all sailing ships tattered by a fierce storm.

At the wheel Captain Head looked up at the sails fully spread as the transport heeled along smartly in the after-storm breeze. He noted the favorable winds with a silent nod. *Everything draws well.* Dawes took the time to demand a haircut from Kikilani. Seated on a bench that surrounded the skylight above the passenger quarters Dawes bragged about his Captain. "The Cap'n hits everythin' he aims at…and naught he daren't want to hit." With lather full and razor in hand Kikilani paused as she thought of poor Duffy Ragsdale. A sudden lurch — or so she imagined — could make her blade slip. Then a small nick to Dawes' ear drew a few drops of blood. "Stupid sea monkey!" The mate pushed the island girl away. Wiped the foam and blood from his face. A cautious glance revealed the harpooner leaned against the galley only steps away. The mate threw the barber's cloth at Kikilani and stormed up the quarterdeck ladderway. She collected her tools and returned them to the barber kit. *Give me another chance and Duffy's death won't go unanswered.*

That evening nestled in the surgeon's quarters with four large candles correspondent S. Thomas Swift put pen to parchment. The terror of Cape Horn. The monster storm. The death of a friend. Her words flowed like a heart pulse. Soon the pages formed a long dispatch.

Special Report to the Brooklyn Daily Eagle
CORRESPONDENT SURVIVED THE HORN!
HURRICANE DROVE SHIP INTO SOUTH PACIFIC!
SAVED BY THE ISLE OF ROBINSON CRUSOE!
NEXT: WHAT MYSTERIES AWAIT IN SANDWICH ISLANDS?

Part Two in a Three-Part Series
JUAN FERNANDEZ ISLAND— The terror of Cape Horn was behind us. Only to be besieged by one of the worst storms in the memory of our most-seasoned mariners. Driven west from our intended haven of Valparaiso Chile our stout ship followed its bowsprit on a single latitude of hope. Now more than four months at sea. Your faithful correspondent and all aboard the Black Cloud *late of New York Harbor eagerly anticipate the opportunity to go ashore on the lonely rock known as Juan Fernandez Island.*

Imagine—Dear Reader—our firewood gone. Thus no hot meals. No warmth below deck. The water in the casks turned green and ropy with algae. One wag instructed us how he strained the water between his teeth—what teeth he still had. Even the barest water ration of a pint a day was not as welcome as a tot of rum. Rats and cockroaches and small vermin reigned supreme on what formerly were provisions. Our fair ship raised Valparaiso for supplies and succor. But destiny had in mind a different turn for your correspondent.

Almost within sight of Valparaiso a great hurricane drove us west into the Pacific sea. The Captain told us to make peace with our God. One stout lad replied: "We left for the Sandwich Islands…and we shall get there." For the rest of us our prayers were answered.

Soon—we pray—we shall freshen our casks with sweet drinking water on Juan Fernandez—360 miles off the coast of Chile. Replenish our wood: neatly baled and stowed. Plus…goats. Wild boars. And fresh fish will soon supplant the wretched monotony of brined pork and stale sea biscuits. Wild fruits and homeland orchards fill our dreams. And some say the huge crawfish of this heavenly isle rival the lobsters trapped by our Yankee brethren from Maine. The chance to bathe in fresh water…do laundry in cool streams…is almost too delicious to contemplate.

Yet imagining our destination—Dear Reader—is not needed. All you must do is turn to your book peddler for a copy of Daniel Defoe's 1719 novel: Robinson Crusoe. *The first novel in English. Inspired by none other than the real-life Scottish castaway: Alexander Selkirk. Marooned on Juan Fernandez Island—some say at his own request—Selkirk survived four years to tell his story. Then enterprising author Defoe turned the tale into a great yarn. Your correspondent has read Defoe from a gloss edition with margin notes to the sailors aboard the* Black Cloud *who have long ago committed Defoe's words to memory. Cannibals! Captives! Mutineers! All came from the inspiration of the island before us—perchance someday to be known as "Robinson Crusoe Island."*

Oddly your correspondent must bid adieu shortly. For these words to reach you this dispatch must be transferred to one of the magnificent clipper ships in Juan Fernandez. These sleek ships of sail and wind ply the tea and opium trade from China—your faithful scribe has been told. You see: In the previous decade England bought too much from China. Tea. Silks. Prized porcelain. In payment more English sterling flowed to China than English goods. Simply put...English payments exceeded exports. What the exchequer termed a "trade deficit."

In solution: England devised a simple substitute...so a man of commerce told this reporter. The empire grew poppies and processed sticky opium paste in the Bengal region of India near Calcutta in the early 1800s. This opium was traded to Chinese factors or brokers in exchange for tea to be shipped to England. In turn the Chinese factors traded the narcotic with inland smugglers for slaves. Or young girls sold by addict parents for opium. Or trafficked by desperate families to avoid large dowry costs.

The growing addiction to opium by millions of Chinese caused grave concern with the Chinese authorities. Ending the trade—as the Chinese government demanded—fell on deaf English ears. The argument grew into the Opium War between England and China in 1839. That war ended to China's disadvantage in 1842. The resulting peace treaty enshrined unfettered foreign access...and the opium trade blossomed. More English opium. More Chinese addicts. More tea in exchange.

Each season when the first Chinese tea is harvested it is exchanged for Anglo-Indian opium. Fast clipper ships stand by to race the first tea delivery to England or New York. These three-masted and square-rigged ships are ideal for high-value lightweight goods...like tea and opium. Rather than bulk commodities like whale oil or grain. Soon to those goods was added the ultimate value: passengers. The need for speedy advantage spawned the majestic clipper ships. Ships with maximum sail and narrow hulls that "clipped" down the wind in record times.

As you read this OFFICIAL REPORT in the Eagle *be it known that your correspondent succeeded to pass this dispatch to a great clipper on Juan Fernandez Island. Perchance the Sea Witch — or another feted wind dancer of her same caliber.*

And know: From the aforementioned isle of Robinson Crusoe — after a refreshing sojourn — we have soldiered on before the mast and the wind toward the Sandwich Islands.

Full sail! On to Maui!

Godspeed to any poor ship caught in the path of that monster storm to our west.

S. Thomas Swift
Foreign Correspondent
Exclusive to the Brooklyn Daily Eagle

Swift folded her dispatch and pressed her signet ring into the melted wax seal. Then gazed at Kikilani as she cut long linen strips for dressings curled in her bunk. A motion in the corner of her eye made Swift look up. Standing in the surgery cabin door was Mr. Flute. She beckoned him inside. The powerfully built man turned sideways to enter. Swift saw his freshly shaved head caught a glint from the deck prism. Then he closed the door behind him. Without hesitation Swift asked the question that for weeks had burrowed into her brain.

"Tell me...Mr. Flute...is there a greater reason for you to be on this voyage than as a harpooner? After all — we are a transport ship... not a whaler."

Mr. Flute hesitated. Then leaned forward as though Swift had perceived the reason for his visit. "There is...Miss Swift...as you may have surmised. My employer has given me a mission." Standing with his back to the apothecary counter their protector turned his knit cap in his hands with a boyish gesture. "As you learned earlier...our Angus Macomber has more fingers in more pies than may meet the eye. I've been sent to get to the bottom of it."

Samantha Swift's eyebrows raised. " 'It'?"

"Fraud and corruption."

Swift capped her inkwell and took a pencil from her writing box. "What exactly is your employer suspicious of?"

"Ah…the list is a tad long." Mr. Flute shot a glance at the examining stool. "Where to begin?"

Swift gestured for him to take a seat.

For the next half hour Mr. Flute outlined the various schemes his employer suspected of Angus Macomber conspiring for his own benefit. Swift gave a click of her tongue as if savoring some delicious morsels. "On the surface the American Consul on Maui ran his general store and ship chandlery called 'Macomber's' in Lahaina. He provisioned and supplied ships: from cordage to sailcloth to barrels and tuns to tar and varnish." Mr. Flute gave Swift an intense look as if he was choosing his words carefully. "His store was the port exchange. Mail was held there. It was a meeting place…a crossroads in the Pacific." The clandestine harpooner looked at Swift for a moment. "Macomber also was the customs collector who levied tariffs on imports and collected mooring fees from the ship captains who came to port to reprovision and recruit."

Kikilani looked up from her berth where she wrapped bandages. Her brow furrowed in understanding. "My people call that a *pahu kālā*. It means iron money box. What you call a safe."

Mr. Flute withdrew his snuff box from the pocket of his peacoat. Placed two large nips on the webspace behind the thumb of the hand holding the box. Then inhaled the healthy pinches of snuff. "When whaler's transferred oil barrels to the transport ships each barrel received a 'hail.' The count of barrels was the basis of each sailor's wages at voyage end. The more barrels…the larger the amount of each sailor's lay or share." The seaman turned aside and blew a howitzer-like sneeze into his kerchief. Then wiped his nostrils. "Whenever a dispute of the count arose between crew and captain…it fell to the 'independent' consul to resolve the count. Captains curried the favor of the consul to ensure the resolutions were in the captains' favor. As they say…a happy consul is a happy captain. Unfair. But it goes on."

Swift tapped her notebook with her pencil. "I've been told ship owners contribute as much as twelve dollars a month per sailor to the Sailor's Relief Fund. This fund pays the sailor's wages in the event they are injured or take sick and must stay ashore at a Seamen's Hospital."

"Right you are…miss." Mr. Flute slipped his well-worn silver snuff box into his peacoat. "The Seamen's Hospital on Maui is a hot iron for my employers. You may also know…Consul Macomber operates that sailor's hospital too. That is: His reports claim he contracted with a doctor and a purveyor…as well as the landlord for the property. In turn Macomber submitted the 'expenses' for those three 'contracts' to the State Department for payment." Mr. Flute arched one eyebrow and gave a short laugh. "What the rag-shop coves noticed—when they got around to comparing the accounts—is the Seamen's Hospital run by Macomber charged almost double the daily average rate as the hospital in Honolulu. Macomber's operations are either wildly inefficient… or wildly overcharged."

Kikilani put down her bandages and joined in. "This is the Seamen's Hospital owned by Joaquin Armas—the King's Mexican bull catcher? North of Lahaina Town about a mile? They say the Hawaiian King and his sacred sister used to have liaisons there before she died."

"Is that so?" Mr. Flute thumped the slatted table in confirmation. "Seems Consul Macomber has many irons in the fire. Not only do we think he cooked the hospital accounts—he also put the sailors' wages from the Relief Fund into his 'iron money box' while they were in the hospital." Mr. Flute gave Kikilani a look of disappointment that was remarkable for its utter sincerity. "Records showed the funds for sailors that have died—and in some cases their wages and valuables while in the hospital disappeared from the books. We suspect Macomber pocketed the relief payments…and also any dead sailor's valuables."

Swift glanced at her notes and muttered thoughtfully. "And the captains turned a blind eye…."

From across the operating table Mr. Flute looked at Swift. "When sailors were reportedly cured—often from scurvy or beriberi or an injury—they waited weeks or months to rejoin a ship. In the meantime: What did they do? They walked to town for work. But Macomber still kept their names on the hospital rolls for full medical and board reimbursement from the State Department. Already we have testimony that Macomber made his patients sign blank service receipts by the stack. Only later did Macomber enter the figure he wanted the State Department to pay."

Swift looked at Kikilani and then at Mr. Flute. "Does your employer have these forged receipts?"

Mr. Flute shook his head. "No. Only the statements of former sailors. Those receipts are on my evidence list to uncover."

"Are all these schemes on top of Macomber's earnings from his chandlery store and the canal marketplace?"

"Aye." The State Department's man acknowledged his affirmation with another snort of snuff. "And don't forget the arrangements Macomber made to barter low-priced local produce — especially potatoes — for imported goods from foreign traders. He then exported the same trade goods and flogged them at higher prices in New York."

"Is there any suspicion of contraband trading?" Swift gave Mr. Flute a look of growing respect. "Such as rum or opium — or even native girls?"

"You have a true compass for how the world works…Miss Swift. Nothing confirmed. That is part of my mission. To find out what is being traded — and by whom…and how — to allow my employer to move more decisively on several fronts at once." Mr. Flute narrowed his eyes before he gave a loud sneeze.

"Someone with Angus Macomber's background would be in an ideal position." Swift counted the connections on her fingers. "Ties to religious missions offer legitimacy. Native connections. His duty and port fee collections. A mercantile monopoly with the chandlery. And a natural coziness with ships' captains whose favor he curries as a mutual benefit society."

Mr. Flute rose to take his leave. Then turned to face the two women. "Now lasses. Remember. Not everyone is a friend on this voyage — as you know. Take care. There's murder in the heart of some aboard. The devil's luck could mean one's life…and Duffy Ragsdale is evidence."

At that moment from above decks came the muffled sound of bell strikes in four pairs. Eight bells tolled — marking the end of the last dog watch.

Mr. Flute settled his cap and closed the door behind him. Soon the comforting smell of his meerschaum pipe drifted from the cable-tier under the cabin's locked door. As the sands of destiny's hourglass ebbed away.

CHAPTER 39

BILLY MACK knew his place. And played it. "Oirish" — as he pronounced his origins. Irish. Catholic. Second class seaman. In that order. He hated piously superior missionaries. And with the same breath loathed anything smacking of the landed class. Mack's dark eyes and dark mouth like a dark bruise gave away precisely nothing. He had sailed out of Brest in February on a China-bound Dutch clipper ship to Pape'ete Tahiti. Like many of his countrymen Mack endured pain stoically. Yet anger simmered perpetually beneath the surface. On the outbound voyage Mack's anger had not come to a boil. Nothing to question his newfound home helping the French. That point arose from a rapturously satisfying bender in the Tahitian mountains with a native girl. The result of an extraordinary ceremony.

One morning beside Pape'ete's Matavai Bay — named in passing by Captain James Cook as Port Royal — young Billy Mack stood outside Fort Venus near a great tamarind tree that — legend held — the English navigator planted over seventy-five years before. Two young island women and their manservant came by. The women were naked from the waist up. They approached Billy Mack — for he was apparently the ranking representative present—as the only foreigner prepared to receive offerings under the tree's shade circle. The threesome appeared to be bearing two dozen plantain-tree seedlings. The roots balled in pandanus leaf sacking. The man bent down and— with the help of the native women—set some of the seedlings in two rows beginning about six meters from Mack's post. When they had finished the two women stood at the end. The leafy balls now formed a lane between Billy Mack and the two women. Then—picking up one of the remaining plants—the manservant advanced up the avenue and stopped before the sentry. Spoke an incomprehensible sentence. Handed the plant to Mack. Then returned down the lane. Lifted another plant. Six times the attendant passed forward and backward. Each time he repeated the presentation to the white man.

The native man returned to the foot of the lane. From a kit he and the two native women had set down when they first arrived the man withdrew a stack of tapa cloth squares and placed them on the bag. He took two top squares of tapa cloth. Then placed them at the end of the lane. Each young women stepped forward upon one of the pieces of bark cloth. Turned once around. Then gradually once again. The servant carried two more squares and placed them before the cloths the lovely women stood upon. Both girls stepped forward. Again performed their slow turning ceremony of welcome. Two more cloths placed. Again the turned greeting. In this way the women advanced over the cloths to face Billy Mack. Upon the last cloth with great innocence the women let their wraps fall from their waists. They turned slowly. Then again revealing their naked beauties. Both stood smiling openly before the sailor. So close the perfume of their oiled skin intoxicated Billy Mack. The manservant followed. Collected the square cloths as he came forward. The naked nymphs made it clear the cloth squares were intended as a present for the white man. The servant handed them to the agog foreigner. Then he stood aside.

The women advanced still farther. In turn both embraced a nirvanic Billy Mack. With gestures and smiles the high-rank maidens insisted: Billy Mack must choose one of them. Both Tahitians had thick black hair. Trimmed short around their ears. Fine white teeth. With great pride and no restriction of modesty they showed the Irishman the tattoo that covered their buttocks. And with pleasure showed the black arched pattern that reached as high as their short ribs. Mack hungrily eyed their lively bodies. *Almost as light-skinned as Europeans*—so Billy Mack thought. He fantasized the two women openly enjoyed the free liberty of love. And that chastity was an unknown idea.

"Hullo." Billy Mack blinked. Then raised his hand and recited: "Eeny. Meeny. Miney. Moe." The chosen woman smiled broadly while the unchosen one moved several cloth squares back and covered herself. Then the manservant handed the smiling young woman an elaborately decorated piece of the tapa cloth which she wrapped around her torso. She took the white man's hand. And led the foreigner down the lane of plantain-tree seedlings. In short…Billy Mack abandoned his post. And himself. Without a second thought. The pair threaded between the palms and pandanus trees. Up the sandy jungle track toward the Fautaua River. Then into the mountains. Into a South Sea paradise valley every sailor savored in his dreams.

The Tahitian sprite led the Irish sailor six kilometers up the incline. Then five kilometers farther up a precipitous path. They climbed vined and rooted trails to the top of Fautaua Waterfall: a free-falling ribbon one hundred thirty-five meters high. Mack trudged on. Up a muddy pass where crude stone walls forced the trail into a narrow defile. There they entered their destination: Fort Fachoda. The last stronghold of Tahitian fighters sat four hundred sixty meters above the sea. Mack had been told the French only months before had crushed the last Tahitian guerilla resistance here on 17 December 1846. Mack raised his eyes to the forbidding double-horned pinnacles of Mount Orohena towering above him. The twin precipitous peaks defined the island's silhouette for all who approached Tahiti by sea.

Panting like a blown horse Billy Mack stumbled inside the stone walls and caught his breath. Then pulled the native woman to him and kissed her deeply. When he came up for air the deserter clasped her to his side as he gazed toward the valley through which they climbed. He surveyed the French Polynesian island that surrounded them below: Shaped like a round rattle with a bulbous handle. The larger western section called Tahiti Nui where they huddled descended from the extinct Mount Orohena volcano. Its peaks encircled the lovers' verdant redoubt. Mack pointed to where he thought Fort Venus and his sentry post existed. Pape'ete and its Matavai Bay hugged the northwest lowland shore of Tahiti Nui far below them. Behind the pair — on the far island side beyond view — the mount's sheer cliffs dropped to the smaller eastern peninsula of Tahiti Iti. Now as far away for Billy Mack as the farthest netherworld.

Without hesitation the chosen maiden made a lovers' nest inside the fort walls. Billy Mack watched as she selected an angled corner in the stone refuge sheltered by a wet sapling-raftered lean-to. Under the cover she righted a bamboo platform discarded against the wall. Behind this makeshift bed she discovered a cache of abandoned supplies. From this cache she pulled a piece of sailcloth. Together they pulled the canvas over the lean-to roof and secured its corners. Upon the bed the native sprite placed layers of palm fronds and large breadfruit leaves and fragrant ferns. Then she finished the nest with a found sheet of *tapa* cloth. Next appeared a large calabash for fresh water which she supported on a ring of flat stones. A stump served as the only stool for the master. Mack breathed deeply of the slightly moist flowery scent that came from the rainbow of vegetation all around them.

The island nymph positioned Billy Mack on his stool. And quietly undressed the breathless sentry. She removed his jacket. His shirt. Made him stand to take off his pants. Then she gently instructed the sailor how to wear the *ahu* or tapa cloth. Mack fumbled the folds with its two or three meters wrapped from waist to knee. Patiently she communicated to the foreigner how the *ahu* would be his sole garment. Next she showed him how to fold an elephant-ear leaf into a sun cap.

Other than buttons the sailor had little to offer in return. Besides the gift of a comb from his jacket pocket and a few white phosphorus matches. The native damsel smoothed her thick short-cropped hair. Then fashioned one of his European buttons to take the place of the single earring she wore of lustrous black pearl. Soon the mountain peak extended an afternoon shadow over their fortified nest. Mack watched as the girl practiced the Tahitian custom of plucking all hair from her armpits. She returned his attention by mocking his body hair as unclean. And led him in the shadows through the watery veils that dripped from vegetation above. Made him bathe repeatedly in the upper icy grotto pool that fed the falls. Then led him laughing down the smooth water-worn slide to the second pool at the falls' break.

Time was suspended.

Under the sapling shelter the native Diana scented her hair with coconut oil from her woven tote. Before making love. Incapable of resistance the Irishman rationalized as he stroked her glossy hair: *Why should I return to ship…where they work us like horses and we live like pigs?* Afterward Billy Mack gathered dry grass. Leaves. Twigs. And sticks. With one of his Lucifer matches he nurtured a small fire in a nook of the stone wall.

The Irishman's clipper sailed without him.

A few short months before Mack had barely escaped the Irish potato famine. And the typhus and cholera that killed tens of thousands in his western County Mayo. The English response to their plight was the conventional wisdom. *The Irish are idlers and caused their own misfortune.* They only tilled "lazy beds" on hillsides to plant their blighted potatoes — even though they claimed the soil was so thin and poor potatoes were all the land was good for. *Misplaced sympathy only encouraged their slothful ways. If there was aid…no aid should be free. Assistance must carry work requirements. No help to spongers!* The self-righteous landed class was convinced the high calling of honest work was the only way. Able-bodied unfortunates must lift themselves from their shiftless poverty into self-sufficiency. All that was needed was to show the rustics the righteous path. As Paul wrote to the church: "If a man will not work…he shall not eat." Mack scoffed. *Says so in the scriptures!*

As the gentry scoffed at the farmers — and exported their tenants' food — entire Irish communities died off. Billy Mack barely survived to the age that attracted the English Royal Navy press gangs. Soon he escaped to Brest in northwestern France on the Atlantic. And volunteered to aid the French. To his astonishment within days he was sent on the longest passage his limited County Mayo world could never fathom: Tahiti. Since that day the dire treatment of his family. His country. And his people by greedy Protestant English landlords festered into vengeful hatred for all Protestants.

On the third evening Billy Mack watched as the princess — for that was how the young Irishman saw her divine loveliness — used the last friction match to kindle a fire. Then they curled under an *ahu* cloth. And watched the glowing embers from their nest.

The next morning in his forest paradise the Irishman discovered he had been abandoned by his island faerie. Gone like a sunbeam in the forest. Haplessly alone the sailor followed the river trail off the mountain. When he reached the flat the Fautaua River made an abrupt turn to the east. Here at the river's deep bend islanders and foreigners filled their gourds and casks at the *pape'ete*: the water basket. The mountain-cold water then traversed the lowland skirt that surrounded the island. Parallel to Matavai Bay one and a half kilometers past Fort Venus to the beach. On this course the fresh stream delayed as long as possible its inevitable union with the salt sea.

Aimlessly Billy Mack shuffled barefoot along the sandy paths that interconnected the dispersed houses: The few Tahitians who survived the white man's diseases did not live in clustered villages or towns. He passed separate plantations of breadfruit. Banana. Plantain. Passed fertile patches of sweet potato. Yams. Passed thorny-woven hog pens. Always shaded by coconut palms.

Mack's bare feet made a beeline to a waterfront groggery. With his last franc — sewed inside his jacket sleeve — he got irredeemably drunk.

Billy Mack stumbled out of the shop into the darkness of Pape'ete. Next morning old Tiki Tieva — the local witch — checked the public hogpen. She found the sailor. His form unconsciously snuggled next to a mucky sow. Not unlike one of her suckling piglets. Tiki Tieva watched as the French governor's gendarme delivered the Irishman to the calaboose jail.

Billy Mack faced an ultimatum. What the French governor of Tahiti Armand-Joseph Bruat called justice. *Une:* Three years in the prison colony of New Caledonia for desertion. Lascivious conduct. And drunkenness. *Deux:* Take the first ship to the Sandwich Islands. Deliver a message to Henri Malbec who schemed with the native rebels to claim the Hawaiian kingdom in the name of France. And keep an assassin's eye for an American agent doing the work of the Protestant American president. This man was the agent of evil. And must be stopped.

"Do this" — so Bruat told Mack — "and the liberty of your Tahitian station wife will be spared."

Mack without hesitation agreed. But not for the maiden's sake. (He couldn't care less.) Nor for the alternative of the French penal colony in New Caledonia. (Ireland had been worse.) He accepted simply for revenge. *Better to serve a Catholic master* — so Billy Mack thought — *than any Protestant oppressor.* He vowed: *If that means sleepin' with the French...I figger so be it. No more consequence than sleepin' with a Tahitian slut.*

Billy Mack rubbed his palms together in anticipation. "As for slippin' a dirk to that Protestant president's agent on my own hook...hullo. Consider it done."

Mack smiled darkly. He rather liked the role of spy inside a Trojan Horse. "If that American traitor crosses me path...it'll be me pleasure to leave that soup-taker as cold as a wagon tire."

CHAPTER 40

GOVERNOR'S RESIDENCE
PAPE'ETE / TAHITI
31 MARCH 1847

THE *BOUNTIFUL* hove to. Dropped anchor on the eastern end of the deep blue Matavai Bay. Pape'ete settlements hugged the northwestern shoreline on the larger of Tahiti's two islands. Both islands were surrounded by the azure necklace of a coral atoll and crowned by the verdant twin peaks of Mount Orohena. The ship's pinnace boat dropped into the water. Captain Hamilton Post — accompanied by a Catholic priest — was rowed ashore.

The American whaler master beat a line directly to the Governor's residency on the grounds of the Queen's palace. Paid the exorbitant mooring fee required of any non-French ship. And presented his formal request to recruit as many as three seamen. Captain Post and Governor Bruat knew the *quid pro quo.* The Captain needed bodies. The Governor welcomed making more room in his calaboose available for additional prospects for Malbec's prison in Nuku Hiva on the Marquesas Islands. Despite the unending scourge of foreign deserters. An "administrative fee" that was triple the bounty paid for French prisoners was arranged for the Governor's pocket. Shortly three sailors — including Billy Mack — were escorted toward the *Bountiful*'s pinnace.

The Governor turned to the priest. "And what brings you to Pape'ete…Father?"

Hamilton Post provided the backstory. "We collected Father Jean-Claude in Samoa. He was sent there by the Marist Fathers based in New Zealand."

"*Mai oui*…of the Vicariate Apostolic for Eastern Oceania." The Governor ran a suspicious eye over the priest.

Post said simply: "Father Jean-Claude has been sent on a scholarly mission."

The Governor frowned slightly in anticipation of another troublesome missionary. "How may I be of service?"

"Your Grace. " The disguised priest began in a distinctly American accent. "Bishop Bataillon…of the Central Oceania region…asked me to visit *votre île*." The priest cleared his throat. "Please pardon my awkward French…as I have been stationed in New Zealand most recently." The Governor nodded for the priest to continue in English.

"As you may know…Your Grace…as Marist Fathers we minister under the name of Mary. We live the Gospel in humble. Modest. And simple ways. We are called to imitate Mary in this way of life and ministry."

The impatient Governor quoted a Catholic dictum. " 'Think as Mary. Judge as Mary. Feel and act as Mary in all things.' I am familiar with the Society of Mary."

"You honor our simple work." The priest was fawning in his praise. "As you know…Your Excellency: As Marist Fathers we are known for our work with island languages — and the flora and fauna of the south seas. That is why I have come. The *Bountiful* will sail soon to the Sandwich Islands. And I must continue as soon as possible to Easter Island. Which brings me to my request."

"*Oui?*" The Governor's tone conveyed only minimal interest.

"Is there — to your knowledge — anyone — perhaps an old chief or elder — who remembers the old language and old ways of Tahiti? It would greatly advance the church's codification of island languages if I could find such a person."

Post gestured toward the priest. "And help sort the migration voyages of all Polynesians by understanding the dispersal of their flowers and animals."

The Governor thought for a moment. Then challenged Post with a direct question. "How long do you expect to be in my harbor...Captain?"

"With the three sailors you've kindly provided we now have a full ship's complement. Today we replenish our water casks. My expectation is to set sail for the Sandwich Islands tonight—with your permission...Your Excellency."

"I will grant the priest can conduct his idle research on two conditions." The Governor spoke officiously. "Only the priest may conduct such research. No sailors. No officers. No one may leave your American ship—besides a four-man water crew—before you leave my harbor at candle lighting tonight. Even removing those three drunken fornicators does not earn a single American liberty in my Pape'ete. Beyond sunset—as protector of the Kingdom of Tahiti— your welcome is not extended. Am I clear?"

"Thank you...Your Grace. And the second condition?"

The Governor looked at Post. "As I said: All priests are meddlesome. But priests that overstay their welcome will not be tolerated."

The priest struck a subservient pose and thumbed his rosary beads.

The Governor gestured as if he were dispensing a beneficence. "Father Jean-Claude is granted a stay in Pape'ete for forty-eight hours. No more. In two days a ship will leave for Easter Island—or Rapa Nui as the natives call it." The Governor's hard look toward the Captain avoided the priest. "If the priest misses that ship to Easter Island...there is a ship to the Marquesas Islands the following day. That ship is a penal colony transport timed to refresh the cells for Commandant Malbec's two months on Nuku Hiva. Henri Malbec passed through our fair paradise only six weeks ago...on his way to 'improve conditions' at the Marquesas prison. He said it was his 'calling.' An unforgettable experience...for all of us."

With the mention of Malbec the Governor's expression had turned dark. A faraway look came into his eyes. *Henri Malbec...That fiend still haunts me!* As the Governor touched his temple his first encounter with Malbec flashed like a nightmare. Two castaways—one European and a large Arab—had stepped into Malbec's path near the harbor. Unintentionally. But Malbec exploded. When he was told they were thieves Malbec had them tied to a palm. Then flogged them unmercifully. Malbec's high-pitched voice still rang in the Governor's mind: "Thieves! *Incos!* Degenerates!" The Governor shuddered as he remembered Malbec's excitement growing with increasing intensity as he tortured the men. The commandant's pleasure had dripped from every sarcastic phrase. *And with every cruel stroke of the lash.* "The sooner" — Malbec lashed the small man — "these undesirables" — he lashed the heavy-set Arab — "are purged from this earth" — again the lash fall — "the sooner" — and again — "their filthy depravity" — and again harder — "will be eradicated!" The Governor shook his head in disgust: Both men were just petty thieves. The big Omani spit at Malbec and called him a son of a pig's whore. Two days later the European died. And Malbec shipped the Arab in chains to end his days on Nuku Hiva.

With a stricken expression the Governor turned to face Father Jean-Claude. "You do not want to know Henri Malbec...not if you value your life on this earth." The official blinked rapidly at the thought of the prison commandant. "Do I make myself clear? Be on the ship to Easter Island in two days — or you will learn the meaning of hell on earth as Malbec's guest." The Governor shook his head as if to clear Malbec from his mind. "Those are my conditions. Leave in two days — or leave now with the American Captain who brought you here."

With those words the Governor seemed to push Malbec's cruelty from his conscious mind. He pointed vaguely beyond the far end of the harbor. "There is only one old witch still living from before foreign contact. They say she is the oldest inhabitant of Pape'ete. And — some say — she knows all the bloodlines. Chants. Death stories. She lives somewhere beyond the eastern side of the settlement. Beyond Matavai Bay. Past Fort Venus and the tamarind tree. Perhaps in the area where the Fautaua River meets the sea. The superstitious say no one comes back from her lair. Ask any passerby. They will know her putrid work. But don't expect more than the feeblest directions. No one will take you there...out of fear for their life. The natives say simply to place eyes on the ancient one is a sentence of death. If you do survive" — Bruat sniffed — "my orders are for you to take the next ship to Easter Island...Father. And leave Tahiti as you found it."

The priest and Post exchanged a surprised glance. Then the priest smiled uncertainly. *After forty-seven years could the old witch the*

Governor described have knowledge of LeGrand?

"What is this witch of death called?" asked the priest.

"Tiki Tieva."

Captain Hamilton Post gripped Father Jean-Claude's hand meaningfully. "I suspect we will never meet again...Father." Within earshot of the Governor he spoke to the priest in a grave voice. "I look forward to continuing the discussion of the afterlife we've been having aboard the ship. Is death a fact...or a perception? Time will tell."

With that farewell Post gave leg to the Governor in a deep bow. Then turned to leave the priest to his fate. The American Captain swiftly returned to the *Bountiful.* But as the crew prepared to sail at sunset something gnawed at him. The Governor had agreed to Dancer's request too easily; Post had expected more hostility from the French. Something was not right...What was really going on?

Even more troubling: Once the *Bountiful* sailed for the Sandwich Islands would Dancer's wild hunch about LeGrand pay off on Easter Island...or would it be another spectacular bust?

CHAPTER 41

TEMPLES OF DEATH
PAPE'ETE/TAHITI
LATER THAT AFTERNOON

DISGUISED AS FATHER JEAN-CLAUDE Dancer lugged his three traveling cases through a labyrinth of sandy pathways. The cases — one along each hip and one across his back — were slung from his shoulders by a canvas-yoke contraption won from a porter in Singapore.

Every Tahitian left old Tiki Tieva alone. No one wanted to give directions to the priest. When Dancer stopped one old woman she whispered that Tiki Tieva followed the Tahitian royal custom of eating the eye of defeated foes. Then the old woman scuttled off in the opposite direction with her hand over her eyes. No one dared test the tale. After several failed attempts Dancer finally located the precinct of the Witch of Death. Less from following his eyes than from following his nose.

On the outskirts of the precinct Dancer came upon a fresh *marae* burial platform. A Temple of Death. Several body lengths before the platform — as if guarding the otherworld in the death garden just beyond the platform — stood a huge effigy in the likeness of a man. Almost three meters tall. Its body of woven basketwork. White feathers stuck in the weave appearing to represent skin. Black feathers signifying…tattoos? Three nobs rose from the effigy's head. More like stumps than horns. Dancer had heard the stories: This was the monster the islanders called *Mauwi*. The deity that had inhabited the earth since the creation of man. His three horns represented the three principal bloodlines of Tahitian lineage.

Dancer's gaze swept the space before him. Here were the platforms for the dead. Well beyond the platforms — set apart in a towering grove of mape chestnut trees draped in vanilla vines — stood the outline of a thatched house. A plantation stretched between where Dancer stood and the grass house. Everyday islanders would have cultivated crops. Fruits. And useful plants there. Tiki Tieva cultivated death. Nurturing it until the spirits joined life forever in the afterworld.

Behind Dancer a fading South Pacific sunset glorified the billowing heavens. Dancer stepped forward in the low gloaming light. His footfalls silent on the sandy ground. When he rounded the effigy Dancer stopped short. Not ten feet in front of him stood the Witch of Pape'ete. She stood tall. Thin. As deliberate as a gray heron. She chanted. Eyes closed in ritual. As her body gently bobbed from the waist her cracking voice gave recognition of the departed soul on the raised death platform above her.

Dancer quietly took a place a body length to the side. Took out his rosary. Touched his fingertips in prayer. And quietly began to recite the Lord's Prayer. Head bowed. Respectful. As his mother had shown her two sons once upon a time in Charleston. For some moments the simultaneous chants mingled in the evening breeze off the mountain. When they had both finished Dancer didn't move a muscle. His rosary beads dangled from his hands. Tiki Tieva turned. Nodded silently. Dancer held her gaze. *Perhaps she believes the arrival of a priest at her* marae *is an auspicious sign?*

Without a greeting — or any words of instruction — Dancer understood he should follow the old woman on her evening rounds. The priestess led the priest as they walked the sacred plantation. Tieva stopped first before a death scaffold. Intoned a message to her gods. The scaffold was supported two meters off the ground by two sculpted posts. One a single phallic post. The other a V-shaped feminine symbol. Above the bamboo scaffold rose a thatched sunshade. Set on the corners of four bamboo poles. The shade was constructed much like the awnings Polynesian chiefs constructed on their catamaran canoes for relief from the relentless sun.

As the pair moved among the raised stands old Tiki Tieva pointed to a bundle placed on each stand. If a platform did not support a corpse then as keeper of the dead the old witch had placed a roasted pig. The stinking bodies and pig bundles similarly covered in a sheer cloth were in much the same stage of decomposition. If not for the steady trade winds the rotting stench would have been intolerable for Dancer. Tiki Tieva plucked a sweet-scented vanilla vine and entwined it with fragrant pandanus leaves. Handed it to the white man. Dancer acknowledged the gift. Then — at each platform — he held the bundle to his face within prayerful hands. And left a priestly blessing to the deceased — whether human or porcine.

Dancer saw neat pyramids of papaya and pineapple-like pandanus fruit stacked beside the human bodies. The ageless priestess explained with gestures to the patient priest. These tempting foods were not afterworld sustenance for the departed. Instead: The offerings were to satisfy the gods' hunger. Dancer nodded knowingly. *Lest the gods eat one's dead relative.*

To Dancer's surprise as Tiki Tieva continued her rounds he realized quiet words sometimes accompanied her gestures. As Dancer listened intently he shortly discovered Tiki Tieva spoke in heavily accented French. Dancer formulated a timely question or two in his mind as they proceeded.

After they passed the third or fourth platform — repeating their combined blessings at each — Dancer realized some platforms were neatly fenced with fitted bamboo. Tiki Tieva opened a small gate in one fence and walked through. Dancer followed and closed the gate behind him. A freshly wrapped corpse lay silently on the platform. The old crone guided Dancer around the space. With a long finger she gestured to the ground. The sand was littered with bloody rags left by relations of the recently deceased who had bled themselves in grief.

Farther on Dancer stopped before what appeared to be wooden boards with relief carvings. These stood about the yard as markers. Dancer laughed morbidly to himself. *A headstone is a headstone…even if you've lost your head.* Soon he observed other markers that resembled cricket wickets or upended wooden forks. Near one such marker stood an image of a bird carved in wood. On the ground next to the bird lay a fish carved in stone. The stone broken in two places. Bleached bones lay beneath every platform — or were tossed carelessly against the bamboo fences. Dancer walked among a great quantity of clean bleached bones. Human bones. Some littered helter-skelter. Some stacked in neat rows. And skulls. Their hollow eye sockets seemed to lock in and follow Dancer's every movement. Dancer reacted by thumbing the beads in his rosary a little more intensely.

From the corner of his eye Dancer observed Tiki Tieva as he and the priestess walked among the bones. The wizened woman moved with familiarity among the platforms and the dead. Her skin shriveled by the sun: The years of toil in her death temple had taken a toll.

As they came to the end of her rounds the Witch of Pape'ete stepped on a sharp bone shard. She stood on one foot as she held the injured foot. Gritted her teeth. And muttered an ancient curse at the sky. Had her gods not returned the care she had given the departed souls? As Dancer helped her to a nearby palm log — he could feel the bones of her spine: They formed a ridge down her back. He tied her wound with a kerchief. Without articulation Dancer sensed a forlorn sorrow in the wrinkled old woman. He studied her mournfully. *When it comes time for your place on a platform who will drape the body? Who will stack the fruit? Who will roast a pig to distract the gods? What will become of the* marae *when Tiki Tieva dies?*

Not far beyond the precinct of death stood the fine house Dancer noticed earlier. From the distance the house looked like all other dwellings of the higher ranks on Tahiti. Oblong shape. Thick thatch roof. Loose bamboo wicker walls that allowed air circulation.

Tiki Tieva pointed. "*C'est ma maison.* It is time. Come."

The priest gave the old priestess his arm and they moved to the house together.

Unlike most dwellings there were no partitions inside: Dancer's eyes grew accustomed to the darkness as he swept his eyes around the dim space. Half the floor was covered in dried balsa pulp. The other half covered in pandanus fiber mats. Only one stool furnished the entire house. At the far end was a shrine that displayed an array of *tiki* sculptures — the craven idols Dancer had read about that were outlawed by King Pomare II to appease the Protestant missionaries

from London. The King's edict ruled all the Society Islands—
including Tahiti. In turn those English missionaries had been banished
long ago by French Catholic priests. Dancer's body gave an involuntary
shiver as his eyes met the saucer-shaped eyes of the squatting figures.
Arms held high with fingers splayed in surprise—or astonishment—
at the misdeeds of the people.

A tired Tiki Tieva directed Dancer to take the lone stool. Like a
great bird she settled on one of the pandanus mats before him.

Was it the priest's prayers? Was it the priest's empathy? His
kindness? As if the priest's coming had broken a great dam the ancient
necromancer talked far into the night by the light of a single torch.
Dancer understood. She must release her story…before it was too late.
If not…her story would disappear on a *marae* without being spoken
into history. Into the oral tradition of her people. She began simply.

"Easter Island was my homeland. My *ariki*—my god-king…
descendant of the great Hotu Matua—erected the massive *moai*
statues along the coastline of the island to protect us. When I was a
teenager the *matatoa* warriors defeated our king. Brought a new god
they called the 'Birdman.' Internal disputes erupted. No longer did one
god-king show us the way. The conquering warriors toppled many of
the *moai*. Trees were burned. Gardens were neglected. The raising of
food stopped."

The ancient elder seemed to read Dancer's eyes and continued:
"Our tribe escaped to Tahiti—with nothing but hate and hunger to
sustain us. We could not go back to Easter Island. Our homeland was
devastated. Yet on Tahiti I was an outsider. What the Tahitians call a
manahune—a commoner. One caste above a slave. Tahitian
oppression drove the refugees—the *manahune*—into the mountains.
There we hid in caves. In the forest. In the shadows. In fact…I was a
princess-in-waiting on my Easter Island. But here I was little more than
a yellow lizard…a *mo'orea*."

The old crone's eyes twinkled. "Survival summons a spirit you may
not know you have. We found ways to be invisible. Being invisible was
our survival."

With that revelation Princess Tieva rose. Moved past the torchlight
toward a dark corner of her dwelling. She rummaged among the
dusty rafters. From a secret place she brought down an ancient

bundle wrapped in waterproof waxed canvas. Then limped back to the torchlight.

Tiki Tieva squatted on the pandanus mat. Blew dust from her trove. And unfolded the stiff canvas carefully. When the last fold was removed the bundle revealed a fragile old volume. Its brittle pages barely resisted crumbling. "A foreigner gave this to me...as captains did at that time. I was young then. Beautiful. He had already lost two ships. Barely reached Tahiti with one unseaworthy vessel. Never knowing if he would die at sea...he wanted his voyage to live on." She softly recalled the words spoken to her long ago. She had kept her lover's log as a memento. A talisman of hope. "As you can see the dead are my witness...Father. I faithfully waited for his return."

Tiki Tieva handed the volume to Dancer.

Dancer saw it was a captain's log. He opened the pages gingerly. In his hands was Gagnon LeGrand's diary. Now almost fifty years old.

Dancer couldn't believe his eyes. As La Pérouse before him LeGrand had sought to immortalize his journey. Dancer turned through the crumbling pages as quickly as the fragile document allowed. Even to Dancer's basic market-French LeGrand's words in the voyage journal clearly stated that LeGrand indeed sailed east from Zanzibar. North of Australia into the Coral Sea. Sheltered at New Caledonia. Struck out to cross Oceania. Stopped in Samoa. Then east to Tahiti....Dancer recognized LeGrand's Pacific ports of call. All stops of La Pérouse...in reverse. LeGrand's next landfall was to be Easter Island. Then challenge Cape Horn.

But after the Tahiti entry LeGrand's log abruptly stopped.

"Take it...Father." With a gesture Tieva indicated that Dancer should keep the log. But despair was in her voice. "A lifetime of hope has sustained me. Please...take LeGrand's voyage with you...see that it gets a new life in your land. Your coming gives me the chance to keep my hope alive."

Dancer took the log. Soon swaddled again in its timeless canvas. Tieva's story had ended. He prepared to depart.

"Father...before you leave...hear the last wish of a dying old woman. I will die soon. Take my holy confession."

"Are you Catholic...my child?"

With the suggestion of a smile the ancient Tiki Tieva answered truthfully. "I am a believer. As was LeGrand."

The priest took her hand in his and smoothed it between his fingers. Looked into her eyes. Held his rosary in his free hand. They knelt in the soft balsa shavings. Beyond Tiki Tieva's figure a faint starlight outside illumined the rotting platforms of her death temples.

"Holy Father...I have sinned." She squeezed Dancer's hand. "When LeGrand landed on this island he was ill and weak. I nursed him back to health. One day the English missionaries coaxed the Tahitian King to send his chiefs to destroy all the *tikis*. 'Purge the craven idols...and the idolaters!' they screamed. LeGrand hid my sacred *tikis* on the death platforms...and protected me." The old woman smiled at the memory. Then cupped Dancer's hand inside both of hers and gave a heavy sigh. "Father...you must know there was a child. I had a son by LeGrand after he sailed away." She paused. "Our son grew to be difficult. Never obeyed me. Lied often. Enjoyed hurting animals. Started fights with the native boys. Once he lit a thatch stack on fire." A tear came to the eye of Tiki Tieva. "To protect the boy from the chiefs...and the missionaries...I gave up the boy to a French priest. And in thanks converted to become a Catholic." Again the woman gave a silent sigh. "I never saw my son again. He was my second lost love. That is why I remain here. Until I die. A woman's duty is to be home should her son...or lover...return someday."

Dancer felt an involuntary pressure from the old woman's hands around his.

The old woman continued. "I gave up my son. Still...a mother never forgets. The boy had a birthmark. A mark on his inner arm. Some said it looked like a turtle with a missing front fin."

Dancer raised his hands to his lips and kissed the rosary. Made the sign of the cross. Blessed the old woman. Then handed the rosary to Tiki Tieva. "You are forgiven...my child." He looked into her face with feeling. Then rose. As Tiki Tieva followed after him Dancer passed through the low doorway of the old princess' house. And shouldered his cases. Then turned back to the doorway. Silhouetted by the torchlight behind her the tall gaunt figure nodded to the priest. Then turned back inside.

Dancer moved toward the river. Away from the death temples. And muttered under his breath: "LeGrand intended to sail east to Easter Island. But he never made it. Where did he end up?" he wondered. "What happened to LeGrand?"

CHAPTER 42

DANCER CLAMPED a kerchief over his nose. Then tried to pick his footsteps through the reeking *marae*. In the darkness his toe struck a skull. The white orb wobbled crazily across the sand. Spun. Stopped. Black holes where eyes once were stared back at Dancer. An involuntary shiver ran through his body. Dancer adjusted his cases in the porter's yoke. Then carefully made his way under the mape trees. Slipped past a canopy of pandanus trees. The top-heavy trunks propped up by odd clusters of stilt roots looking like awkward legs in the sand.

When Dancer reached the fast Fautaua Stream he stopped. Blinked. *Where now?* He clutched LeGrand's log. *What good will it do? Stuck here in the middle of the ocean. The* Bountiful *has sailed.*

Absentmindedly the agent-in-priest's-clothing turned toward the sea. As he moved along the river's edge he heard something. A rhythm. Did it come from where the rush of mountain water met the backwash of salt waves? Dancer keened his hearing. Was that the sound of wood on water? A manmade sound?

At that moment out of the darkness came a man's voice.

"Father Jean-Claude? Are you there?"

It was Hamilton Post.

"Didn't think I would leave you…did you…Father?"

Dancer exhaled. "After the last few hours I could believe almost anything."

Through the darkness a pinnace boat pressed up the river and stopped. Several seamen held it steady. Dancer gave them his traveling cases. Post handed him into the small craft. Soon they skimmed out across the cove. Oars muffled with jute. Through an opening in the atoll. There to Dancer's eyes in a starlit silhouette of mast and spar the *Bountiful* never looked better.

Later that evening—over a box of Dancer's Oscuro cigars and generous pours of Post's wine—Dancer revealed LeGrand's log to Hamilton Post in the privacy of the Captain's cabin. Together they deciphered the entries in the old log…taking care with every brittle page turn.

Soon Dancer brought out Professor Champollion's notebook. And the coin purse. Napoleon's Malta coins given to the American agent by the Champollions in Paris—and later expanded to include Paatel's coins from Zanzibar. All pointed toward the Pacific Ocean. In the notebook Dancer turned to the section with a map of the La Pérouse Expedition. On the edges of a double page Champollion had sketched the coastlines of the Pacific Ocean. In the right margin: South America. Alta California. Lituya Bay in the Arctic north. On the left were Australia. Philippines. China. Japan. And coastal Russia. In the open center Champollion had drawn the image of a large looping letter *H*. The sinuous figure represented La Pérouse's logged course.

Dancer tapped his finger on the map. "From Australia in 1788— for the second time in his expedition—La Pérouse sent copies of his charts and journals back to France. This time on a British frigate named the *Alexander*. By the time the naval ship reached Zanzibar the Captain was fed up with the mission—and with the French seaman who accompanied La Pérouse's documents. Both were castaway on Zanzibar."

"You know this for fact?" asked Post.

"Yes. I met the ancient rascal. He gave his name as Rene LaFleur.

The Frenchman told me about his misfortune. About being marooned in Stone Town. Acted all-fired crazy. Said he hated the British. But something about LaFleur didn't beat the Dutch in my mind. Still can't quite put my finger on it…crazy like a fox. Anyway: LaFleur survived on Zanzibar. Mostly thanks to the Sultan. Then about ten years later— 1798—who sailed into Zanzibar but another Frenchman…LeGrand. At least that's what the balmy beachcomber told me."

Post poured two tots of wine and listened as Dancer sorted his thoughts. "LeGrand was trapped. To the north were pirates. To the south were British patrols. Ultimately LeGrand escaped both. Used the change of the monsoon-season winds. Before LeGrand broke out he gave the Frenchman a letter." Dancer explained the hidden history as he unfolded a copy of LeGrand's letter. "This letter outlined the plan of LeGrand's voyage to the east. Not around Africa's Good Hope."

Post nodded several times. Scanned the letter. "Aye. LaFleur probably gave La Pérouse's charts to his countryman. This letter showed LeGrand knew of La Pérouse's explorations of the Pacific. That meant LeGrand knew about La Pérouse's stops across the Pacific. Spanish Concepción in Chile. Easter Island. Even the North Pacific Sandwich Islands. The Arctic. Alta California on the mainland. And the South Pacific at Tonga. Samoa. New Caledonia."

Dancer stepped over to Post's prized globe that was supported in a leveling gimbal ring. He shot back: "The only way to France is east. Around the Horn. Why would LeGrand go north to the Sandwich Islands? That's crazy. North doesn't make any sense."

"Maybe. Maybe not." Post touched the document before him. "Look at these dates where LeGrand's log ends. He left Tahiti in October 1799. That is the tail end of the Eastern Pacific storm season of April to October." Post took out an old sea-captain's almanac. Slapped the volume next to Champollion's sketch of La Pérouse's voyage.

At that moment a seaman knocked on the closed cabin door. He opened the door a crack. "Sir?" came the Irish voice of Billy Mack.

"Clear the dinner plates…sailor. Bring us another stoup of that Madeira." Post gave his order without looking up.

As the newly rostered Billy Mack cleared the plates Post opened the well-thumbed volume of the *Navigator's Almanac*. He rapidly turned the pages until he found what he was looking for. "Tarnation...October 1799. The Christmas before—in 1798—Spanish sea captains off the coast of South America reported much warmer water temperatures." Post scanned the following almanac page. Then jabbed the tip of his index finger into the book. "That's it! 'Bout the same time—in early 1799—the British in Australia reported exceptionally high air-surface pressure in the western Pacific. The almanac says that created one of the greatest storm seasons for tropical hurricanes in recorded memory. Cyclones raised in the high pressure of the west intensified because of warm oceans...then swept east along the equatorial countercurrents."

"You lost me. Equatorial...what?"

Post explained: "In the South Pacific the currents run counterclockwise. Like this." Post ran his finger counterclockwise on the lower section of Champollion's *H* map. "In the North Pacific the currents run clockwise. Like that. When these two currents try to meet off South America near the equator the south and north currents move west. A third current—the equatorial countercurrent—runs east between them along the equator... keeping the westerly currents apart."

"I get it. Like a doddering old cuckold trying to keep his young mistress and her lover from rolling in the hay together."

Post gave Dancer a wry look that asked whether he spoke from experience.

Dancer shrugged. "It happens." He deflected Post's look. "Currents...countercurrents...what does it all mean?"

Post spread his *Navigator's Almanac* in front of Dancer. "Given the date—October 1799—that means LeGrand sailed smack into one of the biggest hurricanes of all time. At first from Tahiti LeGrand probably beat north against the South Pacific current pushing to the west. His plan was to meet the equatorial countercurrent going east and sail toward South America. What he didn't expect was the countercurrent that year had combined with hurricane-force winds. He was driven northeast instead. Not east. Then the hurricane collided with the North Pacific clockwise-gyre pushing west. The lethal combination of eastbound hurricane and westbound trade winds drove LeGrand north. Uncontrollably. Like a leaf before a storm."

Dancer peered over his friend's shoulder as Post flipped to the next page. "The almanac says the storm's remnants reached as far north as the Sandwich Islands. Look here. This modern footnote says more Pacific islanders were killed in that historic storm than died during the next five decades from white men's diseases." Post tapped the almanac with his finger. "That's it."

Dancer looked puzzled. "What do you mean 'that's it'?"

At that moment there again was a knock on the door. Billy Mack entered the cabin. Again. Deposited a flagon of wine and two glasses. And slipped out again — as unseen as a ghost. Leaving the door slightly ajar.

"If Tiki Tieva's memory is correct…" Post reflected.

Dancer confirmed the Captain's thoughts: "LeGrand left Zanzibar in April 1799." He opened LeGrand's log to the last entry. "LeGrand shipped out of Tahiti six months later…in October 1799…despite Princess Tieva's best attentions."

Post spoke quietly…almost to himself. "LeGrand set sail into what became one of the greatest storms in the history of the Pacific. If he survived — and that's stretching the improbable into the impossible — he would never have reached Easter Island. Instead his rotten down-by-the-head ship was driven off course to the north. Passed the Marquesas. Into the Northern Pacific. Helpless. He fought a battle of survival between his ship and the storm. His only possible landfall would have been raised by dead reckoning…here." Post thumped the map. "The Sandwich Islands."

"You mean with nothing to do but pray…LeGrand had no choice? Once blown into the North Pacific his only option was to limp to the Sandwich Islands?" Dancer speculated.

"Exactly. With nothing to go on but La Pérouse's charts. LeGrand had nowhere else to go….if his ship wasn't dismantled by the hurricane."

"Which is more than likely."

"If LeGrand survived…he had no other port in the storm."

Post leaned back in his chair. Lit one of Dancer's black Oscuro cigars. "There y'have it…Dancer. Your choice. Either you sail with us to the Sandwich Islands…or I put you and your kit back on Tahiti."

Post blew a conclusive cloud of smoke into the air. "Unlikely you'll see a ship going east for a while. Very little trade with Easter Island. Warring native clans are hostile to any attempts to make landfall. Most of the great *moai* statues have been toppled. Your only hope in Pape'ete is to catch a whaling transport returning to the East Coast of America with a hold full of oil and baleen sometime in late June …after the last whaler leaves Maui in May for the summer Arctic whaling."

Post sharpened the horns of Dancer's fateful dilemma: "Or…you can come with us. But the *Bountiful* can't wait. It's paramount to meet the transports in Maui. Miss that rendezvous and our best season ever will be a bust. I can't do that to my men. Or my company. I gave them my word."

"Wait till June? By then President Polk's war with Mexico could be lost! The last penny spent from the American treasury! My whole mission may just be some wild treasure hunt...but I can't sit by and let that happen…No…never again…not since I stood by and let that bastard uncle send my brother Jace off to Texas." Dancer's uncle had been adamant to punish Jace by enlisting Jace and sending him away…but Dancer's own inability to muster the courage to save his brother from his dire fate had long haunted his dreams. "When I didn't step up…look what happened. I'd never be able to hold my head up again…or look Sam Houston in the eye. No. This calls for action… not tilting at windmills."

Both men looked at each other. The choice was stark. Dancer could chase LeGrand's proven intentions east to Easter Island. Then Concepción. And Cape Horn. As he had for months.

Or change course. And fate the dice on the slimmest prospect that LeGrand miraculously made it to the Sandwich Islands.

"It's a long shot at best." Dancer nodded. "But my gut tells me to bet on action…not hesitation."

Post smiled. "Spoken like a man who was born on All Fool's Day. No more crazy than hunting the gowk…that phony cuckoo bird. Happy birthday…Dancer."

The men shook hands heartily and clapped each other on the shoulder.

"Maui it is."

Billy Mack eavesdropped from the cabinway. *President Polk. Treasure hunt. The American agent.* Instinctively he tapped the secret compartment inside his seaman's kit. There the message meant for Henri Malbec — recently of New Caledonia and Marquesas Islands — was still perfectly safe. Silently Mack's hand passed over the straight-bladed dirk in his waist belt. *Hullo.* A venomous look crossed his face. *Time at last for a little Irish justice.*

CHAPTER 43

MAIN DECK/*BOUNTIFUL*
EQUATORIAL PACIFIC/NORTH OF TAHITI
9 APRIL 1847

A WEEK HAD PASSED at sea since Tahiti. On the eighth day the skies above the *Bountiful* abruptly darkened. The equatorial wind rose wet and warm. Captain Post frowned at the onrushing storm. "Feels like we're in for heavy seas." Within minutes a tempest of death enveloped the *Bountiful.*

"Reef the main sails! We'll run head down to leeward! Hold her before the wind!" Post shouted to his first mate to take the helm as he touched the looped rattail behind his neck for luck. The mate braced his feet and took his trick at the wheel. The bosun piped all hands. Every sailor scrambled on deck with a scrape of boots and heavy tread. Each raced to the weather braces and was aloft in an instant as ordered.

"Haul aboard!" roared Post as the wind rose with the sting of first rain. "Get your tack well down...bos'n! Set taut the braces...lads! Steady now. Sheet home! Now hove away there!" All hands were mighty busy aloft and alow.

"Dancer!" Post gripped Dancer's shoulder. His voice almost lost in the rising wind. "Assist Hawthorne on the bowsprit with the forestays'l and inner topmast jib! Leave the outer jib on the t'gallant stay to catch the wind! But reef the forestays'l and inner jib one by one! As I say...leave the outer jib in place! Lay on now! No time to lose!" Then Post yelled into Dancer's ear: "Only the outer jib on the t'gallant stay is needed to keep her before the wind! If we run with all three jibs the cursed waves will drive us under!" Post watched as Dancer worked his way forward along the bulwark as quickly as he could. Post squinted against the spray to see where the three stays were fixed: One ran from the bow to the foremast. A second stay from the bowsprit to the topmast. And a third from the outer jib boom to the uppermost t'gallant mast. He watched as Dancer stepped up on the foredeck. *Not a healthy place to be in a sea.* Each permanent stay held a triangular sail: First the forestays'l. Then inner jib. And finally the outer jib. Each sail was anchored at the mast top by a heavy block and tied off by a halyard that ran perpendicular down the foremast to the deck below. There the halyards were made fast to the clew on the aftermast corner and back to a pin on its rail.

Through the deluge Dancer could see the sailor Hawthorne struggled as he planted one boot on the bow rail and the other on the projecting bowsprit. Beyond the sprit Dancer eyed the jib boom extension — what every sailor called the "widow maker." Below churned the sea as the *Bountiful* raced ahead of the wind. Dancer made his way across the slippery foredeck. No sooner had Dancer reached the bow than the innermost forestays'l luffed and flapped as its leading edge slacked on the stay. Dancer and Hawthorne gathered the wet canvas as best they could. Then furled the smaller forestays'l and secured the sail against the foredeck rail.

The roaring Pacific tempest toyed with man's folly. The ship bucked backward as it climbed the rise of a wave. Then pitched forward as it plummeted down the trough. Half blinded by rain Dancer stepped up onto the bow rail and inched out on the bowsprit opposite Hawthorne. There the two men faced each other. Hawthorne's feet jostled for purchase on the sprit's uncertain under netting.

Dancer shouted to Hawthorne: "One hand for yourself...one for the ship!" The sailor didn't need to be told.

Dancer carefully edged out on the bowsprit. His boots beneath the foot of the inner jib. At the same moment the jib sagged...covering Dancer's head like a ghost. Without warning a huge wave just then slammed into the *Bountiful* amidships. Arms full and hands aching from effort Hawthorne and Dancer were nearly jolted off the bowsprit. Rain. Fury. Wind. Lines whipped. Eyes stung by the salt tempest. Arms overloaded in canvas and line. Both men struggled. In a desperate effort to sort the sagging sail young Hawthorne stepped up from the under footrope onto the bowsprit. Wrapped his elbow around the topmast stay that held the inner jib. Reached with an extended hand to help Dancer clear the inner sail. Suddenly the middle stays'l flogged loose. Then gave way.

Dancer looked up. "Look out!"

Too late. The heavy wet canvas and halyard plummeted down the stay from the topmast head. Slammed into Hawthorne's shoulder. He screamed in agony. The sound almost lost in the wind. The canvas enveloped the sailor. Instantly a heavy halyard block followed. Loosed from the topmast. The block zipped down the stay line like a boulder. Smashed the sailor senseless. Dancer lunged for him. Grabbed at his belt. Dancer's boot slipped. His knee slammed into the wooden bowsprit. Then his leg twisted awkwardly in the sprit under netting. Dancer winced in pain. Desperately tried to hold on.

In the next instant the sailor too lost his handhold. Fell back. His belt ripped from Dancer's fingers. Without a cry the man dropped from the bowsprit. A hollow sound rose an instant later as the ship's bow drove him to his death. Dancer tossed a line into the froth below. Futilely the line slapped against the hull. Ineffectual against the roar of the sea. Dancer strained to right his position. But he was trapped. The tangle of lines and netting and canvas of the inner jib made it impossible to move aft or forward. Held fast like a helpless Lilliputian. Again without warning the ship pitched forward. Drove Dancer under water. His failing hold on the bowsprit and topmast stay involuntarily loosened. The wind slashed a line across his face like a bullwhip. A fading reserve of will was the only thing that held Dancer from meeting his doom.

Raised by a shout from the boatswain Post instantly took in Dancer's distress. Together the two men raced like tightrope artists onto the bowsprit. Grasped lines to keep from being toppled into the sea. Post maneuvered Dancer back to the safety of the foredeck. While the bos'n secured the inner jib to the bowsprit. With its main sails reefed and the outer jib secure on its t'gallant stay the *Bountiful* ran before the tempest wind.

◎ ◎ ◎

Hour after hour. Through the night. The storm toyed with the wooden ship. Shrouds shrieked. Timbers groaned. And the storm drove man's frail folly before the wind. With sunrise the beastly blow released the exhausted ship: As quickly as the storm arrived its wind beat off into the western horizon. Like a workhorse headed to the barn the *Bountiful* again settled back onto an even keel running north toward Maui and the Sandwich Islands.

Post joined Dancer in the master's cabin. Dancer looked out from a blanket that wrapped him where he sat on the Captain's settee. "'Twas a close call…Dancer."

"I did what I could. But we didn't expect the inner jib to flog *and* its halyard to part at the same time."

"The sea is a hard business. We wouldn't be talking now if you and Hawthorne had taken opposite posts. Yet…that's only the second man we've lost in three years."

"Still" — Dancer nodded — "a tragic accident."

Captain Post looked at Dancer out of the corner of his eye before replying. "If 'twas an accident at all."

Dancer's searching eyes looked at his friend for an explanation.

With the air of a forensic Post chose his words carefully. "Before the storm struck…I checked all the rigging. All in place. No one should have expected the inner jib to run free like that. Or for that halyard and its block on the topmast to give way. Much less to release at once."

"You have some suspicions?"

"Nothing I can pinpoint…but it was almost as if something — or someone — had an intention of sending *you* into the sea — not young Hawthorne." Captain Post rubbed his clean-shaven chin. "Aye…blocks and buckets fall from aloft. Sails flog and lines snap. Accidents happen. But this has too many coincidences to be an accident…."

"You're saying…if someone was out to kill me…loosening the jib halyard could have done it?"

"Aye." Post gave his old friend a hard look. "I'd watch your back if I were you. You may yet become fish fodder…if that's their intention."

CHAPTER 44

CARPENTER'S WORKSHOP/*BLACK CLOUD*
EQUATORIAL PACIFIC
28 APRIL 1847

CAPTAIN HYRAM HEAD stepped inside the deck house workshop then closed the door behind First Mate Ratter Dawes.

The Captain crossed his arms and drummed his fingers on his black sleeve. "Have you seen Swift and that island girl in the past hour or two?"

Dawes rubbed his chin. "Now that you ask...no I haven't seen 'em lately."

"Ever since you told me about them snooping around the cargo hold my dander gets up when I don't know where those two women are."

Ratter Dawes picked up a barrel stave from the workbench and hefted it nervously.

"Tell me again...what were those wagtail women looking for in the hold?"

"Said they was checkin' their cargo is all. Wanted to be sure their baggage been stowed." Dawes scratched his hairless forearms. "You know: the brothel equipment they says they're deliverin'. Piano. Crystal glasses. Statues. Paintings. Sea chests of fancy dresses."

"I never swallowed that Philadelphia story from the white woman." Head pulled on his black whiskers. "Doesn't fit her if you ask me. Not with her nosey questions and scribbling in her journal day and night."

The mate shot his Captain a sidelong glance. "And sending off letters on that clipper ship from San Juan Fernandez."

"Never bought for a copper that concocted story they was from Philadelphia...not New York." Head pulled a chisel out of its rack and tested the sharpness of its edge against his thumbnail. "Or that Swift was a brothel investor just chaperoning the island girl back to her adopted missionary parents. Malarky."

"The native is the one that has troubled me memory. At first I'd thought it was some port from some previous voyage. But..." Dawes snapped his fingers. "Now I remember. 'Twas from ridin' the waves of pleasure in New York City. Now almost two years ago." With a sly expression on his face Dawes took out a tobacco twist and cut off an inch with his knife. "She was all painted up. Looked totally different. A parlor hostess she was. All 'em native tramps look the same from the ways I sees 'em."

Dawes gave Captain Head a shifty look as he tucked the chaw into his cheek. "Fore we set out from New York...I had a meetin' in The Tombs with a mystery man. He wore a big green pinky ring." Dawes adjusted the tobacco between his teeth and gum then spit a stream into a pile of sawdust. "Short of it is...he wanted me to kill Swift. Figured if I took care of business — and you weren't involved — it was safer for you...Cap'n." Head gave a sideways nod that suggested he agreed with Dawes. "When I caught 'em snoopin' in the hold... I thought 'twas time to collect on the ring man's offer. I'd dune it too... if it hadnah been for that harpooner named Flute."

The Captain drove the chisel into the thick workbench and sneered. "That Swift woman...She's the one we're best done without. But now — thanks to your bumbling...Dawes — we'll have to bide patient. Now that we've caught the trade winds from the east...there's smooth sailing to Hawai'i. No more commotions like the Horn...or storms to give us opportunities."

Head turned and idly picked up a hammer from the workshop toolbox. On the butt end of its handle were carved the carpenter's initials.

"'Twas the hammer of the dead carpenter." Dawes gave the tool a smirking look. "Swept overboard at the Horn when he came out of the head after tippling some pilfered rum. Lost at sea…like you said. To me he died from his own foolishness."

"Accidents happen." Head had answered Dawes darkly as he seemed to consider another thought.

"What d'ye plan…Cap'n?"

Captain Head paused. Then settled on Swift's fate. "We'll bide our time until we're approaching Lahaina. Sometime when the ship is quiet. No prying eyes. Maybe a Sabbath Sunday will be fitting."

"A double rum ration would keep all hands below."

The Captain nodded in assent as his dark eyes glittered. "We'll make our own opportunity—and feed that meddlesome woman to the sharks with a couple buckets of bloody chum…afore we raise Moloka'i."

Dawes licked his lips. "If the island girl raises a peep…the devil will take her too."

"The native wench doesn't matter." Head fixed Dawes with a black stare. "It's that Swift woman we must be rid of. And I know just the man to get the job done…plus an extra rum ration will put us elsewhere at the same time."

Dawes gave a stealthy look as if his food was threatened.

"Don't worry…Dawes. I'll vouch for your bounty from the pinky-ring man back in New York. Whatever it takes to keep that lyin' strumpet out of my business is all I want. But what about Flute?"

"The pleasure is mine." Dawes shot a brown stream toward a corner and wiped his lips with the back of his hand. "Got a tally to settle with the man." He slipped a belaying pin from its pin rail bracket on the wall. "Me and my friend Billy." He smacked the butt end of the pin into the palm of his hand. "Just leave that bald scum to me."

CHAPTER 45

WORKSHOP ROOF/*BLACK CLOUD*
EQUATORIAL PACIFIC
SOMETIME LATER

KIKILANI personified innocence; Swift observed with envy how the sailors followed her loveliness with their eyes. And how small gifts from admirers were anonymously hung from the latch of the surgery door. Scrimshaw pendants. A ribbon of Parisian silk. Shaved-wood flowers. Even Duffy Ragsdale's former bunkmate—no older than Kikilani's eighteen years—blushingly asked her to read to him after months of screwing up his courage.

Now perched on the workshop's roof Swift and Kikilani felt the warmth of the sunset across their faces. A light breeze wicked away a modest moisture from their suntanned temples. Atop the deck house just aft of the forehatch they huddled between the ship's tender pinnace and the Captain's fast gig boat. Both double-ended boats sat upside down on the workshop roof ready to be rapidly lowered by tackle to the waterline. Between the small crafts folded weather sails and coiled rope at the aft end created a hidden refuge: out of any helmsman's view from the stern. In a moment of contentment both travelers intently stared forward at the northwest horizon. Both hoped to catch that ethereal green flash of a Pacific sunset.

As the sunset intensified a cry came from the lubber's hole at the masthead: "There she breaches! On the lee beam! Sperm whale about one hundred yards off!"

The bosun at the wheel called back: "Sing out when you see her blow!"

"Ay...ay...sir!" came the call from the top mast.

While Swift and Kikilani looked eagerly off to starboard they heard a thundering snore rise directly off the bulwark rail. Followed by a heavy splash. They craned their necks higher just in the nick to see the flukes of an enormous whale sweeping through the air—not more than fifty yards off the side of the *Black Cloud*.

Standing with the bosun on the quarterdeck Mr. Flute paused with the knotted line and chip-log in his hands. The master harpooner gave a rare half smile as he recalled the youthful joy of a wild Nantucket sleigh ride pulled by a lanced whale.

Beneath Kikilani and Swift the daytime workshop was empty. The cooper. Sailmaker. And shipsmith took their ease in fo'c'sle bunks. All three were labeled "idlers" by the common seamen. All because the tradesmen did not stand watch. The Captain and his first mate had taken their scheming treachery to other quarters of the ship. In the fo'c'sle mess supper was being served to the ongoing doubts of the cook's lineage. Only an occasional sailor passed along the deck below the boat skids—unaware the women nestled in their hiding place above.

Swift studied Kikilani. Her eyebrows almost met in the middle over her brown eyes. Her regal nose was unusually straight for an islander. Kikilani turned her head and returned Swift's gaze. Her radiant smile lit up her face with a brilliant naturalness. A tiara of wood-shaved blossoms Kikilani had banded with a blue ribbon rested on her black waves of hair. What looked like a small tortoise design graced the olive skin at the nape of her strong swimmer's neck. When Swift looked more closely she realized the image was not a tattoo but a birthmark.

Kikilani returned Swift's gaze and cocked her head to one side. "You have a question face...as my Auntie used to say."

Swift blushed. She never knew why. But the unexpected rush always annoyed her. She wrapped her arms around her knees. "We come from such different worlds. Yet we share so much." Swift turned her sea-green eyes toward the sun. "We've both lost our parents. Almost a day doesn't go by without me remembering when they brought my mother's body home from the canal. My sixteenth birthday." Swift's voice caught from the loss. "I hid beneath the table. Legs walked back and forth. That image of water falling from the table onto the parquet floor haunts me. At first a stream. Then slower and slower…to a trickle. Then drops. Like tears. It was her soul ebbing away. Along with my father's will."

Swift watched the sunset as her story tumbled out again. "A year ago last January….the headmistress told me not to return. Something about my 'follow me' personality wasn't suitable for their rules of 'deportment and etiquette.' Uncle Jacob was furious. Said he expected to get his money's worth from his tuition payments." Swift bit her lower lip. "The real reason was he stole my inheritance. My parents' home…and my father's newspaper." The expression in Swift's eyes turned angry. *And enriched himself with backdoor deals for equipment and construction.* "Worst of all he arranged for me to marry some half-wit son of a paper buyer at his club."

Kikilani encouraged Swift with an understanding smile.

"I told Uncle Jacob the only man I would marry was one I loved. Do you know what he said?" Swift almost spit out the words: "'A woman can't survive in this world without a husband! The richer the better!'" Swift twisted a length of rope in her hands. "My mother — God bless her — always said to follow my heart first. And that is what I must do." Swift sighed and added softly: "Once I decide what my heart is saying." She squinted at the orange disk of the sun as it edged toward the horizon. "Now I must win my own way in the world. And prove that I have the steel to take back what is mine." Swift's jaw flexed behind her freckled Welsh complexion.

Kikilani looked at Swift and shivered slightly despite the warm sun. "The same for my people — the Pi'ilani of Maui. For generations every large *moku* region and smaller *ahupua'a* area ran from mountaintop to the sea. A stream often defined the land. From the mountain came water and pasture. On the upcountry slopes…we cultivated *taro* in terraced fields. Sweet potato. Sugar cane. And pounded *kapa* bark cloth." Swift watched as Kikilani moved her hands gracefully to represent her words. "All of these we traded for fish. Seaweed.

Breadfruit. And coconuts gathered by our kinsmen near the water. They worked the fishing grounds as far as the reef." She raised her small hands and settled the carved tiara more firmly on her head. "No one owned the land or water. We were all caretakers. The idea of owning land was as foreign as owning your grandmother. Living on the land gave us the *kuleana* responsibility to care for it. And in return the land had the *kuleana* to feed and shelter and clothe us. Our wholeness with the land gave a unity to life."

Swift took off her shawl and gently draped it over Kikilani's shoulders.

"Then white men's diseases came ashore with the whalers and seamen. Took almost everyone in our compound overnight: Mother. Father. Aunties. Uncles. We were orphans. Lost. Many families sold their girls for food to the highest bidder. Other girls ran away. Many visited ships...never to return to the island." The island beauty shook her head slowly as if she looked into emptiness. "Without a familiar world the missionaries pushed their laws and their God on us. For many their foreign scriptures filled a void left when our chiefs destroyed the *kapu*."

"What is *kapu*?"

"*Kapu* was our system of traditions...of laws...of instructions. *Kapu* guided us to understand how to act. *Kapu* informed our elders when judgments needed to be made. Without *kapu* all order was forsaken. Our faith was lost." Kikilani gave Swift a serious look in which a vague disquiet was apparent.

Swift sat up straighter. As if she knew what Kikilani was trying to tell her with absolute certainty. "There is a proverb I have read: 'If the camel gets his nose in the tent...his body will soon follow.'"

"I don't know this thing—this camel. But if it is like a village dog...it is true. My people were no match for the change the missionaries and foreigners forced upon us."

"My editor told me: 'The West brought guns. Disease. And Christianity to the islands. Each equally destructive to an idyllic way of life.'"

Kikilani nodded then pointed to the horizon and whispered: "Make a wish." Both women stared toward the sunset. "Wait. Wait. Right...there!" As the top of the sun's disk disappeared a bright green bolt shot out from the spot. The quick flash crossed the horizon in both directions like emerald lightning — and was gone…like the day itself.

Swift rubbed her eyes and looked beyond the horizon. "Our mission has just begun…my friend." With elbows on her knees Swift entwined her fingers under her chin. "Mr. Flute says Lahaina has become an open port after you left the islands…Anything goes. He said the missionaries lost their grip. That dram shops sprung up like fungus. The only vestige of morality is the sunset cannon. It's a curfew for sailors to return to ship…but he says it is ignored more than obeyed."

"Even before I was taken…you could see the result. The canoes with girls were common moonlight figures. Some even paddled from ship to ship to obtain the highest offer."

As the orange twilight deepened over the Pacific and the sun dropped lower under the clouds an uneasiness fell over both Swift and Kikilani.

Mindlessly the *Black Cloud* beat its way across the calm Pacific.

A cloud passed over Swift's face. Her thoughts drifted to the topic of Kikilani's absence from her home. The *Black Cloud* had been at sea for many weeks. If the voyage took much longer the whalers — and the smuggler's evidence — might have vanished by then…and left Swift's entire mission a complete tatter. Would she even reach Maui in time?

Finally Swift returned to the topic Kikilani had first spoken of. "What version of Lahaina will we find?"

Silence consumed her thoughts again.

After a long while Swift spoke in a quiet voice. "Will it be a return to the Garden of Eden…or as some say: a volcanic Sodom and Gomorrah?"

CHAPTER 46

TAFFRAIL/*BLACK CLOUD*
EAST OF HAWAIIAN ISLANDS
13 MAY 1847

DAY AFTER DAY the *Black Cloud* closed the distance to the Hawaiian Islands. Trade winds from the east filled her sails. And leveled the sea. Onward the old sea pacer ran across the Pacific. Seamen's tally sticks notched nearly five weeks since leaving the island of Robinson Crusoe. Yet tallies weren't needed to sense the rising ardor of almost all aboard to see and smell their island destination: now five-and-a-half months since leaving New York.

The old salts shared a scrimshaw map of Cook's Sandwich Islands with the greenhands in the foc's'le. To the southeast the first island was Hawai'i: The Big Island. This was the home island of the conquering king. As a native Hawaiian the great king had imposed its name on his extended fifteen-hundred-mile archipelago kingdom. Next — to the northwest — came a cluster of four islands: Maui. Moloka'i. Lāna'i. And Kaho'olawe. A narrow channel called Lahaina Roads separated the group.

The cabin boy with freckles across his cheeks pressed closer in the cramped crew quarters and gave rapt attention to the scrimshaw lesson. Maui was the largest of the four. The leathernecks pointed to a peanut-shaped mass formed by two ancient volcanos: From the eastern "wetside" the great Haleakalā rose above the rain forests of Hāna Bay. From the volcano's windswept ten thousand-foot crown Haleakalā's slopes descended to a desiccated valley to the west. The fair-haired youth followed every word with wide-eyed fascination. Into that valley little rain fell under the shadow of Haleakalā. From that dusty desert climbed a second volcanic cluster that created some of the wettest mountains in the world. There constant clouds shrouded the mysterious ʻIao Valley. From that sacred valley the rain-carved slopes dropped down precipitously to the western "dryside" shoreline that sheltered every whaler's haven in the Pacific: Lahaina Town.

The boy reached out and touched the wondrous black lines engraved on the cool white ivory as the old salt continued his narrative. Farther northwest from Maui and her smaller sister islands lay the island of Oʻahu with its great port of Honolulu. Now the King's residence and seat of government manipulated by many forces: Foreigners. Traders. Missionaries. And temperance. The lad imagined the farthest northwest islands inked into the mariner's ivory scrimshaw beyond Oʻahu labeled Kauaʻi and Niʻihau. These remote outposts were the last landfalls—and the last chiefdom to pay fealty to the conquering King Kamehameha a quarter century ago.

Samantha Swift awoke to a nagging dispirit. *Nearly a month overdue. And still no sign of Hawaiʻi.* Swift rubbed sleep from her eyes as daylight seeped through the surgery's glass prisms. *What if I'm too late? Could our shilly-shally pace have been plotted on purpose to block my investigation?* The next moment Swift muttered to herself: "There you go again...Stop fretting over things you can't control." In a show of rationality Swift forced her mind to be hopeful. Despite her gnawing doubts. With resolution she addressed a small mirror Kikilani had tacked to a bulkhead timber. *Today calls for a turn in the sun and being dressed for the Sabbath. Put your best foot forward...as Mother said.* She tried to feel lighthearted as she shook out her long-stowed society dress and dry petticoats. Swift quickly wet and brushed her auburn tresses—now grown out to her natural color since the dark-dyed disguise at the Paradise Palace. She hoped the unruly waves cascading over her shoulders would hang somewhat straighter.

Swift winked at her image in the mirror. *You've done well by yourself so far.* She thought back to how she helped bind the crewmen's wounds. Splint sprains. Treat the cook's worst efforts. Many of the men showed an honest appreciation. *Not only do they trust our cures…but they confide their lives to us.* How she wrote letters. Listened without judgment. Read aloud to the men. Swift gave a silent smile as she realized she had gained an appreciation for the confined fo'c'sle's smell of tobacco. Men. And honest work. And — if they ever got there — had sent those exclusive dispatches to the *Eagle.*

She looked into the small mirror that presented a slightly blurred image of herself. Then forced a smile and gave her rich hair two extra strokes. *The end of the voyage is near.* She felt good this day — despite the unpleasantness with Dawes at the Horn.

Captain Head had formed his plot in the days before the Valparaiso storm: One Sunday he had noticed Swift helping the simple-minded Moses Smidt with passages in his miniature Bible that stumped the seaman. The Captain knew the hulking Prussian obeyed his every command. Ratter Dawes reinforced that view — "as the scriptures say" — by confiding in Smidt that the Captain was the representative of God on ship.

For weeks Head cultivated his handpicked zealot with chapter and verse. "Swift is a wicked sinner." Or so Head whispered in Smidt's ear. "Look how Swift flaunts her flowing locks…no better than Mary Magdalene flaunting her hair to dry tears from Jesus' feet…as the scriptures say in the Gospel of Luke. What blasphemy!" Each passage selected by the concerned Captain painted Swift as the personification of evil…but many times worse. "Look! That vile woman shames every seaman's manhood whenever she wears trousers. Not since the shameless Jezebel in the Book of Kings — as the scriptures say — has there been a more sinful woman!" One day — when Smidt listened as Swift read a Bible passage to another young sailor — Dawes came up behind the Prussian. "Hear that?" he whispered. "Swift is intentionally misreading the passage to corrupt an innocent mind. Cover your ears…she is doing nothing more than 'speaking in tongues.'" Swift promoted the worship of false gods…Smidt must see it…because the Bible says it's so. One day at the helm Captain Head confided in Smidt: "Swift trespassed in the cargo hold and the *lazarette*…where no one can go without my orders. The woman willfully disobeyed me…just like Eve disobeyed God in the Book of Genesis when she ate the apple. As the scriptures say: 'In the day that you eat of it…you shall surely die.'" At each opportunity Head and Dawes worked every susceptibility of the impressionable sailor to poison his mind. Until Smidt's zealous rage rose to righteous hate.

On this Sunday morning as Swift emerged on deck she felt a slight twinge of unease. But put it aside as quickly as it came.

The bosun brought her word that Smidt had a Bible passage question. Would Swift tutor him? The sailor was at the wheel on the quarterdeck. Where he stood while taking his solitary trick as helmsman during a special Sabbath rum ration. With the ship's full complement taking rum in the fo'c'sle below Swift had the main deck almost to herself. She approached the quarterdeck ladderway in her full Sunday fig. Then climbed the three steps and walked past the raised cabin as she ran her fingertips along the varnished rail enjoying the peace and quiet. *Like a stroll in Madison Square Park. It should be opening in May.* She thought of the city finery that would be on display. Petticoats. Stockings. Boots. A light breeze. *Lovely.*

Swift's mind half noted that besides Smidt no one else was on the deck behind the mizzenmast and galley. No other watch. All the crew huddled in the forward fo'c'sle below deck where the Captain lauded their voyage with doubled tots. No one even perched on the far foredeck. Swift smiled with understanding. *Sailors do love their Sabbath rum.*

When Smidt saw Swift approach he looped two lanyards over the wheel spokes to hold the tiller steady. Swift composed a friendly smile as her green silk dress ruffled slightly in the breeze on the raised bridge. "I understand you have a reading question?" she asked the hulking Prussian. "Can I help?"

Smidt grunted. Then took out his miniature Bible and stepped to the aft rail.

No sooner had Swift come within reach than the hulking seaman slammed his fist into her stomach hard as a battering ram. The sudden blow drove the breath from her lungs — as well as her voice. In a blink the big sailor covered her mouth with his huge fleshy hand. Grabbed Swift from behind as he clamped his arm around her middle: so tight the air again left Swift's lungs as her feet rose off the deck.

Smidt stepped away from the wheel. Approached the rail at the stern of the ship. Raised his arms. And with one great effort tossed Swift over the taffrail.

"*Sterben!*" Smidt snarled. "You God-forsaken sinner…die!" The righteous sailor chucked two piggin buckets after Swift's body…each bucket brimming with bloody fish chum. "Now God's sharks vill finish His verk." The sailor crossed himself. Turned back to the wheel. Picked up his small Bible and tucked it back into his pocket. Then returned to his duty as if he had done nothing more than offer a Sunday tithe.

Swift's breathless form plunged into the ship's wake and sea. Quickly distanced by the receding ship. Her petticoats took on water most terribly: like a dead weight.

At that moment Mr. Flute and Kikilani emerged from the workshop companionway. Kikilani followed toward the quarterdeck to help time the harpooner's log line. From a compartment just past the raised cabin skylight Mr. Flute took his knotted line and handed Kikilani the hourglass. As Smidt stood indifferently at the wheel Kikilani knit her brow in concern. *Where is Sam? I heard the bosun summon her to the quarterdeck.* She turned to Smidt: "Have you seen Miss Swift?" Smidt sullenly ignored Kikilani. As her suspicion grew Kikilani glanced over the port side gunwale. Nothing came to view below the ship. With no Swift to be seen Kikilani stepped past Smidt who stood dumbly by the wheel. Kikilani looked directly below the taffrail at the cusp foam. Then with both hands shading her eyes she searched the receding wake. There in the increasing distance Kikilani thought she saw a blotch of green akin to Swift's society dress. Was that a bare arm thrashing helpless beyond the *Black Cloud*'s wake?

"Man overboard!"

Mr. Flute grabbed the helm's pipe. Shrilled the man-overboard alarm.

Instantly Kikilani unfastened the buttons of her Basquine bodice and dress. Stepped out of its folds. Then threw off her Sunday petticoats. Leaving little besides her sit-upons. Without hesitation she scaled the taffrail. And dove into the sea toward Swift.

Mr. Flute raced back onto the main deck as crew appeared from below. "Man overboard! Lower the Captain's gig from the davit cranes!"

Almost simultaneously Captain Head came on deck with Dawes a step behind. "Call all hands!" roared the Captain to Ratter Dawes.

Dawes turned and through his cupped hands shouted down the fo'c'sle companionway. "All hands ahoy!"

In short order every man in the fo'c'sle was on deck.

"Hoist and lower a boat!" cried the Captain to the men as they took their places almost before you could wink.

Standing near the gig boat was Ratter Dawes. Mr. Flute collared him and growled. "You're coming with me…Dawes. As insurance."

Quickly Mr. Flute. Dawes. And three sailors were lowered to the waterline. "Row…you sons of a witch's whore!" Mr. Flute ordered. "Or I'll feed you to the sharks as well." He cast his most vicious scowl at Dawes. Immediately Dawes and three men pulled on the long oars. Mr. Flute took charge from the boatheader's plank at the stern. There he handled the steering oar. Guided the smuggler's gig boat across the *Black Cloud*'s wake. Toward the swimming Kikilani.

Kikilani's powerful strokes brought her to the place where she judged she last saw Swift. All that marked the spot was Swift's white handkerchief floating listlessly on the waves. Kikilani took a deep breath. Dove down below the surface…into the green sea. Nothing. Her bursting lungs soon drove her to the surface. Nearby floated the two chum buckets. Their bloody contents spread like a crimson cloud into the water. The next moment a hand splashed through the surface two boat-lengths away. Then sank. Kikilani stroked hard. Swam to the spot. Dove again. Her wild reach struck cloth. Then a wrist. Kikilani grabbed Swift around the chest. With several great kicks she strained to pull Swift up…the ballast of Swift's water-logged petticoats almost too much. Even Kikilani's desperate efforts were hampered as her kicking feet tangled in the sodden folds. After what seemed like an eternity Kikilani willed Swift to the surface.

Kikilani guided Swift's limp body to the nearest piggin bucket. Turned upside down the bailing bucket formed a rudimentary float. Kikilani propped Swift's arms limply across the floating vessel.

Her chin lifted somewhat by the edge. Kikilani swam to recover the second bucket.

Swift's insensible hold slipped from the wooden bucket. Her long auburn hair spread beneath the surface. Kikilani raced back to where Swift had been. Grabbed a fist of hair. Yanked Swift's head above the water. Swift didn't inhale. Cough. Or even sputter. Her face as still as death.

Terror had gripped Swift's mind. Every synapse paralyzed by her worst fear: Death by drowning. Just like her mother. Just like that horror years ago. A terrible vision had driven Swift into failing consciousness. Her mind saw only her own form laid out. White. Dripping. Dead on the dining room table. Her soul draining away....

With one arm Kikilani used the second bucket as her own buoy. With the other she tried to keep Swift afloat across the other stout wooden bucket. She locked her legs firmly around Swift's unconscious body.

Within moments the gig pulled up to Kikilani and Swift. Mr. Flute moved forward from the boatheader position. Threaded his way past Dawes and the three sailors single-banked with oars alternating from each side. He took the harpooner's station at the bow. From that angle out of the corner of his eye he saw a dark shape slide past below the women's' legs. Then a second shape. And a third. Each passed in ugly menace.

Mr. Flute reached down and grabbed Swift's collar with one hand. Kikilani released her legs. Then let go the bucket float and took hold of the gig's gunwale. With his free hand Mr. Flute took Kikilani's wet wrist. With one great lift he brought her aboard. With the same free hand he grabbed the second chum bucket. Flung the wooden container as far from the gig boat as he could.

Kikilani bent over and with both hands took Swift's wrist. Placed her unresponsive hand on the gunwale. But before they could lift Swift aboard Mr. Flute froze. A dark fin cut across the water...aiming directly at Swift's dangling legs.

"Hold her!" Mr. Flute released Swift's collar. Grabbed a harpoon. The honed single flue sparkled in the sunlight—its razor edge gleaming only inches from Swift's head. Without warning he drove home the spear—casting it deep into the water...where it hit its deadly mark. The handle jerked crazily. Then ran off wobbling across the surface: a trail of blood in its wake.

The shiver of sharks turned and followed. Attracted by the death throw. Even from one of their own. At the same moment Swift's dead weight pulled her limp hand from the gunwale. Kikilani bent low over the water. Reached into the sea. Her fingers collided with Swift's fingers...then Kikilani pulled with all her might. Mr. Flute saw Swift's arm rise above the waterline. He grabbed her elbow. Together Kikilani and Mr. Flute hoisted Swift's form into the boat.

Swift's body convulsed in agitation. A silent wail came from her mouth. Agony constricted her face. Kikilani reached out her warm hands. Grasped her friend's cold fingers. Just then the terror in Swift's eyes went blank. Unconsciousness took her.

Kikilani draped Swift over a cross thwart. Gave her lower back a sharp push. Nothing. Pushed again. Swift gasped. Sucked in air. Sputtered. Coughed. Vomited seawater. Her body wracked by inner terrors. Swift moaned. Kikilani pivoted Swift's exhausted form to sit on the bottom slats of the gig's narrow hull. Swift's eyes fluttered. Then focused. A wet hand rose up weakly. Kikilani's fingers intertwined with Swift's. Slowly Swift's lips mouthed a profound silence: *Thank you.* Then again Swift's lungs were overcome by coughing up seawater. After a moment Kikilani—using both hands—gathered Swift's dripping auburn hair from out of her face.

Swift looked at Kikilani. Mr. Flute. Gave them a brave half smile. "Not what I would call a pleasant Sunday outing. Must say...it brings up bad memories...and my worst fear."

At the back of the gig Dawes' eyes narrowed. *The damn woman is alive.*

His sour expression looked like a man who had lost a fortune.

And he had.

PART 3

PELE'S REVENGE

A SWIFT & DANCER
ADVENTURE

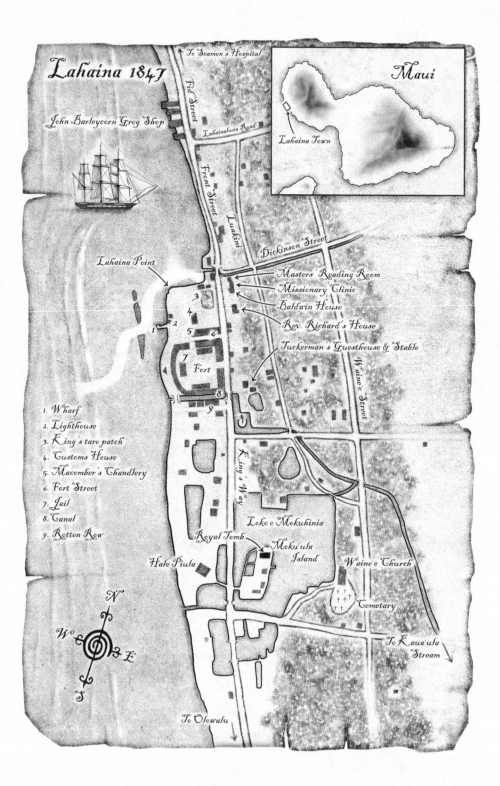

Lahaina 1847

Maui

Lahaina Town

To Seamen's Hospital

John Barleycorn Grog Shop

Fid Street

Lahainaluna Road

Front Street

Luakini

Dickinson Street

Lahaina Point

Masters' Reading Room
Missionary Clinic
Baldwin House
Rev. Richard's House

Tuckerman's Guesthouse & Stable

3

4

2

5   6

1

7

Fort

Waine'e Street

8

9

1. Wharf
2. Lighthouse
3. King's taro patch
4. Customs House
5. Macomber's Chandlery
6. Fort Street
7. Jail
8. Canal
9. Rotten Row

King's Way

Loko o Mokuhinia

Royal Tomb

Moku'ula Island

Hale Piula

Waine'e Church

N
W   E
S

Cemetary

To Kaua'ula Stream

To Olowalu

CHAPTER 47

SACRED MOKUHINIA LAKE
KING'S WAY/LAHAINA/MAUI
MID-MAY 1847

LAHAINA TOWN had more ships in the harbor than the harbor had
buildings. Eager whalers surveyed the forbidding mountains that
formed a dark brow beyond the town. This range was broken by the
Rainbow Valley—cleaved precipitously by the Kauaʻula Stream where
the striking yellow-plumed ʻōʻō bird nested. The lush line of water cut
through the brown foothills as it descended to the Lahaina shore. There
a canopy of breadfruit orchards was punctured by tall coconut palms
near the beach: their trunks rose above the green strip like spindly
feather dusters. In the center for all to see was the flag atop the twenty-
foot coral walls of Fort Lahaina. Situated beside the wharf on Lahaina
Point. A break in the reef directly offshore created the harbor entrance.
The S-shaped break allowed smaller pinnaces. Yawls. Gig boats. And
tenders to come ashore. While all deep-draft ships anchored outside
the reef.

Off the south wall of the fort a canal emptied into the harbor.
From the beach the canal ran inland past the fort to a boat-turning
basin. There a small islet supported a lone coconut tree standing like
a birthday candle. Along the canal native vendors fashioned palm

lean-tos where they bartered Irish potatoes. Sweet potatoes. Sugar cane. Breadfruit. Plus coconuts and some native crafts. In exchange for foreign trinkets. Hardware. And cloth offered by the ship's stewards and cooks.

A short walk north from the canal along the main street — past the fort's rectangular walls on the harbor side and Tuckerman's Guesthouse inland — a natural artesian spring created a constant water source for the ships. Somewhat brackish where the freshet mixed with seawater. But good enough for whalers. Here at the village pump water gangs refilled ships' drinking casks. Then rolled the ponderous barrels into a dripping queue on crowded Fort Street that ran to the boat wharf near the lighthouse tower. This sandy way separated the modest bastion from Macomber's ship chandlery general store and the Customs House. At this exchange captains collected mail and newspapers — and stayed to share gossip of the sea.

While the masters gathered news — and the casks waited to be rowed back to the ships — the thirsty whalers slipped away from the wharf. They passed the lighthouse tower. Passed the seldom-used palace and council-meeting Long House on the promontory of Lahaina Point. Around the King's *kalo* or taro patch. Then back toward Front Street — as the missionaries called it. This main track ran parallel along the beach from the canal north and marked the dusty backbone of Lahaina Town. Quickening their step the whalers turned north. Surreptitiously avoided the missionary houses. Crossed a footbridge at Dickenson Street — where a stream emptied into the sea creating a fine sand beach. Beyond the footbridge a corridor of grog shops beckoned. Some white stucco adobe. Some sawn clapboard. Others nothing more than barrels and a plank between two breadfruit trees. All were temptingly concentrated along the same blocks of Fid Street — as the whalers called it — around Lahainaluna Road and beyond. Here the festivities houses sold grog rum by the fid shot.

When time or money ran out the whalers returned south along Front Street to their boats in the watering canal near the fort with its curfew cannon and calaboose.

At the canal another footbridge crossed the stream. Here the livery and hotel buildings of mainland architecture gave way to native construction. White adobe and stone exteriors were replaced by thatch and high grass roofs. At the bridge Lahaina's seaside thoroughfare continued south along the King's Way—as the islanders called it.

The narrow King's Way passed near the shore as it ran through the royal district. After a few hundred yards winding between fishponds the track formed the levee of the sacred Loko Mokuhinia off to the east. Into the royal district only noble *ali'i* natives were allowed access. The path wound past the most sacred royal island of the Moku'ula. Here the royal compound was forbidden *kapu* to all commoners and foreigners. Beyond this precinct the track continued along the shoreline toward Olowalu Stream half a dozen miles away.

Isaac and Thomas had sampled the northern grog shops since midday. At some point their crawl turned south. Passed the water pump. Passed the fort. Somewhere at the end of Front Street they had acquired an old horse. Perhaps at Major Tuckerman's livery near the turning basin. Or perhaps the horse acquired them. By late afternoon the memories of all three were about equal.

New England's two sons of the sea sat astride their single steed: Back-to-back the two sailors faced opposing directions. Thomas—who steered from the rear—held strands of the horse's tail wide in his hands like reigns. The faithful charger walked steadfastly south along the sandy track. Well beyond the market canal. Past a graceful *hale* house on the inland side. "Never fear-ah…Isaac." Thomas spoke with a Boston accent. "I'll steer-yah! Giddyap…horsey!"

Near the edge of Loko Mokuhinia Isaac slid off the neck of the horse. He stepped unsteadily into the reeds to relieve himself. Thomas tried to steady the horse when it turned suddenly skittish—then grew almost uncontrollable from fright. Thomas teetered this way and that on its bare back like a disjointed manikin. "Steady as she goes…horsey."

The next moment—less than a horse length from where Isaac stood near the lake's edge—the water roiled and churned. The horse's eyes bugged. It reared up high on its hind legs: Thomas shot off its rump like a toboggan jump. He landed more or less feet first. Then planted a header into the sand—a few wisps of horse tail still in his grasp. The next instant another churn came from the water. The horse bolted. Raced back toward town at uncontrollable speed. Isaac tottered at the water's edge. Thomas grabbed his friend's elbow. Pulled Isaac from the shoreline.

"Thomas...did you see that?"

"See what?"

"That...that shadow. That thing in the pond." Isaac unsteadily pointed back toward the lake. "It was huge!"

"Where?" Thomas threw his arm around his friend's shoulders for support and squinted. "In the water?"

"Must'a been big as a whale!"

"A whale you say!" offered Thomas. "This is no place for two old salts at sunset."

Isaac grabbed his friend — and they scrambled away. Tripped. Fell over each other. Stumbled off. Jabbering.

"That is a sign...Thomas."

"A sign from the devil himself!" agreed Isaac.

Together the friends swore off demon rum. "Cross my heart and hope to die!" they both pledged as they capered as fast as their rubber legs could carry them toward Lahaina Town. A solemn oath for as long as they would remember the pledge. The brilliant sunset was full in their faces.

CHAPTER 48

ADAM AKAMU watched the two sailors from atop the ladder of the nine-foot Lahaina lighthouse tower. The two rounded the corner of the fort and stumbled toward the wharf in the tropical dusk. Without warning the fort's eight o'clock curfew cannon roared only a few feet away. The blast shocked the bejeebers out of the drunken seamen. Thomas and Isaac dove to the sand. Covered their heads. Then recovered. Scrambled to the last pinnace boat at the end of the dock. The harbor before them held well over a hundred seagoing sailing ships at anchor beyond the reef. As the sailors clambered into the tender they pointed to the ship with the tallest masts in the harbor. Safe at last. The *Bountiful*.

Adam Akamu turned back to preparing the lighthouse. Checked the oil levels. Wicks. Made sure the stationary mirrors were clean. Years before as a scholarship student at the Lahainaluna School on the slope above town he won the honor to maintain the royal lighthouse. Picked from all the resident boys. That daily honor Akamu had taken seriously for almost six years as a Pi'ilani...and as an orphan. Ever since the King built the boxlike tower as the first lighthouse in the

Hawaiian Islands. Akamu knew boats trying to reach the wharf depended on the waterfront light to thread the crooked passage known as *keawaiki*.

Foreigners saw Akamu as an island Adonis. Tall. Broad shouldered from his enthusiasm for riding the surf every moment the waves called him. His brown skin was clear. His jet-black hair spread in waves over his head. As he turned he squinted into the violet sunset spread across the Lahaina Roads passage. The low light illumed his long lashes and brown eyes. To the whites....they saw a pure man. A throwback with untainted soul. The embodiment of wild nature as the cure for over-civilization. For himself...Akamu felt less sure about his own calling.

Soon the last whaler's pinnace cleared the harbor break. Then Akamu watched as the King's royal yacht from Honolulu entered the harbor. He noted the King's ensign did not fly. Which could mean only one thing. *The King is not on board.* The handsome yacht tied up at the wharf below the lighthouse. Adam descended the ladder. Stood near the yacht. A former missionary and now the King's American advisor—Abner Sisson—came on deck. Sisson seemed to Akamu to always be in a hurry. Even when he wasn't going anywhere. Like a sand flea.

Their eyes met. "You're just the one I was hoping to meet...Adam. Look at you. Now a fine young missionary." Sisson's gaze took in the handsome figure of a young man dressed as a proper New Englander.

"Thank you...Reverend Sisson." Akamu glanced admiringly at the royal yacht.

Sisson noticed the look. "The King has sent me from Honolulu to collect the custom duties and records from Macomber's safe."

"How is the King?" Akamu asked.

"The King...how is the King? Now that is the central question... isn't it. Best not explained at a shout. Come aboard and I will make it simple so you can understand."

Accustomed to the condescension of patronizing foreigners Akamu simply smiled.

Sisson repeated his invitation in an accent that still reflected his Yankee origins. "Come aboard and sit. I'll join you in a moment. It will be a history lesson for you."

The young man stepped aboard and took a seat on the yacht's fan deck. Akamu's gaze looked beyond the lighthouse and took in the King's stone palace and Long House for counsels. Then Macomber's store nearby on the harbor side of Front Street. Across the street were the stone buildings of the missionary doctor and his clinic. One block north Lahainaluna Road ran up a mile and a half into the hills to his Lahainaluna School. Where the headmaster never tired of saying it was the "oldest high school west of the Mississippi"—even though the school only opened in 1831. Sixteen years ago.

Akamu knew this because the same number of years ago—sixteen—the missionary doctor enrolled him in the school's first class. When Akamu was age ten. He graduated four years later and stayed on for the next twelve years as an editor translating English to Hawaiian after the "first newspaper west of the Rockies" was launched in 1834. Now age twenty-six Akamu's memory flicked through the years that had brought him to today.

Sisson took a seat next to Akamu. Then snapped his fingers as a hypnotist would in a cabaret act to revive a volunteer. "To answer your question…sadly the King bends in whatever direction the wind blows. He is desperate. But with our guidance—"

"Whose guidance is that?" Akamu interjected.

"The King's Privy Council. Three American advisors. And—unofficially—the editor of *The Polynesian* newspaper in Honolulu. We made progress with the Declaration of Rights in 1839. But it proved nothing more than words. In July of that year the King again succumbed to French threats and signed that so-called 'Edict of Tolerance' not to persecute Catholic priests. Abominable."

Akamu focused on Sisson's words. "The French forced the King to pay twenty thousand dollars in reparations. They claimed for the mistreatment of Frenchmen and their priests. With my own eyes I have seen the King quake like a child before a storm." Sisson's voice grew more rapid. He clenched his jaw as he spit out examples of the King's weakness. "That is why we insisted the King sign our Constitution in 1840 to install the Legislative Council and the Privy Council to counterbalance the King's temerity. And allow him to rule as a popular monarch."

Akamu considered the facts. "Our headmaster taught us that

Constitution changed the name from Captain Cook's 'Sandwich Islands' to the 'Hawaiian Islands.'"

Sisson nodded. "Yes. Among many other important things." He paused. "That was one small victory."

Akamu stared at him. Sisson looked absently out to sea.

"To validate the Constitution we sent ambassadors halfway around the world. Thank god." Again Sisson paused. "Our efforts eventually secured recognition by America." He sighed. "But America is powerless against the French or English navies. Again the King waffled. He signed a treaty with England—only to have Parliament reject the occupation five months later!" Sisson ran his hand over his head in a sign of frustration. "The King was constantly summoned to Honolulu like an Indian-rubber string toy. That is why we persuaded him to move his throne from Lahaina to Honolulu in 1845."

Akamu shielded his eyes against the sun's last glare as it bathed Lahaina in sunset. Sisson continued. "Last year was the worst whipsaw. In February the King again bowed to English pressure and agreed to allow grog sales of English rum." The privy advisor gritted his teeth. "Then not two months later in April he signed a pledge with the temperance society of American missionaries in Honolulu. With our encouragement…I should add. The missionaries demanded the King set the highest example. So…they dumped his liquor into the sea. It was the only way we could get the King to understand the sin of drink."

Akamu watched Sisson as the advisor's attention hopped to the next idea like a beach biter looking for its next meal. "Not to be outdone by the English—that next month—after the grog sales agreement—the French returned the twenty-thousand-dollar reparation bond. They claimed it was for 'Hawaiian compliance' with the 1839 edict of tolerance treaty."

"Why now?"

"Clearly 'great powers' have designs on the Hawaiian Islands…the French among them. Otherwise why bother to return the money? Worst of all…the entire twenty thousand dollars has gone missing!"

Akamu stared at Sisson. "How can that be?"

"The French Consul made a great show of presenting the strongbox to the King. I watched them as they opened it with two heavy keys. The coins almost spilled over the top. The chest was closed.

The King ordered his guard to take it to the Treasury at the Customs House in Honolulu's Old Fort."

"What happened?"

"Unknown to anyone a transshipment of lead shot had already been laid in at the Customs House. Soon after someone who had the keys — or had copies of the keys — switched the gold in the strongbox for the lead shot. And made off with the gold coins hidden in the two boxes secreted among dozens of shot cases. The King seemed irritated but not unduly concerned. After all...it was money he never expected to see in the first place."

Akamu protested. "There must have been suspects. An insider? Foreigners? Guards? Custom officers?"

"Or maybe all of them." Sisson nodded in agreement. "Customs House records are incomplete and contradictory — if anything. Yet one entry suggests the lead shot may have been forwarded to Honolulu from Lahaina. It's not clear. What is clear is the gold is gone."

Sisson rose to his feet and leaned his backside against the stern rail. "Now there is another problem. The Pi'ilani pretender. The one who calls himself the Great Kahuna of Moloka'i..."

"Maunakili?"

Again Sisson nodded. "Yes. Maunakili. He has forced the Pi'ilani nobles to spread an *inoa* about his ability to throw sacred ashes of a Hawaiian chief into the ocean. The chant said Maunakili is the rightful King of Maui. Rubbish! Maunakili is a pretender. And not to be trusted. Worst of all...these rumblings came when the King waffled at his worst."

Akamu leaned forward. As a student of native oral history he knew the difference between a storyteller's *mele* song of history and an *inoa* name chant composed to honor a chief. Maunakili was falsely promoting himself. Yet either song or chant could push the Pi'ilani to good or evil. "What will happen next?" Akamu asked.

"Who knows? Anything is possible...the worst nightmare is if a world power pressed their expansion designs as a foreign protector. The King is weak. Powerless. We are all powerless...before the vultures. Hawai'i looks like a *mahi-mahi* steak hung out with a sign: 'Eat me.'" The American privy counselor shook his head. "Unless the forces of good can win over the King's ear."

Akamu noticed Sisson looked haggard and anxious as the sun set beyond the ominous outline of Moloka'i Island across the channel. The darkness of night settled and brought a foreboding stillness over Lahaina. Even the lustrous-feathered 'ō'ō birds were silent.

CHAPTER 49

JOHN BARLEYCORN/GROG SHOP
FRONT STREET/LAHAINA TOWN
NEXT AFTERNOON

BULL SHAW AND KAPU THE UGLY walked through the door of the John Barleycorn. It was their fifth grog shop that afternoon on Fid Street.

Snuff Mitchell wasn't pleased to see the two men. He never was. Under his breath he said: "Look what the cat drug in." With a subtle gesture he directed the pair past the long bar to the oceanside verandah. "Bull…wanna drink?" He eyed Kapu. "You know we don't serve Kanackers here."

The English deserter and mercenary for hire ignored Snuff Mitchell. He and Kapu took two corner seats outside on the *lanai* verandah overlooking the water. "You should be glad to see us." So Bull Shaw began. "Kapu here has been working hard for you all week. Real hard." Kapu the Ugly's tattooed shoulder and upper arm bulged with his personal symbols of black *kākau* shapes: triangular shark teeth and cresting waves. As one of the few remaining native storytellers he could recite the lineage of almost every family on Maui.

Snuff Mitchell wiped out one fid glass and grabbed a bottle. Then poured a fid of strong grog and set it in front of Bull before he sat down at the same table. Snuff let Bull Shaw talk.

"Yeah. Kapu's been busting up farmers' stills. You know the potato...melon...sugar cane *hale* brews that give you a run for your money."

Snuff refilled Bull's glass from across the table.

"Do you have our rent payment today?" Bull asked.

Snuff squirmed slightly in his chair. "Bull...ya knowd I wont hornswoggle you. I'll be straight up. We've been laying in supplies for weeks. You know. You made the deliveries with your potato wagon. Just to be ready for this moment when the full whaling fleet has arrived. Those expenses have taken every penny I have. When the sailors leave port...then I'll have your rent easy."

Bull downed the second fid. And put his empty glass out for refill. "Be a shame if those deliveries stopped just when business was peakin'. Happened to the Rising Sun. Old Jolly Fred didn't pay the pony. Closed same day." Bull swirled his glass. Downed the drink. "You got a nice place here...Snuff." Bull's tone turned menacing. "Be a right shame if a bunch of soaplocks got a little too merry and smashed up the place...all because you brought it on yourself by not paying what the Kahuna asks."

"I hear you...Bull. Just a couple more days."

But Bull ignored him. "Or worse still — looks to me that your little unlicensed grog shop here could run afoul of some temperance violations....Certainly be a shame if the missionaries and newspaper editor and dry sea captains were to hear of that. No telling what kind of repercussions might occur from that public press — eh...Snuff?"

"Ya knowd I'll pony up...Bull. Always do. I'm only askin' this once. A little more time while the full fleet's in anchor."

"Now Snuff. You know how this works. The Kahuna gets special rum shipments at the best price just for shops like you. He passes that savings on to you...because he knows you'll return the favor. Kapu keeps the farmers from distilling *okolehao* and *lami* rum and competing with you. Kahuna keeps the chiefs from brewing too much. You know how?"

"I'm sure you'll tell me."

Bull threw Snuff a broad smile. "If some chief doesn't see eye to eye with the Kahuna...the Kahuna arranges for that chief to be suspended from church. Can you believe it? You know that doesn't sit well with the chiefs' wives. Tongues wag. Never seen a chief yet that didn't give up his still to keep his womanfolk happy."

Bull Shaw laughed. Then leaned in closer to Snuff Mitchell's face. "I hear you've mortgaged this shop to our friend Angus Macomber. Shame if that mortgage was called. Double shame right during the spring season in the Hell of the Pacific — that's what they're callin' Lahaina Town now. 'Hell of the Pacific.' Gonna be a good year... my friend."

Snuff Mitchell caved. Dipped inside his shirt. Handed Bull Shaw a sachet of coins.

"Thanky kindly...Snuff. Pleasure doing business with you."

Bull Shaw rose to his feet. Across the verandah a barmaid squealed. Bull watched a moment. Then charged across the space. Grabbed the guilty sailor by the nape and belt. Pulled him from his barrel. Spun the drunken sailor around. And with a powerful heave threw the sailor over the railing. He landed in six feet of water. Realized where he was. And splashed toward shore spitting saltwater.

At a mirror facing the end of the bar inside Bull Shaw spotted the barmaid straightening her dress before her reflection. Brown hair flowed over her light skin.

"Who's this lovely?" Bull asked no one in particular.

Snuff did not mind supplying the answer. "She comes in to boost the afternoon trade. Sometimes the water-gang boys give her a hard time."

Bull Shaw approached the barmaid and laid his hands on the lovely's bare shoulders. Suddenly a sharp elbow came around fast. And cracked Shaw in the ribs. The grog shop fell silent.

"Keep your hands to yourself...sir. Or you'll be in danger of losing something more."

Bull Shaw caught his breath. "I like a little fire now and then." He snatched the barmaid's wrist. With her free hand the barmaid grabbed a rum bottle. Inverted it by the neck. And wound up: ready to land the bottle on the side of Shaw's skull.

Snuff gathered the barmaid in his arms. Kapu the Ugly wrapped a tattooed arm around Shaw and pulled him away.

"What the dickens?" Shaw said. "This shrew got some fight in her."

He grinned at the feisty barmaid. But the next moment stepped back. "Wait. I've seen you before. You're the one down by the pump. The one givin' come-hither eyes to the sailors. Now lookee here…missy. You keep your bottles to yourself and your mama wont never know what I seen here."

"Go crawl back under that rock where you came from." The barmaid hissed from where she stood behind a corner of the long bar.

Bull Shaw feigned a lunge toward the pretty island maid. But Kapu the Ugly pulled Bull Shaw toward the door and pushed him into the glare outside.

"You crazy…missy?" Snuff asked the barmaid at the end of the bar. "That's Bull Shaw. Not one to tangle with without some help. Though ya sure gave him the mitten. And good."

"He doesn't bother me." The barmaid turned back to the mirror and pretended to admire her dress again. "If there wasn't some danger working Fid Street…where's the fun?"

Snuff Mitchell shook his head. "Take my word. Bull Shaw isn't fun. Or anyone's friend." He extended his hand toward the barmaid. "That's enough excitement for one afternoon." With that he handed the young woman her share of the afternoon take.

The barmaid took the coins. Shook out her brown hair. And flounced saucily out the door into the bright low sunset light of Fid Street.

CHAPTER 50

FOREDECK/*BLACK CLOUD*
LAHAINA ROADS CHANNEL
EVENING/19 MAY 1847

SWIFT. KIKILANI. AND MR. FLUTE stood at the fore rail before the mast. A new scent came to them on the light wind at night's first moment. Fresh. Verdant. Yet pungent somehow. The smell of land. Before them on the port side loomed the two great Maui mountains: Haleakalā and Pu'ukukui. Separated by a vast valley and silhouetted by translucent clouds that hung before the moon in a star-cloud sky. With ease the *Black Cloud* cut through the peaceful channel that ran between Moloka'i and Maui...one of the "eight seas" that tradition said connected the islands and their peoples to each other. Soon the transport entered the Lahaina Roadstead — or 'Au'au Channel — between Lāna'i Island to starboard and Kā'anapali beach. During these last four nautical miles of its five-and-a-half-month voyage the ship glided through the roadstead. A gentle wind pushed them toward the harbor of Lahaina.

"Hear that?" Swift said as she looked toward the dark shoreline.

"What?"

She listened again. "Sounded like splashes...like rocks landing in the ocean."

"That is Puʻuokekaʻa at Kāʻanapali." Kikilani spoke with renewed self-confidence. "The Black Rock is a sacred place where our *mele* songs say the souls of the recently dead jump into the sea after sunset to join their ancestors in the afterworld."

Standing at the port rail Swift screwed up her eyes to look toward the island. In the near distance a craggy promontory jutted darkly into the sea silhouetted against the sky. "There it is again…two splashes this time."

Kikilani looked into the dusk as night settled in. "Could be Menehune."

Swift looked at Kikilani blankly.

"The little people." Kikilani smiled before continuing. "The Menehune are to Hawaiians as the leprechauns are to the Irish. The elders say the Menehune are great builders. Stone walls. Bridges. Roads." She stared quietly into the evening. "They only come out at night. That is why you never see them."

At that moment Swift and Kikilani heard another heavy thump and wash arise from the beach. As if a large cannonball had hit the water.

"Menehune love cliff diving…or so the storytellers say."

Mr. Flute scoffed. "I don't believe in ghosts…or leprechauns. Legends and myths are one thing. But little people? No thanks. I'll take my people full-size and real."

Kikilani shrugged. "Maybe it's only waves against the rocks…or the blowholes of whales."

◎　◎　◎

As the three friends talked and eager sailors stood at the ship's rails Captain Head minded the wheel at the far stern of the ship. A week ago—when he had watched Kikilani dive into the water to swim after Swift—he had seen his carefully orchestrated plot unravel. The *Black Cloud* had luffed its sails and slowed its progress as Kikilani swam vigilantly for her companion. The thought had occurred to Head to simply continue course. Leave Swift. The native girl. And the harpooner to fend for themselves at sea in their small gig boat. But Dawes was on board. Which had made Head reconsider. *Dawes will tell all…Can't have that story come out at the inquest.* To cover his tracks the Captain ordered the zealot seaman Moses Smidt to be taken below and locked in the *lazarette* brig—as had been previously agreed upon. Smidt had clutched his small Bible and shuffled off with the pride of the self-righteous.

Now the Captain's concentration focused on the other ships anchored in Lahaina Harbor. Meanwhile…Dawes slipped away from behind the foremast and made his way to the aft quarterdeck to join the master. Yet kept his gaze trained on Swift. In his fists behind his back he held a belaying pin retrieved from the *Black Cloud*'s aft rigging.

"Looks like we are not the first."

The Captain's eyes swept the calm harbor…searching for a prime anchorage near the breakwater. Scores of ships were anchored throughout this crossroads of the Pacific.

At that moment a swarm of outrigger canoes drew alongside the *Black Cloud* to escort the ship into harbor. Every canoe sported several *kukui* torches that made them look like floating fireflies on a moonlit sea. Each craft seemed to hold a small village of girls and young men: Their warm faces beamed in the mixture of torchlight and starlight outside the breakwater of Lahaina Roads. Finally—at his chosen spot—Captain Head ordered the bosun to drop anchor. After months at sea the *Black Cloud* swung to her anchor's flukes in Lahaina Harbor.

Eager sailors standing at the rails leaned over to catch sight of the native girls in the canoes below them. Moloka'i loomed dark across the channel as the giggling girls scrambled up the *Black Cloud*'s Jacob's ladder and climbed aboard. They deposited multitudes of flower *leis* on every sailor and formed groups of gay welcome. General whooping and hollering rose from the deck. One seaman danced a happy jig.

Dawes turned his gaze away from Swift. "Too many witnesses." Dawes slipped the belaying pin he had been holding into a hole in the aft deck pin rail.

"Be patient…Dawes. Good things come to those who wait."

From the largest of the twin-hull canoes alongside the *Black Cloud* a handsome young islander dressed as a missionary climbed aboard the ship. White twill trousers. Loose black cravat. Turned-down collar. Linen vest now a half size too small for his swimmer's shoulders. By now Mr. Flute. Swift. And Kikilani had moved from the foc's'le deck to midships at the corner of the workshop. Swift scanned the innocent faces of the natives around the main deck…but Kikilani's eyes focused on the face of the young islander. The young native woman immediately raced to him. They leaned in toward each other. Kikilani pressed her nose gently against the handsome islander's. The next moment — together — they inhaled quietly. Drawing in each other's breath. The traditional *aloha* greeting. They whispered in their tongue. Inspected each other at arm's length. Kikilani's hands touched the man tenderly. A pang of envy shot through Swift as she watched the genuine tenderness between Kikilani and young man.

Kikilani led him to Swift and presented her visitor. "Akamu…this is Samantha Swift — my friend from…Philadelphia. Sam…this is Adam Akamu — my…"

After an uncomfortable moment Akamu interjected: "Classmate."

"So happy to meet you." Swift gave Akamu a meaningful smile. "And more relieved to be here than you know."

"When you are ready I will take you both ashore." Akamu spoke in a gentle voice that made Swift think of waves on a quiet beach. "If you haven't arranged lodging…Miss Swift — "

Swift touched Akamu on his sleeve. "Call me Sam."

The rote-schooled Akamu hesitated. Uncomfortable with such easy familiarity. "If you haven't arranged lodging…Miss Sam…let me introduce you and Kikilani to Major Tuckerman and his missus — proprietors of the temperance house near the canal. It's the only genteel guesthouse in Lahaina Town. Just across from the fort."

Swift turned to Mr. Flute standing near the gangway.

"Best to go ashore…" Mr. Flute spoke quietly as his eyes flicked toward the helm. "No telling what could happen on board tonight. I'll organize your cargo and kits. You go now."

Kikilani. Swift. And Adam Akamu climbed down the rope-and-rung ladder into the double-hull canoe from which Akamu had emerged. As Akamu and the canoe's three other paddlers turned the craft into the waves Kikilani pointed to the clouds that capped the mountains ahead. "These clouds are not as I remember."

Akamu sat quietly behind Kikilani. "'Iao Valley is always covered in cloud. But the mist never descends to Lahaina."

"Yes…I know." Kikilani shrugged as she shielded her eyes from the moonshine. "But these clouds are darker… ominous somehow. Is a storm coming?"

"Maybe it is the moonlight." Akamu kept his true thoughts to himself: More likely Kikilani's homeland felt strange after she had run away to the white man's world. He sighed. "You've been at sea too long. It's just mountains."

Swift startled when the boom of the curfew cannon came at them from ashore. "Eight o'clock." Akamu gestured toward the shore in the settling darkness. "The blast was meant as a warning to all sailors to return to their ships. And widely ignored. Just like the temperance rules the curfew represented."

Akamu leaned into his paddle. A note of disdain came into his voice: "To most sailors in the harbor the sound is less a warning shot — and more like a starting gun."

CHAPTER 51

QUARTERDECK/*BOUNTIFUL*
LAHAINA HARBOR/LAHAINA ROADS
THAT SAME EVENING

JACK DANCER AND CAPTAIN POST watched the *Black Cloud* arrive in port. Greeted by a swarm of native canoes. Not long after — their torches flickering — the canoes cleared the ship. Soon a lone canoe with its torch extinguished carried a solitary figure from the *Black Cloud* to the *Bountiful*.

In the settling darkness Dancer's gaze ran along the volcanic ridge carpeted in rich green that formed the backdrop above Lahaina Town. His gaze then dropped into the cavernous gulch of the Rainbow Valley. *Looks mysterious once the sun sets.*

Dancer and Post went below.

Within minutes a man with the easy movements of a seasoned mariner came aboard. Clamping a hand to the satchel strapped across his shoulders he was directed to the Captain's cabin by Billy Mack. Dancer looked up. Slapped the table with both hands. "Last time I saw you was Foggy Bottom back in the Territory of Columbia. I'll be damned."

Dancer stood up and shook hands heartily with Mr. Flute.

"Captain Hamilton Post" — Dancer turned to the Captain —

"let me introduce you to Mr. Flute...of our President's secret service."

Mr. Flute nodded to Post without a flicker of emotion. Touched two fingers to his bald head in salute to the Captain. Then pulled the satchel strap over his head. Rested the bag on the table. While Dancer poured a neat rum for his fellow agent.

Mr. Flute opened the pouch and pulled out a curious parcel that appeared to be a spice shipment. Small enough to fit in a captain's cupboard. "This sewn-jute bundle was delivered to me by canoe within the hour while I was aboard the *Black Cloud*. Came via the American consul in Honolulu. Seems to be addressed to you...Dancer." Stencils on the outside suggested the small parcel traveled by way of an East India Company clipper ship out of Calcutta—via Zanzibar. Around Cape of Good Hope...and Cape Horn. To Hawai'i—on its way to Hong Kong.

Dancer cut the twine. Found a message tucked between the baglets of cinnamon and black pepper. A folded paper bore a red signet only Dancer recognized: the Sultan of Zanzibar's imprimatur.

Dancer broke the wax seal. Then scanned the words written in a feminine hand.

11 January 1847...Stone Town...Zanzibar
LaFleur is spy. Sultan's informants learned of plot to take over Sandwich Islands...dominate North Pacific...local Hawaiian conspirators unknown...probably allied with French. Utmost urgency...and danger. Beware.

Inside the folded message lay a gold filigree earring wrapped in blue silk. This earring matched the one Dancer had found when he finally untied the gold-braided ribbons around the blue-silk bundle Shieka Sharife gave him that last afternoon in the atrium of Sultan's palace in Zanzibar. Proof positive of the sender. Dancer inhaled the smell of jasmine and clove. *Shieka Sharife.* She must have written the note for the Sultan. Damned smart of her to send it by China clipper to Honolulu. Dancer's eyes closed slightly as he again brought the ribbon under his nose. *Too bad it wasn't hand delivered.*

Dancer read Shieka Sharife's last words out loud: " *'If this message finds you in Hawai'i...for your sake—and our American friends— identify conspirators and stop plot at all costs.'* "

Just then the *Bountiful* rocked to a set of waves. Dancer looked at

Post. Then Mr. Flute. "Looks like our little *fandango* isn't just a simple treasure hunt anymore."

Mr. Flute gave Dancer a hard look. "Anything learned following Napoleon's treasure?"

Dancer made a frustrated expression then began to pace. "Been on the treasure's trail for months. First Paris. Then Zanzibar. Followed the trail of Napoleon's right-hand man: Gagnon LeGrand. Best we know is LeGrand had a shipload of treasure. An emperor's ransom. Trail led to Samoa. That's where I met up with Post. Then we gambled on Tahiti."

Hamilton Post passed Dancer's last box of black Oscuro cigars to Mr. Flute. "A new chapter in an old friendship."

"My mission was a treasure hunt. Just find Napoleon's treasure… until now."

Post showed Mr. Flute a map open on his chart table. "My best guess is LeGrand sailed from Tahiti for South America. But got caught in the great hurricane season of 1799. All he had were the charts of La Pérouse — a French explorer who charted the Pacific twelve years before. If LeGrand was blown north…"

"That's wishful thinking." Dancer blew smoke toward the low ceiling. "Puts to the test even La Pérouse's goose chase for a northwest passage."

Post looked down at the old map. "Not that many other logical choices. LeGrand may have been shipwrecked on Maui. But we still need to prove it."

At that moment seaman Billy Mack knocked and opened the cabin door. "Will there be anything else…sir?"

"No." The Captain nodded. "That's all for tonight. Tell the mate to set the standard watches."

"Yes…sir."

Mack paused.

Post looked at the sailor.

"Some men want to go ashore tomorrow…sir. Being as we've not had liberty for a while. And the natives seem…friendly."

"Right. Tell the mate. Relaxed rotations. Four hours each by boat crew. In order of catch on this voyage. First crew can go ashore at 08:00 hours tomorrow. All must be accounted for by curfew cannon at 20:00 hours tomorrow night."

"Thank you…sir." Mack retreated. And left the cabin door open a crack.

Mr. Flute asked: "This LeGrand…what would he have found in Maui almost fifty years ago?"

"Besides the hurricane and being shipwrecked LeGrand couldn't have picked a better time." The seasoned Captain explained: "The great Hawaiian King Kamehameha had defeated the King of Maui the second time in 1795. But it wasn't until 1810 that Kamehameha consolidated his power as first king of all the Sandwich Islands. Thus LeGrand would have arrived when the Pi'ilani—the Hawaiian King's most powerful opponents on Maui and O'ahu—were still smarting from defeat. But before the Hawaiian King had taken control. The Pi'ilani would have welcomed a foreigner's assistance. Maybe even protected LeGrand."

"And hid his gold." Dancer lit another black-wrapped cigar. "But now that there's a plot to overthrow the Hawaiian King…finding the treasure is only part of the story." Dancer expelled a worried cloud of smoke. "We must be sure Napoleon's treasure doesn't fall into the hands of someone who could use it to their advantage…like bribe the King to surrender." Dancer looked at the cigar he rolled between his thumb and fingertips. Then lowered his voice as if he was whispering a secret. "The Shieka wrote: 'Stop the plot at all costs.' How the hell am I supposed to do that?"

Captain Post raised his chin toward Mr. Flute. "How about you… Flute? Smooth sailing?"

Mr. Flute described his voyage. The strange death of Duffy Ragsdale. How an island girl and her traveling companion almost got tossed overboard at Cape Horn by the mate Ratter Dawes. "That's the first time my harp came in handy." Mr. Flute shook his head. "Then not a week back—when we were just off the eastern shore of the Big Island of Hawai'i—an oaf of a sailor did toss the traveling woman overboard. Tossed some shark chum after her too. If it hadn't been for quick work and the powerful swimming of the island lass…that city girl would have been in Jones' Locker right now. I reached them just as the tiger sharks began to close. Got one with my harpoon. Gave us time to pull both the woman into the gig boat."

Post picked up the bottle of brandy from the table and topped off Mr. Flute's fid.

"Strangest thing. The oaf was sent to the brig. Seemed proud of his handiwork. That was the last we seen of him. Seems he committed suicide with his scrimshaw blade that night. I never got a chance to hear him sing."

"Did the city girl deserve getting the heave-ho?" Dancer quipped. "Maybe she didn't show the lads a proper good time?"

Mr. Flute turned up his rope-calloused palms. "The city woman used a cover saying she was out of Philadelphia and an investor to some island madam. Got an entire cargo hold of lady's things. Don't think Dawes and Head bought it....She finally confided that she is from New York. Forever working her pencil. Writes for the *Brooklyn Daily Eagle*...I think I seen. Sent back dispatches from the tropics in the Atlantic and Juan Fernandez Island off Chile. Believe she uses a pseudonym."

Dancer started. "What name does she use?"

Mr. Flute paused. "Sounds like a gentleman's name. Probably gives her license to be a scribbler. Doubt you've seen it...S. Thomas Swift."

Dancer's jaw dropped. "The same Swift who scooped all the foreign correspondents at the battle of Matamoros?"

Post and Mr. Flute exchanged bewildered glances. Mr. Flute wrinkled his brow as he cracked his knuckles. "All I know is I had my hands full keeping her alive...."

Post gave his head a tilt with a questioning expression. "What brings you to Lahaina...Mr. Flute?"

The veteran agent ran a hoary hand over his perspiring pate. "The Foggy Bottom Boys put me aboard to treasure hunt in Hawai'i... in case Dancer never picked up the trail." A half smile came to Mr. Flute's sunburnt face as he shot Dancer a look. "Didna take long to see Swift and her Hawaiian friend were on their own...and at the mercy of the sailors."

Dancer asked: "Do you think Head was behind it somehow?"

"Can't pin the donkey on Head. But he's a hoister that'd go the whole hog if I ever smelled one."

"How about Dawes?"

"Definitely Dawes. Came within a blade of skewering the bugger myself." Mr. Flute put his empty fid down near the brandy bottle. Dancer did the honors this time. "Haven't dared get a wink at night since Cape Horn where I hung Dawes over the bulwark until he told us who put him up to it. Said it was a dandy stranger in New York City. Wore a sapphire pinky ring." Dancer and Post exchanged glances. "Swift thinks the stranger was her uncle...a newspaper man."

"Who's the island girl?"

"Calls herself Kikilani. Says she was abducted from Lahaina."

Post remembered the incident. "May 1845. Almost two years now. There was talk among the masters of another girl named Loki."

Mr. Flute nodded. "The whalers called her Rose. Lost at sea some said."

"Never heard what became of either of them." Post frowned.

Mr. Flute gave a long look in which vague disquiet was apparent. "Swift says they were kidnapped and Kikilani was sold into the sex trade."

Dancer chimed in: "Reminds me of my last night in New York City. I stopped by the Paradise Palace to see Queen Tin'a for a tub and a rub...."

"Now the truth comes out." Post grinned broadly at his jest.

"Bit of a hubbub over a missing ledger the madam kept." Dancer remembered the night well. "Ran into Swift. Fortunately we made it out alive...given a Maori rascal with a *moko* tattoo that kept order in the Palace. Seems to me we parted ways in the alley." Dancer rubbed his jaw. "So that was you...Mr. Flute...tending that four-wheeled brougham carriage? Neat getaway with Swift and the island girl — if I'm not mistaken."

"Don't know how you keep your gin joints straight...Dancer." Mr. Flute winked knowingly. "But that's the sum of it."

"I'll be damned. So we meet again." Dancer's utterance was directed at no one in particular. "What's your stunt this time...Swift?"

CHAPTER 52

MACOMBER'S CHANDLERY
LAHAINA POINT
NEXT DAY

ABNER SISSON normally liked the smell of a ship chandlery. Oiled instruments. Machine-spun rope. It smelled of progress. But not today. Sisson walked out of the missionary compound and across Front Street onto Lahaina Point. *Why is it — in this Garden of Eden — that heat. Dust. Fleas. And mosquitoes mar the salubrious climate of Lahaina Town?* A little more than two hundred yards beyond the wharf was the spot where the narrow dog-legged reef break regularly dumped newly arrived seamen into the harbor. Mostly nonswimmers. Only to be saved by islanders. Who terrified the sailors with pantomimes of sharks.

On the street south of Macomber's chandlery heavy water barrels being rolled along Fort Street gave up a dull rumble like far off thunder. As always — day and night — Fort Street was obstructed with casks. Some empties waited in line to be filled at the missionary's pump. Other full casks were continuously rolled back aboard tenders at the landing.

The King's advisor entered the chandlery yards. The King's well-irrigated taro patch — bordered within a low mud wall — ran alongside him. Soon he entered Macomber's warehouses. The long storerooms were filled chockablock. Rope coiled in six-hundred-foot lengths. Hauling blocks and tackle. Turnbuckles. Anchor balls. Hoops. Caulking irons. Copper sheets to keep ship worms from turning wooden hulls into sieves. Barrels of every type and size stacked several rows high. Slack casks and hogsheads made of softwoods for dry cargo. Sisson knew these barrels arrived filled with potatoes on the outbound journey to Lahaina. Apples. Crockery. Huge 256-gallon "tun" barrels bounded by sturdy iron bands stood ready to hold lucrative liquids. Spirits. Molasses. Water. Others contained turpentine. Varnish. Oil. Pitch. Tar. And a noxious fluid inside barrels marked *PAINT OIL* that jolted his nostrils.

As he stepped into the ship chandlery itself and its accompanying general mercantile store Sisson breathed in the smells of commerce and the sea. Everything a vessel or seaman could need was for sale here: The merchandise was especially useful for whalers. Sisson sidestepped bins of salted fish. Beef and pork. Ship's hardtack biscuits. Bags of onions. Flour. And jars of spices. All casting off aromas. Next: Tobacco. Pipes. Cigars filled an entire glass showcase to one side. Beside them candles were arrayed neatly beside boxes of Lucifer matches. Dozens of buckets filled with bolts. Nails. Screws lined the floor beneath the vital goods. Above—on shelves—sat blankets. Clothing. Boots. Knives. Next to tools. Hardware. Glass buoys. Lanterns hung from rafters. Drawers were stuffed with logbooks. Inkstands. Beeswax. Needles. Canvas. Below other tables were baskets of string. Rope. Cloth. And more canvas. On the far wall a board displayed every size and type of brush needed on a ship. The natural bristles as yellow as a virgin's locks. A separate locked glass display—as though guarding the crown jewels—presented polished velvet-lined boxes with a selection of sextants and marine chronometers.

Sisson paused in the northern side doorway under the store's inner verandah. With several long strides he crossed the sandy alley. Stepped onto the covered porch of the Customs House. Lahaina's center of commerce and government was a low fifty-foot-long adobe-brick structure situated perpendicular to the chandlery. Two windows and a center door faced the taro patches near Front Street and the mountains two miles uphill. Beyond the Customs House stood the grass-thatched *hale mua* meeting house. Sisson coughed. A haze mixed with Lahaina's dust. The advisor's gaze took in the thatch longhouse. He mused for a moment how he had guided the Hawaiian Bill of Rights and its attachment of laws in that very *hale* almost eight years ago. That political statement led to the kingdom's Constitution a year later.

Abner Sisson entered the Customs House. He acknowledged three sea captains seated to his left at a simple table against the front wall opposite the customs counter: They scratched answers onto the official forms of his own design. Arrival date. Ship's name. Master. Origin port. Months out. Every port of call during their voyage. Number of men on board. Barrels of whale oil taken this season. Here customs collected 12½ percent duty on every barrel entering Hawai'i. Each ship filed papers before a vessel could unload cargo or put to sea. These in turn were duly recorded in ledgers kept behind glass-doored shelves behind the counter. New arrivals also paid the mooring fee to the Harbor Master—Angus Macomber. Shielded by the counter in the back corner stood the great vault. Its heavy doors ajar. Open for business. Inside…the iron box held the captains' fees. Customs duties. And government papers.

From the entrance Sisson glanced straight ahead through an open rear door that revealed a platform holding a scale. This scale could be carted to the wharf to be taken onboard a ship before the ship's cargo was unloaded. Or taxed. Goods destined for transfer to other ports were brought to Macomber's public stores warehouse. Where they remained until either proper duty was paid to Customs Collector Macomber. The freight was loaded onto another vessel for transshipment to another port. Or the "unclaimed" goods sold at auction. Storage. Drayage. Auction services. And "scale fees" all lined Macomber's pocket as shipping agent for supposedly favored shipping lines. Not to mention "consular fees" to facilitate transactions between sellers and buyers by American Consul Angus Macomber.

Off to the side—opposite the captain's counter: at the far end of the Customs House—Macomber's "mail forwarding agency" garnered even more activity. Captains claimed bags of long-held mail and emptied the contents onto a broad sorting table against the wall beside the entrance. These were counted by the rail-thin clerk. Himself a former missionary teacher. Every ship's master paid the postmaster's two-cent "ship fee" per piece. All other individual travelers—with letters kept scrupulously separate from island residents' mail — had to call separately at Macomber's mail house to inquire after any recently arrived letters. Postage was paid upon receipt. All carefully kept in Macomber's vault.

Outbound postage "single" letter — one sheet of paper — carried a fee of ten cents. Plus the two-cent ship fee. Two sheets of paper were a "double" letter...at double the price. Three sheets of paper were a "triple" letter...at three times the postage. And so on. To economize Sisson himself developed the skill of using tissue-thin paper. Writing first horizontally across each page. Then crosswise vertically to make a cheaper missive. But that solution required head-scratching concentration to decipher. After letters from home: Newspapers were particularly prized. Macomber sold these publications at his own price schedule. Discounted — as a public service — one penny for every month out of date.

The wiry clerk tossed outgoing letters into five neatly labeled bags hanging from frames: Missionary mail. Consular office. Whaler. Customs House/Post Office. And mercantile. Senders insisted their mail not be mixed for fear they might be personally identified with the wrong group. As customary...the missionary bag was empty. To Macomber's chagrin. The missionaries preferred to forward their own mail. In fact four thousand stampless letters had sailed from Lahaina. Sent free by ink-stained island missionaries. In 1845 alone.

Sisson shook his head. His own handiwork from the Organic Act of 1846 had set up the postal system across the kingdom. Rates were fixed. Yet he knew it would be years before the inflamed boil of Macomber's ex-officio monopolies might be lanced and divested. Merchant. Customs Collector. Harbor Master. Postmaster. And Superintendent of the Seamen's Hospital.

The words of the King came to him. "The life of the land is perpetuated in righteousness."

If not greed.

CHAPTER 53

CUSTOMS HOUSE & EXCHANGE
LAHAINA POINT
A SHORT WHILE LATER

ANGUS MACOMBER ushered the last straggler out of the Customs House. Dismissed the two clerks. Closed the doors. Locked his vault. As the sun set across the roadstead beyond the shoulder of Moloka'i his bony fingers made it difficult to light a solitary lamp. While Abner Sisson quietly clenched his jaw as he considered the conversation to come. Joining Sisson and Macomber around the mail sorting table in the privacy of the Customs House was Charlie Pickham: first son of the missionary doctor.

"Maybe we've done all we can for the King." Sisson shrugged. "We supported him. Counseled him. Pushed him for codes of law."

"Yet still some old-faith non-Christian chiefs and foreigners opposed us." Macomber's tone was ingenuous.

Pickham leaned in with his slight unprepossessing frame. He was nearer forty than thirty — and his keen blue eyes gave a shrewd foxlike look as if he was reading your every thought. "Even in Europe traders and the merchant class resisted the political authority of the kings. It is the right of liberty and freedom to be heard."

"There are good people on both sides." Sisson pressed the point.

"Missionaries pushed for constitutional reform. A legislative council. Courts. Rules. Laws. It is why the capital was moved from Lahaina to Honolulu. Because that is where the power is."

"That cracker barrel committee they call the Privy Council did what it could to look out for commercial interests." Macomber was only half joking. "As progress is made it's natural for the patrician classes to want land…Profits. They are the future of the islands."

"Our course is clear." Pickham held no reservations. "As they said in the Legislative Council: All things must be considered. Religion. Economic development. Cultural superiority. Even the difference between the white and the brown races."

Sisson wrung his hands "Bringing order out of chaos is our highest calling. Land ownership is paramount now…a rational… legal…universal system. It is fundamental for a true nation. Without it anarchy wins. There can be no stability without rational land ownership…."

"Look how the natives have died off. Much of the land is unoccupied. Unworked." Macomber's words added to the agreeable echo chamber. "At last a land reform plan has been settled. Next year it will be the law of the islands."

Pickham agreed as he struck a match. He found lighting a cigarette a convenient veil for disguising the quick glances he used to read others' true motivations. "Fairness was the byword behind all changes. The Great Mahele will shape the Kingdom of Hawai'i for generations."

"It is reasonable." Sisson was insistent. "Without reason and rules and law and order—any progress is lost…Civilization falls into decline. The future is bleak without land reform."

Pickham tempered his enthusiasm with a facade of evenhandedness. "The new Land Division laws are just. Out of fairness all lands are now required to be surveyed. Every plot survey must be registered. Every *kuleana* homesteader must bring two witnesses to confirm he works the land. That is logical. Clear. Certification confirms fact. Without verification—there can be no certainty…So it is for all claims. By *kuleana*. Chiefs. Or the kingdom."

Macomber concurred. "Costs should be paid by those who benefit: the chiefs and the native landholders."

Sisson's words betrayed his doubts: "But many surveys were poor.

Boundaries overlapped. Some parcels were separated. Not contiguous. The entire process required the owner to have the ability to read. Understand the written word…"

"Growing pains are to be expected." Pickham dipped his head as a sarcastic little smile hovered around his thin lips. Then watched his cigarette ashes drop to the stained floor. "If the Kanakas can't follow the system…that is their loss. They can dispute the ownership. There is a clear appeal process. That's fair."

"It's as if the natives are being made outlaws in their own land." Sisson shook his head. "Land rights. Surveys. Registrations. Property taxes."

Pickham persisted—which lent his cunning face a momentary earnestness: "Of course—as I said—there will be growing pains. Even infractions. Of course there will be missed deadlines. But without those rules it will never be possible to determine if vacant parcels are occupied or inherited or abandoned without clear claims."

"Yes…there may be a handful that push unscrupulous claims." Sisson was clearly worried. "I've seen that some bad actors approached an extended family. Told them they will be paid for their land—in return for a signature. They don't have to do a thing now. No map. No forms. Nothing. The family does not work the land anyway. To receive the *makana* gift—the family was told—all they must do is sign a paper."

"Trust is essential." Pickham's voice was hard and incisive. "Having a respected name is invaluable. I've learned that. If they don't sign—and don't work the land—how can the government expect any native to prove they own that parcel? Those who do not register—who miss the deadline…or who cannot prove legal ownership—must be evicted as squatters. Don't you agree?"

Macomber examined his fingernails. "If the land is unoccupied or unworked—either from neglect or death or for nonpayment of property taxes—then it's proper that title to that land should be forfeited—and made available to those who do meet the government's requirements. It's simple justice."

"Many natives will never understand that distinction." Sisson muttered his response quietly.

"Land reform is for their own best interest." Macomber nodded firmly. "Everyone wins either way. If they register — they own the land. They can live on it. Work it. They can even sell their land to another Hawaiian or to foreigners. If they do not register — someone else who pays for the title or pays the taxes has a right to register the parcel as theirs. Much of the land is abandoned anyway."

"With the natives killed off in droves and so much land abandoned now is our chance." Pickham gave a dry rasping little laugh. "Only the rule of law — and foreigners — can save these islands from collapse."

Macomber agreed. "Only white men can turn it to a productive use. At least the *kuleana* homesteaders will have steady jobs — whether it's cane or taro or sandalwood or pineapple."

"Steady work will give them steady values. Work is the only thing that will help these savages make something of themselves." In his enthusiasm Pickham thumped the Customs House table. "Like the poor anywhere. Hard work is their salvation. Not the return to their island sloth and pagan profligacy."

"There is one great problem..." Sisson said with a voice not raised above a whisper.

All three nodded with understanding. None of the three trusted Maunakili. But Maunakili's influence with natives was crucial to land reform — and to the trio's plans. They knew Maunakili needed allies to join his rebellion. But they needed him too...specifically to dispose of the young King. Perhaps the most worrisome aspect was the rumored claim by Maunakili that his nobility — as he called it — was a noble claim to Crown land that was a superior claim to others' rights. To tenants. Chiefs. And governments. A right that could not be extinguished by mere rules and laws. The three had heard Maunakili claim the King himself had forsaken his *mana*. His sacred all-pervasive right to the kingdom...a sacred energy given by the old gods. The King's noble *mana* was broken when he embraced Christianity. Or so Maunakili claimed. For Maunakili's followers the Hawaiian King was little more than a forsaken heretic.

"Most of the Pi'ilani chiefs and old believers already treat Maunakili like a king." Sisson stated the fact with a quiet stoicism.

With astute judgment Pickham offered a warning: "Maunakili said he is with us...But never trust the devil until the deal is done. He may have something evil up his sleeve that could ruin our plans."

Macomber added: "Stopping Maunakili will not be that easy...Charlie."

"No. But a rebel king is a necessary evil...Angus. If we want land division to serve the whole kingdom then we must make absolutely certain the King serves all of his subjects. If you get my meaning. Being the son of a do-no-wrong missionary doctor has its privileges." Pickham crushed the remains of his cigarette beneath his fine shoe. "And privilege is on our side."

CHAPTER 54

THE GHOSTS of Pu'uhonua whispered through the Place of Refuge as the soft wind rustled the coconut palms. Maunakili sat serenely beneath a *ti*-leaf canopy. Here Keoua — high chief of Kona from the previous generation — was said to take his favorite rest. Situated on a tongue of black lava that had flowed from the ancient Mauna Loa volcano the refuge protruded into the western Kona Coast. Maunakili's gaze surveyed the place where water. Heaven. And earth met to shelter men. Where the surf and lava flats meant refuge. Isolated beside the shore by a barren slope that inclined three miles before it reached the cooler green hills of the Hawai'i island.

The sacred Place of Refuge formed a small cove off Hōnaunau Bay four miles south from where Keoua's ancestors dispatched the murderous Captain James Cook at Kealakekua Bay. The sparse shade of the coconut palms danced starkly over the white sand and black rock. Here protected were the sacred residences of the old *ali'i* ruling chiefs. Safe behind a great L-shaped black lava wall ten-feet high and seventeen-feet thick built three hundred years before. But it was not the stone barrier that bestowed sanctity to this refuge. Maunakili knew it was the bones of the chiefs buried here. And their *mana*. The spiritual power of the second chance.

The same second chance that fueled Maunakili's obsession.

Maunakili smiled to himself. No blood could be spilled in this sacred compound. That is…if you could survive the gauntlet of the gods. Here noncombatants fleeing death by an enemy devoted to extermination were safe. Here warriors defeated in war were safe. Here offenders of *kapu*—guilty of looking at a chief or walking in a chief's footsteps…or women eating the food of men—were safe. Safe from the penalty of death. A death required to appease the gods whose slightest affronting could trigger violent volcanic eruptions. Tidal waves. Famine. Or earthquakes. Only here. Safety. Absolution. Safe return home. Reasons to give thanks to the old gods.

Landward—outside the wall—stood the royal grounds. Soft sand warmed the feet of workers who harvested fish from the mixed spring water and saltwater ponds. Or pounded taro in *kanoa* bowls carved into the rock. Shelters and temples of *ʻohiʻa* wood tied with coconut-fiber and shaded by *ti*-leaf thatching stood on stone platforms. There Maunakili's chiefs and warriors idled. The Piʻilani King's great voyage canoes lined the sand near the royal cove. The spirit of the *puʻuhonua* refuge was again respected by all.

Maunakili understood that times changed. New ways tried…then abandoned. He also knew it had been twenty-eight years. Twenty-eight years since the King's older brother abandoned the old ways. For twenty-eight years the old temples of the refuge had been left to disappear. Sea. Wind. Sun did their worst. But no more.

The Restorer had come.

Maunakili rose from Keoua's shelter. Made his way along a soft sandy path that ran between beds of razor-edged lava. As he passed the thatched *hale o keawe* temple he touched his feathered cloak. In that temple the bones of twenty-three *aliʻi* chiefs rested. He stood beside the *lele* tower that held offerings to the gods. At that moment Kapu the Ugly came up beside Maunakili.

The royal storyteller cleared his throat tentatively. "Several days ago—before Bull Shaw and I left Lahaina—I saw a native woman in town…she had returned to Maui on a whaling transport. To be sure I asked several trusted spies to observe her more closely."

Maunakili looked down on Kapu with cold eyes.

The storyteller was quick to reveal his discovery. "They also saw what I saw: We believe she is the lost Pi'ilani princess." Kapu hesitated then continued. "She goes by the name: Kikilani."

A slight sparkle flickered in Maunakili's eyes. Then a deep breath swelled his broad chest. *The gods are smiling.* Another piece of his plan had fallen into place.

Maunakili was about to press Kapu to tell him more about the Pi'ilani princess — Kikilani. But at that moment Maunakili's eyes narrowed as he watched outside the cove: A long boat was being lowered from a large French frigate of war. Quickly the foreign sailors stroked the craft toward the royal canoe landing. From the sharp lava of the Place of Refuge Maunakili watched his future come ashore: Henri Malbec. Maunakili had chosen this sacred refuge to meet secretly with the Frenchman.

As Malbec came ashore then walked up the sand toward the temple Kapu the Ugly thought the two men had a similar manner. Malbec older slightly. Tall. Whip thin. Not the muscled giant like Maunakili. Both swarthy. Suntanned. Kapu thought: *In this noon sun the Frenchman almost has an islander's looks.* Maunakili's body tattooed half black looked the fierce warrior. Yet Hawaiian. *Different men. Yet something similar.* Their gait? Their hands? As Malbec and Maunakili faced each other Kapu saw they shared pale gray eyes. Reptilian eyes. Bleached by the unrelenting sun. Kapu felt an unsettling shiver in the strong light.

"Impressive artwork." Malbec gestured with a dismissive wave at Maunakili's tattoos. "Was the artist eaten by cannibals before he could finish?"

Maunakili ignored the insult. He beckoned Malbec to take a seat on the far side of a large *konane* stone. Alternating black lava and white coral stones had already been placed in small indentions to form a checkboard pattern. Malbec understood. *Konane* was part checkers. Part chess. All strategy.

Malbec took a seat to play the black pieces. Without hesitation he made the first move: a single leap-frog capture. Then removed Maunakili's white piece — and smiled to himself. *Not too fast. Let the monkey think he can win.* Maunakili responded: a multiple-capture move that stayed in the required straight line. He scooped up Malbec's black pieces. Gradually a clatter of markers grew in a basket near each man's feet. After multiple turns Malbec hesitated. He was not able to make a move that would capture any white stones. Neither right. Left. Forward. Or back. Stymied. By rule Maunakili won the first game. The tattooed chief smiled. Nodded as if to say: "Again?"

Malbec adjusted his feet wider in the sand. Reset the table. Settled a glare on the island pretender. "Your play…Kanaka."

Bull Shaw joined Kapu the Ugly outside the temple to watch the two men play. As Maunakili and Malbec played—each circling the other's pieces like a shark circles its prey—they talked.

"Your payment must be complete by the end of May." Malbec's words reflected his disdain. "You *do* know what a calendar is… don't you?"

"That is my intention…Malbec."

"Good. If not by Thirty-One May…then no deal. It's that simple."

"You have brought only one warship." Maunakili nodded toward the cove. "And from its look your vessel also does duty as a prisoner ship. Does it not?"

"What you see is the key to your kingdom…Maunakili." Malbec jabbed his forefinger into his palm. "But first there must be payment. Without payment—you will not have the French Navy protecting your back."

Maunakili countered as he captured another black marker from the table: "And without my *mana* and my men to take back our rightful kingdom…your King will not have an island ally who works with the French." He repeated the threat: "The French…instead of the British or Americans."

"Money talks…Maunakili. Without it your little dream will go the way of the steam clouds over Mauna Loa."

The Pi'ilani chief scoffed. "What is most important is land. Land…more than money. I will restore the Kingdom of the Pi'ilani before the land reform pushed by the foreigners takes hold. My pure heirs will rule for generations. Only then will we protect the islands from the American and English vultures—and benefit from French protection in the kingdom's foreign affairs. I know you understand…Malbec."

In the next moment Maunakili pointedly replaced one of his white stones on the *konane* board with a gold coin. Then took the coin in his right hand and made another multiple capture. In a stroke he swept six of Malbec's black pieces off the board. In that movement Malbec spotted a purplish stain on Maunakili's forearm. His left hand grabbed Maunakili's wrist. Bent back the warrior's hand. Simultaneously four Maui warriors touched their *leiomano* clubs. Almost hidden by the warrior-cut-in-two's intricate black tattoo Malbec made out a birthmark. *This cannot be.* For a long moment Malbec held Maunakili's arm. *Ridiculous. I...Henri Malbec...cannot possibly be related to some stupid island half-breed.* Malbec shook his head. *Impoyssible.* Then Malbec dropped Maunakili's wrist.

Maunakili believed the white man had merely been challenging the play he had made on the *konane* board. With an air of triumph the rebel chief picked up Malbec's markers one by one — until only the gold coin remained on the checkerboard stone.

The time had come. Maunakili motioned to Bull Shaw and Kapu the Ugly. The two men ducked into the temple. Then returned in a moment. Each carried a heavy wooden case stenciled *Lead Shot.*

Shaw opened the first case. A small fortune of gold coins lay within. Twenty franc pieces. Fifty franc pieces. An occasional silver franc coin shone through the golden horde. Shaw shook the case gently as he held it: A golden shimmer shot quietly through the sea air.

Kapu the Ugly opened the second chest. Again a small fortune lay inside. He too shook the case. A soft golden shimmer arose from the brilliant sunlight.

Malbec stared. He recognized the coins. They were the monies France returned to the Hawaiian King in Honolulu months before as reparations for their 1839 treaty.

Maunakili no longer smiled. "You may rule the sea today... Malbec. But the Great Kahuna has a long reach throughout the Islands. The reach that you need."

"And only France has the power of their warships to give you what *you* need." He gestured disdainfully at the money. "How did a savage come by this gift to the King?"

Maunakili waved away the question. "What is mine is mine. It only needs to be taken."

In the hot air of the sea Malbec and Maunakili glared at each other.
Then each man stood.

Malbec hissed. "This is only a fraction of our agreed price."

"That is all there is...Malbec."

"You know — and I know — that is not true. No...there is more."
Malbec pointed a long finger at Maunakili's tattooed chest. "Much
much more." He waited a moment. For he knew for certain now.
All those months ago...Admiral Messimer had been right. It was here.
Napoleon's treasure was here! "Bring me Napoleon's treasure and this
stolen down payment will not go for nothing. Only if you provide all
of the treasure will the French Navy be at your back in Lahaina when
the whalers leave the harbor."

Maunakili bent down...smiled...and picked up his winning gold
coin from the *konane* stone. He rose to his full height.

"Your blood money will be ready for you."

"Without it" — Malbec nodded pointedly — "you get nothing."

With a dismissive snap of his fingers Malbec ordered the cases
carried to the long boat. Maunakili's men hesitated. Maunakili nodded.
The men did what their king asked.

Malbec returned to the cove and boarded his long boat. With his
foot upon one of the treasure cases the Frenchman turned toward
Maunakili as the proud chief stood nearby.

"Attendez...metis."

Malbec drew a pistol from his belt. Raised the weapon over his
head. And fired a single shot into the air. Almost simultaneously two
squads of men on the prison frigate in the waters of the cove behind
him put their shoulders to the fore and aft capstans. The great drums
turned. Cables — run from the capstans through pulleys on the
foremast and mizzenmast spars — snapped straight. From out of the
tween-deck cages of the frigate rose a shackled figure: legs first. Even
from a distance Maunakili could see the wretched prisoner wore the
blue-striped long-sleeved blouse and soiled white pants of a French
sailor. His body kicked and twisted in protest as he rose upside down.
Each ankle fettered and hooked to a line that slipped through a sheave
block attached to the farthest ends of two yardarms that extended out
above the water of the cove. The lines then ran taut to the two capstans
being operated by the squads of men.

Across the blue cove a breeze carried to shore the straining creak of the capstans. Malbec faced Maunakili and shouted derisively: "Remember…Great Kahuna! If you do not deliver Napoleon's treasure by the thirty-first of May there will be no French Navy for your kingdom." Malbec pointed his empty pistol toward the yardarms. "And you will beg for my mercy."

Screams for mercy indeed came from the tortured figure. Steadily the bloodless lines running from the yardarms to the prisoner's ankles tightened. Quickly the pain rose in pitch as Malbec's premeditated demonstration proceeded. Soon the sailor's legs were drawn beyond endurance…The screams rose in unbearable agony. The next moment the figure was split in two. The capstan drums snapped against their notched ratchet brakes. From the limp end of each line dangled part of the broken man. Two soldiers cut the loose lines. The ropes whipped through the pulleys. Dropped from the yardarm spars. The larger torso section fell with a heavy splash into the clear waters. Followed by the lighter leg and line. Instantly the blood-red cloud attracted a swirl of shark fins. Followed by a brief frenzy. Then — nothing.

Malbec wet his lips and enjoyed the horrified look on the faces of the natives watching from the shoreline. With his left hand he twisted his right sleeve to ease a strange sensation that radiated from the turtle-shaped birthmark on his lower arm. His high-pitched voice carried a sarcastic sneer as he shouted: "Maunakili! That is the fate that awaits all of you should you not meet Malbec's deadline. Be warned!"

With that cold-blooded ultimatum Malbec's launch shoved off from the beach. From a short distance he repeated his warning: "By the last day of May! Or France will take the islands for herself!"

Maunakili winced. Not from the Frenchman's demand. A searing pain — like a hot iron pressed against his skin — had spread outward from the birthmark on his forearm. He stood expressionless as he massaged his forearm and watched the Frenchman's boat pull toward the diffused red cloud that lapped the black hull. Then climbed aboard the dark prison frigate.

After a few moments Maunakili turned to look at a dumbfounded Bull Shaw and Kapu the Ugly. "Do not be afraid. Fear is the foreigners' only weapon. The Gods know our cause is righteous. Not Malbec's evil."

The great chief pivoted in the sand. Then led Shaw and Kapu back along the fine white-sand path lined by black lava into the sacred *pu'uhonua* refuge. As he walked under the *ti*-leaf canopy his voice was low and determined. "My great-grandmother told me: My father was shipwrecked...blown onto Maui. When he recovered he was in Makena. All had been lost. His ship. Crew. Even the treasure he had protected halfway around the world." Maunakili recalled his great-grandmother's story as if it had happened yesterday. "We must find that treasure or this chance to restore the Pi'ilani and the people's rightful king could slip through our fingers. That must not happen."

"Who could have taken the treasure?" Shaw asked.

Maunakili considered. "It was millions in gold. Jewels. Coins. So said my great-grandmother."

Shaw whistled. "That much treasure doesn't just disappear overnight!"

Maunakili nodded. "I am convinced. The only one who could have stolen the treasure was the King. No one else would have the power."

Kapu nodded in agreement. "Or the ability to hide it."

Shaw wondered aloud: "Where could the King have buried it? Makena? Olowalu? The Seamen's Hospital?"

"The King thinks it is safe. But has not dared to move it."

Bull Shaw and Kapu the Ugly offered to twist some of the old chiefs' arms to obtain the information they were seeking. "Get some answers. Find out what the old men say. Eliminate the obvious."

Maunakili turned again to the waters of the cove. And watched as the French frigate *Némésis* lowered sail. "Now that the King has abandoned Lahaina for Honolulu there is only one hiding place for such a treasure. That place is the royal compound...where all commoners and foreigners are forbidden." He nodded with certainty and touched Kahekili's golden earring. "The treasure is in the *Moku'ula*."

"If it's hidden in the *Moku'ula*" — Bull Shaw smiled knowingly — "the treasure is unguarded."

Maunakili nodded again. "That is true. There are no warriors. No guards. The King thinks it is protected by tradition. And by his royal *mana*. All we must do is take it. That is why the treasure is not our only objective. The Pi'ilani princess is another fruit we will pluck at the same time."

CHAPTER 55

CUSTOMS HOUSE & EXCHANGE
LAHAINA POINT
22 MAY 1847

SAMANTHA SWIFT rode up to Lahaina Point on horseback. Flushed from her first ride onshore. She wore her black flat-brimmed *cordobes* hat. Wide-legged *gaucho* pants to mid-calf. And soft boots. Gifts from Don Carlo Juan Baptiste in Matamoros Mexico just a year before. She pushed the hat back to hang on her shoulders by its drawstring. Wiped her forehead. And smiled broadly as her spirits soared. Swift inhaled a lungful of dry hot air. Then cleared her throat gently of the fine lava dust. Her fingertips stroked the firm leather of her Western saddle. At last she enjoyed the exhilaration of feeling at home. With a horse under her. Not the sea.

Swift patted the livery mount's withers. Then tied the mare's reins to the chandlery fence. A tuneful hum came from her lips as she untied the saddle strings that held her Mexican-textile bag. She slipped the woven band across her shoulders. Then strode toward the low Customs House building.

Swift stepped onto the porch and through the entrance doorway. At the simple wood table two whaling captains leaned over Sisson's forms. Swift moved to the customs counter. Found a cargo form and glanced at the *Entries and Clearances* book. Then stepped to the small table. Swift spoke with confident aplomb: "May I join you gentlemen?" The two New England masters began to rise to their feet. "Please. Be seated." She took the third chair at the worn table against the wall.

"I've just arrived. We sailed on the *Black Cloud* out of New York." Swift nodded toward the customs counter. "If I am not mistaken… after a glance at the Entries log…is one of you Master Page of the bark *America?*"

The bearded captain nearest Swift touched his cap. "Ma'am. William Page from New Bedford. Nine months out." His weathered hands rested on the partially completed Harbor Master form. "One hundred barrels of sperm and three-hundred seventy-five barrels of whale oil. Bound for New Zealand once we transfer our barrels."

Swift shifted her gaze to the tall master across the table from her. "You then…sir…would be Captain Steele?" The stony expression from the clean-jawed master suggested he would weather the interruption… to a point. "Master Gilbert Steele. Twenty-five months out. Thirty barrels of sperm oil. Fourteen hundred seventy barrels of whale oil. Bound for home in a fortnight or so."

"And did the log indicate home would be Sag Harbor on the Long Island Sound?"

The flinty whaling captain settled a questioning gaze on Swift that suggested the young woman introduce herself.

"I'm S. Thomas Swift. Recently arrived. As a writer I hope to record the adventures of the Pacific whaling fishery. I wonder if I might have a word with you?"

Captain Page tapped his papers with his blunt pencil. "Certainly."

Steele studied Swift for a long moment before nodding. "As you wish."

"May I take notes?"

The captains exchanged a sidelong glance. But didn't object.

"I've heard Lahaina described as the 'Hell of the Pacific'…would you agree?"

"A fester of wickedness and sin." Master Page leaned back in his chair. "If the local officials would just prevent the sale of ardent spirits we would all be better for it." The bearded New England captain thumped a thick finger on the table edge. "Stop selling spirits to the men and you will find our crews as peaceable and well behaved on shore as we find them to be at sea."

"Do you share that view…Captain Steele?"

"The *Black Cloud* you say?" The Sag Harbor master's expression suggested an instant dislike for this scribbler. "As far as I'm concerned any outlander should mind their own business."

Swift turned back to the New Bedford ship's master.

"Licentiousness…" The whiskered Captain Page picked at his favorite bone. "Licentiousness and spirits…those are the roots of all evil in Lahaina. The men have been at sea for months…Now these island Jezebels flaunt themselves in a most conspicuous manner…Why wonder the boys go overboard with drink and temptation?"

Master Steele shot the other whaling captain a glare. "Enough loose talk."

Captain Page's expression closed like a window shutter. Then Steele pointed a blunt finger at Swift. "Let me ask *you* a question." Swift stopped writing. "Hyram Head told us he carried a passenger to Lahaina who was a business partner with a brothel in New York. Is that passenger you by chance?"

Swift put her pencil down. "That is correct. I am also a woman of business…and I traveled as supercargo for a shipment consigned to a business associate in Lahaina."

The clean-shaven Steele scoffed. "Which is it? Scribbler or business associate? What Head told us is your business partner is Mama Samoa of the *Ship of Paradise.*"

"You are correct…Captain. The cargo was assembled to interest Mama Samoa."

With a look so hard it could have raised a spark from a flint Captain Steele rose to his feet. "My view is a young woman such as yourself is out of her league this far from her home." He leaned over the table toward Swift. "As Head says…you better stop nosing around this town."

Master Page snatched his papers. Stood up. Slapped the form on the customs counter behind him. And turned on Swift. His expression hardened behind his beard. "And stay away from my crew…Asking too many questions could be unhealthy — for them… or you."

As fast as oil separates from water both captains moved away from Swift. And stomped out of the Customs House back door barely fifty yards removed from the wharf.

Swift pushed back her chair. Her first foray investigating Lahaina whaling captains done. A dark expression passed over her face. *That was odd…Did those captains know more than they let on?*

Swift slipped her notebook and pencil into her Mexican sling bag. Her buoyant mood had evaporated. She moved to the other end of the exchange. Collected her newspapers and letters without a friendly word. Even the bundles waiting for her didn't lift her spirits. She took out her riding crop to make room in her bag and roughly stuffed both bundles inside. Then moved through the entrance onto the porch. Without warning the blinding Lahaina sun hit her face like a slap. She turned away. Rubbed water from the corners of her eyes. Then settled her favorite hat low on her forehead. And stepped off the porch into the blast-furnace heat.

◎ ◎ ◎

As Swift approached the chandlery opposite the King's *taro* patch she stopped short. A man had stepped out on the verandah. Swift blinked. Smacked her boot with her riding crop. Then stepped up into the shade of the overhang.

"Dancer?"

Dancer raised an eyebrow at Swift. And feigned surprise. "Like I said in New York…what the hell are you doing here?"

Swift considered asking him the same annoying question. Then thought better of it. "Same reason everybody comes to the Customs House. To register my cargo for the customs inspector and collect mail. And you?"

Dancer leaned in as he looked about. "This place has ears. Let's get some water for your nag."

Swift led the way off the verandah to her tethered horse. Her face darkened as she tied the saddle strings to secure the bag with letters and newspapers onto the back jockey behind her saddle seat.

Dancer gestured toward the bulging bag. "You must have a large family."

Swift's eyebrows narrowed. "You know my parents are dead…

Dancer." She gave the leather strings an extra tug. "At least I have friends who can—"

"Read?"

Swift's face reddened. "I was going to say...who can write."

Swift mounted her horse. Dancer walked beside. They walked in silence toward the fort. Crossed the footbridge at the canal where the King's Way began. Then turned toward the harbor behind the islander's stalls. What the missionaries called "Rotten Row" due to the bawdy sailor shops. Reached the harbor and walked along the firm beach. Away from town. Partially shaded in the late morning by giant breadfruit trees.

Dancer broke the silence. "Where did you get the horse and tack?"

"Rented her from the Major at Tuckerman's Guesthouse."

"The temperance hotel near the boat turnaround?"

"I heard it's the only genteel *hale* in town."

"As they say...what the *hale*." Dancer chuckled as he tilted his head back toward the jail in the Old Fort behind them. "Sure has the other fleabags in this port beat."

"*Hale* means house in Hawaiian for you philistines that think English is the only language."

Dancer bit his tongue. "So. Mr. Flute tells me you're up to another one of your journalism stunts. What is it this time?"

Swift's head whipped around and she looked down at Dancer. "You know Mr. Flute?"

"Yes...we go way back."

Swift flexed her legs in the stirrups. "We call it investigative reporting...Dancer. I'm here to expose a sex trafficking and opium smuggling ring. That's why I was working the Paradise Palace in New York."

Dancer looked up at Swift with a mischievous expression. "Sure you weren't moonlighting to make a few extra gold shiners?"

"At least I was working." Swift's tone grew testy. "The patron's ledger was very revealing. Appears there's a connection between New York and Lahaina. Something's going on between Five Points and the whalers. Just need to find out what...and who. At least that's what I'm here to do."

"What's your cover this time?"

"I'm undercover as a brothel investor. Here to deliver supplies from Queen Tinʻa."

"You've come a long way...Swift."

"Sometimes you can almost be polite...Dancer." Swift drew her horse up short. "Now it's your turn — if you can be honest for one minute. Why are you here? Has that scavenger hunt your Washington handlers sent you to Paris for turned out to be a bust?"

Dancer held back. "That trail was cold. You know me. Heard there were profits to be made off these islands. I'm here to find land deals for some Eastern speculators before the easy pickings are gone."

"Another race to the bottom...Dancer? Is this a new low?"

"Now I remember just how irritating you can be...Swift."

"Goes both ways."

"Feeling's mutual."

Swift's sea-green eyes tightened. "I've got better things to do with my time than waste it gossiping with you...Dancer. Mama Samoa is expecting me."

Swift wheeled her horse. Planted two well-placed heels to its ribs and bolted off. Dancer's eyes followed her as the horse left deep tracks in the sand. He admired Swift's straight back and easy posture as she galloped down the beach. Her auburn hair glinted in the sun. Accented against the black *cordobes* hat hanging around her strong neck.

After Swift was out of sight Dancer retraced his steps back toward the landing. As he approached the fort a distant but unmistakable tremor shuddered through the earth under his feet. The rolling vibration sent a strange sensation up his legs. *I've been at sea too long.* The thought was as unbidden as it was unwelcome. *Need to get my land legs back.*

CHAPTER 56

PUBLIC STORES WAREHOUSE/NEAR CHANDLERY
LAHAINA POINT
THAT AFTERNOON

MAMA SAMOA was a huge woman. She wore a giant loose-fitting *mu'umu'u* dress of European black silk. A high tortoise-shell comb rakishly held back her elaborately coiffed hair. When she stood up to greet Kikilani and Swift — the two women who had brought her the trade goods on the *Black Cloud* — Swift's first impression was shock. *That dress is large enough to hide an entire family.*

Mama Samoa glowered at Kikilani as soon as she saw her. "You island slut that disappeared with that other slut...Loki."

Kikilani opened her mouth as if to speak but said nothing.

Swift stepped forward. " 'Kidnapped' is more like it." She extended her hand to Mama Samoa. "Good afternoon. I'm Samantha Swift."

Mama Samoa assessed Swift with a quick glance. "You too soft for working girl. What your story?"

"I'm Queen Tin'a's business partner from the Paradise Palace. I brought Kikilani back to Maui." She withdrew her hand. "We have trade goods Queen Tin'a knew you would want."

Mama Samoa frowned. Crossed her tattooed arms over her huge bosom. An emphatic nod of her head told Kikilani to speak...

and told Swift to be quiet.

Kikilani tried to speak with self-assurance. "Thank you…Mama. I am here thanks to Samantha. When she agreed with Queen Tin'a to be supercargo for these invaluable goods…she brought me along. That is how we came to Maui together." As Kikilani spoke the madam detected her longing. "But my family has died."

Mama Samoa looked unmoved. Instead she ran her eye over Queenie's tempting feast of bordello furnishings…which Kikilani had arranged to have attractively arrayed here in Macomber's ramshackle public stores warehouse earlier in the day.

"We talk…on two conditions." Mama screwed up her face. Grunted. The sound made Swift think of a wild sow who had just stuck her nose into a pile of boar taint.

Kikilani and Swift exchanged glances. "Two 'conditions'?"

Mama Samoa planted her large bare feet wider on the warehouse floor and gave Swift a skeptical look. Then crossed her large arms tighter. "Mama's conditions…take or leave. First: I pick and choose. Only take best goods." She gave Swift a best-and-final look. "And second: I get the girl. Kikilani work for me on *Ship of Paradise*."

Swift gave Kikilani a questioning look.

Kikilani gestured toward the full warehouse. "You make a hard bargain…Mama." The island madam gave a softer grunt of acknowledgment as Kikilani drew her fingertips across the knap of several fine Persian rugs. "You are right…Mama. I was taken with Loki. But you must know I am not the island girl I was two years ago. I've learned many things in New York…thanks to Queenie." Kikilani touched a gilded frame that displayed within its borders a voluptuous Rubenesque nude. Then flashed the madam a radiant smile. "If you wish I could show your girls what I have learned from Queenie."

Mama Samoa let her arms loosen. A look of opportunity came into her eyes. Then—like a cobra—her expression changed. She looked at Swift.

"You nothing but delivery woman. Messenger. You no use for me." Mama turned a beefy shoulder toward the outlander.

Kikilani raised and lowered the tamboured curtain of an ornamental rolltop desk. Swift blinked as the cheap reproduction reminded her of when Queen Tin'a's desk almost ruined her Blue Book exposé at the Hall of Paradise.

Kikilani continued: "All these items from Queenie come with one price. All or nothing." Kikilani anticipated Mama's resistance. "Not my price…Queenie's price. Or she says we sell everything in Honolulu." She faced Mama Samoa. "All Queenie asks in return…is a few cans of opium."

Mama's distaste for Queenie's ultimatum showed in her frown. Then Swift saw the madam's eye steal back to the tempting pile of cargo from the *Black Cloud.*

"Opium? No…not Mama. What makes Queenie think I trade in opium? Not the Madam of the Pacific."

Kikilani repeated the offer. "Three cans."

"One." The outsized madam nodded firmly. "One can — and you… Kikilani. You work for me on ship. Teach girls all Queenie's tricks…like she say. Take or leave."

"Promise Queenie two cans — and take the whole shipment. Agree…and your boys can take the goods on consignment. Right now. Or we leave for Honolulu."

Mama eyed Kikilani. "Okay. You bargain like Queenie. Two cans." She put a husky arm around Kikilani's shoulders — and ignored Swift. With a rapid double snap of her fingers she summoned three boys dressed as girls — flowers in their long hair. A fourth boy trailed behind. Swift immediately recognized the *Black Cloud*'s cabin boy. When the freckle-faced youth saw Swift he flushed and dropped his eyes. Mama Samoa saw the exchange. "Captain Head lent me his boy." The island madam directed her four helpers to move the merchandise to her freight launch. Mama Samoa squeezed Kikilani. "Queenie is my *uso*. She be my fine sista."

She gave Swift a what-are-you-good-for look. "You? Not so sure."

The large madam took a wide seat and reviewed every item like they were floats in a Christmas pageant as her helpers carried the irreplaceable gifts past her on the way to the launch. Mirrors. Rugs. Licentious paintings. Crystal glasses. Turkish bell pulls. Fern vases. Water pitchers and basins. As the girl-boys moved each gift to the launch — and the cabin boy ticked off an inventory — the best-known madam in the Hell of the Pacific seemed inclined to accept that the boggling hand-picked assortment came from Queen Tin'a. She clucked with joy. "Only Queenie know what Mama needs."

Then the Madam of the Pacific brightened as she calculated yet another angle. With a slight smile and a blunt pencil she marked *"TARIFF PAID"* in bold letters on the bill of lading. Then stuffed the folded paper into her deep bosom. "You leave custom duty to me — and Consul Macomber."

CHAPTER 57

SHIP OF PARADISE
LAHAINA HARBOR
AS THE SUN SETS

"*SHIP OF PARADISE*...best in Pacific." Mama Samoa's pride was evident in her voice as she began the tour with Kikilani. "Bought transport ship that had two decks and large hold. Outfitted as floating brothel." Kikilani soon learned that Mama Samoa sailed the ship between Lahaina. Honolulu. And Wailuku — "on the other side" — to meet the whaler fleet wherever it landed. "Honolulu too tight now. Too many missionaries. Temperance bad for business. Laughter good. Lahaina more better for Mama now."

As they climbed down the companionway to the middle gun deck Mama paused. "Two seasons now King and his church-wives no longer in Lahaina Town — so sailors are own law. But missionaries still make trouble. Some are as corrupt as the traders."

Kikilani prompted her. "So that's why you retrofitted the transport ship to service whalers as a brothel?"

"You got it...Kiki. We anchor outside reef. Missionaries can't see. Captains shortsighted. No see...no tell. We make best business after sunset cannon shoots....How you say? Make hay while moon shines."

"I get the picture." Kikilani smiled in her revealing hostess outfit as she followed the tent-like *mu'umu'u.* "Your ship goes to the customers...so they don't have to go to you. What do the whaling captains say?"

"Most look other way. Only ship captains who want something make big noise. Mama slip them special favor." The large madam made a small gesture toward several girls lounging on settees in the cable tier saloon amidships. "Others get opium to sell back home. Big hush hush. Small tin bring big price. Then they look other way. Mama's ship can come and go. Island to island. Flow like trade winds. Go where needed. Beyond arm of law and prying eyes of missionaries."

"Where does the opium come from?" Kikilani feigned innocence.

"Where you think...girlie? British. All Chinese opium from British India."

"Who supplies it?"

Mama Samoa gave Kikilani a harsh glance. "You ask too big questions for small girl. None your business."

As they reached the lower hold Kikilani's eyes adjusted to the dim whale-oil lamplight.

"Now Mama show you Hall of Paradise." Kikilani realized Mama Samoa had rigged mats in the center of the cargo deck: they hung vertically to enclose a rectangular area. That area was divided into three rooms. Along each of the two longer exterior walls of the rectangle ran a narrow passage near the hull. The two end chambers enclosed within the rectangle each had three doors. Two that opened onto the outer passages. One that connected the two rooms to the small center dressing room.

"Looks familiar." Kikilani smiled to Mama Samoa. "Queen Tin'a had a similar plan. But she had four guest rooms around a center diamond."

"No!" The madam candidly exclaimed her astonishment. "You say Tin'a use my Hall of Paradise? That rascal." When she laughed several of her chins waggled. "Good idea travel fast....Four rooms? Me show Queenie right way. Then she go big."

As they walked Mama continued to explain her operations: "Mama say...we only sell one thing. The secret is not sell slow to one man. But sell fast to many as possible."

Kikilani nodded as she remembered Queen Tin'a's exact words. But she didn't interrupt.

"Guest come in here." Mama indicated one of the outside doors to an end room. "Enjoy visit. Go out there." She indicated the opposite passageway door. "Last guest never see next guest. They like that. Especially the captains — and missionaries."

"Queenie didn't use beds either."

The madam shook her head. "No beds. Too slow. Much washing. Attendant brings in guest and help him…get ready. Sounds from other room help raise his interest." Mama gave a sly wink as she patted the palm-mat walls and continued: "My best girl on duty that hour enters from her dressing room. When Randy is done she goes back to center room. Attendant take guest up forward companionway to saloon on main deck."

"And your best girl moves on to next guest?"

"You got idea. I see you be experienced Queen Tin'a girl. You natural businesswoman. Village girls take forever. Some take fifteen minute to do two sailors. Best girls take five minute to do pair. After done…bar girls like Loki get sailor to buy rum drinks. Until taxi canoe take customer back to his ship…or to shore."

Kikilani stopped before a small mirror hung on the divider mat and smelled the fresh *lei* that draped the neckline of her revealing dress. "I can show the bar girls some tricks to sell more rum." Then offhandedly asked: "Did you say Loki? She disappeared two years ago."

The tour stopped short outside the open door to the small end room. Mama Samoa turned on Kikilani. Her huge form suddenly menacing. "Now true tell me. Why you come Lahaina side?"

The madam stepped within reach of Kikilani. Kikilani moved back farther into the small room. Bumped against the padded chaise longue. Lost her balance. And sat down hard at the foot of the long couch. She blushed in the lamplight — and crossed her arms over her heart. "I went to find Loki on that whale ship. But I was kidnapped too."

Mama towered over her and gave out a derogatory snort. Then her eyes screwed up in what looked like a realization. She continued in a softer tone. "That missionary son: Charlie…Prickhim — me no say *haole* names…He say to me Loki was island slut. Freelancing on my business. Mama no like competition." She spoke with an edge in her voice. "That missionary man say he had friend...Captain Head... who know whaler master on ship called *Condor*. Whaler promise take care of Loki for me. Next week that whaler make sail. Loki no more problem. Good riddance I say." She shrugged her formidable shoulders above the seated Kikilani. "You just in wrong place... wrong time...girlie."

Mama Samoa cocked her head and gave Kikilani a shrewd look. "Tell me girlie...talk straight now...why you want to work for Mama?"

Kikilani rose from the longue. A deep sigh quaked her shoulders as she faced the formidable Madam of the Pacific. "My people are gone...I'm an orphan now." Kikilani fought back tears. "I have no family to go home to."

Mama Samoa put a fleshy hand on Kikilani's tan shoulder. "You special...girl." An expression of what passed for sympathy crossed the madam's face. "You stay with me. Mama Samoa...she be your good family now." With that revelation Mama Samoa led Kikilani up the aft companionway from the hold's Hall of Paradise to her private staterooms beside the master's cabin on the middle orlop deck.

Perhaps twenty minutes passed...and then Kikilani heard a soft rap on her stateroom door. When she opened the door what seemed a whisp of a figure slipped inside. The sun-speckled cabin boy from the *Black Cloud* held up his index finger. He gave a furtive glance around the master's cabin and closed the door silently. Then jumped into the cabin's berth. His arms wrapped around his knees. Kikilani brought an oil lamp and placed it in a wall holder. When she moved closer to the berth Kikilani realized the boy was shivering. She lifted a wool blanket. Placed the cover over the lad's bare feet and legs.

"You helped at the warehouse today." Kikilani noticed the boy had grown two inches during the voyage but not gained a pound. "My name is Kikilani."

The boy nodded. But did not speak. The answer came so slowly Kikilani wondered what made him so frightened. "They call me David." Kikilani adjusted the warm blanket around the boy's body. In the dim light from the lamp Kikilani saw his expression soften.

The wide-eyed youth gave an imploring look at Kikilani. "I never knew my mother…or father." He spoke hesitantly. "They say I'm a trick baby. They told me my mother worked in the Five Points brothel where I grew up.…" — Kikilani saw his eyes welled with large tears — "… …Before the madam traded me last Thanksgiving to be Captain Head's cabin boy."

Kikilani adjusted the lamp reflector toward where David sat. "I've lost my family too."

"I know. I heard you talking to your friend on the *Black Cloud*." The young boy pulled the woolen blanket under his chin. "I may know a secret."

Kikilani composed her face into a sympathetic expression. "I know I can trust you…and you can trust me. We are friends."

After a long moment the boy leaned forward. "Don't tell anyone I told you…especially anyone on the *Black Cloud* crew…promise?"

"I promise. Friends can trust friends."

"Last night on the *Black Cloud*…Captain Head had a visitor… another master. I brought them dinner and wine in the Captain's Cabin." That admission seemed to strengthen the youth's resolve. "When I took away the dishes…I listened to the two captains talking." Both his freckled hands clutched the rolled edge of the dark blanket. "Captain Head said it was easy money…"

Kikilani leaned closer. "What was easy money?"

"Trading rum for opium."

Kikilani held her breath. "What else did they say?"

"I couldn't hear clearly…but Captain Head said he expected a delivery of opium from the Chinaman."

"This is important: Did you hear where or when he expected the delivery?"

The youth made a face that suggested he wasn't sure. "They didn't say. Only that a delivery was coming…I think Head said…soon."

Kikilani reached out and gave the blond-haired lad a comforting pat on the shoulder. "Do you know who the other captain was?"

"He didn't say his name." The boy bit his lip. "All I heard was the captain was master of a whaler out of some harbor…Bag Harbor? Lag Harbor?"

"Sag Harbor?"

"Yes. That was it." The boy pushed the blanket from his knees.

"Now I remember. His ship is the *Enterprise.* That's all I know." He swung his legs over the edge of the berth. But they didn't reach the floor. "You were good to me…and the other sailors aboard the *Black Cloud.* I want to return the favor."

The boy leaned closer to Kikilani and lowered his voice to a whisper. "Head said two cans of opium could more than double the other captain's voyage tally."

Kikilani touched the boy's shoulder. "You're very brave to come here. But I have another question. Some say in addition to the opium the whalers kidnap island girls."

The boy's eyes widened as Kikilani took him into her confidence.

"Have you heard the captains…or whalers…talk about where the kidnappers keep these girls before they are shipped away? A hiding place?"

The boy blinked. "Hiding place…for kidnapped girls?" He shook his head. "No. But if you want I can keep my ears open." He smiled bravely. "I'm good at that."

Kikilani gripped his shoulder firmly. "Okay. But nothing more. I don't want you to ask anybody directly…that could be dangerous."

At that moment the heavy sound of boots pounded across the raised deck overhead the stateroom.

The boy froze. "Got to get back to the *Black Cloud.*" He jumped out of the berth. Opened the stateroom door and looked both ways. "I'll let you know what I find out."

With that hurried whisper he vanished in an instant out the cabin door.

CHAPTER 58

SHIP OF PARADISE
LAHAINA HARBOR
EARLY NEXT MORNING

KIKILANI COCKED HER HEAD when she heard the loud voices. Without a sound she opened her stateroom door an inch just steps away from the master's cabin.

In the quiet morning stillness Mama Samoa's deep voice was threatening: "No *haole* cheat Mama!"

"None of my ship captains get that much. You know that!" Captain Head's unmistakable voice was adamant.

Kikilani edged around the captain's table in the center of the main salon and moved closer to the open vent above Mama Samoa's expansive quarters.

"What you pay your boys is your business." Mama brought a heavy fist down on her newly acquired oak desk. "If you want to do business in Lahaina Roads…then that is my price. Ten barrels of rum…and four cans of British opium. Only offer. Mama has big expense. Many sailors and missionaries to service these days."

Head threw up his hands. "Four cans! You've never demanded opium before to distribute a rum shipment!"

"Expenses go up." Mama stood firm.

Head gave a distressed look as if he was caught between a hammer and an anvil. "Maybe—not saying I can...but maybe—I can find more rum barrels. Macomber has so many fingers in so many pies he'll probably never miss them."

"Not my problem. Too many sailors. Too many bits go out... not enough bits come in. Three cans is last price. Or I tell the Great Kahuna we find new captain with better head for business." Listening through the vent Kikilani heard Mama snort at her own pun—at Head's expense.

"Alright. One can of opium. But if tonight's shipment is short then there's less for all of us." Head stuck out his hand to close the deal.

Mama slapped Head's offer away. Moved into Head's face. "*Two* cans...no less."

The Captain gave out an exasperated sigh. Then he smashed his felt top-round hat on his head. He could almost feel this trip's smuggling tally tucked into the inside band of his hat. "Two cans it is—this time." Head's boots made a hollow sound as he stomped across the planks of Mama's master cabin. At the door Head turned toward Mama Samoa. "Don't expect that much come next fall."

Kikilani retreated quickly. Slid around the fiddled table and ducked through her stateroom door. She listened as Head's bootsteps crossed the main cabin and ascended the aft companionway to the upper deck. Kikilani let out the breath she was holding. Another piece to the puzzle had fallen into place—Captain Head *and* Mama Samoa were both in on the rum-for-opium trade. And there was to be an opium drop later that night...but where?

She remained quietly behind the thin door until her mind was clear and she understood what her next step would be.

Must get word to Sam.

CHAPTER 59

COMMAND DECK/FRIGATE *NÉMÉSIS*
HĀNA BAY/EASTERN MAUI
AT SUNRISE

A MAN OF THE CLOTH seated at the bow of a *proa* canoe sailed
toward the *Némésis*. Rear Admiral Louis Tromelin—second in the
French Pacific command—watched as a native sternman guided the
double outrigger across the sheltered Hāna Bay at the farthest eastern
point of Maui. From the command deck Tromelin's gaze swept from
the shoreline over the thick vegetation that climbed up the steep
mountainside. Here the great heights of Haleakalā volcano caused the
water in the clouds high overhead to be squeezed from the trade
winds—and the sky to rain mercilessly on Hāna Bay. One of the
wettest places on earth. Except this morning. Any droplet spared by
Haleakalā was carried on the perpetual wind and squeezed from the
clouds over West Maui by Pu'ukukui mountain. There great torrents
fell into the caldera of the mysterious 'Īao Valley. Beyond Pu'ukukui's
peak the exhausted trade winds barely caused the slightest sprinkle to
be dropped upon parched Lahaina Town on the western shore.

The outrigged canoe tied up amidships behind the Admiral's gig.
Judiciously the unannounced priest reached the gangway ladder and
placed his sandals with care on every rung as he climbed up to the

French warship's gangway. On the deck the stooped friar adjusted the rounded crown of his *cappello romano* firmly on his head. The clerical hat offered some protection against the glare of a momentary blue sky. A subaltern greeted the priest. After exchanging quiet words the young officer led the clergyman toward the command deck of the *Némésis'* quarterdeck. There Admiral Tromelin and Henri Malbec took the bright morning air after a night of torrential rain. An annoyed expression formed on Malbec's face as he watched the shuffling priest come toward them.

Tromelin sipped his milky coffee fortified with cognac and noted the hunched priest held his rosary with both hands at the open front of his elbow-length shoulder cape. Beneath the cape the priest wore a black ankle-length cassock and full collar.

The priest approached the Frenchmen and bowed. *"Bonjour... frères de Dieu."*

Malbec gave the man a sour look.

Tromelin stepped forward and greeted the cleric. *"Comment pouvons-nous vous aider?"*

"Assistance?" The priest gave a small smile then answered in French and English. *"Merci non.* I am here to assist you...if at all possible."

The Admiral blinked and put down his morning *café*-and-cognac. "Assist us? How is that possible?" Besides Malbec—as the King's Representative—Tromelin was beholden only to Admiral Messimer in the naval command.

"Of course...forgive me...how rude." The Catholic priest gave an obsequious glance at the two Frenchmen from under the wide black brim of his cleric's hat. "My name is Father Jean-Claude. I am stationed here in eastern Maui. When I received word yesterday that a great French warship had anchored in Hāna Bay...it was my duty as a Marist Father to present my assistance...if needed."

Both Frenchmen eyed the curious fellow with suspicion.

The priest continued. "If I may? Not long ago...I took my vows with the Society of Mary in New Zealand. Although I studied... my French is still not good...that is one reason my bishop sent me to Maui for some time now." The amenable clergyman gave an amiable shrug. "Fortunately...to the natives what language I speak makes little difference."

Henri Malbec directed a distrustful question at the little priest. "You say you are posted by your bishop in New Zealand?"

"Yes…your honor."

"Who is that bishop?"

The priest fiddled with his rosary. "My vicar apostolic is the right honorable Bishop Jean Baptiste Pompallier of Auckland. Do you know him?"

"No." Malbec huffed slightly. "I have only crossed paths with Pompallier's deputy in New Caledonia. A foul excuse for a man of the cloth. No better than Brother Blaise Mamoiton."

The bent cleric nodded gravely and replied. "Ah…my bishop's coadjutor…that would be Bishop Douarre. As you say…not every subordinate can be as skilled as his master."

Malbec bristled at the memory. "When Douarre tried to move his starving New Caledonia mission and supplies from Mahamato in the north to the south end of Grande Terre…those Pouma clan savages murdered Brother Blaise…when the fool tried to guard the provisions with an attack dog."

"You seem to know New Caledonia well…sir."

"Of course. I am Henri Malbec. Commandant of the New Caledonia penal colony. Those blood-thirsty Pouma savages got only my best service." A malicious sneer raised on Malbec's thin lips.

The black-clad priest made the sign of the cross. Raised his rosary. And mumbled an absolution. Then he tucked the rosary into a deep pocket and clasped his hands before him. "God's work can be difficult. All we can do is remain true. And as we say: 'Think as Mary. Judge as Mary. Feel and act as Mary in all things.'" With that maxim the simple priest addressed the uniformed Admiral. "That is one reason I have come today. You can imagine my consternation when Bishop Pompallier's reassignment for this humble servant arrived only days ago. The Vicariate wishes me to transfer to Wallis in the South Pacific."

The Admiral spoke with a tone of surprise. "North of Tonga and west of the Navigator Islands?"

"Yes. Exactly. Do you know it?"

"Near Futuna…at the end of the world."

"Indeed." The Marist Father addressed the Admiral. "My fervent hope is that your fine ship will sail soon for the South Pacific. If that were so...perhaps this humble servant of Mary could travel with you...to whatever destination you design?"

Admiral Tromelin emptied his *café* and waved his hand dismissively. "That is not possible...Father. Our orders take us shortly to Lahaina...on royal business. We will be staying in these waters for some time."

"Pity." The little priest sighed heavily and seemed to slump as if deflated. "So be it. Then I must take my leave."

Half-heartedly Tromelin offered a suggestion to the cleric. "Perhaps you could provide the sacrament of Communion to our crew members?"

Marist Father Jean-Claude joined both hands prayerfully and touched his lips in thought. "I only wish that were possible...but I must go before the weather changes. It is my duty today to lead the holy Mass at a settlement around the headland." He paused. "But I do have time to offer the Eucharist thanksgiving to you two gentlemen as representatives of your fine complement." The Father paused again. "If you are true believers in the Catholic faith...and are not conscious of grave sin."

"My conscience is clear." Malbec turned a shoulder to the priest. "But since childhood I have forsaken such superstitions."

Admiral Tromelin ran his fingers over the naval brocade on his cuff. "And I have sworn to serve my King with my utmost loyalty. Thank you for the offer...and for coming...Father." The Admiral bowed and extended his arm toward the aftercastle break.

The reduced priest turned toward the ladderway to return to the main gun deck. Malbec stepped beside the priest. Caught him by the elbow. The priest turned—and Malbec leaned forward. Then the commandant voiced what seemed like a friendly question. "Before you go...Father...which Vicariate will you serve in Wallis? The Eastern or Western Oceania?"

The priest nodded. Understood. Then answered: "Neither... Monsieur Malbec. As you may know the Eastern Vicariate—Tahiti. Marquesas. Hawai'i—was assigned to the Picpus Fathers. Such a large territory in the west required the creation of smaller districts." The man of the cloth held his hands together in repose under the opening of his shoulder cape. "I will serve as a Marist Father under Bishop Bataillon in what is now known as Central Oceania. That is my calling now."

Malbec's eyes narrowed. Then he straightened and let the priest pass.

The agreeable priest touched his hat brim. "*Au revoir*...Monsieur Malbec." He descended the aftercastle ladder. Crossed the deck. Climbed down to the waiting canoe tied to the ship's tender. In a blink the native pushed off and let the single triangular sail fill. Then steered north toward the black lava of Nānuʻalele Point. Malbec watched the small craft with some unease until it disappeared around the wind-beaten headland.

No sooner than the priest's boat disappeared from the French frigate's sight than a double-ended New England whaleboat pulled through the surf from the Red Beach. Four stout seamen pulled at the whaleboat's long oars while from the boatsteerer's position a bald-headed mariner steadied the craft as it lunged into the waves. Within moments the fast boat pulled alongside the *proa* sailing canoe. Two strong seamen grasped the outrigger and held the small craft to the longer boat. The islander steadied his passenger as the Marist Father slid out onto the boom and extended his sandals to the outrigger float. From there the bald-headed steersman helped the priest aboard.

Moments later the sails filled and the whaleboat picked up speed and heeled as the light craft raced before the easterly trade winds. In short order Mr. Flute's chase boat scudded west along Maui's north shore toward the ʻAuʻau Channel and Lahaina Roads. In the breeze the man of the cloth pulled off his priestly disguise.

Mr. Flute gave a nod to the man facing him from the aft rowing thwart and spoke a rare compliment.

"Well played...Dancer."

CHAPTER 60

SHIP OF PARADISE
LAHAINA HARBOR
LATER THAT AFTERNOON

JACK DANCER climbed aboard the *Ship of Paradise*. Before his boots hit the deck the catcalls began. Several girls seemed to know Dancer. "Hi…Dancer Man!" "What you bring us…Mister Jack?" One sylvan nymph tried to place a *lei* around Dancer's neck. He accepted the flowers. Then placed them on the nymph's shoulders with a whisper in her ear: "Maybe later." She giggled and skipped off smelling the fragrant *lei*.

Dancer stepped to the companionway stairs. Placed both boots on the cargo skid at one side. Then impetuously shot down the skid. Near the bottom he braked his momentum. Caught his balance. Then let his boots slide across the boards of the orlop deck. There Kikilani met him with a purred greeting. "Aloha…Dancer." Kikilani winked as though she had been expecting Dancer — in case anyone was watching — and took Dancer's arm. "Come meet my companion…I believe you might know her? She's overseeing a cargo delivery."

Swift looked up and frowned. "This one needs no introduction."

Kikilani flashed Dancer a not-so-innocent smile. Then climbed the stairs back to the upper deck saloon. Her appearance instantly attracted a chorus of clamoring sailors who applauded the barefoot beauty of their dreams—dazzling in her flowered *haku lei* headpiece.

"Why am I not surprised to see you here…Dancer? You seem to turn up wherever there is profit—or pleasure—to be had."

Dancer looked at Swift. In that moment he decided it was time. He looked left. Then right. Then took Swift down the aft companionway to the lower Hall of Paradise. Ushered her to the pleasure room at the far end. Looked back down the dim passageway again. And closed the flimsy door behind them.

Dancer lowered his voice. "You've stepped in deeper than you know…Swift."

"I'm sure you'll enlighten me." She glanced at his clean upper lip. "Starting with why you shaved off that Lord Byron affectation."

Dancer put the side of a finger to his lips and listened. When no sounds came to his ears besides the old ship's creaking timbers he took Swift into his confidence.

"As you suggested on the beach…I've been on a scavenger hunt since Paris." Dancer sat down on the chaise longue and leaned against the headrest. "A treasure hunt—if you want to know the truth." Swift raised an eyebrow and kept standing. "Both President Polk and Secretary Buchanan are wetting their pants for me to find a long-lost treasure of Napoleon's. Seems the American war chest has hit bottom. Turns out the boys in Washington aren't the only ones in this hunt."

Dancer ran his fingertips across his upper lip. "The night the *Black Cloud* anchored in Lahaina the American Consul in Honolulu sent Mr. Flute a bundle from Zanzibar. Mr. Flute brought it to me on the *Bountiful*." Dancer lowered his voice. "The message warned of a scheme to dominate the Pacific with a takeover of the Hawaiian Kingdom. My new mission is to identify the conspirators…foreign and local…and stop the plot at all costs." Dancer took a deep breath. "While doing some liaison work ashore Mr. Flute overheard Snuff Mitchell talking to a first mate in the Barleycorn. The whaler said a French warship had anchored in Hāna Bay." Swift leaned closer to hear. "Mr. Flute and I did a bit of spying to find out more."

"And that's why you sacrificed your moustache?"

"Didn't seem to fit the persona of a Marist Father." Dancer paused and frowned. "Our fears were confirmed. The *Némésis* warship will sail soon for Lahaina. Plus the gun ports on the lower deck were replaced with bars. Looks like the warship has been outfitted — at least partly — as a prison ship. I also learned the commandant from the New Caledonia prison colony is on board. Nasty piece of work. I get the sense Henri Malbec is on equal footing for this mission with Admiral Tromelin."

Swift sat down on the footrest of the chaise — leaving an adequate space between them. "Sounds like Washington will want somebody to stop it — if at all possible." Swift turned up the wick on a burning oil lamp nearby. "You said you've been on a treasure hunt...what does that mean?"

"It's a long story."

"Trust me."

Dancer tilted his head and listened for eavesdroppers beyond the mat walls. "Ever since Paris I've been tracking Napoleon's lost treasure...Fifty years ago his general — named LeGrand — was sent to return the treasure to France...but he never made it. Best Captain Post and I can figure is LeGrand may have shipwrecked on Maui...at least that's our hunch."

"That could make sense." Swift rubbed her forehead as if to clear her thoughts. "If the French intend to take over the Hawaiian Kingdom maybe the French need the treasure to *buy* local support?"

Dancer nodded as he followed Swift's logic. "In other words... the French need Napoleon's treasure as much as Washington does."

Swift steepled her index fingers together and touched her lips. "Or maybe the locals need the treasure to *pay* for protection."

Dancer crossed his arms and leaned back on the narrow longue. Then he looked at Swift thoughtfully. "No telling if Napoleon's treasure — if there *is* a treasure — is mixed up somehow in this conspiracy. Or who the local conspirators are...or where the treasure is. Mr. Flute and I are working on that."

Swift frowned. "I've got my own worries. On the voyage out here Kikilani and I discovered the *Black Cloud* is smuggling rum. It's marked as paint oil. I don't know if Mr. Flute told you — but Kikilani told me another island girl was kidnapped at the same time. A girl named Loki."

Swift regarded the flame in the oil lamp. "Loki was targeted by Mama Samoa because Mama was told Loki was a threat to her business. The captain who took Loki was a friend of Captain Head."

"Do you think Captain Head is behind this sex trafficking?"

"It gets better…or worse. Last night the young cabin boy from the *Black Cloud* told Kikilani that he overheard Mama Samoa arguing with Head over a spring opium delivery. Sounds like it's tonight."

Dancer unfolded his arms. Leaned forward and touched Swift's arm. "Have you not heard?"

"What?"

"The cabin boy…his body washed up on Moloka'i when Mr. Flute and I were in Hāna. Found by a fisherman. When the fisher brought the body to the landing Captain Post was there. At first it looked like the boy got caught in seaweed and drowned while swimming." Swift's face turned white as Dancer continued. "Captain Post looked closer. He realized the boy was tied by the seaweed and probably dumped into the channel."

Swift heaved a heavy sigh. "That freckle-faced boy risked everything to tell Kikilani about the opium shipment tonight."

The two sat silent. Then Dancer asked: "Maybe he got caught eavesdropping…or asked too many questions?"

Swift choked back a tightness in her throat. Then gathered herself. "I suspect Head is behind the smuggling and maybe the sex trafficking…or has worked with other transports to do it." Dancer gave Swift a quizzical look. "Dancer…don't ask me if there is any connection between my investigation and your treasure hunt. Or the conspiracy. You're out on a limb on that one by yourself."

Dancer turned on the upholstered couch. Brought one leg up and leaned forward on his other boot. "But we need to figure out any connection between the smuggling ring and this conspiracy to take over Maui. And fast." Dancer fixed Swift with a look. "Working together makes more sense than going it alone."

"Let me think about it. In Mexico last spring your idea of fast action was to jump off a cliff then look for a place to land." Swift rolled her eyes at the memory then returned Dancer's gaze. "Fire. Ready. Aim….That's what working with you is like. Not the greatest approach when your country's destiny hangs in the balance…and my investigation." Swift rose from the long chaise with a thoughtful expression. Then kept her voice low. "If we assume there's a connection between the opium trade and Napoleon's treasure…how do we figure that out?"

"Suppose…" Dancer outlined the first thought that came to him. "To avoid being caught by direct contact…maybe transport captains barter rum for opium 'off the books.' But who is the island connection? They would need someone here in Lahaina to arrange all the shipments. Maybe there is an opium kingpin we don't know about?"

"That could be hard to prove. None of the whaling captains will talk to me. They may be in on the trade. Or they're terrified of something…or someone. Shaking in their boots. That's all I know."

They stood. Swift spoke to Dancer in a stage whisper as the chaise backrest remained between them: "Kikilani told me Mama Samoa is involved in the scheme herself—from her toes all the way up to that tortoise-shell comb in her hair."

Dancer leaned on the chaise. "My guess is Head and Mama are just middlemen. There must be a bigger fish."

Swift sighed. "For my exposé I need more than theories. I need evidence."

Just at that moment Swift and Dancer jerked when the door opened.

Kikilani backed into the small room. She called out behind her: "I'll be back on deck in a moment!" Then she closed the door and turned. "What are you two doing?" Kikilani gave Dancer a wry look and gestured to the longue in the lamplight. "Mama Samoa thought you were sampling the goods…for free."

Swift tensed as if her reputation might suddenly be in question. "Just talking."

"Just talking?"

"I told Dancer what the cabin boy told you about an opium drop tonight."

Kikilani's expression darkened. "Lost at sea…same as with Loki. Now the boy makes two we know about."

Swift moved back into the sphere of soft light. "We were just talking about the opium drop tonight." She ran her fingers across her forehead. "Where would a drop take place?"

Dancer thought out loud. "Got to be somewhere secluded...that many rum barrels would take a boat...or two." Then stated the obvious. "Can't have that big an exchange at the town wharf."

"There is one place..." Kikilani stepped into the circle of lamplight. "I remember an *oli* chant that honored an ancestor no one wanted to claim. They called him: Makua Kāne Waiwai... Uncle Money. The song said Waiwai found riches and lost riches like a...how do you say...up-and-down?"

"Like a seesaw?"

"Yes. Like a seesaw." Kikilani's expression brightened. "Waiwai sometimes appeared with bundles of goods...as if by magic."

Impatience got the better of Dancer. "How does that help us?"

"The chant said Waiwai often visited a special place on Kaho'olawe Island...the *oli* poem called it: Smuggler's Cove."

"Where is this...Smuggler's Cove?

"Directly across from La Perouse Bay."

Swift snapped her fingers. "That's it!" Then nodded as a picture formed in her head. "Kikilani...meet me two hours before sunset at the Lahaina Wharf. Bring the fastest sailing canoe you can find...not too big...so it can be hidden. Wear your walking boots and sailor pants. I'll take care of the rest."

Swift turned toward Dancer. "How about you...Dancer. Got any ideas?"

Dancer gave a wry smile. "How's this? I can interview some of Mama Samoa's girls...to pick up any scuttlebutt about the smuggling operation on Maui..." Quickly the mischievous look left Dancer's face as he feigned seriousness. "...Or uncover what I can about the French plot."

Swift gave Dancer an irritated scowl.

CHAPTER 61

ANCIENT RUINS
LA PEROUSE BAY/MAUI
JUST AT SUNSET

THE MYSTERY OF LA PÉROUSE hovered over the ancient ruins.
The first European to set foot on Maui in 1786 had picked one of the
most forbidding places on the island to land. Thirty miles from
Lahaina. South along the coast. Past Olowalu Stream. Past Māʻalaea
Bay. Past the beaches of Kīhei and Wailea to the end of the spit of
lifeless lava known as Mākena Bay.

After meeting Swift at the Lahaina Wharf Kikilani pushed the
sailing canoe into the waves and listened to Swift's simple plan. "We're
sailing to Mākena Bay…and we'll leave the canoe in an adjacent cove."
Without a further word the duo sailed toward the bay. When they
reached the adjacent cove they stowed the mast and boom. Then left
their sailing canoe hidden under the cover of palm branches. Swift
handed Kikilani one of two stuffed knapsacks she had stashed in the
canoe. "These may come in handy." Without being seen the two
companions made their way around a low conical hill. Through a stand
of thorny *kiawe* trees. Then hid behind a ruined ancient lava wall.
Early evening had turned the long-abandoned encampment into a
shapeless labyrinth.

Only yards from where the walls concealed Kikilani and Swift endless waves crashed against the lava flow. Spumes of salty froth shot into the air. Followed by a hollow subterranean cough like a ghost clearing phlegm. Kikilani whispered as a ghostly geyser shot up from a blowhole in the lava: "That's where the mystery of La Pérouse takes over."

"What do you mean 'mystery'?"

"The *oli* that tells of Makua Kāne Waiwai — Uncle Money — mentions whalers. Native divers. Even opium. But then all that disappears...like magic...there's no mention of whalers or divers again. *Poof.* Nothing. Nobody knows what happens next."

"Because there's no proof." Swift nodded toward a black lava flow that sloped to the bay. "But who controls the trade on Maui? Some mysterious middleman?" She stared off into the distance. The next instant everything made sense to her. "There must be a connection between rum. Opium. And trafficking island girls...It would make somebody rich! Very rich."

Swift swept her gaze across the channel toward Smuggler's Cove. There an anchored catamaran with two or three men smoking cigarettes seemed to patiently await something. The men's laughter drifted on the breeze across the bay. Beyond the tender loomed the treeless island labeled Kahoʻolawe on navigator's charts. The island was an isolated hump of lava even a castaway would curse. As the seamen said: *Not fit for anything more than target practice for navy gunners.*

A breeze circled around the downwind slopes of Haleakalā. The sweet sea scent of the early evening mixed with the melancholy murmur of the waves upon La Perouse Beach. Swift felt the rising freshet tickle strands of hair against her neck. She pulled a spyglass Dancer had lent her from her knapsack and looked into the twilight. She trained the spyglass across the bay and examined the shores of Kahoʻolawe Island. Waves sprayed the rocky shoreline: Smuggler's Cove. Just then — Kikilani elbowed Swift. Then pointed toward Kukui Point illumined by the glow of dusk and overlooking Smuggler's Cove.

"Look."

Swift shifted the spyglass. Through the lens she watched as torches on the beach were lit one by one. For some minutes Swift scanned the torches: their flames danced in the quiet breezes. Then a small outrigger canoe appeared in the cove's windward waters near Kukui Point. And another. Then another. Four canoes converged in the cove. Not far from the large double-hulled catamaran. Swift trained the glass on one of the four canoes. Watched as the small craft pulled up alongside what looked like a buoy. The dark form of a man stood on the canoe hull and outrigger boom. In a graceful arc he dove into the water beside the buoy. Several long moments passed. Nothing. Then in a burst the diver emerged…holding a large object in his hands.

"What is it?" Kikilani whispered.

Swift adjusted the spyglass. "It's too far away. I can't tell. Whatever it is…it's too heavy to hold above the waves."

Swift strained to see the man place the dark object against his hip. Gather the buoy. Then swim toward the large catamaran waiting in the cove. "Looks like the buoy is roped to the object. It may be a large cannister?" When the diver got to the tender he reached up. Handed the buoy to another man in the tender. The second man fed the wet rope tied to the buoy through his hands until he held the large cannister. Placed it on the gunwale. Took out a knife. Sliced the rope. Lifted the large cannister and placed it on the platform between the hulls. Then cast the buoy back into the water. The diver swam quickly back toward his canoe.

As Swift watched the process repeated. Each diver reached his canoe. Climbed in. Seemed to rest a moment. Stood. Then all four — as if by a signal — dove into the water. Moments passed. Each retrieved a cannister. Brought it to the waiting tender. Again and again they pulled cannisters to the catamaran. Too many times to count.

Kikilani spoke in a hushed tone. "Could be the opium…."

Swift followed the divers until all the buoys and cannisters were collected. And delivered to the large catamaran canoe. Minutes after the final buoy had been retrieved the catamaran canoe unfurled a sail. Moved away from the cove. And started across the channel toward the leeward shore of La Perouse Bay. Swift nudged Kikilani. "The catamaran is coming this way. Right toward the beach. Stay low."

Just then noises arose from the brush behind them. Kikilani cocked her head. "Did you hear that?" The next moment the duo watched as a wagon pulled by six natives trundled out of the bush to their left. Swift saw the men struggled to pull the conveyance over the ancient lava. Then another wagon followed. And another. And another passed the ancient lava wall where Swift and Kikilani hid. A single torch attached to the lead wagon revealed the men's faces for an instant. Kikilani pointed and whispered to Swift. "I know those two men! Bull Shaw and Kapu! They were always hanging around Lahaina Town. Making trouble and pawing at Loki and me!" She whispered the two men's names with loathing: Bull Shaw and Kapu the Ugly!

Kapu brought the first wagon to a stop alongside a flat table-like lava-stone. From the catamaran tender a man dressed in a Chinese robe stepped onto the beach. He approached Shaw. In the torchlight the Chinaman gestured with five fingers. Five times. "Twenty-five opium cans!" Swift muttered in a low voice.

Shaw pulled out a heavy purse. Counted out twenty gold coins and dropped them onto the table-like stone. Then Shaw pulled the drawstrings closed. The smuggler shook his fist at Shaw. Leaned in. Then gestured again. Five times with five fingers in Shaw's face. Then again. Twenty-five fingers. The robed Chinaman folded his arms across his chest. His chin rose slightly.

Shaw laughed derisively. Spit a tobacco stream into the black sand. Swift saw through the spyglass five more Golden Eagle coins dropped onto the stone. The Chinaman collected the money. Bowed. Signaled to his canoe.

Quickly the canisters in the tender were offloaded to the beach. Through the spyglass Swift saw the tin containers looked like the tea chests on the China clipper ship she had seen at Juan Fernandez Island. On the side was printed the crest of the East India Company. Below the crest one word was stenciled: *Calcutta*. Fifteen opium cans were put in the lead wagon. Then covered by a canvas. Ten cans remained on the beach like orphans.

A few minutes later a longboat cut through the surf toward the beach at La Perouse Bay. Drove its bow member up on the sand next to the Chinaman's double canoe. The transport crew pulled a tow rope. And brought a small lighter beside the larger longboat.

Kikilani again lightly prodded Swift. "Look who's here!"

From the longboat stepped Captain Hyram Head and Ratter Dawes.

After a brief consult with Bull Shaw the Captain directed a gang of island laborers to offload the cargo on his longboat and lighter. The native men silently offloaded a hundred large barrels. Large stenciling on each barrel identified the contents held inside: *PAINT OIL*. With a nod from Captain Head the laborers then moved the ten cans of opium from the sand into the longboat. Head spoke a few words to Shaw. A rising wind carried the words into the twilight. Shaw gestured inland toward the forbidding great hulk of Haleakalā silhouetted above them.

Head and his hired gang climbed aboard his longboat. And Shaw. Dawes. And Kapu pushed the longboat into the bay. In no hurry the catamaran canoe also pushed into the surf: The Chinaman stood in the bow as he drew the purse strings holding his white man's money tight. The lighter rested on the sand alone beside the wet slashes left by the two other boats' keels.

Shaw and Kapu climbed into the lead wagon with its torch. Now loaded with fifteen opium cans under the canvas tarpaulin. And filled out with barrels of paint oil. Presumably. Shaw cracked his whip at the six natives in the traces. They strained like mules to rock the loaded wagon forward. Like a native overseer Shaw stung one of the natives viciously with his whip. Gradually the wagon wheels followed a track that skirted the nearly impassable lava fields and led upcountry toward the dark volcano. Three more loaded wagons followed. Dawes rode in the last wagon also lit by a solitary torch as the train vanished noisily up the mountain track.

Questions ricocheted around Swift's mind. She murmured her thoughts to Kikilani. "Sam Hill! What was it Walt Whitman told me before we left New York?" She began working out the logistics of the smuggling operation. "Whaler captains return to Lahaina from winter killing waters in the Sea of Japan. When they return they bring British opium disguised as tea from China: I wrote about it in my Special Dispatch after the *Black Cloud* rounded the Horn! Then the whalers drop the opium here. At Smuggler's Cove. The Chinese collect it. Deliver the cans to Bull Shaw. Head barters rum for opium." Swift stopped. She was certain of her conclusions—to a point. "But what happens to the New England rum on Maui? And the fifteen skimmed cans of opium? Who is the mastermind behind this smuggling empire? Surely not Hyram Head."

Before the groan and rattle of the wagons faded up the mountain track Swift and Kikilani followed them into the shadows. They moved silently into the deepening darkness.

CHAPTER 62

SMUGGLER'S CAMP
KULA HILLS/UPCOUNTRY MAUI
LATER THAT NIGHT

SWIFT AND KIKILANI trailed the rum wagons at a safe distance. At that moment the last wagon's torch disappeared.

The pair ran forward. Nothing. The wagons had evaporated. *Where did they go?* Swift swept her gaze left and right. Kikilani dropped to a knee and touched the red dust. Then Swift looked past Kikilani's shoulder. Before them she spotted a half-hidden mouth to a large cave and pointed.

"Lava tube." Kikilani followed the lines of wheel impressions at the entrance. "There are tubes all over these islands. Whenever Haleakalā erupted the lava flowed toward the sea and melted the exposed rock as it went. The top layer of lava cooled and formed a roof. With every flow the hot lava cut deeper into the earth. The result is a lava tube — a cave often big enough to drive a wagon through it." Again she pointed to the impressions of the wagon wheels.

Swift nodded. "We didn't come this far to stop now."

From her knapsack Swift pulled two small whale-oil lamps. Each lamp had a hood that directed the lamplight downward. She strapped one tin light to Kikilani's knee-high walking boot. One to her own leg.

Then lit them both with a friction match. "You can see where you're putting your step. But nobody else can see the light if you keep this hood closed." She demonstrated the ingenious lantern. "At least that's Dancer's theory: He gave the lamps and the spyglass to me before I met you at Lahaina Wharf."

Kikilani and Swift entered the lava cave unseen. They followed the only path they could find—the path taken by Bull Shaw and the rum wagons. Each step took them up a steady rise that paralleled the mountain's slope. The air was moist but not cold. The cave floor was almost flat in the center. Runoff channels ran along each side. Faint wheel tracks cut into the packed pumice floor.

After a half hour of silence Swift grabbed Kikilani's arm. "Hear that?"

Up ahead a collapsed ceiling formed a ramp rising roughly from out of the cave. When Kikilani and Swift followed the ramp they found it led them through a large skylight. They snuffed their lamps and emerged onto the Kula hills that overlooked La Perouse Bay. Without making a sound they darted into the cane growth beside the track. Within a few steps—while still remaining carefully hidden behind the foliage—they discovered a camp lit by torches arranged as for a Tahitian *luau*. Scores of barrels marked *PAINT OIL* stood stacked on a large platform under a grass roof. A storehouse squatted nearby.

Bull Shaw and Kapu's laden wagon had apparently arrived in the camp only moments earlier: They stopped beside the platform. Several coolie figures with long braids lined up beside each other. Fire-brigade style they passed the rum barrels one by one to each other as they unloaded the barrels from the four wagons. As soon as the wagons were emptied the laborers moved several jute bags filled with potatoes near the wagon. Unexpectedly one Chinaman lifted his head and made a distinctive bird call in the torchlight. A shadowy figure shifted his weight under the storehouse beneath the grass roof.

"Potatoes?" Swift whispered. "Is that the cover for the activity from Smuggler's Cove?" Something did not make sense. "But why has Dawes risked coming to the Chinaman's camp?"

At that moment Dawes and Bull Shaw walked into the ring of torchlight outside the covered platform. Then a large man stepped from the shadows. Kikilani gasped.

"Maunakili! Before I was kidnapped…I heard storytellers say he bears the royal blood of King Kahekili."

The rebel chief gestured to Dawes and the two men sat down on stumps with a hogshead barrel between them. Bull placed the bag of gold coins—what remained in it—on the barrel. After a nod from Maunakili Bull Shaw wrote two figures in chalk on the barrelhead: *10. 100.*

Kikilani whispered as she squinted from her hiding place: "Looks like ten opium cans for one hundred rum barrels."

Swift nodded. "That's the transaction with Head. That's not even forty percent of the opium for all the rum." Swift calculated aloud. "Head got the short end."

Almost simultaneously Maunakili snapped his fingers at a figure standing outside the reach of the torchlight. From out of the darkness stepped a Chinese man wearing a skull cap and quilted jacket.

"That's Chang Fu—headman of the Chinese laborers." Kikilani maintained a low tone.

Chang Fu gave a slight nod. From out of the darkness four Chinamen dragged two Chinese girls. The girls stumbled. Swayed. Could barely stand. Swift murmured: "They look drugged!" Swift and Kikilani watched as the Chinamen half carried the two compliant girls with some effort over to Dawes' wagon. Then roughly lifted each girl and deposited her inside. And tossed a tarp roughly over the girls. Then placed potato sacks around the unprotesting forms as if they were so much produce. Kapu climbed into the wagon's board seat and played nervously with the reins.

Dawes took out five coins. Then counted them on the barrelhead with exaggerated slowness.

Kikilani strained to see. "Dawes just bought two girls…!"

Swift squeezed Kikilani's hand. "Shaw paid twenty-five coins to the Chinaman for the opium—which bought one hundred barrels of rum from Head. Five more coins is another nice profit for Maunakili."

Without a glance at the money Maunakili stood up. With an outward flick of his wrist he dismissed Dawes. Dawes lost no time: He immediately climbed into the wagon. Kapu cracked the whip. The wagon of potatoes lurched forward on the lava-cave track: heading down toward La Perouse Bay and the awaiting lighter.

Swift muttered to Kikilani: "Let's get out of here."

Instantly Kikilani saw their dilemma. "The wagon is headed into the lava tunnel. We'll have to cut through the canebrake aboveground."

Kikilani had taken no more than twenty steps when the tin lamp strapped to her shin dropped around her ankle. The flopping lamp clattered like a cow bell.

Chang Fu instantly jumped up. After a moment he spotted the two forms in the canebrake. "Intruders!" He pointed. "Get them!"

The shadows of the two spies disappeared into the wild grass. A few moments later a gang of cutthroats raced toward the edge of the dry canebrake.

Swift whispered hoarsely: "They'll never be able to follow us in here."

As the two stumbled and pushed through the tall blades they all at once realized they were being followed. Not by men. But by hot white smoke.

"They've set the dry grass on fire!" Swift called out. "Run for it — or we'll be cooked alive!"

Behind them the roar of the all-consuming blaze filled the night. Without warning the pair were no longer alone. Their feet were surrounded by hordes of spiders. Rats. Centipedes. Helter-skelter the poisonous vermin landed on their arms. Scurried across their feet. Tangled in their hair. Amidst the swirling sparks.

"I *hate* bugs!" growled Kikilani as she scraped a coating of spiders off her arm.

"They don't want us!" Swift coughed in the smoke then tried to shout as her partner desperately flailed at the swarm. "They want out of here before they're burned alive!"

"Me too!" Kikilani murmured through clenched teeth.

The cacophony of terrified insects and screeching rodents was quickly drowned by the roaring fire coming for them. To Swift the racing sound was like a hundred oncoming steam engines. The inferno consumed everything in its path. Cane grass and *kiawe* mesquite trees burst into flames. Pine trees exploded like bombs. All whipped by the southeast venturi winds that circled around the volcano. Then roared north across the isthmus valley between the two great volcanos.

"Follow the fall line!" Swift shouted.

The two women plowed their way through the thick cane blades. Face. Arms slashed by the *kiawe* thorns. A torrent of rats crowded underfoot. Kikilani's sandal slipped on a wave of scurrying insects. Swift's walking boot flattened a rat. The rodent squealed in agony. Kikilani slapped embers from Swift's sleeve. And a poisonous-looking centipede. The fire roared close by. Smoke choked every breath.

Without warning Swift's feet went out from under her. Kikilani crashed on top. Entangled together — before the women could stand — they were covered by a tide of rats. Hundreds. Skittering over their arms. Legs. And faces. Like a wave. Before the horde swarmed away into the darkness.

Kikilani grabbed Swift's hand and pulled her up. From the red-orange inferno behind them came the roar of oncoming annihilation. Hand in hand the pair turned in the direction the rats had disappeared. Swift and Kikilani moved instinctively from the flames and heat…and stepped over the edge. Into a pit. Both fell forward. Tumbled down an incline. Beneath their hands they sensed the slippery gravel slurry of a ceiling cave-in.

At the bottom the duo checked for injuries. Nothing more than their pride. "This way." Kikilani coughed as she led Swift farther down the incline. Deeper into a cave. "We're in another lava tube…I think."

Hidden by the cave Swift untied the oil lamp still attached to her shin. Moved the reflector away and lit the wick again. The battered light shined a small cone of brightness on the cave floor at their feet.

Kikilani pointed to her companion's shin. "You would have made a nice Roman candle if that oil had spilled."

Swift gave her a half smile in the darkness. Then slapped a huge spider off her arm. "Where does this cave lead?"

Kikilani looked about the darkness lit by the meager lamplight. "Could it run toward the cove?"

"Shit and lava flow downhill…Dancer used to say." Swift pointed ahead. "Follow the rats. Wherever they go to escape is better than going back up there."

Sharing the lamp between them the two women staggered along the tube. Down into the darkness.

When they came out near the small cove Swift gave a relieved sigh. Kikilani held up her hand. "Dawes and Kapu will be at the lighter by now. We must wait until Dawes sails past our hiding place. If we launch now he'll see our canoe sail in the starlight and overtake us."

After what seemed like an eternity the duo saw the lighter's sail raise the peninsula that hid them. And then watched as the lighter increased speed across Māʻalaea Bay toward Lahaina.

Kikilani took charge. "We'll paddle at first. Silently. When Dawes is upwind he won't hear us. Once he passes Papawai Point at the headland we'll raise sail too."

Against the night chill and the adrenaline of their close escape Swift and Kikilani pulled on sweaters retrieved from their knapsacks. Together the pair pushed off into the rough surf. Overhead a galaxy of stars sparkled like countless diamonds.

Swift grabbed a paddle. A vision from only a year before of capsizing in the torrent of the Rio Grande River twisted her gut. She set her jaw. *No way to tip over a sailing canoe equipped with a boom and float…is there?*

CHAPTER 63

CAPTAIN'S CABIN/*BOUNTIFUL*
LAHAINA HARBOR
NEXT MORNING

SWIFT AND KIKILANI stood in singed and torn clothes beside Captain Post's map table. Mr. Flute looked on. No steam rose from five pewter mugs of Kona coffee in the warm morning light.

Jack Dancer entered the cabin. The last to arrive—and looking tired. He nodded to the two men and Kikilani. "Morning...Swift."

"Do some partying last night...Dancer?" Swift chided.

"Undercover interviews can be exhausting." Dancer took a mug of strong coffee from Captain Post. "And you and Kikilani?"

"A little caving and caning." Swift sipped her coffee. Sweetened with cane sugar. "You're late."

Dancer surveyed Kikilani and Swift's scratched arms. "Looks like you got the wrong end of a mad cat—or tangled with a Maui thorn tree."

Swift forced a smile as she reached into the medical bag from the *Black Cloud* Captain Post kept for her. Then massaged turmeric salve on her forearms...and passed the salve to Kikilani. "Mostly cane grass. I had enough of mesquite in Texas. Best not to fight with a sister tree on Maui."

Dancer pressed his advantage. "Some say the missionaries planted the *kiawe* to teach the islanders the benefits of wearing shoes."

When Swift threw Dancer a scowl Captain Post changed the topic. Before Swift and Dancer could scratch each other's eyes out.

Post's tactic worked. Swift swallowed her retort to Dancer. Then pointed to the map of Lahaina Roads. She explained to Post and Dancer how the opium was dropped at sea. "Whalers fresh from the Orient drop the opium at Smuggler's Cove. The Chinese collect the opium cans and bring it ashore. They're met by Bull Shaw and Kapu at La Perouse Bay. Shaw pays a pittance in Golden Eagles for the opium. Then Shaw barters the opium for rum with Head and Dawes. Shaw and Kapu escort the rum upcountry to Chang Fu's camp."

Dancer raised his coffee mug to toast Swift's discoveries. "You were right…Swift. That rum on the *Black Cloud* is at the heart of this scheme."

Mr. Flute nodded. "Head and Dawes will get a hundred times the price for their opium back in New York City."

"And as the sole supplier of rum to the American whaling fleet in Lahaina the smuggling ring can sell its rum — watered down — at exorbitant prices to the grog shops." Dancer unsuccessfully tried to stifle a deep yawn.

Post nodded. "Nothing like a monopoly to keep prices high."

Mr. Flute poured Swift another mug of sweetened coffee.

Swift gestured toward the Customs House on the waterfront. "That so-called paint oil — Captain Head's rum — should be recorded in the collector's duty books. If there is no logbook record then Head bypassed customs and outright smuggled the rum ashore. My guess is our friend Angus Macomber has his finger in this pie too."

Dancer emptied his metal mug. And poured another strong coffee. "Scuttlebutt from Mama Samoa's says Macomber skims a share. But he's an Indian — not a chief — in the smuggling ring. No one let slip who's the mastermind." Dancer's eyes flicked from face to face around the cabin.

Swift tapped two fingers on the chart table. "Kikilani and I scored on that one too. Tell them…Kikilani."

Dancer and Post turned toward Kikilani. "The kingpin behind the entire Maui smuggling network — rum…opium…girls — is no other than His Royal Highness: Maunakili. He's the rebel Pi'ilani from Moloka'i who the storytellers say wants to be king."

"Kikilani is right." Mr. Flute addressed the group. "My sources at the grog shops and gossip on Rotten Row confirm that Maunakili has his hands in the entire operation."

"The Great Kahuna?"

"One and the same." Swift confirmed the information with a nod. "Looks like Maunakili has more irons in the fire than just becoming the king of Maui."

Dancer turned to Kikilani. "What else do the native chants tell about Maunakili?"

"The *oli* say half his body is covered in black tattoos. That's why the storytellers call him the man-cut-in-two." Kikilani felt a sharp prickle at the back of her neck under her long hair. She reached up and kneaded the area around her birthmark. "The *oli* also say Maunakili is a fierce warrior..." As she spoke an expression of dark presentiment passed over her face.

With those final words a heavy silence fell over the group. While unseen outside the cabin's air vent Billy Mack held his breath. Eavesdropping.

CHAPTER 64

THE FRENCH NAVY CAPITAINE stood stiffly beside the Admiral. His hands clasped behind his back. He waited to be addressed. There was a knock on the door. A lieutenant entered. Walked over to Admiral Messimer and handed him a scrolled message. Messimer's eyebrow arched. He tapped the rolled dispatch from Tahiti in his palm. Smiled slightly. The lieutenant retreated from the room. And closed the door behind him.

The capitaine stared at the French Naval Commander of the Pacific questioningly. "A new development...Admiral?"

Admiral Messimer scanned the dispatch. "Our spy was placed on the whaler *Bountiful*...He sailed to Maui to kill the American agent on board. The American was convinced LeGrand sailed toward South America. But the American had no choice but to take the *Bountiful* to the Hawaiian Islands." Messimer handed the dispatch to the capitaine.

"What can one man do alone?"

"A mosquito inside our net...nothing more than a distraction." Messimer sneered. "If the American is not swatted away by our spy then Malbec's prison frigate will do the job. The Americans are helpless against the naval power of France."

The capitaine placed the scroll on the table. "The agent has less chance than an American beaver caught in his own trap."

The Admiral smirked. "Probably wears a coonskin cap and Indian moccasins. What do the Americans call those simple-minded rustics?"

"Frontiersmen."

"I can almost see the painting. A beaver trapper with nothing but a knife and a mule — and a heathen squaw suckling a runny-nosed naked half-breed." The Admiral laughed.

"The American doesn't know what he's sailing into."

"Our trap is set." Admiral Messimer stepped with supreme confidence to the aft gallery of his flagship as a cloud darkened Noumea Harbor. "We've sent Malbec to the *puʻuhonua* — that abandoned Place of Refuge on the Kona Coast — to make final arrangements with Maunakili."

"Do you think King Philippe's twenty thousand dollars was wasted on the King in Honolulu?"

"Not at all. My subterfuge worked perfectly. First the simple King was impressed by French generosity. Then it was child's play to manipulate Maunakili to 'steal' the coin chests from the Customs House for his own Treasury."

"Only to have Maunakili pay the money back to Malbec."

"Everything ends up in King Philippe's pocket after all… with one twist. We bought Maunakili without spending a sou." Messimer smiled.

"Brilliant…Admiral. You have outdone yourself. The only better use would have been to invest the coins yourself in the opium trade."

"*Peut-etre*…Capitaine. Perhaps. Soon much more treasure will be ours. But now Malbec must stay the course and steer his ship toward King Philippe's grand design to rule the Pacific. If anyone can run the board for our attack it is Malbec and Commander Tromelin. By now the frigate *Némésis* should have reached Hāna on the windward side of East Maui. From there Malbec will be ready to race west to Lahaina when the time is right to strike."

The capitaine smiled. "California will be next."

"And all Nouvelle France — from California to the Mississippi River!"

CHAPTER 65

HALE PIULA — KING'S HOUSE
ROYAL DISTRICT/LAHAINA/MAUI
SAME DAY

A TAWNY HAZE hid the dim sun. A long shudder passed through the ground. Soon the rank smell of slime belched from the uttermost depths of the sea only three canoe-lengths away from shore. Onto the beach swept a line of floating pumice: White ash spewed by Pele herself.

In the air the taint of sulfur made spit hard to swallow. Where the acrid pall settled over the greeting piazza that surrounded the palace the vapors smothered the fragrance of gardenia and tuberose in an ominous and deathly combination.

Around the Hale Piula — the King's palace — the old wives and young men were in turmoil. All knew the ancient chants of the storytellers that foretold eruptions — and the lava and tidal waves that followed the eruption itself. Soon the gods would release convulsions from the ocean floor. What fissures would split the world asunder? Who would be swallowed first by the sea? When would the end come?

Huddled inside the Hale Piula palace the Pi'ilani nobles and old men sat transfixed. In their terrified silence Maunakili seized his opportunity. "You!" he shouted towering over the old men. "It is you that brought on Pele's anger!"

The old believers squatted and sat close packed on the fine pandanus floor mats. Their thoughts imagined the monstrous scene that would engulf their paradise at any moment.

"You turned your backs on our traditions. You embraced the poison kiss of the white man's religion. Now our gods — our Pele — is angry. Pele has come to take reckoning."

The nobles and old men squirmed. Forlorn glances exchanged. Murmurs of acknowledgment. Several hugged their knees and rocked. Bull Shaw and Kapu the Ugly hovered over the scene.

Maunakili crossed his arms angrily in front of his chest. "Pele's anger is great. Not even the bones of our ancestors will appease Pele." He spread his feet and planted his hands emphatically on his hips. "But there is one hope. Only one thing will cool Pele's rage."

All faces turned up toward Maunakili.

"Pele's volcano will claim you — unless we offer her the treasure collected by our ancient chiefs. We must give up the lost treasure. Now! Or all is lost. Only sacrificing the foreign treasure — the treasure shipwrecked at La Perouse Bay in the old days…before the seduction of the Christian ways sapped the strength of our forefathers: The treasure is the only way we can calm the anger of our gods and save our island kingdom…The only way to return to the true *mana* of the Great Kahuna.…We must give up the blasphemous white man's treasure to Pele." He made a gesture toward the inland valleys. "If we do not do this? We die. Speak now to live!"

At that moment another savage explosion from deep within the earth jarred Lahaina.

An old *ali'i* noble raised his hand in the back. Maunakili waved his hand. "Pass him the Talking Stick."

Kapu the Ugly handed a carved wooden staff to the old man. The elder placed both hands around the Pi'ilani totems and shell inlays of fish and crops and mountains. Then used the stick to rise to his feet. The chief's crest at the top stood taller than the old man's white head. "There is an old *mele* that has been chanted many years now by the truth tellers. The *mele* says the Menehune — the little people — took the Frenchman's gold and secreted it in the 'Iao Valley."

"Rubbish!" Maunakili shouted as he plowed his way through the chiefs. The warrior jerked the Talking Stick from the old man's hands.

"Don't waste our time with that claptrap…old man!" He bellowed as he threatened the chief with the carved staff: "Tell us facts we can act upon — not tales of leprechauns and Menehune! Who can tell us something true? A true believer must speak." Maunakili relinquished the Talking Stick to Kapu who stood amongst the seated *ali'i* elders.

The oldest chief of all rose unsteadily to his feet. Kapu gave the Talking Stick to a gray-haired chief squatting in the second tier. Hand to hand the Talking Stick passed through the crowd of elders until it finally was handed to the noble elder. At first his mumbled words could not be heard.

"Speak up!" barked Bull Shaw who paced like a guard dog near the only door of the meeting chamber.

The chief began haltingly. "Many years ago…when the King's sister died in childbirth…" The old noble gathered inner strength. Coughed. Then continued more confidently as he grasped the speaker's staff. "The King ordered a shrine to be built. I know. I carried stones to the causeway of the Moku'ula."

"We all know that story…old man." Maunakili continued to bully the chief.

"What no one knows is…that tomb is not merely a tomb for the dead. The shrine contains more than the King's dowager queen mother. His sacred sister. And their child." Kapu and Bull Shaw exchanged a look then leaned in. "To this day the King prays not only to his sacred sister and lover…but to the golden spirit of the Moku'ula."

Maunakili shouted at the old chief: "Stop speaking riddles… old man. Does the royal tomb contain treasure? Speak plainly!"

With everyone's attention riveted on him the old *ali'i* thumped the Talking Stick on the matted floor. "The sacred tomb is also a sacred treasury." The old chief held firmly onto the Talking Stick. "Entrance to the King's island is strictly *kapu*. No one — not even myself — is allowed on the island except as the King's chosen guest."

"There are no guards now." Bull Shaw growled. "We can enter anytime."

The old chief smiled. Shook his head. "You are wrong. There is a guardian…The goddess Khawahine. She is the supernatural spirit of the lake. A great royal *mo'o* — the largest in all the kingdom. She is always watching…always vigilant. She devours any intruders that violate the sacredness of the Mokuʻula. This restriction is enforced on all the uninvited." The old man stared quietly into Maunakili's eyes. And nodded. "Be warned."

With that the old man relinquished the Talking Stick to Kapu. Bowed. No more was to be said. He walked backward toward the low door in the long wall of the Hale Piula. Then shuffled backward into the piazza outside. All the other nobles soon followed.

At the mountain-facing *mauka* end of the Hale Piula a throne stood before a tall screen. Maunakili stepped behind the screen to a garderobe area. From this cloakroom he selected a priceless mantle of ancient *mamo* feathers. And placed it over his massive shoulders. Resting on this cloak he placed a necklace of shark's teeth suspended by braided human hair. A royal necklace of the supreme rank. Finally the Piʻilani chief settled on his head a magnificent helmet crested in yellow feathers. Maunakili stepped out from behind the alcove screen. Took his place on the throne. His fearsome black tattoos ready for war.

"I knew in my bones the treasure is on the Mokuʻula. Now you heard it." Maunakili nodded to himself even as Bull Shaw and Kapu the Ugly stood nearby. "But if the treasure is not in the mausoleum…then my *mana* gives me the power to force the King to tell me where he hid it. The remains of my ancestor Kahekili gives Maunakili that power."

"What do we do now…Kahuna?" Bull Shaw asked.

"We must lure the King back to the Mokuʻula. He will lead us to this sacred treasury."

Kapu the Ugly nodded. Yet the idea of breaking the taboo and angering the lake spirit left him unsettled. He bowed deeply to hide his uneasiness.

"We can kill two birds with one stone." Bull Shaw snorted. "And we'll all be rich."

Maunakili took hold of the royal *koa* spear in a stand beside the throne. He planted it erect beside him. "And Maunakili—the Great Kahuna—will be the rightful King of Maui."

CHAPTER 66

A SOLITARY MAN drenched by a continual deluge pulled himself up the gangway ladder to the French warship. The torrential downpour made him almost invisible. A native with a double-outrigged *proa* and crab claw sail had carried the dark figure seventy-five miles from Lahaina to Hāna Bay at the eastern tip of Maui. The taciturn islander waited in the rain for the white man to return.

The man's boots splashed across the warship's deck with some familiarity. He rapped sharply on the captain's cabin door. Without waiting he then stepped into the cabin. He shed a sodden hat and dropped his rain-soaked oilskin cape.

Billy Mack saluted Rear Admiral Louis Tromelin. At that moment the Irish spy saw a second man — dressed from head to toe in black — turn from the window to face him. The Admiral gestured toward the figure. "*Permettez-moi de presenter…Envoy Extraordinaire…* His Excellency…Henri Malbec."

A chill ran up Billy Mack's spine. He nodded. At a gesture from Tromelin Mack handed Malbec the *bona fide* letter from Tahiti Governor Bruat. Then began his report. He told how he signed aboard the whaler *Bountiful* in Tahiti. As the Captain's steward Mack shadowed the American agent. That was how Mack learned the agent had run out of options. On a hunch the American agent and the Captain of the *Bountiful* sailed for Lahaina. They guessed LeGrand had been blown off course while carrying Napoleon's treasure. The American agent and the whaling Captain bet everything that LeGrand made landfall on Maui.

Malbec examined his fingernails with great interest. "And the name of this American agent?"

The Irish spy spit out the words with a slight disgust. "Jack Dancer."

Malbec took a pinch of snuff from a small tin lifted from his pocket. Offered none to Admiral Tromelin. And gave more attention to a fly buzzing around the cabin than to the Irish agent.

Mack continued: "Last night the agent's acquaintance—an American correspondent named Swift—and her island friend Kikilani investigated how opium is smuggled onto Maui. That led Swift and her companion to observe Captain Head trading rum for opium with Bull Shaw. Then they followed Shaw to Chang Fu's upcountry camp." Mack paused as he shot the Admiral a quick glance. "Maunakili was also there."

"*Merde.*" Admiral Tromelin frowned. "If the Americans learn we are using Maunakili to take over the Hawaiian Islands it will add another enemy to our plans."

Malbec continued to watch the fly. Then—faster than an eye can see—he raised his hand and snatched the fly from the air.

The commandant of Camp Blood opened his fist slowly. Held the fly by one wing and methodically plucked off its other wing and legs. Then placed the insect on a chart upon the plank table. And studiously watched the fly as it did its best to raise itself from off the table. *Interesting.* He smiled to himself. *It tries to fly…even with only one wing.* The next instant Malbec crushed the insect with his palm. Then dragged his hand across the back of a chair to scrape the carcass off his skin.

A drop of icy sweat ran down Mack's ribs in the humid air. "All the Americans know is that Maunakili is the kingpin behind the opium and trafficking cartel."

Malbec hissed. "Just another annoying American fly to be crushed!"

The French commander interjected. "We cannot let rum and opium turn Maunakili's head from wanting to be king of Maui."

"Maunakili needs us more than we need him." Malbec spoke through his clenched jaw. "Without France's naval power his plan will be nothing more than a rustle in the wind. Soon forgotten. Without Maunakili the Hawaiian King is just as needy of French protection. Yet we will complete our mission for King Philippe most easily if Maunakili is our puppet king. Then Maunakili can play at imposing a new domestic rule. While France rules all foreign affairs. Just as in Tahiti and the Marquesas."

Malbec stared quietly at Admiral Tromelin. Billy Mack watched the two men tensely. At that moment the downpour stopped.

In the silence the three men heard a deep rumble in the earth. A few moments later a rogue wave rocked the warship.

Malbec's lip curled into a sneer. "That is not thunder…Comrades."

The three men stepped to the gallery windows at the stern of the cabin. Their eyes took in the dull red glow of an angry horizon under a receding thunderhead.

A smile began to form on Malbec's thin lips. "Pele seeks revenge on the Hawaiians. For their sloth. And the Americans and British for overreaching in their greed." His eyes narrowed with a faraway look as he gazed out the aft-gallery windows.

After a long moment Malbec began to laugh aloud. "Pele's eruption will be our ally in our just and righteous mission."

CHAPTER 67

JOHN BARLEYCORN/GROG SHOP
FID STREET/LAHAINA TOWN
AS DUSK FELL

ISAAC PLACED his fat fingers on the bony shoulder of his equally drunken companion.

"If the end is near…Thomas…we should enjoy it!"

"Pele? Schmaylay. Gods are nothing but superstitious horse hocky." Thomas slurred as confidently as a drunken scarecrow. The other drinking companions at the table hardly seemed to notice. "It's the leprechauns of Maui that are making this fuss. Mind my words…Isaac. What we need is to find 'em and tell 'em… 'nough's enough."

"Yessiree Bob"—Isaac swayed—"tell 'em the joke's gone far enough."

They waved a cheery goodbye to their barmates. With many slaps on the back and "Godspeeds" the comical Don Quixote and his Sancho Panza led the nag awaiting them up the hill rising above the town. Up toward the volcano. Suddenly the earth shook.

"Here…'ave another swig…Isaac. It'll steady your feet." Both sailors sucked a long draft from a brown clay rum bottle.

"What are they called again?"

Thomas answered: "Menehune."

Isaac took a second slug. "Niver heard of 'em."

Thomas pulled Isaac up onto Rocinante's back. And settled his plump friend behind him.

Unsteadily onward the duo rode double: up the darkening slope toward the Kaua'ula Stream ditch. "Here Menehune… Here Menehune…" the tall drunken sailor called as the air cooled. "Come to Thomas…."

◎   ◎   ◎

From the harbor grog shop far below onlookers watched the two riders on horseback. Then — as dusk set in — followed the two whale-oil sea lanterns the sailors carried as they climbed the winding mountain trail. Soon darkness left little to see except the sailors' lamps. The lanterns made a sharp right-angle turn toward the south. The twinkling lights traversed the hillside as the pair seemed to follow a track beside what — in the thin light — looked like a bright line: an irrigation ditch. The onlookers knew this was the mother ditch that brought water north across the foothills from the Kaua'ula Stream. Eventually the two lights reached an elevation where the stream exited a gulch. From out of nowhere a flickering light appeared. Then three. Then a dozen. A hush fell over the drinkers below. One pointed toward the dark mountainside. The fainter points of light seemed to surround the two brighter whale-oil sea lanterns. Steadily more flickering lights appeared. The tiny lights encircled the sailors like fireflies.

Every eye from the grog shop was riveted on the strange scene. The circle of lights seemed to steadily close on the two seamen. For a long moment the seamen's whale-oil lamps seemed to halt by the gulch. Then the two lanterns swung in this direction. That. Front. Behind. As though the two lantern carriers were looking for an escape route — or were trying to frighten away small rodents that had surrounded them. The rapidly redirected lantern beams seemed to make the circling lights pause. To the onlookers' surprise the circle of needlelike lights tightened. Closed around the two stronger lamps. All at once the two sea lantern lights went dark. A gasp arose from the grog patrons. Looks of did-you-see-that burst on every face. And then the needlelike lights moved away. Like fireflies taking flight.

Then the lights entirely disappeared.

All night the grog shop waited. Two full jugs were placed on the bar. A sign beside them read: *Lost & Found.* One corked jug marked in candle soot with an *I* and the other with a *T.* Yet that night along Fid Street only the sailors' nag wandered into town. Isaac and Thomas never returned.

Next morning a handful of Boston shipmates retraced their comrades' path up the mountain. They found no sign of Isaac or Thomas. What they did find — lying next to the path — were two flattened sea lanterns.

The crushed lanterns lay beside two stone pillars. Like twin sentries. One tall. One short. The pillars stood beside the Kauaʻula Stream at a place that appeared to guard a hidden entrance to the distant Rainbow Valley.

In honor of their own effort — and their missing comrades — a Bunker Hill whaler uncorked the stoneware jugs marked *I* and *T* he had cradled all the way up the trail. In solemn ceremony the shipmates passed the finger-hole jugs one to another in grave communion. Soon the empty crocks rested near the guardian stones. And the party began to think about returning to their grog shop.

Just then a violent rumble convinced the search party to run for their lives back to Lahaina Town below.

CHAPTER 68

QUARTERDECK/*BOUNTIFUL*
LAHAINA HARBOR
EARLY NEXT MORNING/25 MAY 1847

DANCER. SWIFT. POST. AND MR. FLUTE stood on the *Bountiful*'s quarterdeck. All four companions shared Swift's disconsolate feeling of inevitable doom. Helplessly they peered up into the yellow sky. Toward the advancing hell. The air was heavy with sulfur. The sea a stench of slime. The water almost still as glass. Then Captain Post pointed down at the green water. Reverse wavelets pushed away from the shore and ran toward the *Bountiful*. Post expected the Maui volcano eruption would turn into catastrophe at any moment. *The harbor looks like a pincushion.* A sea of needlelike masts bobbed gently in the waves.

Moments later the delayed sound of a deep threatening rumble reached the foursome's ears.

From out of the thicket of masts a small outrigger made its way toward the *Bountiful*. The canoe's sole occupant maneuvered between the dark hulls and anchor lines. Swift's gaze quietly followed the craft. *Is that Kikilani?*

Within minutes Kikilani brought her canoe up on the far side of the *Bountiful*. Swift ran to the gangway and climbed down the ladder nearly to the waterline.

"What's the matter?"

Kikilani steadied her small craft at the bottom of the ladder. "Bad news."

Swift bent her knees and drew closer to Kikilani. With an arm hooked around the rope between rungs she shot Kikilani a concerned look. "Tell me."

Kikilani pointed with her chin in the direction of the *Ship of Paradise*. "Got to get back. But you must know…" Kikilani bit her lip. "I tried to talk to some of the captains when they came aboard the *Paradise*…to find out about Head. Dawes. Loki. And anything they knew…like what happened to those two Chinese girls at Chang Fu's camp."

"Did you learn anything?"

Kikilani swallowed then continued. "Word got back to Mama Samoa that I was asking about her private business for you." Kikilani wiped salt spray from her eyes. "Mama Samoa told all the captains to shut up…not talk to you—or me—about her operation." Kikilani stood up in the dugout. She held onto the ladder. "I heard one captain tell Mama: 'Only thing worse than a meddlesome missionary is a nosey scribbler. Mum's the word.'"

Swift couldn't believe her ears. "Sounds like my exposé has hit a wall."

"Sorry…Sam." Kikilani lowered herself back into the canoe. "Maybe I tried to help too much…"

With those last words Kikilani pushed off from the *Bountiful* and sailed back in the direction of the *Ship of Paradise*.

Swift climbed back on deck. Made her way slowly to the quarterdeck ladderway. Then rejoined Dancer. Post. And Mr. Flute at the side rail as they watched dumbfounded. First one. Then a pair. Then several whaling ships hoisted sail. The sound of capstans raising anchor chains rattled across the harbor. A veritable regatta began to file past the *Bountiful*. Out the Lahaina Roads. Around Kāʻanapali Point. Toward Kahului Bay. Into the yellow bank of volcanic fog hugging the northern shore. Swift's gaze followed the line of ships as it was swallowed by the pall of ash and cloud that hung over Lahaina Town.

A look of concern crossed Swift's face. She watched through the Captain's spyglass as a desperate line of abandoned missionaries onshore slowly made their way toward the Royal District along the King's Way. She saw — after a gap at the end of the line — a stooped missionary and his wife coming slowly along: the Reverend Jedidiah Wise and Mrs. Wise — who had sailed to Maui aboard the *Black Cloud*. The pair shuffled slowly. The Reverend's arm around his wife's shoulders: Mrs. Wise — Swift knew from surgeon's cabin chats — was almost five months pregnant...counting from New Year's Day at the equator. The entire line moved with the certainty of the condemned. A death march toward the Waine'e Church grounds. And its graveyard. The church's low square steeple still under construction. Its Normanesque outline barely visible between the palm trees. At a glance Swift realized the church on the inland shore of the King's sacred Loko Mokuhinia was the zealots' last refuge.

Captain Post spoke out loud...but softly. "Time is running out. I doubt even God can save them." Then Captain Post pointed toward the breakwater. Two islanders approached his vessel in a voyage canoe.

"Mauna Loa! Mauna Loa!" the islanders shouted. And pointed toward the sky of fire to the north.

Swift looked at Dancer questioningly. He raised his hands in bewilderment. And they both turned toward Captain Post and Mr. Flute.

Post's eyebrows raised. His voice spoke slightly above a whisper: "They say the volcano is Mauna Loa. It's the great Hawaiian volcano that erupted...Mauna Loa is on the big island of Hawai'i."

Mr. Flute responded almost immediately. "The eruption is almost a hundred miles away."

Post's shoulders relaxed. "That means the earthquakes and ash don't come from Maui's volcanos. They come from Pele's cauldron on the next island. Not here."

Dancer cracked a wry smile. "Looks like this isn't Maui's last call after all."

Post explained. "The trade winds brought the volcanic cloud over Maui from the Big Island of Hawai'i. The tremors we felt came from

Mauna Loa…not Haleakalā…or the caldera of the ‘Īao Valley on Maui. We're not doomed."

Swift looked stricken. She turned to face the others. "All this was a false alarm?"

Post and Mr. Flute nodded their assent.

Swift didn't share the others' relief. The departure of the whaling fleet had shattered the entire purpose of her mission. Now she could never gather the evidence she needed. Her project was finished before it got started. No sources. No proof. Just supposition and hearsay. Defeated. Nothing more than a naïve girl's laughable stunt.

Swift's gaze swept the harbor. Only three ships remained in Lahaina Roads. The *Bountiful*. The *Black Cloud*. And Mama Samoa's *Ship of Paradise*. Unable to sail because her "crew" had abandoned ship for the opportunity to follow the whaling fleet.

Mr. Flute shook his bald head. "Now that the whaling fleet has decamped…we are defenseless. We have no allies."

Swift stared at Dancer. Then Captain Post. And Mr. Flute. "This couldn't be worse." She gestured toward the empty harbor. "What do we do now?"

PART 4

KINGDOM OF MAUI

A SWIFT & DANCER
ADVENTURE

Moku'ula/King's Island

CHAPTER 69

A SMALL GROUP of elder chiefs filed from the Hale Piula. Then walked inland along a sandy causeway toward the King's Way. Several chiefs carried tall drums. All wore bunches of dried *kukui* nuts tied behind their knees. Soon before them—across a moat—ran another short causeway. This raised path was blocked by a stone wall and sentry gate that guarded the royal grounds of the most sacred place in all the Hawaiian Islands. The Mokuʻula. The King's island.

Beyond the island lay the legendary lake. The great seventeen-acre Loko Mokuhinia. Into this lake projected the sacred peninsula. The soil solely reserved for the King. Noble *aliʻi* over the years fortified the entire perimeter of the island with a low wall of lava rock. Not long ago open areas on the peninsula were maintained as vegetable and food gardens. Now they had turned to weed from disuse. Ever since the King abandoned the island as the site of the royal court two years before.

Every chief bowed his head momentarily in respect as he approached. *Mele* chants telling of generations of royals passed through their minds…back to King Piʻilani in the sixteenth century. Royal lines that made the revered islet their residence. It was a symbolic *piko*—

an umbilicus—that connected their highest chiefs to the islands'
ancient creators. A place of sacred red mists. An oasis. A retreat. Cool
and secure.

At the causeway—where they could not proceed over the moat
blocked by the sentry gate—the chiefs turned north. Padded along the
King's Way toward Lahaina Town. On the inland side they passed what
remained of fish-pond enclosures and watered taro fields. Now filled
with reeds in the elbow of the island between the King's Way and the
sacred space.

The elders knew without looking the sacred peninsula was shaped
like a giant boomerang. The compound supported three grass houses
for the royal family. One to the side of the gate. And one directly
opposite: on the far side of a ceremonial space. The third was the King's
sleeping house midway along the long axis of the island. Here a small
dock on the mountain side jutted into the lake. Two unused royal
canoes were tethered there. In days gone by the King's mother was
paddled across the pond for Sunday service at the Congregational
Waine'e Church. Its low square steeple and grassy grounds had
welcomed thousands. Back in a happier day.

Farther from the sentry gate at the northern tip stood a large stone
building. Part house. Part mausoleum. Designed in a European style.
Complete with pedal organ. Here the King kept the remains of his
mother. His sister. Their child. Close ancestors. And other treasures.

The chiefs moved farther along the road: perhaps twenty-some
canoe lengths toward Lahaina Town. Then gathered at the northern
edge of the sacred Mokuhinia lake. Along this shoreline the royal court
had once kept residences. Among them had been one of the finest grass
houses in the islands. The Hale Pili. A royal house built for the King's
sister—who was also his sacred wife. Nearby she had built a stone-and-
mud tomb for her mother—who died in 1823. In 1836 the princess'
first-born died weeks after birth. And the princess followed in death
within months the same year. Now both structures were abandoned.

Huddled beside the lake the elders raised a chant toward the
Rainbow Valley. Cut from the mountains in the upcountry distance.
The chant thanked Pele. Goddess of fire. Lightning. Wind. Volcanoes.
Ka wahine 'ai honua...the woman who devours the land. Creator and
destroyer. From a flat stone that projected into the water one elder

released a dog into the pond. The dog swam in a manic zigzag. Then struck out across the black-water lake. The men chanted. Watched. The mutt paddled: his head and neck bobbed along the surface.

The chant rose in pitch. Joined now by the chiefs' drums. The men stamped their feet in unison. The dried *kukui* nuts tied behind each chief's knee amplified the chant. The drums rose louder. The voices reached across the pond to the great breadfruit trees planted near the Moku'ula.

Without warning the dog yelped. The next moment the dog was pulled under the water. Then resurfaced.

The voices. The rattles. The drum's crescendo reached higher to the gods. A second time the dog was jerked below the surface. The chant peaked...and the dog disappeared.

"Oh...Kihawahine goddess..." The oldest chief intoned the ancient song: "Spirit of the lake...protect us. Oh...Sacred One: Take this small sacrifice to your sister goddess Pele. Take with it our thanks for not destroying the world."

Moments later the chiefs moved on toward the footbridge where the fresh mountain water flowed.

CHAPTER 70

WAINE'E CHURCH
OVERLOOKING LOKO MOKUHINIA
LATER THAT DAY

MAUNAKILI WALKED with his guard beneath the towering coconut palms along the southern inland trail around the Mokuhinia. Pele's revenge had passed. Now the Waine'e churchyard was empty. Except for Charlie Pickham. Angus Macomber. And just-arrived Abner Sisson. The three white men prepared to greet Maunakili under the great palms as he entered the churchyard. The Pi'ilani king swept past them. He wore a full-length *ahu'ula* cape: To a base of netted twine the brilliant-colored feathers had been expertly attached. The solids broken by black and yellow patterns of *'ō'ō* black-bird feathers. The broad cape made Maunakili's imposing size even more threatening.

The Pi'ilani's gaze moved over the walls of the simple Congregational Church. The Mokuhinia Lake stretched toward the seashore. And the grassy area where thousands of parishioners could gather. A contemptuous snort passed from the warrior's half-tattooed face. Macomber stiffened. Adjusted his place slightly behind Pickham's shoulder.

Maunakili turned and faced the threesome. Abner Sisson took a deep breath. Began. "As you know…I had just come from Honolulu before—before the Mauna Loa eruption. The day I left the palace the King confided in me that he planned to sail to Lahaina soon."

Maunakili managed a disinterested look.

Sisson read Maunakili's mood. "The short of it…is that the King secretly yearned to come to Lahaina."

"Why do you waste our time with this?" Maunakili demanded as his feathered cape seemed to flutter in the breeze.

"It is critical because the King plans to travel incognito. And…alone."

Pickham's foxlike face seemed to have grown ebullient. "That is exactly what the King did five months ago. It was the ten-year anniversary of his sister's death after childbirth. As we know…she died 30 December 1836."

Maunakili raised a hand for silence. "Now is the time to strike. We must trap the King on the Moku'ula. If he travels alone…all the better. That will make it that much easier for me to force him to reveal where the great treasure is held."

Macomber instinctively fondled his gold watch. "The King moved the royal throne and court to Honolulu two years ago. As you can see the royal compound—the Moku'ula—was left abandoned. Guarded only by tradition and superstition."

Pickham cut him off. "We know…Angus. No one goes to the island now. Even the old chiefs are afraid to get closer than the road for the occasional ceremony."

Maunakili halted further talk. "We trap the King on Moku'ula Island." He nodded to indicate the island several hundred yards across the lake. "We must rid our land of the usurper King—and force the usurper to reveal where in the sacred compound he keeps the treasure. Only then will the Pi'ilanis' lost kingdom be restored and our rightful treasure found. Nothing less will reestablish my true line to the throne." Maunakili let his demand sink in. "That is also why I must personally see he meets the same fate his father showed my people at the battle of Kepaniwai in the 'Iao Valley. The Battle of the Dammed Waters. Where the bodies of my Pi'ilani brothers blocked the bloody stream. Revenge will be mine."

"An eye for an eye." Pickham slyly muttered the old adage.

There was a pause. Then Sisson continued: "It is unfortunate that it must be this way. But we can no longer stand by while the King waffles over the future of the kingdom — and our future as well."

Maunakili raised his index finger. "To ensure the outcome we all want we must stand ready to take over after the King's death."

Macomber nodded reflexively.

Maunakili stepped forward in the grass. He stood between Sisson and the other two men. "Sisson: At my direction you will create a provisional government. As your first act you will muster a militia under the command of Captain Head and Mate Dawes."

Maunakili fixed them with a determined glare. "The militia must protect the fort and the Customs House to guarantee peace and order."

"And the chandlery." Macomber paused then added: "And the Seamen's Hospital."

Cold calculation crossed Maunakili's brow. "As the new king of Maui I will rule from the royal compound of the Moku'ula — and the Hale Piula will be my court." He spread his tattooed feet wider. "My spies tell me a native girl was returned by the *Black Cloud*. They say she has a birthmark on her neck that resembles a sea turtle. Your first responsibility is to bring me that soiled Pi'ilani girl. She will be my sacred queen." The rebel chief's glare swept the group. "Then our allies — the French — will guard our shores. Those arrangements have been made. The French Navy will protect us from retaliation from the British or Americans."

Sisson stared at Maunakili. Realization and shock registered on his face. "What is needed beyond the militia?" Sisson stammered unsure of himself.

Maunakili held Sisson with a stare. "As your king I shall name you my prime minister…Sisson."

Sisson blinked. *The King…or Maunakili?* His plans with Pickham and Macomber always assumed Maunakili would depose the King and claim the throne for himself. Only then could he see a clear path for their property grab to be implemented. But now he found his loyalties in turmoil.

"And for your support…gentlemen" — Maunakili nodded toward Pickham and Macomber — "you will have first choice of Crown lands and water sources abandoned by the King and his Hawaiian *ali'i*. For that opportunity you will pay my kingdom one half of the land's value to hold ownership. Your other petty schemes will remain untouched...as long as I say so. Understood?"

Pickham and Macomber expressed their acceptance silently.

"Then we are agreed. You will soon have a new king—and sacred queen. At last the righteous line of Pi'ilani royalty will be restored. And the Hawaiian usurper will be dead."

Maunakili turned and left the churchyard. His palm-carrying entourage then led their high chief around the south side of the Mokuhinia: back toward the Hale Piula.

@ @ @

Sisson's gaze followed the warrior king. *Am I nothing more than a traitor...a Judas Iscariot to the Hawaiian King?* His turmoil continued to force the questions into his mind. He checked his pocket watch and grimaced. "Must leave...Angus. Charlie. Other affairs require my presence. Excuse me."

The King's advisor—and soon to be undoer—hurriedly retraced his steps along the path on the inland edge of the lake. He made his way through the breadfruit grove toward Lahaina Town.

CHAPTER 71

WAINE'E CHURCH
LOKO MOKUHINIA/LAHAINA
MINUTES LATER

PICKHAM AND MACOMBER gloated over their good fortune as they moved inside the church nave for more privacy.

"We win either way...Macomber." Pickham's shrewd eyes fixed on the ex-missionary and he smacked a fist into his palm.

Macomber looked quizzically at the renown missionary's son. "What do you mean?"

"If Maunakili's rebellion is successful...you and I get first pick of the best lands."

"At one-half the land value for payment?" Macomber winced. Then rubbed the tips of his fingers with his thumb as if that price was too high.

"One-half...One-third...Even double the value. It doesn't matter. The key is who sets the value. Picture this. Land seized for taxes. Or for unpaid survey fees. That value is only pennies. Or take abandoned land. That land is worthless until it is worked. We'll register our claim at minimal present value. Especially if the land is dry. Water directed from the mountains will enrich the value...in the future." A cunning smile crossed Pickham's thin mouth. "All we need is title."

Greed showed in Macomber's gaunt smile. "Grab free land…
assemble large parcels." His brow knit. "But we don't set the value.
That's done by the Commission to Reform Land Titles…isn't it?"

Pickham rubbed his little hands together. "Yes. Exactly. And every
ex-missionary and trader on the commission is our friend. In fact…
our ally."

"What if Maunakili fails? How do we win?"

"The Hawaiian King is committed to going ahead with the land
division already in motion. That is the only way he can disenfranchise
the Pi'ilani *ali'i*—and annex their lands for his kingdom. Once
foreigners can buy land—and hold title free of any royal
chicanery—then we have won. We will be able to sell the lands we
hold—and transformed with the diverted streams—to foreigners
for unimagined prices. Against our web of laws. Rules. And
ordinances Maunakili's old ways will be even more futile than the
Hawaiian King's mistakes."

"But who can make that happen?" Macomber questioned.

Pickham's eyes glittered in the light from the church windows.
"Watch me. Except for Sisson…every member of the Privy Council is
licking their chops to expand the land division rules already passed by
the Honolulu Legislative Council. No problem. We will make those
rules so fiendishly complex—so convoluted…so byzantine—no local
kuleana—no land tenant or witless native—could hope to comply."
Pickham smiled with satisfaction through clenched teeth. "Land
division will change everything…forever."

Pickham laughed to himself. "The Great Mahele." He stated the
name without irony. "To divide…or to portion. That is the best
translation." A crafty expression crossed his face. "Of course Sisson in
his naïveté thinks it will bring order out of chaos…Provide secure title
to the islanders…."

"The road to hell is paved with good intentions." Macomber's joke
fell on friendly ears.

"Divide and conquer. Literally." Pickham paused as the intrigue
seemed to give him strange pleasure. "Gone will be the idea of squatters
possessing the land as caretakers. Gone will be the influence of kings.
And with them their heathen gods."

"Once the educated and the elite own the land…someday they will call it the 'Great Taking.'" Macomber joked. His comically large ears belied the avarice behind his grin.

Pickham pounded his small hand on the back of a pew in resolve. "At last we will save Hawai'i from the Hawaiians themselves!"

Macomber licked his lips. "We'll make the rules...then use the rules against them."

"Exactly."

The men shook hands. Clapped each other on the shoulder.

Macomber tipped his hat mockingly toward the simple wooden cross behind the church's altar. "It's the burden of the white man."

They both laughed like misers as they left the church.

Samantha Swift crouched as quiet as a church mouse in the nook behind the church's pulpit. Until the two schemers left by the side door. Once the shadows from the palms lengthened over the church graveyard Swift slipped outside. Undetected she made her way along the Waine'e church path. Ducked into the groves. Then turned left toward her guesthouse just beyond the bridge: over the stream that fed the Loko Mokuhinia waters.

CHAPTER 72

CAPTAIN'S CABIN/*BOUNTIFUL*
LAHAINA HARBOR
SUNSET

DANCER GREETED Samantha Swift and Mr. Flute as he entered Captain Post's cabin. The late-afternoon arrival nodded to Kikilani and Adam Akamu. Only Captain Post was missing. Mr. Flute stepped forward and shook Dancer's hand. Dancer dropped into the Captain's seat at the table opposite where Swift stood. He took a brief glance at some sheafs of paper and stacks of receipts lying beside Swift but then leaned back and turned his eyes to Swift.

"I brought you all here with a purpose." Swift held each onlooker's gaze. "That purpose...is our survival."

Dancer let his eyes travel around the cabin. Kikilani and Akamu: youthful and eager. Mr. Flute: ironclad and reliable. His gaze stopped on Samantha Swift. His eyes imperceptibly narrowed.

With a determined look Swift continued: "The volcano drove the entire American whaling fleet off to Kahului Bay. We're helpless." Then it struck her. "Where is Captain Post?"

Dancer tapped the toe of his boot impatiently. "You're right... Swift. It's only us. The fleet is gone. We can expect no help from that quarter. As for Captain Post...Doctor Pickham beseeched Post to take the good doctor to the Big Island. To check on the missionaries: Reverend Asa Thurston. Reverend Elias Bond. A rancher named John Palmer Parker. And their families."

Mr. Flute filled in the blanks. "Their stations are all on the northern-most Kohala Coast of the Hawai'i Island. About sixty nautical miles southeast as the gull flies—but farther if you tack around the north shore of Maui fighting the trade winds. You can almost see the Kohala headland and the harbor of Kawaihae from the *Bountiful*'s crow's nest."

Dancer picked up on Mr. Flute's explanation. "The missionaries live in the shadow of the Mauna Loa volcano. No word has come. They may have perished. Captain Post could not say no to Doctor Pickham's request. They left early this morning in a double-outrigged sailing canoe. If you want to go ashore and scribble notes in your temperance hotel you're free to go any time."

Swift set her jaw. Took a deep breath. Shot Dancer a hard glance. "As far as I can tell we're all in this together…what's left of us. Your shoot-first-aim-later style could risk the entire mission…Dancer. Here is how I see it. Tell me if I'm wrong."

Swift took a seat on the edge of the table. Dancer leaned back in the chair at the end.

"Kikilani was kidnapped two years ago. Taken to New York. On the way Loki was either killed or committed suicide. Together Kikilani and I investigated the Paradise Palace. We found out Queen Tin'a had lots of low friends in high places." Swift shot Dancer a disapproving look. "Besides the need to bring Kikilani back home we came to Lahaina to find a connection between trafficking island girls for rum and Chinese opium…and where the whalers fit in. Thanks to our night work at La Perouse Bay we know Head and Dawes trade rum for opium… and buy girls."

Dancer nodded. "And that the kingpin behind it all is Maunakili."

"As I said…our night work paid off."

Dancer gave a satisfied half smile remembering his rigorous contribution on the *Ship of Paradise.*

Swift continued: "My mission is to expose the traffickers and prove the tie-in between Atlantic rum. Pacific girls. And opium. That's why I used the volcano panic to do some midnight research in the Customs House."

"Good thinking…Swift." Dancer's tone conveyed that he was impressed.

Swift shifted her gaze. "You'll remember the paint oil barrels… Mr. Flute?"

Mr. Flute nodded.

"The cargo from the *Black Cloud* was entered in the Harbor Master's ledger…as you'd expect. But when I studied the log I discovered it recorded only half the quantity of barrels Kikilani and I counted in the hold."

"Sounds like a hugger-mugger in the Customs House." Dancer leaned forward with greater interest. "That suggests Head had an accomplice."

"Even more telling: I was able to scan the tariff receipts book. Head's paint oil was never taxed. Yet on the previous page another rum import from Nantucket paid a temperance tax of nearly ten dollars per gallon."

Mr. Flute whistled. "Sounds like protectionism to me. That's how Head maintained his monopoly in the grog shops."

"Exactly. Head's no-taxed rum undercut any other imports. Plus…half his cargo wasn't reported at all."

"But that just makes Head a smart trader…not a traitor with a 'T'. He can't do it alone. Who is part of his scheme in Lahaina? Who is Head's accomplice?" Dancer asked.

Swift looked at Dancer and smiled. "That would be our friend…Angus Macomber. General consul of Lahaina. Harbor Master. And custom collector."

"How do you know?" Kikilani asked.

"On a hunch I followed Macomber to the Waine'e Church this afternoon. Macomber met Sisson and Pickham outside with Maunakili and his troop. I couldn't hear what they said. But afterward Pickham and Macomber went inside the church. They started gloating about how they would grab land no matter what happens regarding Maunakili's plot to overthrow the King."

"Nice work again…Swift." Dancer gave the journalist credit.

"As I learned last night in the Customs House: Every cargo entry has Macomber's initials in the ledger book. Every tariff receipt is signed by Macomber. But he slipped up. In the back of the book I found a batch of tariff receipt forms. Signed. Stamped. Made out to Captain Head for paint oil. But without any received cargo...or revenue. In short: faked receipts to paper over their scheme. And that is what I have here."

With that Swift picked up several of the sheafs of official-looking parchment lying on the table. Waved them quietly. And passed them around.

Dancer muttered: "Got him."

"There's more." Swift nodded. "Under the tariff receipts were forged receipts from the Seamen's Hospital. Doctors' contracts. Supplies. Rent. Food. Laundry." Swift picked up the receipts and handed the forgeries to Mr. Flute. "Doesn't add up...especially because I rode by the Seamen's Hospital and discovered the hospital is not in operation. Empty as a graveyard."

Even the tight-lipped Mr. Flute acknowledged Swift's results with a nod. "What you said earlier corroborates your lava tube adventure too. You and Kikilani saw Head and Dawes transport the rum and barter it for opium with Bull Shaw. And then you watched Dawes buy the girls. From my grog shop visits I know Bull Shaw and Kapu enforced the monopoly in the grog shops and collected protection money on the side."

"But Bull Shaw and Kapu don't work for Head and Dawes..." Swift said.

Dancer snapped his middle finger with his thumb. "Behind it all is Maunakili. Maunakili is the bigwig...the Opium King of the Pacific. He directs the flow of opium to Maui and takes it in through one powerful beak. Like a giant squid!"

"That fits." Swift nodded. "We saw Maunakili at the Kula Camp of Chang Fu. Maunakili *is* the bigwig behind the operation. And his henchmen — Bull Shaw and Kapu — do his bidding."

Silence fell over the group as the revelations sank in.

Dancer broke the quiet. "After my chat with Malbec and Tromelin in Hāna Bay...my instinct tells me there's no end to the mischief they might be up to. It seems possible" — he caught himself — "no...*probable* that they have planted a spy amongst us. He most likely blended in...unobserved. But a cutthroat...not a

trained assassin. My guess is that spy may have tried to kill someone…
or was successful."

"Tried to kill someone? You mean someone like Duffy Ragsdale?"
Swift gasped. "Could the spy be Ratter Dawes?"

"Unlikely." Mr. Flute's tone was as stoic as ever. "Dawes is a thug.
Hired to kill you on the outbound voyage."

Dancer concluded: "No…this spy would be working in concert
with the foreign power plotting to take over the islands and dominate
the Pacific."

Swift interjected. "Dancer…weren't you almost killed on the
Bountiful after Tahiti? Could the spy have been on board with you
traveling to Maui?"

Dancer pondered Swift's question. "We lost a sailor in a storm
when he and I were taking in the staysails and storm jibs…" He
frowned uncertainly. "Whoever the spy is we'd better figure it out
before it's too late."

A few moments passed in silence. Kikilani whispered something
into Akamu's ear. He cleared his throat before speaking. "On the day
before the *Black Cloud* and the *Bountiful* arrived in Lahaina I was filling
the lighthouse oil. As is my custom every evening. The King's yacht
was docked at the wharf. Abner Sisson invited me aboard the yacht.
He told me twenty thousand dollars was missing from the Customs
House in Honolulu. Someone had laid in a shipment of lead-shot cases.
The money was exchanged for the shot—and the cases removed from
the Customs House."

"Any suspects?" Dancer asked.

"Sisson wasn't sure. But he suspected Maunakili. I must be
honest. This disturbs me greatly. For years I have studied the
Christian ways of the missionaries. They told us our King had
accepted their teachings. That we—in turn—must also accept the
foreign way. Now I hear of Maunakili. Chants and *mele* songs say he
is Maui's true king. That his bloodline is pure Pi'ilani. More pure
than the Hawaiian King. The Pi'ilani chiefs say Maunakili will restore
the Kingdom of Maui. The kingdom that the Hawaiians took from
us by force. But—if it is true Maunakili has profits from rum
and opium smuggling—why would he risk stealing from the
Customs House?"

Dancer stirred uncomfortably in his chair. "The only reason is that Maunakili needs the money. Or he needs much more money. Really *big* money. Not just a down payment...but enough money to buy complete protection. To buy the protection of a foreign navy."

Akamu knit his brow and put a gentle hand on Kikilani's shoulder. With a slight squeeze he encouraged her to speak up. She cleared her throat. "The other day I saw my cousin. He said he sailed a foreign seaman to Hāna Bay. There was a great storm. But the sailor went aboard a foreign ship. It had a flag of three colors. I wish I knew more."

Dancer rose to his feet and came beside Swift. "The pieces are falling into place. This is what has bothered me. The powers that be...marshalled by your editor Mr. Whitman and your friendly banker Mr. Penrhos...sent Mr. Flute to protect Swift. And the President and Secretary of State sent me to find a lost treasure. But that was in November. Little did they know that a major foreign power would hatch a plot to control Hawai'i—and the entire North Pacific."

Mr. Flute hesitated and then spoke slowly. "Washington is probably still clueless. It isn't the British who are trying to control the North Pacific. They had second thoughts about canceling their protection treaty with Hawai'i. And wanted compensation for the loss of the Oregon Territory to the United States."

Dancer addressed the entire group. "What nobody knew until I followed the trail left by Napoleon's treasure—a Paris notebook— a Zanzibar letter from LeGrand: LeGrand followed La Pérouse's charts across the Pacific from Samoa to Tahiti—"

"And then the hurricane shipwrecked LeGrand on Maui." Swift recalled the information Dancer had told her aboard the *Ship of Paradise.*

Mr. Flute ran his calloused palm over his mouth and chin. "Now Dancer's spying has confirmed the mystery ship Kikilani's cousin saw in Hāna Bay....is the French warship *Némésis.*"

Swift threaded the beads. "Everything points to one conclusion. There is only one tri-color flag behind this plot. The French."

"What does that mean?" Kikilani asked.

"It means Maunakili is plotting to use the French Navy to take over Maui and Hawai'i." Dancer nodded to Swift. "That's why Maunakili stole the twenty thousand dollars: as a down payment for French protection. And why our spy met the French ship in Hāna Bay."

Mr. Flute stared at Dancer. Realization and a grim look on his face. "This is bigger than all of us...."

Swift bit her lip. "When Walt Whitman sent me out here it was to get the story about rum and opium smuggling. Now I see that's part of a much bigger story. But I still need to thread the beads on the sex trafficking. Where did Dawes take those Chinese girls when he left Chang Fu's camp?"

Dancer took a deep breath. "More than a story...Swift." His eyes swept the room. "This could be the end of America's brief—but doomed—seventy-five-year history."

Mr. Flute pushed both of his leathered hands over his shaved head to wipe away a gleam of sweat. "If we don't stop the French now— here in Lahaina—they could rule the entire Pacific."

Dancer spoke his worries out loud: "If we don't stop them America could be facing a Third Empire on our west coast. Or worse." He sank back into the Captain's chair. "The French. Maunakili. And their allies must be stopped."

Mr. Flute nodded. "As Swift said...our survival depends on it."

As the harsh Lahaina sunset poured through the *Bountiful*'s stern gallery Swift spoke evenly. "To save America we must save Hawai'i. We're on our own. We are the only ones who can save Hawai'i now...and America." The young correspondent frowned. "There is no turning back. We cannot let America's destiny die here."

CHAPTER 73

FIVE DESPERATE FIGURES stood over the Captain's table. Mr. Flute spread a map of Lahaina Roads and Lahaina Town on the wooden surface. Akamu lit the gimbaled lamps. Swift and Dancer took charge.

Swift leaned over the maps. "We need to buy some time. Soon the French will be sailing around the south shore of Maui to Lahaina Roads to take advantage of the trade winds."

Dancer traced the route on the map. "We need to keep them out of the harbor — beyond cannon range of Lahaina…if at all possible."

"Leave that to me." Mr. Flute nodded. "I will take a fast whaleboat to Kawaihae on Hawai'i and try to locate Captain Post. It's a long shot — but if I can find him…and if we can return to Kahului Bay — he may be able to bring back what's left of the whaling fleet."

Dancer muttered: "That's a lot of ifs…It could take days — if you find him at all. But success would give the French something to think about."

"When can you leave?" asked Swift.

"We can shove off in the darkness before dawn rises to attract the least attention. With the *Bountiful* still at anchor no one will suspect."

Swift turned her gaze to Kikilani. The island maiden was biting her full lower lip. "I'll redouble my efforts at Mama Samoa's." Kikilani plucked a fragrant tuberose blossom from her flowered headpiece *lei*. "If there is any place that can turn out a spy it's the *Ship of Paradise*. And whoever the spy is maybe he'll lead us to where Head and Dawes hide the kidnapped girls. I haven't had any luck on that yet…though I've worked a lot of whalers at the bar."

Akamu cast a glance at Kikilani as if to say she shouldn't enjoy herself. Then thought better of it. His voice carried concern for a different worry. "I will gather my friends and brothers. Among them are some fierce warriors. We may need some help once Maunakili's men and the French get serious."

"Place some of them as lookouts on Mama Samoa's ship." Dancer eyed Akamu keenly. "Never can be too safe. If Kikilani uncovers a spy we may need to neutralize whoever it is before the spy kills one of us."

Swift nodded to Akamu in acknowledgment and gripped Kikilani's hand. "We know Head. Macomber. And Maunakili are profiting from their smuggling network. Greed and opportunity. But it stands to reason there are more actors." She began to rattle off the remaining questions: "Who is influencing the King? Why has he isolated himself in Honolulu? And why is the King so intent on giving up the royal lands that belong to the kingdom? The whole idea of the land division — the Great Mahele — troubles me. Who has the King's ear? Who is manipulating the King?" She frowned. "We are missing an important piece of the puzzle. While Mr. Flute is searching for Captain Post on the Hawai'i island I'll do some more digging in Lahaina Town."

Swift paused. Mr. Flute shifted his gaze. "What are you up to…Dancer?"

Dancer wrestled with his thoughts for a moment. "I promised Post I'd stay with the *Bountiful*. But I didn't promise to stay in Lahaina." Dancer spoke his words emphatically: "I'm going to sail to O'ahu for a quick turnaround visit to see some friends. Let's pray for fair winds."

CHAPTER 74

KIKILANI POURED Billy Mack a fourth rum cocktail with bitters. Lime. Sugar. And very little water. A soft wind caressed the elevated deck of the *Ship of Paradise*.

"Show me a real Irishman and I'll show you a man that drink cannot affect." Billy Mack balanced unsteadily on a stool facing the sunset.

Kikilani beamed a lustrous smile at Mack. "Not every Irishmen… only the strongest." She practically cooed her compliment.

Mack puffed his chest like a barnyard rooster. Kikilani freshened Mack's drink with more rum. Stroked his shoulder. Looked fascinated with every word the sailor spoke.

"Soon I will be a very very rich man…my lovely."

Kikilani smiled and touched the back of Mack's hand. "Kikilani likes rich men." She adjusted a spray of fragrant tuberose behind her ear.

With a furtive glance Mack watched Kikilani's young breasts rise under her gauzy shift. He took a long pull on his rum. Then bragged again that the French would soon make him rich.

Kikilani smiled. "Rich men are best. But sometimes"—she pouted—"their talk is bigger than their action."

Billy Mack swelled even more. He motioned with an index finger for Kikilani to come closer. As if he had a secret to share only with her. Kikilani leaned in. "Take me to the Hall of Paradise...and I'll tell you a secret."

Kikilani moved her body closer. Pressed her thighs against Billy Mack. "You tell me your secret...and I'll show you mine." Kikilani touched the back of Mack's neck and laid her lips on his ear. "You tell me...and I'll show you my secrets. Promise."

Mack teetered drunkenly. "Promise?"

"Promise." The beauty of Lahaina threw Mack a dazzling smile.

Mack leaned forward on the bar: He used the crook of his elbow to shield his secret from prying ears. "I work for the French...you see." He tittered drunkenly. "I was undercover when the *Bountiful* sailed from Tahiti. They wanted me to keep a watch on that American agent...and that self-righteous Captain Hamilton Post. I did more than that." Mack confided his claim conspiratorially.

Kikilani played along. "What did such a strong man like you do?"

"Dancer almost met his maker. Would have. But that fool sailor Hawthorne got in the way. Would have meant a big bonus too." Mack's vehemence grew as he ran on: "But just you wait...Dancer. Your tears will be sorry...but they'll be too late. You see...I've got Dancer's number. And while I'm at it that pompous Captain Post will get his high and mighty payback too. You'll see. My French pals will blow them to smithereens...and that will make me a very rich man. Very very soon. Then you can be my prinssess." Mack slurred the final word.

"You're like no man I've ever met...Billy." Kikilani continued her soft whisperings into the sailor's ear. "How do you know so much?"

Mack laughed self-importantly. "I know because I delivered the message in person to Hāna Bay. Let me tell you...that Dancer cracker...he's no profiteer...no trader....He's a secret agent for the Americans! They'll go down together...all because of me...you'll see." The Irish sailor still tittered to himself. "Not only that...but I know another secret."

Kikilani whispered: "If you tell me...my friend...I'll show you more. Would you like that?"

Mack looked left. Then right. Leaned back deeper into one elbow on the bar. Then pulled Kikilani closer. "I know where Dawes and Head keep their girls…before they sail for New York…"

Kikilani turned her ear with the tuberose blossom closer to the sailor.

Mack breathed deep. "Smells like paradise."

Kikilani touched his cheek in encouragement.

Mack whispered: "They keep 'em in the storeroom at the grog shop." The Irishman hiccuped. Then under his breath began a sing-song boast. "Mack ain't no gimp. No…not Billy Mack. Take a gander…prinssess. Here you see a rich man…a very very rich man. Grand Billy…theys'l call me…Touch their hats… Curtsey low…Yes…a very very wealthy man…that's me!"

Kikilani slipped Mack a last drink. This one laced with a hefty potion. A cocktail courtesy of the Shanghai crimps that trolled for unsuspecting dregs at the Paradise Palace. The Irishman's face stiffened. Then he went limp. Two warriors carried his form to the gangway and placed it in a canoe taxi: Billy Mack was fated to wake up on a remote beach beside the Olowalu Stream south of Lahaina Town. Memory-less. And with a roaring headache.

But a free man.

CHAPTER 75

FOOTHILLS CAMP/OLOWALU STREAM
SOUTH OF LAHAINA TOWN
NEXT DAY

THE OLOWALU FOOTHILLS overlooked Lahaina Roads. From a hidden outpost Henri Malbec's gaze took in the Olowalu Point below. Where the stream entered the sea. There the reefs were inhabited by manta rays and blacktip reef sharks. These denizens patrolled beyond the ancient Olowalu *heiau* and its sacred Place of Refuge. Here in days past common islanders entreated their gods for good fishing. An adobe Congregational church with three-feet thick walls stood near a one-room Catholic school established the year before by Father Modest Favens. Both buildings already showed decay.

Six miles to the north Malbec could just make out three ships anchored off Lahaina Town.

A suffering Billy Mack hovered like a sentry in the shade not too near Malbec.

Below the well-positioned camp Malbec surveyed Olowalu's alluvial plain: the taro fields and fishponds. There the stream fed irrigated terraces that hugged the foothill slopes. Planted successively with breadfruit trees. Sweet potato. Coconut. And *kukui* candlenut. On the plain — beyond the taro plants — mulberry grew to make *kapa* cloth. There was grass for *pili* house thatch. Sandalwood once grew here in plentiful groves.

Malbec waited as he leaned into the carved back of his wooden campaign chair.

The camp's level ground with its canopy of shady hibiscus was an old resting place at the mouth of the trail that led into the mountains: up to the Olowalu Pass and 'Iao Valley. Up the hillside path from the lookout camp — near the base of a cliff — eons before the rushing Olowalu Stream had carved a natural rock overhang. It was along this trail — fifty-seven years ago — that the son of Maui's King fled after the Battle of the Dammed Waters.

Soon Maunakili appeared below. Carried toward the hillside camp in his litter by his *ali'i* followers. Six subservient steps behind Maunakili's palanquin Bull Shaw and Kapu the Ugly attended their chief. The Great Kahuna was carried to the back of the camp near the largest hibiscus tree. Kapu glanced at the valley trail across the stream. Then at Bull Shaw as he eyed Billy Mack…who stood rubbing his eye sockets and sweating in the shade near Malbec.

Maunakili rose to his full height from his litter. Then strode toward Malbec…who insolently did not rise from his foldable scissors chair deep under the shade tree.

Quickly bored Malbec spoke bluntly. "Here is what must happen." His words dripped demeaning insults with every phrase. He presented the French ultimatum: France would protect King Maunakili. In return France would control foreign affairs. And shipping. Maunakili would control internal affairs. Tax collection. Landownership.

"Do you understand?"

The price was fixed. Maunakili must supply payment of Napoleon's treasure. Payment of the treasure was paramount.

Maunakili demanded the rum monopoly. The opium. And the trafficking trade. "That belongs to me. The King of Maui."

"What you do on your little island is of no interest to the King of the French." That — however — was a lie. Malbec secretly imagined himself as the kingpin of the opium. Rum. And slave-smuggling trade in the Pacific.

Malbec repeated: "Payment of Napoleon's treasure is everything. No payment and we'll blow your paradise away for sport."

Maunakili shot Malbec a fierce scowl. "You will have your treasure. I know exactly where it is." Another lie.

"Just so you understand. Your absolute deadline is sunset three days hence."

Maunakili's nostrils flared. His eyes widened slightly. The whites showed like a searchlight in his tattooed half-black face. His jaw clenched. *When I am king you will prostrate yourself before me.*

"In the meantime..." Malbec's voice was unconcerned. "The French frigate will sail soon from Hāna into La Perouse Bay. On the night of the deadline I—Malbec—will station myself in this Olowalu outpost. From here I can see Lahaina clearly. When I hear the eight o'clock cannon I will signal the warship in the bay to the south to advance." Malbec pointed toward La Perouse Bay.

Through a tight jaw Maunakili said: "You can count on the Great Kahuna."

Malbec snorted contemptuously. "I never trust natives. Least of all half-breeds."

Maunakili flexed his fists.

Malbec rose. Stood eye to Adam's apple with Maunakili. "When you have the treasure and the King is dead—you will not light the lighthouse that night. It must be dark. Do you understand? *Keep the lighthouse dark!* Darkness in the lighthouse will be the signal that the Hawaiian King is dead—*and* that you have the treasure." Still...Malbec saw the need to repeat his instructions: "Do not burn the white light. When I see no light I will direct Commander Tromelin to keep his cannons covered." Malbec paused. "If there is light I will know your coup has failed. Then King Philippe's powerful warship will arrive at full battle stations with cannons primed and fuse punks burning."

Maunakili nodded in agreement.

Bull Shaw and Kapu the Ugly moved to stand a step to the side and behind their Pi'ilani patron.

Malbec repeated: "If you fail and the lighthouse burns...we will blow Lahaina off the map. Let me be clear. Kill the light...and I will know the King is dead. If there is light...all Lahaina will suffer. But darkness or light—either way—France will control Maui that night. Be it known that France is interested in the larger picture. First Lahaina and Maui. Then Honolulu to displace the Americans and British—

and rectify the ill treatment of our priests." Malbec saw no need to reveal France's grander plans. Ruling the Pacific. Colonizing California. Liberating the lands of the Louisiana Purchase. And restoring French Canada. "And—when you do as I say—you will have your little kingdom…Maunakili. Your little kingdom here in the French Pacific."

"The Hawaiian King is a dead man." Maunakili snarled. "Leave him to me. I will take care of him. My plan is in place. And I will have your treasure."

Bull Shaw rubbed his hands together. "I'll take care of the lighthouse." Shaw sneered. Then added. "And Mr. Flute is mine."

Malbec closed the exchange. "How you do it is your affair. But do it. Deliver the King's head and Napoleon's treasure—and you'll get your kingdom…Maunakili. Remember: Darkness means the King is dead and France will make you king."

After Maunakili's litter left the compound—flanked by Bull Shaw and Kapu the Ugly—Malbec spoke over his shoulder in a low malevolent voice to Billy Mack. "Bring me Dancer's head. King Philippe will reward you as a true champion of France. You will be *commissaire* governor of these islands with riches beyond your dreams."

Billy Mack pulled the heels of his hands out of his aching temples. Straightened and croaked: "Dancer will be no problem."

CHAPTER 76

STOREROOM/GROG SHOP
FRONT STREET/LAHAINA TOWN
NEAR MIDNIGHT

SWIFT AND KIKILANI silently paddled toward the black pilings. The sharp lava rocks supported the grog shop's storeroom that jutted over the water. Waves curled by the coral reef farther out at the breakwater rocked their canoe. Then hit the stone seawall with a thump and rush of foam. The small craft rose and fell with the waves.

Kikilani timed her strokes. The canoe glided under the overhang. Swift used her paddle to parry the current and prevent being slammed against the stone piers. Then she reached out and grabbed the slimy side rail of a ladder that extended down from the building above. The canoe pivoted into pitch darkness on the landward side. Kikilani reached and grabbed a low rung of the wet ladder. A moment later the next swell hit the ladder. And then the canoe. But the women's grips held.

Without warning a trapdoor above the canoe abruptly opened. Light dropped down from the storeroom above and illumined the ladder's rungs. Swift and Kikilani froze. Then recoiled behind the ladder outside the light shaft's purview. Meat scraps from a piggin bucket splashed into the water not a canoe length away. Sharks made fast work of the offal. Both women held their breath. And braced their paddles against a black piling. The trap slammed shut over their heads. Again. Darkness. Above them only cracks of light between the storeroom's warped floorboards showed through the black barnacle-encrusted underbelly.

Swift jockeyed onto the ladder and climbed the slippery rungs. Kikilani tied off the canoe behind the ladder then followed Swift. At the top Swift shouldered the trap open an inch. Slowly eyed the floorboards. No boots.

First Swift — then Kikilani — entered the dim storeroom. A door stood midway along the back wall: The doorframe was outlined by streaks of light. From the bar in the grog shop beyond the door loud noises filtered through the wall. The redolence of stale alcohol mixed with the sharp tang of saltwater. Kikilani pointed to racks of rum barrels labeled *PAINT OIL* that flanked the door. Tucked behind one barrel was a metal canister from the East India Company. The canister was marked: *Calcutta.* Swift raised an eyebrow at Kikilani. Both women recognized the storeroom was the transfer point for rum from transport ships. And Maunakili's opium. Kikilani nodded but threw Swift a questioning look. Was the storeroom also used to send girls out to the whaling ships?

Swift and Kikilani crept toward a small chamber at the storeroom's far end. At its door they removed the lock pin. Eased back the slide bolt. Then slowly entered the space. Two islanders and two Chinese girls huddled in opposite corners. When the terrified native girls jumped to their feet Kikilani put her finger to her lips. She whispered in their language: "We won't hurt you. We're here to help." The girls quieted. From a cut half-barrel table Kikilani brought the cell's only candle closer and looked in their eyes. Then checked the girls' wrists and ankles for signs of abuse. The heavier island girl assured Kikilani they were all right. With a sad shake of her head she pointed to the Chinese captives cowering in the corner. Swift tiptoed across a filthy mattress and knelt before the two Asian girls. She raised both hands to calm the two captives. Then spoke a Chinese phrase she had heard at the Paradise Palace in Five Points. "*Bùyào hàipà.* Don't be frightened." Kikilani held the light higher. Swift noticed the bloodshot eyes. Dilated pupils. Drowsiness. "Looks like they've been drugged...." The taller

Hawaiian girl pointed to several small bottles scattered on the floor. Swift recognized the blue-glass containers: "Laudanum." She picked up an empty whiskey bottle from the half barrel. Sniffed. Her nose wrinkled from the odor. "There's enough opium powder dissolved in this alcohol to stun a mule."

The drugged Chinese girls wobbled onto their legs like shanghaied sailors. Swift gestured to the native girls to prop them up while Kikilani searched the small room. Quickly she uncovered evidence of other girls: Messages on folded papers tucked into cracks. Names and dates carved in wooden objects. Decorative Chinese hairpins. In a corner Kikilani uncovered a beaded necklace. She brought the candle closer and immediately recognized the beads and shell spacers. "Loki's necklace!" She blinked. Swift held open a discarded sling bag. Kikilani dropped her findings into the pouch. Then hung the bag across her shoulders.

Swift cracked the door leading back to the storeroom and peered outside. "All clear." Then she gestured for all four girls to join hands to form a chain. Kikilani then led the captives to the trapdoor; Swift propped the door open with a barrel stave. Kikilani went down first. Pulled the canoe around to the bottom of the ladder and placed one foot in the craft to steady it. The canoe rose and fell with the nighttime waves. The two island girls climbed down the ladder while the Chinese girls remained with Swift. Without a word the island girls moved to the middle of the canoe's long hull. Kikilani gestured for them to lie still under the sail cloth so they could not be seen from above.

As Kikilani whispered her instructions to the native girls Swift watched beside the Chinese girls from the trapdoor above. The next instant she heard the barroom door to the rum room crack open. "How many bottles yah want?" the barman shouted back to the bar. Swift quickly closed the trapdoor. Then pulled both Chinese girls stumbling like frightened birds back toward the small room. Where she pushed the girls inside and locked the slide bolt behind them. Then she stepped away from the cell door. Stood beside the rum rack.

No place to hide.

The barman turned. Pushed the barroom door fully open. And entered the storeroom. He took one surprised look. Lunged—and grabbed Swift. Dragged her forcefully back into the grog shop. Pushed her into a side room. Where Head. Dawes. And Chang Fu were seated around a small table. The barman roughly shoved Swift in front of the men. "Look what I catch'd in the storeroom."

The expression on Head's face tightened. "Sticking your nose where it don't belong again...little missy? Time your big city ways came down a peg."

The barman released his hold.

"'Don't belong'?" Swift bluffed as she looked down at the Captain. "From Boston to San Francisco I've put money into a lot of saloons and brothels. And made them a lot of money—I might add. Seems like—more than anything—we're in the same business."

Head gave Swift a hard smile. "Not according to what Dawes here tells me. He says you've made some enemies too—like your fancy pinky-ring friend in New York."

As her mind raced Swift stuck with her cover story. "Probably an unhappy investor...goes with the territory." She tried to ignore the icy bead that trickled down her ribs. "But it's true. Not all my partners are as successful as you...Captain."

"Hah! You're no more a brothel investor than I'm a choir boy!"

Head slammed his palm on the table as he rose to his feet. His chair tumbled backward.

At that moment—as silent as a shadow—Chang Fu rose and slipped from the room.

Swift looked straight at Head and began again. "So...what's it going to be?" She gave Head a steady look. "Can you supply my houses in 'Frisco and Philly with opium and girls? My syndicate pays top dollar."

Head grabbed Swift. Shoved her onto a chair. "So...you saw our little rum store." Head cocked his head toward the storeroom. "Nothin' wrong with a little side business. Anyway...my owners know all about it. Everyone gets their share."

Swift thought quickly. "Then why bother with the paint oil cover?"

Head sneered. "Cuts down on paper forms."

"And maximizes profits...deary." Dawes spat his interjection with ruthless candor.

No sooner had Dawes uttered the last word then Chang Fu returned like a deadly snake and whispered in Head's ear.

Head turned on Swift. "Two island girls are missing! You let 'em lose…you little witch! You'll pay for this!"

Head grabbed Swift by the throat. Lifted her off the chair. And pushed her against the wall. In the same motion he brought a nasty dagger with a curved blade against her cheek. Fire burned in Swift's eyes as she clutched Head's iron grip at her neck.

"You…little missy…will make fine food for my sharks."

The barman licked his lips. "That I'd like to see."

Head slammed Swift against the wall then released his grip on her throat.

Swift coughed. The realization hit her like a hammer. Trying to escape was hopeless. Again she coughed. Words failed to rise from her throat. She swallowed hard. "A lot of people know I'm here." She croaked the words and tried to sound confident. "If I go missing… they'll know who did it. And your little rum-for-opium-and-girls scheme will evaporate."

"I'll take that chance."

Head grabbed Swift's open-collared shirt in his fist. Then thrust his face into hers. And stood nose to nose. Swift blinked at the whiskey and garlic on the Captain's breath. In his other hand Head held the razor edge of his dagger against her jugular.

Dawes stepped forward. Grabbed the Captain's knife arm. "She's right…Cap'n. She's more trouble to us dead than alive. Plus…if Swift breathes a word…her little friend Kikilani 'ill be known as used goods. The slut won't have any future on this island."

Head released Swift. Sheathed his dagger.

Dawes sensed a standoff. "I say let her go…Cap'n. Swift won't be any trouble here — and it's unlikely she'll make it back to New York."

Head grunted. "It's your loss." And jerked his head toward the door.

Dawes grabbed Swift behind the neck. As he pulled upward Swift's long hair lifted her chin. Quickly the *Black Cloud*'s mate two-stepped her across the smoky grog shop. Through the bat-wing double doors. Into the night air.

In the lamplight outside the tavern Dawes hissed in Swift's ear. "Our ledger balance from Cape Horn is now even…Swift." Then he pushed her forward and spat a large mass of tobacco into the sand of Fid Street. "There won't be a next time."

CHAPTER 77

"THE MISSIONARIES brought this on themselves." Henri Malbec hissed. Venom subsumed his voice. "The American Protestants pressured the Hawaiian King to persecute French Catholic priests. I have seen it myself in Olowalu. Our tiny church is a shamble. While the Americans plan a new tower for their Lahaina church. Despicable. This treatment was an insult to France. To our King."

He turned while pacing the aftercastle deck alongside his French commander. Rear Admiral Tromelin. "We should exterminate them all." The Royal Envoy's complaint fell on sympathetic ears. "Not just the Americans and the British...but the entire Hawaiian race. They are all savages. Uncivilized savages! Nothing compared to a Frenchman."

Malbec turned and paced again as the French warship dropped anchor off La Perouse Bay. The frigate's gundeck cannon and stern chasers at the ready. Without a sound Admiral Tromelin followed Malbec up to the poop deck of the large prison frigate.

"We will burn both ends in this fight to see which begs for mercy first." Tromelin flinched: He was slightly surprised by Malbec's voice. "Already the Maui pretender has sworn to accept a French protectorate in matters of foreign affairs. We will make him sign a treaty protecting Catholics. And allow French merchandise to be traded freely. Not overtaxed or banned. Especially our wine and brandy." Malbec warmed to the sound of his unreasonable demands. "We will make the same treaty demand of the Hawaiian King. After all—when it comes to vassal kings…one savage is no different than the other. For either one our ultimatum is ironclad. If the Hawaiian King submits to France— we protect him from Maunakili's plot. If the Hawaiian King refuses— we let the Maui rebels kill him. And deliver the entirety of Napoleon's treasure to us for the privilege."

Tromelin nodded. "Brilliant…Commandant."

As the King's Envoy Malbec instructed the French commander to wait at battle stations in La Perouse Bay. "Be ready to advance directly on Lahaina. The harbor is empty. You'll have no problem forming a line of battle at the breakwater. My signal will direct you to present the treaty—or reduce every building in Lahaina to dust and ash. Remember. Watch the Olowalu foothills for my signal at the curfew cannon tomorrow night."

Rear Admiral Tromelin saluted. "Once we take the harbor we will command Lahaina Roads. No ships will enter without French permission."

Malbec wrung his hands in anticipation. "Excellent."

"Do your spies expect resistance? Any bystanders with dreams of glory?"

Malbec snorted dismissively. "We can expect no interference from the Americans. The whalers have run off to Kahului Bay beyond the Kā'anapali Point. Left the field to France like scared rabbits. They are beyond worry. Already our allies among the rebels have summoned the King from Honolulu. When he comes the rebels will force the King to abdicate. Then Maunakili will sign our treaty. And turn over Napoleon's treasure." Malbec wiped saliva from the corner of his mouth.

"What if the King doesn't sign the treaty—or Maunakili doesn't pay us Napoleon's treasure?"

A cruel smile formed across Malbec's face. "Then the bombardment begins by eight o'clock tomorrow…That will be the last day of May Lahaina ever sees. In the name of King Louis Philippe—

we will destroy Lahaina. Blow the fort and buildings to rubble. Burn every miserable grass hut to the ground...."

Malbec spoke over his shoulder as if to a lackey. "Treaty or resistance." He licked his lips as he envisioned the destruction. "Either way we will establish French dominance across all the Sandwich Islands — and France will rule the Pacific at last." In that moment a sharp sting like a nettle being dragged across his forearm caused Malbec to knead the area around his birthmark. He found the pain exciting even though it caused a strange numbness to radiate down his arm.

CHAPTER 78

DANCER LISTENED as the *Bountiful*'s anchor chain rattled off the capstan until the anchor's great flukes bit into the coral of Lahaina Harbor. When he looked up he saw a sailing canoe gliding over the reef shallows toward the *Bountiful*. The whaling ship had just returned from an overnight sail from Honolulu.

A crew of powerfully built warriors drove the sailing canoe toward the ship. First in the bow were Swift and Kikilani. Behind them two island girls peeked over the polished *koa* wood hull. At the stern Akamu steered the sleek craft. Quickly the three companions — Swift. Kikilani. And Akamu — climbed aboard the *Bountiful* and shepherded the two girls down the steerage stairs. When the trio came back on deck Dancer waved them aft to the bridge deck.

Swift told Dancer about Head. Dawes. Chang Fu. And the previous evening's incident at the grog shop. Kikilani reported the two island girls were safe for now. "But the two Chinese girls have gone missing...or so a *Paradise* barmaid told me."

Dancer shared his news: No word from Post or Mr. Flute in two days. Did Mr. Flute find Post? Was he still searching on Hawai'i?

"Anybody's guess where they are." Dancer assumed the worst: Mr. Flute's attempt to get help had failed.

For a long while no one dared speak. Their melancholy faces looked from one to another. Then across the roadstead…The *Bountiful* was the lone ship that remained in Lahaina Harbor—besides the *Black Cloud* transport and Mama Samoa's love boat.

Akamu shook his head. Then told how Maunakili and his Pi'ilani henchmen before dawn that morning herded every Hawaiian islander they could find…the King's kinsmen…into a holding pen like cattle on the Olowalu beach. "All know that is the site of the Olowalu Massacre—now fifty years ago—where an American trading captain killed more than one hundred villagers over the loss of a small boat. No one doubts Maunakili would do the same." Akamu's expression looked as desperate as his words. "Maunakili made his demand: The King must come from Honolulu and sign the French protectorate treaty to return the Maui kingdom to Maunakili. If the King does not sign the French will destroy every building in Lahaina in two days. And Maunakili will kill all his captives."

Dancer added to the gloom when he shared the news gleaned from the *Bountiful*'s turnaround run to O'ahu. "When we reached Honolulu…I was too late. The King had already left for Lahaina." A murmur of disappointment came from the group.

Akamu's gaze drifted to Lahaina Town. "The only place he would go is the Moku'ula Island."

Dancer pounded his fist into his palm. Action was the only answer.

"Akamu and Kikilani: After sunset take your canoe with your warriors and race to Māla Point. Try to avoid being seen by the *Black Cloud*—and any of Maunakili's cretins. If you can work your way around Lahaina Town by foot—along the edge of the groves near the foothills. Go to the Moku'ula Island. Try to get word to the King. Beseech him to return to Honolulu. If not—make sure he remains on the royal island. The King must *not* leave the island. For his own sake. And the sake of the Kingdom of Hawai'i."

Akamu agreed with what Dancer had learned for himself: "If Maunakili cannot assassinate the King—then Maunakili cannot take over the royal throne. If the King leaves the *kapu* of the royal island the kingdom could be lost."

Swift added the final word. "If you reach the King—or not—return to the Seamen's Hospital. It's closed and will be a safehouse for you. Someone will send word tomorrow."

As darkness fell Dancer and Swift watched as the outrigged sailing canoe cut through the surf in the Lahaina Roads channel and grew smaller in the distance.

Swift grasped her arms against a chill breeze. "Now what?"

Dancer scuffed the gray teak deck with his boot. "Not much we can do—but cross our fingers."

CHAPTER 79

CARGO HOLD/*BLACK CLOUD*
LAHAINA HARBOR
BEFORE SUNSET

HEAD AND DAWES watched unconcerned as the *Bountiful* returned and soon swung on its anchor chain in the empty harbor. Already the sealed cannisters of opium — minus two paid to Mama Samoa — were stowed in the *Black Cloud*'s hold. Each container secreted inside an empty barrel labeled *PAINT OIL*. The eight mislabeled barrels covered with a tarp. Then concealed between rows of filled whale-oil barrels. Before they left the hold Dawes checked the two drugged Chinese girls locked in the *lazarette* where Smidt had met his maker.... When asked upon arrival by the Harbor Master eleven days earlier about the hulking sailor's suicide by hanging — a particularly curious death given the low space available in the *lazarette* — Captain Hyram Head lifted his shoulders dismissively as if to suggest the cause was obvious. "No doubt driven by guilt and Christian remorse."

The Captain's entry in the Harbor Master's roster was as official as it was terse: *Lost at sea.*

Now that the day's job in the cargo hold was done the *Black Cloud* was prepared to sail for New York as soon as the winds were right. With a confident air the ship's master directed the first mate to join him in the Captain's cabin.

"We may have lost two island girls"—Head pulled out a secret drawer from under his velvet settee—"but the two Chinese are something at least."

From the drawer the Captain lifted a strongbox. Unlocked it. Then withdrew an Oriental-silk drawstring bag. "For your work… Dawes. You deserve a bonus." Head handed Dawes a pouch of gold coins. *The fool.* The Captain smiled to himself. *He'll never know how much his bonus could have been.*

Dawes hefted the pouch. "Thank ye…Cap'n. It's a pleasure doing business with you."

From the weight Dawes knew the pouch was light. The coins jingled as he put the bag into his seamen's kit. *Head thinks he has cheated me again. We'll see who gets the last word.*

Head clapped Dawes on the shoulder. "Let's celebrate on Fid Street."

Minutes later Head and Dawes climbed into a waiting longboat and were oared ashore. Head leaned toward Dawes. "Tomorrow we collect the paid tariff receipts from Macomber that prove our delivery—and add an official stamp to our efforts. With Maunakili king we'll be sitting pretty for years to come…Dawes. Sitting pretty."

CHAPTER 80

MR. FLUTE SQUINTED back toward the distant harbor of
Kawaihae on the Hawai'i Island as it brightened in the early morning
sun. Within minutes the whaleboat disappeared around Kapalua Point.

Mr. Flute and Captain Post turned their gaze away from the dry
Kohala Coast of the biggest Hawaiian island. Their world was once
again an open twenty-eight-foot New Bedford Beetle whaleboat.
Doubled-ended. Strongly built. The light craft designed to hunt whales
cut through the water in desperate search of the greatest prize of their
lives. Mr. Flute's four hand-picked sailors pulled on their long oars with
a vengeance. Even Mr. Flute — at his honored position as harpooner at
the bow — leaned his shoulders and back to a fifth oar to supplement
the thrust supplied by the fore-and-aft-rigged sails.

Captain Post scanned the chase boat as he looked for excess weight
still to be jettisoned. No line tubs with their nine hundred feet of coiled
hemp met his eye. No harpoons or killing lances. No waif flag to mark
a kill. No dragging float to tire a whale. No fluke spade to tow a carcass
back to the *Bountiful.* No anchor. Buoy. Hatchet. Nor water or lantern
keg with bread and tobacco. Even the doctor had volunteered to stay

behind to calm frayed nerves of the Big Island missionaries. Only the weight of a second fore-rigged jib sail had been added.

Post rested his hand on the boat's gimbaled compass. Speed was everything. The Captain tacked into the easterly trade winds. The New Bedford whaleboat cut fast through slight chop. Precious time ticked away.

In short order the craft raised Hāna Bay of east Maui. Then along the northern shore the Beetle swept past the Kāwe'e Point and its ancient royal grounds on Ke'anae peninsula. Soon the whaleboat rounded Kapakaulua Head. In the late-morning distance — arrayed like a flock of resting seabirds — lay the entire Pacific whale fishing fleet anchored en masse in Kahului Bay. The dark shapes aligned roughly parallel into the wind. The great whaleships held in position by the strain of their anchor lines. Just outside the harbor the floating blubber factories rested a safe distance from the yellow cloud that still clung to the central valley due south between the twin volcanos of Maui.

Quickly the Beetle closed on the fleet. Post steadied the lion's-tongue tiller and reached under the after cuddy. He withdrew a distress flag. Handed the signal to Mr. Flute. Who raised the distress flag up the solitary mast. As the sleek whaleboat neared the anchored whaleships Mr. Flute semaphored an urgent message from the harpooner's bow position: "M-e-e-t_C-o-l-u-m-b-i-a_N-o-w." The *Columbia* — one of the largest Nantucket whaleships on a four-year run — acknowledged Mr. Flute's message. The hulking whaler repeated the signals to the entire fleet. Captain Steele of the *Enterprise* barked orders: Quickly a tender crew slid his ship's gig boat along skids to the davits. Connected the craft. Just as quickly the granite-jawed master climbed aboard with six oarsmen. In moments the tender crew lowered the men and sleek boat into the water. As the seamen pushed off from the Sag Harbor whaleship other whalers across the bay dropped tenders from their davits. The whaleboats smacked into the water. Raced with crews and captains toward the *Columbia*. One young lad rose in a bow to try out his semaphore skills. No sooner than he stood but a rogue wave toppled him — tossing him into the sea. His mates backwashed their oars and came about. At the same moment another tillerman on a collision course abruptly tacked. He swung his boom and knocked an oarsman into the drink. With a rending crash the second tender sideswiped the first whaleboat. Sending several more oarsmen into the sea. Mr. Flute shook his head at the scene. As two more tenders glided up to pull the floundering sailors aboard their whaleboats. Nothing injured but their pride.

Shortly Captain Post guided the Beetle to the *Columbia*'s gangway ladder. His quick gaze judged more than a hundred captains had converged on the *Columbia*. Captain Post climbed on board and warmly greeted the ship's master. "Old Hammerhand…if I knew you were coming I'd have swung out the gamming chair for yah." The *Columbia*'s dark-complexioned captain smiled broadly and gave Post a manly thump on the chest. Post returned the compliment. "Thank you kindly…my friend." Then gestured to his old friend's healthy waistline. "You have the largest deck in the fleet…and perhaps the largest middle. Hope we can all come aboard."

The Nantucket captain's face turned grim. "Serious business to call a convention at such short notice."

"Aye." Captain Post returned his stern gaze. "As you shall soon see and hear."

Within half an hour scores of masters and mates gathered around the great mainmast on the *Columbia*'s wide main deck. The New England captains greeted each other familiarly while the sailors gathered in small groups talking boisterously among themselves. One Pacific Islander mate stood aloof by the aft gunwale. Captain Hamilton Post faced them with his back to the cold tryworks furnace while standing on a water cask. Around the barrel the high sun cast no shadow. The *Bountiful*'s master projected his voice past the mainmast to the afterdeck break as he laid out the facts. "Our livelihoods are in peril…gentlemen. We must act now. Or our industry — and America — may never recover."

In a straightforward voice Post quickly outlined the situation. "The volcano was a false alarm. Nothing more than harmless ash from the Big Island of Hawai'i." Standing at Post's side Mr. Flute looked across the assembly of upturned weathered faces. He felt a twist in his gut as his instincts sensed the crowd was not of one mind. Post continued: "A more dangerous enemy has arrived." His words gripped the men's attention. "French warships have landed in Hāna Bay. They are now over anchor along the southern shore of Maui — at La Perouse Bay.

Objective unknown—but we must assume Lahaina."

A rumble of concern passed through the captains. Several old salts gathered near the mainmast demanded: "Tell us straight!"

Captain Post spoke in a clear voice that travelled to every man present. "Our only hope—America's only hope—is if you all return to Lahaina. Now."

A negative mood spread across the deck. "We're provisioned and ready!" The objection raised by Captain Page of the New Bedford whaleship *America* was shared by many. "It's time to leave for New Zealand or the Arctic fishing grounds!" The severe Captain Steele advanced a similar idea in a contemptuous tone. "Our hull is chockablock with whale and sperm oil. The time has come to take our treasure to New York!" Other captains said they planned to sail to Honolulu—instead of Lahaina—for final repairs. Still others— Mr. Flute observed a pale Dutch captain and a flamboyantly coiffed Spanish master—wanted nothing to do with the American problem.

One Norwegian captain voiced a common argument. "American greed has brought this on your heads. You think whales are nothing but floating oil wells to be drained. Now your greed has attracted an even greedier enemy. France." He leveled his cold blue eyes at Captain Post. "That is your problem. Not ours."

Yet Post's reply appealed to the whalers as a whole. "If we let the French win in Lahaina your nations will never sail freely in the Pacific." He cast his gaze out to the captains gathered around and looked each captain in the eye. "Yes. It is time to sail for the Arctic grounds. Or your homeports. But if you leave without helping in this fight you will not be allowed to return. You and your investors could lose everything in the coming seasons." Mr. Flute released his clenched hands at last and looked up at the Captain on the hogshead. Post steadied himself with a hand on Mr. Flute's shoulder and jumped down to the deck. Where he landed on two feet. Then worked his way through the captains. Cuffed a shoulder here. Shook a hand there. Reached the gangway opening. And turned to fill the egress. Mr. Flute stood at his elbow. With a steadfast look Captain Post played his trump card. "Today this may look like an American fight. For Uncle Sam. For your future harbor rights. For every American on your crews." He paused as he sensed his words had seized the crowd and held it fast in agreement.

"Yes. We fight for America. But we fight for all of you. For every captain. For every crew. For every investor." From the midship railing his voice bellowed loudly. "United we stand! Divided we fall! Today we must stand together. We must stand for the freedom of the seas!"

An old New England salt known to every whaler in the Pacific stepped forward from his perch on the starboard rail and shook Post's hand. Then turned and in a booming Irish brogue he shouted for all to hear. "When Old Hammerhand tells me to stand up…I for one say…Aye. Aye. Captain!"

With that appeal a handful of American captains and whalers raised a ragged call. "Freedom!" Soon the ragged call swelled with more cries rising from around the *Columbia*'s deck. "Freedom! Freedom!" The rising chant passed from the captains on the deck to the sailors cheering along the gunwales to the tenders bobbing in the water below. From tender to tender the chant spread gloriously. Moments later the battle cry swelled from the crews anchored in the harbor. "Freedom! Freedom!" Quickly the resolve of many forged itself into a single cry: "Freedom! Freedom! Freedom!"

Post stepped to the center of the deck. "Captains…gather round." He gestured to the whalers to move closer. Mr. Flute herded a couple outliers into the huddle. "Here is our mission…."

◎   ◎   ◎

Moments after Captain Post had disclosed his plans the assembled captains and first officers pushed toward the gangway and in turn climbed down the ladder to their waiting tenders. In rapid succession each whaleboat pushed off—quickly replaced by the next tender—and set its oars into the sea. The Norwegian captain shook his head at the American mistake in the making. And climbed down a cargo netting on the opposite hull to his waiting whaleboat. Followed by a handful of other doubters.

Within minutes the first tenders reached their mother ships. Even before the masters climbed aboard their shouted orders snapped crews into action. Soon seamen raced up the ratlines. Then danced outward onto the yard footropes. Mr. Flute watched the figures untie gasket lines from the Jackstay cables that held the heavy canvas. On every crosstree he saw a sailor reach the Flemish horse at the outermost yardarm. One after another great sails dropped into position.

At the *Columbia*'s bulwark gangway the ship's master and Captain Post stood shoulder to shoulder as the fleet's sails blossomed like canvas clouds. The master shook hands heartily with Captain Post. Not a word was spoken. But both understood the look of gratitude the Nantucket captain gave Captain Post. Within the hour nearly eighty whaleships prepared to sail past Kā'anapali and return to Lahaina Roads.

As the midday sunlight glistened on the billowing sails of the *Columbia* Captain Post and Mr. Flute stood beside each other near the afterdeck helm. The black ribbon that held Post's looped rattail fluttered in the wind as he pointed to the foremast. There Mr. Flute's chosen four-man whaleboat crew worked the shrouds alongside the ship's complement. Mr. Flute nodded. Then tapped Captain Post on the arm and confidently gestured toward the *Columbia*'s wake. The *Bountiful*'s speedy Beetle whaleboat bobbed in the waves below them: towed by a cable from the *Columbia*'s stern. Satisfied expressions formed on both their faces as they surveyed the horizon behind them. As far as the eye could see sailed a diminished but determined whaling fleet out of Kahului Bay. The wind was at their backs. Their course was clear.

Under the brilliant Maui sun the salty air blended in the wind with the earthy smell of Pu'ukukui's precipitous green slopes a few miles west. Mr. Flute smacked his palms on the polished taffrail. Then reassured Post with his self-confidence. "No French warship will come within range of Lahaina Town if these whalers have anything to say about it."

CHAPTER 81

DANCER'S GAZE swept across the 'Au'au Channel to the north. Scores of whaling ships led by the *Columbia* sailed toward him through the narrow straits off Kā'anapali. From Dancer's vantage at the *Bountiful*'s bow he watched the armada approach. Immediately behind him at the breakwater channel the *Ship of Paradise* — then the *Black Cloud* — floated at anchor. He raised his brass spyglass and saw at the front of the line of whaleships the *Columbia* led the way. On her afterdeck stood Captain Post and Mr. Flute.

As the ships entered Lahaina Roads a deep misgiving came over Dancer. He watched as the whaleships sailed past Lahaina and headed toward Lāna'i Island. He muttered out loud: "Are they sailing away to Honolulu? Are we being abandoned again?" Dancer lowered his glass and for long minutes stared with his jaw open. Onward the fleet sailed past. Pushed before the northeasterly trade winds…away from Lahaina. As his spirits sank Dancer shook his head in disbelief. Ship after ship passed by Lahaina Harbor as they swept far across the roadstead.

Dancer's open astonishment sank into despair when the *Columbia* raised Lāna'i — roughly ten miles from Lahaina Town. Then unexpectedly the sound of a salute cannon echoed across the water. Dancer grimaced: "A last farewell?"

At that signal something quite singular took place.

The *Columbia* turned in a great arc back toward the sheltered Olowalu shore. Soon the fine ship tacked into the gentle leeward coastal wind toward Lahaina. Then the other ships in the armada turned to follow the same course as the lead vessel threaded the needle beyond the coral reef.

Within the hour the *Columbia* approached Lahaina Harbor. Then passed close to the *Bountiful*—whose crew sent up a reverberating *Huzzah!*

Sailors in the *Columbia* downhauled sails to shorten canvas. "But why shorten sail now?" Dancer wondered out loud. Nimble crew furled the sails snug against the spars. Soon he saw only the top gallants propelled the great ship.

Dancer raised the spyglass again. Then lowered the telescope's view circle down to the *Columbia*'s deck. There an anchor crew stood close to the capstan on the foc's'le. The great iron flukes—Dancer saw—were suspended from the projecting cathead timber on the landward side of the bowsprit. The ship still ran close to the coral reef. Yet continued past the *Bountiful* anchored near the harbor access channel. Following behind in a parade of canvas came what looked like the entire Pacific whaling fleet.

Dancer turned his glass to the leading whaleship as it came abreast the Seamen's Hospital a mile north of Lahaina Town. He saw the *Columbia*'s captain shout an order. The bosun blew three short blasts on his pipe. The shrill sound drifted to Dancer on the light wind. As he watched first the anchor shackles were released. Dancer saw the heavy chain run out through the hawsepipe in a blur. Then splash into the shallow surf. In a moment when the anchor bit into the coral the capstan drum stopped. The crew jammed rachets into place to hold the chain scope from running longer. Simultaneously the crew clewed up sail and furled canvas to the yards. In a moment the ship's progress died against the wind. Then gradually the wind carried the ship back to the end of its anchor scope. At last the *Columbia* lay at anchor close to the frothing breakwater waves. At rest. Bowsprit pointed north.

Onward behind the *Columbia* came the column of ships. Not far behind the mother ship another captain marshalled his crew. Dancer recognized the old New England salt with the Irish brogue: He had overheard him at the *Ship of Paradise*. He watched the captain through his glass. Again the master ordered the sails lowered to minimum. His ship slowed into the wind. Came abreast the *Columbia*. Then glided past — perhaps a ship's length. At that moment the veteran captain shouted the order: "Let go the anchor!" Again the anchor splashed into the bay. Again the crew set the capstan. Again the sailors furled the last canvas. Dancer saw the Irish captain's whaleship pause in the wind. Then be carried back against its anchor chain. As its fluked anchor bit into the sea floor the vessel came to rest with its bowsprit not quite — but almost — abreast the *Columbia*'s stern.

Dancer watched in awe as ship after ship attempted the same maneuver. One by one the flotilla formed a row of ships. Without warning the bosun on one following ship rang the ship's bell frantically. Dancer swung his glass to see. From gestures of the crew Dancer immediately saw the disaster unfold. The anchor flukes did not bite the coral. The ship drifted backward with the wind. Then swung around abeam the ship behind it. Sailors from both ships extended long poles and whaleboat oars to fend off the imminent collision. A rending sound of timber and plank ran across the harbor to Dancer's ears. The following whaler slammed into the poorly anchored ship. The force tore the first ship's capstan loose from its deck. The anchor chain snapped...sending the chain like a whiplash back through the hawsehole toward the capstan. A shirtless sailor screamed. Crushed by the iron snake that slammed into his body. Dancer watched in horror as the rigging — then the spars — of both ships tangled. Shrouds pulled from their bolts. Cables fell to the deck. Two men splashed into the sea. Quickly safety lines were tossed. With his glass Dancer saw the two ships were entangled as one.

Next came the *America* out of New Bedford: Captain Page stood at the helm. Dancer saw the danger. He watched as the captain he knew from Macomber's chandlery altered course. Steered his ship farther from the shore. Passed close by the entangled ships. Then let go its anchor roughly opposite the *Columbia*...nonetheless several ship lengths farther from the reef. Thus the captain established a second arc of ships around Lahaina. Dancer saw how the maneuvers were not a precise exercise. Regardless of the captain's or crew's experience.

More oncoming ships formed rows in long arcs around Lahaina Harbor. The bow of one of the great ships nearly touching the stern of the preceding ship. Others separated by the length of an anchor chain. Each successive vessel in a column hove outside the previous ship. Onward the whalers sailed into the harbor. Like a swarm of bees intent on a single destination. One by one they worked for position. Set staggered ranks. All struggled to position themselves parallel to the shore. In what seemed like a tedium of slow motion to Dancer the whaling ships doggedly let fall anchors into the wind.

Dancer turned to see Captain Steele of the *Enterprise* shape his sails against the wind. Even from his viewpoint Dancer could see the Sag Harbor master's maneuver between the anchored rows was risky. A gap had appeared between ships in the inner arc: Captain Steele guided his whaleship to fill the space. With miraculous timing—just as he had sailed his ship almost abreast of the *Black Cloud*—the flinty master signaled his anchor drop. The precision left a noteworthy impression on Dancer.

When Dancer ran his glass along each column in the harsh afternoon light he further marveled at the seamanship. Each ship in its arc was offset bow to stern with the whaleship beside it. "Like alternating domino tiles…" Dancer murmured in admiration. He counted with a pointed finger as many arcs as he could make out. "Three…Four…Five." His eye noticed how each row formed a great semicircle of ships. Each ship faced north as it swung on its anchor chain. Each semicircle ringed the harbor entrance in what seemed to be a crude web of anchor chains and wooden hulls. "They've formed a defensive dome outside the reef."

As the relentless sun blasted the harbor Dancer heard a cheer rise from the fleet in unison. At first the hurrah pleased him. Then Dancer knit his brow. "Sounds like French revolutionaries at the barricades of Paris. Spirits high…before the storm."

Captain Post heard the loud cheers rise from the whaling ships as he paced the quarterdeck of the *Columbia* anchored just north of the last grog shop on Fid Street. He leaned toward Mr. Flute beside him. "If the French truly intend to take Maui by force...then blockading their path could be the whalers' death sentence. Particularly for the wooden ships with their oil-soaked decks."

Post clenched his teeth. "The whalers will be sitting ducks for French guns primed with incendiaries."

Mr. Flute nodded in begrudging agreement. But did not say a word as the afternoon sun cast a fireball of blinding light over the bobbing fleet.

CHAPTER 82

MOANUI — SEAMEN'S HOSPITAL
NORTH OF LAHAINA TOWN
MIDAFTERNOON

SWIFT RACED toward the appointed rendezvous. She gripped the polished outer hull and stared at the rough dugout ax marks under her feet. Only four paddlers propelled her outrigged canoe forward through the bay. Unseen by the Provisionals or any prowling French warships. The muscular gleaming men drove the canoe on to the beach at Pu'unoa Point just over a mile north of Lahaina Town.

Swift jumped onto the firm sand. Effortlessly the Maui warriors dragged the outrigger under a stand of coconut palms. Quickly hid the craft beneath dried feather-like palm fronds fallen on the beach. For a moment the lead warrior hesitated as he settled his feathered war helmet on his head. Hefted his shark-tooth *leiomano* club. Then struck up the beach and turned toward a spot where a gap appeared in the dense-growing shrubs. He pushed aside the salt-air loving branches and hurried through the gap. Followed by the three other warriors. Swift ran behind the men through the cool understory. Within moments she stood on a sandy path. Where the powerful lead warrior had stopped. They waited a beat as he listened. Then in dappled shadows the small party followed as the warrior sprinted south along the dusty track toward the *Moanui* or Seamen's Hospital. The dry land air was scented by the entwined undergrowth that blended with wafts of sea breeze. Within several hundred yards the hard-breathing troop closed on the hostel. There Akamu's orders had established a cordon of native irregulars who stood guard like disciplined sentries surrounding the shuttered two-story stone building.

The helmeted chief led Swift around to the shady backside of the stone building. Then bounded ahead of her up the exterior stairs. At the top the leader burst into the second-story chamber. Where they found Akamu and Kikilani standing over a wooden table. Kikilani gave Swift a warm heartfelt hug. Then with her arm brought Akamu into the group. Swift caught her breath. "New developments." Kikilani handed her a cloth to wipe away the sweat. "The whaling fleet has returned and blockaded the harbor." Her voice was vibrant with earnestness. "A provisional government has been sworn in by Abner Sisson...a catchpole militia was formed under Captain Head and Mate Dawes...Front Street is barricaded at Lahainaluna Road a mile away."

Kikilani's expression looked as if bad had gone to worse.

"What is it?" Swift asked as a feeble breeze penetrated the shuttered balcony windows that faced the ocean.

"Akamu and I tried to reach the King. But the ways around Lahaina Town were blocked by militia patrols...as you say. We can only guess the King made his way to the sacred Moku'ula Island. But he has no guards."

Swift bit her lip as if she contemplated a series of chess moves. "I've got an idea."

Kikilani gave Swift and Akamu a doubtful look. "Whatever it is are you sure it will work?"

Swift fixed them both with a determined glance. "Better than charging the roadblock head-on."

Quickly Swift outlined her plan to Kikilani. Akamu. And Akamu's lead man-at-arms. Within minutes the four descended the board steps to the ground. The warrior dashed around the hostel to collect his men. Then Kikilani from behind the Seamen's Hospital stable led Swift's horse — already saddled — under the palms. Swift gently extended her open hand. The mare returned the greeting by touching her palm with its muzzle. Swift swung up into the saddle as Kikilani stood beside the settled mare.

At the same time Akamu divided the warriors into two groups. Akamu and his squad followed Swift and Kikilani around the stone building toward the dusty path in front. Swift turned the mare south toward Lahaina Town. While a dozen fighters led by the helmeted warrior trotted up a narrow path. This track ran along Kanahā Stream at right angles to the shore toward Waine'e Street. Soon Swift knew the fighters had reached the street that ran south toward Waine'e Church. Through the breadfruit grove in the near distance — as they worked toward Lahainaluna Road — she heard the warriors beat their battle drums. Pounded their spears and clubs together in rhythm. As the fighters moved slowly at a measured pace they raised a battle chant that sounded like ten score men.

At this signal Swift turned her mare south toward Lahaina Town. Kikilani. Akamu. And Akamu's small band fell in well behind her.

Back in town a motley provisional militia of Pi'ilani elders milled about the barricade at Front Street and Lahainaluna. Their leader repeated Captain Head's orders: Block passage from the north along Front Street. Do not let anyone — or anything — unchallenged pass to the fort or beyond to the royal Moku'ula compound a half mile south. Behind the makeshift barrier the elders and Moloka'i hangers-on milled about. One wore an ancient feather cape that had seen loftier days. What looked like a pirate pistol tucked into his belt. Several old chiefs brandished ceremonial spears with died hemp tassels. Two other old men marched back and forth with century-old flintlock muskets behind the hasty breastwork. As a group the militia huffed and bluffed and peered over the debris piled across Front Street at the southerly corner nearest to Fort Lahaina.

Into this sundrenched scene two drunken sailors spilled out from a grog shop on Fid Street. With some mystification they approached the fortification. The spear-carrying militia leader clambered around the barricade. Almost tripped over a broken wagon wheel. He blocked the corned whalers' way. Growled a harsh rebuke...or order...or challenge. Then the elder — holding his adorned spear like a prod —

shooed the flabbergasted seamen around the barricade.

The sailors stumbled along Front Street toward the wharf—none too sure if the greater danger was behind them or in front. At the end of a long block when their sea boots clomped over the footbridge at Dickenson Street one of the sullen sailors gestured lugubriously toward the missionary clinic. There several wide-eyed islanders huddled on the clinic porch overlooking Front Street only a dozen musket lengths away.

Far behind them—as the sailors clumsily continued toward Rotten Row—Swift trotted at a fast cantor along the shoreline road toward the barricade. As she came within range muskets raised. Pistols pointed toward her heart. Swift held up her hand at the bristling barrier to present the sign of a peaceful greeting. She slowed her mare. The militia's appointed leader stepped forward. He composed his face into a severe expression. Over his bare chest he wore a faded British redcoat that once fit a much smaller man. His large girth barely supported by his bandy legs. Around his neck the elder wore the *kukui* nut necklace of command.

Swift addressed the stern commander. "A troop of the King's warriors are getting past along Waineʻe Street! Listen…"

As soon as she said the words a cacophonous martial chant and drumming sounded through the breadfruit groves.

"They are marching around you! They are marching toward the Mokuʻula on the back road! You must stop them!"

A fierce-looking tattooed noble tapped the leader's arm and pointed beyond the groves. The entire squad gathered behind the two men.

"We can still stop them! Let me show you!" Swift gave the squad a dramatic follow-me gesture as she shouted. Then wheeled her horse onto Lahainaluna. "Come! Quickly!"

The commander hesitated. Swift reigned in her eager horse. The militia leader turned to the tattooed *aliʻi* beside him. They conferred in hushed tones. When the redcoat leader turned to face Swift he swelled his chest. Raised his palm. "You. Wait." The fierce noble disappeared between two shanties. In a moment he returned leading a saddled horse. Swift squinted in the glaring sunlight. Then recognized the small horse from Tuckerman's Stable she once passed over. As the tattooed chief held the bridle his leader stepped up from the road onto a large stone. Part of the retaining wall of a small drainage ditch that ran beside the unpaved street. The leader mounted his steed from the wrong side. Then the chief turned the horse to face up the road. The severe leader shouted a native command. Waited while his militia assembled in formation around him. Then gave a gesture: Forward...march! Swift released her spirited mare and trotted inland up the dusty road. The militia leader trotted after Swift. The entire squad loosely formed behind their leader. All followed Swift up Lahainaluna Road. Her mare's hooves raised small red puffs as they fell silently on the sandy ground. Swift heard several militia elders cough in the dryness of the dust. As the troop approached Luakini Way the commander called to that side-street picket to join his men. Quickly the gaggle of conscripts left their position to fall in behind the first formation. Their common objective whispered gravely by the barricade squad to the newcomers. All were now intent on confronting the warriors on Waine'e Street. The barricades were abandoned.

Just as Swift was halfway to Waine'e Street a cannon boomed from the fort. The whistle from the cannonball could be heard sailing out over the harbor. "The rebellion has begun!" Swift wheeled her horse about. Then jerked to a halt at the side of the track beside the militia commander. With one arm she pointed to the sound of the advancing warriors. "They are coming! The rebels are moving quickly!" Warlike sounds filtered through the breadfruit orchards that surrounded them.

Swift touched the red sleeve of the leader and pointed emphatically. "There! They are approaching Lahainaluna Road. Not a moment to lose! Hurry!"

The commander patted his *kukui* necklace as if for luck and ordered the tattooed noble to march forward up the path. As every rank passed he held his horse in check. Then moved up the street supporting the last man of the magpie militia as the troop moved forward. Front Street at their backs. Faces frozen in expressionlessness as every step took them closer to harm's way.

As the militia men moved up the sandy track Swift rode abreast of the commander's horse then gestured in the direction of the fort. "If the rebels break through...the fort could be surrounded!" Swift stood in her stirrups. Craned her neck toward the advancing horde along

Waineʻe. Leaned closer to the commander. "Got to warn the militia at the fort! Before itʼs too late!" The militia leader gave a distracted wave as his horse veered toward the drainage ditch. Swift reined her horse around. Jabbed her Mexican spurs into the little horseʼs flanks. The horse bolted into action.

Kikilani. Akamu. And the rest of Akamuʼs foot soldiers darted in and out of hiding along Fid Street. Ducked behind parked freight wagons. Stayed low around hogshead casks. Silently they zigzagged up Front Street. At the Lahainaluna corner Akamu looked up the road at the disappearing militia. With a gesture his men and Kikilani scrambled around the deserted barricade. Akamu followed as they sprinted toward the harbor. Just before the missionary doctorʼs compound at Dickenson Akamuʼs soldiers crouched at the corner. Kikilani cast a quick glance up the street. Then signaled to Akamu to lead the others forward across the footbridge to the fortʼs main gate. Kikilani touched Akamuʼs forearm and blurted out: "Iʼll circle around and stand lookout at the turning basin bridge beyond the fort." Akamu looked surprised. Kikilani squeezed his arm."Donʼt worry. Iʼll be careful." With that revised plan Kikilani pivoted left. Separated from the others. Ran up Dickenson past the Mastersʼ Reading Room. Then at the first opening sprinted to her right onto Luakini Way and disappeared. Around the corner she paused. Looked back north along the Luakini path under the groves in the direction of the Lahainaluna Road. Then cast her eyes forward in the direction of the turning basin. Her path was clear.

Swiftʼs mare galloped back down Lahainaluna. Through the breadfruit orchard. Past Luakini. The barricade loomed ahead. Swift held rock solid in the saddle as she approached it. The next moment the horse jumped the abandoned barrier: Only a trailing hoof rapped the debris. With the balance of a barrel racer Swift leaned hard left onto Front Street. Pounded toward the waterfront wharf....

Kikilani worked her way along the soft track behind Tuckerman's stable. Then moved toward the ocean and crept along the edge of the turning basin. There she took up her lookout: where the Front Street footbridge crossed the canal at Rotten Row.

⚙ ⚙ ⚙

Swift bounded past the missionary clinic. Passed the taro patch. The Long House and Customs House blurred to her right at Lahaina Point. Her flat *cordobes* hat flapped wildly by its neck cord against her back. At Macomber's Chandlery Swift cut hard right. The quadrangular coral-block fort stood just ahead.

No sooner had she beat the corner than Swift's horse reared. Twisted sideways. Slammed all four hooves to the ground. Swift almost toppled to the dirt. But gripped the mare with her knees. Two rough-looking seamen held her mount's bridle. Swift recognized one scared face belonging to a Shanghai thug she'd seen up at Chang Fu's camp laughing with Ratter Dawes. The second bearded tough snatched Swift's reins from her hands. Yanked so hard the mare whinnied in pain. The horse's eyes bulged white. Pulling bridle and reins Dawes' recruits quickly manhandled the pony into submission. Two more Provisionals grabbed Swift's arm and vest. Tried to drag the rider from her saddle. Swift kicked with her boot. Her Spanish spurs raked a bloody track across the Shanghai thug's cheek. "Let go...you idiots. I'm on your side!" But her protests were ignored. Her boots hit the packed sand of Fort Street. Rough hands pulled off her prized Spanish hat and stomped it into the dust. Then pushed Swift through the fort's north-wall gateway near the landing. Into the one-acre parade ground. Then hard against the inner wall. The rough coral jabbed her back as she was thrown against the stone. Cutlasses. Daggers. And muzzles encircled Swift.

Through this ring stepped Captain Head. Dawes a step behind him.

"Tie her hands...boys. She won't be needin' 'em when she goes for a swim off the end of the wharf."

Before a rope was produced a ragged burst of pistol shots and musket fire came from Waine'e Street in the distance. Then silence.

"Forget that...boys!" Head hissed. "It's nothing." He gestured to Swift. "Tie her up!"

The bearded tough pinned Swift's arms behind her back. With a gasket line in each hand the Shanghai rat moved closer to Swift. Blood trickled down his chin. Swift tried to kick him in the crotch. But he parried her boot. "Hold her!" shouted the thug. The bearded one spun Swift. Pushed her against the coral wall with his shoulder. Then grabbed her hands and extended her exposed wrists to Dawes' thug. Quicker than a cat's eye the wharf crimp knotted a line around both wrists.

At that moment from around the corner of the fort's jail marched Dancer and Akamu. Behind them was a ferocious gang of tattooed Maui warriors. Clubs. Spears. Throttling lines. Each man held his weapon of choice tight in his powerful hands. In their center the helmeted warrior who led Swift to the Seamen's hostel gripped his shark-tooth *leiomano* club. Head's provisionals instinctively backed away: They took a few steps toward the fort's main gate on Front Street.

Head clamped his arm over Swift's shoulder and grabbed her armpit in his vicelike grip. With his other hand he held his razer-honed rigging knife — its serrated edge pressed to her throat. Dancer saw the knife blade rested taut against Swift's jugular. Head dragged Swift in front of him as a shield. She raised a boot and tried to stomp Head's instep. But missed. Repositioned on Head's hip Swift's boots were useless weapons. Head cinched Swift even more tightly against his hip.

Just then several warriors burst through the fort's covered main gate on Front Street. They stood ten abreast — blocking the gate from the safety of the road. Then more Maui men-at-arms sprinted through the gate. They too blocked the egress. Head and Dawes were trapped. Almost simultaneously overhead — along the fort's ten-foot-thick rampart walls — Captain Post's men rushed. From their killing vantage point each man raised a musket and quietly but deliberately pointed their barrels at the provisionals below.

The provisionals separated themselves from Head and Dawes like water from oil.

"This fight ain't worth dyin' over."

Ratter Dawes muttered his observation to Captain Head from the corner of his mouth: He spoke loud enough to be certain the militia would hear. He dropped his saber. A metallic clatter broke the stillness.

More weapons hit the packed red earth. The rebels raised their hands in the air.

Head tightened his grip around Swift's torso. Stepped back toward the wharf gateway. Swift twisted. Kicked at Head's shins. Tried to sink her teeth into his upper arm. Anything to slow Head's retreat. But still he held her in his desperate grip. Head shuffled back three steps toward the wharf. Unseen Mr. Flute stepped from the street into the shadow of the fort's wharf-side gate. Silently he took position in the path of the retreating smuggler and trafficking ringmaster. The smooth wood and black steel of his harpoon held at the ready. One hand supported the shaft. The other cupped around the butt for leverage. The tip's sharpened barb glinted in the sun.

Dancer stepped forward. "Look behind you." He nodded toward the open ground behind Head.

Head laughed. "I won't fall for that."

"You'll be sorry."

Head hesitated. Mr. Flute's muscles tightened like a lion preparing to pounce. Then he reflexively rotated the barbed single flue. Sighted down the black shaft. In that instant Swift threw her arms over her head. Mr. Flute shifted his weight backward. Swift dropped her full weight to the ground. Mr. Flute set his jaw as Swift's body slid under Head's grasp. Head's body twisted slightly around. Then with the strength of the god Neptune Mr. Flute threw his weight into one great thrust: The razor-tipped harpoon flashed. The shaft struck Head center chest. The harpoon traveled out the back of Head's pea jacket behind. His rigging knife fell to the ground as Head grabbed the shaft with both hands. Disbelief in his eyes. Then blood bubbled from his mouth.

Head staggered. Stumbled sideways over the red-spattered earth. Slammed into the coral stone wall. Then — his body crumpled. A puddle of crimson spread rapidly in the packed dust near Swift's face.

"That's for Kikilani." Mr. Flute flexed his grip on the harpoon shaft. Then gave the blade a sharp twist. "And Loki. And all the other girls."

The helmeted Maui warrior took hold of Dawes. Bent his arm behind his back. At the same moment pairs of tattooed fighters grabbed the provisionals. When the Shanghai thug attempted a run for the Fort Street gate a shot rang out from the rampart. The ball caught the thug squarely in the back of the head. He jerked down into the dust. Half his head gone. Moments later pairs of Akamu's warriors cat-walked the militia men. Dawes. And Head's henchmen to the four dark jail cells beneath Fort Lahaina.

Long afternoon shadows cast by a line of palms crossed the parade ground inside the twenty-foot-high walls of Fort Lahaina. Akamu and Mr. Flute comforted Swift. Whose body shook with an unnatural chill. A tear streaked her cheek. "Where is Kikilani?"

Mr. Flute and Akamu looked at each other. Both shook their heads. No sign.

Captain Post hurried down the stone stairs from the ramparts. He gathered his men and Dancer in a huddle. Gave them brief instructions. Immediately Post's men took up picket positions on the ramparts. At the fort's front and side gates. The jail. And along the seawall outside on both flanks of the landing wharf. Then Captain Post and Dancer joined Akamu and Mr. Flute to console Swift.

"Have you seen Kikilani?" Swift gave Post an imploring look. Post shook his head.

Swift shot a glance at Dancer...and Mr. Flute...and Akamu in turn. Worry constricted her face.

Akamu pointed vaguely toward the canal and the King's Way beyond. "Last I saw her she was headed that way. Said she was going to post a lookout at the footbridge."

CHAPTER 83

KING'S WAY
ROYAL DISTRICT
LATE AFTERNOON

BEYOND THE CANAL and its marketplace. Beyond the vendor's empty stalls and thatched market house. Beyond the point where the King's Way became a causeway through the fresh inland waterways of the royal precinct. Maunakili smiled as if his hostage was a sign of his true destiny. Surprised near the footbridge Kikilani had scratched and clawed like a hellcat and butted her forehead into Billy Mack's cheekbone. A move she had seen the gangs of New York employ around Five Points. But she was quickly overpowered by the rebel's henchmen. Bull Shaw and Kapu the Ugly dragged Kikilani — bound and gagged — toward the royal compound. Billy Mack trudged along behind as he nursed his swollen face and his damaged pride. Maunakili followed only a few steps back. His dark eyes watched Kikilani's long hair sweep back and forth over her bare shoulders like a mare's tail. Then Maunakili passed his tongue over his lips. *First kill the King. Then Kikilani is mine.*

The would-be king smiled with anticipation as he watched his storyteller and Bull Shaw march his prisoner along the sandy way. Before they reached the reedy edge of the lagoon Maunakili moved quickly forward. "Stop." He held up his hand. Then turned to tower over the others. "Kapu's spies confirmed the King is on his little island. But there are no guards. He is alone." Maunakili's lips curved in a half smile. "He can see us if we approach along the causeway. We will cut through to the beach. Then turn inland at the Hale Piula." Kikilani twisted her body to break free but Bull Shaw and Kapu held her in their grips. "From the Hale Piula Bull and I will take the princess through the shade bower at the back of the island. Then Bull will stand guard in the grass house near the causeway gate….The King cannot see us from the far end." He paused to direct orders to Kapu and Billy Mack. "You two continue along the beach. Then take up a lookout on the south side of the island."

Kapu the Ugly dipped his head in understanding. "Along the Olowalu path between the beach and Waine'e Street?"

"Yes." Maunakili gave an emphatic click of his tongue. A spark of excitement came into his eyes. "Be ready. When the King is dead… take the news to the Olowalu camp. Do you understand?"

Billy Mack moved his jaw back and forth to test if it still worked. "Aye. We will be ready."

Maunakili turned toward the sea and made his way through the dense salt-air shrubs. Bull Shaw and Kapu the Ugly lifted Kikilani roughly under both arms. Then half carried her toward the beach. Billy Mack glanced back over his shoulder. No one followed them.

Several minutes passed before the rebel king paused where the Hale Piula path met the causeway. Here Maunakili eyed the entry gate to the royal *sanctum sanctorum* that stood across the narrow path opposite them. Stately coconut palms rattled like swords above the Hale Piula behind them. He crouched as his narrowed eyes swept the long narrow island. Then studied the large stone building at the island's far northern reach. White lace billowed through the open windows. "See the curtains?" The warrior pointed a finger then closed his hand into a fist. "The King is in his house…counting his bones. We have him."

Together Maunakili and Bull Shaw carried Kikilani across the causeway as quickly as her struggles let them. Through the open heavy wooden gate. And onto the sacred island's greeting area. Immediately to their right they dragged their prisoner behind a fine grass house. Forcefully Maunakili and Bull Shaw pulled Kikilani to the end of the building. Directly before them stood another steep-roofed native house. This second grass house — Maunakili saw — formed the backside of the greeting space. While Bull Shaw held Kikilani Maunakili moved to the corner of the first house. Then swept his gaze past the greeting area along the length of the royal island. As he looked toward the stone mausoleum the warrior's shoulders tensed slightly. A red dust devil rose from the sand of the King's Way just beyond the borders of two fishponds. Dark clouds gathered. Maunakili glanced to the sky and recognized the signs. The specter of a windstorm threatened Lahaina — devastating westerly Kona winds colliding with easterly trade winds.

Now shielded from view behind the grass house the sweating captors ducked under a low bower of hibiscus trees that created a cool shade. Here a clean white hammock was suspended next to a small *ti*-leaf hut built for a queen. Newly mown grass covered the floor of the hut. The trio moved forward on the lakeside behind the second grass house. Labored along the long axis of the island. Came to a fine third grass house. Maunakili cast his warrior eyes over the King's sleeping *hale*. And canoe pier behind. Moved to the end of the thatch house. And fixed his gaze on the end of the island. There sat a large stone building designed in a European style. The royal residence and mausoleum.

Bull Shaw pushed Kikilani inside the King's empty sleeping house. Roughly threw her down against a support post. Kikilani groaned in pain. Maunakili pressed the girl's shoulders against the pillar while the English mercenary tied Kikilani's torso to the timber with lengths of thatch cordage. With a commanding gesture Maunakili dismissed Bull Shaw back to stand watch at the grass house close to the causeway gate.

Maunakili knelt beside his princess. Tested Kikilani's binds. Then reached out and touched her damp skin. Kikilani jerked away. Growled through her gag. Maunakili frowned but there was an amused gleam in his eye.

Like a great cat the warrior-cut-in-two slipped silently outside. Unseen — as if hiding beside a game trail — Maunakili settled behind the thatch to await his moment.

CHAPTER 84

KING'S ISLAND
MOKU'ULA/LAHAINA
SHORTLY AFTER

THE HAWAIIAN KING — dressed in a blue double-breasted
roundabout and white pantaloons — looked about the splendid
sea-view room. In this stone retreat he had enshrined the bones of his
sacred sister. His queen mother. His son. And *ali'i* ancestors of the royal
line. Complete with pump organ.

Around this holy tomb the King walked thoughtfully. A place of
origin — a symbolic *piko* or umbilicus — most holy in all the chants
and history of his beloved islands. The King gave a relaxed sigh in what
seemed to be a sense of relief. In his upturned hands before him he
held an offering of food and flowers. His attention turned inward to
lost love.

Stealthily Maunakili closed the short distance to the stone tomb
and royal residence. As the delicate curtains riffled in the breeze the
rebel's glare followed the King as he moved inside the mausoleum
room. Maunakili whispered to himself: "Got you....Now you cannot
escape. At last you will show me where Napoleon's treasure is hidden in
the false tomb of your sister...before I kill you."

Maunakili crept silently forward. The warrior took care to stay hidden from view from the King's Way. And hidden from the King should his eyes turn.

The King paused in his grief before the European window. Then moved around the tomb chamber closer to the doorway to the anteroom at the end facing the inland lake. At that moment Maunakili leaped forward with the silence of a panther: He stole through the door to the tomb house. The King's back to his assassin. Then — in the blink of an eye — Maunakili looped a strangling cord around the King's neck. Pulled the two wooden handles of the cord tight. The King gasped. The flower petals in his palms dropped to the floor. He grabbed at the heavy *olona*-fiber cord. Maunakili dragged his victim deeper into the small reception room. Kicked the outside door closed. Heaved the King by the killing cord and dropped him onto a gilded sofa.

Terrified — the King gasped for breath. Before him towered a monster. Half black tattoo. Half human. All at once the King recognized Maunakili. The two stared at each other for a long moment.

"Tell me where the treasure is hidden!" Maunakili bellowed as he towered over the King.

Dizzy from lack of oxygen the King blinked. Took a moment to recover his bearings.

"Tell me!" Maunakili smacked the King on his shoulder. "Or I will kill you!"

"What do you mean…treasure?"

"Don't play with me!" the increasingly wild warrior frothed. "I am the Great Kahuna! I will be King!" He paused a beat. "You will die — and the dust of your sister and mother's bones will be scattered to the winds — if you do not tell me where you have hidden the treasure of Napoleon! The treasure my father brought to this island. The treasure that is rightfully mine!"

The King looked stricken. Rubbed his throat. "You do not understand. This is my home. And the resting place of my ancestors. There is no treasure here."

Maunakili charged the King. Lifted him off his feet by his roundabout coat. Slapped him twice. Hard. A brass button fell soundlessly to the fine mat beneath the King. "Show me where you hold the treasure!"

Maunakili dragged the King into the adjacent mausoleum room.

Doors on the far side opened onto a piazza with a view of the harbor and Lānaʻi beyond. Maunakili's wild eyes scanned the large chamber. Ornate chairs and tables sat around the perimeter. Large mirrors had been placed incongruously beneath the splendid tables. Against the interior wall that ran opposite the piazza sat an imported harmonium pedal organ. In the center of this large and splendid room was a raised platform. Like a large bedstead. On this platform rested three coffins. Each covered in scarlet velvet and draped in a gossamer rose and peachblow cloth. Over all three lay a deep-blue netting embroidered with black figures. The spectral net was held down against the sea breeze by a collection of solid gilt ornaments. On the long wall beyond the coffin bier stood a broad glass-door cupboard that displayed a silk dress and white satin shoes. Surrounding the platform were numerous wooden *kahili* royal staffs. The stout shafts were topped with feathers. Red. Green. Yellow. Black. Some staffs no taller than the coffins. Others almost as high as the twelve-foot ceiling. A fine Chinese matting covered the mausoleum floor.

"It must be here!" Again Maunakili shook the King like a mute doll. With one thunderous backhand blow he knocked the King senseless. Then cast the King aside in a crumpled pile against the pump organ pedals. "You've hidden the treasure in the tombs!"

Maunakili stepped up onto the raised platform and ripped the gossamer covers of the coffins away. Golden ornaments sailed around the room like missiles. A mirror shattered. He tore the velvet covering from the first coffin. Jammed a blade under the sarcophagus lid. With his powerful arms he wrenched the lid aside. Tipped it between the tombs. Then pried open the lead and zinc inner coffins. A noxious mist rose from inside. The Great Kahuna reached down and dug with his hands in the dust and bones. Dug frantically…looking for treasure. He rummaged deep into the crypts. Tossed remnants of bone. Cloth. A necklace. An ornamental gourd. Threw fists of dust into the air. Like a mad dog scratching the ground. He leaped to the second coffin. Repeated his destruction. Then the third.

Lying beside the pedals of the pump organ the bloodied King silently gathered himself. He looked stealthily at the debris scattered around him. Anything he could use as a weapon. Slowly he reached for a bludgeon club. An ancient weapon kept near for his ancestors' afterlife. As he closed his hand around the grip again he marshalled his strength. Then rose and positioned both feet under his weight. Enraged — he rose and charged Maunakili. Club raised over his head. At the last moment Maunakili turned. Grabbed the club's handle. Wrenched it from the King's grasp. Then shoved the King backward toward the corner of the coffin room.

"Enough!" A demented look spread over the rebel King's half-black – half-brown features. "Your father killed my people in the 'Īao Valley! For his crime...you must die!"

With a fiendish roar Maunakili lunged forward and swung the club at the King. The blow landed hard to the King's head. The King grabbed a curtain as he crumpled to the floor behind the pump organ. His body shuddered. Blackness overtook him. As the funeral shroud fell over his still form.

CHAPTER 85

DANCER. MR. FLUTE. AND SWIFT ran along the King's Way. The Americans were followed closely by Akamu. They approached the entrance gateway to the Moku'ula Island. Akamu held back—something froze him in place. "Commoners are forbidden...I cannot enter." He leaned over his toes but his feet would not move forward.

A frantic look of concern for Kikilani flashed across his face... Somewhere deep in his being an undefinable force seemed to forbid Akamu to break the ancient *kapu* despite his fear for Kikilani. Gone was his missionary education. Travel. Exposure to foreign ways. Like a lightning bolt all that personal history did not matter. Akamu turned away from the gateway and paced the King's Way. Isolated outside the sacred precinct. Whatever came—he could only watch.

Before them Bull Shaw appeared from the shadows of the *hale pili* grass house nearest the entrance. He blocked the causeway.

Mr. Flute stepped forward.

Shaw extended a stout *koa* spear in his hands. Mr. Flute brandished his harpoon shaft: naked without its detachable metal point. "Your day is done...Shaw. Step aside from the gate."

Bull Shaw laughed as he filled the narrow entrance. "Is that so? I reckon I'm going to enjoy this."

Shaw swung unexpectedly. Mr. Flute parried with his shaft. But the blow caught Mr. Flute's fingers. He recovered.

As the two fighters' wooden shafts resounded in quick succession a gaggle of Pi'ilani elders gathered in the Hale Piula causeway opposite the two men. Bull Shaw landed a vicious blow to Mr. Flute's ribs. Then connected with a roundhouse to Mr. Flute's knee. Mr. Flute doubled over in pain. Shaw smashed the harpooner's back with a downward blow.

Mr. Flute tumbled to the edge of the causeway. Cheers erupted from the Pi'ilani elders.

Dancer pulled Mr. Flute to his feet. "Get up. Move quicker."

Mr. Flute thrust high. Then stepped behind Bull Shaw and swung lower. Landed a crushing blow across Shaw's back. Bull Shaw staggered. "We're not through yet." Mr. Flute snarled as he limped slightly.

"Alright…you old fool." Shaw painfully sucked air into his lungs. "You want another good walloping? You shall have one!"

Rat! Tat! Tat! The sound of two shafts of solid wood colliding with great force rebounded across the King's Way. After a furious exchange Mr. Flute managed to smack Bull Shaw on the side of the head. Shaw went down on one knee. Blood ran from his ear. Mr. Flute kicked Shaw hard against the gate post. Bull Shaw staggered backward. Stopped midway into the courtyard. Leaned on his spear balanced across his knees.

Dancer looked down upon the deserter. "Seems like we made it past the gate…Shaw. How are you enjoying this now?"

Bull Shaw again attacked Mr. Flute. Blow after blow. Moved to his left. Shaft glanced off shaft. Mr. Flute grunted and whistled the air with a sweeping blow of his shaft. Shaw ducked. Then parried and caught Mr. Flute with a vicious uppercut of his spear shaft. Mr. Flute stumbled back. His mouth bloodied. He touched his lips. Charged.

Another furious exchange of batons. Mr. Flute landed a blow to Shaw's head. Shaw staggered near the edge of the fishpond. Mr. Flute smashed him again viciously across the jaw. Shaw's body teetered. Motionless. Mr. Flute drove the butt of his harpoon into Shaw's belly. Pushed him hard into the air. Shaw's limp form hit the shallows with a splash. Floated in the reeds. Motionless.

"Swimming time with the fish…old chum." Mr. Flute breathed hard.

Mr. Flute waded into the shallow pond. Grabbed Bull Shaw by his collar and dragged him over the black lava wall that edged the fishponds. Holding Shaw face forward Dancer and Swift each pulled one of his arm's back. Then Mr. Flute slipped his harpoon shaft behind Shaw's back at Shaw's elbows. In a moment Mr. Flute pilloried Shaw by using braided rope to tie his hands together in front like handcuffs.

Mr. Flute shoved Bull Shaw along the King's Way as they headed toward the fort. Then shouted over his shoulder: "I'll deliver this rascal to Captain Post." Mr. Flute's prisoner stumbled forward. "Then be back as soon as I can."

Dancer and Swift ran past Akamu. Who paced on the causeway outside the sacred island in his long white trousers and loosely knotted cravat-tie. Indecision racked his face. Swift and Dancer raced onto the island. Instinct made Dancer run toward the far stone residence. Where else would they find the King?

At the mausoleum's front door Dancer charged inside. Flower petals scattered. Floor mat askew. No one.

As Dancer swept his gaze around the coffin room Maunakili crouched silently behind the coffin platform. He had heard Bull Shaw's cries as the strongman fought the bald American out on the causeway. Then he had ducked behind the platform a moment before this other American—this man with the odd buckled boots—had come rushing into the mausoleum. Now the rebel king rose silently from behind the platform. Raised his lethal *leiomano* club. Poised to strike.

Just then—having followed Dancer—Swift stepped inside the mausoleum room doorway. She gasped. "Look out…Dancer… behind you!"

Maunakili rose up and moved quickly toward Dancer. Dancer looked back. Instinctively dropped to the floor. Rolled into the blow. The *leiomano* sliced past his head. Struck the organ cabinet. Shark's teeth exploded in all directions like a grenade. Maunakili discarded the broken weapon. Dancer picked up one of the royal staffs that surrounded the elevated platform.

Dancer knew Maunakili's powerful hands could crush him to death. And he knew his only hope was to show no fear of the tattooed warrior-cut-in-two. As Maunakili faced Dancer the strong chief grinned demonically: The black swirling *kakau* bird-of-prey design ferociously rose across the right side of his neck. His face. And head. As if the bird of prey took the place of the man. Dancer smiled — matching the Kahuna's demonic grin. Then he moved to circle Maunakili. A look of anticipation came into the Pi'ilani's eyes.

Maunakili sidestepped with his back to the coffin platform. Dancer aimed his first swing at Maunakili's knee. The blow smashed the chief's kneecap. Maunakili grunted in pain. He recovered in the blink of an eye — and leaped at Dancer. The impact knocked Dancer to the stone floor. The breath knocked out of him Dancer nonetheless managed to twist away. Came to his feet. Stood still for a moment. Sucking painful breaths of air.

The two men circled each other. Dancer holding the staff before him. Maunakili limping on a broken knee. Swift reached for the fallen *leiomano* club. Maunakili caught the movement. Stepped on the club. Swift retreated to where the King lay.

Dancer lunged forward. Swung. The shaft ordinarily would have hit Maunakili on the side of the head — but Dancer's boot had slipped in the bone dust on the Chinese matting of the mausoleum: The arc of his blow was off. Maunakili simply raised his powerful forearms and deflected the impact. In that moment Dancer's eyes glimpsed a strange mark on the great chief's tattooed forearm: A birthmark in the shape of a turtle?

The staff quivered in Dancer's hands as if he had struck an anvil. Maunakili lashed out. Grabbed the end of Dancer's shaft with both hands. Leveraged the shaft under his armpit. Heaved like a giant. Dancer's body lifted into the air. He landed halfway across the room: His body crashed awkwardly against the corner of a heavy coffin.

Maunakili inhaled slowly. He took his time approaching Dancer's form on the coffin platform. A triumphant glow came to his half-black face. His white eye shown like a fiendish beacon. His mouth opened like a shark ready for the kill.

Dancer rose to one knee. Maunakili stopped. Incredulous. Dancer rose up. Like a phoenix rising from the fiery ashes. Then he stepped down from the platform and grabbed a stout wooden *kahili* staff at his feet. Advanced to meet the fearsome warrior. Feigned a swing right. Then left. Then with all his might tried to thrust the butt end of the royal shaft into that sneering face.

Again Dancer misjudged. Maunakili sidestepped. Met the shaft with his huge paw. Violently yanked the shaft toward him. The tattooed warrior used Dancer's momentum to pull him forward. As quick as a snake catcher Maunakili hooped his heavy strangling cord over Dancer's head. Then spread his elbows wide and pulled the wooden dowel handles outward with bloodthirsty strength. Dancer twisted violently. His neck in a noose. Victim and executioner struggled face-to-face. Dancer kicked his boot high into the Great Kahuna's groin. The blow would have doubled over another man. But not Maunakili: He gasped slightly. Blinked. Then increased the crushing pressure on Dancer's throat with his executioner's garrote.

Maunakili stood a head taller than Dancer. He ground his jaw as he strained. Blinked in rage. His white eyelid turned inside out. The demonic half-black–half-human face quivered intensely. The veins in his face seemed as if they might pop. His only expression was to kill.

Maunakili lifted Dancer off his feet by the strangling garrote. His chest muscles quivered from the effort. One arm extended for more leverage. The trained warrior anticipated the pleasure of watching Dancer's life fade as the end came.

The blood was shut off from Dancer's brain. The room began to spin. The pain behind his eyes erupted in agony. Blackest oblivion began to fog his vision. Death was only a moment away. Dancer's instincts were all that remained.

Dancer thrust his hands upward. Within the giant's wingspan. Smacked both palms hard against Maunakili's earlobes. Then grabbed the warrior's ears. Yanked the monster toward him. Smashed Maunakili's nose with his forehead. The warrior shuddered in pain. Dancer's left hand ripped Kahekili's gold ring from Maunakili's ear. Crimson spread over his tattooed neck. Summoning his last strength Dancer thrust his right thumb into Maunakili's eye. Drove the digit its full length inward. Deep into the socket. Then cocked his wrist. Twisted. Suddenly Maunakili's eye popped out. Dangled from nerves and vessels. Blood sluiced down his face as Dancer's right thumb momentarily wedged itself between skull and nose bones.

Shock wiped the sneer from Maunakili's face. The great warrior howled. Dropped the garrote handles. Then threw his hands up to his blinded face. The black tattooed features contorted: Maunakili's face was now covered in black and crimson. Dancer's thumb dislodged from the great warrior's eye socket as the rebel chief fell to the floor.

The giant stumbled. Disoriented from pain. Disbelief. He careened forward. Stumbled over Dancer's body. Kicked Dancer a punishing blow to the head. Caught his balance...his depth perception gone. He crashed about the sanctum like a wounded bull; but kept his feet despite the agony.

Swift knelt over the body of the King behind the pump organ. She saw Dancer lay inert on the dusty floor. Watched as in crazed desperation Maunakili turned to face the room. The rebel king bellowed in a voice that made Swift's blood jump. He moved forward. Turned toward the crouching figures. Caught himself. Stumbled forward through the door of the small entry room. Then hurried out into the yard. Maunakili lurched unsteadily toward the King's sleeping house. Inside he ripped off the ropes that held Kikilani to the post. Dragged her to her feet and from the residence.

The Great Kahuna roared in defiance. Cinched Kikilani to his hip as if her weight were nothing more than a bundle of thatch. He lurched forward. Crazed. But the causeway was blocked by guards coming from the fort: a large contingent led by the bald American. Maunakili saw another young man — the one the missionaries called Akamu — standing uncertainly outside the causeway gate. He reeled toward the canoe pier. On the small jetty he threw a woozy Kikilani into a canoe.

Ripped the painter rope lose. Then leaped into the craft—launching the canoe out onto the water with his weight.

Blood stained his body red. Sweaty gore spattered Kikilani's gagged face as she pushed herself up in the canoe. Then scrabbled inches away from Maunakili.

Maunakili paddled furiously over the black waters. Kikilani took a few breaths. Then leaned her bound hands over the edge of the canoe. Reached to the dark waterline. Cupped her hands. Splashed the stream-fed water into her face. Cold as a waterfall. She gasped. Repeated the refreshing splash. The shock revived her consciousness. Blood shot into her brain. She gathered her thoughts. The danger registered on her face. Beside her hip she felt a paddle. Slowly she twisted her hands held by the wet ropes and worked the paddle free. Placed the flat tip on the canoe. Pushed up to one knee. Slid her hands to the grip. Leaned her weight back. Then with both bound hands Kikilani swung the paddle at her captor. Maunakili grabbed Kikilani's arms with one hand and shook her like a plaything. Kikilani felt her hands slip free of the loosened paddle. She scratched at the warrior's face in desperation. Her fingers snagged the dangling eyeball. As if plucking a plum she gave a yank. Maunakili roared. Blinded by agony. He lunged. Lost his balance. His huge mass splashed into the lake—the canoe twisted into the air as Maunakili fell in…rocking the canoe violently. Head over heels Kikilani fell overboard too. Disoriented she quickly sank into the dark lake. But she calmed herself. Raised her bound hands. And pulled the gag from her mouth. It dangled around her neck as her feeble kicks churned the dark water.

The low afternoon sunlight—dimmed by volcanic ash—filtered dully over the dark waters of the sacred Mokuhinia. Across the lake a deathly quiet fell. Wavelets from Maunakili's heavy body thrashing and Kikilani's kicking moved toward the King's Island. These ripples spread to the middle of the deep lake. There they seemed to stir larger eddies in the dark water. Soon these eddies amplified as something unseen moved under the water. Faster the water swirled. Soon a great movement roiled the calm surface. Brown froth whipped up. What seemed like a giant being awakened from its depths. Faster the water churned. Round and round circled the unseen menace. Soon the water virtually boiled with disturbance. Then without warning an enormous being broke the surface. Black-scaled body. Nostrils like slits. A sloped black head. Quickly the creature's head rotated. Its blank eyes searched the lake. Its nostrils snorted spray. The beast's black forked tongue searched the air to detect the scent of any nearby prey.

The great *mo'o* lizard goddess Kihawahine darted her eyes — her dexterous tongue now flicked in anger. The monster arched its back out of the water — rows of thick scales trailed murky strands of grass along the creature's spine — then dove under. Circling waves revealed its path as it slithered its way across the lake. Again the monster raised its head: eyes hungrily trained on the bloody water around Maunakili's body. As it approached it spread its jaws and opened its great mouth. Just then Maunakili seemed to sense the goddess' presence. He lifted his arms to prevent the lizard's jaws from closing around him. The lizard again arched her back — raising her head out of the water before bringing her teeth down on Maunakili's arms. With her teeth flashing the great goddess shook her head back and forth: shaking her prey violently. Maunakili's arms tried to punch back but were pinned. The monstrous jaws of the goddess opened momentarily — but only to bite harder on the great warrior. Shook Maunakili's form like a wet rag. Bit again. Adjusted her prey above her monstrous gullet. Then devoured the tattooed warrior. Whole.

Kihawahine sank beneath the red-bubbled surface. Circled.

Then turned toward Kikilani.

Akamu stood outside the causeway gateway. He gripped his head between his hands: indecisive even as he saw the lizard goddess turn for Kikilani. His pacing outside the gate had quickened as events unfolded around him. He looked up. There along the King's Way Mr. Flute jogged toward him. Akamu saw he carried his harpoon balanced easily at his side in a loose fist. The razor-sharp single flue glinted. At that moment the haze opened and the sun again broke free. Akamu felt the sun's warmth wash across his face. It bathed his skin. It calmed his nerves and instilled a quiet reassurance in his soul. He breathed fresh air into his lungs. Mr. Flute pulled up before him.

Akamu spoke quickly. "Swift and Dancer went into the mausoleum—after some time Maunakili appeared in the yard." Mr. Flute strained to listen as he caught his breath. "Then he ducked into the King's sleeping house. When Maunakili came out he carried Kikilani to a canoe. Tried to cross the lake. Now Kikilani is struggling to escape the *mo'o*—the great lizard goddess Kihawahine."

Akamu closed his eyes to calm himself. Felt the cool breeze of the sea on his skin. Heard a voice in his head...Sisson? What had he said? "Worst of all: The King waffled..." Akamu felt his heart quicken. His entire body began to shake. He wouldn't do it—he wouldn't waffle like his King. He opened his eyes. "*Kapu* or no *kapu*...I must do this!" Akamu turned and raced through the entrance. Mr. Flute posted his guards at the gateway and followed Akamu a stride behind.

Within moments they came to the floating pier at the water's edge. Before them—some distance out in the lake—Kikilani took a deep breath. Slipped beneath the surface. And yanked her hands free from the wet *olona* rope. She surfaced. Gulped air. Pain shot through her one shoulder; hurt when Bull Shaw threw her against the post in the sleeping house. The lizard's thrashings had pushed the canoe farther from the shore. She kicked hard toward the canoe. With a grimace she gripped the carved gunwale with one hand.

Kikilani turned her head. At that moment Kihawahine charged. Terrified Kikilani shoved the canoe toward the monster. The giant lizard took the wooden canoe in its jaws. Squealed a primordial cry. Then crushed the canoe like kindling. Again Kikilani sank under the water's surface.

Akamu ran to the end of the wooden dock and dove into the lake. In a moment he reached Kikilani. Pulled her to the surface. Then supported her on his hip and with strong side strokes propelled both of them toward the pier.

The black waters churned in the settling twilight. Roiled waves belied the huge creature just below the surface. Then the ripples calmed. As though the protector of the Mokuhinia had swum away from the Moku'ula. Away from Kikilani and Akamu.

In an instant a bulging wave formed again on the surface. Heading for Kikilani. The monster rose up out of the water and drove its dark body straight for the struggling swimmers.

◎　◎　◎

Three figures hobbled toward the island's edge. When Dancer regained his senses in the mausoleum one look about the room recalled what had happened. Maunakili had nearly killed him. A wary glance about the shattered room told him the warrior was gone. Dancer grabbed his throat. His windpipe felt like it was on fire.

Just then Swift reached out. "Are you okay?"

Dancer looked up. "I've had better days."

Swift ignored him. "Help me with the King. We must get him to his sleeping house to recover."

At that moment from the lake they heard a great commotion. Shouts. Cries. Swift and Dancer supported the King and made their way into the yard. They followed the sound of the shouts outside. Swift looked toward the small boat dock. Then glanced at Dancer.

"Go ahead. I've got him."

Swift supported the Hawaiian King as the two of them walked around the sleeping house beside the edge of the lake. With her arm around his waist — his roundabout torn and dust-covered — the King lowered himself to a small bench and leaned back against the thatch. Swift found a box of friction matches inside the grass house and lit two *kukui* torches like sentries stuck in the sand outside.

Dancer joined Mr. Flute at the brink of the island.

Mr. Flute pointed. Akamu struggled to bring Kikilani ashore. Then Dancer saw the wake of something large and black — and advancing fast toward the swimmers. He held his throbbing head as he limped back to the grass house. "Grab all the *pili* thatch you can carry!" Dancer. Swift. And Mr. Flute grabbed armfuls of grass thatch. "Bring that torch!" They raced back onto the pier. Dancer hobbled behind them. All three dumped straw bundles into a second canoe. Swift ignited the tinder with a *kukui* torch. Then Dancer extended his leg and with a great kick sent the flaming canoe out into the lake. The canoe glided away from where Akamu swam with Kikilani still held fast against his hip.

From the dock Dancer and Mr. Flute gathered stones at the water's edge and lobbed them toward the retreating canoe. Coconuts. Burning torches. Swift brought them whatever came to hand near the sleeping house. The missiles splashed as far from the swimmers as possible. Anything to distract the Kihawahine.

Angered the giant lizard turned toward the burning canoe. Charged the flames. Her black eyes flashed. Her forked tongue darted from her grotesque mouth. Kihawahine opened her great jaws and splintered the *koa* wood with a single bite. Then searched in vain for another morsel. With a roar the monster turned again toward Akamu flailing in the water.

Mr. Flute found a line attached to a dock post. Dancer tossed the line. Short. Tried again. With the fingertips of his free hand Akamu snagged the rope. Hand over hand Dancer and Mr. Flute pulled on the rope and stepped backward to the shore—drawing Akamu and Kikilani toward them—and avoiding further unbalancing the rickety dock. Akamu scrambled up onto the dock. Then pulled Kikilani by her wrists onto the boards. Akamu tried to help Kikilani stand on the wobbly pier. They turned and took several desperate steps toward shore.

Simultaneously the giant monster arched its back and with a thrust of its long tail launched itself into the air. Heavily-armored forelegs flexed five-taloned claws to both sides. The reptile's full weight landed on the end of the flimsy boardwalk. Her huge chest crushed the planks: upended the pier under Kikilani and Akamu's feet. They fell to their knees as the dock elevated under the lizard's weight. Kikilani and Akamu scrabbled for a handhold. But slid backward toward the lizard's jaws.

Mr. Flute and Dancer lunged to grab the dock. But came away holding only one loose board. The forked tongue darted from the *moʻo's* evil mouth. The monster's teeth still dripped crimson slather—and Maunakili's flesh. The islanders tried to scramble up the inclined pier. Akamu pushed Kikilani ahead. Again the forked tongue shot out like a bullwhip. Wrapped around Akamu's ankle. The young commoner lost his balance. And was pulled backward toward the monster's wide-open gullet. While Swift pulled Kikilani onto the island.

◎   ◎   ◎

As Akamu struggled against all odds Mr. Flute stepped to the end of the jetty. His harpoon gripped tight in his bloodied hands. His seaman's blouse stained red beneath his ear from his contest with Bull Shaw. The harpooner braced himself against the dock post at the water's edge. With steely determination he set his weight. Drew his arm back. Put all his might into the throw. Like an arrow of the Gods Mr. Flute's lance drove deep into the monster's neck: up to the shaft's cord grip. The angry monstrosity released Akamu's ankle. Distracted. But unfazed. Akamu's foot glanced off into the lizard's snout.

In the blink of an eye Swift and Kikilani brought from a rack on the side of the sleeping house two long *pololū* spears. Dancer and Mr. Flute grabbed the thrusting spears. Braced the spears against their sides and gripped the spears' knob at the base. Then raced forward onto the splintered remains of the dock. Dancer jammed his spear into the back of the lizard's gaping mouth. Mr. Flute's shaft drove home into the monster's dark eye socket. The monster gave a sudden writhing hiss. Then reared back. Mr. Flute and Dancer grabbed Akamu and pulled him ashore.

All eyes were fixed on the throes of the goddess Kihawahine. The exhausted group caught their breath as the monster shook off the spears. Like so many pinpricks. The lizard's black eyes contemplated the group for a moment. Then retreated. Pushed off from the broken pier. And disappeared into the black water of the sacred Mokuhinia.

Kapu the Ugly watched from his hiding place: a raised path behind windblown rushes that formed the southern bank of Mokuhinia Lake and the sacred Moku'ula Island. Beside him Billy Mack winced from the pain that still lingered where Kikilani had butted her head against his cheek. The Irish spy pressed a pineapple poultice against his bruised skin. Without a word the misfit pair slipped into the darkness along a sandy path that ran away along the shoreline toward Olowalu. Away from Lahaina Town.

The King lived.

Maunakili the imposter was dead.

CHAPTER 86

LAHAINA FORT
LAHAINA TOWN/MAUI
EIGHT O'CLOCK THAT EVENING

MR. FLUTE HAD RETURNED to help Captain Post check on their prisoners in the fort's jail. The harpooner rattled Bull Shaw's cell. "All's well here."

Post clapped Mr. Flute on the shoulder. "Then it's time to light the lighthouse."

Bull Shaw grunted as he grabbed his bruised ribs. "You fools! You're signing your own death sentence." The deserter pulled himself up by the rusty iron rods. "Don't light the damn lamp...I tell you."

Mr. Flute smacked Bull Shaw's bars with a belaying pin. "You'll get used to the dark soon enough where you're going...Shaw."

"Fools. Fools! If you light the lighthouse lamp we'll all die!" Shaw gave Mr. Flute an imploring look. "The French will blow Lahaina to smithereens! Me. You. The whole damn place!"

Post and Mr. Flute climbed the jail's stone steps to the parade ground. Then walked quickly out the Fort Street gate toward the lighthouse on Lahaina Point. Post nodded to the pickets standing along the seawall smoking. When they reached the lighthouse beyond the wharf Post realized his picket was not there. At a glance—looking up at the light tower—Post saw two of the light's mirrored panels were broken.

"The lamp has been tampered with." Mr. Flute pointed toward the sandy grass near the light's base. "See the stain on the ground? The whale oil was drained."

"That's strange." Post's voice was muffled as he surveyed the tower. "As if someone didn't want the lighthouse to be lit tonight."

"Here's more oil." Mr. Flute hefted a small barrel from a niche in the base of the lighthouse. Climbed the ladder and poured the oil into the lamp reservoir below the mirrored magnifiers. Just then the eight o'clock curfew cannon roared from the fort's ramparts less than a hundred yards away.

"Wait." Post looked up at Mr. Flute. "The whaling fleet has blockaded the harbor."

Mr. Flute nodded. "And the entire Lahaina Roadstead to the north and south." He gestured toward the harbor channel crowded with whaling ships.

Post took a deep breath. "All are in position. No ship will be entering or leaving the harbor this evening. The winds have lessened. Why light the lighthouse...Mr. Flute?"

Mr. Flute considered the question. Head and Maunakili were dead. Dawes and Shaw were in irons. Order had been restored.

Mr. Flute shrugged half-heartedly. "Because we promised Akamu we would do his job for him?"

Post considered that idea. And nodded. "A promise is a promise." Post spoke matter-of-factly as he ran his hands over his black hair. Reflexively his fingers checked the storied ribbon that held his braided rattail in a loop behind his neck.

"What was that gibberish Bull Shaw tried to sell us?" Mr. Flute speculated out loud as he descended the lighthouse ladder. He returned the oil barrel with one hand and withdrew a cold tinder from the storage niche with the other.

"Something about a death sentence...and us being fools if we lit the lighthouse lamp."

Post shrugged and struck a lucifer match to put a spark to the tinder. Cupped his hands and blew gently on the rising flame. Mr. Flute pulled a black Oscuro cigar from his inner pocket. Then used the flaming match to ignite Dancer's gifted cigar. Mr. Flute took two short puffs. Then a long draw. Exhaled like the release valve from a steam engine. And again climbed the nine-foot lighthouse ladder. At the top of the boxlike wooden tower he refreshed his tinder. Touched the burning punk to the cold lamp wick. The whale-oil lamp steadily grew brighter. Mr. Flute closed the faceted cover. And climbed down.

The two men looked out over the moonlit breakwater toward the tropical harbor. Then turned toward the fort.

"If anything will drive away the French it's one of Dancer's cigars." Post smiled broadly.

Mr. Flute took another deep drag. Blew the smoke into the air from the sweet foul-smelling cigar.

The lighthouse beamed bright. Like the center of a bull's-eye.

CHAPTER 87

FOOTHILLS CAMP/OLOWALU STREAM
SOUTH OF LAHAINA TOWN
MOMENTS LATER

"MAUNAKILI HAS FAILED!" Malbec roared as his face turned white with anger. The Lahaina lighthouse lantern burned bright. The light told the story. Maunakili's uprising *had* failed. No payment was to come for protecting the rebels.

The curfew cannon resounded in the distance. "Signal the commander to fire on Lahaina." Malbec gave his demands without preamble.

Sails at full rig the French warship returned the semaphore. Scudded south past Kahoʻolawe and Smuggler's Cove. The prison frigate rounded the island in little time. Then bore down directly on Lahaina. The whalers in the harbor watched as the French ship appeared. White canvas turned bloodred in the last rays of sunset. Closer the frigate advanced. Closer still. The dark-haired Nantucket captain aboard the *Columbia* whispered the Lord's Prayer. With deft seamanship the single warship closed outside the five loose arcs of anchored whaleships. Swept directly opposite the harbor entrance. Struck sail. Dropped sea anchor. Then swung taut just outside the center gap between the whaling ships. The Americans literally stared down a double-tiered broadside. Caught between the French cannon muzzles and the fort Mama Samoa twisted and untwisted clammy hands aboard the *Ship of Paradise.*

Shortly from the French frigate's gun deck came a plume of white gunpowder smoke. Then a boom. The Americans nervously held their ground. From the warship's longest gun a cannonball arced high against the western sky. The whistling ball hurtled over the masts of the whalers. Tethered to each other like floating target practice. Then the volley crashed down on the fort's twenty-foot wall. Ripped a corner off the rampart nearest the canal. To a man the whalers held their breath. Within minutes the French frigate's silent guns had revealed the commander's plan.

The broadside was merely a warning shot.

In the settling darkness Rear Admiral Tromelin sent ashore his ship-of-the-line senior officer. The longboat easily maneuvered the dogleg entrance to Lahaina landing. A troop of French marines marched between Post's pickets toward the fort. Tight order. Red epaulets on blue tunics matching the red trousers of the Grenadiers. A red plume danced atop their black Albert shako hats. Emblazoned with their King's golden-eagle plate. Sabers rattled. A drum beat out a call to arms.

Captain Post. Abner Sisson — the King's advisor. And Angus Macomber — United States Consul — met the officer on the fort grounds. Stiff introductions were exchanged. The French captain came to the point. Take his ultimatum to the King. Capitulation and payment of the treasure — or bombardment would begin. Time was running out. The men must tell the King he had only a few hours of grace remaining. The King must comply — or die — in twenty-four hours.

Post bluffed for time. "We must do anything you ask...Captain. But carting such a large treasure to Lahaina is not a fast process. It comes from many places. Some from a great distance. You will have your money. But we must have forty-eight hours...if you want full payment."

The French captain regarded Post coolly. "This is not a negotiation...Captain." He flicked an imaginary spec from his braided cuff. "Twenty-four hours. By this time tomorrow night. Payment and capitulation. Or every building will be leveled and burned."

With a smart salute the French captain turned on his heel. Led his squad back to the ship's longboat.

In the camp on the Olowalu foothills Kapu the Ugly kept silent. Billy Mack nursed his bruised cheek and stood near Malbec. He had earlier pointed out the palace called Hale Piula. *Visible from the harbor... Too large to miss.* A semaphore signal had been sent to the frigate. Now Tromelin watched as the squad of French marines made ship. As ordered by his King's representative the naval commander raised his saber. His blade cut sharply down. In the next instant a stand of six long-range cannons roared. Shells arced high over the whaler's decks. Slammed to earth. Exploded. Direct on target. Sparks from red-hot shrapnel traced the darkness as the Hale Piula shuddered from the violent impact. The iron roof of the King's house spun crazily high in the air. Fell into the piazza. A twisted snarl of smoking metal. Then three fused incendiaries exploded into fireballs. And a pair of nearby palms showered sparks like Roman candles.

Malbec had made his point.

Comply...or die.

PART 5

THE LOST CITY OF THE PI'ILANI

A SWIFT & DANCER
ADVENTURE

CHAPTER 88

ROYAL HOUSE/KING'S ISLAND
MOKUʻULA/LAHAINA
SHORTLY AFTER

SAMANTHA SWIFT shivered in the night breeze. The horror of watching Kikilani being attacked by the giant Kihawahine lizard left her body drained. Her own suffocating nightmare of death by drowning flooded her mind. Closing her eyes as she sat at a safe remove from the lake made it worse. Despite her own ordeal Kikilani found the strength to wrap her friend in dry *kapa* cloth. Dancer tried to comfort with words. As uncomfortable as they sounded. Akamu stood apart questioning whether he belonged in the presence of the King at all.

Silence soon enveloped the tired group. They sat. Exhausted. On the edge of Loko Mokuhinia. Swift's attention fixed blankly on the black waters of the Mokuhinia. The image of her mother's body — dead and dripping on the dining table — brought mist to Swift's eyes. Beyond the tall palms the black outline of forbidding mountains riveted Dancer's thoughts. A chill wind from the mountain valley licked across the lake. Like witches' tongues the *kukui* torches lit the night.

The Hawaiian King rocked on his knees beside the black waters of the Mokuhinia. With an ancient *mele* chant he acknowledged the goddess Kihawahine.

Moku'ula...home to mo'o *Kihawahine.*
Guardian spirit. Goddess to our origins.
Moku'ula is our piko *hole and central source.*
The source of our divine power.
Our mana.
Hear...the spirits of earth and water rely on Kihawahine.
Hear...High Chief Kahekili...unifier of Maui...served the
true ancient Gods.
Hear...all Hawaiians share the origins of the same goddess...
Kihawahine.
Her appearance embodies the true reign of our traditional
ways.
Hear...today one Son of Hawai'i lives on to save us.

As the King ended the chant Swift and Dancer held back in reverent silence. Then the King beckoned Swift. Dancer. Akamu. And Kikilani to follow him to his royal retreat. Upon entering the royal house Kikilani and Akamu both prostrated themselves before the King.

"Rise up. You have earned my respect."

All stood silently. Then followed the King into the inner sanctum. At length the King said in a quiet voice: "We have won the battle. But lost the war."

The words stirred the others to listen.

"It is inevitable. I must sign a treaty with the French...the same as the sovereigns of the Marquesas and Tahiti. At least Hawai'i will have a King for internal affairs within a Hawaiian kingdom. There is no other choice. The British rejected any alliance. The Americans are powerless. Unless we accept the protection of the French...all is lost." The forlorn King cast a worried glance toward the smoking ruins of the Hale Piula not a hundred yards away.

Akamu and Kikilani stirred in protest. But no words came. Their features were shrouded in sadness.

Moments passed. The King moved to put his hand on the pump organ. "Please...can you help?" He gestured to move the heavy inlaid instrument. Dancer and Akamu slid the cabinet away from the wall. From a secret compartment in the tomb's wall behind the organ the

King removed a heavy bottle gourd wrapped in a leather casing. The leather carrying case had a strong handle. Then the King carried the heavy object with both hands back to the smaller anteroom overlooking the lake. Set the gourd down with a hollow thud as the four visitors gathered around. Then took seats. The King in his armed chair. Dancer and Swift righted the torn sofa and sat down. Kikilani and Akamu sat cross-legged on the fine mat.

The King removed the handle and opened the gourd's leather cover. From the hollow gourd the King pulled golden gifts. Handed a jeweled brooch to Swift. A precious ring to Akamu. Another ring to Kikilani. And a golden buckle and several coins to Dancer.

Dancer examined the ancient coins in his palm. He raised his gaze: his eyes met Swift's.

Dancer turned back to the King. "Your Highness…where did you get this buckle? These coins?"

"These shiny things appear." The King's tone was simple. "Sometimes at the edge of the Mokuhinia. Other times in a royal fishpond or *kalo* paddy."

Dancer leaned forward. "They just *arrive* in the sacred lake…?"

The King nodded. He pointed to the far northeast corner of the lake. "There—where the channel refreshes the Mokuhinia. These treasures arrive. Not uncommonly on occasions of great significance. We have saved them all." He indicated the heavy gourd. Held it for all to see. Inside were coins. Gems. Small jewelry. A wealth of treasures. "The same as we do to protect our ancestors' ashes."

The King again gestured toward the gourd: He seemed to invite them to have a closer look. Swift reached out and sunk her hand into the gourd's hollowed-out interior. Her fingers dug knuckle-deep in the trove. "These treasures just appeared where the cutover canal from the Kaua'ula Stream feeds the lake?"

The King nodded. "Sometimes the washer women bring them to me. Other times children playing on the banks of the Mokuhinia lake. Mostly in ones and twos. But sometimes in handfuls. As if the gods left them as gifts. A sign we had made them happy."

Dancer lifted an embroidered antimacassar cloth from the sofa back and spread the square fabric onto the room's floor mat. Tilted the gourd. And allowed a splash of gold and silver to spread across the white cloth. He marveled at the collection. "These are clearly from Malta. Ottoman Turkey. Egypt."

Swift examined several coins in a separate pile of the lucre. "And these are Napoleonic coins...."

"Could it be...?" Dancer asked looking at Swift's surprised face.

Dancer turned back to the King. "When did these gifts from the gods first come to the Moku'ula?"

The King turned some coins over in his fingers. As if they were of no more value than bead-like *puka* shells picked from beach sand. He tilted his head. "It has been many years. Most of my life. But not all. They have come since I was a boy."

"Your Highness is now what age?"

The King gave Dancer a puzzled look.

Akamu raised a finger. "At Laihainaluna School they taught us you were born in 1813...Your Highness." He blushed slightly at his brashness. "On the English Calendar...you are thirty-four this year."

Dancer exhaled a deep breath. "1813 was some years after LeGrand shipwrecked on Maui."

Swift gave Dancer a long look. "What does that mean...Dancer? Do you think there is a connection?"

Before Dancer could form a reply Akamu asked a question. "Will this treasure—and Maunakili's death—be enough to buy off the French?"

Dancer shook his head. "Maunakili's death will not stop the French. He was their pawn. Only a means to an end...not the key to their scheme. And this small gourd will only whet their appetite."

One by one the King looked into the four gathered faces. His expression forlorn. Almost defeated. "The French bombardment begins in twenty-four hours." As Dancer had explained to the King.

Swift took a deep breath. "There must be something..." Then she looked at Dancer.

Dancer straightened. Smiled his instinctive smile and said simply: "There is one last hope...."

All eyes turned toward Dancer. *Here we go again.* So Swift thought to herself. *Shoot first...aim later.*

Dancer rose from his kneeling position. Returned to the edge of the sofa. Flipped a gold coin in the air. Caught it. Then leaned forward and repeated. "There *is* one last hope."

The King turned toward Dancer. "But there are only twenty-four hours remaining in Malbec's ultimatum. What choice do we have?"

Akamu found his voice. "We must do something."

"Even if it doesn't work." Swift conceded the point with a glance toward Kikilani.

Kikilani nodded agreement.

Dancer flipped the coin again. Caught it. And smacked it onto the back of his other hand. *Heads.* He nodded. *That's a start.* He swept the faces with his glance. "I have an idea...."

Dancer briefly outlined the scheme that was partially formed in his mind. The four of them must go up into the hills...find the source of the treasure...that seemed to drift down from the slopes above the sacred lake. "It must come from somewhere." Dancer paused as if for a reply. But none came.

The King rocked forward and back. "All is lost." He repeated the phrase. Then added: "Unless you can work your miracle."

Dancer nodded. "It's a long shot. But at least it's a shot."

"Better than waiting for the inevitable without trying." Swift gave a half-hearted smile with a touch of desperation in her voice.

Dancer recited a short list to his trio of companions. "Get your backcountry kits together. Clothes. Boots. Canteen. Cold food. Akamu...come with me. We'll grab some gear at Macomber's. There's not a minute to lose. We'll meet everyone in two hours at Major Tuckerman's. Swift...arrange for four horses and a wrangler from the Major's livery. We must reach the mountain trailhead above the Lahainaluna School print shop before dawn!"

All four stood up. Each in their own way honored the King with a gesture or a bow. Then they raced across the Moku'ula Island. And along the King's Way. Toward Lahaina Town.

When the group reached the canal footbridge Dancer shouted over his shoulder to the others: "Bring bags of *kukui* nuts. As many as you can carry."

"Did he say *nuts?*" Swift shook her head. Then disappeared with Kikilani into the darkness toward Tuckerman's. Akamu and Dancer ran ahead.

CHAPTER 89

TRAILHEAD/KAUAʻULA STREAM
LAHAINALUNA/ABOVE LAHAINA TOWN
BEFORE DAWN

THE PARCHED HIGHLANDS retained their twilight coolness. For now. Five riders trooped up the steep mountainside trail above Lahaina: a group of four close-knit companions followed by a wrangler. The only sound was the soft grind of horseshoes on gravel wash. And the occasional rattle of gear as the riders ascended the slope. Roosting Nene geese quietly called a drawn-out *NAY-nay* cry as they passed. Then scattered into the scrubland in the first glow of dawn.

Behind the cantle on each rider's saddle Dancer had strapped a knapsack. The bulging packs contained hastily gathered essentials. Lanterns. Lamps. Ropes. Paraffin-canvas pancho. Padding to be bound to knees and elbows. Seamen's gloves used to tar and varnish. Straw hats with extra padding. Food to be eaten with dirty hands. A pipe whistle. Jackknifes. Short lengths of cords. Candles. Matches. And grabs of miscellany. All jammed into waterproof ditty bags.

Dancer's pack had a short-handled shovel tied to it.

As daybreak outlined the dark ridge above the riders followed the Kauaʻula Stream into a gulch. Lush leaves and giant ferns brushed them as they passed. The winding trail took them across the stream. And back. They moved upward. Onward.

At a pool Swift caught a sparkle out of the corner of her eye. *Probably a sunbeam.*

Kikilani saw it too. She slid off her horse. Bent over the water. Reached into a narrow crevice just above a cascade. She straightened with a broad smile across her lustrous white teeth. To the group she held up a gold coin. "Look!"

Dancer came over. Examined the coin. "Egyptian. Keep your eyes peeled for more. We're on the right track." Then dropped the coin into his pouch with the other coins.

Around the far side of the pool the horses could not go farther: The rocky trail was too narrow. Here two streams merged into one.

Dancer helped Kikilani with her pack. While Akamu hoisted a knapsack on Swift's shoulders. The mist coated the surrounding rocks in moss. Unbalanced by her pack Swift slipped. Scraped her shin on hardened lava. She winced but quickly got back on her feet. "I'm okay." Kikilani explored the stronger fork of the two streams. In a minute or so she found another coin. "This way!" A short distance farther the path stopped at a deep pool in a dead-end canyon.

Akamu scrambled around the pool's edge. In the cliffside he discovered dense foliage draped in shorter ferns and roots. Behind this curtain he found a smaller pool. Scoured by a small waterfall that dropped from the mouth of a half-hidden lava tube. From the sand of the clear pool Akamu retrieved a sparkling red gem. Held it up to the others. "Looks like our first ruby."

Dancer collected the coins and ruby. Tied the pouch to his belt under his shirt. Then returned to the horses. Gave two cigars to their wrangler. Then added a message. "This is for you. Return with the horses in twelve hours. Got that?" Watching the wrangler guide the horses back down the trail he thought: *Where we're going we won't be needing horses for a while...if at all.* He called before the wrangler disappeared back into the green gulch: "Twelve hours from now. Without fail!"

Swift gauged the sylvan terrain with a careful eye. "Clearly the coins and gems were pushed down by the stream."

"Probably during storm runoff." Kikilani made sense of their finds:

"That's what carried the gifts into the Mokuhinia...like offerings from the gods."

Akamu gave the two woman a look of bewilderment. "But where did they come from?"

Dancer checked everyone's gear. "My guess is we're going to do some crawling." He instructed the others to strap on their padded hats. Strap on their coconut-shell elbow and knee padding. And wear a longer jacket to cover any gaps where their shirts and pants met. "To keep out the dirt." He hung a candle strung on a lanyard around each of their necks. "In case you're separated from your lantern...you won't lose your light source." Akamu removed a *kukui* necklace and *puka*-shell bracelet from Kikilani. Put them into her pack with a brotherly look. "So nothing gets snagged."

Kikilani looked teasingly at Akamu. "In your vest and belt and twill trousers...you look the proper missionary off on a picnic."

Akamu blushed. Removed his cravat tie and opened his collar. But kept his jacket and vest.

Everyone knew they were in a race against time. The clock ticked relentlessly toward the French ultimatum. Their timetable was set. Find the treasure. And beat the clock. Or perish.

"Good thing we've got this trail of coins all to ourselves." Dancer swept a glance at the three cave hunters. "All we have to do is follow the breadcrumbs."

Swift muttered under her breath: "Sounds easy...unless it rains."

CHAPTER 90

FOOTHILLS CAMP
OLOWALU STREAM
AT DAWN

"THE MYSTERY of what happened to LeGrand's treasure was never solved. He took that puzzle to his grave." Kapu spoke in an impassive tone as he tutored Malbec. "Maunakili thought the treasure was hidden at the Moku'ula. That mistake cost him his life."

"*And* the kingdom. The stupid half-breed bunga!" A slight sneer curled Malbec's lip as he spoke dismissively of the dead rebel.

Kapu gazed quietly at Malbec. "He was indeed a half-breed." He paused as though considering whether to continue. "When you first came ashore at the refuge to meet Maunakili I noticed you have the same birthmark as he. An old *mele* speaks of this matter." A dead silence followed. "You are Maunakili's half-brother...Malbec."

Malbec shuddered in rage. "You—Kapu the Ugly—storyteller and fabricator of the Pi'ilani...you think you know the truth?" Like a long-smoldering volcano he clenched his teeth with fury. But refused to explode before Kapu. "*Non. Non. Non.* That I—Henri Malbec—commandant of the New Caledonia Prison Colony—carry the same blood as that polluted Pi'ilani? A bloodline no better than you? *C'est grotesque.*"

Kapu the Storyteller gave Malbec a neutral look. Then calmly changed the subject and shared the details of LeGrand's mystery passed from generation to generation. "LeGrand's treasure was taken away at night. The old *mele* chants said Napoleon's gold was stolen from La Perouse Bay. Taken to Olowalu. Then carried up Olowalu Valley trail. The shortest route into the 'Iao Valley." Kapu recited the old myth. "The ancestors say the 'Iao Valley is where the treasure was hidden." Kapu managed a faraway look. Paused. Then continued. "All this was done by the little people...the Menehune."

Anger again flushed Malbec. Kapu had told him long ago of Maunakili's rage at the suggestion that the Menehune—a people no more than three feet tall—had taken Napoleon's treasure.

"Little people? What do you mean?" Malbec growled. "Don't lie to me! *Mon Dieu!* You'd need an army for that much gold."

Kapu held his ground. "Legend says they carried the treasure on their backs along a seldom-used trail." He vaguely gestured toward a dark valley cut from the mountain above the camp. "There. See for yourself. The trail runs through a lava tube."

Malbec paced. Stopped. Looked at Kapu with the blank expression of a sadistic bully. "Impossible."

Kapu's gaze greeted Malbec with equal stoicism. "The *mele* says the Menehune worked wonders at night. Built walls. Castles. Then disappeared before dawn."

Malbec scowled. Unsure if he was hearing the truth. Or just another heathen myth.

"The Menehune also protected the sacred sites of our ancestors." Kapu seemed to be warning Malbec.

"Protected? Hah!" Malbec mocked the storyteller. "What protection are old bones and stupid superstitions? Nothing! Give me real gold and I'll show you what's truly sacred."

Kapu read Malbec's mood. "An old chant told of some Pi'ilani who escaped from the Great Conqueror after the battle of Kepaniwai. The great Battle of the Dammed Waters. The waters of the river ran red—blocked by the bodies of Maui's fallen warriors. But a handful of the highest chiefs and their chiefesses made their way out of the 'Iao Valley. They traveled along an ancient trail to Olowalu. Then Moloka'i. That is why LeGrand was taken to Moloka'i years later.

And why Maunakili was sired on that island."

Malbec nodded. *So that is how LeGrand ended up fathering Maunakili.* The next moment he gave Kapu a belittling look. "What more do the chants of these old wives say?"

Kapu knelt down and sketched a rough map in the dirt. The diagram showed how the Olowalu Stream diverged from the Kaua'ula Stream in the 'Īao Valley. "The one who follows the Olowalu trail is the one who will find Napoleon's *waiwai*. Napoleon's treasure."

Malbec weighed his options. He had sent Tromelin the evening before to demand payment and tribute in twenty-four hours. A smile crossed his thin lips as he thought of his calling card: the Hale Piula. *That table is set. And I hold all the power. The deadline runs out this evening at eight o'clock.* But now Kapu's spies had brought word the Americans had set out on the Kaua'ula Stream trail after meeting with the Hawaiian King.

"There is one way to beat the Americans to the treasure." Kapu stated the situation matter-of-factly. "Take the shorter Olowalu trail. Find the lava cave. And reach the 'Īao Valley first."

Malbec's eyes narrowed.

Kapu persisted. "Beware. The stream and caves split into many forks…Over the years many have been lost without returning. But there is one guide…." Kapu paused. And nodded knowingly. "An old *ali'i* who is a bird-catcher. His life has been spent gathering feathers for royal clothing. He knows the Olowalu trail like no other. Only he knows the true path from the false forks…if he will guide us."

A crooked sneer raised Malbec's thin upper lip. *Why wait to get what is mine?* He had decided. Quickly he mobilized an expedition party. Malbec. Kapu. Billy Mack. And a hand-picked squad of French mercenaries. Each man armed as a fast-moving skirmisher. Light bivouac rations. Field canteen. Lantern. Powder and ball. Within the hour Kapu moved up the Olowalu Stream trail. Followed by Malbec. Billy Mack. And a troop of villainous-looking hirelings. Only one objective stood before them: beat the Americans to the treasure.

Malbec accepted the challenge with relish. "The Americans don't know where the treasure was taken…much less where it's hidden. Unless the Hawaiian King told them the same fanciful story you've told me…Kapu."

Malbec understood his greatest advantage: surprise. If the Americans showed their faces they still wouldn't know Malbec would be lying in wait for them. "Even if the poor bastards overcome every obstacle and trip over the treasure…we will take it from them. Either way we are invincible."

Malbec pushed his troop to conscript the bird-catcher guide and intercept the unsuspecting Americans in the deepest mountain valley. "At last we will trap them where there is no escape." He laughed icily. "Napoleon's gold will be returned to the emperor. And France will rule the entire Pacific. That is to be. That is France's manifest destiny."

Malbec withdrew a fragment of an American flag Billy Mack had taken from the *Bountiful.* And spit on it.

CHAPTER 91

CAVES OF FIRE
KAUA'ULA STREAM
AN HOUR AFTER DAWN

DANCER LED HIS FOURSOME into the lava tube. The cave had been cut through the mountain by eons of molten lava on the north side of the Kaua'ula Stream. Within a few steps a screeching horde of bats flew from out of the blackness. Bats by the thousands! The small animals flapped past the group's heads. The mammals' needlelike claws smacked against their upheld arms. A pair tangled in the strands of Kikilani's hair that flowed from beneath her padded caving hat. She let out a shriek. Froze in place. Paralyzed by fear.

And then just as suddenly the screeching cloud was gone. Swift moved close to her friend. Handed Kikilani a fragrant sprig of sandalwood leaves she had picked earlier along the stream. "Very rare these days. When you hear or see bats…crush a leaf. The scent keeps them away."

Swift's words comforted her friend. Kikilani regained her composure. Moved forward following Akamu's lantern.

Dancer spoke to Swift. "I never knew that about bats."

Swift whispered so only Dancer could hear. "Neither did I…but the hills these lava tubes run through are her homeland. She seems determined to learn all she can from it. She took the lead — and now we need her to keep going."

Over their heads the cave's ceiling arched fifteen feet. The sinuous lava tube snaked through the mountain. Like a great frozen river. The air dank. But not cold. Not a sound came to their ears. Except the scuff of their soles on the smooth unbroken lava floor. Not a hundred yards along Akamu heard Kikilani shriek behind him. When he turned his lantern behind him he saw Kikilani pointing to a pile of dark slender objects on the floor of the cave. "Are those…bones?" Akamu took three steps forward into the darkness. His right shoulder hit what seemed to be one of four upright poles set on the hard stone floor. The support gave way. Quickly Akamu swung his lantern around as the pole clattered at his feet. Without warning from a *marae* platform just above his head a corpse slipped off the scaffold. A macabre bundle dropped suspended in the darkness beside Akamu. Held by its rotten shrouds. At the same moment Kikilani raised her lantern. Into its beam the skeleton danced beside Akamu like a ghoulish jester.

Kikilani screamed.

Swift snapped her light forward to see Kikilani stumble backward. "Look out!" Swift shouted.

Too late. Kikilani's foot stepped into a dry rib cage lying on the cave floor. The bones closed like a bear trap around Kikilani's calf. Again she screamed in terror. Her cry echoed away into the darkness. She toppled backward. Clutched her lower leg.

Akamu pushed the skeleton aside. The wrapped bones fell in a pile at his feet. He turned his light on Kikilani as Swift leaped to her side. Kikilani shrieked again. Wrestled with the white bone cage clamped around her leg. Swift bent down. Put a hand on Kikilani's thigh to settle her. Then spread the brittle bones apart. Leathery tendons stretched easily. Several rib bones broke off in Swift's hand. With a terrified look Kikilani scuttled like a crab away from the grotesque trap.

Gradually her breathing slowed as she recovered.

Dancer stepped up to where Akamu stood. Together they cast their lanterns about the area. Around them lay a scatter of bones. Nearest the two men lay a host of animal bones. Goats. Cattle. Rib cages. Then farther on their lights revealed more white bones. And human skulls. These remnants glowed in the lantern light like ghostly apparitions.

Swift and Kikilani joined the two men. Soon their lanterns revealed the full extent of the deathly scene. Skeletons wrapped in decaying twine. Gourds that once held food sat beside them. Drink. Scraps of decorated *kapa* cloth lay all about. Sooty burn marks rose above miniature shrines.

Akamu cast his lantern over a cluster of human bones. "This is a boneyard. The ancients honored their dead in these caves."

Kikilani breathed evenly as her light slowly passed over the burials. "Our people place their deceased here because they will be safe."

Dancer tapped the lava wall with the heel of his metal lantern. "Plus it's easier than digging graves out of the lava rock outside."

Soon Akamu led the group beyond the silent boneyard. Swift. Kikilani. And Dancer followed. Careful not to disturb the spirits of the dead. Or trigger the retribution of a curse.

They pressed forward up the meandering passage. In places the lava-stone floor running down the center of the passage was as smooth as a wagon track. In the lantern light Swift noticed that when the bulbous lava solidified it had formed a wide curb on both sides of the lava tube. Beyond the stone curbs the black stone had formed gutters. Ahead a glow appeared. As they rounded a curve all saw a heavenly light descending before them. A thick mass of snakelike roots hung down within the circular glow. A single waterdrop glistened at the bottom of each root — making it seem like a fang glistening with poisonous venom.

Kikilani pointed toward the light shaft. "A *puka* hole....Long ago the ceiling crust collapsed here to open a skylight window."

The lush rain forest vegetation virtually closed the hole above them with green growth. A loose cascade of crust from the ceiling had broken down and fallen to the floor below: Walking was difficult. Surface moisture coated the sharp rocks with moss and slippery slime as the group passed.

Around the curve another pinhole ceiling break had occurred. Through this tiny *puka* came a pencil-thin beam of light. The beam fell directly on a strange stalagmite. Swift examined the column's drippy shapes that looked like a pile of giant worms. Frozen in stone. The angelic beam made the shapes sparkle as if the gods intended the column to serve as an omen.

Step-by-step the hunters followed their whale-oil lanterns as the passage straightened and the ceiling rose higher — as if the lava had flowed at a higher speed and began cutting a straighter passage. Their footsteps became more assured on this lava road. Soon Akamu shouted: "Watch out!" He pointed a few steps ahead. There the floor of the lava tube dropped off sharply. Before them stretched what looked like a hardened lava lake. Yet their lights revealed wide cracks in the stone floor. Dancer tossed a rock into one of the largest cracks. The stone dropped for several seconds. Silence. In time a distant rattling rebounded from far below: a deep well. All realized the floor was treacherously thin. A long drop would be their last.

"Best work our way around the ledge."

Dancer pointed to a narrow passage and led the way. Swift got down on hands and knees. Then crawled around the apron — glad to have pads on her knees. At the far side the ledge abruptly ended. The heavy humidity of the cave felt stifling.

Kikilani lifted her lantern to reveal another passage entering from just above their heads. "Lava fall." Her voice sounded grim. "We'll have to climb it." With the agility of a mountain goat she ascended the cascade of solidified stone. Dancer was the last to arrive at the top. Shortly beyond where the lava once flowed over the lip of the falls the height of the dark passageway was reduced to little more than bathtub depth. Dancer balked. "I hate small spaces." His taut jaw remained unseen outside the cone of his lantern light. "It's not the dark. It's getting stuck that gets me."

Swift stated a practical solution: "Kikilani and Akamu will go first. They'll shine their lanterns on the sides of the passage. I'll come behind you...Dancer. My light will show you the way."

Dancer swallowed. Inhaled deeply. Lowered himself onto his belly. Then crawled forward. Shark-toothed stalactites jabbed down from the ceiling. Dancer's pack ripped loudly in the silence. He stopped crawling. Then carefully. Slowly. Slipped out of the pack's straps. Pulled the load beside him.

"Breathe." Swift's whisper was emphatic: They had fallen behind Kikilani and Akamu. "You'll make it. The least we can do is show a little courage — especially after Kikilani's little swim in the Mokuhinia."

As Swift inched forward behind Dancer the oily smell of lantern smoke hung in the still air. Swift frowned in the darkness. *Anybody will know we've been here with a single sniff.* Just then a loose fragment of rock wall fell and clattered on the stone beside her. Dancer's crawl quickened.

Soon Dancer and Swift joined Kikilani and Akamu where the passage opened up and the ceiling climbed higher. When they stood up they realized they were inside the largest chamber they had seen so far. The floor was littered with huge balls of solidified lava that rose up to their waists. Akamu explained that the balls were chunks of ceiling that had broken down. After they had fallen to the floor of the lava tube subsequent lava flows had coated them over and over again until they formed molten boulders. All four scanned the sides of the high chamber with their lanterns. A rainbow of shapes and textures met their gaze. Mineral colors boldly stood out in the beams of light. Iron red. Yellow crusts. Ghostly white shapes. Moisture coating the green and chocolate rock bounced the light back.

On the far side of the cathedral chamber the mouths of three passages loomed dark and identical.

"Which way do we go?" Swift asked.

Kikilani reasoned out loud. "None of these can be the wrong way."

"How do you know?"

"Because the lava flowed downhill toward us. If it was blocked above the lava would have closed the passage."

"You mean if these are tubes they must connect with another branch farther on?" Dancer's skepticism was reflected in his doubting tone.

"Exactly. Of course…I could be wrong. But I say we take the largest passage: the one in the middle."

"And cross our fingers." Dancer followed Kikilani into the middle passage.

Here the ancient lava flow had cut a deep trough in the stone floor. Water filled the trough: cool but not icy. The lava-stone trough ran between two stone levees — one on either side. Soon Akamu spotted a sparkle in the shallow water. He dropped his pack. Stripped off his jacket. Vest. Shoes. Shirt. And rolled up his twill trousers. Then waded into the pool. Walked several careful steps and reached up to his shoulder deep into the trough. He came up holding a strangely carved black gem.

Back on the levee Akamu brought the stone under Kikilani's lantern. The black object almost filled his palm. "Odd...It's shaped like a keyhole." Kikilani ran her finger over the highly polished stone. "A very large keyhole." On the stone's polished black face a clockwise spiral design had been delicately etched. Kikilani touched the spiral. The dull area felt rough — like sandpaper — and contrasted with the polished surface. "Looks feminine. And very old."

Akamu pointed to the stone's oblong top end — where a small hole the diameter of a wire was visible. The gem felt heavy for its size: As Kikilani wiped the water from the mysterious onyx a rising sense of strength filled her with confidence.

Dancer gestured to move ahead. "More treasure up yonder. Time's a wasting."

Kikilani handed the gem to Swift who wrapped the heavy stone in dressing gauze. Then placed it in the medical kit Dancer had put in her pack.

Akamu shivered slightly. Pulled on his shirt. Then stuffed the missionary's jacket and vest into his pack. His black hair glistened with water droplets. Swift turned her light on Kikilani's face. Her friend's expression had a distant air — as if her thoughts had drifted far away. Swift watched her carefully. "Kiki...?" she asked. "What are you thinking about?"

Kikilani did not answer.

"Are you alright...?"

Kikilani touched her temples. "Just feel a little faint. Must be the altitude."

Dancer led the way forward. Ahead the height of the passage constricted. Akamu dug into his pack for the coconut kneepads and strapped them over his trousers. The others followed suit. All four edged on their knees along the levee apron. Their shoulders brushed the cutbank wall. They approached another shaft of light shining down through a *puka* hole. Then from out of the darkness ahead they heard a rumble coming toward them. The sound increased as if a dammed reservoir had been released.

"Flash flood!" Dancer shouted as he pointed toward a narrow incline formed by fallen debris. "Move! Akamu...climb that breakdown. *Fast!* If we can reach the skylight before the water rises we'll have a chance!"

Akamu scrambled up the loose scree of the breakdown as the others quickly followed behind him. Near the top he extended a hand to a struggling Kikilani. Swift clasped an arm around Kikilani's rump and pushed her upward. The water rose steadily beneath the group. Suddenly the water surged like an underground river rising up toward them. A cresting wave pushed the water rapidly higher. Dancer's snake boot slipped — both feet plunged into the torrent. Akamu yanked free a knotted rope attached to his pack. Tossed one end toward Dancer — who was still unbalanced and struggling to maintain a hold on the breakdown. The floodwaters rapidly filled the passage around Dancer. He grabbed the line Akamu had thrown him. Akamu pulled with all his strength even as Dancer found his footing. Then climbed up the collapsed rocks.

The foursome grabbed ahold of roots. Rocks. Scrambled upward toward the light. Beyond the clutches of the cold flood below. Climbed higher. Through the skylight. And emerged into the sunlit warmth of a natural Eden.

CHAPTER 92

TRAIL OF THE BIRD-CATCHERS
OLOWALU STREAM
SHORTLY AFTER SUNRISE

KAPU LED MALBEC. Billy Mack. And Malbec's troop of mercenaries up the rain-swollen bed of the Olowalu Stream trail. After following a faint track up a narrow defile between sheer cliffs for a considerable distance the trail opened. They came upon a grassy open space with houses. Food plots. Storage racks. And home to the father of all *kia manu*—the bird-catchers of the Pi'ilani kings. From this point only the *kia manu* knew the climb to the Olowalu Pass and 'Iao Valley.

Across the grassy space a small man approached the waiting trio. He was almost as thin as the long *kia* pole he carried upright before him. At the top of the pole shone a *kano* crosspiece. To Billy Mack the native looked like an acolyte carrying the crucifix at the entrance procession for a Catholic mass.

As the strange man walked toward the visitors he made a clear trilling sound. Almost a processional hymn. The man noticed Billy Mack and Malbec staring at him as he approached.

"*Kahekahe.*" The old man's voice cracked with age.

Malbec laughed contemptuously.

Kapu explained what the old man was trying to say. "*Kahekahe* is an ancient technique for catching birds." He nodded. "Watch."

The small man leaned his long pole against a storage platform. Billy Mack realized only now that the crosspiece was stained brown with gum. Soon several stunning flycatcher birds hovered over the crosspiece: A forked branch held sweet *lehua* flowers. Eager for a taste the birds pecked each other for first rights. One hopped onto the crosspiece. Malbec watched with dark curiosity as the bird soon became glued to the gum. The small man reached out to the flycatcher and began ruffling the bird's feathers.

Kapu again explained: "The bird-catcher prunes back the flowers in the blooming season from the branch of a felled tree. The bare branch is spread with sap of the breadfruit. Birds come for the honey-laden flowers: It intoxicates them. Meanwhile their feet stick to the sap."

"Sounds like Maunakili trying to trap the King on the Moku'ula." Malbec snapped his words impatiently. "Didn't work for him."

The bird-catcher continued to feel the bird's feathers. He all at once plucked a fine feather free. Then applied a salve on the bird's flesh to speed its recovery. Next he used *kukui* oil to remove the gum from its feet. As Malbec reached for the bird the King's bird-catcher released it into the air.

Kapu nodded. "Without the spirit of life the colors are lost. The best birds are very rare. True *kia manu* spare the young birds."

Malbec reached the end of his attention span. Flexed his knuckles. Paced petulantly. Impatient. He stared at Kapu as if the storyteller were mad. "Tell him I will pay for a guide."

The royal bird-catcher bowed to Kapu. And Malbec. And Mack. After a short conference in native tongue Kapu announced Kaikano—the King's bird-catcher—had agreed to guide them. On one condition.

"What does he want?" Malbec spat. "Name the price."

"He doesn't want money—or payment of any kind." Kapu gazed at the commandant of Camp Blood without expression. "Kaikano only asks that the first bird captured be released as an offering to the gods."

Malbec flexed his grip on his sword hilt. "More *kanaka* superstitions…"

Kapu read Malbec's mood and turned to Kaikano. "He agrees." Then indicated to the others to follow the bird-catcher. "We go now."

Without hesitation Kaikano turned. Led Kapu. The foreigners. And Malbec's small troop of soldiers across the stream and along a bypath on the north side of the stream to the 'Iao Valley-Olowalu Pass. Within a few hundred yards the troop reached the entrance to a lava cave. They scrambled up the breakdown rubble. Lit their lamps. And moved forward in single file.

They had not gone thirty yards when Kaikano held up his hand.

"What is it now?" Malbec asked in an irritated voice.

"Listen."

From the cave overhead came a single sound: chewing. At that moment the hired soldier at the rear screamed. They turned. Around him scores of colorless almost translucent string worms descended from the darkness. The eyeless worms hung from long filaments. A single worm could be brushed away. Perhaps. But this onslaught consisted of scores of worms. Teeth like piranha jaws sunk into the soldier's flesh: Each worm took hold of its victim's skin with a fiendish grip. Then stunned him with venom. The man's struggles attracted more string worms. Arms. Legs. Heads. Nostrils. Every appendage was fair game.

Malbec's lantern cast a feeble light on the dangling worms. After striking each string worm appeared to separate from its teeth. As bees do when leaving an imbedded stinger. When a second lantern focused on the worms Malbec realized the teeth were not in fact detached. The cave worms instead had a grotesque adaptation: Their jaws swiveled on their necks like a pulley-block and hook. As if by silent command the worms reversed rotation. Quickly their dangling filaments wrapped around their spinning bodies. To the intruders' horror the curtain of worms—their teeth still buried in the soldier's skin—spun like bobbins and lifted the man off the floor. Malbec raised his lantern and followed the soldier as he rose to his doom. Gradually he realized the illuminated ceiling revealed above was covered in a viscous cluster of cocoons. The silk sacs bulged oddly with the bones and flesh of animals in various stages of digestion.

"Nothing can be done." Kaikano shook his head simply. "There is no medicine for their poison. The only comfort is the string worms always live near the entrance to a cave. Where prey may wander in. As you see."

As the group stared the paralyzed mercenary's body gave a last twitch. The man's canteen fell to the cave floor with a hollow thud. His body elevated farther. And disappeared into the string worms' seething lair.

"Enough." Malbec's order was terse. "Move forward. We've wasted a lot of time already."

The soldiers huddled closer together. Disoriented in the blackness. Then found their way along the path.

"They call this the Menehune Highway." Kapu's words were volunteered. "It's easy going. Here the lava flowed quickly. Straight. The gutters forced the lava to erode the middle. That is why the way is smooth...as I told you it would be."

"Smooth enough for a wagon." Mack stated the observation flatly.

At that moment the mountain quivered. Through Mack's feet he felt a gentle movement. Gradually the cave floor shuddered — then shook. Mack stumbled. Caught his balance. Lanterns flashed wildly about in a dizzying kaleidoscope. Mack shuffled sideways and placed a steadying hand against the moist cave wall. A deep rumble came from overhead. Mack cast his lantern up and back at the rocky ceiling. With a sudden fracture a section of the roof collapsed behind them. Large chunks of lava-stone fell across the road they had just stepped. While Mack held his breath after a moment the fall stopped as if a shaft had been completely filled. Kaikano and Kapu approached the debris slide. Passed their light beams along the walls. Mack fixed his eyes on the moving lights as the beams met at the top of the rock fall. Tons of loose debris blocked the track. Kapu stepped up on a large boulder for a closer look. Escape was possible he reported. But would mean heavy scrambling over the debris. Unless there was another tremor.

In the silence Kaikano spoke. "This is the work of the cave snakes."

"What do you mean 'cave snakes'?" Mack asked.

"An old myth." Kapu's voice was slightly unsettled. "Some believe that giant snakes inhabit the caves. And protect the bones of our ancestors. But no one has reported actually seeing the snakes...or at least lived to tell about it."

Kaikano nodded. Then fingered the talisman around his neck. "The only way is forward."

Increasingly whispers grew among the hired men-at-arms. Their imaginations had been released. Venomous worms. Earthquakes. Giant snakes. What else lived in the caves? Gargoyles? Trolls? Demons?

As the group of soldiers marched forward holding their lanterns Kaikano guided them along a ledge that circled an old lava lake. Pieces of breakdown lay scattered about the passageway. Two of the soldiers ignored Malbec's order to stay close: They fell behind the others. Soon a screech like the cry of a banshee broke through the darkness. The two laggards raised their muskets and fired toward the sound. Bolted. Ran back across the lava lake. Then froze uncertainly. A sound like breaking glass rose around their feet. Then both men fell through the thin lava floor. Their screams were heard for a long moment. Then silence.

An icy calm seemed to settle over Malbec. He turned to the others gathered before him. "March on." He pushed the remainder of his troop along the ledge. And up a short lava fall toward the next passage.

Kapu turned. Lifted his arms toward the black chasm behind them. Then let his arms drop dejectedly.

"I have seen this before." Kaikano nodded as he looked back. "The cave and its dark lure will drive even the bravest man mad in the end."

An hour or so passed as Malbec and his men progressed through the lava tube. They passed skylights. Colored formations of ghostly rock shaped by fire. Bottomless pools of groundwater. Yet they pushed on. Kaikano showed them the way. Without the trial and error of false passages and mistaken assumptions the troop soon arrived at a spot where two passages merged into the one tube they had followed.

Always impatient Malbec pushed past the bird-catcher. "We go this way." He pointed toward the right passage. Huddled into a group — no longer marching single file — the men advanced down the passageway. One man thought he saw a light ahead. Or was it an apparition playing in all of their minds?

From out of nowhere a rumble filled the passage. The noise rose as the group sensed some great object gaining speed as it came tumbling down the passageway. The sound thundered toward them. At the last moment—before the great object reached them—Kaikano. Kapu. Malbec. Mack. And four soldiers squeezed into a side alcove. But the other dawdling mercenaries hesitated—then turned and ran back down the passage. Their jostling lanterns illuminated the scene with crazy gyrations of light as they ran. One of the soldiers fell. Two tripped over him. While the fourth stumbled on.

In that moment the deafening noise reached the alcove where Malbec and the others were huddled. They watched in horror as three huge boulders—frozen balls of lava-stone—careened down the tube. The heavy boulders bounced off the walls. Shattered stalagmites and stalactites in their path. Ricocheted down the passage. The four men were nothing more than human pins: The boulders crushed the four figures like so many ripe berries. Then thundered onward. In another moment the giant boulders dropped into the plunge where the two soldiers had earlier fallen to their deaths. Leaving bloody death in their path.

Billy Mack squatted against the cave wall. Malbec pointed his lantern down into his face. The Irish spy's face was ashen. Shaken. He begged that the group return to Olowalu before they all were killed.

Malbec snarled. He grabbed Mack by his shoulders. "Go! Go on now!" He pushed Mack up the passageway. "Shine your light ahead. Malbec will never surrender. Never admit defeat!"

The smaller group moved forward. Kapu led the way. Then Mack. Followed by Malbec. And the remaining four ex-legionnaires. Kaikano followed last. Around the next curve the glow of a light opened ahead of them. Malbec's troop jogged forward. Moments later Kapu led them out onto a dark apron of rock.

Before them spread the mist-soddened green of an upland valley. Steep rocky cliffs dropped from all sides. Below them what Kapu guessed to be the Olowalu Stream's white headwaters cascaded past over jagged black boulders. The small troop advanced along a narrow trail into the lush vegetation. Kapu turned for directions from the bird-catcher. But Kaikano was nowhere in sight.

The bird-catcher had disappeared. As silent as a bird in flight.

CHAPTER 93

SWIFT AND DANCER...Akamu and Kikilani...stepped into the brilliant light. Kikilani stumbled as though she was suddenly tired. Swift shaded her eyes. The others squinted as their gazes adjusted to the lush upland paradise before them. Sunlight. Wind. Birds. A riot of plants presented the foursome with a dreamland. A lost world. Dancer guessed no Europeans had ever ventured here. And that few Pi'ilani probably had passed this way within living memory. Reaching the valley felt like a supreme triumph. Who could have guessed the paradise would prelude disaster?

Akamu and Kikilani moved on to another overlook. Dancer and Swift found themselves gratefully sucking lungfuls of sweet air as their gaze spread over the sheer valley. Below raced the headwaters of the Kaua'ula Stream. Fed by a stunning waterfall directly across the valley. Some distance away an equally powerful waterfall created the raging Olowalu Stream. Between the torrents a spur range opposite the waterfalls separated the two streams — splitting the life-giving waters that ran to the shoreline at Lahaina and Olowalu. It was at the foot of the spur range that they had just emerged from the Kaua'ula Stream lava tube. The waterfalls surged from what appeared to be a curved crater that formed the opposite wall of the verdant valley. Steep and unclimbable mountainsides rose thousands of feet above both streams. These precipices shaped a green bowl so steep even mountain goats with wings would have feared to scale them.

Swift admired the view for several long moments while Dancer joined Kikilani and Akamu. The air Swift breathed was warm… somehow its heady ozone seemed more exhilarating than the cave air she had long been breathing. As she stood looking over the valley Swift thought she saw movement on the path ahead. There — looking back at her — stood a small person. No taller than a shrub. The humanlike creature seemed to wear a mantle of scaled plate armor made from leaves. When Swift pointed toward the apparition the nimble phantom ran ahead and ducked around a bend in the trail. Swift touched her forehead. What was that? She muttered to herself: "Maybe Kikilani isn't the only one affected by that lava tube…."

Swift moved to join the group that stood at an overlook. Their gaze followed the Kauaʻula waterfall up the green slope where it burst from a plateau. Dancer calculated the cataract's freefall dropped perhaps forty feet from brink to pool. The slopes of the great surrounding massif were moistened with mists. Random streams spewed from the preternatural green. High over this extinct crater hung a dense cloud cover. In the far distance behind it another eastern range rose even higher.

"Puʻukukui." Akamu pointed toward the high peak beyond the crater sides. "That is the highest point in West Maui. Almost six thousand feet. Only the great Haleakulā to the east of the central valley is higher." He screwed up his eyes as if he tried to make out a deeper meaning. "Puʻukukui is one of the wettest places on earth — so the storytellers say. Since our origins the rain has carved steep valleys from these peaks and sharp ridges. That water feeds the pure streams that flow to the sea and shape the fourteen *moku* districts of Maui."

Swift followed Akamu's gaze and a thought formed into words. "Is it possible the treasures we've been gathering from the Kauaʻula Stream washed down from these mountains?" She then shifted her attention and pointed to the moisture over the plateau. "Are those clouds?" The moisture looked like rising columns of smoke.

Dancer squinted. "Hard for me to tell. Seems to be mixed with white plumes...almost like geysers."

"Or steam." Swift paused. "Like the forge-fired chimneys of New York's riverfront."

The next moment Kikilani held up her hand. "Listen." Her voice hushed. "Hear that?... Someone is coming."

From the far side of the spur range near the Olowalu Stream came the sound of voices. Did the voices move directly toward them from the valley? Or did they echo off the promontory between the streams?

Kikilani looked confused and dropped her voice into a low whisper. "Which way should we go?"

Akamu pointed straight ahead. There a plunge pool formed below the great waterfall made by the Kaua'ula Stream. Quickly the foursome sprinted along a game trail. Raced around the pool. And ducked into a shallow space carved behind the waterfall. Instantly the roar of the falls enveloped them — but the cavern behind the falls was surprisingly dry.

"Everybody...quiet as a wet mouse!" Dancer said in a hush.

Dancer pressed his back into a crevice. Then pulled Swift's back against his chest. His arms encircled her body. Her hands rested lightly on his bare forearms. Beside them Kikilani tripped slightly on a wet stone. A worried look came over her face: This was the second time she had stumbled since emerging into the lush uplands. Earlier she had been willing to lead the group through the lava tube — but now she felt a sudden exhaustion. *Where are we?* She wondered. *It's not too late to turn back.* Akamu wrapped Kikilani inside his unbuttoned shirt for warmth. And she pressed her shoulders into Akamu's body as they stood in the next gap in the rock cliff. Kikilani's eyes fluttered slightly. A warmth rose in her cheeks despite the chilled air. *I must try.*

From their hiding place in the darkness Dancer caught a glimpse through the veil of the falls: A troop of tall men was marching by. He saw several were armed with short-barreled skirmish rifles and field canteens. In a moment his limited view was lost. Had the troop passed along the trail that followed the stream?

Several minutes passed. Dancer whispered: "Let's get out of here while the getting is good. I think I saw a way."

Dancer led the party to the side of a cliff a short way from the falls. Running up the cliff — somewhat hidden by the foliage of the waterfall mist — was a crude ladder: Someone had placed wooden pegs for hand grips next to toe holes cut into the lava rock. A coil of rope was partially secreted under a bush near the base.

Dancer gestured toward the cliff face above them. "A removable ladder." He picked up the rope and turned to Akamu. "You're the strongest…you go first. Take the rigging rope. Show Kikilani how it's done as you climb. Then lower the rope for her."

Kikilani eyed the steep cliff. Looked at the ladder. Then laughed out loud. "You want me to climb *that*?" She shook her head. Dropped her pack. Then plopped down on a grass mound and wrapped her arms around her knees. "It's pointless." She threw a vague gesture at the surrounding slopes. "This whole thing is a wild-goose chase." She snatched their last water canteen from Akamu and drank it dry. Then flipped it with a haughty gesture onto the ground.

Swift frowned. Then sat next to her. "What's going on? You were so confident earlier?"

Kikilani squeezed her knees in a defiant pout. "Who cares?"

"*We* care. We can only do this together."

Again Kikilani shook her head. "This is your treasure hunt. Not mine. I don't care."

Nevertheless Kikilani reluctantly stood up. Swift took her by the shoulders. "Akamu will have you from the top with the rope. Can you make it?"

Kikilani craned her head back. Swallowed. "We'll find out." *You may be sorry.*

"You can do it. I know you can. I'll be right behind you all the way."

Dancer took Swift aside. "When you climb the ladder…remove all the hand pegs as you go. Leave two for me. I'll go last and bring the two pegs with me. That way no one can follow."

Swift frowned. "How'd you know that?"

"Read about it once in the penny dreadfuls we sold in Charleston. Story about Kit Carson — he came across some cliff dwellers who used ladders like this to give their enemies the slip." Dancer raised his shoulders matter-of-factly.

"Glad you believe everything you read." A half smile accompanied Swift's retort.

Akamu dropped the coiled rope over his shoulders. Stepped to the cliff. Grabbed one peg. Then another. Using these two pegs set slightly wider than his shoulders he inserted a foot into the first toe hold in the center. Using pegs and toe holds he pulled himself up. Then grabbed the next peg with a free hand an arm's length higher. Hand over hand. Toe after toe. Akamu moved up the well-worn ladder. Near the top the sun and strain made his hands sweat. Carefully Akamu wiped his palms against his twill trousers. Flexed his grip. Then moved up the cliff side. Like a born cliff climber Akamu reached the top and rolled onto the grass panting hard. After several breaths he looped the long rope around a *koa* trunk several steps back from the cliff edge. Tied off the loop. Cinched the triple knot tight against the tree. Tested the knot with his weight and dropped the line over the edge.

Meanwhile Dancer retrieved a loose rope skein from his pack. Measured a length twice Kikilani's wingspan. Tied the ends together with two interlocking overhand knots. Leaving a hand span extra on each tail. Dancer put the circle rope around Kikilani's body. Made a twist for her left hand. Then another twist for her right. Next Dancer opened these twists wider: pulled one over Kikilani's far shoulder; then the second over Kikilani's other shoulder. The rope formed an X across Kikilani's torso in front and back. Dancer lifted the front loop hanging near Kikilani's waist and brought it up to the X across her chest. With the end of Akamu's rope he tied the front loop to the X. Then signaled Akamu to take up the slack. In a moment Kikilani was almost lifted off her feet in the chest harness.

Dancer curled his hand around the safety rope. "The harness rope will keep you safe." She gave him a doubtful look. "You'll be okay. Use the hand pegs and the toe holds to walk up the cliff. Just like Akamu. The rope will make it easier." Kikilani took a deep breath as Dancer dropped to one knee. She put one foot on his thigh as Swift pushed Kikilani up from behind. Kikilani reached the lowest hand pegs and then placed one foot—and the other—into the first toe holes. Swift supported Kikilani from below and whispered into her ear. "You can't fall." Dancer gave Akamu a hand signal to pull gently. Peg by peg Kikilani climbed the primitive ladder beside the waterfall as Akamu kept the safety line taut.

After Kikilani was safely at the top Akamu lowered the rope and harness. Dancer untied the long rope. Helped Swift with the contraption. And retied the long rope at the X. An amused smile crossed Dancer's face. Swift shot him a look. "Keep your mind on your work…Dancer." Within moments Swift moved up the cliff ladder. Hand over hand. As she moved she levered the wooden peg near her hip loose. Slipped the carved handhold into her sling bag. Soon she found a good rhythm. Worked hand over hand as the safety harness squeezed her breath. Methodically she climbed the ladder one peg at a time and removed the pegs as she went. Near the top her arms trembled as she lost strength. She took a deep breath. *Kikilani made it. So can you.* When she reached for the last peg Akamu reached down and grabbed her wrist. With a groan he lifted Swift over the precipice. In her sling bag Swift brought all the hand pegs with her. Except for the pair in the first set of holes so Dancer could use them as the last man.

Akamu again dropped the rope and harness. Dancer tried to wiggle into the harness. The loops were too small. He quickly untied the circle rope. Retied the overhand knots but left almost no tails so the harness was larger. Dancer slipped the wrist twists over his head. Knotted the safety rope around the X at his chest. Signaled Akamu with two gentle tugs. Then started up the cliff. As he climbed he used the last two handhold pegs — inserting one peg into the hole above him then leveraging his hold on that peg to remove the other peg and set it into the next hole. Soon he had made it halfway up the cliff. Then while reaching for the next peg hole he made the cardinal mistake bemoaned by novice rock climbers and greenhand sailors. He looked down. And missed the hole. The whittled wood bounced from his grasp. He snatched for it as it twisted in the air. The safety rope stretched taut. The peg landed noiselessly on a moss-covered ledge below him — too far to retrieve. He stared at it while supporting himself by one hand peg and two toeholds on the cliff. His other hand on the safety rope.

At that moment on the trail beside the waterfall pool far below the voices returned. The troop had doubled back. But facing the cliff Dancer still could not see who — or what — was looking for them.

Dancer froze. His hand quivered on the peg grip. In desperation he jammed the fingers of his free hand into the next highest peg hole. Pain shot up his arm. He clenched his jaw. Pressed his forehead against the rock to forestall crying out. After what seemed like an eternity the last figure passed along the trail below.

Dancer breathed deeply. "Only one way to go." Dancer set his foot holds. Pulled the peg. Stabbed for the next opening. Missed. Pain shot through his other arm like a lightning bolt. He almost slipped. Stabbed again. This time the peg slid cleanly into the hole. He pulled himself up. Reflexively he reached with his injured hand for the safety line. To his horror the line flapped in his hand. The short tails of his overhand knots had slipped through the knots themselves. The chest harness loosened. Then slipped away. The length of harness rope fell like a dead snake to the ground below. He tightened his grip on the remaining hand peg. The agony in his other hand lessened. He gathered himself momentarily. Shook out his joints. Then jammed the fingers of his free hand into the next open hole. The pain almost made him faint. But the move worked. With extraordinary will he pushed himself up with his legs and pulled with the hand on the peg. Grasping the peg he jammed the fingers of his other hand into the next hole. As the pain pounded his brain like a steam hammer Dancer pulled himself upward. Painful step by painful step.

Soon Dancer reached the top. Barely. Hands grabbed him under the armpits. Dragged him from the brink. He rolled onto the mossy surface of the cliff's summit. "Whose idea was that anyway?" The American scout breathed heavily even as he mocked himself. "Maybe next time I'll bring a real ladder." He flexed his right hand. Slowly. Blood trickled down from his lacerated knuckles. Swift brought out the gauze-wrapped onyx from her kit. Handed it to Kikilani—who gently raised Dancer's wrist with one hand. Her face brightened as she held the gem in her hand and dabbed Dancer's knuckles with the gauze. Within moments the blood dried…almost as if something had pulled the heat out of the wounds.

"Extraordinary." Swift watched as Dancer's knuckles continued to clear. Then she placed the wrapped stone back into her kit. Again a faraway look came into Kikilani's eyes.

After a moment Swift asked the obvious. "Where are we?"

"Not sure." Dancer surveyed the valley below. "Either we reached a sacred place…or we're lost." Just then a breath of mist rose from the waterfall's brink just beyond the grassy summit and cooled their faces. "Did you see anything?"

They all shook their heads while exchanging glances.

"Maybe we're just on edge." Swift paused. "Chasing a treasure can do that."

After a short rest Akamu led Kikilani on. Swift hung back and whispered to Dancer: "Where is that troop now?"

"From the cliff I saw them come back along the trail. Then they slipped into the vegetation around the promontory."

"Did they see us?"

"I don't think so. Definitely not just a bird-catching party. If they don't know a way up the promontory they'll stay down in the valley. Nowhere to go but back to the sea."

From far within the mountain came a deep rumbling. The ground under them shook.

Swift gave an anxious look. "Did you feel that? Could that be the foreshock of an earthquake still to come?"

Dancer tilted his head in speculation. "Maybe that party on the trail will think so...and run back down the mountain."

"We couldn't be so lucky. Could we?" Swift muttered.

She and Dancer turned to follow Akamu and Kikilani up the steep path.

CHAPTER 94

HIDDEN CRATER
LOST CITY OF THE PI'ILANI
MIDDAY

WITH NO SIGN of the intruders Akamu and Kikilani soon came upon a narrow stone stairway that climbed toward the crater's crest. They were followed by Swift and Dancer. Single file the group passed terraced fields bordered by fitted stone. Yet no sign of human habitation. Or the troop seen in the valley.

"These walls were not built for military purposes." Dancer ran his fingers along the finely hewn stone. "Although it's a highly defensible location."

"Maybe a religious sanctuary?" Swift suggested as the late morning sun made her sweat.

Well before the small group reached the summit the steps ended. Before them the worn path led toward an opening in thickly grown vegetation. Akamu pushed vines aside and moved through the canopy. The others followed him into a dark passage carved into the mountain. Within a few steps the passage opened onto a landing. In crouched positions they advanced to the edge. The view they beheld stunned them.

Before their eyes lay a great chamber. As large as the curved crater seen from outside. In an instant they realized they were—in fact— inside a caldera: Its sides formed an ancient volcanic cone. High overhead from the crater's roof dangled tap roots. Vines. And stalactites. The solid roof appeared to be thickly interwoven as a result of the continuous growth promoted by the wet hothouse air. They looked again and saw the domed ceiling had been ingeniously constructed. Flying buttresses rose from the sides of the crater to support great vaults of vegetation that formed the roof. Arches that seemed alive with roots and vines rose from the crater's floor to abut the roof. Matted vegetation covered large portions of the roof like frescoes. The roots. Vines. And vegetation interconnected to create a wondrous architectural hybrid: a cross between a basilica and a hanging garden. Everywhere dangling roots dripped—creating a sensation almost like rain. Water released by the vegetation collected at the edges of the roof and cascaded down the volcanic walls. Stone spouts extending down from the dome directed threads of water to pools below. One falls dropped a hundred feet from the ceiling.

Akamu pointed toward shafts of light that illumined swaths of the scene below. Smaller sunrays fell on specific stones. Fountains. And terraces like spotlights. Rising in counterpoint were columns of steam that erupted from several places. The white columns rose up to meet the cooler vegetation of the dome—where their droplets collected like clouds before exiting through small openings in the ceiling. Swift whispered: "Steam chimneys...That must be what caused the strange clouds I saw from the valley outside."

The foursome breathed in the humid atmosphere. Warm. Verdant. As rich as a botanical garden conservatory.

From their elevated landing their gaze took in the contours of a large city spread out before them. The ancient city—whoever had built it—was roughly circular in shape. A multitiered system of waterways channeled the constant seepage and rainfall: Terraces. Channels. Ditches. Canals. Aqueducts. Control points. All channeled excess water into cascades. Waterfalls. Master storm drains. Drain water landed in basins. Always getting larger and wider as the waters descended. Until the final voluminous spill water dropped smoothly into a tranquil central basin. Here great gates separated the basin from the city's other structures.

Lost City of the Piʻilani

The central portion of the city was built on multiple levels. Along narrow passageways neighborhoods of small row houses stood in a line. All manner of vegetation grew on their sod roofs. Every surface—pitched or flat—created a space for gardens. Diminutive dwellings were set along twisting paths and stairs. Other apartments were tucked into the arches of the interconnected system of aqueducts and viaducts. Several houses clung dangerously close to steaming volcanic vents. Others precariously butted against channeled waterways racing past in torrents. The undersized neighborhoods were tied together by a labyrinth of stairways. Courtyards. And walls. The system of aqueducts. Retaining walls. Terraces. Channels. Stairways. Fountains. And pools left the hidden city perfectly dry.

Swift smiled. The impression was of a grand estate whimsically organized—and serendipitously planned. A vast garden city built inside a waterworks. The design was masterful and somehow high-spirited if not downright playful.

Akamu pointed out two rivers that coursed through the crater and hugged either side of the city like the wings of a wasp. One immediately below them. One on the far side. "My guess is the near stream is the Kauaʻula Stream. The far river is the Olowalu Stream. This must be their headwaters."

At a glance they saw that a narrow two-arched stone bridge stretched over a calm lake and then over the Olowalu Stream. It came to an end at a stone pier. Then a second and longer span of the bridge gracefully extended over the reservoir basin. Dancer saw that larger structures were placed haphazardly around this basin. Storerooms. Food depositories. A guardhouse. And even what looked like a jail. The walls of the buildings appeared to be slightly sloped: the bases were wider than the upper portions. The stonework seemed to be fitted by a dry-stone technique. No mortar. All carved from readily available lava-stone.

Dancer looked more closely. Most of the stone blocks were relatively small. Intricately fitted. The colors ran from black. To chocolate. To red. To sulfur yellow. Some stones sparkled with what seemed to be quartz nuggets.

"There's nobody here." Dancer had only now realized the city appeared empty. Abandoned. "Where are the people who built this?

What happened to the people that lived here?"

Swift shook her head. "Maybe they evacuated ages ago....Some calamity like Atlantis—or Memphis in Egypt."

"Or Mesa Verde." Dancer rubbed his right hand. It had suddenly started aching again.

Swift again swept her gaze over the lost city. She realized the city was odd in another way. All of the steps were short. The doors low. Passageways narrow. Even sitting benches were diminutive.

It dawned on each member of the foursome at the same time: The city was built by—and for—little people.

"Menehune?" Akamu offered.

"Why didn't I think of that?" Kikilani replied absently. "Yes. The Menehune. Of course..."

Dancer scoffed. "If they exist."

Swift gave a puzzled look. "But how could they build this city? It seems ancient; the Menehune could not have known the wheel when they built it."

"The Aztecs did not know the wheel either..." Akamu responded.

With little interest in her voice Kikilani added: "Some legends say the Menehune used long lines. In the style of brigades." She pressed her eyes closed tight—fighting an unseen inner battle. "They moved vast amounts of stone hand to hand."

The group continued studying the city before them. They soon spotted several grander buildings arrayed around a great plaza. The plaza contained a *heiau* platform as a place of worship.

Dancer gestured toward the larger buildings. "They look more official...Perhaps council chambers?" One large stone building especially stood out: Monumental parallel columns defined its entrance. Strangely—behind the columns—the space looked more like a three-sided walled scallop shell than a building. For it had no roof. Nor a rear wall. Instead a column of steam surged dramatically like a giant locomotive at the far end. The steam glowed an ominous red—as if it billowed from the bowels of Hades. The building seemed to Dancer to be an open-air temple—or a tribunal. His eye followed the side walls of the structure until they stopped: rising high over an aisle that ran along the back and dropped off into a red caldron of lava. The bottomless pit smoldered.

Steamed. And glowed with the bubbling fire of Pele.

◎   ◎   ◎

Unknown to the foursome another party also stood looking out over the lost city. Malbec and his troop had followed the Olowalu Stream after emerging from the darkness of the lava tube. Under Kapu's guidance they had ascended a narrow trail through the green valley. Passed waterfalls. Through thick foliage. Around steep cliffs. And finally through a dark passage that led them to the city. Now Malbec stood on an opposite landing watching the foursome — who had just recently arrived. He noted every step. Tracked their movements through the lost city. His gaze had the frozen concentration of a predator.

◎   ◎   ◎

The presence of the foreigners defiled the sacred sanctuary. Both the small foursome and the party that had brought soldiers. Somehow they all had avoided the lava tube traps. The worms. The snakes. The ancient and thin-crusted lava lakes. The thunderous boulders. Seeing this the Menehune were agitated and angry: The creators of the lost city had been hiding themselves — quietly watching the foreign intruders for several minutes. But they were content to bide their time...to play hide-and-seek. For now they were willing to give the false appearance that they had left the city abandoned.

Until the moment to strike presented itself.

CHAPTER 95

PELE'S CAULDRON OF SACRIFICE
TRIBUNAL/LOST CITY OF THE PI'ILANI
A FEW MINUTES LATER

AFTER THE TRIALS in the lava cave the discovery of an abandoned city made the group almost giddy with relief. Along a path that led from the overlook a trio trotted down winding switchbacks toward the crater floor. Listlessly Kikilani came along behind. Swift eyed her carefully even as she breathed deeply in the dense humid air. A lingering damp earthy smell filled her nose. Soon the foursome wandered over a delicate arched bridge. At its middle Akamu smiled and spread both arms over the stone railing to acknowledge the raging torrent. "The Kaua'ula headwaters." A fine mist cooled their flushed skin. Several crude reed boats were tied to stone pylons along the riverfront. Farther up the bank stood clusters of quirky houses. Narrow alleys ran between the small dwellings. Swift stopped at one of these sandy runs. Cocked her ears. "Hear that?" Dancer shook his head. "There is no birdsong... or buzzing insects." The only sound they heard was a soft moan — the mournful murmur of rushing water. With a counterpoint of waterfalls splashing into pools. And the incessant bass of rain-scented streams dashing down stone spillways.

Soon the group rounded a low tongue of lava — its black surface pocked by earth-filled depressions of green plantings: the rocky flow projected into what seemed to be a broad plaza. On the plaza's cinder surface they stepped easily over a network of stone-lined gutters. Before them stood the curious roofless building that seemed like a theater or tribunal. The small band stepped over a runoff flume. And moved toward the columned entrance of the building. Dancer noticed a small thatched lean-to stood to one side. Scattered about were an upset coconut shell — rice had spilled from the overturned container — and a squashed banana. Dancer looked again at the lean-to. Was it a sentry post? If so: The guard was very short. Dancer looked again at the scattered food. Had the lookout been surprised by an unseen enemy?

The group passed through the undersized doorway between the columns of the tribunal building and entered the roofless semicircular chamber beyond the entryway. Before them terraced rows spread out in a wide fan. The fan grew wider — and the rows grew longer — as they ascended. Three ramp-like aisles cut through the risers. One ran through the center. The other two ran up along either end of the terraces. The foursome took a step forward and were immediately hit by a blast of humid air. Swift almost gagged at the smell: overcooked hard-boiled eggs. Kikilani continued on. She crossed the half-moon space that fanned out before the first of the terraced rows. Tired. Out of breath. And hardly caring. She sat on a stone slab. The length of a child's body. The stifling arena gave off the feeling of a venue where solemn rituals were performed. The pitched terraces faced a raised altar at the bottom of the semicircular area.

Swift touched her friend's shoulder. "You look more tired than I've ever seen you."

Kikilani abruptly pushed Swift's hand aside. "You always think you're the boss. Well…I'm tired of it. And tired of you treating me like an orphan."

Swift held her stance. "You're not thinking straight."

Kikilani shrugged. "I give up."

"Give up?" Swift stared at Kikilani. "After we've come this far?"

"We followed your trail of jewels — and look where it got us." She turned away. Closed her eyes. And thought of nothing but sleep.

Akamu came over and tried to tend to Kikilani. Meanwhile Dancer strode up the center aisle that ran through the terraced rows. The closer he drew to the topmost terrace the more the heat increased. When he in fact reached the uppermost terrace—which was no wider than a spear length—he set his arm before his face to ward off the tremendous heat rising from below. Beyond the terrace the stone floor ended abruptly: a terrifying precipice dropped into a fiery cauldron of bottomless lava.

Breathing shallowly in the stifling steamed heat Dancer retreated down several rows. Sat on one of the risers of the middle terraces. He tried to make sense of the space. His gaze fell on Akamu attending Kikilani. As he watched Akamu's attention was drawn to something curious in an alcove off the altar space. Akamu briefly left Kikilani and Swift to examine what he saw. When he returned he carried an ornately painted bottle gourd he had retrieved from the alcove. Not unlike the gourd in the King's mausoleum.

Akamu indicated the alcove to Kikilani. "There must be a half dozen similar vessels in there."

With some effort Kikilani withdrew a *kapa* cloth from her pack and spread it on the altar. Akamu removed the leafy cover from the gourd. Tipped the contents of the vessel onto the cloth. Out spilled handfuls of gold and silver coins. And jewels. Yet when he looked inside the vessel he saw that three-quarters of the container was packed with straw. The value of the treasure was certainly impressive—yet the amount was mystifying. Swift wrinkled her brow. *Why would the bottom be falsely padded?* The vessel at most held less than a fraction of a chest from Napoleon's treasure.

Swift fingered a few of the coins. "This is not treasure beyond imagination...."

Just as the trio was examining the contents of the gourd they heard a loud commotion behind them. Without warning Malbec. Billy Mack. Kapu the Ugly. And the troopers stepped through the entrance door of the tribunal building and marched into the chamber. Three of Malbec's mercenaries drew their swords. Ready to strike. A fourth pushed a bushy-eyebrowed hostage against the wall of the first terrace: The short captive was bound and had a gag stretched tightly across his mouth.

He seemed hobbled. Trapped between the altar and the stepped seats of the terraces. Akamu. Swift. And Kikilani froze.

Dancer had spied Malbec's men from his spot on the center terrace. Then he glimpsed the bound hostage. He blinked. Was that one of the Menehune?

Dancer bolted. The sound of his boots as he leaped up several rows of the terraces drew attention away from the others. A trooper with a broken nose tracked Dancer in his rifle sight.

Malbec snapped to the mercenary: "You've got powder for only one shot...Make it count."

As the marksman squeezed the trigger a deafening explosion rose from behind the top terrace: A plume of lava spurted high in the air before molten splatter fell on the back levels. As loud in the confined space as a bomb blast. The booming report bounced off the walls behind the soldier. He flinched. His point-blank shot missed.

At the topmost terrace Dancer skidded to a stop before the precipice. Looked down between his boot toes. *Crap.* The heat from the fathomless cauldron of lava hit him in the face like a blast furnace. He dropped to all fours. Just below his face—under the lip of the terrace—ran a stone spillway trough. The current seemed to flow toward the plaza side wall. Blebs of lava from the eruption had fallen all about him. Dancer lifted his hands off the terrace. Rocked back on the balls of his feet. Tried to avoid the hot mounds. Then watched as one lava bleb that fell near him seemed to stretch out. Elongate into the shape of a short sword. A blade formed. Then a hilt. Dancer reached out tentatively—lest the sword's handle be too hot to touch—and picked up the sword. *What the hell?* The small sword was like a toy miniature. Dancer grasped the tiny grip. Winced as the grip jammed his fingers— raw from climbing the peg ladder—against the cross guard.

Watching from below Malbec drew his saber. Sprinted up one of the side aisles through the terraces. Blocked Dancer's path. Malbec looked at Dancer and blinked. "You've come a long way... for a Marist priest."

Dancer returned a mocking smile. "Farther than you know... Malbec."

Anger spread across Malbec's face. Then he charged and slashed at Dancer's throat as though to decapitate him. Dancer ducked. Malbec swung the saber in a backhanded arc. His blade collided with Dancer's short sword. Sparks flew off the two blades.

Malbec held the height advantage. Dancer tested his reach. Feigned an attack. Then lunged suddenly to learn how Malbec would react.

Dancer moved left. Right. Waited for his enemy to make a false step.

Malbec knew he had the advantage. He grinned sadistically. *Out-muscle. Out-smart. Out-last...All are in my favor!* He lunged powerfully. Sliced the air with an overhead thrust of his sword. Then again with a backstroke. The short sword flew from Dancer's weakened hand. It rattled against a stone step behind him as Malbec closed in.

Dancer rolled away from his combatant. Regained the small sword. Tripped Malbec's heel with the cross guard.

Malbec kicked Dancer's arm away. Dancer rose to his feet. Rounded on Malbec. Malbec thrust. Dancer parried. Malbec extended the longer saber before him — used its length to his advantage: Dancer was forced to step back closer to the cauldron's edge. Dancer felt the heat on his back. Malbec drew a second knife — a short sticking knife — from his belt. Dancer wrapped both his hands over his small sword's hilt. Then desperately raised the blade and lunged with a furious downstroke. Malbec crossed his two blades to parry the attack. Then shoved the two crossed blades with all his strength against Dancer. Dancer stumbled back. His rear boot reached the brink of the terrace: Only the toe of his boot found purchase above the fiery cauldron. Dancer dropped to all fours. In the next instant Malbec threw a roundhouse kick. Slammed his instep into the American agent's temple. He crumpled. With a final push Malbec rolled the body over the edge. Dancer disappeared into the abyss.

Malbec stood gloating malevolently over the cauldron. Seeing Dancer's executioner was distracted Akamu raced up the center ramp. Rushed Malbec. From the arena below Billy Mack screamed: "Malbec...look out!" Akamu shoved Malbec to the edge of the precipice before the French commandant recovered. He turned and thrust a vicious knee to Akamu's groin. Akamu collapsed to the ground. Malbec kicked him in the ribs. Akamu's body tumbled down the aisle. Malbec followed. When Akamu finally came to a rest Malbec kicked him in the throat. The young warrior's body crumpled against the stone altar. Then lost consciousness.

Kikilani had watched the fight from below. Her strange exhaustion had made her too weak to move. Now she knelt beside Akamu and drew his body from Malbec.

Sensing a pause in the fighting Swift dashed up the center aisle. Then raced to the cauldron precipice. Screened her face from the heat blast. "Dancer!...Dancer!" Her voice choked in the sulfurous smoke. Enraged. And helpless.

Malbec shot the threesome a sneer of triumph. "No one defeats Malbec! Not Maunakili! Not you!"

The mercenary with the broken nose ran up the terraces. Quickly subdued Swift as she stood crying at the precipice. Then brought her down to the altar. As Akamu slowly regained consciousness Kikilani drew him closer. Soon they stood with Swift beside the altar. Malbec ordered Kapu the Ugly to bring the Menehune hostage: the little man's large eyes bulged beneath overgrown eyebrows. Malbec's men then grabbed the half-dozen treasure vessels. "Take him from the tribunal!" Malbec and Billy Mack held the three remaining captives at bay with sabers before following Malbec and his troop from the chamber.

As Malbec passed through the entrance he reached out to release a brake connected by thick braided ropes to two large counterweights on either side of the narrow doorway. As the weights rose the heavy stone door of the tribunal descended in weightless balance. Steadily with a grinding rasp the tall stone began to slide down along finely cut grooves. The ornate slab lumbered lower until it settled into its fitted bottom track and sealed the threshold tight. With both hands Malbec then lifted a rounded timber leaning against the wall: He thrust the horizontal locking pin into place through the stone jamb.

Immediately beyond the entrance door two of Malbec's soldiers walked over to a short stone lever that operated a sluice gate across a run of steaming water. Columns of steam rose from the spillway as it ran several hundred yards parallel to the lava cauldron at the back of the lost city. Then turned sharply into the plaza area. There the deep spillway split into several branches. Each branch connected to stone aqueducts that crisscrossed the city. Malbec paused. "Lava vents." He admired the design malevolently. "That Menehune sentry we captured told us all we needed to know." He explained the clever design to Billy Mack. "The vents heat the water. By the time the water reaches the aqueducts it's still scalding."

Billy Mack smiled. "All we have to do is redirect the water into the tribunal...."

Malbec's men pushed on the stone sluice-gate lever. Even though the lever was short they needed all their strength to move it. Moments later the searing waters were redirected into the tribunal.

Trapped inside the locked tribunal Swift. Kikilani. And Akamu watched as the stone altar slowly descended into the floor. Stone ground against stone as a hole opened up where the altar had been. In its place rose a trickle of scalding water. This puddle gradually grew until the opening became a bubbler of boiling water and steam. As the water flowed toward the trapped trio they felt the heat on their legs and faces. Quickly the water grew into a raging font as the three tried to back away. The roiling torrent inexorably pushed up into the tribunal amphitheater. As hot as cooking oil.

Swift dragged an exhausted Kikilani and then Akamu's woozy form from the boiling fountain. She pulled them up the terraces. Up the inclined pitch. Row by row they feverously retreated. As the scalding water advanced. Just as Malbec intended. The rising tide pushed them closer and closer to the lip of the cauldron. Swift took only short breaths through clenched teeth in the suffocating steam heat. No escape was possible over the chamber's smooth stone walls. Swift realized their three short lives soon would be anonymous offerings for Pele's cauldron. Certain death was just a matter of time.

CHAPTER 96

MAIN VIADUCT
TRIBUNAL PLAZA/LOST CITY OF THE PIʻILANI
WITHIN MINUTES

MALBEC STROKED one of his half-dozen vessels of coins and jewels.
Triumphant. The four mercenaries carried the vessels up a stairway to
the main aqueduct near the tribunal plaza. They loaded the treasure
into three egg-shaped reed boats tethered at the aqueduct's edge. Three
men climbed into the first boat and took up the paddles that lay inside.
Kapu and a soldier climbed into the second boat. Malbec held the line
to the third boat — in which Billy Mack controlled the squirming but
bound Menehune hostage.

"Take the aqueduct and drainage channels as far as possible.
Then we'll raft the treasure the rest of the way to Olowalu." Malbec's
voice boomed over the din of two nearby waterfalls.

The bearded mercenary muttered to the pug-faced trooper:
"Beats carrying the loot by foot." The barroom brawler looked at him
with hard eyes and simply grunted.

The three men in the first boat untethered it and pushed off.
Entered the aqueduct stream — which worked like a liquid roadway.
The current took them. Controlling the oval boat proved difficult:
There was no bow or stern. And no keel. Even powerful paddling

gave them little control.

Unexpectedly the aqueduct split into two channels. The boat careened to the left channel. More waterways joined in. Sending the light boat spinning wildly in the eddies. Malbec held his boat onto the bank as he watched his soldiers' stupidity with a smirk. *Imbeciles.* The speed of the water increased. As the three fortune hunters clutched the sides of their tiny craft they rounded a sharp corner. Ahead flowed a cascade that descended steeply over several stone steps. The flimsy boat bounced down the liquid terraces. With every step the bow of the boat crashed angrily against the stone — rattling the mercenaries' teeth.

The torrent spun the frail boat toward a stone abutment. The whiskered mercenary held up his paddle like a jousting pole. Trying to prevent the boat's momentum from smashing him against the stone. The boat spun around wildly: Without warning the third soldier's head smashed into a protruding fountain spout. His body was ejected from the boat. Unbalanced the boat shot uncontrollably into an open junction. Here a waterspout descended from the dome far above: A stupendous volume of water thundered into the channel. Swallowed by the thick mist of the falls the frail boat was instantly lost from Malbec's view. But the two mercenaries remaining in the boat tried to prevent it from being pulled under the falls. Into the hideous foam they went. The boat quickly listed to one side. The broken-nosed mercenary in the bow lunged to grab the treasure vessels before they slipped overboard. The shift of the soldier's weight flipped the boat over. Both men and treasure disappeared. Sucked into the violent drain hole beneath the falls.

Behind the first boat Kapu and the last mercenary paddled madly to avoid the same fate: They had untethered their boat shortly after the first boat left the wharf. Now the boat careened around a curving channel. Faster and faster their unbalanced eggshell was thrust down the waterway. Without warning water flowing through a gap in the stone levee formed a spout. The current forced them through the gap. Wide-eyed they clutched the gunwales of the flimsy boat. Like a giant water chute the torrent pushed them spinning wildly into a large basin. Kapu and the mercenary tried to paddle madly toward safety.

Ahead yet another cataract spilled down a shoot. They paddled harder. Without warning a hidden side current catapulted the boat into the cataract. Down the deluge the reed boat raced. At the bottom Kapu's eyes popped wide. Not a dozen boat lengths before them was a terrifying glow: Another cauldron of Pele. The water swept them on at a faster rate. They redoubled their effort frantically. To no avail. Kapu looked in horror at where the torrent tumbled over the edge: The water was instantly vaporized by the molten lava. A horrendous chimney of steam thundered upward. Seeing the lava ahead of them the terrified mercenary jumped for the rock wall that rose beside the channel. Desperately he tried to claw some advantage. But was swept under.

The current pushed Kapu helplessly toward the brink. At the edge his boat elevated. Hung in the air briefly. The Storyteller rose to his knees. Held his hands wide. He accepted the power of the Ancients. In a blink he was lost in the roar of the steam column — devoured at the intersection of time and eternity.

CHAPTER 97

MAELSTROM
CENTRAL PLAZA/LOST CITY OF THE PI'ILANI
SOME MINUTES LATER

MALBEC HELD BACK. His cunning eyes watched the other boats plunge into the hydraulic tempest. With a fiendish effort Malbec and Billy Mack muscled the third craft toward a side spillway. The swarthy Menehune watchman cowered between the two outlanders. At a junction of the spillway and the Olowalu Stream that flanked the lost city on the far side—Malbec and Billy Mack hung to the stone bank and caught their breath. Before they entered the waterway Malbec looked up. There in the near distance—beyond the Olowalu current and the central basin—across the plaza a figure stood. His hands on a wooden shaft inserted into the heavy sluicegate that directed the Kaua'ula Stream. Holding the lever. Was Dancer.

Before Malbec or Mack reacted Dancer put his shoulder to the stout staff he used as a sluice lever. With his legs under him his entire body pushed with all its strength. Slowly the heavy floodgate lowered into its stone grooves against the Kaua'ula current. Slowly the wooden gate cut down through the stream. Until the heavy flood weir closed shut into its seat at the bottom. In an instant the entire current of the Kaua'ula Stream shifted direction. Shot angrily into the reservoir.

Dancer shielded his face from a gust that rose like a waterspout. He withdrew the lever staff from the gate socket. Then sprinted over the arched bridge by which he had entered the city not long before. In one hand he carried the strong wooden shaft balanced next to his hip. He raced across the plaza to the graceful two-spanned arch over the Olowalu current. Far overhead the dangling vines shook. A shower of droplets spattered the plaza.

As he ran Dancer's eyes flicked ahead at the slender two-arched bridge before him—supported by a center pier above the Olowalu current. Just downstream from the narrow stone bridge the now redirected Kaua'ula current slammed into the Olowalu Stream. With an appalling noise—half thunder...half roar—the two currents combined. Dancer watched the rising waters circle at their vortex like fighting pythons. Steadily the spinning whorl of water accelerated. A monstrous whirlpool opened within the expanding funnel—encircled by the maelstrom's widening rim. The brink of the liquid vortex fell away into a black abyss.

At first Malbec thought he could slide past the bridge pier. Then he saw. His escape down the Olowalu Stream to freedom was closed by the maelstrom. When his boat reached the dividing pillar they beached the boat in the upstream pier eddy. Mack jumped onto the stone platform and tied off the painter line beneath where Dancer was standing. Then dragged their small hostage by his leaf collar onto the stepped stones. Malbec followed.

Malbec looked up at Dancer. "Come for more punishment?" His high-pitched voice rose with excitement.

Dancer shrugged. "All in a day's fun."

The expression on Malbec's face silently inquired how Dancer had survived the tribunal cauldron.

"Nifty little bathtub. Easy to miss below the back terrace. Seems whoever made this city liked their bathwater warm. There's a spillway trough that runs under the back of the tribunal and out the side. Quite a fun ride. That is...until you threw the altar lever to send scalding water onto my friends."

Malbec calculated his options like a cold-blooded Marquis de Sade.

Dancer spoke calmly as he hefted the stout wooden shaft in both hands. "The diverted bubbler gave me the idea to redirect the Kaua'ula

Stream into the central reservoir."

Malbec realized the whirling sides of the murderous funnel were strangely smooth. Horribly black. Like polished marble. Round and round the vortex swept. Deep in its maw the bottom of the maelstrom gulf could only just be heard. A bottomless pit that moaned like demented spirits.

Malbec grabbed the small manlike hostage by his long hair. Pushed Billy Mack forward up the bridge pier steps. Toward Dancer. Dancer thrust the end of the pole into Mack's shoulder. And smashed the other end of the rod across the spy's shin. Then Dancer gave ground. He backed his way quickly up the stairway built into the pier's retaining wall. All the time he kept his gaze trained on Malbec. *Show no fear. Just like Maunakili.* Billy Mack raced up the stairs. Closely followed by Malbec. The hairy hostage held captive by Malbec struggled and ripped off his gag. But was dragged up the steps in Malbec's fist like a bunch of bananas. Floodwater from the whirling vortex quickly inundated the pier behind Malbec.

Billy Mack and Malbec faced Dancer barely two staff lengths away as they squared off on the narrow stone bridge that connected the divider pier to the plaza. Dancer's staff extended beyond the low guardrails on both sides of the narrow width like a balancing pole. Malbec pushed Billy Mack forward while he maintained control of the hostage who gave out a blood-curdling banshee scream. Malbec smashed his fist twice into the little man's face until blood appeared over one hairy eyebrow.

Like a duelist Billy Mack advanced with his saber drawn. He had taken only two steps when his back foot slipped on a loose paver: a booby trap. The narrow bridge all at once shuddered violently. The sharp movement unbalanced Dancer. He retreated along the trembling viaduct. Fitted stones jostled from the low guard walls. Under Billy Mack's boots the flat pavement stones danced. The Menehune sentry gave a satisfied deep grunt. His one large unswollen eye sparkled in pride. The trap had been sprung. Before Billy Mack's front foot a crack opened in the slender bridge. Beneath the Irish spy unseen stones dropped into the maelstrom. Malbec realized Mack was caught. *You must attack...fool.*

The viaduct shuddered again. Without warning the opening

widened. Mack twisted his body as he fell back. Clawed at the stone edge. Then extended his hand toward Malbec. His desperate plea was met by a sneer. A flash of pleasure came into Malbec's eyes. As Billy Mack flailed the words of his own epitaph came from his mouth: "God will save me..." Then the Irishman's fingernails slipped and he yelled: "...It says so in the Scriptures!" His voice trailed away for a moment as he disappeared into the whirling abyss.

Dancer extended his staff toward Malbec over the widening gap.

Malbec laughed. "What do you take me for...a frog to your scorpion? If I take your staff you'll drop me into the whirlpool."

"Suit yourself...Malbec. You can die now...or later. It's the same to me. But spare your hostage."

Malbec clutched the Menehune watchman hard in both hands. Raised the little man to his chest. Backed up. Took a running leap toward Dancer. Landed on the far side of the crack like a long jumper: his legs outstretched in front of his body. But his wet boots hit some of the loose pavers. He extended the hostage in front as if for ballast. With a violent twist the potbellied man wiggled free and landed on the stones. Dancer pulled the small watchman from the gap. Malbec tottered. Dancer again extended his wooden staff. This time — desperate — Malbec grabbed the rod with both hands. Dancer pulled Malbec slowly toward him. For just an instant Dancer's gaze fell upon the turtle-shaped birthmark on Malbec's right forearm.

"Your birthmark..."

"So?" Malbec demanded dismissively. "It means nothing." At that moment the birthmark burned hotly and the strange numbness he had felt once before radiated down his arm. In another moment he could hardly feel his arm at all. Malbec saw Dancer sensed the weakness and attacked.

To Dancer's surprise Malbec tucked the staff under his left armpit. Then pirouetted — driving his back along the shaft. In the same motion with his free hand he tried to sweep his dagger toward Dancer's head. Then leveraged his weight against the staff. Dancer ducked the slow blade as Malbec's shifting weight unbalanced them both. They were thrust toward the brink. Staring into the chasm Dancer released his grip on the pole and grabbed the side wall near his toes. Malbec dropped the pole. Grabbed his dagger hilt with both hands.

Then cracked Dancer's temple with a hammer-like blow of the handle. Dancer sank to his knees. Stunned. The pole tumbled into the chasm.

Just then the bridge shuddered again. Malbec staggered. His foot caught against the low guard wall. Malbec eyed Dancer with a hateful look. *Death before weakness.* Without warning the last keystone of the bridge broke away. A look of astonishment came into Malbec's eyes. The bridge beneath him opened. Malbec tumbled; his dagger flew from his hand. And into the thunderous funnel Malbec fell—like one of the incorrigibles dropping out of the *oubliette* cage at Camp Blood. His terrified scream dropped away. Dancer watched as Malbec disappeared into nothingness. Darkness consumed by darkness.

Dancer quickly righted the terrified Menehune. Then retrieved Malbec's dagger from the stones where it had clattered. And tucked the dagger into his boot sheath. A moment later a massive eruption rose from behind the tribunal building. The sentry and Dancer turned to watch a cloud of steam rise violently behind the structure. Then spread rapidly out over the entire plaza. Overhead buttresses and arches trembled. Vines and large sections of matting fell from the ceiling. One struck the arched bridge they had just abandoned…tumbling the remaining structure into the maelstrom vortex. The violent steam spread a dense cloud that smothered the air. What shafts of light lancing from the skylight dimmed. Sending a hush over the lost city.

Dancer and the little watchman ran out onto the level plaza. Dancer leaped over a gap. Then turned to help the Menehune who—to Dancer's amazement—seemed to soar over the opening in one bound. Before them a roiling gutter of boiling water forced them to move closer to the bank of the Kaua'ula torrent. Beneath Dancer's feet he felt the stones give way: the embankment crumbled. The Menehune grabbed Dancer's sleeve. Pointed another way. Just then the stones behind them dropped into the raging current. They zigzagged around gaps in the remaining viaduct. Then pulled up short before a narrow bridge over a runoff trough. Now steaming with bubbling hot water. The small sentry wiggled his bushy brows. Tilted his large head. And led the way. They tightroped over the last arched section of the bridge. Leaped onto the level plaza. Blebs of hot lava covered the sandy surface. Carelessly Dancer tripped. Fell to his knees. His hands slid over the brink into a scalding rivulet. The watchman skidded to a stop. Helped Dancer stand up. Together they raced toward the deafening sound from the tribunal. Then slowed. Almost to a halt.

The roar of the steam explosion before them could mean only one thing.

Dancer was too late.

CHAPTER 98

SCALDING WATER CONTINUED TO POUR into the tribunal chamber. The rising level pushed Swift and Kikilani closer to the cauldron mouth. Holding his ribs and throat Akamu limped beside them. Now the boiling waters rose more slowly as the wider chamber filled. In vain the desperate trio looked for an exit. They shielded their faces with their elbows from the burning steam. From the far side of the cauldron a sudden geyser of red steam blasted into the air. Swift and Kikilani cupped their hands over their ears: The roar was deafening. Kikilani tripped. Her lower leg slipped over the cauldron's edge. She reached up even as she felt her body falling farther toward the lava. At the last moment she was grabbed by Akamu and Swift.

As they pulled Kikilani from the brink Swift peered into the boiling cauldron of red lava that had almost swallowed her friend. Then looked toward where the altar had been at the rising tide of superheated water. She muttered: "The irony of fate. Live to die."

The searing water continued to rise. The trio pressed up against the side wall between the cauldron lip and the boiling bubbler below. In the corner of her eye Swift saw movement on the wall high above her head.

"What's that?" Her words were lost in the cauldron's roar. She grabbed Akamu's shoulder and pointed emphatically.

Someone had thrown what appeared to be a rope ladder over the high wall. But as Swift watched a muscular young man—no more than three feet tall and sporting rope-like braids coiled atop his head—climbed over the top of the wall then lowered himself by holding tightly to the wrists of a bearded man who had already scaled the wall. After climbing over the bearded man the muscular man lowered himself down to the next rung. But the rung wasn't a rung at all—it was another small strong-armed man. With a gasp Swift realized the ladder wasn't a ladder—it was a string of Menehune! The second strong-armed man was as short as the first—but this Menehune wore a short cape of thick leaves like plate armor.

Already a third Menehune came scrambling down the ladder. This one wore only a loin cloth and had oiled hair that stood up straight as if he had just run against the wind. Then a fourth Menehune crawled down: His powerful wrists and ankles were covered in colorful bangles. And then a fifth with a sinewy body: His movements were quite nimble. Each Menehune scuttled quickly down the ladder then held onto the ankles of the man who had just preceded him. Swift saw each Menehune wore a fishnet cape tied over his shoulder and under an armpit. The sinewy last Menehune planted his feet against the wall—as much for an anchor as to keep the potbellies of all the other Menehune away from the sharp lava-stone.

In this way the curious little men created a living ladder stretching down the wall. But it stopped short of Swift. Kikilani. And Akamu. After a long moment—over the top—came Dancer. He clambered down the squirming ladder. He placed his bare feet gingerly on the muscular shoulders of the strange little warriors—but grumbling protests arose. In a moment Dancer's feet came to the shoulders of the last sinewy Menehune while he hung by one elbow from the Menehune just above. Almost within grasp of Swift. Kikilani. And Akamu. He reached his open hand as far as he could. "Throw me your belt...Akamu!"

Akamu stripped off his belt. Buckled it. Then tossed the leather belt to Dancer. Dancer caught it. Twisted the leather into a figure eight. Stuck his wrist through one loop and grabbed the center crossing.

Holding this extension Dancer strained to reach Swift's outstretched hand. And pulled her up.

"Climb up the nets tied to the Menehune! Put your feet on their shoulders!"

Swift pulled herself up. Placed her feet on the bottommost Menehune's muscled little shoulders. And climbed up the peculiar ladder — to sharp complaints. Over the top and out of harm's way. Then Akamu formed a boost for Kikilani by locking his fingers together and letting Kikilani step into his hands. He grimaced as Kikilani pressed her boot against his fingers and extended her arm to Dancer. Then Akamu finally ascended himself from the swirling steam of the tribunal floor.

Dancer climbed to the top. His height and reach spanned two small men at once. Quickly in reverse order the nimble little people scrambled up their living ladder and dropped back over the wall. Just then the full bubbling tide in the tribunal cascaded over the brink. Collided with the fire of Pele's cauldron. A tremendous force blew from the cauldron. Steam from the thundering geyser filled the dome overhead before venting through the vegetation and mixing with the perpetual 'Īao Valley cloud cover. The entire lost city quaked.

CHAPTER 99

THE MENEHUNE PUSHED Swift. Kikilani. Akamu. And Dancer a short distance across a puddled plaza on the other side of the wall. The steam geyser dissipated behind them. As they marched the Menehune pressed the flat sides of short swords against the intruders' backsides. The insistent warriors herded the intruders into a thick-walled building made of fitted dark red lava-stone with narrow arrow slits for windows. The squat structure faced the ritual *heiau* platform on the plaza. Once they were inside a thick stone door again lowered and closed behind them.

Dancer cast a sidelong glance at the area around them. Four stone walls. Stone flat ceiling. *Here we go again.* He sighed tiredly. *Out of the steam bath and into the oven.*

But something felt different.

The foursome was pushed forward by several Menehune guards. Facing the four captives stood a phalanx of fierce manlike beings.

"Friend or foe?" whispered Swift to Dancer beside her.

Steam seeped through the slits of the deep embrasure bays. Torches in wall crevices and column sconces cast a dancing light through the rectangular greeting hall. Only occasional relief came to the stifling air from a myriad of spillways and fountains. Instinctively the foursome stood together in the center of this confined space. Unsure what to make of the ominous turn of events. Before them the Menehune buzzed. Swayed. Studied the intruders with agitated gazes.

At length a fierce-looking warrior holding a wooden staff stepped forward. This wild chief stood out from the others. Or perhaps his helmet merely added to his short stature. He brandished a shining two-edged sword. One edge a honed razor. The other a jagged necklace of shark's teeth. The chief planted himself on large bare feet before them. Held up a fist to the crowd that had formed a semicircle behind him. The Menehune quieted. Leaned in. Swift noted every detail of the muscular and hairy chief. He wore a palm-leaf helmet. Settled rakishly on his sweeping mane — which fell with authority down a woven pandanus cape that almost reached his large feet. A banana-leaf collar around his neck rested on his potbelly. Bushy eyebrows hung over large eyes and a short nose. The Menehune chief stared at the interlopers sternly. Brandishing his blade he pointed at Akamu and Kikilani.

Akamu stood calmly. His island Adonis figure now dressed simply in a *kapa* cloth wrap. Despite the heat Kikilani rubbed her upper arms to calm the strange coolness that had begun creeping along her skin. Then she held her arms across her chest as if a nervous chill had fully gripped her. The chief approached the pair. In unison they knelt on one knee before him. Their heads bowed momentarily. Dancer and Swift saw they knelt respectfully: They were now at the same eye-level as the three-foot-tall chief.

The chief closed the short distance between them. First placed one hand on Akamu's shoulder. Then leaned forward. He and Akamu touched noses on one side. Breathed out and inhaled at the same time. The two then exchanged *ha* breath. Akamu spoke the honorific greeting of his native islanders. "*Alo'ha.*"

"*Alo'ha.*" The Menehune chief had responded in kind.

The Menehune chief turned to Kikilani and repeated the ritual greeting. Swift gasped even as Kikilani whispered to herself: "In the presence of the life force. Love…the breath of life."

The chief tapped his Talking Stick three times for silence. His deep gravelly voice was difficult to understand. Akamu translated his words into English.

"For many seasons"—Akamu's solemn voice rang quietly through the hall as he repeated the chief's words—"since the conquest of the Hawaiian King—our storytellers have sung a prayer to us. Oft they repeated the *mele*. Oft we listened that someday—when our hearts were pure and our bodies strong—a trail of jewels and gold would lead a renewal of the Pi'ilani people to their Lost City. If we were strong— the tellers said—and if without fail we kept the trail fresh…it must be that true Pi'ilani would find their way home to us."

A low hum of agreement came from the Menehune gathered behind the chief. With a tap of the chief's Talking Stick the excited ones quieted.

"We have been patient." The great Menehune chief's voice was deep as Akamu continued his translation. "You have not seen our hand in these affairs. But we've made sure to keep the trail fresh—as the *mele* told us. This ensured fortune smiled on the trail."

The kneeling pair nodded.

"You see…following the trail to the Lost City was only the first test." The high chief paused. "Now comes the true test."

◎　◎　◎

A general silence filled the greeting hall. Only the sound of Akamu's and Kikilani's gentle breaths disturbed the quiet as the chief continued to address the foursome. "Did you find the carved black stone along the Kaua'ula Stream or on your path through the lava tube?"

Dancer turned his gaze to Swift. Swift reflexively touched the shoulder strap of her pack. Kikilani turned back and smiled to her.

The chief intoned his meaning as Akamu continued to interpret: "The ancient origin *mele* songs of the Menehune tell that a black onyx pendant carved with a spiral is meant to be worn by the true princess of the Pi'ilani. If any impostor approached with the stone the life force of the true princess would drain away as the impostor approached the Lost City."

The Menehune warriors began to move out from behind the chief. Even as Swift and Dancer faced the chief they glanced sideways—only to realize the Menehune had surrounded them. A worrisome hum rose from the crowd packed shoulder to shoulder.

Swift reached into her pack. Located the medical kit. Inside the kit her fingers found the gauze wrapping. She withdrew the black stone Akamu had found in the lava cave stream. Then stepped forward and presented the white-wrapped object in both hands to the Menehune chief.

The chief nodded with an expression of foregone knowledge. Delicately he raised the package in his hands. The gauze fell away like a foreign object. By his fingertips the chief lifted the black onyx and turned slowly in a full circle: He held the gem and its carving aloft for all to see—including the ancient gods.

When the chief completed his presentation he stood before Kikilani again. "We suspect you may have felt the stone's power. Perhaps a loss of will? Trials of confidence? Indecision? Even a loss of control or bad choices."

Kikilani nodded assent. She raised her joined hands to touch her chin.

"You felt the power of Father Sky and Mother Earth." The Menehune chief turned and cast a disapproving frown toward Swift. "Now we must cleanse this sacred stone."

The chief held the heavy stone in two hands. Brought the gem near his face and exhaled short forceful breaths through his nose. He then turned. His chief advisor stepped forward. The advisor was a rotund little man with a beard so large the bush covered his ears and mouth. Then spread to the strained belt of his loin cloth cinched below his potbelly. In his hand he held the sundried *ule'ulu* breadfruit leaves tied with thread into a smudge stick. A thin stream of smoke rose from the bound incense. The chief held the stone in the smoke for perhaps a half minute. A third Menehune then handed the advisor a bottle gourd filled with rainwater while another Menehune handed the chief a large scallop shell. The chief placed the stone in the scallop shell—and the chief advisor tipped the bottle gourd over the shell. A steady stream of water slowly rinsed the outstretched offering.

Again the chief raised the sacred black stone over his head in his fingertips and repeated the presentation for all who were gathered in the greeting hall.

Swift glanced at Kikilani. The black onyx explained Kikilani's strange behavior. While Swift carried the stone her friend had battled her ever-increasing demons. Only Kikilani's willpower had allowed her to push forward.

Swift looked again and saw her friend's shoulders square. Her chin rise. Her breathing deepen. Soon Kikilani's poise and color — her full strength — had returned.

Akamu glanced at Kikilani and gave her a warm smile.

"Akamu and Kikilani" — the chief intoned his greeting as everyone breathed deeper — "you have arrived. Welcome."

CHAPTER 100

TREASURY
LOST CITY OF THE PI'ILANI
MOMENTS LATER

A JOYFUL RELIEF broke through the dark cloud of everyone's mood. The Menehune *ali'i* warriors relaxed. Still shy but more playful. Several pairs danced a tentative jig. From unseen passages more warrior men appeared: The mischievousness of tricksters permeated their expressions. All wore banana-leaf skirts or *malo* cloths with front flaps flapping to their knees. Many carried short swords like the one that had formed out of molten lava for Dancer in his duel with Malbec back in the tribunal. One elder Menehune with gray hair and a great beard that surrounded a bulbous nose stood in front: He held a banana-stalk walking stick. The bulb at the end glowed with fireflies.

At once the chief turned on the gathering: It had become overly boisterous. He clapped his hands twice. The happy-go-lucky air settled down. With purposeful gestures and three deliberate nods the chief beckoned Akamu. Kikilani. And the two others to follow him. He led them from the greeting hall. Toward another large stone door. As the door raised and the group entered the chief moved to one side. The foursome moved forward to the top of steps that led down into a lower area. From this edge their eyes were met with the most incredible and joyous sight.

A treasury chamber.

Before them—heaped in gleaming profusion—was the bulk of Napoleon's treasure. Piles of gold coins tumbled out of chests. Gems overflowed from barrels resting on sacks of coins. Some spilling their treasure onto the floor. A slope of silver and gold coins was mixed with jewel-encrusted goblets and ropes of golden chains. To one side a pyramid of treasure boxes was almost covered by slopes of more golden coins. Medallions set with jewels shimmered in the angular light slanting from the arrow-slit windows. Everywhere were objects of uncounted wealth. In gourds. In crates. Under tables. Piled in corners. Riches beyond imagination.

Swift walked down the steps and along a narrow path between the golden slopes. Before her—under a center skylight—was a carved pillar. About her height. From the top water cascaded down over successively larger tiers—each awash in gold coins—then flowed into a shallow pool around the fountain's base. She knelt down. Passed her fingers across the shimmering surface. A layer of gold and silver coins covered the bottom of the well that sparkled with starbursts of scintillating light.

Dancer wandered over to a treasure chest on a sturdy bamboo table. Reached his hand into the chest. And pulled out a fistful of coins. Slowly he let the coins slip through his fingers: Greek. Assyrian. Lebanese. The coins Champollion recorded in his notebook. Dancer bent closer beside the table to scan the glittering mounds more carefully. *No question. This is Napoleon's treasure!* The American agent realized there was enough riches before them for the President's men in Washington to pay for their Mexican War...and several more wars as well. Dancer played with the coins thoughtfully.

Swift eyed the mountains of coins. Gems. And jewelry that filled the treasury room. Silently in her chest her blood throbbed like a drumroll. In a low voice almost unheard by Dancer she spoke her thoughts: "This is the treasure Maunakili coveted to grow his opium-rum-trafficking scheme in the Pacific—and to dominate Maui."

The Menehune chief came before the foursome as they stood around the central fountain and executed an expansive gesture with both arms that encompassed the chamber trove. Akamu translated in a respectful low voice: Generations ago—when LeGrand shipwrecked at La Perouse Bay—the Menehune had brought the treasure here. On holidays and during important Menehune celebrations gold and jewels were given to the Menehune children. The children made wishes. Tossed the treasures from the aqueduct into the Kaua'ula Stream. One special celebration called for all Menehune to honor the great *mo'o* Kihawahine of the Moku'ula. Kikilani privately shuddered as she remembered that fateful confrontation. Now but a few short hours before. She almost had failed to survive the monster lizard of Loko Mokuhinia.

"That is how the treasures ended up in the Loko." The potbellied chief untangled strands of his hairy mane that had become caught in his woven cape. "The King saved the treasures as propitious omens. Blessings from the gods. And he held them close in the tomb house of his sacred sister and wife."

Swift turned to Dancer. "That's how the King knew about the treasure trail. He knew the Menehune had lain the trail for us to follow." She reflexively touched the strap of her pack. At that moment two Menehune nobles eagerly ran around the illumined fountain: Their helmets sported crests made from orange hibiscus. The nobles scampered along the narrow path between the treasure piles to the far end of the treasure chamber. Then tiptoed along a wide ledge that connected the arrowslit embrasures. Their cavorting forms silhouetted against the outside light that turned the red lava bays a dark crimson. At a near corner they jumped onto a large pile of gold—gleefully sliding down the slope of coins on their backs. All four watched as several Menehune wearing *ti*-leaf *kihei* capes played in the riches as if the treasures were golden rain puddles.

Without anyone noticing Dancer made his way to the far corner. He stepped up to one of the chests filled with treasure. Reached into his pack and removed the bag that contained the coins from Champollion and the Sultan. Along with the discoveries they collected in the lava cave. Then gently set the objects onto the piles of treasure.

Swift appeared at his side. "What are you doing?"

Dancer pulled the cord tight on his empty pouch and stuffed it into his pants pocket. "No doubt you'll find this amusing...Swift. But while listening to that Menehune chief just now I actually found myself asking: Who is the rightful keeper of this treasure?" But the next moment Dancer shook his head dismissively. "I must be going soft." He looked Swift in the eye. "Doesn't sound like the Jack Dancer you've come to know and love — does it...Swift?" His gesture swept over the golden horde around them. "Who should have this?" Again Dancer shook his head. "Not the boys in Washington...for their wars. Not the French King...to buy an empire." Resolve came into Dancer's voice. "Not Maunakili's rebels ...or even Napoleon...who stole the treasure for himself." For the first time Swift heard a note of something other than self-interest in Dancer's voice. His quest had ended...successfully. Now he patted his empty pocket. "No...The treasure's rightful place is with the trustees of the treasure...the guardians of the lost city...the people of the Menehune."

CHAPTER 101

THE HIGH CHIEF guided his captives across the chamber and through a vault-like stone door. Led by the glow of a single torch the foursome and the crowd of Menehune passed along a hidden hallway. The hallway gradually transitioned into a passageway that was quite warm — as though it had been carved from the molten magma that lived beneath it. They moved into a larger inner sanctum. The space was brilliantly lit. A heavenly shaft of light from a skylight far above flooded sunlight throughout the cavern. The chamber was filled with bones. Bundles of desiccated bones wrapped in *kapa*. Several long *kapa*-wrapped skeletons had been lain into two- and three-man canoes. Painted bottle gourds rested everywhere with remains of generations long-ago dead.

Akamu and Kikilani stopped in their tracks. Swift and Dancer held back two paces. The two island natives bowed their heads in respect. Kikilani took Akamu's elbow to boost her courage: They had entered the Cave of the Ancients.

The Menehune chief raised his hand in supplication. "For time forever…in this sacred cave…we have collected the earthly remains of our greatest chiefs. In their deaths…from old age…or from violence in the wars between the islands…we gathered them here whenever possible…and their possessions." He hesitated for a moment and gave a bitter smile. "Many were brought here after the Battle of the Dammed Waters in the 'Īao Valley." The chief gave a heavy deep sigh. Then all stood in silence for a long moment.

In the torchlight Dancer made special note of the arsenal of weapons lying around the remains: Possessions left for the departeds' use in the afterworld. His gaze fell on rusty old flintlocks. A single ivory dueling pistol — curiously without its lavish mate. Impractical English fowling pieces. Several British "Brown Bess" muskets with worm-eaten stocks. Boxes of Minié balls and percussion caps. Two hand-to-hand Elgin cutlass pistols in a case beside a telescoping English gadget cane. Paired with a captain's spyglass of wrapped baleen and a ship's hourglass. All dusty and ancient.

The foursome walked among the illuminated artifacts. Admired war canoes. Feather cloaks. Polished *koa* spears. Ancient drums. Royal *kahili* standards festooned with feathered plumes. Wooden litters inlaid with shell and ivory and bone. *Lei niho palaoa* necklaces with whale-ivory pendants styled like a hook or orator's tongue suspended from braided human hair. Capes and *leis*. Helmets and cloaks. All priceless.

Akamu supported Kikilani — who looked pale. They took care not to touch the ancient relics for fear they might crumble into dust.

The Menehune chief gestured to a large drum and spoke in a low tone. "The drum came from Tahiti with the first travelers. The canoe people brought the *'ula* breadfruit. The royal *kalo* taro. And the *'uala*…what you call sweet potato." The high chief tapped a storage gourd with his Talking Stick. "And the *ipu* bottle gourd. The *mai'a* banana. The sugar cane they called *kō* to relieve their hunger…."

He paused. From deep in the earth the mountain rumbled.

As the tremor rose through their feet a light fall of pumice filtered down from the cave roof. Everyone paused. After a moment several warriors let out a low drone as if to say: *All clear.*

Finally the high chief of the Menehune gathered the foursome before a large whale-oil cask that had been cut in half to form a low table.

The table was covered in fine dust. Kikilani. Akamu. Dancer. And Swift leaned close as the chief used his fingertip to draw a great arc in the powder. Inside the arc he drew four ever-smaller arcs. Below the last of the four arcs he drew a prominent semicircular space. The fifth level. The Menehune chief then drew radiating perpendicular lines between the arcs as though to mark off discrete compartments within the arcs. The overall effect was a design that looked like a great fan.

Akamu whispered to the group: "The high chief shows us the lineage of the Pi'ilani ancestry. Each arc represents one generation. Each compartment in the fan marks ancestors and their matriarchal lineage. Each compartment holds the mother and father. In the next arc the chief shows the offspring."

At the center top compartment of the outer arc the chief placed an Egyptian jewel the size of an egg. Then he faced the group. "Back in the time when history began the Gods smiled on these islands. Our storytellers passed on that history in great poem chants." He gestured to the jewel at the top. "Kahekili — King of Maui…descendant of the original *mo'oinanea* lizard spirit — was defeated by the Great Conqueror at the Battle of Kepaniwai. Kahekili and his sister-wife — Queen Pi'ilani — escaped the 'Iao Valley with two granddaughters." The chief indicated the two granddaughters with two gems of different sizes placed at the center of the third arc. "These girls the Queen Mother nurtured on Moloka'i. One was raised in public view. One was kept in secret from the entire world. The Hawaiian conqueror wanted to blend his Hawaiian line with the Maui Pi'ilani line. That is why he came to Queen Pi'ilani to capture the Pi'ilani princess as his wife."

Akamu and Kikilani nodded in understanding.

"Queen Pi'ilani delayed her answer to the conqueror. Yet before she died Queen Pi'ilani agreed to the conqueror's demand. She instructed her court to give the princess to the Hawaiian conqueror upon her death. But only if the Great Conqueror honored the queen mother's death properly. He did that. And he was allowed to take away the younger girl. The public princess." The chief lifted the smaller gem from the dusty chart. At that moment Kikilani swooned.

The Menehune chief paused. Straightened his banana leaf collar. And directed his comments toward Akamu and Kikilani.

"Queen Pi'ilani never told the conqueror there was another

granddaughter. A first-born older princess." The high chief touched the larger gem still in place. "That is why he did not take the secret princess. This secret princess was more sacred. Her Pi'ilani bloodline was pure. The older girl was the true bloodline. Unknown to the conqueror the Queen Mother's court presented him with the younger second granddaughter to be his 'sacred wife.' That younger princess gave birth to three children. The two sons became the second and third King of Hawai'i; the daughter is their princess sister. The younger of the sons is the third Hawaiian King today." As the chief said this he drew the conqueror's lineage off-center in the dust of his chart.

Just then a commotion arose among the circle of chiefs. Swift and Dancer looked toward the disturbance. The chiefs grumbled. Heads turned. Chiefs jerked straight. Warriors parted as if a small bowling ball was passing through the crowd. Even the fireflies in the gray-haired elder's walking stick all lit at once. A commanding voice seemed to be approaching. "Look out!" the voice said. "Move aside... fatty! Coming through!"

In a moment what appeared to be the Menehune queen popped out of the circle. Swift stared at the female figure and made mental notes. A tight topknot accentuated the queen's outsized ears: It seemed to lift her bushy eyebrows higher above her large eyes. Her double chin was hidden by her banana-leaf collar upon which rested a brown *kukui* nut and red *ti*-leaf *lei*. Her bark-cloth tunic fell from her shoulders down to her calves and concealed a stout figure resting on thick ankles and splayed feet. Not to be denied the Menehune queen straightened her tunic. Adjusted her collar. And surveyed Akamu and Kikilani with an accusatory gaze. Then pushed past the Menehune chief and excitedly interjected in a deep voice: "That is why—when the conqueror came years later to Moloka'i to receive the blessing of the priests for his marriage to Kahekili's granddaughter—the priests refused."

With a thump of his Talking Stick the high chief subdued his queen—who stopped talking. Momentarily. The chief continued as Akamu translated.

"The priests talked with two tongues. They said they refused to give their blessing because the conqueror had taken the princess by force. Yet they knew the real reason why the conqueror's Maui princess was not a sacred wife. That was because the conqueror's Maui wife was not the highest princess in the bloodline."

The Menehune queen elbowed the high chief and took possession of the Talking Stick. She ignored his irritation and spoke again. "The oldest and purest first granddaughter was raised in secret by Queen Pi'ilani's sister...the girl's grand aunt. The secret princess was a young girl when LeGrand arrived in 1800. The grand aunt knew the Pi'ilani were no match for the Great Conqueror and his foreign allies with their cannon that licked fire. Thus the aunt and the other Pi'ilani *ali'i* nobles welcomed LeGrand as a savior."

Again the Menehune chief took the Talking Stick. At the expense of a withering glare from his queen. "To cement the alliance LeGrand was wed to the secret granddaughter. They had a son. Maunakili. Maunakili was born before the current King was born in 1813."

"That means Maunakili did indeed have a true claim to the Pi'ilani throne..." Swift whispered to Dancer.

Dancer replied in a hushed tone. "*And* a legitimate claim to all the Hawai'i Kingdom."

The Menehune chief pointed to the fourth arc of the origin chart just above the outsized semicircle at the base of the dusty fan. "The secret granddaughter also had a daughter by LeGrand. Maunakili and that great-granddaughter were the highest descendants direct from King Kahekili—the greatest Pi'ilani noble." The chief's gesture indicated the direct line on his arc of ancestors. "That great-granddaughter of Kahekili was the mother of Akamu...and Kikilani."

Kikilani's eyes grew big. *Is that why Maunakili carried me to the Moku'ula? Can it possibly be...?* She gasped. *I'm his niece.*

Swift turned to Kikilani. "That means you are Queen Pi'ilani's great-great-granddaughter."

Dancer pointed at the chief's dusty arcs. "And Akamu is Queen Pi'ilani's great-great-grandson." Then—with a look of uncertainty that gradually changed to understanding—Dancer whispered to Swift: "Kikilani is Akamu's sister?"

"Yes. His sacred sister. Kikilani carries the purest female bloodline of Queen Pi'ilani."

After a moment Swift and Dancer turned back to the Menehune chief. The chief pulled a pendant from a small pouch strapped across his tummy. In his hands he held a carved ivory fishhook strapped to a leather thong. With ritual slowness the chief paraded around the Cave of the Ancients to display the fishhook before the crowd. Then he placed the ivory fishhook onto the center semicircle of the ancestral table.

Next the queen demanded the black onyx gem with the engraved spiral that the chief had cleansed in the antechamber. The chief held out the sacred stone to the queen. She took the heavy keyhole-shaped pendant. Inserted a peg-bail eyelet into the pinhole in the oblong top. Then bent over and rapped the eyelet home with a small stone.

The queen tested the eyelet bail. Then placed the black onyx spiral beside the ivory fishhook in the center semicircle. The two magnificent masculine and feminine symbols — equal in size — represented Akamu and Kikilani in the matrilineal fan.

Once again the chief's queen held the superior rank. "Akamu's mother — the great-granddaughter of Kahekili — realized she couldn't protect Akamu from the zealots of the Hawaiian kings — or from Maunakili — if her secret came out. She left Akamu with missionaries to be sure Maunakili would not kill him. Kikilani was raised as a common *maka'ainana*...not the royalty she is."

Akamu and Kikilani looked at each other in silence. Swift saw a current of intensity grow between them that she had not seen before.

Into the silence of the sacred cave came a collective breath of exhalation. Every Menehune knew their fate — and their destiny — now was secure. At last the longlost relics — and the true prince and princess of the Pi'ilani — had returned.

At that moment the Cave of the Ancients filled with a throaty hum that rose from the gathered Menehune. The hum grew into a chant as the syncopation of the Menehune's deep voices melded into one. The mellifluous sound filled the burial cave. Louder and louder the rhythm rose until it became a pulsing throb. Surrounding the intruders the short warriors intensified the chant as they pushed Akamu. Kikilani. Swift. And Dancer closer to each other. The chanting crowd moved as one out of the ancient burial chamber. The four captives were held at the center: They stood half-again taller than the irresistible Menehune crowd. The mass shuffled out of the burial cave. Passed through the golden treasury. Through the greeting antechamber. Emerged onto the open *heiau* platform in the plaza beyond. In a low voice Dancer muttered to Swift: "Do you see the angle of the light shafts from the dome?"

Swift nodded. "It must be midafternoon."

"Exactly." Dancer clenched his jaw. "Time is running out for Lahaina — and the King."

"Not to mention for us *haole* intruders right here in this lost city."

CHAPTER 102

HEIAU PLATFORM
MAIN PLAZA/LOST CITY
SHORTLY AFTER

THE MENEHUNE HERDED the four roughly onto the sacred *heiau* platform. Akamu and Kikilani were shown to the far end of the *heiau*. There a throne with two seats sat on a raised dais. The dais was covered by a tent of red *ti*-leaf chains hung from a bamboo pergola. Swift and Dancer watched as the Menehune ushered Akamu and Kikilani onto the double-seated throne like royalty. A pair of Menehune brought forth a feathered *mahiole* helmet and red-and-yellow *ʻahaʻula* cloak for Akamu. Then for Kikilani the Menehune queen brought forth a plaited-flower crown intended only for the highest *aliʻi* royalty.

Prince Akamu and Princess Kikilani were to be coronated.

Two guards separated the two outsized lowlanders from the crowd: They prodded Dancer and Swift toward the other end of the *heiau*. There a stone slab and two timber posts with L-shaped seats awaited.

"Front row seats?" Swift muttered.

"Looks more like garrote chairs to me." Dancer scowled at the predicament. "A bit medieval...but effective."

The bearded warrior who Dancer recognized from the top of the living ladder pushed them toward the place of sacrifice. Dancer stood with his back against the stone slab. "If the Menehune are setting a table" — Dancer whispered to Swift as the warrior returned to the palaver — "something tells me we are the menu."

Swift and Dancer watched as a huddle of Menehune chiefs gathered in the middle of the *heiau*. The two Americans stared as a mystifying scene developed before them. First came the deep-voiced hum of fast chatter. Much commotion. Banana-leaf collars and capes rattled. Menehune heads popped up from the huddle. One gave a throat-cutting gesture while looking at Swift and Dancer. Then dropped back into the huddle. Heads bobbed up. Down. Angry expressions shot toward the foreigners. The debate raged. One Menehune seemed to rub his hands together in anticipation of the fun.

Swift edged closer to Dancer. "This doesn't look good."

Again the chiefs huddled. Pointed. Counseled. This time the gestures took an even more threatening turn of garroting and head bashing. Soon the group reached agreement. The humming stopped. The huddle opened. The high chief stepped forward. With two raised hands he quieted the crowd as a large contingent of Menehune surrounded Dancer and Swift at the far end of the *heiau*. The mob pushed the foreigners before the sacrificial stone slab.

The high chief spoke to Dancer and Swift. "You have soiled our sacred place of refuge with violence. You have broken the *kapu* as the only *haole*'s ever to enter the Lost City of the Pi'ilani. You have observed the resting place of our ancient chiefs. For those crimes you must be sacrificed." Swift clutched Dancer's arm.

Dancer touched Swift's hand. "Looks like we are the appetizer before the main event."

Into the hush Akamu's voice rang out clearly from the dais. "Or be spared." The chief's rotund body spun around and he paused as if contemplating a new idea. Akamu and Kikilani rose from their thrones. Stepped down from the dais and sat on the edge of the platform. Akamu gestured for the high chief to come closer and parlay eye to eye. From the wings the Menehune queen — not to be denied — came forward and joined the three others.

Dancer watched as the chief's banana cape shook in what seemed to be anger. An emphatic gesture. Arms crossed in disagreement.

A negative head shake. As the pair watched from the opposite end of the *heiau* the Menehune warriors pressed closer around them. Among them a glint of short swords appeared. Swift felt the hard coolness of the sacrificial slab press against her back. Dancer looked down beside him and his gaze was met by a scornful look from the muscular Menehune with the short cape. Dancer saw the thick leaves of his plate armor quiver as he revealed a sword hilt protruding beside his potbelly. A menacing deep hum rose from the warriors surrounding the place of sacrifice.

Then all attention turned toward the royal dais.

Akamu and Kikilani rose to their feet. Akamu raised one hand and hushed the crowd of Menehune. The Menehune queen handed Akamu the Talking Stick. "The high chief and his queen have spoken. Now hear their words." As the crowd quieted Akamu in his royal robes lowered his gaze to Swift and Dancer and gestured that the two come forward. When Swift and Dancer came within two wingspans he addressed them directly. "Now is the time of decision." He paused for effect. Perhaps enjoying the moment. "*You* must decide." He paused again and looked at the foreigners solemnly. "If you agree to make one sacred promise you will not be sacrificed. Do you understand?"

When disappointment rose in a rumble from the Menehune warriors the Menehune queen shot the gathered elders a harsh look. Akamu handed the Talking Stick to Kikilani who thumped the carved staff three times. Soon all the Menehune gave the royals their utmost attention.

In a strong voice amplified by resolve Kikilani spoke next to Swift and Dancer. "If you promise never to reveal what you have seen or learned here…never to tell the world of the ancestors' cave…never to reveal the location of the Lost City. Never to speak a whisper about the gold treasure…then the high chief and his queen have agreed…to spare your lives."

Both Swift and Dancer inhaled for the first time in several minutes.

Dancer and Swift exchanged a quick glance. Nodded.

The high chief took back the Talking Stick and thumped it once. Then faced the two outlanders. "Do you accept those terms?" thundered the chief.

Swift and Dancer relaxed. Then Dancer replied: "It has been our honor...your Highnesses."

Swift gestured to the royally caped companions. "And our privilege to protect Prince Akamu and Princess Kikilani."

Both outlanders laid a hand over their heart and spoke in unison. "We will honor your secrets...Your Highnesses. As you and your queen have decided...we resolve to never tell."

The chief acknowledged the foreigners' words. Then stepped closer and took Swift and Dancer by their elbows. Moved them to the front edge of the throne dais as Akamu and Kikilani took their seats on the thrones above.

The Menehune queen pulled Swift by her sleeve and whispered in the stranger's ear. "Most important—you protected Akamu and Kikilani."

Then the high chief mounted the dais and stepped in front of Akamu and Kikilani dressed in their royal garb. "Stand." The prince and princess rose to their feet. At the same moment the Menehune elders on the *heiau* moved forward and the rest of the city's upturned small faces pressed closer to the place of worship. In a booming voice the chief spoke these words. "Prince Akamu—will you take your rightful place as the next Pi'ilani King?"

"I will."

Akamu bowed low. The chief placed the sacred ivory fishhook necklace around his neck.

Next the chief addressed Kikilani. "And...Princess Kikilani—will you be Prince Akamu's sacred sister and wife?"

"I will."

The Menehune queen stepped forward and with her hip moved the chief aside. Then extended her hands to him. The chief grumbled but passed the royal keyhole necklace to the queen. Kikilani bowed down wearing the plaited crown and yellow *lei* of the highest *ali'i*. Around Kikilani's neck the queen hung a skein of tiny white *ni'ihau* shells worn only by royalty. Kikilani pressed the carved black onyx pendant to her heart. She felt a warm glow of belonging emanate from the back of her neck. Then reached up with her fingertips and gently caressed her sea turtle birthmark.

Akamu took Kikilani's hand. Together they stepped to the edge of the royal dais. The Menehune looked at them expectantly.

"With this honor we pledge our allegiance." Akamu spoke his words clearly. "But not to the restored Kingdom of the Pi'ilani."

All talk among the Menehune halted. The plaza fell silent. A questioning murmur rose from the people.

Then both royals raised one hand as Akamu spoke: "With this day we pledge allegiance to the Kingdom of Hawai'i. Let us put the divisions of separate kingdoms aside. Lock them into the ancient cave of sacred ancestors. Never to be brought into our world again. From this day forward may we stand in unity. Unity for all our islands! And may we stand together against all outside enemies."

The effect Akamu's words produced upon the Maui Menehune was electric. All stood and gazed at Akamu and Kikilani in reverence: their hands raised before their faces with fingertips touching in prayer. Their previous look of expectation had changed: Their eyes glistened as though they had heard the inspired voice of true royalty.

Following Akamu and Kikilani's pledge the chief thumped his staff again three times. A deep bass cheer reverberated off the walls of the Lost City of the Pi'ilani. Their new leaders had come.

CHAPTER 103

MAIN PLAZA
LOST CITY OF THE PIʻILANI
WITHIN THE HOUR

THE MENEHUNE NEEDED little excuse. Lively old men with even livelier tummies traipsed into the plaza. Young men whistling tunes with a good-natured air swaggered about. Women holding tender infants six inches tall in their arms. Older girls sporting cowrie shell necklaces around their slender necks sashayed about. Or flirted as they skipped to make their anklets jingle. A trio of young brothers clung to their mother's fiber skirts. Into their midst came the white-bearded elder who danced with a sprightly step around his firefly walking stick. Swift noticed he had donned a wicker helmet from which a tiny banana plant sprouted. Throngs of fun-loving little people joined in playful celebration. All the while happily communicating in their strange humming voices.

Dancing. Singing. Happy Menehune set narrow tubes of wood below their noses and played merry tunes on the nose flutes. *Ti*-leaf trumpets. Small sharkskin drums. Young and old warriors competed in archery. Hand wrestling. And races of all kinds. Still: Two knots of whiskered men spoke among themselves. Another group watched Swift and Dancer with wary looks. Their deep voices again made the sound of a low hum as if to enclose themselves in a protective vibration. Swift called to Dancer over the rising din: "Kikilani told me some Menehune fear owls. That is why they hum. To keep away the owl god...Paupueo."

The next moment a slow movement near the base of the lava-stone wall above the Lost City caught Swift's and Dancer's gaze. A group of teenaged Menehune had begun climbing up the lava-stone wall. When they reached the top two teenage boys separated themselves from the group. They wore matching red *malo* robes. They confidently approached the edge of the wall overlooking the river below. Silently stripped off the robes. Extended their hands into the air before them. Bent their knees. Then dove confidently into the river below.

"Ah!" Swift said aloud. "So the splashes Kikilani and I heard as the *Black Cloud* approached Lahaina were Menehune cliff divers. Not waves or whales!"

"Your Highness." Dancer approached the high chief of the Menehune as the boisterous festivities proceeded. "As you may know...our time is short. The day is almost gone. We've given our word and by our honor we will never reveal your lost city. But it has come time for us to ask your leave."

The chief rubbed his potbelly. Which was now more prominent than before: He had been enjoying a great banquet that was still being served in the midst of the plaza. He nodded. And spoke simply. "The French cannons do not share our jubilation—as we all know." He rose to his feet. Signaled his closest advisors to gather round the four outsiders.

Dancer addressed the chief so all could hear. "Thank you. For a memorable welcome. And for a wonderful celebration. We couldn't be more pleased the way this has turned out...but we must leave you. We are sorry to do so. But the clock is ticking. We have no time to spare."

The chief indicated his disappointment to end such a grand festival. His advisors concurred.

At that moment a light tremor shook the citadel. Several loose stones fell from the arches supporting the aqueduct. A heavy cloudburst above the crater sent a torrent of water through the spouts in the ceiling. Then spilling down into the canals below.

Akamu and Kikilani had been sitting with the chief at his banquet table. Now the royal pair turned to the chief and his warriors. They gracefully confirmed their personal request to leave. A hush fell over the Menehune. As if the serious concerns of life had overshadowed a holiday's end.

Akamu asked the chief: "What is the fastest route back to Lahaina?"

The chief responded briefly in a deep voice. Kikilani explained the chief's words to Swift and Dancer. "A Menehune scout will guide us through the lava tube cave and along the Kaua'ula trail to Lahainaluna. That is the fastest route."

Akamu carefully lifted off his royal helmet and slipped out of the red-and-yellow cape. Kikilani removed her feathered crown. They placed them in the arms of the queen and the chief's advisor. Then turned toward the high chief and presented the royal fishhook and black onyx necklaces. "For safekeeping in the Cave of the Ancients." Akamu and Kikilani bowed to the chief in agreement. Kikilani stood forthrightly before the high chief. "We shall come to the Lost City again...after a lasting union of a united Hawai'i has been formed." Then the royal siblings joined the others again.

Akamu. Kikilani. Swift. And Dancer stood shoulder to shoulder. Clasped hands like a theater troupe. Bowed to the king and queen. Bowed to the crowd. The Menehune bowed back in unison. A note of melancholy came to their low humming.

The foursome crossed to the edge of the plaza. Where a powerfully built warrior with a long spear and helmet of hard green plantains stood proudly. He gestured for them to follow him.

The group moved toward the scout. Alongside him a steep stairway dropped from the edge of the plaza. All four turned back at the stairs. Akamu and Kikilani held hands then waved farewell. Swift and Dancer each raised one hand in parting. "Let's get out of here before they change their minds!" Dancer muttered to Swift in a low voice.

In the blink of an eye the small party trotted down the steps. And within moments were lost in the rich vegetation that hid the Lost City of the Pi'ilani.

CHAPTER 104

GUN DECK/FRENCH FRIGATE *NÉMÉSIS*
LAHAINA HARBOR
THAT EVENING

REAR ADMIRAL LOUIS TROMELIN paced the main gun deck. Nervously he fingered his admiralty signet ring. Looked down an 18-pounder long gun aimed toward Lahaina Town across the harbor. His spies had told him Maunakili was dead. The King lived. Now Malbec was missing. No signal from Olowalu. The ultimatum hour had arrived. Scores of whaling ships rocked in the harbor. Hardly any of the American whalers had fled. *A few incendiaries will clear their nuisance away like a Fourth of July fireworks.* Yet the lighthouse burned bright as ever.

Tromelin signaled his gunners. The sailors used a rammer to pack the black powder charge down the muzzle of the cannon. Then followed with a wad of cloth rammed tightly behind it. A heavy cannonball followed. And was rammed into place. Followed by another wad to prevent the cannonball from rolling out of the barrel. The gunner poked a sharp picker through the hole: the picker broke through the packet of gunpowder. Then a suntanned sailor adjusted the cannon's elevating screw to the precise elevation. The gun in its carriage was then run out as the gun crew heaved on the tackles until the carriage was hard against the ship's bulwark. The black barrel protruded out the gun port: the Hawaiian flagpole was dead center in its sights.

"Fire!" Tromelin bellowed.

The gunner held the lighted fuse at the end of a long pole to the touch hole. Instantly the gunpowder primer flashed. Then the long gun roared. And bucked in recoil restrained only by its ropes.

The murderous ball blew a hole in a front corner of the coral rampart of Lahaina Fort. "The end is near!" prisoners shouted from the basement. Where Bull Shaw fingered a scrimshaw carving of Jesus — and cursed Maunakili.

A screaming second cannon blast shattered the Lahaina lighthouse. A cloud of burning splinters shot into the air then fell to earth. What remained of the whale oil reservoir ignited in a fiery ball of flame.

Then — with Malbec's whereabouts unknown — the Admiral on the French warship hesitated. His capitaine filled the void with questions. What if Malbec appeared any moment? What if Malbec had found Napoleon's treasure? What if he were bringing it now to Olowalu miles away? Gold is heavy…slow to transport.

Tromelin smacked his signet ring against the warship's taffrail. As he often did when making a decision. "Let that be a warning. We will not attack Lahaina…until tomorrow."

Rear Admiral Tromelin dispatched his capitaine with a cryptic note. The capitaine stuffed the note inside his red vest under his royal blue jacket. Saluted. Then climbed into one of the ship's tenders. With his hand inside his vest buttons the capitaine stood at the bow while four sailors rowed through the crooked entrance channel. At the landing the capitaine took his time climbing out of the boat. Then marched the note to its intended recipients at the fort. Who opened it and stared wide-eyed at the words:

Deliver payment. Or…face your execution at noon tomorrow.

CHAPTER 105

AFTERCASTLE/FRIGATE *NÉMÉSIS*
LAHAINA HARBOR
NEXT MIDDAY

FOUR HORSES POUNDED down Lahainaluna Road. Raced along Front Street. And deposited their riders at the wharf. Within the hour Dancer. Swift. Kikilani. And Akamu boarded the French flagship. Joining the foursome were Royal Minister Abner Sisson. U.S. Consul Angus Macomber. And the wily people's representative — Charlie Pickham. A glance at the sun revealed only a few minutes remained before high noon. On Lahaina Point the Hawaiian King's royal party was clearly visible beside the thatched longhouse.

Dancer. Swift. And their entourage were presented to Rear Admiral Tromelin. Sisson and Macomber bowed slightly in what they imagined was a diplomatic gesture. Dancer and Swift stood firm. With expectant scorn Tromelin looked down his nose at them. Dancer stepped forward. From his boot he presented Malbec's dagger. Malbec was dead. Mack. Kapu. The mercenaries. All dead. Dancer had not spoken anything but the truth. Thus far. Then he said: "They were killed by cave-ins and flash floods in a vain search to find Napoleon's treasure." Tromelin's capitaine translated as Dancer spoke.

Minister Sisson declared that the King of Hawai'i was very much alive. In clear words he stated the King rejected the French treaty of protection.

"This is the decision of the King...as you see." Sisson pointed toward the King on shore. Where the old searchlight once stood near Lahaina Point a torch now burned on top of a bamboo pole.

"The legend of the treasure is not true." Dancer reported his lie matter-of-factly — his words again whispered to Admiral Tromelin by his capitaine. "It's a myth. Nothing more than old stories told by old men. Malbec lost his life looking for it. He found nothing. We found nothing. Napoleon's treasure does not exist. At least not on Maui. The legend of Napoleon's treasure is nothing more than an old story... as mythical as the bones of ancient chiefs."

"You have no gold? No payment?" Tromelin repeated.

"Not a coin. Not a penny." Dancer spoke slowly and distinctly.

For a long moment Tromelin glared at Dancer. *France no longer has an ally among the Pi'ilani.* The French Admiral knew the truth. He twisted his royal navy ring. His jaw twitched. The decorated French commander chewed his dilemma. Whether the Hawaiian King would ever turn over any treasure as payment for French protection seemed doubtful. But he held the upper hand nonetheless.

Tromelin barked a litany of island injustices at the French. "The King charges high tariffs for French brandy. The missionaries shut out our Catholic priests and our trade." He fumed. His eyes narrowed as he shot an icy glare at Sisson. "Our priests' homes have been violated by the King's police. Our hotel keepers are not paid for damages by American whalers. Even native schoolboys are impious in our churches."

Sisson uneasily withstood the tongue-lashing.

Sticks and stones...went through Swift's mind.

At that moment a shout came from the lookout on the top mast of the French warship. All eyes followed the lookout's outstretched arm. The sails of a two-masted gun brig rounded the tip of the Moloka'i Island. In minutes a larger sloop of war came into view. Then a massive three-masted heavy frigate — every inch of canvas straining against the wind. The polished muzzles of the ship's 42-pounder short-barreled *carronades* bristled from its forecastle and quarterdecks: cannon designed for deadly close work against enemy vessels. As the squadron bore down on Lahaina all could see the insignia of the British Navy streamed from each of the three ships. Across the narrowing distance a sharp whistle and drumbeat called the crews of the British flotilla to battle stations.

Dancer turned and addressed Rear Admiral Tromelin directly. "Appears the cavalry has arrived from Honolulu."

At that instant a chorus of cheers erupted from the decks of the American whalers. One New Bedford captain brazenly fired his salute cannon. Only to be answered by a solo boom from the blank curfew gun on an undamaged section of the Lahaina Fort's rampart.

Tromelin spat his last invective. "Mark my words...we will be back. Today Lahaina is not important. But France will be back when the Hawaiian King has more to lose than his life. On that day France will rule Hawai'i and French will become the language of commerce between our citizens and the Hawaiian government. Mark this down. We will be back."

Dancer exhaled to himself. Today was not the day of judgment.

Tromelin had the last word. "Maui is little more than a worthless pile of lava." Then the French Admiral rapped his ring against the railing. "Not worth wasting French gunpowder to blow it off the map. In the name of Louis Philippe — King of the French — tell your King that his day will come. He will meet Tromelin again. Soon. Very soon. In Honolulu."

With that threat Rear Admiral Tromelin dismissed the entourage from his flagship. As they made haste to their whaleboat Tromelin ordered his captain to set sail at once. "South past La Perouse Bay. Then sail for Tahiti." With a snap of canvas and shouted orders the French frigate *Némésis* weighed anchor. Beat a course around the American whalers. And fled into the open channel.

Meanwhile Dancer. Swift. And the others returned to shore. They joined the King. Akamu. And Kikilani beside the lighthouse debris. All eyes turned toward the harbor. The full sails of the French warship caught the trades. Moved south past Olowalu. Then — empty-handed — slipped behind the lava flats of La Perouse Bay in the high afternoon sun. All the while taking care to stay beyond the cannon range of the oncoming British squadron.

CHAPTER **106**

SOUNDS OF CELEBRATION reverberated across Lahaina Roads. From the guesthouse Swift looked toward the harbor at the *Ship of Paradise* — lit like a Christmas tree in June. Whale-oil lamps burned from every cross spar. Candle lamps hung from the ratlines. Lively fiddle and accordion tunes blended with sailors' laughter. Released from the threat of French cannons the seamen danced into the night. Even the grog shanties along Rotten Row spilled forth whalers like so many cornucopias. Gathered under the great breadfruit tree in the clinic yard — a few hundred yards from Tuckerman's hostel — a bedraggled group of missionaries whispered to each other and clutched their worn Bibles. When the fort's evening cannon rent the night with a thunderous roar Swift faintly heard a wit's-end cry come from Reverend Jedidiah Wise and his shattered nerves.

Minutes after the eight o'clock curfew Swift caught sight of a muscular figure as he slipped from the fort's main gate and crossed Front Street. A few moments later Mr. Flute stepped onto the porch of Major Tuckerman's hostel. Within a few strides he joined a huddle of people seated at one end on sack back Windsor armchairs. Swift.

Dancer. Kikilani. And Akamu greeted the bald mariner from their seats. Dancer handed Mr. Flute one of his last Oscuro cigars. With a nod Mr. Flute tucked the black-wrapped smoke inside his coat pocket. Without hesitation he made sure he gained their undivided attention. "The two kidnapped Chinese girls..." He turned to Swift and Kikilani. Who exchanged glances. "They are being held on the *Black Cloud* in the *lazarette*."

Dancer asked before Swift could form her words: "How do you know?"

Mr. Flute shot Dancer a bemused look. "I heard it first from my sources on Fid Street." He paused and let what passed for a smile form on his mouth. "Ratter Dawes confirmed it when we...chatted... in his cell."

Kikilani stood slowly. "We've got to rescue them."

Mr. Flute turned to Swift. "With Head gone and Dawes in the calaboose...my guess is the *Black Cloud* is abandoned."

Dancer chimed in. "And with the whole fleet celebrating...now may be the best time."

Swift looked around at everyone. Then rose to her feet beside Kikilani. "Kikilani's canoe is on the beach next to the market canal."

Akamu stood up next. "I'll gather a long canoe with my warriors and standby near the breakwater if needed."

Dancer exhaled cigar smoke before answering. "Somebody better stand lookout on the *Ship of Paradise*...just in case."

With a wave of her hand Swift gave Dancer a sideways glance. "And I suppose you'll volunteer." She rolled her eyes. Then turned to the bald harpooner. "Where will you be...Mr. Flute?"

"My duty is at the fort...to keep the prisoners out of trouble." Dancer flashed Mr. Flute a nod of approval.

A moment later Swift and Kikilani sprinted toward the beach. Together the pair pushed the outrigger canoe into the waves and swung aboard. Kikilani whispered loudly toward Swift in the bow as they both dipped their paddles deep into the water. "Better swing wide of the *Ship of Paradise*." Swift twisted partially around and nodded her assent. Then muttered: "Take us around the far side of the *Black Cloud*. We can tie up at the ladder...and not be seen from the *Paradise*." Swift cast a look at the dark outline of the *Black Cloud*.

"Looks like Mr. Flute was right. Our old ship looks as dead as a stone."

Silently Swift and Kikilani paddled up to the dark hull. Tied up their canoe. Swift climbed the gangway ladder. Followed closely by Kikilani. At the bulwark Swift listened. Then pulled herself into the gangway opening. Again she cocked her ears. Nothing. A quick scan of the deck revealed no one on watch. Swift moved to the main mast and surveyed the quarterdeck and trunk house. She saw no crew or lamplight from the skylight.

Kikilani scampered past Swift and hurried across the deck to the cable tier companionway. "Good thing we know our way around in the dark."

"Six months on board ship will do that." Swift frowned. *I'm starting to sound like Dancer.*

Swift eased the workshop companionway doors open. First Kikilani — then Swift — climbed down the ladder. At the bottom they paused to listen in the cable tier passageway. Kikilani touched Swift's arm in the darkness. "I'll get two lights from our cabin."

"Bring some matches...and a camphor jar for the stench."

A minute or so passed before Kikilani returned. She handed Swift a lighted lamp while keeping the second lamp unlit. "No one can see the lights outside the cable tier." When Swift glanced around the storage area amidships she saw the space was mostly empty. All signs of the sailors were gone. No seamen's chests. No foodstuffs. No hammock where Mr. Flute slept.

"Feels deserted." Swift moved along the passageway and lowered her lamp light to the forward cargo grate. "Mr. Flute said the Chinese girls were in the *lazarette*. The fore hatch ladder will be our best path." Together the pair slid back the hatch cover. Swift dropped first into the darkness. Then shined her light upon the ladder for Kikilani. Standing at the bottom on the center aisle planks Kikilani struck a match and lit her lantern. While Swift dabbed camphor beneath her nose. Then held out the jar to Kikilani.

Rats scampered from their lights. From the ship's tarred old timbers came a slight groan as the *Black Cloud* rocked in the harbor. Yet the dank hold's bilious air did not turn their stomachs as it once did. Swift looked into the hold's black maw. Then raised her lamp to show the way toward the stern. The pair stepped carefully along the narrow boards. Barrels of whale oil were packed on both sides. Smaller barrels of sperm oil filled niches in between.

Swift swept her lantern light over the stacked barrels. "Tight packed. And braced. Looks like Head and Dawes were ready to sail back to New York at any moment."

Kikilani paused and gave Swift a serious look. "I can't say I'm sorry his plans were cut short."

After dozens more careful steps Swift and Kikilani reached the after hold. Ahead were the closed doors of the *lazarette*. Memories of Duffy Ragsdale's lashed back and Smidt's suicide — if not murder — filled them both with misgiving. Swift slipped the bolt and opened the brig slowly. As she moved her light around the room she saw two figures. Huddled in the corner. Eyes wide in silent terror.

Kikilani turned her lamp upon herself. Then Swift illumined her own face and gestured toward the girls to be calm.

"*Bùyào hàipà.*" Swift's voice was calming. "Don't be frightened. We're here to help you." Swift thought she saw a flicker of recognition cross the older girl's face. Kikilani moved close to the two girls who blinked in the light and sat up. She checked their pupils. Then wrists and ankles for bruises. "Looks like the drugs have worn off." Kikilani rose to her feet in the low cell. Then gestured to see if the girls could stand. The taller one rose to her feet first. Her black hair loosely gathered in a twist at the back of her head. She bent down and helped the younger girl to rise: the girl's twin braids framed her face and revealed her pale forehead.

Kikilani whispered to Swift. "See those braids? Traditionally that means the girl has not reached her fifteenth birthday." Kikilani put her arm around the waist of the young girl. While Swift took the hand of the taller girl and led her from the *lazarette*. At the front of the small cell Swift lifted her lamp higher to show the way. "Watch out. Some of these boards are slippery." Kikilani directed her lantern lower to guide their footsteps. Halfway into the cargo hold Swift stopped. She directed her lamp down a narrow alley between barrels. "That's odd." The barrels were stacked on end under a tarp...as if the canvas was hiding something. Swift directed the taller Chinese girl to sit on a protruding cask. Kikilani did the same with the young girl in braids.

"Shine your lantern back there." On hands and knees Swift worked her way into the barrel space. Sat back on her haunches. Kikilani watched as Swift lifted the tarp and shone her lamp light underneath. "These barrels are stenciled *PAINT OIL*. No reason to ship rum back to New York." She started counting the barrels. "One…two… three….Looks like there are only eight paint oil barrels. What does that make you think of?"

Kikilani's voice was low but clear. "Head traded rum for ten cannisters of opium at La Perouse Bay." She connected the dots. "Mama Samoa demanded two cans from Head for him to do business in Lahaina…that leaves eight cans of opium."

"My thinking too. This could be important evidence when Ratter Dawes comes to trial." Swift dropped the tarp. Worked her way backward out of the cramped space. Swift had the Chinese girls hold hands. Just as they tried to do in the grog shop storeroom. Linked in a chain Swift led the way to the forward hatch ladder with Kikilani at the end: holding the young girl's hand while elevating her lantern with the other.

From the dark hold the foursome climbed up to the cable tier. Then ascended the companionway to the main deck. Swift and Kikilani let their lights show the way for the two former captives. Within a few steps they reached the open gangway. "Kikilani…take the girls to the canoe. I'm going back to the surgeon's cabin to get the medical bag. The girls may need it."

"Don't be long…Sam." Kikilani's face looked hopeful in the rising moonlight.

"Don't worry. I know just where to look."

With a gesture Kikilani indicated to the Chinese girls the canoe tied at the bottom of the ladder. She climbed backward down two rungs of the *Black Cloud*'s Jacob's ladder then beckoned the youngest girl to follow. When the Chinese girl came onto the rung above Kikilani…Kikilani wrapped the girl with her arms: Together they climbed down the ladder. Once settled in the center of the canoe Kikilani returned up the ladder. At the top she looked the hesitant taller girl in the eye. "We can do this…together." Kikilani smiled at the Chinese girl encouragingly. "Come."

In the canoe the two kidnapped girls hugged each other while Kikilani returned up the ladder. When she poked her head over the gunwale she stopped short. Squinted. In the ghostly moonlight— across the deck...just outside the workshop companionway— Swift stood stock still. Her medical kit in one hand. Before her loomed a dark figure. Slightly crouched. At that moment Swift's lamp shone on the man's face. Chang Fu.

The Chinese smuggler gestured toward the companionway. "I'm here for the girls. Stand aside." His hands were raised before him. As if he was about to attack Swift. "They belong to me."

Swift bluffed. "All yours...my friend. I'm here only to collect my medicine bag." Swift slowly moved sideways away from the companionway: toward the landward side of the deck. As she moved her eyes followed Chang Fu as he circled toward the ladderway. Then he stopped. "Witness no good. Like Mama Samoa say: You in wrong place...at wrong time...girlie."

In a blink Chang Fu charged. Grabbed Swift around the waist. Lifted her into the air. Swift dropped the medical kit. Pounded Chang Fu's head with the heels of her fists. Tried to knee the smuggler in the stomach. But his grip didn't allow any space. Swift felt herself being carried backward toward the bulwark. She scratched and clawed at Chang Fu's face and ears. His sinewy arms held her fast. Without warning the Chinaman rammed Swift's back against the railing. Driving much of the air from her lungs. A paralyzing memory of Smidt tossing her overboard flashed before her eyes. She kicked again with desperation. This time her toe caught her attacker in the knee. He wobbled. Then lifted her atop the railing.

From the corner of her eye Swift saw Kikilani spring across the deck: silent as a tiger. In her fist a belaying pin raised high. With a thunderous blow Kikilani smashed the wooden pin against the back of the Chinaman's head. His knees buckled. His fingers released Swift. Swift fell to the deck boards and collapsed on top of Chang Fu. The smuggler groaned but quickly began to recover. Kikilani raised the heavy oak pin with two hands above her head like an ax—then struck another blow across Chang Fu's head. The smuggler rolled and sank to the planks on his back.

"Quick...hold him down!" Swift cried. "I need the medicine bag."

Kikilani leaped on top of the smuggler. Pinned his wrists to the deck while Swift brought the heavy bag beside them and dug inside. "Where is it? Where is it?"

"Where is what?" Kikilani asked.

"The chloroform! We used it for seasickness."

"In the side pocket!"

Swift jammed her hand into the pocket. Lifted out a bottle of the anesthetic. Grabbed a wad of dressing. Uncorked the sweet-smelling colorless liquid. Emptied the bottle onto the cloth. Then with both hands held the soaked rag over Chang Fu's nose and mouth. The smuggler's eyes opened wide. He struggled against Kikilani's strong arms. Swift pressed home the rag. What seemed like minutes passed. "Hold him." With one hand Swift reached back into her medicine kit. Withdrew a bottle of ether. Uncorked the green bottle with her teeth. Dowsed the damp cloth again. Then pressed it over Chang Fu's face.

Gradually the Chinaman's struggles lessened. Then ceased.

Kikilani grabbed several short gasket lines looped over a pin rail along the bulwark. She quickly tied Chang Fu's limp hands and ankles. Kikilani gathered the precious medical bag. And Swift grabbed the belaying pin from the deck. When she reached for the lamp the wick flickered and died. Together in the faint moonlight they moved toward the gangway ladder.

At that moment two nimble figures came over the rail from the landward side. Swift spun. Kikilani dropped the medical bag. Swift gripped the oak pin from the deck and raised the bludgeon to strike the intruders. The two dark forms stopped. Then a third figure vaulted over the bulwark. Kikilani stepped beside Swift's shoulder. Apparently not noticing the two women the stealthy troop advanced without a sound. Then almost tripped over the bound body of Chang Fu. The third man dropped to a knee. Felt the Chinaman's binds with his hands. "He's not going anywhere." From the corner of her eye Swift saw Kikilani relax her stance. "It's okay…Sam. I think we both know that voice."

The dark figure rose. Strode across the deck. And clasped both Kikilani's hands. "Are you okay?" She gave him a warm smile. "Yes…Akamu. We're okay." With relief in her voice Swift spoke succinctly: "We've got the Chinese girls in the canoe." She tilted her head toward the gangway. "Can you take Chang Fu to the fort?"

In moments Akamu's two men lifted the bound Chinaman over the rail. Lowered him into the hands of two more warriors waiting in the double-hulled sailing canoe. Swift touched Akamu's wide shoulder. "We found opium hidden in the cargo hold. It proves Dawes is guilty. Can your men guard it until tomorrow?"

"Certainly." Akamu spoke quickly to his two men. They took up positions at the cable tier companionway.

Kikilani moved close to Akamu. Then rose on her toes and gave him a kiss on the cheek. Even in the moonlight his blush was obvious to Swift.

Kikilani moved to the gangway and climbed down to the girls in the canoe. At the rail Swift looked back at the empty deck. The workshop. The gig boats stowed on top. The sailor's bench facing the rail. The companionway to the cable tier. A smile crossed her face as she imagined the stir her dispatches would cause in New York. "Time's a wastin'...."

Swift clambered down with the medical bag into the bow of the canoe. Without another word Kikilani and Swift pushed off. Paddled the outrigger with the two Chinese girls rapidly back toward shore. As they passed the *Ship of Paradise* Swift scanned the silhouette. The impression was somehow less threatening than before. The oil lamps were extinguished. The lanterns dark. The gaiety subsided. She guessed only the serious work in the Hall of Paradise carried on. Yet the sex-trafficking ring and the rum-for-opium operation had been shattered. A shiver ran up her spine as Swift recalled the encounter with Chang Fu. It could have ended differently.

A slight smile appeared on Swift's face as she looked ahead over the gentle waters on which the full moonlight formed a silver ripple across Lahaina Roads. Swift turned and smiled at Kikilani. Who looked up fleetingly and gave a relieved expression. Then bent into her stroke. Together the duo made good headway toward the canal turning basin nearby Tuckerman's Guesthouse.

CHAPTER 107

TUCKERMAN'S GUESTHOUSE
LAHAINA TOWN
INTO THE NIGHT

S. THOMAS SWIFT turned up the whale-oil lamp. The flame flickered in the moonlight on her balcony. Even the chattering night birds in the surrounding breadfruit trees had stopped gossiping. For a moment the correspondent for the *Brooklyn Daily Eagle* paused to imagine the sensation her investigative series on smuggling and trafficking would cause. Swift smiled at the discomfort she knew the newspaper's surging sales would afflict upon her insidious uncle: Jacob Swift. Bold type would feature the traveled reporter's pseudonym. Exchange newspapers would clamor to beat their competitors to get all the investigative reports in the series. Newsboys would please their immigrant mothers with the sound of unexpected tips.

Swift savored a thought: Exactly six months had elapsed since she set sail to plumb the events to be recorded in her exposé series. The interval mostly spent tossing about on the wide ocean. Swift opened her copy of Melville's *Typee* that sat on her desk and turned to the preface for a memorable quote: *Sailors are the only class of men who now-a-days see anything like stirring adventure.* She paused. Shook her head in disagreement. Closed the book. Then spoke out loud.

"Except for a woman — nay — a woman correspondent on the scent of a story of greed and injustice. Now *that* is adventure."

Swift lifted a nib pen from her writing box. Dipped the tip into her ink bottle. Soon her words flowed like the incessant trade winds outside her balcony.

SMUGGLING SCHEME SHATTERED!
EXCLUSIVE EAGLE INVESTIGATION
RUM-OPIUM-TRAFFICKING KINGPINS
EXPOSED BY YOUR CORRESPONDENT

Your Faithful Correspondent's Concluding Dispatch in a Three-Part Series
LAHAINA — MAUI — HAWAIIAN ISLANDS — The far-reaching tentacles of the New York-Lahaina-Canton-Calcutta smuggling and trafficking ring that traded rum for opium and girls has been shattered. Yes — Dear Reader — the exclusive news that follows is the result of your correspondent — and a legion of faithful allies — diving to the deep bottom of a wicked scheme.

Though threats to life and limb have hunted your scribe — quite literally like a shark in chum — the truth is here revealed as a beacon to liberty. Freedom. And the inalienable rights of women and the citizens of these fair isles.

But first — good Reader — as I live let me begin with the facts. With customs documents. Forged logbooks. And eyewitness reports your Eagle *correspondent proved — beyond a doubt — that a network of whaleship captains and their henchmen has for some years bartered rum — often in barrels mislabeled as* PAINT OIL — *for opium in these Pacific Islands. The vile black balls of sticky resin are the product of British factories in Calcutta and Patna in India. Then fed — for that is the most accurate description — to Chinamen in exchange for tea. When the addicts cannot pay for all opium their cravings demand they are known to barter — nay — sell their daughters to feed their habits. But that did not slack the appetites behind the China opium trade.*

With excess supply the opium merchants paid American whalers to transport their poison across the sea—and dropped it from buoys off the Bay of La Perouse in Maui. Your special correspondent witnessed this operation in person. Chinese middlemen retrieved the whaler's perfidy and immediately exchanged the opium cannisters—emblazoned as "Tea" with the symbol of the East India Company—for tax-free rum brought here by at least one American whaling captain. This rum carefully passed duty-free into the Kingdom under the consideration and foreknowledge of the American Consul in Lahaina. A man your fearless correspondent shared passage with for five and a half months to reach these shores. The many ways he lined his pockets became clear when my investigation of forged customs documents proved the practice. Further sleuthing uncovered how the consul's smuggling compatriots further stuffed their purses: Watered rum. Excessive prices. Monopoly. Extortion.

This is the underbelly your correspondent risked life and limb to penetrate. Upon making landfall in this idyllic paradise of volcanic mountains and warm winds your correspondent penetrated the schemes of the Madam of the Pacific by making use of her direct contacts—both of the professional and sisterly kind—with the Madam of New York: Queen Tin'a of the Paradise Palace. [Editor's Note: Regular readers will recall the Eagle's *exposé our special correspondent filed last December that raised the hackles of so many comfortable folk in our fair city.]*

What did the Pacific Madam—known to every sailor on these seas as the infamous Mama Samoa—profess? What did she propose as a means of further enhancing her greed? Nothing less than to demand an even higher share of opium than she typically extorted from the kingpin American captain—the late Hyram Head—former master of the whaling transport: Black Cloud. *What reason did the Madam argue—as overheard by my confederate—in confidence? That her bordello expenses were high and she simply needed more from the captain for him "to do business in Lahaina." As my fair* readers may well know: The port of Lahaina—once the seat of the Hawaiian King's throne but not so since His Highness moved his Crown to Honolulu in 1845—is the greatest whaling port in all of the Pacific Ocean. Bar none.

Yet—Dear Reader—you be the judge of the following revelations.

If a monopoly of rum and extortion were not enough for this loathsome ring of smugglers…some captains kidnapped young natives and Chinese women and hid them aboard ship. One aforementioned captain who met his end—Hyram Head of the Black Cloud out of New York—locked his living contraband in his "lady's cabin" aboard ship—as your intrepid investigator can attest with my own eyes. Only to sell his victims to the highest bidder in New York's Five Points' brothels and misery houses. As you must know your faithful Eagle correspondent went under the blanket to discover where—and how—these villains held the young women. Only to learn their grog houses in Lahaina were the captives' prisons before they were shipped to New York.

These discoveries came to a head—and your scrivener uses the term with razor precision—when the smugglers and local Provisionals tried to mount a fishhook rebellion against the Kingdom of Hawai'i. Again your investigative scribe— and my allies among the honest whalers and visiting American agents—cornered the kingpin in the parade ground of Fort Lahaina. There the culprit was skewered with a harpoon— thrust not inches from my face—during the arrest of his first mate and several ineffectual militia men. All with the aid of the native constabulary wardens. Final tally of hostages released by these honest efforts: two native girls. And two kidnapped Chinese maidens.

That—fair Reader—is the succinct summary of your correspondent's work to get to the bottom of this investigation. No longer is the rum-for-opium-and-girls smuggling and trafficking ring in operation. Yet understand—my Dear Reader—that this correspondent is under no illusion the breakup and arrest of this nefarious network will do more than *put a momentary kink in the hose of these clandestine operations in other cities and ports. Whispers from Rotten Row suggest Mama Samoa will soon move on to calmer waters. And two whaling captains from Sag Harbor and New Bedford — suspected of illicit complicity — have this eve already set sail — destinations unknown — before the ink of this report is dusted.*

Yet rest assured — as you are…my faithful Readers — the Eagle's campaign has just begun. And your special correspondent will be there — wherever the next assignment may take me — to shine a light on these and other heinous wrongs — as no doubt you shall see.

S. Thomas Swift
Special Correspondent
Exclusively for the Brooklyn Daily Eagle
Reporting from Lahaina in the Hawaiian Islands

CHAPTER 108

ROYAL HOUSE/KING'S ISLAND
MOKUʻULA/LAHAINA
EARLY NEXT MORNING

COOLED BY THE MORNING SHADOW of Puʻukukui volcano the King gathered a select group to his royal house. All took their seats on the soft screw pine mats spread on the mausoleum's piazza at the tip of the Mokuʻula. Clusters of night-blooming Cereus at the water's edge still lent a light cactus scent to the rising dawn. The King's first thanks were to Dancer. Swift. Akamu and Kikilani. Together they had foiled the French plot. Captain Post and Mr. Flute—temporarily stepping away from their jailor duties overlooking the prisoners in the fort—received special thanks.

Dancer summed up the affair. Just as he had done with Tromelin. Malbec and his henchmen were dead. Billy Mack the Irish spy served his Catholic master before his adopted country. Maunakili had a true claim to the throne through Queen Piʻilani.

The King nodded as he toyed with his red-feathered whisk. Then Dancer continued in a frank tone: "We learned that the coins in the lake were—indeed—signs from the gods. Or so the Menehune believe. As you suspected…Your Highness." He paused to choose his words carefully given Swift's and his promise to the Menehune high chief. "The myth of Napoleon's treasure is just a myth...as far as the Menehune are concerned. But they will continue to pay tribute to the lizard god in the Mokuhinia by tossing occasional jewels and coins from the treasury into their aqueduct. In that way they will maintain the native myth. At least...that is my understanding."

Again the King nodded.

"We did make one important discovery. Malbec and Maunakili were half-brothers."

The King sat farther upright.

Dancer explained how he learned the truth. He had gleaned the first piece of the puzzle from the wizened princess in Tahiti. She had told him she had given birth to a boy with a birthmark on his right inner forearm...the same as his father. LeGrand. But she had given up the baby to a French priest and never saw her son again. The next piece of the puzzle Dancer had learned only recently: He had observed the mark of a tortoise on Maunakili's inner arm during their battle in the royal house on Moku'ula island: The shape of a turtle with a missing fin had been etched into his brain. Then only a short time ago he had observed the same strange birthmark on Malbec's inner forearm during their battle above the whirling vortex in the mountains near the 'Īao Valley.

Dancer concluded his story: "Maunakili and Malbec shared the same father. LeGrand. But Maunakili's threat to the throne died with him. And so the Kingdom of Hawai'i lives on."

The King accepted Dancer's truth.

Next the King turned to Akamu and Kikilani. "You are the rightful heirs to the Kingdom of Maui...Prince Akamu and Princess Kikilani."

The pair rose and stepped before the seated King. As they did on the *heiau* of the Lost City. Now Akamu stood shirtless. And both wore the traditional *kapa* wrap. Yet Akamu and Kikilani had the countenance of *ali'i* nobility. In a display of their sincerity they prostrated themselves before the King. Their faces rested flat against the mat in the ancient manner of the *ali'i* nobles. To show their allegiance to their King.

The King motioned for Akamu and Kikilani to rise. They both rose to one knee. Akamu put their mutual thoughts into words. "From this day forward—Your Highness—you shall have our personal allegiance…and the allegiance of all the Pi'ilani of Maui to the one Kingdom of Hawai'i."

The King assented as he rose to his feet. "Stand…my friends." When the Prince and Princess stood up the King brushed both in turn with the red feathers of the royal plume. After a long moment he spoke solemnly: "Your oaths — and your bond of sacred brother and sister — are accepted. Be it known by all heretofore the King of Hawai'i gave his blessing for the union of Akamu and Kikilani."

Akamu and Kikilani bowed. Then Akamu took Kikilani's hand in his. Kikilani's ecstatic smile displayed a radiant brilliance against her bronze skin.

"May you and your children — and your children's children — be great protectors of native rights and traditions." The King intoned his blessings with another flick of his royal whisk. Then extended his arms over the gathered company. They all bowed their heads as he spoke. "*Ua mau ke ea o ka aina i ka pono.*"

Akamu and Kikilani translated in unison: "*The life of the land is perpetuated in righteousness!*"

QUO VADIS?

DEAR READER: Although all was safe in Hawai'i—thanks to Jack Dancer. Samantha Swift. And their friends' dramatic success—back in Washington DC there was much nervous second-guessing and hand-wringing. Every penny of any treasure—real or apocryphal—was sorely needed for the Mexican War—and the Inner Circle knew they could not provide even the humblest naval support in the Sandwich Islands. While our heroes had their hands full in the Pacific two months earlier in March American General Winfield Scott stopped dithering and finally landed at Veracruz in Mexico. From that beachhead Scott and his Army advanced along the old "Cortez Route" on Mexico City…outnumbered two-and-a-half to one. Outcome unknown. Fortunately Old Fuss and Feathers' young officer corps was outstanding. Robert E. Lee. George Meade. Ulysses S. Grant. James Longstreet. Thomas "Stonewall" Jackson. From whom we will hear much in the future. For now suffice it to say the group of military men distinguished themselves on the road to the Mexican capital.

Meanwhile in Washington: Polk. Buchanan. Walker. Houston were preoccupied. Opponents to the Mexican–American War like

Abraham Lincoln and Frederick Douglass resisted the effort and feared the captured territory would become additional slave states. While expansionists demanded "All Mexico" as a prize. The boys in Washington were distracted. No word from Hawai'i. Should they fortify Los Angeles? Monterey? Sonoma against attack? Houston summed up the situation. "Let's pray Jack Dancer and that correspondent woman — S. Thomas Swift — have our backs in Hawai'i. Otherwise we could lose California before we win it!"

Quo Vadis? Where to now?

As we look ahead…you'll be pleased to learn S. Thomas Swift's exposé — when it finally appeared — ended trafficking between the Pacific and New York City. Although the smugglers' trade in opium continued. At the *New York World* — the *Brooklyn Daily Eagle*'s newspaper rival across town — publisher Joseph Pulitzer was reputedly heard to say: "If any of my reporters sold as many papers as S. Thomas Swift I'd give them a prize."

After Captain Hyram Head's abrupt death at Fort Lahaina First Mate Ratter Dawes was found guilty of attempted murder and kidnapping. Transcripts indicate although he never finished the hit job Jacob Swift hired him to perform Dawes never confessed. What occurred after Dawes' trial is unclear. The historic records are sketchy. One researcher's account suggests Dawes ended his days soon after in Honolulu's notorious prison. Apparently it was rumored that other prisoners tied him to his bunk and smeared Dawes with bacon fat — where upon he was eaten alive by rats. Although Dawes died in prison — the use of bacon fat could not be verified. As for the *Black Cloud*: The ship was claimed from impound later that fall for harbor fees and nominal fines by two officers of the whaling ship *Condor*. To avoid the *Black Cloud*'s unpleasant reputation Captain Hunter rechristened the ship as the *Huntress* and sailed from Lahaina in the dead of night. By Christmas Captain Hunter and Red John had relocated Hyram Head's rum-for-opium-and-comfort-girls operation to San Francisco's Chinatown. Just in time for the Gold Rush of 1849.

Despite Akamu's pledges and best efforts — Charlie Pickham and Angus Macomber fanned the dangers of native rule. They promoted the bogeyman of a nonexistent crisis. Manufactured by Abner Sisson. At every turn the trio conspired to demonize islanders. Every native complaint was painted as a disastrous threat of "inexhaustible" Pi'ilani land rights tied to royal bloodlines. Their ginned-up reports reinforced the fabricated conclusion by the Legislative Council that land division must go forward. Surveys were required. Procedures must be established. Sworn verification of boundaries made mandatory. Deadlines created. Fee schedules inflated. Convoluted appeals. Hearings. Paper filings. Missed deadlines. Technical errors gave plausible reasons for the Land Commission — and its chairman Abner Sisson — to deny most claims from exhausted and befuddled land occupants.

Sisson was fond of the higher ground. Yet…in one of the ironies of fate poor Abner Sisson fell ill in the summer that year and died a few months later in the colder November season. His life's work never seen to fruition. As he would have said with cool New England logic: "We shall bring order out of anarchy. Law and order must prevail. Logic and reason must triumph over tradition and chaos."

Within a year the stage was set in 1848 for the Great Mahele: the Great Division. Six short years later an amendment to the Great Mahele allowed foreigners to buy up "unclaimed" commoner lands from the government for one-third the value. Great land barons soon emerged to claim upstream water rights on Crown lands. And introduced an era of sugar cane and imported labor. Interlocking boards of directors often controlled by renowned names entailing ex-missionary scions soon controlled most of the Hawaiian Islands' economy. Wealth. Finance. Construction. Agriculture. Transportation. Shipping. The family names held sway into the 1960s — when the Era of Plantations gave way to the Era of Tourism.

Mama Samoa moved her Hall of Paradise to Honolulu. There she quickly established the most famous land-based brothel in the Pacific — just off Hotel Street. As always it prospered. Primarily thanks to her handpicked star attractions of the season who worked an expanded four-room bullpen. Island lore has it that no one in the Hall of Paradise ever equaled Queen Tin'a's record of six minutes twenty-seven seconds to complete a circuit of four sailors back in the Paradise Palace.

Year after year the entire whaling fleet shifted from Lahaina to Honolulu. Soon the age of whale oil harvesting declined: Petroleum was discovered in Pennsylvania in 1859. Within a few short years Lahaina returned to being a sleepy outpost in paradise. Over time the moated palace of Moku'ula fell into disrepair. By 1919 the county overfilled the Mokuhinia Lake and turned the sacred land into a park. The Friends of Moku'ula—a nonprofit organization dedicated to restoration of the sacred site—formed in 1990. The future of the Moku'ula's preservation is unclear.

To this day two mysteries remain. No one has ever found the Cave of the Ancients or the Lost City of the Pi'ilani—even after extensive searches by several Hawaiian kings over the years. Some say it is hidden forever by the clouds of the Pu'ukukui summit. A lost city all but inaccessible—perhaps in some upland valley. Guarded by the mythical—and sometimes invisible—little people of Maui. The Menehune.

And no one has ever found Napoleon's Malta treasure. Not in Aboukir Bay. Not in Egypt. Not in Zanzibar. Nor on Maui. Napoleon's treasure is still a mystery...wherever it may be.

AUTHOR'S NOTES

MORE THAN ONE HUNDRED SEVENTY-FIVE YEARS have elapsed since the occurrence of the events recorded in this volume. Yet — notwithstanding the familiarity of many readers with aspects of this history — this novel is intended completely to be a fictional account. That said: Napoleon's Malta treasure. Locations. Historical characters. Travel distances. Modes of travel. And details from weapons to clothing to customs — are real. Every effort was made to purge all words not in use before 1847. Where the story touches on historical fact we tried to be invariably accurate. However: Only you can form your own opinion and be your own judge. In this regard no one can be more sensible of his deficiencies than the author. We trust you weigh them with the understanding that the work was driven by the desire to put down a truthful adventure — both entertaining and historical.

Yet for the sake of the tale some facts have been shifted. In New Caledonia (for example) the penal colony details are correct. Yet the first prisoners arrived in 1864. A time-telescope was needed to move Malbec's Camp Blood back to 1847.

The opium smuggling plot was inspired by a *Maui News* supplement from July 1989 (*Haleakalā Ranch: One Hundredth Anniversary*) that detailed the opium drops in Smuggler's Cove on Kahoʻolawe Island made in the early 1900s. The buoy and pickup process described here became part of this story including carting the opium up the mountainside to Kula camps. Only the date was shifted fifty years or so.

For the fictional character of Shieka Sharife the author took inspiration from the 27th child of Said bin Sultan of Zanzibar: Sayyida Sharife whose younger sister (36th child of the Sultan) — Sayyida Salama (Salme) married a German merchant in 1867 and later published her history: *Memoirs of an Arabian Princess: An Autobiography* (1888) under her married name Emily Ruete. Ruete described Sharife as the daughter of a Circassian woman and a "dazzling beauty with the complexion of a German blonde. Besides, she possessed a sharp intellect, which made her (Sharife) a faithful advisor of my father's."

Jean O'Hara — one of most famous madams of the Second World War in Hawaiʻi — is the inspiration behind the "bullpen" or "bullring" setups of the Paradise Palace and *Ship of Paradise* brothels. As a Hotel Street madam in Honolulu's red-light district — and an Irish Catholic native of Chicago — O'Hara is credited with the arrangement of three flimsy-walled cubicles where a single prostitute worked three rooms in rotation: One for a waiting client. One for an engaged customer. And the last for a man dressing. With as many as 30,000 sailors daily in 1941 through 1945 visiting 20 registered Honolulu brothels and their 250 licensed "entertainers" — and paying a fixed rate of three dollars for three minutes regulated by military and local police — the historical record informed the fictional bordellos of Queen Tinʻa and Mama Samoa: Time is money. Jean O'Hara published her 56-page memoir as *My Life as a Honolulu Prostitute* in 1944 (later republished as *Honolulu Harlot*). Her story is said to have inspired William Bradford Huie's 1951 novel: *The Revolt of Mamie Stover* about a feisty Honolulu madam in which the 1956 movie adaptation starred Jane Russell. On the last page of O'Hara's typed and mimeographed epilogue she wrote that a lack of room kept her from including all the names she wanted to mention. "I have finished writing a sequel to this book. It will lay the rest of the criminal ring open like a crisp biscuit. Watch your newspapers and observe the frantic efforts that will be made to keep me from printing it. But it will be on the streets as soon as the first suit is filed against me." That sequel is yet to be published.

For the fictional names of sailing vessels the author drew on several actual ships. The French frigate *Némésis* was in fact a French naval ship launched in 1847 at Brest. Yet that modern ship was a screw-powered 50-gun second-rate frigate of the *Artemise* class that served as the flagship of Admiral Rigault de Genouilly during the Second Opium War (1856–1860). As for the *Black Cloud* the inspiration for that ship design was a combination of two whaleships. One was New Bedford (1841) whaleship *Charles W. Morgan* which visited Lahaina six times on whale fishing voyages between 1849 and 1862. The *Charles W. Morgan* is now faithfully restored at the Mystic Seaport Museum in Connecticut and is "America's oldest commercial ship still afloat." The other deck-plan model was the Nantucket-based American whaleship *Essex* which was rammed by a whale in 1820 and sank providing the climactic scene in Herman Melville's classic *Moby Dick* (1851).

The age of whaling owes a large deal of its aura to Herman Melville who signed onto the New Bedford whaler *Acushnet* in 1841 and sailed for five years — including five to six months in Hawai'i with possibly a landing in Lahaina in 1843 — then returned to Boston and wrote five books in five years about his adventures: *Typee* (1846). *Omoo* (1847). *Mardi* (1849). *Redburn* (1849). *White-Jacket* (1850). Melville moved to the Berkshires in 1850 where he wrote *Moby Dick* (1851) — a critical and commercial failure. The book marked the end of Melville's career as a successful novelist although he published five more standalone novels. *Moby Dick* today is considered one of the greatest American novels. The author confesses a special place in his heart for the *Typee* adventure which was the first book his mother gave him at age ten.

The idea of a French plot to control the Hawaiian Islands may stretch credulity. Yet at the time the geopolitical maneuvers of England attest to an unvarnished true story. And include France and the United States as well. In fact Rear Admiral Louis Tromelin did return to Honolulu in 1849 aboard the frigate *La Poursuivante (The Pursuer)* as promised. The incident is known today as the Sacking of Honolulu or the Tromelin Affair. The year before the French Consul Guillaume

Patrice Dillon in Honolulu had written his superiors that the presence of a warship could "force concessions from this devious and hypocritical government." On 12 August 1849 Admiral Tromelin arrived with a corvette and frigate. The French were angered by Protestant missionaries' efforts to shut out Catholic priests and French trade. Tromelin and Dillon presented ten demands to Hawaiian King Kamehameha III. When the demands were not met Tromelin sent ashore 140 marines with field pieces and scaling ladders. They took the Honolulu Fort from the two men defending it. Spiked its coastal guns. Tossed its gunpowder into the harbor. And proceeded to wreck destruction in town — reportedly to the tune of $100,000 in damages. To add insult Tromelin confiscated the King's yacht — the *Kamehameha III* — which was subsequently sailed to Tahiti and never returned. Tromelin held Honolulu for about 11 days then left Hawai'i on 5 September 1849. At first the French government condemned the attack on Honolulu. But upon receiving the personal account of Tromelin and Dillon — who sailed away with Tromelin — the French government reconsidered the incident as justified and never paid reparations for damages.

For the commercial conspiracy and fictional character of Angus Macomber — former missionary supply agent turned merchant and greedy American Consul in Lahaina — inspiration came from a long history of Lahaina consuls who skimmed from every plate they could reach in the period of 1840 to 1860. Corruption took many forms: Confiscating "shore wages" paid to hospitalized sailors by the Seamen's Relief Fund; keeping money deposited with the consulate by seamen who died; overcharging the State Department for physician services and supplies and rent; and taking bribes from whaling ship captains to shade the "hail" count of loaded whale oil barrels in favor of the captains to the detriment of the crews' lay share — to name a few schemes. For this avenue of research I relied on past-president of the Maui Historical Society Dorothy (Riconda) Pyle's *The Intriguing Seamen's Hospital* (Volume 8 of Hawaiian Journal of History dated 1974) originally researched for the Lahaina Restoration Foundation. Also of great value was Peter von Buol's work: *Abner Pratt and Michigan's Honolulu House* (Volume 38/Number 3 of *Prologue* of the Journal of the National Archives dated Fall 2006).

Peter von Buol is an adjunct professor of journalism at Columbia College Chicago.

The historic fort at Lahaina plays an important role in the story. Yet today Fort Lahaina is a ghost of its original self. Built in 1832 in a similar design to the fort in Honolulu: Fort Lahaina's 15- to 20-foot-high walls were constructed of coral blocks. For the sake of the story the author shifted the *makai* ocean-side gate (facing what is Wharf Street today) to the corner nearer the landing facing Fort Street (today named Hotel Street). By 1842 American naval officer Charles Wilkes described the fort as "of little account" as a defense. The fort's role was primarily as a calaboose to confine unruly sailors—most often overnight until their captain paid a fine the next day. Although the fort was restored in 1847 and the Governor of Maui James Young lived in the fort in 1848—the fort was demolished in 1852—twenty years after being constructed. Many of the recovered coral stones were used to build a "new" prison—*Hale Pa'ahao* or "Stuck in Irons House"—that opened at the corner of Prison and Waine'e Streets in 1853. When the Hale Piula palace was destroyed by a fierce Kaua'ula wind in 1858 the old palace's stones were used to rebuild the Lahaina Court and Customs House in 1858–1859. The Old Lahaina Courthouse has seen several restorations since. On the *mauka* mountain side of the courthouse is Lahaina Banyan Court. Its majestic banyan tree—that today dominates the fort site—was planted in 1873 as a seedling about eight feet tall. The India banyan memorialized the 50th anniversary of the first American Protestant mission in Lahaina (1823) and is reported to be the largest banyan tree in Hawai'i and one of the largest in the United States.

On 15 December 1854 the longest ruling monarch of the Hawaiian Kingdom—King Kamehameha III (Kauikeaouli)—died. Unmarried. Heirless. But he and his consort Kalama had adopted (*hānai*) a toddler cousin whom the King decreed heir to the throne and raised as the crown prince. The future Kamehameha IV (Alekanetero 'Iolani Kalanikualiholiho Maka o 'Iouli Kūnuiākea o Kūkā'ilimoku; anglicized as Alexander Liholiho) was the biological son of one of Kamehameha I's brothers: Kehuanaoa and Kinau; thus Kehuanaoa was King Kamehameha III's uncle. Kamehameha IV died of chronic asthma 30 November 1863 also without an heir. He was succeeded by his brother who took the name Kamehameha V. The royal house continued to Liliʻuokalani ("Liliʻu". 1832–1917)—Hawaiʻi's last queen—who ruled until the overthrow of the Hawaiian Kingdom in 1893. For a richly detailed history of this period readers will enjoy Julia Flynn Siler's *Lost Kingdom: Hawaii's Last Queen, the Sugar Kings, and America's First Imperial Adventure* (2012).

As for the land reform drawn up by the King and his Privy Council and Hawaiian Legislature the ultimate resolution to this day is complicated and controversial. The Great Mahele or great land division occurred in 1848 and was followed by the Kuleana Act of 1850. Essentially a feudal system of land rights—where no one owned the land and upon death the King could redistribute land to anyone he wanted—was replaced with an allodial system of ownership where land was not subject to an overseer lord and carried value greater than its yield of produce. After 1850 all *aliʻi* high chiefs and *konohiki* chiefs and *kanaka* commoners—although granted their land—had to apply for title through the Land Commission. They had to prove occupancy and boundaries and pay a commutation fee. When claims were not filed or filed incorrectly the lands could be sold to natives or foreigners. To this day land rights raise high emotions and legal claims. Were commoner's traditional land rights extinguished in 1848 to 1850—or are they available to descendants today? How those battles over land rights—and by extension even statehood and sovereignty—play out may still be determined. Yet title to all land in Hawaiʻi today can be traced back to the land divisions created by the 1848 Great Mahele. The year after our tale takes place. Which is one inspiration behind our story being set in 1847—and why the ending left the question open: *Quo Vadis?* Where to next?

But back then—back in 1847—the outcome of our story could well have been different. Indeed: dramatically different. When history is spun as a tale the truth behind the real events enriches the bones of history. Who is to say that Swift and Dancer's strategies and achievements did not make history what it is?

And that is why…Swift and Dancer will return again.

ACKNOWLEDGMENTS

My aim is to entertain…and at the same time share the exciting history from the time of Swift and Dancer. Simply put: The purpose of this work is historical fiction not fictional history. Every effort was made not to fight the facts and instead to be inspired by them.

For this narrative actual events and the lives of historical figures inspired several fictional characters. Any motives and actions of these fictional characters are entirely the author's imagination. Any resemblance to current events or locales…or to persons living or dead…is entirely coincidental.

Only the most accurate language can reflect real history. That is why I am immeasurably indebted to the Merriam-Webster.com Time-Traveler dictionary. With it I tried to time-check every word and phrase and idiom as best I could to weed out anachronisms. When modern words failed the test — by entering the English language after 1847 — they were rejected. A special acknowledgement goes to the Hawaii Board on Geographic Names' May 2018 report that we used as the official guide for spelling Hawaiian place names and features. We hope this historical and cultural authenticity is a pleasure to readers. Please let us know what was missed.

For research and history of Lahaina and Hawai'i in 1847 I am indebted to the unfailingly helpful Lahaina Public Library Branch Manager Alayna Davies-Smith. Her library's Hawaiiana collection particularly on whaling history and island flora and fauna was invaluable with books dating back to 1872. In particular her assistance uncovered the world-building details of whaleships in Maxine Mrantz's *Whaling Days in Old Hawaii* (1976) and R.M. Ballantyne's *Fighting the Whales: Doings and Dangers on a Fishing Cruise* published by Porter & Coates (1876); plus W. Arthur Whistler's *Plants of the Canoe People* by National Tropical Botanical Garden (2009); and renowned botanist Beatrice H. Krauss' paper on *Ethnobotany of Hawaii*—to cite a few. Also of great assistance was the Lahaina Restoration Foundation and particularly Theo Morrison (Executive Director) and Kimberly Flook (Deputy Executive Director). The foundation's work to restore and preserve the history of Lahaina—and some of the town's most significant sites—is an inspiration to cultural preservation anywhere. In my attempt to locate accurate maps of the time the aid from Director of Operations Elizabeth Po'oloa with the Hawaiian Mission Houses Association in Honolulu went far beyond my hopes. As well as essential research guidance generously provided by Ju Sun of the Hawai'i State Archives located on the 'Iolani Palace Grounds in Honolulu. The State Archives collection of maps is unparalleled and highly accessible.

The author gives particular acknowledgment to the outstanding historical scholarship of P. Christian Klieger's *Moku'ula: Maui's Sacred Island* by Bishop Museum Press (1998); Jill Engledow's *The Story of Lāhainā* by Maui Island Press (2016); Dave Bunnell's *Caves of Fire: Inside America's Lava Tubes* by National Speleological Society (2008 & 2013); Gavan Daws' seminal work: *Shoal of Time: A History of the Hawaiian Islands* by University of Hawai'i Press (1968); the richly illustrated three volumes of maps and artwork by Riley M. Moffat and Gary L. Fitzpatrick in their essential works *Surveying the Mahele: Mapping the Hawaiian Land Revolution* (1995) and *Mapping the Lands and Waters of Hawai'i: The Hawaiian Government Survey* (2004) published in limited edition were a gold mine. For the worldview of President James K. Polk and Secretary of State James

Buchanan I depended on Arthur M. Schlesinger Jr.'s *The Age of Jackson* by Little Brown and Company (1945). And for a fresh perspective on Hawai'i I often return to Jack London's *Stories of Hawaii* by Mutual Publishing (1986) and the Lahaina Mysteries Series by Barbara E. Sharp (2001–2005).

A work of this scope takes a village. Without the unfailing and professional help of an incredible group *The Fishhook Rebellion: Hawai'i 1847* would not have made it to print. First acknowledgment goes to my wife—Synnöve Granholm—whose love and support made completing this project possible. Accolades to my editor— William Oppenheimer—who persevered through manuscript evaluation to line edit to revision review with unflagging encouragement and sage suggestions. William axed every anachronism and story hiccup he found. To my marketing guru— Amy Hausman—who stuck with this tale since 2017 I offer my profoundest gratitude. I couldn't have done it without you. To the best book mapmaker in the business—Rhys Davies—I owe the adventure of accurate and inspirational maps that illustrated every section. My invaluable page proof editor—Barbara Uebelacker— immeasurably improved the final page proofs with her eagle eye. David Wu—who designed the book text and always makes me look good—I have unending respect for. And to Richard Ljoenes Design LLC whose book covers for both *The Good or Evil Side: Matamoros 1846* and *The Fishhook Rebellion: Hawai'i 1847* made the Swift & Dancer Adventures jump off the shelf.

For nomenclature and ship design in the many chapters set aboard sailing ships I turned to longtime friend and tall-ship captain J.B. Smith who has literally sailed the world. Captain Smith's experience includes years as master in the Brig *Unicorn* (used in the filming of the *Pirates of the Caribbean* as well as the series *Roots*); Washington State's official tall ship Brig *Lady Washington*; Brigantine *Gazela* of Philadelphia; Coasting Schooners SSV *Harvey Gamage* and SSV *Spirit of Massachusetts* and Staysail Schooner SSV *Westward* with the Ocean Classroom Foundation as well as various schooner yachts. In 2009 Captain Smith was awarded the Lifetime Achievement Award by the American Sail Training Association (now known as Tall Ships America).

And finally to my niece Katrina Dorman whose knowledge and insights on the qualities of everything from gems and crystals to flower essences and astrology pointed me in the right direction to find the black onyx for our magical pendant that crowns the climax of our story. We always look forward to visiting her in Maui. Thank you.

ABOUT THE AUTHOR

Dan Gooder Richard's love of adventure stories began as a boy. The first two novels his mother gave him at age ten are still on his shelf: Margaret Armstrong's *Trelawny* and Herman Melville's *Typee*. That boyhood love of a good tale was reinforced as Dan listened to his father weave cowboy yarns during family trips from Iowa to his father's childhood home in Montana. After earning a bachelor's in history Dan blasted water wells in India  with the Peace Corps. Ski bummed in Taos Ski Valley. Motorcycled across the Sahara. Then earned his master's in journalism at Missouri.

Dan's middle name comes from his maternal grandfather: Leslie MacDonald Gooder who was a publisher in Chicago from the early 1910s through the 1950s. Dan carried on the family name in publishing. After he and his wife sold their marketing/publishing business in 2016 Dan turned his full-time attention to writing historical adventures. Dan lives in Virginia with his Swedish-speaking Finnish-born wife who also loves adventurous travels. Their 40+ year life/work partnership — without the loggerheads — inspired the Swift & Dancer Adventures.

In Dan Gooder Richard's previous life as a publisher and one of the real estate industry's leading authorities in marketing and lead management he wrote two top-selling books on real estate marketing: *REAL ESTATE RAINMAKER®: Successful Strategies for Real Estate Marketing*, and *REAL ESTATE RAINMAKER®: Guide to Online Marketing*; both published by John Wiley & Sons. Dan also authored two nonfiction books in the popular SMART ESSENTIALS series: *SMART ESSENTIALS FOR COLLEGE RENTALS: Parent and Investor Guide To Buying College-Town Real Estate*, and *SMART ESSENTIALS FOR REAL ESTATE INVESTING: How To Build Wealth In Real Estate Today*. You can follow Dan's recent work at www.DanGooderRichard.com.

DON'T MISS THE NEXT
EDGE-OF-YOUR-SEAT READ
FROM DAN GOODER RICHARD

CODE DUELLO: PARIS 1848

CODE DUELLO follows journalist-adventurer Samantha Swift—a sister in spirit to Nelly Bly—and secret agent Jack Dancer—a rogue in the mold of Harry Flashman—when Swift is assigned to report on democracy-torn 1848 Europe and Dancer is independently dispatched to win France's clandestine support for America's westward expansion.

But on their Atlantic crossing a book antiquarian is found dead leaving behind a mythical chronicle of all human history with unimaginable powers to know the future. Soon Swift and Dancer's separate but entangled missions are drawn into a swirling plot of rare books. Deadly duels. Back-stabbing royalty. Occult legerdemain. And the bloody June Days Uprising in France. From Manchester to London to Paris Swift and Dancer attempt to solve an age-old riddle with little more than a Masonic optic lens and a miniature locked book.

If their strained relationship doesn't destroy both their quests— Swift and Dancer must stay one step ahead of their enemies as they face a maze of death traps and betrayals in a race to solve a mystery as ancient as civilization itself. But when a handsome revolutionary connected to Dancer's past joins Swift in the hunt—all the rules change. In this life-and-death game—Swift and Dancer's next move may be the most dangerous one of all. Until they find themselves in an unknown world beneath Paris—both wondrous and horrifying— where the ancient Devil of Death has kept his secrets—until now.

DISCOVER AN ADVENTURE
175 YEARS IN THE MAKING!
CODE DUELLO: PARIS 1848
by Dan Gooder Richard

THE ADVENTURE THAT STARTED IT ALL

THE GOOD OR EVIL SIDE
MATAMOROS 1846

BY THE SPRING OF 1846 — the tinderbox of the Mexican-American War needs only a first spark to explode. Two powerful enemies plot Mexico's defeat for diabolically opposing reasons.

President Polk enlists secret agent Jack Dancer for a suicide mission to single-handedly expose the Southern slavocracy's plot to steal victory from the American Army and claim new territory for slavery — as America's Manifest Destiny hangs in the balance.

On a collision course with her own destiny the headstrong war correspondent Samantha Swift races to the Rio Grande to report exclusively on the looming battles from behind Mexican lines. Failure risks forfeiting her vast — and stolen — newspaper fortune.

But as their lives collide from New York and Charleston to New Orleans and Matamoros — Swift and Dancer are thrust into a struggle against all odds to unscramble a grisly murder — outwit a mysterious organization intent to kill them — and decipher the key to a lost treasure — before war destroys everything.

9 781939 319340